T. Csernis

GREYKIN VALLEY
GREYKIN CHRONICLES VOLUME TWO

GREYKIN VALLEY
Greykin Chronicles | Volume Two

Copyright © 2024 by Tate Csernis (T. Csernis).

All rights reserved. No part of this book may be used or reproduced in any form whatsoever without written permission except in the case of brief quotations in critical articles or reviews.

This book is a work of fiction. Names, characters, businesses, organizations, places, events, and incidents either are the product of the author's imagination or are used fictitiously. Any resemblance to actual persons, living or dead, events, or locales is entirely coincidental.

For more information on the world, this series, other books, or to contact the author, head to:
https://www.numenverse.com/

Cover designed by Julia Bland

Internal art page designed by Tate Csernis
Internal art page drawn by Simon Zhong
Internal art page edited by Julia Bland

ISBN – Paperback: 978-1-917270-10-6
ISBN – Hardcover: 978-1-917270-11-3
ISBN – E-Book: 978-1-917270-12-0

THE GREYKIN CHRONICLES is a work written by

Tate Csernis (T. Csernis) involving some characters created by Julia Bland (Julia B.)

Each Party retains ownership over their respected Intellectual Property created outside of this collaboration, including but not limited to names, characters, stories, etc. All Collaborative Intellectual Property shall be jointly owned by the Parties, and each Party shall have the right freely to use all Collaborative Intellectual Property for all purposes and uses.

GREYKIN VALLEY
Greykin Chronicles | Volume Two

GLOSSARY

Ethos [ee-thos] - The energy within someone that can be used to create or manipulate other energies

❋

New Dawnwood [dawn-wood]
(aka, New York)

❋

Ascela [as-kella]
(aka, Alaska)

❋

Dor-Sanguis [door-san-goo-wis] - Translates roughly to Pain *[Portuguese]* and blood *[Latin]*
(aka, Romania)

❋

DeiganLupus [day-gan-loo-pus] - Translates roughly to 'refused to turn to the wolf' *[Icelantic, Latin]*
(aka, UK)

❋

Aegisguard [ee-gis-guard] - The world
(aka, Earth)

❋

Proselytus [pros-elly-tus] – A heart-like organ which creates ethos inside a body

❋

Numen [noo-men] - God-like beings that chose to show themselves to the world rather than remain anonymous

❋

Aegis [ee-gis] - The Dragon Gods, children of Letholdus

❋

Caedis [kay-dis]

❋

Zenith [zee-nith]

❋

Zalith [zay-lith]

❋

Daimon [day-mon]

❋

Caius [kai-us]

❋

Nyssa [nis-ah]

❋

Strămoş [struh-mosh]

❋

Zanthé [zan-thay]

The Months and Currency

Months

January – Primis
February – Cordus
March – Tertium
April – Aprilis
May – Quintus
June – Iunius
July – Quintilis
August – Tria
September – Novem
October – Decem
November – Undecim
December – Clausula

Currency

Copper – Equivalent of $0.01
Bronze – Equivalent of $0.20
Silver – Equivalent of $2
Gold – Equivalent of $10
Coronam – Equivalent of $100
Cidaris – Equivalent of $1 million

GREYKIN VALLEY
Greykin Chronicles | Volume Two

CONTENTS

1	In Pursuit of the Target	Pg11
2	Retreat	Pg19
3	Humanoids	Pg27
4	Debrief	Pg34
5	The Conspiracy	Pg40
6	A Mate's Worry	Pg49
7	Decisions	Pg55
8	Ulterior Motives	Pg64
9	But Then I Found You	Pg73
10	The Infected	Pg82
11	Ucigaş in Wolf's Clothing	Pg90
12	Check Out	Pg101
13	The Mission Begins	Pg110
14	Kingslake Pass	Pg116
15	Debts	Pg125
16	A Wolf in the Dark	Pg135
17	Silver Traps	Pg143
18	Onwards	Pg151
19	That Ominous Feeling	Pg158
20	The Woman in Silver	Pg164
21	Sixteen Hunters	Pg171
22	Inimă	Pg179
23	Asmodi	Pg186
24	Lock and Key	Pg195
25	Report	Pg201
26	Back on Track	Pg207
27	The River	Pg215
28	Stop	Pg222
29	Doctor's Orders	Pg229
30	Burial	Pg236
31	Fire	Pg243
32	Hounds	Pg252
33	Warning	Pg258

GREYKIN VALLEY
Greykin Chronicles | Volume Two

34	Declaration	Pg264
35	War Plans	Pg271
36	Wait Out The Storm	Pg279
37	Fangs and Blood	Pg286
38	The Ambush	Pg292
39	Metamorphosis	Pg299
40	Evolving Danger	Pg306
41	A Missing Piece	Pg314
42	Exes	Pg319
43	Waiting on Fate	Pg328
44	The Great Lake	Pg335
45	Final Warning	Pg342
46	Bloody Glade	Pg347
47	Kane Ardelean-Blood	Pg355
48	The Arena	Pg363
49	The Last Option	Pg370
50	Don't Look Back	Pg377
51	Wait	Pg382
52	Patrol	Pg388
53	Friend or Foe?	Pg395
54	Reiner Manor	Pg401
55	Bloodlines	Pg409
56	Liberation	Pg415
57	Hunt for the Inimă	Pg421
58	Butcher	Pg426
59	The Missing, The Found	Pg432
60	Cat and Mouse	Pg438
61	To The Pit	Pg444
62	Siren	Pg450
63	Blood and Stripes	Pg455
64	A Long-Awaited Call	Pg462
65	There Are Laws	Pg468
66	Talk of Ancestors	Pg474
67	Greymore, Greyson, Greyblood, Greykin	Pg479
68	Lines	Pg486
69	Conference Hall	Pg494
70	A Few Hours' Rest	Pg503
71	The Redblood Line	Pg509

72	Demon Name	Pg515
73	Wolf's Rite	Pg521
74	An Impending Choice	Pg528
75	Moving Out	Pg533
76	Winner Takes All	Pg538
77	Antlers	Pg543
78	The Perfect Vessel	Pg549
79	Victor	Pg555
80	The Phantom	Pg561
81	It Will Always Be Him	Pg566
82	Guilt and Shame	Pg571
83	Mate	Pg577
84	Sequoia Point	Pg584
85	Shrieker	Pg590
86	Plan A, Plan B	Pg597
87	Greykin Valley	Pg603
88	The Lab	Pg609
89	A Sea of Red	Pg618
90	Black Files	Pg624
91	Patient Zero	Pg633

GREYKIN VALLEY
Greykin Chronicles | Volume Two

GREYKIN VALLEY
Greykin Chronicles | Volume Two

Chapter One

In Pursuit of the Target

| Daimon, before the chase |

Daimon despised hunters. As he watched each man and woman laugh, drink, and clean the weapons they clung to so dearly, all he could think about was tearing them apart. They spat at the Caeleste locked in cages and grinned proudly at their latest catch. But not one of them had any idea what was about to happen; no hunter in that camp could fathom the idea that they were now the prey.

He waited in the cover of the brush for the signal, watching Ethan's every move. Daimon's hatred for the hunters swiftly shifted to Jackson's friend; he wanted to tear *him* to pieces, too. But Jackson cared about him, so Daimon was going to have to do his best to control his protective, possessive feelings.

Ethan walked out of the tent and started talking to one of his comrades, and when they discussed what bounties were left to capture, Ethan's comrade mentioned something…strange.

"Saw it with my own eyes. Fucking massive this thing was."

"And you're sure it was a corpse?" Ethan questioned.

"Certain. The *smell* that came from this thing…ugh." He spat and retched.

But then came Tokala's piercing howl.

There was no time for Daimon to ponder. It was starting. Everyone in the camp stopped what they were doing and listened.

The howls of Wesley, Brando, and Enola followed, and with their calls, the hunters burst into action. They yelled orders at each other, hurrying around, snatching their pathetic little weapons, and starting up their vehicles.

Daimon began his prowl. He stayed low to the snow-covered ground, moving silently, keeping his eyes fixed on Ethan. However, he needed to remind himself that he couldn't kill Ethan; he had to ignore the growing urge to dispose of him before he could become a threat to his and Jackson's relationship. But he loved Jackson too much. He couldn't take his friend away from him.

His target loaded up on arrows, checked that the silver revolver on his side was loaded, and climbed onto one of the motorbikes.

At least he wasn't in a jeep; he'd be much easier to single out now.

The hunters moved out. First, a wave of those on bikes sped into the murky woods, followed by several jeeps, and then the rest of the bikers drove off. *Ethan* drove off.

Daimon sprung forward and began his pursuit. He swerved through the trees, focusing his sights on Ethan, and when he was joined by the rest of his hunting party, he waited for the perfect moment to begin the attack.

That moment came when Brando's second howl told him that they were a klick away from the hunter camp.

He looked to his right. Rachel, Dustu, and Leon nodded. He looked to his left. Ezhno, Lance, Bly, and Alastor nodded. They were ready.

"Go!" Daimon called.

On his word, Rachel caught up to one of the bikers and lunged at him. She pulled him off his bike as he screamed in shock, and when the rest of the bikers turned their heads and saw her kill their comrade, the rest of the wolves moved in.

All of the bikers swerved and tried to drive after Rachel—who was now running deeper into the woods—but Dustu and Leon cut the man driving beside Ethan off, letting only four of them chase her.

At the same time, Lance jumped out of the murk and pulled the biker furthest to the left off his bike, and when the bike crashed into a tree, the explosives in the saddlebags went off, shaking the ground at their paws.

What remained of the backline fell for it. They turned away from Dustu and Leon and started chasing Lance, Ezhno, Bly, and Alastor.

To keep the jeeps from turning back, Dustu and Leon raced forward and grabbed their attention, and just as Rachel did, they raced off in a different direction, taking half the jeeps with them.

When Daimon was sure that his packmates were fine, he veered left and caught up with the bikers Ethan was amongst.

But gunfire echoed behind him. Rifles and machine guns, yelling voices, and another fiery explosion. His wolves could handle it.

He fixed his eyes on Ethan. The brown-haired man was in the centre of the chase, following directly behind Alastor. There were seven other bikers to deal with first, though. As much as Daimon wanted to adorn his Prime form and slaughter the lot of them, he had to keep his wolves in mind. He wasn't going to risk them.

With a short burst of several snarls, he let his packmates know that it was time to separate these hunters from their target.

Simultaneously, Bly ran to the west, Ezhno to the northwest, Lance to the east, and Alastor to the northeast. The hunters immediately split to chase after them, but Ethan didn't budge. He kept driving forward, seemingly unshaken by the breaking pack *and* by the fact that he was now on his own.

A sudden chill ran down Daimon's spine, his instincts screaming that something was off. The air around him seemed to pulse with tension, and just as the realization hit, Ethan whipped around with deadly precision, his bowstring already drawn. In a blur, the arrow sliced through the air straight toward the Alpha.

But Daimon's reflexes were honed beyond human capability. He twisted his body in a flash, dodging the arrow by mere inches. The sharp whistle of the arrow passed his ear, but he had no time to think—Ethan was already spinning his bike around, the wheels skidding in the snow as he aimed for another shot.

Daimon launched himself at a nearby tree, using its sturdy trunk as a springboard. The force of his leap was like a thunderclap, and before Ethan could even blink, Daimon was upon him. He crashed into Ethan with the full force of his body, sending the hunter and his bike careening across the ground. The bike collided with a fallen log, flipping over and crashing into the snow with a metallic clatter.

The Alpha tumbled through the snow, but his powerful paws dug into the earth, slowing his momentum. In one fluid motion, he was back on his paws, muscles coiled, eyes locked on Ethan. The hunter scrambled to stand, snow flying around him as he regained his footing. As Ethan rose, he drew his revolver with a quick, practised motion, his eyes narrowed in cold determination.

Daimon bared his teeth, a low growl rumbling in his chest. The standoff lasted only a heartbeat, but Ethan's little revolver wouldn't do him any favours; Daimon wouldn't give him a chance to aim. The Alpha burst to the left, and when Ethan fired, his bullet hit the tree Daimon just passed. The hunter fired again and again and again, but Daimon effortlessly dodged each bullet, and when he reached Ethan, he lunged at him—

Ethan's body suddenly transformed, and when Daimon collided with him, he found himself brawling with a beast his own size. It roared and hissed, managing to slam its huge paw against his muzzle in his moment of confusion, and when it went for his throat, he used his back leg to kick the striped creature's neck and backed off.

And then he saw what his target had become.

In Ethan's place stood a tiger just as big as him, its blue eyes shimmering in the dark as it glared right at him. Orange, white, and brown-striped fur, sharp and tall lynx-like ears, and a jaw full of teeth as sharp as Daimon's.

Ethan was a muto tigris.

And things just got a whole lot more complicated.

When Ethan roared ferociously, Daimon responded with a vicious snarl; his loathing for this man drastically increased, and he now felt even more protective of Jackson. He didn't want to let this creature near him—a creature that had long been rivals of wolf walkers. There was *no* way Ethan was going to accept Jackson.

↔ ≼ 13 ≽ ↔

They charged at each other, and the moment they clashed, the tiger went for Daimon's throat again—how predictable. Daimon slammed his paw against Ethan's face, sending him to the ground; he pinned the tiger before it could get up, but that was when he hesitated, keeping himself from sinking his teeth into the beast's throat. Muto or not, this was Jackson's friend—*this* was the target he needed to deliver to the Venaticus.

Ethan took Daimon's moment of hesitation to throw the Alpha off him, kicking him away with his back legs. Daimon's back hit a tree, and with a pained grunt, he landed on his stomach.

But he had to get up. The muto was coming.

Daimon got up in time to dodge Ethan's claws. He backed off with each of the tiger's swipes, calculating the brief moments between attacks, and after Ethan's next strike, the Alpha lunged forward and gripped the tiger's neck with his teeth.

The tiger yowled painfully and tried to pull away, but Daimon held his ground. He bit harder—but not hard enough to kill him—and tugged with each of Ethan's yanks. They fought in Daimon's lock for several moments; the tiger was getting weaker as Daimon injected his venom into its bloodstream and attempted to attack with its claws, but the Alpha avoided each swing. And finally, the muto's strength declined, and it collapsed under Daimon's bite.

Daimon released his jaws, and the tiger's head thumped against the snow. It groaned quietly as it slipped into unconsciousness, and when it was out, the Alpha snarled victoriously and shook his head, spraying the blood from his teeth.

He then roared fiercely at the muto's face, stomping his paws into the snow. The tiger's body morphed back into Ethan, who lay still and silent.

It was done, and now it was time for everyone to head back to the van.

Daimon lifted his head towards the sky and let out a loud, rumbling howl, letting his pack know to retreat. Once he was done, he shifted into his Prime form, picked Ethan up and threw him over his shoulder, and then he headed for the Venaticus van.

But as he raced through the woods, a sudden feeling of apprehension gripped him and constricted tighter and tighter with each step he took.

Something was wrong.

He focused on what his instincts were telling him, and the moment he realized that it was in fact his connection to Jackson that was warning him, his heart started racing, and his body was filled with dread.

Daimon wanted to call to him; he wanted to ask him what was going on, but Jackson didn't know how to communicate through their mated connection, so he wouldn't get an answer. The only way he'd know was if he got to him, and that was exactly what he was going to do. His mate was in trouble, and Jackson was more important to him than getting Ethan back to the van.

↔ ≼ 14 ≽ ↔

The Alpha changed his course. He veered left and followed Jackson's scent, racing through the murk as fast as he could with Ethan still over his shoulder. It was becoming harder for him to remain composed, though. His worry for Jackson grew heavier; he had no idea what was going on, but when he caught the rotting stench of cadejo, he became certain that he knew why his mate was in trouble.

"Alpha!" came Tokala's voice.

Daimon looked to his left, setting his sights on Tokala and the rest of his pack. If he was going to be able to help Jackson, he needed to make sure that his hands were free. So he skidded to a halt, and as his pack hurried over to him, he put Ethan down. "Tokala, Rachel, get Ethan back to the van. The rest of you, on me!" he ordered and then morphed into his normal wolf form as he started running again.

He moved as quickly as he could. The cadejo stench grew thicker once he passed the empty hunter camp, and when he focused the rest of his senses, he didn't only pick up the sound of two savage, snarling beasts…but he could also hear something else. Something humanoid.

Then he saw it.

The figure of what looked like a man slowly dragging his left foot through the snow while he groaned and growled.

Daimon slowed down in case the guy was a hunter, but he obviously heard some of his packmates treading in the snow and turned to face them.

That wasn't a man. Not a living one. The creature's face was pale and rotting, and through its torn clothes, Daimon could see its insides hanging out through several deep, wide slashes. It smelled just like a cadejo and possessed the same red eyes, too.

"A-Alpha…what the hell are we looking at?" Wesley breathed.

The creature suddenly snarled aggressively and charged towards them.

Daimon scowled and lunged at it; he clamped his jaws around its head before it could try to attack him, and when he tore it off, the creature's body didn't collapse. It kept moving towards his horrified pack, reaching its hands out as if it was trying to grab something.

The fact that it was still walking confirmed Daimon's suspicion—a suspicion he'd hoped was no more than that. But now it was a fact. That creature was infected with the same virus that was driving wolf walkers nearer to extinction.

With a furious growl, the Alpha launched himself at the headless corpse, pinned it on its front before it could reach his frozen, mortified pack, and plunged his jaws into its back. He tore its rotten heart out and chucked it into the murk, and then he turned around and kept running, his desperation to get to Jackson increasing. He could hear more of those undead humanoids, and among the snarls and growls, he heard voices.

Jackson's voice.

"Jackson!" he called.

It was hard to see through the thickening fog, but Daimon could make out the shadows of two wolves up ahead surrounded by human figures, and he was certain that those wolves were Jackson and Julian.

As his heart raced in his chest, Daimon burst through the darkness and into the midst of the corpse horde. He tore the head off the first zombie he saw, kicked a second one away, and hurried to Jackson's side.

"Daimon!" Jackson exclaimed with both relief and startle in his voice.

"They're coming from everywhere!" Julian cried.

"Go for their heads first!" Daimon called. "Don't let them get their arms around you!"

His pack immediately got to work and fought off the groaning, undead monsters, tearing them apart and avoiding their arms and teeth.

"Are you okay?" Daimon asked Jackson, and when Jackson nodded, the Alpha looked around for the guy who was supposed to be helping him. "Where's Sebastien?"

"I-I don't know, he was just…I…" Jackson answered, shaking his head and looking around.

There wasn't any time to look for him, and despite that his wolves were making quick work of the undead humanoids, the horde wasn't getting any thinner. He also spotted Lalo lying still in the snow, and the only way he could see getting everyone out alive was to run.

He scowled in frustration and told Jackson and Julian, "Stay behind me." He adorned his Prime form, picked Lalo up and held him over his right shoulder, and then called to his pack, "We're retreating! Make a hole together—Wesley, lead the way!"

Wesley finished executing the corpse beneath his paws, and with Brando and Enola at his side, he hurried over and started clearing a path through the horde in front of Daimon. The rest of his wolves helped, and once there was enough space, Daimon ran forward, and his pack quickly followed.

The Alpha used his free hand and all the force he could to shove away any corpse that came at him. His wolves tore apart whatever got too close, and once they were free of the horde, they raced back towards the van.

"Did you get Ethan?!" Jackson asked anxiously.

Daimon didn't want to overthink the fact that *his* mate seemed more concerned about a friend—a friend who had just tried to kill him. "Tokala and Rachel should be back at the van with him."

"What the hell were those things?!" Julian panicked.

"They looked like people!" Lance breathed.

"Humans?" Leon questioned.

"Let's focus on getting back to the van," Daimon called. The last thing any of them needed right now was to be distracted by questions that no one could answer.

But he couldn't help wondering: where the hell did those humanoid corpses come from? How long had the virus been infecting them? Did the Venaticus know? And what did all of this mean? Was it possible that the virus was progressing, and if so…how much worse was it going to get?

"How much further?" Ezhno asked from the back.

"What about Sebastien?" Jackson then asked him.

But Daimon didn't answer. He heard them, but he was also hearing something else. The horde they'd left behind was catching up; somehow, those corpses that had once been people were catching up to a pack of *running* wolf walkers. "We need to pick up the pace," he called.

Everyone ran faster, following him through the woods, and after a few more moments, he spotted the van headlights.

"There!" Brando announced.

The pack rushed towards the light, and when they got to the van, Tokala and Rachel—in their human forms—pulled the back doors open for them.

"Everyone, get in!" Daimon ordered, handing Lalo to Tokala.

Each wolf morphed into their human form and climbed into the van, and once Daimon was inside, he pulled the doors shut.

"What are you waiting for?!" Tokala exclaimed, leaning past the passenger seat so he could look at the driver.

"Where's Sebastien?" the man asked.

Daimon shouted, "We lost him in the woods—he'll find his way back—"

"Did he tell you that?"

"Just go!" Tokala insisted.

"I can't leave without him!" the driver insisted angrily.

Daimon focused on the noise outside the van for a moment.

The undead were getting closer.

He snarled angrily and stormed to the front of the van. He reached around and gripped the driver's collar. "Either drive us the fuck out of here or I'll throw you out the fucking window and drive myself!"

With a nervous nod and terrified expression, the man twisted the keys and started the engine.

Daimon turned around, but before he could get back to his seat beside Jackson, he heard a ferocious roar and the driver shriek—

The van jolted, its tyres squealed as it skidded on the road, and Daimon was thrown to the side when the vehicle tipped and rolled.

Everyone shrieked and yelled in horror as they were chucked around inside. The glass smashed, the engine sputtered, and when the van landed on its roof, the sound of the incoming horde grew closer and closer.

A sharp, searing pain spiralled up Daimon's spine, forcing a tortured grunt from his lips. His muscles locked up, his body refusing to respond; whether it was the throbbing agony in his back or the weight of his packmates pressing down on him, he couldn't tell. He felt trapped, pinned by both the ache and bodies around him.

From his limited vantage point, he could see out of the open back left door, and what he saw sent a cold wave of terror crashing through him. A swarm of at least a hundred corpses was surging toward the van, their dead eyes fixed on them with relentless hunger. His heart pounded in his chest, each beat drumming louder than the last as the horde closed in, and for the first time in a long while, true fear gripped his heart.

How the hell were they going to get away now?

Chapter Two

⌐ ≼ ☽ ≽ ⌐

Retreat

| **Jackson** |

The smell of ash and blood filled Jackson's nostrils. His ears were ringing, and the world was spinning. He opened his eyes, and although his vision was a little blurred, he could make out the faces of the people lying around him. His packmates grunted and groaned, gripping their heads as they slowly sat up. Jackson's first thought was Daimon, but in his search for the Alpha, his eyes instead located the incoming horde.

Fear ensnared him like a starved snake, constricting tighter and tighter as each second raced by. There were too many of them, and the swarm wasn't just made up of humanoid zombies, but of cadejo, too. And they were coming in *fast*.

"Daimon!" he called, but when he tried to get up, pain shot through his leg, and he grunted in startle. He looked down and saw a large shard of glass sticking out of his ankle and a puddle of blood at his foot.

"Jackson," came Tokala's voice. "Are you all right?"

Jackson looked at the orange-haired man, who just helped Rachel and Dustu sit up. "Y-yeah, I..." he answered but then shifted his sights to the horde. "W-we gotta go!"

Tokala looked over his shoulder and out the open van door. "Holy fucking sh—"

"Alpha!" Lance called in a panic.

Jackson saw Lance trying to help Daimon up. With an irritated grunt, he pulled the glass from his ankle and moved past the recovering pack, trying to get to Daimon. But that was when he saw Ethan. His best friend lay unconscious close to the doors; his wrists and legs were bound in rope, and there was a small cut on his forehead.

No one was helping him. Why would they? He was just the target.

Lance and Bly tried to help Daimon sit, but the Alpha *whined* in agony as they moved his body.

"Put him back down!" Tokala exclaimed, hurrying over there.

"They're getting closer!" Julian called, pointing out the open door. "What the fuck are we supposed to do?!"

"Calm down!" Alastor snapped.

"Oh, shit... guys," Wesley stammered.

Jackson was about to head over to Ethan, but when everyone started gasping and panicking, he looked at Daimon again. Wesley had moved the Alpha onto his side, revealing the hilt of a dagger sticking out of his back... and the blade could only be inside.

"D-Daimon?!" Jackson exclaimed in horror, desperately pushing past his packmates to get to his mate. "W-what happened?!"

No one answered him.

"Don't move him!" Bly said, pulling Lance away before he could try to move the Alpha. "If we don't pull that out properly, he could be and remain paralysed."

"Then what the hell are we supposed to do?!" Julian shrieked, waving their hand out at the horde, which was mere moments away. "Sit around in here and wait to be eaten?!"

What *were* they supposed to do? A cold sweat spiralled through Jackson as he watched the blood ooze from Daimon's back while Bly and Lance argued about what they should do about the blade. How the hell did it happen? A part of him wanted to suspect that someone had left a knife out or one had come flying from somewhere when the van flipped... but he knew that wasn't it. His instincts told him that someone did this on purpose—someone *stabbed* Daimon... but who?

Jackson frantically glanced around as his breaths became stifled. If Caius or Nyssa were there, then he'd *know* that it was one of them, but there wasn't anyone around him who would want to do this to Daimon.

He looked down at his mate, his heart racing. Was Daimon going to be okay? They'd be able to help him, right? He'd heal—he *had* to heal!

"Is he gonna be okay?!" Jackson begged Bly.

She stuttered, looking overwhelmed. "I-I—"

Tokala shook his head and held up his hand, silencing everyone. "Someone help me pull this door shut—now!"

Jackson took his eyes off Daimon and hurried to the door with Brando and Alastor, gripped one of the two handles, and as he prepared to pull, he stared in horror at the tsunami of corpses. Where the hell had they all come from? There were too many for the pack to handle—what the fuck were they going to do?!

"In three," Tokala said. "One, two, three!"

They all pulled on the door, forcing it back into shape as they heaved it shut.

Jackson tried his best to keep as calm as he could; there were already too many of his packmates freaking out. "What about the windshield?" he asked, looking at it.

Tokala moved past everyone and grabbed one of the pistols which must have fallen out of someone's bag. "We'll kill whatever crawls in, and enough of their dead bodies will block access."

"And then what?" Leon asked. "W-we just…we just sit in here and wait for them to tear the van apart and pluck us out like worms in a log?!"

The Zeta didn't seem to have an answer.

But then Daimon grunted and panted. "The…the d-driver."

"Don't talk," Jackson murmured worriedly, placing his hand on the side of Daimon's face.

Everyone looked around for the driver.

Something hit the van. Something *scraped* at the metal and thumped the outside walls.

Savage growls and pained groans began surrounding them.

And an undead humanoid stumbled in front of the vehicle and started crawling in through the broken window.

Without a moment's hesitation—and as if this wasn't his first time using a gun—Tokala shot the creature's head, and when it flinched violently, exposing its chest, Tokala shot its heart, and it fell silent. "Four of you, get up here and help me," the orange-haired man commanded. "Jackson, do you see the driver?"

Jackson looked around, but there was no sign of—

Horrified screaming came from outside the van. Something hit the snow with a thud, and then several savage roars accompanied the sound of tearing, oozing flesh.

"I…think *that* was our driver," Jackson shivered.

Daimon then grunted and coughed. "Ch-check…the dashboard."

"Fuck," Wesley uttered through gritted teeth as two zombies crawled in through the windows.

Tokala's group shot them, and once they were down, the Zeta moved closer to the front seats and searched around. It looked like he found something, and as he reached for it, a snarling, hissing cadejo burst in through the window beside him— "Shit!" he shouted as several of the pack whimpered in fear.

Wesley and Brando unloaded several bullets into it as Tokala kicked its face, and after a few more shots, the monster whined and backed off.

Tokala quickly returned to the back of the van, and as he did, Jackson watched as a thick sea of humanoid and wolf legs flooded the view through the windows.

They were surrounded…and the ocean of corpses was probably growing thicker and thicker by the second. How the hell were they going to get out of this?

"Chief," Tokala said. "You think we can call for backup?"

Jackson turned to face the Zeta, and when he saw that he was holding a radio, a slither of hope struck him. "Here," he said desperately, moving over to Tokala. "I can probably work out how to use it."

Tokala handed him the radio.

Jackson desperately switched it on as Wesley, Brando, and Enola shot at the corpses trying to crawl past the lifeless bodies which were starting to block the windows, just as Tokala said they would.

The radio clicked and made a static noise.

Jackson pulled it to his face. "Hello?" he asked, holding down the broadcast button. "Is anyone there? Hello?!"

The radio beeped. "*Uh... this is Silverlake Home receiving. Who is this? Over.*"

"Oh, thank God," Jackson breathed as several other relieved murmurs came from his packmates. "Uh, this is the, uh...the group that Lord Caedis sent out! We need—"

"*Uh, please specify via codename, sir. We have too many groups in the field to—*"

"The group with Sebastien!"

The guy on the other end went quiet, and the corpses outside began banging so fiercely against the walls that the van shook.

"Hello?" Jackson pleaded.

"*If Officer Huxley is present, please pass the—*"

"He's not here! We got attacked by a swarm of zombies and we need backup!" Jackson interjected. "They're everywhere!"

"*Where is Officer Huxley? Over.*"

"We lost him in the woods. Can you send help?!" he exclaimed, almost shouting into the radio.

"*Uh, that's a negative on that. We can't authorize anything without command from Officer—*"

"*Give me the fucking thing,*" came Heir Lucian's voice, and after the sound of a grunt, a struggle, and disapproving mumbles, he spoke to Jackson. "*What's your location? Are you in the van?*"

"U-uh, yeah, but it's flipped over, and we're surrounded," he answered.

Something *huge* then collided with the van, and as everyone screamed and yelled, the vehicle skidded across the ground and hit something else.

"What the fuck was that?!" Ezhno called.

"We can't get out!" Jackson told Heir Lucian.

"*All right, I'm sending over reinforcements now. Do you have the target?*"

Jackson glanced at Ethan, who was still unconscious by the closed doors. "Yeah, he's here."

"*You get anything out of him?*"

"No, we were attacked before we could."

"*They'll be with you soon. Do whatever they tell you and don't try to defer. Understand?*"

"Y-yeah, we got it."

The radio then beeped and went silent.

For a moment, Jackson stood there and stared at it, expecting to hear something else. But that was it.

"How long are they gonna be?" Julian asked desperately.

"I don't know how much longer we can leave this in his back," Bly called, shaking her head as she stared at the blade in Daimon's back. "Alpha, are you still with me?" she asked, looking down at him.

Jackson looked at him, too, and watched him nod with a pained grimace on his face.

Something collided with the van again, and again, and again, like it was bashing its head against the side in an attempt to break it open. And then a creature started clawing at one of the doors like a cat. The bodies blocking the windows were shifting, and when one of them was yanked out, a seething, snarling cadejo burrowed through and tried getting inside.

"Tokala!" Brando called as he and the others shot the beast.

"Keep shooting!" Tokala said as he crouched beside Daimon. "Alpha?" he asked.

Daimon grunted in response.

"Help's on the way, okay?"

Jackson kneeled beside Daimon, but when he saw the puddle of blood beneath him, he scowled in dismay and gently took hold of the Alpha's hand. "Daimon?"

The Alpha opened his eyes to look at him.

"It's gonna be okay," he told him. "They're sending help."

But Daimon didn't grip his hand in return. In fact, for the first time ever, the Alpha's skin felt cold to the touch, and Jackson didn't understand why—he didn't want to *know* why. He just wanted to focus on the fact that Heir Lucian had sent help. But the suspicion that someone had done this to Daimon purposely crept back into his mind. He couldn't help but glance around and eye his packmates closely, but he felt wrong searching them all for signs of guilt. Why would they hurt their Alpha?

He glanced at Julian. Would they...?

No. He shook his head and focused on Daimon. "I'm right here," he told him, moving as closely as he could without touching his body. He didn't want to risk hurting him more. "They're gonna get here, and then we're—"

The creature outside crashed into the van again; the pack yelled fearfully, and Daimon groaned in pain as everyone was abruptly flung around. Whatever was doing this started *pushing*, and the left wall began bending around the tree that it was stuck against.

"We're gonna die in here!" Julian panicked, backing into a corner. "We're all gonna die!"

"Shut up!" Wesley yelled.

"Calm down!" Tokala ordered.

But Julian kept panicking. "They're gonna get in here! They're getting in!" they cried as Wesley and Brando kept shooting the cadejo trying to get inside the van.

"Shut up!" Dustu insisted, gripping a fistful of his hair as he gritted his teeth and looked around frantically.

Jackson's heart was racing. His fear was increasing as he watched everyone panic in their own way. The creature was still banging, the van was bending, and now another cadejo was trying to burrow in through the dead corpses.

But then he heard Daimon mumble something. He didn't catch it, so he looked down at him and frowned. "Daimon?"

The Alpha's eyes were closed, he looked paler than he did a minute ago, and his jaw was moving as though he was trying to say something. "I…I can't…" he whispered, his voice breaking.

"You can't…what?" Jackson asked anxiously.

"Can't…breathe."

Terror struck Jackson. "C-can't you do anything?!" he exclaimed, looking at Bly. "Help him!"

She shook her head and stammered, "I-I can't risk it! If I pull this out wrong, it could kill him or paralyse him for life! I'm not going to—"

"He can't breathe!" Jackson insisted as Daimon started suffocating.

"Alpha," Bly said firmly, moving closer to his head. "I'm going to move you a little so it's easier to breathe, okay?"

Daimon grunted in response, gritting his bloody teeth, and when Bly gently adjusted his head and pushed his body so that it was slightly titled, Daimon choked and gagged. Blood sprayed from his mouth, splattering all over Jackson's trousers, and then he groaned painfully.

"W-what did you do?!" Jackson snapped worriedly, tightening his grip on Daimon's hand…and this time, he felt the Alpha grip back. He took his eyes off Bly—her reply drowned out when his terror was pushed aside by relief—and he stared at Daimon's face. "Daimon?"

The Alpha slowly moved his eyes until they locked with Jackson's. "Don't…don't leave me," he breathed.

Jackson frowned in confusion and shook his head. "I…. Why would I leave you, Daimon?" But that probably wasn't what the Alpha needed to hear right now—that *wasn't* what Jackson wanted to say. "I love you. I'm not going anywhere, ever. I promise. Just…hold on, okay? They're coming."

"Ethan," the Alpha said through gritted teeth. "He…he's…." He exhaled shakily, and when he grimaced, blood sept from his mouth again.

"Why is there blood coming from his mouth?" Jackson questioned desperately, looking at Bly and Lance.

Bly frowned and said, "I-I don't know, I can't tell until I can get a better look at him, but—"

"Jackson," Daimon pleaded.

Jackson stopped listening to Bly and stared at the Alpha.

Daimon scowled painfully as he grunted, "Your friend, I... *know*... what... what he—"

The banging creature smashed into the van once more time, and the wall behind Jackson gave way. As the metal split and the tree trunk cut inside like a blade into flesh, Jackson was launched forward, and all he heard when he hit the floor were screams, snarls, gunfire, and a horrific roar.

But there was something else. A thumping sound grew nearer and nearer. At first, it sounded like a creature running through the snow at lightning speed—either that or it had a dozen legs—but once the disorientation he received as a result of his collision with yet another wall, Jackson was sure that the noise was helicopter blades.

Helicopters.

The sound was over them in seconds, and among the confused voices of his packmates, he heard soldiers barking orders at one another... and deafening gunfire.

"*Jackson,*" came Heir Lucian's static voice. "*Hello?*"

Jackson shook his head and scrambled over to Tokala, who handed him the radio. "Y-yeah!" he spoke into it.

"*You're gonna feel a bit of a jolt, so tell your friends to hold on to whatever they can.*"

There wasn't any time to ask questions. The second Heir Lucian finished talking, the sound of something metal wrapping around the van sliced through the commotion. Then, what sounded like a wire tightened, and the van started shifting.

"What's going on?!" Julian demanded.

"We're moving?" Leon questioned as he gripped one of the handlebars.

"Everyone, grab on to something!" Tokala called. "Bly, Lance, make sure the chief's secure."

They did as they were told and gripped whatever they could, and when the corpses started slipping out the windows, Jackson looked outside. The helicopter was lifting them away, and below, at least *fifty* soldiers were fighting off the horde.

He looked down at Daimon. "It's gonna be okay, just hold on." Then, he glanced at Ethan, who Tokala was holding down to keep him from slipping as the van moved.

Everything *was* going to be okay, wasn't it? They'd get back to the Venaticus and they'd help Daimon, right? They *had* to.

He couldn't lose Daimon; if he died because of this stupid mission—if he died because of Jackson's selfish need to find Ethan—then not only would he never forgive himself, but he also felt like he'd have nothing left to fight for.

⇝ ≼ 25 ≽ ⇜

He couldn't go back to New Dawnward; his life was *here* with Daimon. And if he lost him, what more did he have?

Chapter Three

⌐ ≼ ☽ ≽ ⌐

Humanoids

| Sebastien, during the retreat |

Sebastien watched while Jackson and Julian helped Lalo out of his cage. Once the three of them joined him, he hastily led the way out of the hunter camp and into the trees. All they had to do now was get back to the van and wait for the rest of the wolf walker pack to join them. He just hoped that Daimon managed to capture Ethan.

"Are we heading back to the van?" Julian called from behind.

"That's where your Alpha told us to regroup, so yeah," Sebastien answered, glancing back at them.

But his eyes shifted from Julian to Lalo. The brown-furred wolf was limping and struggling to keep up with them.

"We need to slow down," Jackson said and then looked back at Lalo. "Are you okay?"

Sebastien sighed to himself and rolled his eyes. But he couldn't sense any incoming danger, so he slowed down enough for Lalo to keep up.

Lalo panted as he responded to Jackson, "Y-yeah... just... been stuck in that cage a while. S-so... what's going on here?"

"It's a long story," Jackson answered. "But the short version is that we made a deal with the Venaticus, and in exchange for whatever we want, we need to help them find a laboratory."

Sebastion felt a little disgruntled. He wished he'd been as cautious as Jackson when he signed *his* deal with Lord Caedis. Now, he was paying the price for being an idiot... but at least he got what he asked for. Being stuck working for a demon god wasn't *so* bad, but it was at times like these that he found himself wondering why he was there. He was a creature that could communicate with phantoms and spirits, not some chaperone.

"Do you need to stop?" Julian asked Lalo.

Sebastien snapped out of his thoughts. "No stopping. We keep going."

"We need to stop," Jackson insisted, slowing down.

Sebastien snarled irritably. He just wanted to get back to the van, but clearly, things weren't going to go as smoothly as he wanted. He slowed when the others did, and while he turned back and moved over to where they were, he said, "We can't hang around out here. Some of those hunters could come back."

As he wheezed and collapsed, Lalo shook his head. "N-no. If... if they're herding, n-no one's getting away. Alpha... Daimon's herding technique, it's... it's perfect."

"Are you all right?" Julian asked worriedly. "You... don't look too good."

Lalo huffed and puffed as he rested his head on his paws. "I just... need a minute, that's all."

Sebastien looked around cautiously. A minute could be all it took for something he couldn't detect to pounce out of the fog; he might not be able to smell or hear anything rotting coming their way, but he'd seen enough surprises to be so naïve as to think that everything was going to be fine.

And there it was. That rotting, disgusting stench.

"Shit," he growled, setting his sights on Jackson, Julian, and Lalo. "We need to move *now*!"

Lalo tried getting up as everyone prepared to run, but he fell again.

Sebastien growled angrily, "We have to leave him." There was no other way. He wasn't going to risk losing a valuable asset because of some weak wolf.

"What?!" Jackson exclaimed. "We're not leaving—"

"Oh, for fuck's sake!" Sebastien yelled. He moved closer and stood in front of Lalo. There wasn't any time to argue, and if Jackson wouldn't leave without this guy, then he'd have to do something he vowed *never* to do in front of people. "Shift back," he told Lalo.

"W-wh—"

"Shift back!"

Lalo groaned and did as he was told. He shifted into his human form.

Sebastien crouched down and ignored the feeling of embarrassment that was beginning to consume him. "Get him on my back."

Jackson and Julian helped Lalo climb onto his back, and once he was securely between Sebastien's wings, Sebastien got up and started running.

But the rotting stench was closing in on them. Sebastien tried picking up the pace, attempting to outrun the cadejo on his trail, but he could hear the savage snarls and pounding footsteps. Whatever was coming was *big*, and as much as he wanted to get back to the van, he couldn't risk their only transport back to Silverlake—he had to ensure that *Jackson* got back to the Venaticus.

He stretched out his wings, but before he could take off and grab Jackson, something huge burst out of the fog and smashed into him, throwing Lalo off his back as the force of the collision sent him tumbling across the snow and away from Jackson.

With a pained grunt, he hit a tree, but before he could even try to get up, the creature which threw him off course sunk its teeth into his front leg and threw him through the air.

Sebastien yelled painfully as the monster's venom entered his bloodstream, ensnaring him in agony. He hit the ground, tumbled through the snow, and came to a halt after rolling through some brush.

Thumping footsteps were coming his way.

Despite the burning, throbbing pain, he grunted and climbed to his paws. He turned to face his incoming enemy, and it was unlike anything he'd seen before. It looked like a bear with a wolf's head, and just like the cadejo, it was rotten and missing huge chunks of flesh, exposing its bones and organs.

The creature was charging at him faster than any other cadejo he'd faced, and the sounds it made were distorted and similar to those of a bear. But whatever the hell it was, Sebastien was going to have to fight and kill it. He couldn't risk it getting anywhere near Jackson or Ethan.

When the creature reached him, Sebastien used his wings to propel himself up, and as the beast skidded in the snow and tried to turn around, he descended and dug his claws into its back. Before he could try to lift it, though, it reached its head back, gripped his left wing with its teeth, and pulled him off.

Sebastien yelped but recovered the moment he hit the ground. He got back up, turned to face his foe, and dodged its charge; he swiftly swung his right wing around and sliced the beast's side with his carpal spike. The creature shrieked and howled as its body tore, and when it abruptly turned to face and try to attack Sebastien, he pulled his carpal from the monster's flesh and leapt onto a nearby tree. He dug his claws into the bark, enabling himself to grip the tree and remain there while the rotting bear-wolf tried to reach him.

But something else snatched Sebastien's attention. A flurry of dark blurs was moving through the fog below, and the longer he focused, the clearer they became, and he wasn't sure what to make of it.

They were *people*. Groaning, stumbling human figures shifted through the murk; some of them were missing limbs… and he spotted one of them with its insides hanging out through its stomach.

And they were heading in Jackson's direction.

Sebastien snarled in frustration. He needed a little longer for his wounds to heal, but he couldn't risk the Venaticus' asset. He looked down at the bear-wolf, which was trying to climb up to him, but its huge, heavy body wouldn't let it get further than a few inches off the ground. Then, he glanced at each tree around him. Flying wasn't an option with his injured wing, so he was going to have to use the trees.

He took a deep breath, set his eyes on his target, and jumped. When he reached the first tree and dug his claws into it, his healing wounds tore a little, but he didn't care. He had to get to Jackson before the swarm of disfigured humanoids. So, he jumped again, and again, and again, and when he reached a tree right on the edge of the horde, his nostrils were filled with the rotting, sickening stench of cadejo.

Confusion ensnared him as he set his eyes on one of the people below, and it turned out that that swarm he was looking at wasn't of people at all... but of *undead* humanoids. Their skin was dark and peeling, their eyes were as red as blood, and they walked in the same strange way that cadejo did.

His greatest fear had come to pass. The cadejo virus was evolving; what he was seeing was evidence enough that it had spread to humans. It had grown beyond the sickness he'd witnessed ravage an entire town two hundred years ago and was somehow turning people into the same undead monsters it was turning wolf walkers into.

He had to get back to Lord Caedis. He had to tell him about this before it was too late.

But what about Jackson? What about Ethan?

Sebastien scowled as he watched the humanoid horde move through the forest. Where *was* Jackson? He looked around frantically, but there was no sign of him or anyone else. He was quite sure that the bear-wolf hadn't dragged him too far away from where he'd left Jackson, especially not far enough that he wouldn't be able to see him from up here.

He concentrated his senses. The only life force he could detect was at least a mile away and getting further with each second. Could that be them? He stretched out his injured wing and checked on his wound. It was still healing, but he was sure he could fly now. So he extended both his wings, and as he pushed himself off his perch, he curved his body upwards and began gliding towards the sky.

Once he broke through the treetops, he followed the life force he'd locked onto, but the chorus of painful groans and gurgles sent a chill down his spine. He looked down at the horde; there had to be hundreds of them. Where did they all come from? How long had the virus been affecting more than just wolf walkers?

Something else cut through the sound of the swarm. Helicopter blades rumbled through the clouds, and when Sebastien stared in the sound's direction, he spotted a trio of Venaticus birds. Someone called for backup, which had to mean Jackson was in trouble.

Sebastien flapped his wings harder, picking up his pace. But when he saw the helicopters stop, he watched two of them drop troops and the other lowering its cargo hooks. In a matter of moments, the helicopter lifted the battered, upside-down Venaticus van, and started heading back the way the birds had come. The life force Sebastien was following moved with the chopper, so he felt it was safe to assume that Jackson was inside.

Since Jackson was on his way back to base, Sebastien would make himself useful. He descended and landed beneath the troop helicopters and joined the soldiers who were trying to destroy the swarm of infected humanoids *and* cadejo.

He spat blue flames and cut down as many of the corpses as he could, assisting the Venaticus troops.

"It's Officer Huxley!" one of the soldiers called.

The commander hurried over to Sebastien. "Sir, we're here to extract you."

But somebody then screamed painfully, and Sebastien turned his head and set his eyes on one of the soldiers; a humanoid corpse had sunk its teeth into his arm and tore away a huge chunk of his flesh. One of his comrades shot the creature's head and then plunged his bayonet into its chest, freeing the bitten man, who fell to his knees, gripping his bleeding arm.

"We need a medic!" the other guy called.

But if these humanoids were infected with the cadejo virus as Sebastien suspected, then no medic was going to be able to do anything.

Sebastien sliced the corpse in front of him in half and then hurried over to the wounded soldier. Before the medic could try to tend to his wound, Sebastien mercilessly forced his wing carpal into the bitten man's chest and tore out his heart.

"What the bloody hell did you do that for!?" the medic yelled.

"We don't know what the fuck these things are," Sebastien called, "and the last thing I'm going to do is risk something spreading back in Silverlake!"

Every soldier who heard him stopped shooting and started glancing at the humanoid creatures.

"Whatever infected them could infect others," Sebastien called. "We need to get the hell out of here and get this news back to Lord Caedis."

"On me!" the commander called, and then he began slowly retreating towards the helicopter ropes.

Sebastien took out the corpses which lunged and tried to attack the troops, and once all the soldiers were safely off the ground, Sebastien took off and flew up into one of the helicopters. The moment he morphed into his human form, he made his way over to the commander. "Did Jackson get out?" he asked desperately.

"Yes, sir," the commander confirmed. "His pack and the target were extracted when we arrived. They're headed back to base now, perhaps fifteen minutes ahead of us."

"Good, good," he breathed, relieved. "I'm sorry about your man. We can't risk something like that getting back to the city," he said, looking out through the window at what was left of the humanoid swarm in the forest.

"What were those things, sir?" one of the other soldiers asked.

Sebastien glanced back at him. "I'm not entirely sure, but from what I saw, they looked like they were infected with the same virus that's been infecting wolf walkers. Before now, all this virus did to people was make them sick and die, but now it looks like all of that is changing." He looked around at the soldiers. "Did any of you get a close look at them? Did you notice anything that might tell us who they were or where they came from?"

No one spoke up. They all shook their heads and looked utterly horrified.

"So...if *we* get bit, we'll turn into one of those...*things*?" one of them asked.

"We don't know for sure," the commander said before Sebastien could speak. "The best thing to do is get back to base and inform Lord Caedis."

"Well, of course *you'd* say that," the medic said, glaring at the commander. "You're a *demon*. You don't have to worry like the rest of us little humans."

"Hey!" Sebastien snapped before things could escalate. "Like he just said, we don't know anything yet. The only thing we *do* know is that we need to relay this information. You're all going to be debriefed, so sit there and make sure you're ready for that. And you," he said, looking at the medic, "demon or human, you're Venaticus. Lord Caedis *and* the Zenith will do whatever they can to protect *all* of us. Our greatest strength right now is the fact that we're united. Let's not lose that, all right?"

Although the medic looked aggravated, he nodded and calmed down.

"You got a radio? I need to speak to the wolf walkers," Sebastien asked the commander.

The man nodded and handed him a radio.

Sebastien held it to his face. "Jackson?" he asked. "Are you there?"

The radio beeped and cracked. "*Sebastien?*" came Jackson's voice.

Relief flooded through him. "Thank fucking God. Is everyone okay?"

"*Y-yeah—well, no. Daimon's hurt; he's paralyzed—*"

"Paralyzed?"

"*W-we don't know if he's gonna make it back to base,*" Jackson replied, his voice breaking.

Sebastien's heart beat a little faster. They *needed* Daimon for all of this to work out. But the guy was an Alpha—a *Prime*. He'd make it...right? He sighed and tried to keep himself from freaking out. "What about Ethan? Did you get him?"

"*I...yeah, Daimon got him.*"

"Good. I'll see you back at base." He handed the radio back to the commander. "Thanks."

"What do we do about those corpses, sir?" the man asked, nodding out the helicopter window.

"Nothing as of yet. Lord Caedis will tell us what to do when we relay the information. Silverlake's defences are in place if anything comes so much as five miles in range."

The commander nodded. "Yes, sir."

"I need to sit my ass down and rest. I'll be over there if you need me," he said, gesturing to an empty seat. Then, he headed over to it and sat down.

What he'd seen tonight reminded him of the time he'd first ever laid eyes on a creature infected with the cadejo virus. Up until now, he'd been sure that the virus didn't turn humans, and if he was wrong about that, then what else was going to change? Would it evolve to infect demons? Would it soon become unstoppable? Would it become something that even Lord Caedis and the Zenith couldn't deal with?

He shook his head. No. He'd seen those two men conquer much worse than a virus. But… what if the virus mutated into something that could affect even them?

Chapter Four

Debrief

| Jackson |

Jackson held Daimon's hand, trying his best to stay composed. But the Alpha's blood covered most of the floor, and there was no way to tell whether they were close to Silverlake or still in the middle of the forest. He glanced around the van, and the harrowing suspicion that someone had stabbed the Alpha on purpose lingered in the back of his mind. His eyes fixed on Julian again; he wanted to trust them, but what if he'd got it wrong? What if Julian was still Kane's wolf? What if they'd been sent to gain Daimon's trust…and then kill him?

Daimon grunted weakly.

"Daimon?" Jackson asked shakily as he looked down at him; he watched the Alpha's eyes close. "You have to stay awake," he insisted.

Daimon groaned painfully in response.

"Can't we do anything?" Jackson pleaded, looking at Bly.

She shook her head. "The best we can do is hold him on his side like this until we get back to the Venaticus. They're going to need to have everything ready for surgery."

"Can you get that Lucian guy again?" Tokala asked, holding the radio out to Jackson. "Tell him what's going on."

Jackson nodded as he took the radio. He held it to his face and pressed the button on the side. "Uh…hello? Heir Lucian?"

There was no reply.

"Hello?!"

"*Yeah, I'm here. What is it?*" Heir Lucian replied.

"Uh…i-it's Daimon. When we crashed, a knife…impaled his back. Our Theta says he's gonna need surgery. Can you—"

"*We've got a med team standing by already. Can you tell me more about his injury so the team can be better prepared?*"

Jackson looked at Bly.

She took the radio from him. "From what I can see, there's a dagger through his lumbar region. He can't move and he's losing a lot of blood. If he's not in surgery in the next few minutes, he might bleed out," she explained quickly, shaking her head.

Her words struck Jackson with horror. A *few* minutes? Were they going to make it? He couldn't lose Daimon—not now. Not because of *this*. Not because he'd dragged him and his pack out here on some stupid mission to find *his* friend.

"*All right, we've got a neurologist on site. You're just a few moments out, so I'll see you all for debriefing soon,*" Lucian said as Bly handed the radio back to Jackson.

But Jackson didn't say anything else to him. He put the radio down and moved his free hand over his other one, which he was still holding onto Daimon's hand with. "It's gonna be okay," he told the Alpha quietly. "We're almost there."

It *would* be okay, right? Daimon was strong—he was an *Alpha*. He had to hold on. He *had* to make it. It was only a few more moments.

The van began descending; it felt a lot like an elevator moving to a lower floor, and when they landed, the van shook a little, and something clanged above them.

Several voices broke through the sound of the helicopter blades. Tokala and Wesley moved over to the back doors to push them open, but just as they reached them, the doors opened from the outside, and several soldiers peered in at everyone.

"There!" a woman in a white coat called, pointing at Daimon. "Get him on the stretcher."

Two men hurried into the van; they ushered everyone away from Daimon, and then they carefully picked the Alpha up and placed him on the stretcher.

"I wanna go with him!" Jackson insisted.

But that was when Sebastien appeared. He stood in front of the doors and set his eyes on Jackson. "You're coming with me." He looked down at Ethan, who was still unconscious. "Get him into an interrogation room."

"Wait!" Jackson insisted, trying to reach Ethan as a man picked him up and threw him over his shoulder.

But Sebastien grabbed his arm and stopped him from following. "You'll get to see your friend later. You're needed for debriefing."

Jackson stood there and watched the medical team carry Daimon inside the double doors at the end of the helipad, and then he looked at the man carrying Ethan. *He* went through a different pair of doors, taking away Jackson's best friend before he'd even had a chance to talk to him.

"The rest of you will follow Commander Frances here," Sebastien instructed. "He'll take you down to a room we've prepared for you all to clean up and rest in."

Tokala stepped forward. "Don't you need us for debriefing, too?"

"Yeah. You'll be summoned one by one. For now, go rest."

"What about our Alpha?" Alastor asked. "Is he going to be okay?"

"Can we see him?" Wesley asked.

"Yeah, isn't there a waiting room?" Bly asked.

Sebastien opened his mouth to speak—

"Lalo needs help, too!" Julian announced.

Everyone stepped aside, revealing Julian and Lalo. Lalo lay on the floor, panting and struggling to breathe.

Jackson felt anger building up inside him when he set his eyes on Julian once again. He wasn't sure whether they were genuinely concerned for Lalo or if it was all some act, a ploy to keep the pack from suspecting that they'd stabbed Daimon. But Jackson wasn't going to let his guard down. He *knew* that someone stabbed his mate, and he was going to do whatever he had to to prove it.

With a quiet sigh, Sebastien looked at Commander Frances. "Make sure that guy gets down to medical," he said, pointing at Lalo.

"Yes, sir," the commander said.

Sebastien then pulled Jackson with him as he headed across the helipad. "Don't worry, all right? Your Alpha will be fine. We've got the best medical team anywhere else in the world."

"Why can't I just...go with him? You can debrief me after," Jackson complained sullenly as Sebastien led him through the double doors and down a wide, white, empty hallway.

"You can't watch a surgery, kid. You can go to the waiting room after we're done with Heir Lucian and Lord Caedis, though."

Jackson kept a despondent frown as he followed Sebastien into an elevator, and when Sebastien let go of him, Jackson crossed his arms. His heart was beating *hard*; he wanted to believe what Sebastien told him, but knowing that Daimon was moments away from bleeding out horrified him—it made him want to *scream*. All he wanted to do was be with him; he wanted to *see* him. But he wasn't going to get to do that for a while, was he?

He turned his head to look at Sebastien. "Can I just...see him for a sec, *please*?"

Sebastien sighed and looked at him. "Look, kid. He's going to be fine. The surgeons here have saved me from much worse than a knife in the back, all right? I promise you. Now, just focus on what you're gonna tell the boss man."

Jackson wanted to share his suspicion about Julian and the knife, but what did he mean by what he just said? He frowned and asked, "What do you mean?"

"We saw some weird shit tonight, man. I'm gonna warn you now, Lord Caedis might flip a table or something."

His frown thickened. "What...you...you mean the people zombies?"

He nodded. "As far as we knew, the cadejo virus couldn't turn humans or humanoids into undead. A mature demon's immune system fights the virus off, and it just kills humans. But as far as the human fact goes, it seems like shit's changing."

Jackson took a moment to absorb it, and when the elevator arrived, he followed Sebastien out. "Wait, so... if a demon's immune system fights the virus off, why not just use whatever part of a demon does that to manufacture a cure?"

"Do you think we haven't tried that?" Sebastien mumbled.

"What... happened?"

"Humans and demons don't go together unless they're born a cambion. You can't just... *make* a human-demon hybrid out of a human that's already walking around. All the attempts our scientists made ended up in death or Neophytes, and some of those deaths were really gnarly, man," he mumbled, heading through the offices and towards Lucian's corner office. "No, this whole thing started with wolf walkers, and that's how it's gonna end."

Sebastien pushed the office door open.

Jackson immediately set his eyes on Lord Caedis, who was sitting on the black leather couch by the window. Then, he looked at Lucian, who just stood up from his chair and made his way over to the couch.

"'Ow are your vounds?" Caedis asked Sebastien.

"I'm all right," he answered with a nod, closing the door behind them. "Look, we saw some pretty fucked up stuff out there, and you're not gonna like any of it."

Lord Caedis raised an eyebrow.

"Zombies," Jackson uttered.

"*People*," Sebastien added. "Turned people."

Both Lucian and Lord Caedis adorned the same concerned frown.

"Turned by the cadejo virus?" Lucian asked.

"I believe so," Sebastien answered. "They looked the same way all things do when that virus takes them, and they smelled the same, too. There were *hundreds* of them."

Lord Caedis scowled irritably—it looked like he was going to flip the coffee table in front of him as Sebastien said—but he shook his head and exhaled quietly. "Ve can't be sure until ve get samples. Vor all ve know, zhis could be someving else. Whoever created zhese cadejo could be creating ozzer vings, too." He looked at Sebastien. "You zidn't so 'appen to bring vone of zhese turned 'umans back vith you, did you?"

"Uh... no, My Lord. Sorry," Sebastien answered, shaking his head.

With a sigh, Lord Caedis turned his head and gazed out the window. "Ve're going to need to tighten security 'ere. Ve'll 'ave to do medical screenings vor everyvone coming and going. Ve can't visk vhatever you saw out zhere getting in."

Sebastien nodded. "I already took precautions, My Lord. One of the troops was bitten. I had to kill him."

Lord Caedis nodded as he turned his head to look at Sebastien and Jackson. "And zhe mission vent vine apart vrom zhis?"

"Yes, My Lord. We extracted the target. He's in an interrogation room downstairs. We're going to try the personal approach first, and if Jackson can't get him to reveal where the laboratory is, we'll get someone else to extract the information."

"You're still going to let me talk to him?" Jackson asked, surprised.

"Yeah," Lucian said. "If we can avoid force, then we will. Sometimes, though, force is the only thing that tends to work."

Jackson shook his head. "He'll talk to me."

Lord Caedis sighed as he stood up. "Vell, you better get to, zhen." He moved closer to Lucian and muttered to him, "I need to share zhis vith Zaliv. You're in charge vhile I'm gone."

"Like always," Lucian replied.

Then, Lord Caedis pulled open one of the windows. "Ve'll veconvene vonce I 'ave more invormation." He morphed into a cloud of vermillion smoke and raced out the building.

Jackson shook his head and frowned strangely. What the hell just happened?

"Come on," Sebastien said.

"What just happened?" Jackson asked, following him out of Lucian's office.

"What?"

"Lord Caedis. He just... turned into, like... smoke."

"It's an ancient form of demon travel. Dude is probably already on the other side of the world by now."

A part of Jackson wanted to ask if he'd be able to learn to do that, but he didn't have any motivation for absorbing information right now. He wasn't only entangled with worry for Daimon and anger and suspicion towards Julian, but he was also scared about what those human zombies meant for the world. "What happens if the virus *has* evolved?" he asked Sebastien, following him towards the elevator.

"Cadejo were never a problem to humans, but if the virus is turning humans, we're going to have to up our defences *a lot*. Not just here, but everywhere. As far as we know, the cadejo are only here in Ascela, but all it takes is one infected person to get on a plane and carry it elsewhere. It's now the Venaticus' job to stop the spread before it can start," he explained. "This also means you're really going to have to step up and get this information out of your friend. We need to find that lab so we can stop this thing once and for all."

Jackson exhaled deeply and tried to calm himself down. He had to believe that Daimon would be okay and focus on what he was going to say to Ethan. But what *was* he going to say? He had so many questions: why was he working with hunters? Why was he *acting* like a hunter? But his need for answers was going to have to wait, wasn't it? The Venaticus wanted to know where the laboratory was.

The elevator arrived, and as he followed Sebastien through the hall, Jackson glanced inside every empty room. When they stopped outside that which Ethan was in, though, he tensed up. His friend was handcuffed to the table, and he was sitting there with his head in his arms.

But then Jackson noticed that Ethan's clothes were torn and bloody. "What happened to him?"

"He's a little roughed up. Maybe from the van crash or whatever happened out in the forest when your pack captured him. Do whatever you have to to get the location of that lab out of him," Sebastien answered.

"What…what if he doesn't tell me?"

Sebastien shrugged. "Then we take over."

He didn't want that to happen. The way demons pried information from someone sounded painful, and as much as he wanted to find out where that lab was so that he could fulfil his part of the bargain with Lord Caedis, he didn't want his friend to be subjected to such a thing. So, he was going to have to do his best to get Ethan to tell him where they needed to go.

When Sebastien pushed the interrogation room door open, Jackson watched through the window as Ethan lifted his head and glared at him.

"What's going on?" Ethan called. "Where the hell am I?!"

With a deep exhale, Jackson did his best to shove aside his feelings and slowly made his way past Sebastien and into the room.

And the moment Ethan saw him, his face lit up, but then a frown stole his surprised expression. "Jackson?"

Chapter Five

⌐ ≤ ☽ ≥ ⌐

The Conspiracy

| Jackson |

A flurry of emotions raced through Jackson as he stared at Ethan. Relief gripped him tightly and he didn't stop himself from running over to him. Ethan chuckled and stood up, and when they clashed, Jackson wrapped his arms around him. Ethan tried to do the same, but his restraints stopped him.

"What are you doing here?" Ethan asked, stepping back so he could look Jackson up and down.

"Well, it's a long story, actually," he said as he heard Sebastien close the door, leaving them alone. He pulled out the chair across the table from Ethan and sat down. "But the main part of it is that I came looking for you."

A shocked expression appeared on Ethan's face. "It worked?"

Jackson frowned. "What…worked?"

"You had a perception filter on—you're probably not hearing any of this—"

"No, I hear you," Jackson assured him. "I know all about the perception filter and demons and wolf walkers. I took the sensus stone off a few days ago."

Ethan scoffed in what looked like amazement. "Huh…."

Jackson shuffled around; he couldn't help but feel a little wary. But why? It was *Ethan*. This man was his best friend. He still looked and sounded the same. He was still the same guy he knew before he disappeared, right? And knowing that brought his feeling of relief back. He thought he'd never see him again, but there he was…right in front of him. Jackson wanted to hug him again, but there was too much at stake for him to waste time.

"Well…if you know about the perception filter, then you must know I'm an asmodi demon, right?" Jackson asked.

"Yeah, I knew from day one, man."

Jackson scoffed amusedly. *Of course* he knew. "I learned that…asmodi demons' ethos doesn't fully awaken until they make their first kill, so…when I accidentally killed someone, it woke up my demon…stuff…and *that* started fighting the perception filter. I began to remember things."

"Makes sense," Ethan said. "You killed someone?"

Guilt began consuming him. "I didn't mean to."

Ethan sighed. "Don't feel bad about it, Jack. It wasn't your fault. Demons, they just…gotta kill sometimes."

With a confused frown, Jackson looked at him. "What did you mean when you said it worked?"

Ethan rested his arms on the table. "I kinda figured you had a perception filter when one night we were talking about wolf walkers, and the next you were acting like you had no idea what they were. I knew Eric was an asshole, but *that* was a move I wouldn't have thought he'd take." He sighed and shook his head. "After I figured it out, I had to do *a lot* of digging around in old books, but I found a way to sort of…hack perception filters."

"Hack?"

"Yeah. I couldn't remove it because it would find its way back to you, but I *could* mess with it so that you'd remember wolf walkers and that they're in Ascela."

Jackson nodded. "And that's how I got here. So…is that what you've been doing this whole time? Looking for wolf walkers?"

Ethan shrugged and slouched back. "Nah, I didn't make my own way here." He fixed his eyes on the camera in the corner of the room and then set his sights back on Jackson. "Where are we?"

He wasn't sure if he was allowed to share that information. "A police station."

His friend scoffed. "Oh, Jack. You're still such a terrible liar."

With a quiet sigh, he leaned a little closer. "Do you know what the Venaticus is?"

Ethan scowled and shook his head. "You're working with *them*?"

Jackson frowned at him. "And *you're* working with hunters?"

Ethan tried to stretch out his arms, but the cuffs stopped him. "I had to make my way out here, Jack. This place isn't like New Dawnward. You gotta know how to hunt and fight off a million different creatures. I stuck with a group of people I knew I could rely on to make sure I made it through to tomorrow."

"I saw you dragging that unicorn, Ethan. The Ethan I knew would never—"

"The Ethan you knew died the moment I was torn out of my apartment and shipped off to wolf country!" he exclaimed, banging the table with his fists.

Jackson flinched in startle and pulled his hands off the table and into his lap. Ethan had never done anything like that before, he seemed so *angry*….

Ethan held up his hands and leaned back in his seat. "I'm sorry. This whole thing has just been a huge shock, you know?"

With a nervous frown, Jackson asked him, "What happened? Why did you just suddenly disappear?"

"Let's just say I dug a little too deep, upset some people, and the next thing I knew, I was locked up in a shipping container in the middle of the ocean. I had no idea where I was going."

"Upset what people? Who would do that?"

Ethan exhaled sharply. "Come on, Jack. You're smarter than that. Work it out."

His frown thickened as he stared at Ethan's expectant face. What was he talking about? All he knew was that Ethan was digging up information about wolf walkers and illegal experiments happening on them out in…. "Oh…."

"Yeah."

Was that it? Had the people experimenting on wolf walkers found out that Ethan was looking into them and somehow kidnapped him? But… why send him to Ascela? Why not just kill him? He thought about it for a moment. Hiding a body would be hard, right? So… they used a cover story. The journalists… the promise of a promotion. "Is… you mean… your uncle?"

Ethan shrugged. "Only thing that makes sense. And I wasn't the first, was I? All those people who just so happened to come out here looking for the *same* thing before me?"

"But…." Jackson was lost for words. Was this all some huge conspiracy? Was Ethan's uncle involved in some sort of ploy?

For a moment, Ethan glanced around the room. Then, he leaned closer to Jackson and whispered, "Something fucking weird is going on, Jack. Holt must be involved. It's odd that all these journalists before me went missing when they were looking into the same thing. There are people experimenting on wolf walkers, and for whatever reason, my uncle is helping them keep it covered up. I don't know why, and I don't know what he's getting out of it, but it's the only thing that makes sense. Especially after I dug into all the articles he's been releasing."

"What articles?"

"I did a little good old journalist digging. Weird, off-book shipments, unmarked vans, and shipping containers. People were getting sus, said they were hearing weird noises and shit. All those rabid, wild dog reports. Holt was onto us for weeks to write about it, remember?"

Jackson thought to himself for a moment… and nodded. "Yeah, I… I remember that. He gave us notes. He—"

"He was *insistent* that we write some articles to assure the people that all these shipments were just a silly little mistake on the courier records. That they were shipping in materials from overseas for, uh… what's that place? El'Vorian Industries."

"The pharmaceutical company."

"Yeah. *That's* what I was digging into before a bunch of masked dudes broke into my place and carried me off."

Jackson shook his head. "So...you think El'Vorian is a front for...for what, exactly?"

"Lyca Corp."

"I've never heard—"

"Why would you have?" Ethan interjected. "I only found out because I came across the word in one of those old blogs, which was gone the next day. I started looking up Lyca Corp., and here we are."

"And...Lyca Corp. are the ones doing experiments on wolf walkers?" Jackson questioned.

"Yes," Ethan said, tapping the table. "And you remember that lab we were gonna come out here and look for?"

Jackson shuffled in his seat and leaned a little closer. *Finally*, they were on the subject he'd been sent in here to gather information on. And he couldn't help but feel a little excited. He missed Ethan so much, especially when they sat down like this and talked about whatever article they were working on or what shady company they were looking into. "Yeah, I remember."

"I've been trying to get out there so I can gather some evidence. They might have shipped me off to no man's land hoping I'd get eaten by something, but that isn't gonna stop me. I wasn't the first guy they sent out here and I won't be the last. And whatever they're doing in their labs is wrong. I'm gonna find out what they're up to...and I'm gonna bring them all down, Holt included."

"So...you didn't get to the lab yet?"

Ethan shook his head. "No. I've been waiting for the right moment to ask Riker—the leader of the hunters I was with—but I've been trying to prove myself."

"That's why you were dragging that unicorn?"

He nodded slowly...but then a frown appeared on his face. "How do you know about that? Were you out there?"

Jackson leaned back a little and scratched the side of his face. He wasn't sure how Ethan was going to react to finding out that he was a wolf walker, so he was going to have to tread carefully. "I...before I say anything else, I need to ask you something."

"Okay?"

"Wolf walkers: how do you...feel about them?"

Ethan tapped the table as a look of pondering appeared on his face. "Why?"

"Just tell me."

He exhaled deeply and shook his head. "Curious," he answered. "But only because they're tied into this conspiracy. If Lyca Corp. is experimenting on *them*, then maybe they're experimenting on other Caeleste, too."

Jackson nodded slowly. His answer didn't make him feel like revealing that he was a wolf walker was a good idea. "So, you still wanna find this lab, right?"

Ethan laughed quietly. "Yeah, but it ain't looking like that's gonna happen now. What do these Venaticus assholes want with me?"

There was no point in lying; it would probably make things worse. "They're looking for the lab, too."

With a scoff and shake of his head, Ethan slouched and scowled at him. "Of course they fucking are. They're probably in on this whole—"

"They're not," Jackson interjected. "You've seen the cadejo, right?"

He didn't respond. He just glared at him.

"The Venaticus are trying to find out where the virus came from, and they think that the answers are at that lab."

"So?"

"What if this is all connected? What if the Lyca Corp. experiments created the cadejo virus? It started in wolf walkers, right? And it's wolf walkers they're experimenting on."

Ethan stared at him for a few long, tense moments. It looked like he was thinking. And then a skeptical frown stole his pondering gaze. "Why are you here, Jack?"

"Because if you don't tell me where that lab is, they're gonna send a bunch of demons in here to dig around inside your brain," he urged desperately. "I don't—"

"No, I mean why are you *here* with the Venaticus?"

Jackson shrugged. "They picked me up not that long ago. I was using this…old demon amulet and they detected it."

Ethan slowly shook his head. "Nah, there's more to it, man. Tell me."

Jackson took a deep breath and looked at the table. He didn't want to keep it from him; the sooner he knew, the better, right? "Just promise me you won't freak out," he pleaded, looking at him again.

"I can't promise that until I know what—"

"Just promise!" he insisted.

"All right, sheesh."

Jackson exhaled deeply, fighting the building worry that Ethan would hate him once the words left his mouth. "When…I first got to Ascela, I…was attacked by a cadejo."

Ethan frowned and waited for him to continue.

"And…because I'm a demon—well, when it happened, I wasn't a like…fully…mature demon, I guess—so the virus didn't turn me into a cadejo, it—"

"—Turned you into a wolf walker?"

He nodded cautiously. "And I was picked up by the Venaticus because I found a demon amulet and I was able to use its ethos. And then when I got here, instead of sending me to wherever they send illegal hybrids, they started telling me that there might be illegal wolf walker-demon hybrids being made using the virus. They think that whatever is at this lab will give them some answers as to where the virus came from and how to stop it—or create a cure or vaccine, at least," he explained quickly, refusing to let Ethan get a word in until he finished. "They also took some of my blood and tested it, and they said that it helped them understand that the virus might have been created using demon blood, too. There's this whole other part about them looking for a hybrid. At first, I was scared it was me—maybe they thought it was me, too—but then they said that this hybrid they're looking for was *created* using the virus, not like…bitten in the way I was. Created by illegal experiments and stuff. So *that's* why we need to know where the lab is."

Ethan looked like he was taking a moment to absorb everything he'd been told. "So…my uncle might be covering up this whole cadejo virus demon-wolf walker hybrid thing?" he drawled.

It was hard for Jackson to tell whether the expression on Ethan's face was one of disbelief or confusion. Perhaps it was both. "Yeah," he said with a nod. "And…I…." It suddenly hit him. If human-turned zombies were showing up, what if Lord Caedis' attempts to stop the virus from spreading were futile? What if the virus or people infected with it had already been shipped across the world?

"What?" Ethan asked. "You what?"

"Did you…ever find out what was in those unmarked shipping containers that Holt was trying to cover up?"

"No. It was like they just completely disappeared."

What would be the point in infecting everyone, though? Something like this could cripple the entire world. Someone like Holt wouldn't have anything to gain from that…would he?

"Jack?" Ethan questioned. "You're making that face you make when you're onto something. What's going on?"

His throat felt dry, and his body went stiff. "You…know your uncle better than anyone, so…do you think he'd gain anything from helping Lyca Corp. spread the virus?"

Ethan frowned strangely. "Uh…well, the dude is obsessed with money. If he's involved, they're probably paying him." But then he shook his head. "So…Lyca Corp. might be using wolf walkers and demons and whatever to create hybrids. But why?"

"Because Lyca Corp. works for the Diabolus," came Sebastien's voice.

They both looked at the door as the white-haired demon came into the room and approached the table.

"And the Diabolus are currently at war with the Nosferatu," Sebastien continued. "So, it looks like Lyca Corp. is creating weapons for the Diabolus to use against us. And your uncle—Holt—is helping cover it up, which makes sense since New Dawnward is one of the main cities the Nosferatu works out of. They've been right under our noses this whole time."

"And *you* are?" Ethan demanded.

"Sebastien Huxley, pal. I'm the guy who's gonna be supervising the trip to this lab. So, where is it?"

Ethan scoffed. "I ain't telling you sh—"

"Ethan, please," Jackson pleaded. "These guys wanna help. And I'm sure they'll let you get whatever evidence you want and expose Holt and everyone else involved."

Sebastien nodded. "To be honest, I'm betting on it. Press is power, nowadays."

With a conflicted frown, Ethan tapped his fingers on the table. But he took his eyes off Sebastien and looked at Jackson. "Those wolves that led Riker's group out into the woods—"

"Yeah, I…I'm with them." And before Ethan could respond, he added, "And…I'm actually mated to one of them."

Ethan went a little pale. "Mated?"

He nodded. "Y-yeah, I…I was—"

"Which one?"

Jackson shrugged lightly. "The Alpha."

With a derisive laugh, Ethan sat up straight and looked around the room. "Damn, Jack. I wouldn't expect any less if I'm being honest." There was a hint of sadness in his voice, though. "Your Alpha, uh…" he said, looking at him, "he's the big white one, right?"

He nodded.

Ethan exhaled deeply. "Yeah, uh…that dude just tore me off my bike. He could've killed me, you know."

"He wouldn't have killed you, I promise," Jackson assured him. "The objective was to just capture you. But then everything went a little haywire when those zombies turned up."

Ethan sighed to himself and smirked slightly. "Where is the crazy son of a bitch? I thought he'd be in here beating the shit out of me—"

"He's in surgery," Sebastien said.

"Surgery?" Ethan questioned.

Jackson nodded sullenly as his heart ached in his chest. "When we were driving away, the van crashed, and…he was hurt." He lightly clenched his fist. He needed to interrogate Julian.

Ethan leaned forward to drag his hands over his face. "Shit, Jack. I'm sorry."

"He's gonna be fine," Jackson said firmly, refusing to let the worry and despair consume him. "Right?" he asked, looking up at Sebastien.

"Yeah. Don't worry, all right?" Then, he looked at Ethan. "Now, the location of the lab?"

"What's gonna happen to me after I tell you?" Ethan asked.

Jackson looked up at Sebastien and waited for his answer.

Sebastien said, "Well, that depends. Lord Caedis was going to leave it up to you two. I mean, it looks like you're still pals, right?"

"Why wouldn't we be?" Ethan grumbled.

"Well, Jackson here became a wolf walker," Sebastien said as he placed his hands on Jackson's shoulders. "And we saw *you* hanging out with a bunch of hunters."

"I already said that I was only with them and waiting for the right moment to ask their leader to take me up to the lab."

"Right, like you're waiting for the right moment to tell Jackson that you're a muto."

Jackson had no idea what that was, and he was sure that the look on his face reflected his confusion. "Muto?"

Ethan looked a little confounded, too. "Didn't you take the perception filter off?" he asked Jackson.

"Yeah, but…I guess there's still some things I don't remember…."

"He's a tiger shifter," Sebastien said, taking his hands off Jackson. "And wolf walkers and muto, once upon a time, were enemies. So, we were a little worried you guys might be at each other's throats. But lo and behold, friendship prevails."

Ethan scowled at Sebastien. "And what do *you* know, huh?"

"How do you know what he is?" Jackson asked.

"Everyone that comes into this building through any entrance or exit gets scanned," Sebastien answered.

Ethan shook his head and scoffed quietly. "Look, I honestly couldn't give a shit if you were a dolphin," he said to Jackson. "Nor do I care what you are or what anyone else is," he muttered, glancing at Sebastien. "All that really matters is that I trust Jack; he's been there for me for more than fifteen years, and I have no reason to doubt him. So, I'm going to tell *him* where the lab is, and whatever he wants to do with that information is up to him," he said firmly. "So *you* can get lost," he snarled at Sebastien.

Sebastien smirked amusedly in response but didn't snap back. He turned around and left the room, pulling the door shut behind him.

"I want to come with you," Ethan said the moment the door closed.

Jackson frowned. "Huh?"

"To the lab. I want to come."

He didn't see any reason why he couldn't tag along, and a part of him wanted Ethan to come; he'd just found his best friend and he didn't want to have to say goodbye again. "I mean…*I* want you to come, but I have to make sure it's okay with the pack. And you need to tell me where it is."

Ethan shrugged. "All right. Well, I'll tell you after you've asked your pack. I guess I gotta wait here, right?"

As Jackson stood up, he nodded. "I mean…yeah, I think so. It shouldn't take me too long, though. But…are you saying…if you *can't* come, you won't tell me?"

His friend nodded. "Terms and conditions, man." But before Jackson could go, he reached out his cuffed hands. "Hey, Jack."

"Yeah?"

"It's uh... despite all of this weird shit, it's good to see you. I honestly thought I was never gonna see anyone from home again."

Jackson smiled at him. "Come on, Ethan. You had to know I'd come for you... or at least *hoped* so, right?"

He shrugged. "I didn't hope because I didn't want you to get involved in all this crazy stuff. But... a part of me knew you'd come anyways—that was if my little hack of the perception filter worked," he laughed.

"Well, it did, and here I am."

He held out his hands and smirked. "Here you are."

Jackson smiled and headed to the door. But his worry quickly returned. What if his pack didn't want Ethan to come? What if they couldn't find a middle ground? The fate of Ascela was relying on Ethan's knowledge, and Jackson had to do whatever it took to get his pack to agree.

Chapter Six

A Mate's Worry

| Sebastien |

Sebastien watched Jackson leave the interrogation room as he clenched his fists in frustration. He made sure that Ethan stayed in his seat and didn't attempt to break his cuffs, and then he stepped out into the hall just as Jackson was about to reach the door.

"What the hell was that?" he asked before the kid could speak.

"What do you mean?" Jackson questioned.

"You were supposed to find out where the lab was, not make deals."

Jackson frowned at him. "He's gonna tell me where it is, he just wants to come with us. And I thought this would be a good thing. The higher our numbers, the higher our like… defences and whatever, right?"

He'd like to believe that, but he had a strange feeling about Ethan. That guy was up to something—he had ulterior motives—but Sebastien wasn't yet sure what. He was going to have to bring this to Lord Caedis, too, and there was no doubt in his mind that his boss would accept Ethan's offer and then make *him* babysit both Jackson and his muto pal.

"We don't know anything about him, Jackson," he said, shaking his head. "Why does he want to find this lab so bad? *So* bad that he's willing to work with hunters? Did you ever think of asking him that?"

"He wants to expose—"

"Expose the conspiracy, write a ground breaking story," Sebastien mocked, waving his hands around. "I'm not buying it. Your friend in there is up to something—he's getting something else out of this; that's why he's so desperate to come with you despite being a species of Caeleste who *despise* wolf walkers."

Jackson's frown turned into a scowl. "I don't know what you're trying to say, but I know Ethan better than anyone. He wants the story. He *loves* exposing corruption, and he's been looking into this wolf walker Lyca Corp. stuff for *ages*. I trust him…and you should, too."

"Kid, I don't trust *anyone*. If he signed a deal with Lord Caedis, then it'd be a different story. But right now, your friend is holding valuable information, and the fact that he was hanging out with hunters makes him a prisoner. We won't be making any special exceptions or bargaining with him."

"Just let me talk to the pack, please," he pleaded calmly. "I *know* they'll agree to it—"

"But it's not up to them or you. The choice is ultimately Lord Caedis'." He sighed and dragged his hand over his face. The last thing he wanted right now was to be standing around arguing. This was the only free time he was going to have in what might be weeks, and he wasn't going to spend it working overtime. So, he said, "You know what? Whatever." He looked over his shoulder at a guard standing down the hall. "You, get over here."

The man left his post and hurried over. "Yes, Officer Huxley, sir?"

"Take Jackson down to see his pack. I've gotta run an errand, so make sure no one leaves the room until I'm back. Got it?"

"Yes, sir."

"Wait, you said we could see Daimon," Jackson insisted.

Sebastien sighed again. His free time was ticking away. "Yeah, fine. After he's done talking to his pack, take them all to the medical wing waiting room. Their Alpha's in surgery and one of their other guys is getting patched up."

The guard nodded. "Yes, sir. This way," he said to Jackson.

Then, Sebastien headed down the hall. He navigated the building's long, winding corridors, and once he reached the ground floor, he walked out the revolving doors and onto the street. Although it was the early hours of the morning, there were cars on the roads and people making their way up and down the streets. There was *always* noise in this city.

He slipped his hands into his pockets and crossed the road. But as he headed for his apartment, every time he saw a man or woman within his line of sight, he examined their faces and the way they walked. After seeing those undead humanoids out in the woods, he was afraid that the infection had already found its way into Silverlake.

But he couldn't let his fears eat him up. He trusted Lord Caedis and the Venaticus. They'd do whatever it took to protect Silverlake and every other civilization they could from this. Sebastien had his own priorities, though. Just like everyone else involved in this mission, he had someone to protect.

When he reached his apartment building, he hurried inside, up the stairs, and to his door. The moment he got inside, he called, "Babe? Are you awake?"

But there was no answer.

He locked the door behind him and made his way through to the lounge. When he flicked the lights on, he looked around for anything that might suggest something happened here, but everything was in order.

Sebastien exhaled deeply and relaxed. He pulled his coat off, threw it onto the couch, and went down the hall to the bedroom. He didn't turn the lights on once he slowly and quietly opened the door. As silently as he could, he moved over to the bed and sat on the edge. "Hey?" he whispered as he gently leaned over to see Clementine's peaceful, sleeping face. "Babe?"

Clementine murmured in response.

"Sorry, I just got in."

With a quiet grunt, Clementine rolled over to face him. "You finished work?" he asked tiredly.

Sebastien shook his head as he ran his fingers through his mate's tousled, blonde hair. "No, I just snatched an hour away."

Clementine opened his eyes and gazed up at him. "Just an hour, huh?"

"Well… forty-eight minutes," Sebastien said with a smirk as he glanced at the clock.

"You better get your ass in bed then," Clementine said, tugging on Sebastien's shirt.

But as much as Sebastien wanted to crawl into bed with him, he needed to put his mind at rest. "Actually, babe… I came to check on you."

"Check on me?"

"Yeah. There's this…. You know the cadejo virus shit we're dealing with right now?"

Clementine nodded.

"Well, we think it might have evolved and spread to humans. I was scared that maybe we discovered it too late, and people were already infected here. I was… I was worried something might have happened to you."

"I'm okay," Clementine said softly as he lifted his hand and placed it on the side of Sebastien's face. "You know you don't have to worry about me."

He huffed quietly. "Yeah, but I do anyway."

Clementine gazed at him for a moment… but then shuffled over to the other side of the bed and made Sebastien lay down beside him. He caressed Sebastien's ashen hair as he asked, "What happened out there?"

"A lot," Sebastien said with a sigh, staring into his mate's piercing blue eyes. "The hybrid I told you about—"

"Jackson?"

"Yeah. We found his friend. We should be getting the location of the lab any time tonight. I don't know how long I'll be gone for once we set out to find it… but a part of me wants to ask Lord Caedis if I can sit this one out."

"Why?"

"Because I want to stay back here and protect *you*. We've lived long enough to know that shit always finds a way in," Sebastien lamented. "No number of walls or guards are gonna be able to stop it. Sooner or later, someone's gonna get infected and bring it into the city. I want to be here when that happens. I'm not going to let anything happen to you, Clem."

Clementine smiled as Sebastien pressed his forehead against his. "Sebastien, you know Caedis won't let you stay here. And they need you out there. You've seen first-hand what this virus does." He stroked the side of Sebastien's face. "You're also the only kludde left in the world; they're going to need you if you come across the Diabolus."

Sebastien grunted and closed his eyes. Frustration gripped him tightly as he remembered what Ethan and Jackson talked about. "Yeah…there's a super high chance the Diabolus will be at the lab. We think Lyca Corp. might be creating demon-wolf walker hybrids for them to use against the Nosferatu."

"That would make sense. Wolf walkers can kill a vampire with a single bite…and with the strength of a demon, Caedis' covens wouldn't stand a chance."

"But why the cadejo?" Sebastien mumbled. "That virus can't infect mature demons or vampires. Using them to take out the rest of the wolf walkers makes sense, sure, since they were one of the Nosferatu's most powerful allies, but would the Diabolus really go so far as to create a virus that could potentially wipe out *everyone*?"

Clementine adorned a look of pondering, and after a few moments, he slowly said, "What if they're trying to draw Greymore out?"

That was a good point. Could the cadejo threat have been created as an attempt to draw Fenrisúlfr out from wherever he was? The Diabolus had been working very hard to take out the Nosferatu's most dangerous allies; they'd used the Holy Grail to hunt down and kill the asmodi demons, they'd killed enough wolf walkers to force the Zenith to send what remained of them out to the secluded tundra of Ascela, and now…could they have their sights set on the strongest wolf walker to walk this world?

It felt like his brain was throbbing. He was tired, overworked, and aching from his fight with that cadejo monster. "Maybe," he said. "I'll bring it to Heir Lucian and Lord Caedis later. See what they have to say about it." He frowned at Clementine. "You know, I really don't get why you don't just come and work with me. You've got the smarts for this kinda stuff, babe."

Clementine shrugged dismissively. "No offence, but after the weird devil-deal that Caedis roped you into, I'm gonna stay far, *far* away from any job remotely *close* to the Nosferatu."

"I don't blame you. But it's not all bad. The pay's good…I get to boss people around. And every once in a while, I get to meet these crazy hybrids and ancient Caeleste species." He smirked because he knew Clementine was going to enjoy what he said next. "We brought a muto in today."

His mate's face lit up with curiosity. "A muto?"

"Yeah. The little hybrid's friend turned out to be a giant tiger. I never thought I'd see one."

"Did you see him shift?"

"No, but Jackson wants to bring him along when we go to the lab, so I'm sure I will."

"I read that they have this sort of golden shimmer to their fur," Clementine said with a fascinated expression. "It's one of the reasons they were hunted so much."

Sebastien nodded slowly. "I feel like this guy is up to something, though. Jackson's convinced he's in this for the story, but it feels weird."

"Weird how?"

"Like there's something more to all of this. I just…." He exhaled in frustration and rolled onto his back. "I suck at piecing things together, man. There's all these pieces floating around in front of me and I'm just grabbing random ones and trying to force them into place," he exclaimed, reaching out and grabbing the air as he spoke.

Clementine reached up and grabbed one of Sebastien's hands. "That's why you leave the piecing things together to the investigators, Seb. You're the muscle. You go places and kill things."

"I know, I know."

"Just tell Caedis. They're gonna read his mind anyway, right? So they can find out what he's really up to."

"I don't know about that. Lord Caedis seems to want to let Jackson choose what to do. If it were my choice, yeah, I would've just got straight to mind reading, but we went with the personal approach first."

Clementine shuffled closer and rested his head on Sebastien's shoulder. "Shh," he mumbled. "This is supposed to be your time away from work, right? Just stop thinking about all of that for a little while and get some rest."

As much as he might want to lay there and try to figure out all the answers, he knew that wasn't going to happen. There was so much he didn't know, and no matter how hard he tried, he wasn't the best at thinking up possibilities or grasping at straws. Could all of this cadejo business be the Diabolus trying to draw Fenrisúlfr out by mass slaughtering his wolves? Maybe. But it could also be a million other things, and there were a *billion* things he didn't know about Lord Caedis and the history of the Nosferatu and the Diabolus.

No. Clementine was right. He should wipe this off his mind and leave it up to the investigators. *His* job was to ensure that Jackson did as he was told and found the Lyca Corp. lab.

He sighed away his thoughts and nuzzled Clementine's soft hair. "You're right," he said quietly. "Sorry. I don't mean to bring my work home with me."

"It's okay," Clementine said. "How long do you have left?"

Sebastien looked at the clock. "Thirty-two minutes."

"Good," Clementine said, pulling the blankets over them both. "That's enough time for you to get some sleep."

With a slight laugh, Sebastien made himself comfortable. Then, he closed his eyes and let himself rest. There was a long mission ahead of him, and he wanted to enjoy what time he had left to spend with his mate before going weeks without him.

But then his worry returned. "Clem?"

"Yeah?" his mate replied.

"If...things get bad here while I'm gone—"

"Seb—"

"Just...listen, please."

Clementine waited.

"If things get bad...if the virus *does* get inside the city, promise me that you'll go to Heir Lucian. I know you don't want to be anywhere near that building, but it'll be the safest place if something were to happen."

Although he didn't sound very happy, Clementine said, "Okay."

Sebastien kissed his mate's head. "Thank you."

"Now let's get some sleep."

He smiled and wrapped his arms around Clementine. "Sounds good."

Sebastien closed his eyes and held Clementine closely. He knew how dangerous this mission to get to the lab was, but he couldn't help but wonder...what if this was the last time he saw Clementine? What if this was the last time he got to hold and kiss the man he loved?

He scowled in dismay, trying to dismiss the thought of it. But he couldn't. What if he was walking to his death? He had a bad feeling about all of this, and that feeling got worse with each passing moment. What if he left to go and find the lab...and the zombies got into the city? What if he wasn't here to help Clementine get out if the place was overrun?

Sebastien held Clementine a little tighter. No, Clementine was the smartest person he knew other than his superiors. He had to trust that he would get out if something happened. But...what if he didn't? What if leaving to get to the lab was a horrible mistake? There was no way for him to know. But he had to go. He had to be brave...for himself and Clementine. And he had to believe that in his absence, the man he loved would be okay.

Chapter Seven

Decisions

| **Jackson** |

Jackson followed the guard through the halls, down in an elevator, and then towards the end of an empty, door-lined corridor.

"I'll be out here," the guard said, pushing the door open.

When Jackson stepped inside, the pack—who were all sitting around on several leather couches—jumped to their feet and hurried over to him.

"Jackson!" Julian called.

Jackson wanted to scowl at Julian, but he didn't want the entire pack to swarm them. He'd rather interrogate them by himself.

"Is Alpha Daimon okay?" Tokala questioned.

"What happened with Caedis?" Alastor asked.

Jackson held out his hands as everyone threw a flurry of questions at him. They were all making him feel overwhelmed already, and the mere mention of Daimon ensnared his heart in pain and worry.

"Give the man some space," Wesley insisted, pulling some of his packmates back.

After taking a deep breath, Jackson moved through the crowd and headed over to one of the couches. He slumped down and watched the pack sit around him, and then he dragged his fingers through his hair. "I haven't seen Daimon yet," he told them, glancing at their anxious faces. "I *did* see Ethan, though, and there's something we need to talk about before we can go and see how Daimon and Lalo are doing."

"What is it?" Tokala asked.

"Well…it's a lot, actually," Jackson drawled, trying to work out where to start; he was desperate to find out if Julian was the one responsible for Daimon's condition, but he also needed to tell the pack what Ethan said. "Do you all know what a muto is?"

Some of them looked confused while others appeared disgruntled.

"Tiger shifters," Lance muttered.

"Annoying fuckers," Brando added.

Jackson sighed quietly. This wasn't going to be easy, was it? "It turns out that Ethan is one of them—"

"A muto?" Bly questioned with a frown.

"Seriously?" Julian asked. "I thought they were extinct."

Jackson had to hold his tongue again; he had to keep a scowl off his face. But it was becoming increasingly harder for him to bury the anger that Julian infected him with.

"Muto and wolf walkers were...*are* natural enemies," Rachel explained, looking around at everyone. "Years ago—back when Fenrisúlfr walked this world—the muto royals decided to wage war against our kind. Something happened, but I can't recall what."

Tokala patted the couch arm. "It was about...three hundred and seventy years ago," he said as everyone looked at him. "Some of my ancestors knew the story of Marquess Adrian. The Zenith and his kingdom of demons settled in Uzlia, which was known as The New World in wartime. However, there was an uncharted island in Uzlia; of course, the Zenith had people scout the island out, but...muto are near impossible to detect."

Jackson nodded slowly; he was trying his best to absorb the information, but he couldn't stop thinking about Daimon.

The orange-haired man continued, "Eventually, the wolf walkers working for the Zenith needed their own space. You know how it is. We need trees and places to hunt. So, Fenrisúlfr was given permission to take his wolves over to this uncharted island. When they got there, though, they discovered they weren't alone. *Muto* lived on that island. They left their usual home in Samjang because they were hunted for their fur."

"Why?" Leon asked.

"Because it has powerful ethos properties. It's a muto's fur which allows them to go undetected," Tokala answered. "Anyway, just like wolf walkers, muto are very territorial. Fenrisúlfr's wolves and the muto got into a fight, where some on both sides were killed. Fenrisúlfr wasn't just going to sit around and let their deaths be in vain, so he hunted down Marquess Adrian—Alpha if you will. But ultimately, the choice of what to do with these muto was the Zenith's. *He* didn't want back-to-back territory disputes or fights breaking out in his kingdom, so he proposed a truce. Adrian refused. Instead, he challenged Fenrisúlfr to a winner-takes-all battle."

"Fenrisúlfr won, right?" Julian asked.

"He did, and killing Adrian sparked a feud that would last forever. The muto were no match for Fenrisúlfr's *hundreds* of wolf walkers, so they fled. But since then, whenever a muto and wolf walker cross paths, they fight to the death."

Everyone glanced around at each other.

Despite Tokala's story, though, Jackson didn't feel hesitant to ask his question. "We need to find that lab for Lord Caedis, and Ethan knows where it is. He'll only tell us if we agree to let him come along with us."

A few scoffs echoed around the room.

"I don't think that's a good idea, Jackson," Rachel said.

"I already told him that *I'm* a wolf walker and he was fine with it," Jackson explained. "I told him I'm part of a pack—I even told him that I'm mated to Daimon. He's *fine* with it. Whatever this ancient feud is, I honestly don't think Ethan cares. He just wants to find this lab as much as the Venaticus does."

They all looked around at each other with unsure, conflicted expressions on their faces. But eventually, the pack set their eyes on Tokala.

With a quiet sigh, Tokala shrugged. "If you trust him, Jackson, then we all trust your judgement. But the decision is Alpha Daimon's…and he's not here right now. We can't make a decision without him."

Jackson nodded as he looked down at his lap. Angst began to enthral his heart, twisting and digging its claws deeper and deeper. He wanted to see Daimon. He wanted to know if he was okay. And since the pack couldn't give Ethan an answer until Daimon was back…the only thing left to do was wait.

He looked at Tokala. "Sebastien said that we can go and wait in the medical wing's waiting room."

"Really?" Ezhno asked.

Jackson nodded.

"Can…we go now?" Brando asked.

"Yeah, I think so," Jackson said with a nod. "He said once we were done here."

Everyone started standing up.

"Then let's go," Alastor insisted.

Jackson stood up, and as he headed for the door, everyone followed. Once he reached it, he pulled it open and set his eyes on the guard who escorted him down there. "Can we go to the medical waiting room now, please?"

The man nodded. "All of you?"

"Yeah," Jackson answered.

With a nod, the man started leading the way down the hall.

The pack followed and filed into the elevator.

As it headed down, Jackson glared at the back of Julian's head. If he questioned them, would they even answer? Would they tell the truth? Jackson didn't know how to tell when someone was lying; he knew that he *could* do it…he just had to listen to someone's pulse. He had to try. If Julian had stabbed Daimon, then he needed to find out before they left to find the lab.

Once they reached a lower floor, the guard led them towards a pair of white double doors with a sign above it that read Medical Wing.

Jackson clenched his fist in an attempt to manage his worry; when the guard pushed the doors open, Jackson started grinding his teeth. It smelled of pharmaceuticals, bleach, and coffee. The bright, white room was empty apart from a nurse behind the reception desk and a cleaner mopping the floor outside the bathrooms.

"Wait here," the guard said.

Everyone stopped when Jackson did. They waited, watching the man as he made his way to the reception desk and got the nurse's attention by tapping the wood.

"Can I help you?" she asked him.

"We need an update on the Prime wolf walker brought in earlier."

She started typing on her computer. "Hmm...Daimon Greyblood?"

"Yes."

"He came out of surgery ten minutes ago. Doctor Laurent and Doctor Kowalski are currently with him in the ICU."

The pack started whispering nervously to one another.

Jackson's heart ached—it felt like a weight in his chest. The ICU? Why was Daimon in intensive care? Did the doctors not manage to heal him?

"This way," the guard called.

Everyone eagerly hurried after him. They went through another pair of double doors and down a long corridor. Once they emerged into a large, open sitting area, the guard took them through a locked door and into a small waiting room.

Jackson looked around desperately. A small reception desk sat to his left, several couches were lined around the room, and to the right...was a patient room.

He rushed over there, and when he got to the window, he peered through the slightly parted blinds and saw Daimon in the bed. There were also two doctors in there; he recognized the black-haired man—that was Doctor Kowalski—but he'd never seen the blonde doctor before. The nurse mentioned that Kowalski was in the room with another doctor—Doctor Laurent—so that must be who that was.

Without hesitation, Jackson pushed the door open and stepped inside.

"You can't be in here," the blonde doctor immediately said.

"How is he?" Jackson asked, looking at Daimon, who was unconscious but breathing.

"You need to leave—"

"It's fine, Sinclair," Doctor Kowalski said, holding his arm out before the blonde man could move towards Jackson. Then, Kowalski sighed and glanced down at his clipboard. "Your Alpha's a tough guy," he said, looking at Jackson. "He pulled through the surgery. We removed the blade without causing any permanent damage. As far as we can tell, he'll regain use of his legs pretty quickly. His body's healing kicked in, too, so...he *might* wake up soon."

"Might?" Jackson questioned as he heard the pack grouping up outside the door behind him.

Kowalski looked at Sinclair.

With a sigh, the blonde man said, "These things are touch and go. He was severely injured and lost a lot of blood. He could wake up, or he could stay comatose. There's no way for us to tell, and we can't wake him up with anything, either." He looked at Daimon. "He has to fight, basically."

Dismay filled Jackson's tense body as he stared at Daimon. There was a chance he wouldn't wake up. Jackson couldn't—no, he *wouldn't* let himself wonder what they were going to do without Daimon…or what *he* would do without him. Daimon was going to make it. He was going to fight and wake up. He had to.

"Look," Sinclair said, "you really can't be in here. You can wait in the waiting area, but we all need to leave this room."

Jackson didn't want to leave. He wanted to go and sit at Daimon's bedside. He wanted to hold his hand and tell him it was going to be okay. And he wanted to be there when the Alpha opened his eyes. "Can't I sit there?" he asked, pointing at the chair beside the bed.

"N—"

"Just you," Kowalski said, cutting Sinclair off.

"What about us?" Bly asked.

"You lot are going to have to wait out there. You can see in through the window, but no one comes in here except Jackson," Kowalski said firmly.

Disappointed mumbles came from the pack, but they followed Tokala over to the waiting area while asking each other what they were going to do if Daimon didn't wake up.

"We'll be back to check on him in a few hours," Sinclair said. "Don't touch anything."

Jackson nodded and walked over to the chair. He sat down and stared at Daimon's pale face; he looked terrible…and as Jackson stared at all the wires and IV lines, he began to succumb to guilt. This was all his fault. He dragged Daimon and his pack into that stupid mission. And now the man he loved was suffering. He might not even wake up.

When he heard the door close, Jackson carefully gripped Daimon's hand. His skin was cold to the touch; the usual warmth that came from the Alpha's body was gone, and his hand felt stiff instead of soft.

"I'm sorry," he said sullenly as his throat began tightening. "I…I can't…." He gritted his teeth and shook his head as he looked down at the floor. "It should have been me. You don't deserve this." He stared at Daimon's face again. Although he knew the Alpha couldn't answer, and despite not knowing whether he could hear him or not, he still wanted to say what he needed to say. "You have to wake up," he pleaded, tightening his grip on Daimon's hand. And as selfish as his words made him feel, he said, "Don't leave me. *Please.*"

Jackson rested his head on Daimon's arm and closed his eyes. There wasn't really anything else he could do but sit there and wait. So, that's what he did. He held Daimon's hand... and waited.

| Daimon, fifteen years ago |

Something woke Daimon from his sleep. He opened his eyes to the darkness of his room and a repulsive smell which turned his stomach. He had no idea what it was, but it stunk like an animal had crawled under his bed and died.

He sat up, holding his hand over his nose. But when he tried to concentrate and find out which direction the smell was coming from, he couldn't pinpoint it. It was coming from everywhere.

Daimon climbed out of bed and pulled on a pair of trousers. He headed over to his balcony door, pushed it open, and stepped outside. He could still smell it, but it wasn't so bad out here.

Just as he was about to head back inside, though, he noticed that the Etas weren't at their posts. His eyes shifted from the estate's gates to the watch towers, and then to the gardens. The whole place was deserted. He even leaned over his balcony to look down at the building's patio. But Kira and Elena weren't there.

Where the hell was everyone?

That was when a cold shiver of trepidation spiralled down his spine. He tensed up, and his instincts started telling him that something was wrong, and he needed to be alert.

With a confused frown, Daimon headed back into his room and to his door. He went out into the hall and to the room next door. He knocked—he didn't wait for Alaric to answer—and pushed the door open just enough to peek his head in.

"Alaric?" he whispered.

His brother groaned from across the room.

Daimon went inside and walked over to his brother's bed. Then, he nudged Alaric's arm. "Hey."

"Ugh, what?" Alaric complained, rolling onto his back so that he could look up at Daimon.

Nyssa, who was sleeping next to him, shuffled around and pulled on the blanket, ignoring Daimon's presence.

"Something's wrong," Daimon told him. "The Etas aren't at their posts."

Alaric frowned in confusion. "What?"

"I looked outside. They're all gone."

His brother sat up and looked around.

Daimon knew Alaric was using his senses to try and locate his Etas, but when he saw a horrified expression steal his tired face, Daimon tensed up again. "What?"

Alaric shook Nyssa awake. "Baby, we gotta get up."

"Alaric, what?" Daimon insisted.

"Get everyone up," Alaric told Daimon as he climbed out of bed and immediately shifted into his wolf form.

Daimon backed off and watched as Nyssa shifted, too.

"Alaric?!" he insisted.

"I can't feel them; something's going on. Come on," Alaric said, hurrying out of his room.

As his heart started racing, Daimon shifted and followed his brother and Nyssa out of the room and down the hall. Alaric let out a loud, bellowing howl, and Daimon howled right after, summoning the pack.

The wolves came running out of their rooms, following Alaric downstairs into the estate's large entrance hall. Once everyone was grouped up, they stared at Alaric, waiting for him to speak.

Daimon waited, too. That rotten stench was getting stronger, and his heart beat faster. He looked to his left and right—he seemed sure he might find something—but there was nothing there.

"Our Etas are missing," Alaric announced. "We must search the grounds, the woods, and if it comes to it, the rest of our territory. I cannot sense them, so either something has happened or they're out of range."

"Where would they go?" Tokala asked worriedly. "My mother didn't say anything about leaving."

"I don't know," Alaric answered as he turned around and pulled the front door open with his teeth. "Come on."

As Alaric led the way, Daimon followed everyone outside. But the feeling of dread which gripped him so tightly didn't let up. It constricted him like a starved snake, making it hard for him to breathe. He looked around frantically as he followed the pack down into the gardens, and that was when he saw it.

Something shifted through the falling snow. A dark blur moved behind one of the towering hedges.

But when he looked ahead and went to warn Alaric, his brother came to a halt. The pack stopped, too, and as they all set their eyes on what Alaric was staring at, everyone gasped, panicked, and asked what the hell they were looking at.

"What the hell is that?" Caius questioned.

Daimon gawped at the creature before them. It looked like a wolf walker, but its body was rotting and missing huge chunks of fur and flesh. It snarled and growled as black blood sept from its gaping jaw, and its eyes were bright crimson.

"Cadejo," Tokala breathed with fear in his shaky voice.

"What?" Maab questioned, stepping back.

But then another rotting wolf stepped out from behind a hedge. And another... and another, and in a matter of moments, there were just as many rotting wolves as there were pack members.

"Who are you?!" Alaric called. "This is our land!"

The creature didn't reply. It growled lowly, standing its ground.

Alaric growled in response and prepared to fight.

And everything happened so fast.

The rotting creatures charged forward, and Alaric ordered his pack to fight. Alaric's wolves clashed with the hostiles; Daimon went for the throat of his first target, but when he tore it out, the creature didn't fall. It kept moving, trying to sink its teeth into him. He dodged every attack, and when he knocked the monster onto its side, he mercilessly tore into its body and ripped out its heart.

That killed it.

"Go for their hearts!" he called, but when he turned to face the battlefield, what he saw filled him with horror.

His bitten packmates were writhing around in the snow, screaming, and crying out in agony.

"Go for their hearts!" Tokala relayed after killing one of the creatures.

Daimon hurried to help his brother. He grabbed the monster's leg with his teeth and pulled it back just as it was about to bite Alaric, and then his brother ripped its heart out.

"What the hell are these things?!" Daimon exclaimed in panic.

But his brother froze up. He was staring at the bloody battlefield, watching his injured packmates convulse and shriek painfully. And that was when he uttered, "We have to fall back."

"What?" Daimon asked.

"Fall back!" Alaric yelled.

The pack kicked away the rotting creatures and started running for the house, but a swarm of the same monsters came from around both sides of the building and charged towards them.

Alaric stopped and turned around, but what remained of the creatures they'd been fighting were running their way.

"Alpha, what do we do?!" Sani asked.

"They're coming!" Fala cried.

"Alaric?!" Nyssa insisted.

Alaric grunted and morphed into his Prime form. "Go!" he instructed. "I'll hold them off. Daimon, get them out of here!"

Daimon stared up at his brother. He knew what he was saying, and he knew what he had to do. But how could he? He could leave his—

"Daimon!" Alaric yelled.

He snapped out of his thoughts. There was no time to grieve—no time to argue. He did as his brother asked. "This way!" he called and darted to the right.

The pack followed him through the hedge archway and into the towering maze of thin bushes. But as Daimon led the way, he looked back and watched his brother clash with the swarm of rotting wolves. He wanted to go to him—he wanted to help him—but he had to get the pack out of there.

He gritted his teeth and ignored his emotions. He shoved aside his pain and focused on the exit. But the fact that he was never going to see his brother again ate away at him. His legs started to feel numb, tears formed in his eyes, and the worst pain he'd ever felt electrified through his body.

And then came his brother's voice. "Daimon." It echoed through his head.

Daimon connected with his brother. "Let me come back and help you!"

"No. Listen to me." He grunted and snarled. He was struggling. "It's going to be up to you now. Promise me... promise that you'll take care of Nyssa. Lead the pack... get them somewhere safe."

As he shook his head, Daimon looked back again. "Let me—"

"Promise me, brother!"

"I—"

Alaric's pained cry echoed through Daimon's head.

"I promise!" Daimon called aloud as tears trickled down his furred face. "I promise," he breathed, leading the pack out through the gate.

He stopped outside as the pack passed him and raced into the woods. But the falling snow was getting too thick for him to see through.

"Alaric?" he called, trying to connect with his brother.

But there was no response.

He couldn't even feel him anymore.

As much as he wanted to deny it, he knew his brother was gone.

Everything was up to him now. He was responsible for the pack. He was going to have to lead them, protect them, find them a new home, and most of all, he had to fight for them. He had to fight off the dismay which was quickly pulling him deeper and deeper into a dark sea of grief and sorrow.

He had to be strong.

And he had to wake up.

Chapter Eight

⌇≤ ☽ ≥ ⌇

Ulterior Motives

| Sebastien |

The streets were empty when Sebastien left his apartment. He still found himself looking over his shoulder at the few people he saw, but as far as he could tell, they weren't infected.

He felt like he needed to get over himself; Lord Caedis had already begun setting up security measures to ensure no one brought the virus into the city. But his lingering worry for Clementine made it hard for him to stop panicking.

With a quiet sigh, he hurried into the Venaticus building and nodded at the security guards on his way to the elevator. While he waited to reach his floor, he tapped his foot and stared at the pin pad. He wasn't sure if Lord Caedis was back yet, but he knew Heir Lucian was still here. That kid spent more time in this building than anyone else.

When the elevator doors opened, he walked to the office space. He saw Heir Lucian in his corner office, but there was no sign of Lord Caedis. This conversation wasn't going to go as smoothly as it would if Lord Caedis was here to keep his nephew in line…but Sebastien couldn't avoid it. Clementine came up with a good point, and he needed to share it.

He knocked on Heir Lucian's door.

Heir Lucian didn't look up from his laptop. "What?"

Sebastien stepped into his office. "Heir Lucian, I have something that Lord Caedis might want to hear."

He still didn't look at Sebastien. "*Might?*"

"I was thinking about what the reason for this virus being created might be. What if it's supposed to draw Greymore out? We have *no* idea where he is, right? And neither do the Diabolus. So, what if slaughtering wolf walkers is the Diabolus attempting to bait Greymore? They already took out the asmodi, so it would make sense for them to go after another of the Nosferatu's strongest allies…right?"

"What's the likelihood of Greymore even knowing that this isn't a normal disease that's just floating around?" he mumbled but didn't sound very interested.

Sebastien frowned. "A normal disease doesn't turn wolf walkers into undead monsters…sir."

"Okay, well how is *he* supposed to know that? Is he a scientist?"

Sebastien tried his best to keep calm, but this arrogant kid was pissing him off. Where was Lord Caedis? This would be a whole lot easier if he was here to tell Lucian to stop being an annoying little…. No, no…this was *Heir* Lucian. He couldn't disrespect him, not even in his thoughts.

He exhaled quietly. "I don't know. Do you know where Lord Caedis is?"

Heir Lucian finally took his eyes off his laptop and looked Sebastien up and down. "Maybe."

"Where is he?"

"I'll tell him. You don't have to worry about it." Then, he spun his laptop around to show Sebastien his notes.

Sebastien moved closer so that he could read them, and he saw that Heir Lucian had already come to the same conclusion.

"Are you emailing Lord Caedis?" Sebastien asked.

Heir Lucian adorned an irritated glare. "No. These are my personal notes." He turned the laptop back around. "He probably doesn't even know how to use email; he's like a million years old."

Amused, Sebastien smirked. "He knows how to use a phone, and if you don't send this to him right now, he's gonna flip a table at both of us."

"I haven't had a chance yet because you keep talking," Heir Lucian muttered, rolling his eyes as he typed on his laptop.

As his irritancy returned, Sebastien turned around and headed for the door. "Just send it."

But he wasn't done. The thought of Clementine being in danger because this mission was going to take too long urged him to try and speed things up. So he sighed when he reached the door and turned to face Heir Lucian. "What should we do with Ethan? He won't tell Jackson where the lab is until his Alpha wakes up and decides whether Ethan can travel with them. This whole thing is a ticking time bomb; we can't afford to wait. And…I think Ethan has ulterior motives. He seems a little *too* desperate for simply wanting to uncover evidence to write a story and expose some shady companies."

Heir Lucian looked at him again. "That depends. If I read his mind, are you gonna go running back to Daddy Alucard to tell him I'm being bad again?"

Sebastien scoffed, but Heir Lucian had a point. He *did* tell Lord Caedis when Heir Lucian was acting up and doing things he shouldn't be…but that was one of his jobs. However, he wouldn't tell Lord Caedis *this* time because *someone* had to make this call.

"Okay, A: he's not my daddy, and B: I wanna get this shit done as much as anyone else. So I don't care how we get the answers."

"Oh, really? Because that wasn't the attitude you expressed previously."

He sighed and crossed his arms. "I'm not going to tell anyone, okay? I just think we should get the answers ourselves in case their Alpha doesn't wake up or whoever's next in charge decides that Ethan can't go with them, which is incredibly likely because Ethan's a muto tigris."

"Obviously," Heir Lucian grumbled. Then, he waved him off as he said, "I'll do it in a minute."

"I'm coming with you," Sebastien said firmly. Despite saying that he wasn't going to tell Lord Caedis about this, he was still going to do his job and supervise Heir Lucian.

Heir Lucian sighed as he closed his laptop. Then, he got up, headed over to the door, and passed Sebastien.

Sebastien followed him through the building. Once they reached the room Ethan was being held inside, however, he looked at Heir Lucian and said, "Just don't hurt him."

But Heir Lucian responded with a devious smile and headed into the room.

"Who the hell are you?" Ethan asked. "Where's Jackson?"

Sebastien watched as Heir Lucian approached the table.

"Out of respect for my colleague," Heir Lucian said, stopping beside Ethan, "I'm giving you one last chance to tell us what we want to know. Decline and things will get very uncomfortable very quickly."

Ethan scoffed. "I already made my deal with Jackson. Go and talk to him."

"Okay, decision made—"

Heir Lucian snatched a fistful of Ethan's hair and forced his head down onto the table. Ethan tried to fight—he tried kicking and writhing around—but there wasn't anything he could do.

"Fighting is only gonna make this worse for you," Heir Lucian muttered as he placed his free hand's middle and index fingers on Ethan's temple.

"Get off me, you demon scumbag!" Ethan growled.

"You knew what you were getting into," Heir Lucian replied.

And then Ethan stopped struggling. He fell still and silent, his eyes glazed over...and there wasn't anything he was going to be able to do to stop Heir Lucian.

Sebastien started to feel a little guilty, though. Yes, they needed the information from Ethan sooner rather than later so they could start planning their trip to wherever the lab was, but this move was most likely going to compromise Ethan's friendship with Jackson. Sebastien was supposed to be keeping Jackson on his side...and this was going to prove to him that he couldn't trust him or the Venaticus to live up to their promises.

He sighed quietly and dragged his hand over his face as he leaned back against the door. Heir Lucian let go of Ethan, who groaned and grimaced. He didn't make much of an effort to try and attack Heir Lucian, either. He just sat there and moved both his hands over his head.

"Someone will come down with something for the headache," Heir Lucian said, wiping his hands on his trousers as he made his way over to the door.

"So, what did you find?" Sebastien asked him as they stepped out into the hall.

"Well," he said with a smirk as they slowly walked up the hall. "It turns out that when this guy was a kid, his parents were taken by a couple of masked men. He saw the van his mother and father were tossed into." He paused and looked at Sebastien. "El'Vorian Industries. The pharmaceutical company acting as a front for Lyca Corp. We all know that Lyca Corp. has been into some shady shit for a long time, experimenting on Caeleste, kidnapping rare and endangered Caeleste. Muto are both those things. Anyway, this guy has been looking into them so much because he thinks they still have his parents. He thinks he's going to go out to this lab and either find them or find something that might tell him where they are."

Sebastien nodded slowly he followed Heir Lucian into the elevator and pressed the button to head back up to his office. "I mean, it all makes perfect sense. To be honest, I'm kinda glad that's what he's doing. I was a little scared he was going to turn on us or something. He kinda has the vibe."

"The only malicious thoughts in his head were towards Daimon."

"The wolf walker Alpha?"

"Dude *loathes* him," Heir Lucian revealed. "Probably because he's mated to Jackson."

"Do you think it's gonna be a problem?"

"Probably. Muto and wolf walkers hate each other. But as long as they get the mission done, who gives a shit?"

Sebastien nodded. "Yeah, that's true. And the lab?" he asked as the elevator arrived.

Heir Lucian led the way out and towards his office. "He *suspects* the lab is up in Greykin Valley."

"Suspects…so he's not a hundred percent sure that it's there?"

"That's what suspects implies, yes."

Sebastien held back a sigh and followed Heir Lucian into his office. "All right, so do *you* want to pass this on to Lord Caedis, or should I? Shouldn't he be back by now?" he asked, looking around.

"I can do it," Heir Lucian said as he sat behind his desk.

He nodded. "Okay. Well…I'm gonna go check on the wolf pack. That's where I'll be if I'm needed."

"Okay," he said, opening his laptop.

Sebastien left and started making his way to the hospital wing. It was going to take him a few minutes to get there, so at least he had time to work out how he was going to tell Jackson that he had Heir Lucian look into Ethan's mind for the information they'd promised Jackson could get without harming his friend. The kid was probably going to freak out, but they needed to know. Now, they could begin planning the mission to get to Greykin Valley, which meant they could set out sooner.

All they had to do was wait to see if Daimon would wake up.

| Jackson |

The beeping monitors echoed inside Jackson's head. He listened to the ticking clock, and as each minute passed, he sunk deeper into despair. He knew it would take longer than an hour for Daimon to wake up…but there was a part of him that was beginning to *actually* believe that might never happen.

He lifted his head from Daimon's arm and stared at his lifeless face. Was there nothing the doctors could do? They'd managed to remove a knife from his *spine* without killing him; surely, waking him up couldn't be impossible.

No. He was letting his emotions get the better of him. If there was anything, those doctors would have tried it already.

He frowned and looked down at Daimon's hand. "I don't know if you can hear me," he mumbled sullenly. "But you gotta wake up, Daimon. I don't know what I'm supposed to do without you."

His heart ached. He couldn't picture the next *hour* of his life without Daimon. He'd never felt this way about anyone, and he had no idea how to cope with the pain. Daimon was a part of him now; he *couldn't* lose him. Nothing would be or feel the same.

But no amount of pleading would wake him.

He heard some commotion outside. With a confused frown, he peered out through the blinds. The pack were standing in the waiting area, but they were following someone with their eyes as they shot a volley of questions about Daimon's progress in their direction.

And then the door to Daimon's room opened.

Sebastien stepped in and closed the door behind him. "Jackson."

"Yeah?" he asked but almost choked on his response. Was he here to tell him something he didn't want to hear?

"Look, I understand if this makes you mad, but just…." He dragged his hand over his face. "All right, look. Heir Lucian looked into Ethan's mind and—"

"What?!" he exclaimed. "You said that—"

"I had my suspicions that—"

Jackson stood up as his grief quickly transformed into *rage*. "You told me you'd leave it up to me!" he interjected. "And now Ethan's probably going to think he can't trust me!"

"Calm down!" Sebastien snapped.

"Calm down?!" he mocked, taking a step closer to him. "He said he was gonna give me the location!"

Sebastien held out his right hand. "You better stay where you are, kid."

Jackson stopped moving. His heart was racing, and anger was *burning* inside him. It was getting harder and harder for him to contain—hell, he didn't want to contain it. He'd *finally* gotten Ethan back, and now he was probably never going to trust him again because of this.

And that was when he let his anger rule him. He snarled in frustration and dismay and lunged at Sebastien.

But Sebastien snatched hold of his throat and pinned him against the wall in the blink of an eye. "I said calm it!" he growled.

Jackson stared at him. He didn't try to break free—he was too stunned to do that. Why did he lunge at him like that? He wasn't entirely sure what came over him, but now that his rage was settling, he felt nothing but confusion and regret. "I didn't…mean to do that, I'm sorry," he said, shaking his head.

With an irritated huff, Sebastien let go of him and stepped back. "You're lucky I'm not some other random demon or your head would probably be on the floor."

"I'm sorry," he mumbled. The anger was returning, but he was starting to feel…sick? He frowned and took a deep breath, trying to calm himself down.

"Forget it," Sebastien mumbled. "You gotta learn to control yourself, though. Others might not be so forgiving."

He nodded and took another deep breath. As he set his sights on Sebastien again, he did his best to keep calm and collected. But he was still pissed off. "You said you'd let me get the information from Ethan. He's gonna blame me for this."

"We'll smooth it over with him, all right? And if he doesn't come around, hell, we'll get someone to make him forget all about it—"

"Are you kidding me? No!"

"All right, all right. It was just a suggestion," Sebastien exclaimed. Then, he huffed again and crossed his arms. "Look, the whole reason I roped Heir Lucian into doing it was because I felt like your buddy Ethan was hiding something."

Jackson adorned a confused stare. "Why would you—"

"And it turned out that he was. He ever tell you about his parents…or mention anything about them?"

He thought to himself for a moment. "Only that they disappeared when he was a kid. It was actually one of the things we bonded over."

"Well, when Heir Lucian looked through his mind, he found that Ethan's parents were actually taken by Lyca Corp. He thinks—"

"He…thinks that he'll find them at the lab," Jackson realized. "That's why he's always been so into all this wolf walker Lyca Corp. stuff, isn't it?"

"That's the way it seems, yeah. The fact he didn't already tell you makes it look like he wanted to tell you himself…or maybe not. So, I'm sorry for exposing your pal like this, but I wasn't going to keep this from you and let him explode at you when you next see him."

Jackson shook his head as he sunk into his seat beside Daimon's bed. "No, it's…I'd rather you tell me than not, to be honest. I just…this all makes so much sense now. I knew Ethan was like me with all this love for uncovering mysteries and exposing corruption, but I never thought his motivation for it all was to find his parents. And…yeah, muto were hunted for their fur, right? Is that why Lyca Corp. took them?"

"We don't know for sure, and I'm not sure that Ethan does, either. But…if he gets around to telling you, I suggest you *don't* act like you don't know. I, uh…might have been in a similar spot once or twice," Sebastien admitted.

Taking his eyes off the floor, Jackson looked at him. "Really? I wouldn't have guessed," he mumbled sarcastically.

"Hey, no need to be a dick about it, all right?" he grumbled.

"Sorry," he said with a sigh. He didn't mean to be so rude; he was letting his emotions get to him again. "What did you do?"

Sebastien leaned against the wall by the door. "Well…it was a long time ago. When I was in school, actually. I met this kid—Clementine. I was into him the moment I saw him kill some other guy and hide his body in the library—"

"Wait," Jackson interjected, shaking his head. "What? He just killed some other kid?!" But then he remembered. "Oh. The academy where they all fought over the New World or something, right?"

He nodded. "Of course, Clementine had no idea I saw. He had no idea I was following him around until I showed myself," he said with a quiet laugh. "Anyway, I was a nosy piece of shit back then—still am, actually—so I snuck into his dorm room while he was in class. I found these little pills stuffed in the back of his nightstand. I didn't know what they were at first glance, but I kinda…pieced it together eventually."

"Pieced what together?"

"I'm not this like…snippy snappy detective like you, but I did find enough clues after a few days. The pills, and the fact he smelled this certain kinda way. Like how humans smell when they're dying."

Jackson grimaced. "I…can't say I know it."

Sebastien waved his hand dismissively. "I saw him out in the woods picking these little mushrooms—and I'll add that there was a leshen in those woods and no kid in their right mind would go out there." He laughed again and shook his head. "You know, that's another thing I loved about him. He led this group of other kids out there to distract the leshen while he got what he came for."

Where was this going? This guy was getting side-tracked like he had ADHD or something.

"Uh…anyway, yeah, the mushrooms. Those, the pills, the smell. He was sick. He had colligo-interitus."

Jackson frowned unsurely. "What's that?"

Sebastien sighed. "Hmm. Terminal disease. You know about the one-hundred-year-long war that happened over two hundred years ago, right?"

He nodded.

"A lot of the history books say it ended in 1126, but it was still going on in smaller parts of the world for another fifty-ish years. Somewhere in those fifty years, someone unleashed this poisonous fog in some parts of DeiganLupus. Clementine's village was hit, and everyone got sick. He knew he was going to die, but he wasn't going to go out without avenging his sister first. That's a whole other story. But my point is, I regretted snooping around and learning something about him before he told me himself. I had to act like I had no idea…and I wasn't sure if I convinced him, but I felt like total shit the entire time."

Jackson looked down at his lap. He wouldn't do that to Ethan. Not because he didn't want to feel like shit but because his friend deserved to know that he now knew. "What happened?" he then asked, glancing at Sebastien.

"With what?"

"To Clementine."

"Oh, he's fine."

"What? But you said—"

"Oh, yeah. He died. In my arms actually…. I was broken. But then I hunted down Lord Caedis and made a deal. I became his little errand boy, and in exchange, he brought Clementine back to me. We're mated, actually. Well…I imprinted on him. I wish I could bond with him, but he's not a demon, so," he said with a shrug. "We're gonna get married, though."

That made Jackson smile. "When?"

"Sometime. I dunno. We're always too busy working to plan anything. Anyway, yeah. Sorry I had to tell you Ethan's motives."

Jackson shrugged. "Did you find out where the lab is?"

"We did. We'll keep you updated, all right?"

He nodded and stared at Daimon. "Okay."

"I'll come by again later." Then, Sebastien left.

Jackson's dismay quickly returned. Sebastien's story about Clementine made him crave Daimon's affection—he just wanted to kiss him and feel his arms around him. But he couldn't. And he had no idea when he'd get to again.

Chapter Nine

⌐ ≤ ☽ ≥ ⌐

But Then I Found You

| Daimon |

*I*n the murk of the early morning, Daimon closed in on his target. After a week without a good meal, he could finally bring something larger than a couple of rabbits and squirrels back to his pack.

There it was... a male pronghorn chewing the grass with its head buried in the snow. It had no idea he was about to pounce, and although it wasn't an elk or moose, it would still feed his wolves enough to give them the strength to carry on for a few more days.

He prowled closer... and closer, keeping his eyes on where he would sink his teeth.

But then he felt it.

Something he thought he'd never feel.

His focus was immediately stolen; his senses went haywire, urging him to turn around and follow the source of this strange, enticing feeling. An entwining flurry of desire, longing, and desperation twisted around inside his body, striking him so hard that he forgot everything he was doing momentarily. He needed to follow—he wanted to—but a part of him thought this might not be real.

Why would it be real? Nyssa claimed him. He was hers. And he'd promised Alaric he'd look after her.

But... the feeling wasn't getting any weaker. It was only getting stronger, like someone had thrown a rope around his body and was now tugging on it, and the more intense the urge became, the less resistance Daimon found himself putting up.

He had to go.

Daimon abandoned the pronghorn and sped off through the forest. He ran as fast as his legs would carry him, swerving past boulders and trees. The feeling reeling him in was soon accompanied by an enthralling scent; it was like coffee and roses with the slightest hint of citrus, and when Daimon burst out of the forest and followed a vast white field, the scent became so overwhelming that he stifled a few breaths.

He knew he was close but didn't want to throw himself at whoever he was being led to. Before revealing himself, he wanted to see who he was about to come face to face with. He didn't want to risk starting a fight if they were from another pack. This was his territory, but he was alone, and if a pack were invading, he'd need backup.

So instead of continuing his mad sprint across the opening, he turned left and hurried up a hill. He crouched, using his white fur to keep himself shrouded in the snow, and then he scanned the area below with his eyes.

There. He spotted someone stumbling through the white, naked and confused. The guy looked dazed, there were streaks and splotches of blood all over him, and he seemed to have no idea where he was, where he was going, or what he was doing.

Daimon knew at first glance that this man had just gone through his first shift, and the fact that there were no signs of other wolf walkers around made it evident that he was bitten, not born. No Ascelan human would willingly wander out to the mountains at night, either, so this guy was either a total moron... or not from Ascela. But that was all Daimon could tell from where he was. He wasn't ready to reveal himself; he needed more information. He had to be sure that a pack wasn't looking for that man.

The Alpha crept through the snow, trailing him to a river. That was where the guy collapsed and passed out.

Daimon waited. He kept his eyes on the unconscious man while the sun rose over the mountains. Was that really supposed to be his mate? A bitten, lost outsider. A rogue. Someone who would have no idea what it was to be a wolf walker. Essentially a clueless, helpless child.

It made sense, though. Of course it did. His grandfather's mate was an outsider from another land, and his father's mate was, too. It fit the bill perfectly that his mate would be someone from somewhere else.

His feelings of uncertainty began fading. The man's scent ensnared him, and his senses begged him to move nearer. He might be a lost rogue, but he would need Daimon's help. And Daimon wanted to help him. He wanted to get closer. But he had to be cautious. He had a pack to consider, and there was no way for him to know whether this rogue was a threat. He couldn't let his feelings rule him here.

The man started waking up.

A strange eagerness shot through Daimon's body, and in response, he tensed up. He eyed the man closely as he came around, noticed the blood on his tawny-brown skin, and hastily cleaned it off using the river. He seemed a lot more lucid now, so perhaps Daimon could read him easier than when he was stumbling through the snow.

The guy got up. He started walking. So Daimon followed. He shadowed the man as he trekked through the snow, went over a ridge, and down a hill towards a village.

Why would he go to a village? Those humans would figure out what he was in a matter of moments and slaughter him! Daimon couldn't let that happen.

He hurried after him, but he was too late. The man had already stolen and pulled some clothes on and hurried deeper into the village.

Daimon snarled in frustration and left his wolf form. He did just as the rouge did and snatched a pair of trousers and a shirt from a nearby clothesline. As he got dressed, he stuck as closely as he could to the man using alleys and the shadows. He watched him go into a tavern... and when he saw all the humans get up and confront him, Daimon's heart started racing.

He wanted to burst out of his cover and go in there and pull the kid out before the villagers could hurt him, but there were too many of them. He had no idea what weapons they possessed—

But then he heard one of them yell, "He's infected!"

The humans took out their weapons and began chasing the rogue through the village.

Daimon wasn't going to let them kill him. This rogue was supposed to be his mate, so he would protect him. He would give in to his urges and instincts and do whatever he had to to get this man to safety.

He hurried through the alley, and when he spotted some loose planks above him, he climbed up and moved along the balconies, following the rogue's trail. He watched the panicked man run into an alley, so Daimon made his way along the roofs of several buildings until he could see the man below.

"Up here," he said, holding out his hand.

The man sharply turned his head and looked up at him. His eyes were bluer than the sky, and he was easily the most beautiful man Daimon had ever seen. But there wasn't time for him to stand there and admire the man who was his mate.

For a moment, the rogue seemed to consider whether taking Daimon's hand was a good idea, but he took it, and then the Alpha pulled him up onto the planks. Then, as the villagers yelled and waved their precious weapons around, Daimon started leading the way to safety.

But as he descended the stairs towards the forest, the world around him became a haze.

Everything went black.

He could hear a voice in his head.

It was a voice he knew.

And beeping. Slow, steady beeping.

He was cold. For the first time in a long, long while... he could feel the cold biting his skin.

Someone was holding his hand. The warmth of their skin against his was comforting, and when his senses slowly returned to him, he was met with the same enthralling scent of coffee, roses, and citrus which led him to the man who changed his life.

Jackson. He was right here... but Daimon couldn't see him.

The Alpha tried to move. He attempted to grasp Jackson's hand, but his limbs didn't respond. His eyes wouldn't open, and he couldn't speak a word. He wasn't able to make a sound.

Where was he? What was going on?

And why couldn't he wake up?

He had to wake up. Jackson was waiting for him. His pack needed him. He couldn't leave them—he couldn't leave the man he loved. All those years ago, he'd promised Alaric he'd take care of his pack; he might have lost half of them because of Nyssa, but those left relied on him. He had to fight whatever this was for them, and he had to fight for Jackson. He'd only just found him—he'd finally found the wolf he would spend his life with... and he wouldn't let him go.

| **Jackson** |

The sun was rising. As light crept in through the blinds, Jackson lifted his head from Daimon's arm and stared at what he could see of the city outside. He was tired, fatigued from all his dismay and worry, and as the monitors beep-beep-beeped... he sunk a little deeper into despair.

Although the night was over, there were no signs of improvement. The Alpha was still unconscious. He hadn't moved an inch. Jackson knew it took longer than a day for someone to come out of a coma, but it already felt like he'd been waiting forever. Every minute he spent sitting there staring at Daimon's still, pale face made him believe more and more that he might never open his eyes.

He slipped his hand into Daimon's, but with his sadness came the anger. Outside, he could hear his packmates talking, and among the voices was Julian. Jackson scowled as he stared out through the gaps in the blinds; he wanted to go out there and grab Julian; he wanted to question them and find out if they were responsible for this... but as the anger boiled inside him, he started feeling nauseous.

With a sickly grunt, he lowered his head and took a deep breath, but it didn't help. In fact, it made it worse. The nausea intensified, so much that Jackson felt like he was going to throw up, and when he retched, his heart started racing, and he scrambled to his feet. He darted into the bathroom, and just as he reached the toilet, he threw up with a painful groan, his body tightening, his breaths stifled. He breathed frantically in an attempt to cope with the sickness and pain enthralling him; when he thought that he could pull away and rest his back against the wall, though, he threw up again...and again, wincing feverishly as he did.

Someone knocked on the door.

Jackson groaned and glanced over his shoulder.

It was Tokala. He stood in the bathroom doorway with a concerned frown. "Are you okay?"

He took a deep breath and waited, but the discomfort ensnaring his body was lifting. Was it over? With another exhale, he slowly stood up, grabbed some tissue, wiped his mouth, and then tossed it into the toilet before flushing. "Fine," he grumbled, lurching past Tokala and back into Daimon's room. He slumped down at the Alpha's bedside and exhaled deeply, trying to relax.

"Are you sure?" Tokala asked.

Jackson nodded.

The Zeta's eyes slowly shifted to Daimon. "No improvement?" he asked.

"Nothing," Jackson answered sullenly.

Tokala sighed sadly. "I, uh...I'm sure this is a silly question, but are you hungry? The nurse said they're bringing some food down for us. You should probably try and eat something."

He shook his head and took a sip of the water from the cup on the cupboard beside him. "I don't want anything."

"You need to keep your strength up, Jackson," Tokala said with concern in his voice.

Not only had he just thrown up and had no appetite whatsoever, but Jackson didn't want to leave Daimon's bedside in case the Alpha woke up while he was gone. He wanted to be there the moment he opened his eyes. "I'm fine," he mumbled.

"Jackson," Tokala insisted. "Do you really think he'd want you to sit around starving yourself?"

"I don't know what he wants," he grumbled. "No one does. He's unconscious. He can't tell us anything. He can't hear us saying anything. He's just...there."

"J—"

"Leave me alone," he mumbled despondently, resting his head on Daimon's arm again.

Tokala didn't say anything else. He pulled the door shut and left.

Jackson knew Tokala was only trying to help, and he didn't mean to be rude, but he didn't want to eat or do anything that would involve leaving Daimon for even a moment. He had to stay right where he was.

He closed his eyes and huffed sadly, trying to keep himself from crying. But all he could think about was Daimon not waking up. He had no idea what he was going to do. Who would be in charge? Tokala?

With a sullen scowl, he buried his face in the blanket wrapped around Daimon. He tightened his grip on his hand and listened to the sound of his heart. All he wanted right now was to hear his voice. But instead…his ears focused on another man's voice.

Sebastien was outside.

He turned his head and stared out the room's window. The white-haired demon was talking to Tokala and the pack, and Doctor Kowalski was with him. Jackson listened to them talk, but they weren't saying anything interesting, only asking how everyone was doing. And then Sebastien asked where Jackson was.

Jackson sighed deeply and prepared for whatever conversation he was about to be roped into. He was still mad at him for letting Heir Lucian read Ethan's mind, but he didn't want to lash out again, so he was going to have to control himself.

The door opened.

"Hey, kid," Sebastien greeted.

He glanced at him and grumbled, "Hey."

Doctor Kowalski stepped into the room, too. "Hey, Jackson. Uh…Tokala out there told us that you threw up. Everything okay?"

Jackson sighed. "Yeah, I'm just…I don't know. Worried."

"Well…grief can do all sorts of things to a person," Kowalski said.

Sebastien cleared his throat. "I know you want to stay here with him," Sebastien said, nodding at Daimon, "but we can't put this mission on hold for too long. The cadejo virus might be evolving—as we've all seen—and we need to get to that laboratory. Heir Lucian emailed Lord Caedis last night, and he sent his orders over this morning." He looked at Doctor Kowalski.

The doctor clapped his hands together. "So, I hear you're going to be training with Lucian, and I thought I'd remind you that I can repair those fangs of yours. I highly recommend that you accept the offer because they could come in handy. I can also explain—to the best of my knowledge—what you can do with them."

Jackson sighed and looked down at Daimon's hand. "I don't want to leave him."

"Jackson, I know this is hard," Kowalski said, "but you need to get yourself ready to head back out there."

"I'm not going back out there until Daimon—"

"Kid, this mission is more important than him, okay?" Sebastien interjected.

Jackson scowled angrily. He wanted to snap, but he contained himself.

"I'm sorry, and I know it's horrible for me to say, but it's the truth," Sebastien said. "The longer you sit around here waiting for him to wake up, the more people could die. You and your pack are the only capable people we have right now to head out there and get to this lab. You need to do what's best for everyone."

Jackson turned his head and glared at him. He wanted to argue—he wanted to yell all the reasons why he needed to stay here. But none of them were good enough to dismiss

Sebastien's statement. He was right. If he didn't get to that lab and find the information the Venaticus needed, then a lot more people could die. The virus could even spread further than Ascela. He didn't want that to happen, and he didn't want to be the reason it happened, either.

He looked at the floor and scowled in dismay. "Fine," he muttered, his voice breaking a little.

"Great. I can do it like…just next door if you don't wanna be too far away from your pack," Kowalski said.

"After you get your fangs fixed, you'll spend a few hours training with Heir Lucian," Sebastien said. "Once he's satisfied that you're ready, we'll head to a meeting room and discuss the plan. If your Alpha hasn't woken up by this time tomorrow, then I'm sorry, but you're going to have to go ahead without him."

They were only giving him twenty-four hours to wake up. That made Jackson so angry that he wanted to jump to his feet and argue, but he didn't have the strength. The nausea was returning, and he knew that if he burst out in a fit of rage, he'd probably throw up again.

"Meanwhile, I'll be taking a team out to capture one of the infected humans we came across in the woods," Sebastien continued. "So, if you need anything, you can ask Stan over there," he said, pointing to an armed guard outside in the waiting room. "He'll be escorting you around the building."

Jackson nodded. Whatever.

"Right, that's me done," Sebastien said. "I'll see you later, Jackson. And I hope Daimon wakes up."

As Sebastien left, Jackson huffed quietly and glanced at Kowalski.

"You, uh…ready to go? I think there's a room just across the way there that'll have everything I need," the doctor asked.

Jackson looked at Daimon again. He couldn't go. But if he *didn't* start preparing to head out to the lab, then he'd be contributing to the virus' spread. *He* would be postponing the invention of a cure, and he wasn't going to get anyone else killed. Not when he had the power to stop it. So he exhaled shakily, dismissed as much of his dismay as he could, and stood up. But when he tried to walk away, he couldn't pull his hand free from Daimon's.

As Jackson turned to face the Alpha, he looked down at his hand. Although he'd let go, *Daimon* was holding on. Daimon was grasping his hand, and he was gradually tightening his grip.

"D-Daimon?" Jackson exclaimed excitedly.

"What is it?" Kowalski asked, moving closer.

"He…he's holding my hand," Jackson said as his heart started beating faster. His dismay was quickly replaced by a feeling of hopefulness, and as he watched a frown flicker across Daimon's pale face, he smiled and exhaled in relief. "He's waking up!"

Everyone seemed to hear him speak. A flurry of voices echoed from outside, and as Jackson moved closer to Daimon's bed, the pack started filing into the room.

"Daimon?" Jackson asked quietly, squeezing his hand. "Can you hear me?"

Daimon frowned again, and a muffled grunt came from his mouth.

Jackson very quickly became so overwrought with joy and relief; he tried to keep as calm as he could, though. As much as he wanted to fling himself at Daimon and cry into his neck, he didn't want to do that in front of everyone or risk hurting the Alpha. So, instead, he placed his hand on Daimon's cheek and moved his face closer to his.

Daimon was no longer cold to the touch. He wasn't only waking up, but he was getting better, too. His skin was back to being warm and soft, and although he still looked pale, he didn't appear utterly lifeless anymore.

"Hey," Jackson said softly as he watched Daimon slowly open his eyes. "You're okay," he told him, trying to keep himself from crying, but he was so overwhelmed that it was impossible.

When Daimon's eyes met Jackson's, the Alpha's confused frown quickly transformed into a sad but relieved expression. "Jackson?" he asked, his voice a croaky whisper.

Jackson nodded as a tear trickled down the side of his face. "Yeah."

"Well, I can see you guys are gonna be busy for the next while, so I'll come back in a little, all right?" Kowalski called.

No one replied to him.

The pack moved closer to Daimon's bed and started asking him if he was okay and how he felt.

But Daimon didn't respond to them. He kept his eyes on Jackson and tightened his grip on his hand. "Jackson," he said weakly.

"It's okay," Jackson said, caressing the Alpha's hair. "You don't have to say anything."

Daimon grimaced and closed his eyes. He looked like he was in pain.

"I-I think he's in pain," Jackson panicked, looking over at the pack. "Someone go and get Kowalski."

Julian nodded and hurried out of the room.

"It's okay," Jackson said softly as he gently stroked the side of Daimon's face.

"What's wrong?" came Kowalski's voice, and as he came into the room, everyone moved out of his way.

"I think he's hurting," Jackson answered.

The doctor moved around to the other side of Daimon's bed and fiddled with one of the monitors. "No worries, I'll just up his painkillers a little more. That should help."

Jackson watched the pained grimace slowly disappear from Daimon's face.

"Look," Kowalski said. "I know you guys wanna see him, but he should be resting. He just woke up and his body's been through a lot. Give him a couple hours."

Although he didn't want to leave Daimon, Jackson considered what Kowalski said. The last thing he wanted to do was slow Daimon's recovery by being clingy. But he wanted to sit there and hold his hand. He wanted to talk to him and let him know that everything was fine.

"It's…okay," Daimon murmured, squeezing Jackson's hand. "I'll be fine."

Jackson frowned hesitantly. What if he left and Daimon suddenly slipped back into a coma? He looked at Kowalski. "W-what if we leave and something happens?"

"Don't worry," Kowalski said with an assuring tone. "There will be a nurse out there at the reception all the time, so if anything happens—not that it will, he looks pretty stable to me—or if he needs anything, she'll get to him. Dr Laurent will be down in a few hours to check how he's healing, too."

With his reluctance settling, Jackson sighed and set his sights on Daimon again. "I don't wanna leave you," he mumbled sadly.

Daimon turned his head to look up at him. "I'll be okay," he told him. "Go."

Jackson nodded as Daimon let go of his hand. "Okay. I'll be back as soon as I can."

"Okay."

Then, Jackson stepped away from the bed and exhaled deeply. He looked at Kowalski. "We can, uh…go do the fang thing."

Kowalski nodded. "All right, everyone. Let's clear outta here and give your Alpha some space."

As the doctor ushered them out, everyone complained quietly.

Jackson looked back at Daimon one last time, and as the Alpha smiled weakly at him, he smiled back. Then, he followed Doctor Kowalski. There was a lot to do today, and he was dreading the dental surgery more than training with Heir Lucian. But both had to be done, and he'd do his best to cooperate.

Chapter Ten

⇝ ≼ ☽ ≽ ⇜

The Infected

| Sebastien |

There was something about the woods that always creeped Sebastien out. Even in the early morning, not much light pierced through the treetops. A flurry of snow crept in where it could, and that which had already set crunched beneath Sebastien's boots as he led the way forward.

He glanced at the squad of six soldiers following behind him, grasping their guns tightly as they searched through the murk. They carried large rucksacks on their back containing the equipment needed for the job, and although it looked like it weighed a ton, none of them complained.

Sebastien couldn't smell anything nearby—at least nothing that would pounce at them and try to tear their insides out. Once he reached a small opening, he halted and looked around. "This is good," he said, pointing at the ground.

The soldiers nodded and started setting up tripwires and the cage that Sebastien hoped would hold the infected human they were after.

Sebastien leaned back against a tree and watched. Whenever he heard something move through the snow, he searched for anything that might be a threat, but all he could see were foxes, rabbits, and a few deer in the distance.

"We're all set up, sir," Captain Barkley said, gesturing to the laid trap.

"All right." Sebastien sighed, standing up straight. "We stick to the plan," he said firmly, glancing at each soldier as they stood behind their captain. "You guys are vulnerable to this thing's bite, so you remain in your cover, and the *only* time you break it is if I need your help or something enters this area and may compromise the trap. Got it?"

"Yes, sir," they replied.

"Good." Sebastien took a communication collar out of his pocket, clipped it around his neck, and put a small earpiece into his right ear. "You keep your radios handy. Keep me updated; I'll do the same. We ready?"

"We're ready, sir," Captain Barkley confirmed.

Sebastien shifted into his kludde form. He stretched his wings out, shook his head, and prepared to head into the woods. "Let's get this thing done," he mumbled, and then, as the soldiers took their positions behind the trees, he raced deeper into the forest. He waited until he was a good distance away before saying, "Can you all hear me all right?"

"*We hear you loud and clear, sir,*" Barkley replied through the earpiece.

"Right. I'll let you know when I find a target."

"*Understood.*"

Sebastien slowed when he approached a hill. Once he emerged from the woods and reached the top, he carefully scoured the land below. Trees shrouded the landscape, and the falling snow made it hard for him to see. Flying and searching from overhead wouldn't be any better, either.

With a sigh, he headed down the hill and moved silently through the forest. He sniffed the ground and air, scanning for the slightest hint of the rotting stench the infected gave off, but what his nose picked up instead made him tense.

Humans…and wolfsbane. There were hunters nearby.

He frowned cautiously and took cover behind a fallen log. If it were night, he'd use his demon ability to shroud himself in the dark, but it was daylight, and the best he could do to hide was use the environment.

Should he investigate? What if they were the same hunters they raided last night? Lord Caedis would want to know about that, especially if they were looking to find their missing comrade and avenge those he and Jackson's wolf pack killed.

Hunters might be human nine times out of ten, but that didn't mean they were stupid. Sebastien had learned never to underestimate them, especially since many soldiers who worked for the Nosferatu's subdivisions were human. They could be smart, tactical, and even a little devious. He wouldn't make the mistake of shrugging them off and telling himself they'd never track the pack back to Silverlake.

He was going to have to investigate.

Sebastien kept low and prowled through the woods. He followed the wolfsbane scent, and when he heard voices, he covered behind a boulder. "Barkley, we got hunters in the perimeter," he whispered.

"*How far out, sir?*" Barkley replied.

"Half a mile, maybe a little more." He peeked around the rock and focused on a trio of armed men standing by a jeep. "I can see three and a jeep, but I can hear several voices."

"*Do you need us to move in and back you up, sir?*"

Sebastien pondered. The hunters were near where his squad set their trap, and there was no way they wouldn't hear the trap go off and the infected human screeching. However, he couldn't tell what they were doing. Were they tracking? Were they waiting for someone or something? "No," he replied, keeping hushed. "I'm not sure what they're doing, but there's a chance they might be the same hunters we extracted Ethan from last night. If they are, and they're looking for revenge, we might have to bring this to Lord Caedis. They could interfere with the mission, and that's something we can't have."

"Of course, sir. We're on standby."

Sebastien scanned his immediate area. There were enough trees and bushes to get closer without being seen, so he started moving nearer, ensuring he stayed hidden. The closer he got, the more hunters he could see; there were three by the jeep and four others *skinning* a dead arieto. They cut the moose-looking beast's cat-like tail off, sawed away its moss-covered antlers, and laughed as they did it.

These men didn't deserve to live—

No…he couldn't let his anger consume him. He had to keep composed and figure out whether these guys were just hunting or stopped to strip the arieto on their way elsewhere.

"Oi, Frank!" one of the men by the jeep called.

The hunter standing over the others while they skinned the arieto looked at the man, tossing his cigarette into the snow. "What?"

"How much longer is this shit gonna take? We gotta get back to camp."

"As long as it fucking needs to take, Bill," Frank replied.

Bill scoffed, looking at his two friends. "Guy's a fucking party, ain't he?"

The men laughed.

Sebastien scowled as they loaded the arieto's severed parts into their jeep. They were headed back to camp, and since the jeep looked like the one Ethan's group was driving, it was safe to assume that these guys *were* part of that hunting party. Why were they in such a hurry to get back, though?

He couldn't follow them. The mission to capture an infected human was more important. So he waited. They got into their jeep and drove off, and once they were out of Sebastien's line of sight, he left the brush cover and headed in the opposite direction. "They've gone east," he told the squad. "Looks like they're heading back to their comrades. I'm getting back on task. Contact Lord Caedis and let him know Ethan's band of hunters might be getting closer to Silverlake."

"Roger, sir," Barkley replied.

Sebastien prowled through the woods. He searched for what felt like *hours*…until he finally picked up the scent he was looking for.

Decaying flesh and rotting blood.

Every time he inhaled that smell, it brought him back to the first moment he caught a whiff. The memory of the place where he initially encountered the disease cursed him. He'd never forgive himself for getting Caleb killed or forget what happened that day.

He didn't want to think about it, though. The last thing he needed was to become a victim of his past. He needed to concentrate and find the source of the smell. It guided him through the woods into a thinner part of the forest. There was more space and less cover, but fog was beginning to ensnare the area, so it wasn't hard for him to hide.

The smell became stronger when he approached the base of the cliff. But it was accompanied by gunpowder, gasoline, and old stew. He frowned and stalked closer. Once he moved around a protruding boulder, a small camp came into view. There wasn't anyone around, but the fire was burning with a pot of stew hanging over it. All three tents were shredded, the snow was red with blood, and a snowmobile was turned over with fuel leaking onto the ground.

Something growled. A wet, deep gurgle came from inside the camp, and it didn't sound like a cadejo. Could it be an infected human?

Sebastien climbed onto the boulder—high enough to keep him safe from whatever was down there—and moved closer.

The sound of grinding teeth and cracking bones made Sebastien grimace, and he felt sick when he set his eyes on the creature inside the second tent. It was a woman with long brown hair; her white fur coat was covered in blood and something black, and she was kneeling beside the corpse of a man, pulling the flesh off his body and shoving it into her crooked mouth.

He frowned in disgust. The sound, the smell…seeing the thing feast on human flesh forced him to recall when he'd first encountered these undead things. Part of him wished he didn't have to take part in a mission where he'd be so close to the cadejo and whatever else was infected with the virus; it reminded him of the things he'd much rather forget, but he couldn't refuse Lord Caedis' orders. Whatever that demon told him to do, he'd abide.

Sebastien took a deep breath, composing himself. He focused on how he'd get the zombie back to the squad's trap; it wasn't a cadejo, so he'd have no trouble picking it up and flying it back, and it was still snowing, so if hunters were lurking in the woods, they wouldn't be able to see him above. But he wasn't sure how infected humans reacted or if it would be fast or slow or able to escape his grip. There was only one way to find out.

He spread his wings, swooped down, and grabbed the zombie by its arms. It grunted and groaned, reaching up to bite, but Sebastien kept his paws far enough away. "I'm inbound with the target," he said.

"*Roger that, sir. We're ready and waiting,*" Captain Barkley replied.

As the falling snow thickened, he carried the snarling zombie back to his awaiting squad. He swerved and plummeted towards the small opening, dropping the zombie a few feet from the ground. As he raced back up, the tripwires triggered, and four walls of bars rose from the snow and clamped around the zombie.

Sebastien landed near Barkley as his men hurried to secure the cage.

"Watch its teeth!" the captain warned.

The zombie tried reaching through the bars, but the soldiers dodged its attacks and locked the cage.

"All right, good work, men," Barkley called.

"We should get this thing back to the truck before something or someone comes to investigate," Sebastien said. He walked to the cage and turned his back to it. "Get it over with."

The soldiers took several chains and a thick leather harness from their bags. While one attached the harness around Sebastien's hound-like body, the others connected the chains to the cage, linking them to Sebastien's harness.

"Let's go," Sebastien muttered. He didn't want to think about how humiliated he felt being a workhorse. He just wanted to get it over with.

The soldiers followed as he dragged the cage through the woods. They didn't have far to go; the truck was only a few minutes away.

But a few minutes was all it took for everything to fall apart. The sound of approaching tyres signalled that things were about to get a lot more complicated.

"We've got incoming!" Captain Barkley announced, swinging to point his rifle toward the oncoming vehicle.

"For fuck's sake," Sebastien grumbled. "Get this shit off me."

The soldiers hurried to get the chains off. Once he was free, Sebastien joined the squad's defence line. The fog was too thick to see what was coming their way, and he didn't like what the rest of his senses told him.

"There's at least ten of them," he said. "Humans with weapons—no...twelve of them."

"Defend Officer Huxley," Barkley ordered.

"Protect the fucking zombie," Sebastien corrected as the soldiers took position around him. "I'll deal with these assholes." He waited as he felt the humans' auras get closer.

Something dark appeared inside the fog. It grew nearer, revealing several *jeeps* when they came close enough that the fog didn't shroud them. The four vehicles came to a halt thirty feet from Sebastien and the squad, and four geared-up hunters climbed out of each vehicle.

"Well, well, well," came a man's voice. "What do we have here?"

Sebastien set his eyes on the speaker. The bearded man was wearing the skin of a wolf walker on his back; there were gauntlets made of antlers around his wrists, and a tiny taxidermy fox head dangled from his rifle.

"This is Venaticus business," Captain Barkley called. "You have—"

"I don't give a shit whose or what's business this is—"

"Carlos, that's the thing we saw leaving our camp last night," one of the hunters muttered to their leader.

Harry set his eyes on Sebastien and pointed. "You killed my men," he accused. "You and your little wolf scum buddies. And you Venaticus cunts were in on it, weren't ya?"

"Get back in your vehicles and leave," Barkley warned.

But Harry chortled, looking to his men. "Riker's fucking livid at you lot. But when he sees that *I* brought them the people responsible for taking all his critters away *and* killing his men, I'll be his next general like that." He clicked his fingers and smiled smugly.

Sebastien eyed each of them. They looked just as eager as their leader to attack but were clearly holding back because they weren't sure whether they could deal with him. After all, he *was* the last kludde in this world, and likely the first they'd ever seen. They didn't know what to expect. He could use that to his advantage.

"*Or*," Sebastien said, stretching his wings out ever so slightly to reveal the long, jagged spikes on their carpals, "I kill every single one of you right here and all you'll be is food for the undead things living out here."

"Holy shit, the thing speaks," one of the men scoffed.

Harry flexed his weapon. "I think… the only ones dying out here will be you lot. You might be part of that Nosferatu nonsense, but we out here don't give a flying fuck. We *hunt* Caeleste, and that government of yours is *all* Caeleste. You see where I'm getting with this, right?" he asked, looking at Barkley and his men. "I'm a lenient guy, though. We humans gotta stick together. So, I'll tell ye what. You guys come over here and help us capture this…thing—" he gestured to Sebastien, "—and we'll let you join our ranks."

Barkley and his men cocked their guns as Barkley replied, "Humans and Caeleste must stick together. *That* is the only way either of us survives. Your way will only get you all killed."

The zombie in the cage behind them beat its hands against the bars.

Harry scowled at Barkley, shifting his sights to the zombie. "What do you lot want with that thing?" He scoffed and looked at his men. "You know, *that* is a perfect example of why *our* way is the right way. Humans are getting sick now because of something those Caeleste started."

Sebastien was getting tired of them. "Last warning," he growled.

"Your call, sir," Barkley said.

As Harry aimed his weapon at Sebastien, his men aimed at the squad. "Don't be stupid, now," he drawled. "There's more of us than there is of you."

Sebastien needed to think carefully. The last thing he wanted was for Barkley's men to die; they couldn't afford to be standing around out here. They needed to get the zombie back to headquarters so Doctor Kowalski could look at it. He glanced at Barkley, who was already waiting for orders, and said, "B." Then he burst towards the hunters while Barkley and his men took cover.

The hunters yelled and started firing, but Sebastien was faster. No one got remotely close to hitting him with their flurry of bullets as he raced forward, pushing off a tree and colliding with three men. He tore them apart before they could fight back and then dove behind a jeep as Harry and his men came after him.

Sebastien watched through the jeep's windows as Barkley's squad hurried towards the cage and picked the chains up.

"Don't let them get away!" Harry yelled.

While they were distracted, Sebastien pounced from cover and executed one of the men about to shoot at the squad, but the other men started firing. Their bullets hit the bars and ricocheted; some of their shots hit the zombie, but they didn't kill it.

Sebastien moved quickly, taking out three more men, leaving just Harry and two others.

But then one of the soldiers yelled painfully when Harry's shot hit him. He tripped and fell, holding his hands over the wound in his thigh.

"Take him out!" Harry yelled.

With a ferocious snarl, Sebastien jumped and landed on one of the hunters, who screamed and fired his weapon. Two bullets hit his body; although it hurt like hell, he couldn't stop. He winced painfully but sank his teeth into the man's body, ending his miserable excuse for a life.

The squad started firing to protect their injured man. Harry and his remaining comrade darted behind a boulder, and Sebastien took cover behind several trees.

"Give it up!" Barkley yelled.

"Sir, he needs medical attention," one of the soldiers said, examining the injured man's wound.

Sebastien couldn't let the last two men get away. If they got back to their camp and shared the news that Sebastien was seen *once again* killing their men, those hunters would come looking for revenge. But first, he needed to examine his wounds.

The bullets burned inside him; this wasn't the first time he'd been shot with silver, and his injuries wouldn't heal until the bullets were removed. But he wasn't bleeding out, so he knew he could kill the last two men without straining himself too much.

"Let's talk about this," Harry called.

There'd be no talking.

Sebastien peeked out from behind the tree, seeing the other hunter whispering into a radio. He couldn't let them tell the other hunters; he hastily widened his jaws and spat a ball of blue flames towards them. The moment the flames hit the man's hand, the radio melted, and the fire travelled up the man's arm as he screamed and shrieked. He scrambled to his feet and stumbled out from behind the boulder, and then one of Barkley's men shot his head, ending his life instantly.

Now it was just Harry.

Sebastien prowled out from behind the tree as silently as he could and approached the boulder. He could hear Harry panicking and fiddling with his rifle, but before he could do anything, Sebastien veered around the rock and sunk his teeth into the man's arm.

While Harry shrieked, Sebastien pulled him out into the open. He tore his gun from his hands and pinned him on his back.

"You're going to answer my questions, or you'll be begging me to kill you," Sebastien growled.

Harry struggled, trying to pull free, but he was no match for Sebastien.

"What were you and your men doing out here?"

The man spat at him.

Sebastien snarled and harshly stabbed his right wing's carpal spike into the man's shoulder.

Harry groaned, gripping the spike with his hand. "Tracking!" he exclaimed.

"Tracking what?"

"The…fucking…wolves who attacked us last night!"

Sebastien snarled. He was right. These hunters *were* going to be a problem. He moved away from Harry, who immediately attempted to get up, but Barkley shot him and ended his life.

"We need to get moving," Sebastien grumbled.

"Sir, you're hit. We need—"

"I'm fine," he interjected. "Get these things attached and let's get moving," he said, kicking one of the chains. "We need to get back before he bleeds out," he added, nodding at the wounded soldier.

Barkley nodded and attached the chains to Sebastien's harness. Then, once the other soldiers helped their wounded comrade to his feet, Sebastien began leading the way back to the van. Lord Caedis was going to be furious when he learned about the hunters, but Sebastien was sure that he'd devise a plan to deal with them. He *had* to. They couldn't let anything stop them from reaching that lab.

Chapter Eleven

⇌ ≼ ☽ ≽ ⇌

Ucigaş in Wolf's Clothing

| **Jackson** |

Jackson watched Doctor Kowalski like a hawk. He twiddled his fingers while he waited on the examination bed; Kowalski was grabbing all kinds of things that sent a shiver down his spine. He took something that looked like a pair of pliers and filled two syringes with different liquids—one clear, another purple.

"Uh…what are those?" he asked as Kowalski made his way over to him.

"These are extraction forceps," he said, shaking the pliers. He stopped beside Jackson and looked down at him. As he held up the syringe with the clear liquid inside, he said, "This one is anaesthetic; it'll make it so you can't feel a thing." He held up the syringe containing the purple liquid. "And this is a healant. It'll kickstart and speed up your healing process so your new fangs come through much faster."

Jackson's eyes widened a little as he stared at the sharp needles. "That's gonna hurt though…right? Injecting it."

"You'll feel a little scratch, yeah. But that's it."

His heart started beating a little harder. But he did his best not to freak out. He was used to needles, after all. "O-okay." He turned his head and looked up at the ceiling.

Kowalski handed Jackson what looked like a pair of sunglasses. "Put these on."

He did as he said and put the glasses on.

The doctor then placed his things down on the nearby table and adjusted the light so that it was shining down on Jackson's face. "All right, I'm gonna do the anaesthetic right now. You ready?"

"Mm-hmm," he mumbled nervously.

"All right, just open your mouth and we'll get this done in no time."

Jackson opened his mouth and clenched his fists as he closed his eyes. He frowned when he felt the anaesthetic needle pierce his gum, but it worked faster than any anaesthetic he'd had before; in half a second, his entire jaw went numb.

"You feel this?" Kowalski asked.

He tried to reply, but his attempt to tell him that he couldn't feel a thing came out as a bunch of jumbled words, and so did his attempt to tell him that he was surprised at how fast it worked.

"Good," the doctor said. "So, you're gonna hear a crack or two, maybe feel a tiny bit of pressure, but that's it."

Jackson nodded. He heard a crack a few moments later, and when he felt the pressure, he frowned and tried his best not to grunt and gag. He hated every second of it. All he wanted to do was get up and—

"All done," Kowalski said.

He opened his eyes and looked at him. "Ca I coe ma muth?" he asked.

"No, no," the doctor said as he placed the pliers down and then picked up the syringe with the purple liquid in. "I still gotta get your new fangs to come through. It'll just take a sec."

With a nod, Jackson closed his eyes again. He didn't want to see what the guy was doing.

"Okay," Kowalski drawled. "And…we're done."

Jackson opened his eyes. "Re-ey?"

Kowalski nodded as he put the empty syringe down. "You're gonna be numb for a little. Oh—" he snatched a mirror and offered it to him, "—you can watch them come in, if you like."

"Uh…" Jackson uttered as he sat up, keeping his mouth open.

"Here."

Jackson took the mirror from him. He felt hesitant to see the state his mouth was probably in, but he *was* curious to see his fangs appear. So, he slowly lifted the mirror to his face…and stared at the two holes where his canines once were. At first, he felt horrified, but then he spotted the sharp tips of *new* teeth gradually making their way through.

"Pretty cool, huh?" Kowalski said with a smirk, standing beside him. "You know, it was a common practice a few hundred—maybe a thousand—years back for people to capture demons and farm them for fangs and venom."

Jackson grimaced uncomfortably as he looked at him. "At's awul."

"It is awful, yeah. But demon venom and fangs were a very expensive ingredient—very hard to come by. It's used in a lot of medicine today. Of course, we get the stuff from much more humane—I guess you'd call it—methods. Just like humans donate blood, demons and vamps and whatever else donate what's needed."

The anaesthetic was starting to wear off. Jackson could feel a little of his tongue, and when he looked in the mirror again, he stared at his new fangs. They looked like canines, but they were slightly longer and much sharper. If he didn't know he was a demon, he'd assume he was a vampire.

"Ca I…r…retrac em?" he asked, glancing at Kowalski.

"Uh no. Only some vampires can retract their fangs. Sorry. But hey, at least you don't have four…or six. I don't know how Alucard does anything with a mouth full of fangs," he mumbled, rubbing one of his own teeth.

"Alucard?" Jackson questioned.

Kowalski adorned an expression which made it look like he'd said something he wasn't supposed to. "Uh…shit. Lord Caedis." He sighed heavily and waved his hand around. "It's hard to remember all these names, man. I ain't a demon. I don't have to use his title, but I'm supposed to do it around outsiders." He looked at Jackson. "Whatever you do—if you wanna keep the skin on your body—you'd better forget you heard it."

Jackson nodded slowly. "Wight…yeah. Ne'er 'eard it."

"Good. All right, you wanna rinse?"

As Kowalski handed him a cup of mouthwash, he took it and carefully tipped some into his mouth. He swished it around, and once he spat it out into the sink, he stared in the mirror again. "Wa…what…" he struggled, trying to fight the fading numbness. "What…do I…use them for?"

"Lucian's probably the one who'll teach you this stuff. What I *can* tell you, though, is that you should never underestimate the use of your fangs. Your venom can do a whole bunch of different things. When you bite someone, you gotta do it with intention to get the right effect, you know?"

"Like…what?"

"Well, if you wanna cause someone the worst kind of pain they're ever gonna feel in their life, that's one thing. You can use it to knock someone out…or cause *extreme* pleasure," he said with a smirk and a wink.

Jackson rolled his eyes, trying to hide his embarrassment.

"As for the blood…well, you need to feed on it, and then after some training, you might be able to learn to do what Lord Caedis does and use the blood to either heal yourself faster, replenish your ethos faster, or even use it to manipulate others. That's blood magic, though. I don't know shit about that. I'm sure Lucian does, though. He'll get you up to spe—"

"Kowalski," came a man's voice as the door burst open. "Silver."

They both looked over there to see a man helping Sebastien walk into the room. But Sebastien looked *terrible*. There were two bullet wounds on his right side, his blood was spilling onto the floor, and he looked like he was moments from passing out.

"Fuck," Kowalski said as he ushered Jackson out of the way. "Get him on the bed."

Jackson backed off and watched as the soldier helped Sebastien get onto the bed. Kowalski rushed around gathering medical stuff, and Sebastien groaned in a way that made him sound annoyed. The bullet wounds were *smoking*, though. Why?

"No exit wounds," Kowalski uttered as he examined Sebastien.

"Is he going to be okay?" the soldier asked.

"Yeah, yeah," Kowalski said, waving his hand dismissively. "Go."

The soldier nodded and left, pulling the door shut behind him.

"All right, Sebastien. This is gonna hurt like hell, but I gotta get them out now before they cause permanent damage; your body's gonna burn off any anaesthetic I got on me right now, so I'm sorry," Kowalski explained hastily as he grabbed a pair of tweezers and moved them towards one of Sebastien's wounds.

"Just get it over with," Sebastien growled.

Kowalski didn't hesitate. He pushed the tweezers into Sebastien's bullet wound and started fishing around.

Jackson grimaced and looked away as Sebastien grunted and yelped painfully. He didn't want to stick around and watch or listen; he wanted to go back to Daimon, but just as he was about to head for the door, it opened again, and this time, it was Lord Caedis who walked in.

"'Ow bad is zhis?" he asked, stopping a few feet from Kowalski.

"Not…too bad," Kowalski answered slowly as he pulled a shimmering silver fragment from Sebastien's body. "That's one. Not sure how many more to go."

Sebastien groaned and dragged his hand over his face.

"Captain Barkley said you 'ad a vun in vith 'unters out zhere," Lord Caedis said, looking at Sebastien. "I need zhe details."

Jackson frowned. Wasn't he going to *at least* let Kowalski finish taking the bullets out?

"The same group we took Ethan from," Sebastien answered through gritted teeth.

"Riker's group?" Jackson asked.

"Yeah," Sebastien confirmed. "They're looking for us. They want revenge or something, I don't fucking kn—hey!" he snapped angrily as Kowalski yanked a silver fragment from his wound.

"Sorry," the doctor mumbled.

Sebastien exhaled irritably. "One of the guys managed to radio something back to the rest of their hunter buddies, but I didn't hear exactly what. It's probably best to assume that they're gonna cause problems on our way to the lab."

Lord Caedis snarled quietly. "Zhat's all ve fucking need. All vight. Kovalski, you vix 'im. Jackson, talk to your Alpha about zhis mission and your vriend, Vilson. I'll come up vith a vay to deal vith zhese 'unters. Per'aps your vriend might know somezing zhat could 'elp us," he suggested, looking at Jackson.

Jackson frowned unsurely. "Uh…like what?"

"Zheir plans, zheir numbers, and vhatever veapons zhey 'ave."

"I mean...maybe," he said as he glanced at Kowalski, who pulled another piece of shrapnel from Sebastien's wound. "He's not gonna tell me anything until I can convince the pack to let him come with us."

"Do vhatever you 'ave to. I vant invormation by two." Then, he turned around and left the room.

Jackson felt a little confounded. He had to convince Daimon to let Ethan come with them—well...he didn't *have* to anymore. Heir Lucian already got the information from him. But he *wanted* Ethan to come. He only just got his best friend back and he didn't want to lose him again.

Sebastien suddenly exhaled in relief. "God...fucking damn it," he grumbled. "Remind me to never get shot with silver again."

Kowalski chuckled. "At least it wasn't salt."

"Right," he muttered.

Salt? Was that what Sebastien's species was most vulnerable to?

"You best get to it," Kowalski said to Jackson.

He frowned and shook his head. "Uh...yeah. I'll get that guy to take me back to Daimon."

"I'll close these up for you," the doctor said to Sebastien. "They ain't gonna heal until the silver's poison wears off."

"Whatever," Sebastien mumbled.

Jackson left the room and looked around for Stan. Daimon's room was literally a minute or so away, but he didn't want to be caught walking around without his escort and get in trouble. "Oh, Stan," he said as he set his eyes on the guy, who was standing by a vending machine.

A vending machine.

"Wait," he insisted as he hurried over to the guard and then gawped at all the snacks and sodas inside the machine. "Do you have a half silver?" he pleaded, looking up at Stan.

The guard fished around inside his pocket and pulled out a silver coin.

"That works," Jackson said excitedly. He could get *two* things with a full silver. "Thanks," he said, glancing at Stan as he put the coin into the machine. Then, he eyed each item and tried to decide what to get. But he already knew. He selected the options for a can of soda and a bag of chips, and once he fetched them from the drawer, he smiled contently and started following Stan back to Daimon's room.

When he got into the waiting area, those of the pack who weren't sleeping looked over at him.

"How'd it go?" Tokala asked as he made his way over.

Jackson stopped walking. "Uh...okay, I guess. I didn't really feel anything."

"Can we see?" Julian asked excitedly, standing beside Tokala.

"Uh...." Seeing Julian brought back the anger and nausea.

"Come on, show us," Wesley insisted.

Jackson felt hesitant but he grinned, showing them his new fangs.

"Ooh, so cool!" Julian exclaimed.

"They look pretty threatening," Tokala said with a smirk.

Wesley asked, "Can you like...tear people's throats out now? Like...as a person, of course. You can already do it as a wolf."

Jackson frowned unsurely. "Well...I guess...if I needed to?"

"Are you still going to train with that Lucian guy?" Tokala asked as Julian and Wesley started comparing their canines.

"I think so, yeah," Jackson said with a nod. "I just need to talk to Daimon about something. I kinda just...wanna spend some time with him, too," he said quietly, looking down at his can of soda and chip packet.

"Oh, yeah, sure. I don't mean to keep you. Everyone's just..." the Zeta paused and looked back at the rest of the sleeping pack. "They're getting a little on edge being cooped up in here."

Before Jackson could reply, Stan said, "Someone will be down here to advise soon."

Tokala looked at the guard. "Oh, all right. Thanks."

"I'm gonna...go see Daimon now," Jackson said.

Tokala nodded and stepped aside. "No worries. See you in a bit, yeah?"

He nodded. Then, he followed Stan over to Daimon's room, and when he headed inside, the guard pulled the door shut behind him, leaving him alone with the Alpha.

Jackson didn't immediately head over, though. For a moment, he stood there and stared at Daimon. He was asleep—at least...that was what Jackson hoped. A part of him dreaded that he might have fallen back into a coma, and it kept him from calling Daimon's name...because what if he didn't respond?

He exhaled deeply and tried to calm himself. Then, he headed to the bed and put his things on the bedside table. "Daimon?" he asked softly as he slowly took hold of the Alpha's hand. His skin was warm again—as warm as it should be—and he had his colour back, too. "Hey," he then whispered when he saw Daimon opening his eyes.

It took the Alpha a moment to come around, but once he set his eyes on Jackson, he smiled a little. But his smile quickly faded, and a confused frown appeared on his fatigued face.

Jackson frowned, too. "What?"

"What...happened to your teeth?"

"Oh. Uh, Kowalski—the doctor guy—fixed them. He said I had my demon fangs filed down when I was a kid or something, so he had to pull the old ones out so some new ones could come in. And look." He grinned so Daimon could see them better. "Pretty cool, right?"

Daimon raised an eyebrow but nodded as best he could. "Why would someone have your fangs filed down?"

"To hide me or that I was a demon or whatever." He sat down and squeezed Daimon's hand. "How are you feeling?"

The Alpha turned his head so that he could see Jackson better. "I don't know," he mumbled. "It doesn't hurt anymore, but I feel…tired."

"Do you want me to let you get some more sleep?"

"No," he said with a sigh as he turned his head to look up at the ceiling. "I keep having these…dreams, I guess," he grumbled.

"Dreams?" Jackson questioned.

"Of my past. I think something is trying to tell me something…but I have no idea what."

"Like The Herald?"

Daimon shook his head. "It's not The Herald. The next Herald isn't until…I don't know. What day is it?"

Jackson thought to himself for a moment. "Uh…Tertium…sixteenth, I think. You were only out for…I think a few hours."

"The last full moon was on the thirteenth, so The Herald started on the sixth."

"So…if it's not The Herald, then could it just be normal dreams?"

Daimon sighed again.

"What are you seeing? If you don't mind me asking," Jackson asked.

The Alpha *did* seem to mind, though. He grunted dismissively and glanced at him. "How's everyone doing?"

Jackson wasn't going to pry where Daimon didn't want him to. "Most of them are asleep. I think Tokala's keeping watch. They're all getting restless or something, though."

"They would be," he said quietly. "There's nothing we hate more than being cooped up inside for too long."

Jackson didn't really know what to say to that. In fact, he was supposed to be asking if Ethan could come when they left this place to find the lab. "Daimon, there's actually something I need to talk to you about."

Daimon frowned and looked at him. "What?"

He wasn't sure why he felt so nervous about asking; maybe it was because Daimon had been a little weird about Ethan from the very start. "Well…I talked to Ethan last night—to try and find out where the lab is—and he asked…if he could come with us."

A *hostile* look appeared on Daimon's face. "Come with us? No."

Jackson frowned. "Why not?"

"Because he's a muto, Jackson. Taking a creature that is a natural foe to wolf walkers with us is the worst idea imaginable," he exclaimed irritably.

"But he's my friend, Daimon."

"I don't care, Jackson. He can't come wi—"

"I *just* got him back…after *all* of this," he interjected as he started feeling a little distressed by Daimon's reaction. "I came all the way out here to find him and I'm not going to leave him now."

Daimon frowned at him. "Isn't knowing that he's alive and well enough? He's not one of us, Jackson. If he were a demon or a wolf walker, then maybe I'd consider it, but—"

"Consider it? What's that supposed to mean?"

"We can't just take anyone we want with us," he said sternly. "We have no idea who Ethan is or what he's capable of. We don't know his motives or—"

"Actually…we do," he interjected again.

Daimon waited for him to speak.

Jackson glanced at his lap and huffed in an attempt to calm himself down. "Heir Lucian went through his head and found out that Ethan's parents were taken by some El'Vorian Industries people, and that's the pharmaceutical company that's a front for Lyca Corp., the people who are responsible for this cadejo stuff, trying to create hybrids for the Diabolus, who the Nosferatu are currently at war with. Ethan thinks that—"

"—He'll find his parents at this lab."

"Or at least an indication as to where they are."

Daimon sighed heavily and glared at the ceiling again. "This isn't a good idea, Jackson."

"Please, Daimon," he pleaded, standing up so he could see his face. "He's my best friend. I know him. He isn't going to do anything that could ruin the mission or get in the way. He just wants to find his parents."

The Alpha looked reluctant. He scowled and frowned, evidently thinking it over. But he soon relented, huffed irritably, and glanced at Jackson. "I'm not going to pry you away from your friend. But if he starts anything with any of my wolves, I'm going to have to teach him to behave himself."

Jackson smiled a little, relieved that he said yes. "He isn't going to start anything, I promise."

Daimon grunted quietly. "I'll believe that when I see it."

He had to go and tell Ethan the good news, as well as inform Sebastien and Lord Caedis. But before he did that, he wanted to spend a little more time with Daimon. He sat back in his seat and relaxed. He'd go tell everyone in an hour or so.

And he hoped that Ethan would behave. He knew how his friend got sometimes, especially around the people Jackson used to date. But Daimon was different. Daimon wasn't just some fling. And *that* might make Ethan act worse. He was a very cautious, protective friend. However, there was no need for him to feel that way about Daimon, and Jackson hoped he'd see that.

He tried to make himself comfortable, but then he heard Julian's voice. He looked out through the window, and he saw Julian's face. They were smiling and talking to the pack as if nothing had happened, and that made Jackson clench his fists.

"I'll be right back," he told Daimon as he stood up.

"Where are you going?"

"I just need to talk to Julian. I'll only be a few minutes," he said as he headed for the door, and then he left the room. "Julian," he called as he approached the couches where the pack was resting; he glanced around for Stan, but the guard was busy talking to the receptionist.

Julian stopped talking to Wesley and smiled at Jackson. "What's up?"

"Can I talk to you for a sec? In private."

"Oh…yeah, sure," they said as they got up and walked towards him.

Jackson led Julian into the hallway, and the moment the doors swung shut, he grabbed Julian's collar and pinned them against the wall.

"Woah, what the hell?!" they exclaimed, grabbing Jackson's wrist.

But Jackson held on firmly and scowled at them. "Did you stab Daimon?" he growled.

Julian scoffed in confusion. "What?"

"Did you stab Daimon?!" he repeated, quickly losing his patience.

"Are you crazy? Why the fuck would I—"

"Because you're still a part of Kane's pack," Jackson accused. "Did he send you here to tear us apart from the inside? So you chose to try and take Daimon out first."

Julian's confused frown grew thicker, and they stammered, "Jackson, I have like…no fucking idea what you're talking about!"

Jackson wasn't convinced. "There's no way that knife just so happened to hit Daimon *exactly* where it could have paralyzed him!" he snarled. "Someone did it to him, and you're the only person with a motive."

They shook their head. "Jackson, I swear to fucking God, I didn't do it! H-he welcomed me into the pack—I have the mark! Why the hell would I try to hurt him?!"

With a furious growl, Jackson moved his hand from Julian's collar to their throat and let his rage slowly consume him. "I'm warning you now; if you did this…I'll do worse to you than Kane ever would."

Julian looked astonished, choking as Jackson tightened his grip. "I-I…Jackson, c-come on. I told you how it was with Kane. W-why the f-fuck would I ever wanna go back there?!"

"To prove yourself," he hissed. "Maybe you're hoping he'll bump you up to Beta or Gamma or something."

"Even if he made me an Alpha, I'd much rather be a fucking rogue. I didn't hurt Alpha Daimon."

Jackson glared into their panic-filled hazel eyes. He listened... and when he located Julian's racing pulse, he concentrated on it, remembering what Sebastien told him about being able to tell that someone was lying. "Did you stab that knife into Daimon's back?" he asked firmly.

"No!" Julian insisted.

Their pulse didn't skip or change. That meant they were telling the truth, right? But if Julian wasn't the one responsible... then who was?

Julian huffed and quietly said, "Jackson, I promise. I didn't—"

"Then who did?" Jackson interjected with a confused frown, slowly releasing his grip on Julian's neck. And for a moment, he stared at his hand, and the burning rage inside him withered. He really did need to make sure he got his anger under control before he did more than strangle someone for a few moments.

"Are you sure that's what happened?" Julian questioned. "The van rolled, man. There was glass and stuff all over the place."

"Glass, not knives." He shook his head. "No, someone did it. I *know* they did."

"How? Couldn't it just—"

"I just know!" he insisted. "It's like... like a feeling, okay? When I think about Daimon getting stabbed on purpose or just falling on a knife, my instincts tell me that it was on purpose."

Julian stared at him for a moment but then turned their head to look through the small window on one of the doors. "Okay, so... if someone did this on purpose, then... that means that... someone in that room... they tried to *kill* Daimon." They looked a little pale. "Who the fuck would do that? That's not only fucking insane but that's like... *illegal*. Wolf walkers aren't supposed to kill each other—that's like Kane—that's like... like... we have an Ucigaș among us?" They looked like they might be sick. "Dude, this shit is gonna keep me up at night."

"What's an Ucigaș?" Jackson questioned.

"Like... the name of a wolf walker that purposely kills other wolf walkers... like murder. Killing wolves in defence doesn't make you one."

Wolf walkers, werewolves, Ucigaș.... Jackson might just lose track.

"Who, though?" Julian breathed.

Jackson glanced through the window, too. "I don't know, but... we have to find out."

With a deep exhale, Julian rubbed their neck and straightened their collar. "I'm sorry you thought it was me, man—like I get it, but... you believe me, right?"

He stared at them for a moment but nodded. Their pulse confirmed that Julian was innocent.

"Do you have any other suspects?"

"No, but I gotta tell Daimon."

"Yeah, that's probably a good idea," Julian mumbled. "What about the others? Maybe we can see how they all react."

Jackson shook his head. "No. I don't want any of them to know that I know. It could make us both targets and put Daimon in even more danger."

"So...like...should *I* do anything? Like...secretly interrogate or—"

"No," Jackson snapped. "Just...don't say or do anything, and don't bring it up with me until I come to you, okay? We don't know who might be listening."

Julian exhaled deeply and dragged their hand over the back of their head. "This is fucking crazy."

"Tell me about it," Jackson muttered but then sighed. "Okay, uh..." he paused and looked around. He set his eyes on the vending machine, but he had no money on him. "Come on," he said and started walking towards it anyway. And when he reached it, he saw Doctor Kowalski in what looked like a blood lab. "Wait here," he told Julian.

"All right," they said.

Jackson went to the lab door and knocked. "Hey, Yuri," he called.

Doctor Kowalski put down the vials that he was reading and opened the door. "What's up? Teeth giving you issues?"

"Uh, no, it's all fine. Actually, I was wondering if I could borrow a piece of silver for the vending machine."

Kowalski glanced at the machine and smirked amusedly. "Yeah, sure." He handed Jackson a coin.

"Thanks," he said. "Is, uh...Sebastien doing okay?"

"He's fine. He'll be ready to head out with you guys when it's time."

Jackson nodded. "Okay, cool. Thanks again."

With a nod, Kowalski went back to his work.

"So, this is like...our cover story, right?" Julian asked as Jackson put the coin into the machine.

"Yeah. What do you want?"

Julian stared in at all the snacks. "Hmm...ooh, chocolate. Can't tell you how fucking *long* it's been, dude."

Jackson pressed the button for the Dreamer Bar, and then he selected the Rockie Wafer for himself. Once both bars dropped out, he handed Julian theirs and then headed back towards the doors. "Remember what I said, okay? Say nothing to no one about nothing."

"You got it," Julian said with a nod.

Chapter Twelve

Check Out

| Jackson |

The next hour was distressing. Jackson sat at Daimon's bedside, trying to work out who would want to try and kill their Alpha, but he couldn't begin to suspect *anyone*. No one had any reason to want to hurt him, and he even let himself doubt his instincts. What if he was wrong? What if he just wanted someone to blame?

He sighed deeply and glanced at the window.

"You've been brooding since you got back, Jackson," Daimon said with a frown. "Are you going to tell me what's wrong?"

Jackson glanced at the Alpha's skeptical face and exhaled quietly. He couldn't keep it from him. Daimon deserved to know…even if it was just him freaking out, he didn't feel right keeping his suspicions from the man he loved. "I just…I've been…thinking about something, and…you can't freak out."

That didn't make Daimon look any calmer, though. "What?"

"It's just…a feeling I've had since the van crash. That knife stabbing you was just a little *too* coincidental; it hit you right where it could've killed or paralyzed you, and…I don't think it was an accident."

Daimon's eyes widened a little. "What?"

"I know it sounds crazy, and I thought it was Julian at first, but…well, I asked them, and Sebastien kinda told me how to tell that people are lying, and Julian wasn't the one who did it."

The Alpha scowled confusedly. "No one would want to hurt me, Jackson."

"I know, I just…it's eating away at me," he insisted, frowning in dismay. "This feeling that someone did it on purpose. I can't…shake it." He shook his head. "What if someone *did* try to kill you, Daimon? We can't ignore the possibility."

Daimon scoffed, still looking confused. "Who?" he exclaimed. "If Caius or Nyssa were in the van, then maybe I'd suspect it, too, but nobody in that van would do that." But then he frowned. "There's your friend Ethan."

"No," Jackson said firmly, shaking his head. "He was unconscious, wasn't he?"

"*Was* he?"

Was he? "I…well…even if he wasn't, his hands were tied."

Daimon huffed and closed his eyes for a moment. "It was an accident. I landed on the blade; if someone attacked me, I would have seen or felt it."

Jackson wanted to believe that, but the biting suspicion wouldn't loosen its jaws. "I can't believe that, Daimon. It's too coincidental."

Before Daimon could reply, the door opened.

Jackson took his eyes off the Alpha and looked over there to see Heir Lucian. The white-haired demon stood there with an aggravated expression on his face, a look that made it seem as though he was being made to do something he didn't want to do again.

"What do *you* want?" Daimon growled, also glaring at Heir Lucian.

Heir Lucian didn't look at Daimon, though. He set his blue eyes on Jackson. "There's been a change of plan. You're heading out today—"

"What?" Jackson questioned, confused. "But…aren't you supposed to be training me to use my demon stuff or something?"

"There isn't time for that anymore. Sebastien will teach you what you need to know on the way. The hunters your little muto friend was hanging around with are looking for you, and we think it's a good idea to get you out of the city and on your way to Greykin Valley before the hunters track you here."

Jackson frowned. "The lab is in Greykin Valley?"

"Why are you only just telling us this?" Daimon snarled.

"Because it wasn't important to you until now," Heir Lucian replied as he shot a hostile glare at the Alpha.

Jackson shook his head. "We can't go today. Daimon still needs to rest, and I literally just saw Kowalski pulling pieces of silver bullets out of Sebastien, so—"

"Stop with the damn noise," Heir Lucian complained, moving his hand to imitate a talking mouth. "A doctor's coming down to check him out," he said, glancing at Daimon. "Is your little friend staying here or going with you?"

By little friend, Jackson was sure that Heir Lucian was talking about Ethan. "Uh…he's coming with us."

Daimon grunted irritably in response to his answer.

"Can I go and tell him?" Jackson asked.

"You'll see him when you get to the loading bay. A van will take you as far as it can, and then you'll have to navigate the forest on your own. Sebastien will be able to contact us, so if you have important updates, share them with him. When you get to the lab, you *don't* go inside or anywhere near it. You wait until Sebastien calls us in," Heir Lucian explained sternly.

"And the hunters?" Daimon questioned as he sat up.

"We've got some people keeping an eye on them. They're going to lead the hunters away from you and keep them away. Your priority is getting to the lab, so I'm sure I don't need to tell you this, but I'll tell you anyway: don't stop for anyone or anything. Get the job done."

Jackson glanced at Daimon. The Alpha looked like he was about to throw himself at Heir Lucian, and it was understandable why. This guy was rude as hell, and he was incredibly vague sometimes, too. Although Lord Caedis' accent made it a little hard to understand what he was saying, Jackson felt as though he'd rather have *him* explaining all of this right now.

"Got it?" Heir Lucian asked expectantly.

"Y-yeah," Jackson said with a nod.

"Good. All your gear is out there," he said, nodding to the waiting room. "Get ready." He looked at Daimon. "The doctor will be here in a sec." Then, he left.

Jackson exhaled deeply and shook his head.

"Asshole," Daimon growled quietly.

"He can't be serious," Jackson said worriedly. "You've only been here for a day; you *just* had surgery."

"I'll be fine," the Alpha said, turning his head to look at him. "My body heals fast."

He shook his head. "I don't wanna go out there with someone who wants to kill you, Daimon," he insisted. "Can we at least find out—"

"Jackson," Daimon said firmly, frowning at him. "No one is trying to kill me. I trust every single one of my wolves with my life, okay? Please, just…drop it."

"But—"

"I understand that you want someone to blame or someone to be angry at—so do I— but it was just…a stupid accident," the Alpha grumbled. "Okay?"

Jackson pouted. He trusted Daimon's instincts and judgement, but he still couldn't just dismiss the persistent feeling that it was attempted murder. Daimon was asking him to let it go, though, and the last thing Jackson wanted to do was stress him out, especially now. So he nodded and mumbled, "Okay."

The Alpha exhaled deeply. "The sooner we get this mission over with, the better. We help them find a cure, and we get what we've been looking for since losing our packhouse fifteen years ago," he said, changing the subject.

Jackson nodded. He knew that Daimon wanted someplace safe for his pack to live— somewhere free of cadejo—and Jackson was going to demand whatever information the Nosferatu had about his parents. They *had* to know how his mother really died.

Despite the suspicions and frustration, though, he was curious to know more about what Daimon wanted, and since they had to wait for the doctor, he felt as if now was a better time than any to ask. "What are you going to ask for? Like…what do you picture?"

Daimon shuffled back down into his bed and rolled onto his side so that he was facing Jackson. "I see...something similar to where we lived before. It was this *huge* mansion—Greyblood Mansion—and it had these massive gardens, tall walls to keep anything from the woods out, and it was surrounded by the forest. Alaric and I were born there; it was where we grew up, where we learned to fight, hunt, everything. It was safe," he explained, but there was a despondent tone in his voice.

"It sounds wonderful, to be honest," Jackson said, taking Daimon's hand. "Eric's house was huge like that, too. It wasn't in the middle of a forest, though. It was in the city, kinda on the outskirts a little, so there wasn't much greenery. There were all these rooms that were never used for anything, too."

"There were a lot of rooms in our old packhouse, enough for everyone to have their own and then some. I shared with Alaric until we were older. When he married Nyssa, he moved into our parents' old room. It sat empty for a while after they died; he only moved in there because Nyssa convinced him to."

Nyssa's name forced a feeling of anger and dismay into Jackson's heart. He despised her, yes, but he still felt guilty. She left and took Daimon's nephews with her; she took away the only part of Alaric that Daimon had left, and all because he'd come into their lives and turned out to be Daimon's mate. "Do you miss her?" he blurted without even thinking about it.

"No," the Alpha replied. "I miss Rom and Rem, though. I miss Kajika; he was like a nephew to me, too. I don't know how Nyssa and Caius are going to get him his medicine. I have no idea where they are or if they're...." But he didn't finish that sentence. He frowned sullenly and rolled onto his back.

Jackson got up and sat on the bed beside him. "It's not your fault, Daimon," he told him softly. "And I'm pretty sure that no one else blames you, either."

He sighed deeply and dragged his hand over his face. "I don't want to talk about it right now," he mumbled.

"Okay." He wasn't going to force him to talk about something he didn't want to. Of course, he was concerned; Daimon seemed to be letting this eat him up. He was blaming himself for Nyssa leaving, but there wasn't anything else he could have done to stop it. He rejected her, and in doing so, the packs split again. The only way Daimon could have stopped that would have been to reject *Jackson*...but the Alpha chose his happiness over the feeling of entrapment that Nyssa made him feel, and he had every right to do so.

But Jackson felt as if he shouldn't be sitting there thinking about it. Daimon needed him, and he tried to come up with something that might take his mind off it. What if they talked about the packhouse some more? He smiled at Daimon and asked, "Do you know *where* you'd want the new packhouse to be?"

Daimon shrugged. "Someplace new. Maybe on the other side of Greykin. This place...it feels...."

"Old?"

"No. It's…cold. Empty. Cursed."

"Because of the cadejo?"

The Alpha looked up at him. "Maybe."

"Do you think there's a place out here where the cadejo haven't been?"

"I don't know. They've spread further than I thought, so there's no way to tell."

Jackson nodded. "Well, maybe Lord Caedis will know of a place. He's the one who'll be giving us all this stuff, right? Maybe he can find or even *make* a place for us to go."

A smirk flickered across the Alpha's face. "You're not going back to your city in Nefastus?"

He hadn't thought about that. Daimon had been all he could think about lately, and the thought of being without him made him feel depressed. A part of him *did* want to go home, but…perhaps his home was here now—*Daimon* was his home. But now that he was thinking about it…*could* he hack life out in the middle of nowhere? All forest and no city. No internet, no TV, no takeout or restaurants or pizza.

With a conflicted frown, he looked down at Daimon's hand. He gently rubbed the Alpha's palm with his thumb as he pondered. Would Daimon compromise? "Well…" he said nervously, "I want to be with you, but I'm not sure I could live out in the forest forever."

Daimon frowned but waited for him to finish.

"Maybe…we could get the new packhouse someplace that isn't too far from civilization. I mean…it doesn't have to be near *here*; I know you want it to be somewhere else, but what if we could live somewhere near a city or town where there are other Caeleste? A place *like* Silverlake."

"You'll always be a city boy, huh?" the Alpha said with a small smile.

Jackson shrugged as he started feeling flustered. There was something about Daimon's smile that made him feel a little mousy. "I guess."

The Alpha's smile evolved into a smirk; he reached towards Jackson and pulled him closer to him, making him rest his body over his. "We can talk about it more when it's time," he said as Jackson rested his head on his shoulder. "I'm not going to force you to move out into the middle of nowhere. If we can find a place that suits us all, then we'll take it."

That made Jackson smile. "Thank you."

But the Alpha then scoffed amusedly. "You know, I'm still getting used to this."

"To what?" Jackson asked, dragging his left hand over Daimon's chest, and then he placed it on the side of the Alpha's neck.

"To talking about things like this. When I was with Nyssa, most of the time I tried to talk to her about things—when we had to come to an agreement—it was just…shouting and cursing. It always ended with one of us hurt. I'd have a bruise from her slapping my face more than half the time. But you actually listen. You let me talk, and what you say to me isn't a bunch of shit."

His explanation made Jackson feel despondent. He didn't know the ins and outs of Daimon and Nyssa's relationship, but whenever Daimon shared a little more, Jackson grew to hate Nyssa greater each time. She treated Daimon like shit. She didn't deserve him, and Jackson was admittedly glad that he'd turned up and pretty much *saved* Daimon from her. He would ensure that Daimon knew he was loved; he'd never do anything to hurt him, and when it came to discussions like the packhouse talk, he'd always make sure that he let Daimon tell him how he felt.

But when he started thinking about how he'd always be honest with Daimon, he was hit with the dismaying fact that he was holding back a very horrible lie. He killed Elsu back when he first joined the pack; everyone thought it was a cadejo—he made it *look* like it was something else—but he'd never forget that *he* was responsible. He was going to carry it around with him forever, and as much as he hated keeping it from the man he loved…he *had* to. What if he told Daimon and it ruined everything? He didn't want to lose him…. But what was worse? Keeping this from him and living in constant fear and guilt, worried that he might somehow find out…or telling him now?

He frowned in frustration and closed his eyes, trying to dismiss the thought. It wasn't his fault. He didn't mean to kill her. He couldn't control himself. Would Daimon understand, or would he brand him an Ucigaş and lose the man he loved and his freedom?

"What's wrong?" Daimon suddenly asked.

"N-nothing," he lied, shaking his head.

Daimon started caressing Jackson's hair. "I'm sorry if what I said was too heavy—"

"N-no, no," he assured him, leaning up on his arm so he could look down at Daimon's face. "I was just…thinking about how she never deserved you. She treated you like shit, and I'm just…well, I'm not like her. I want you to know that. I'm never going to disregard your feelings or make you feel like your feelings about something don't matter. I love you, and all I want to do is make you happy."

The Alpha's smile grew as he moved his hand to the side of Jackson's face. "You're nothing like her. You make me feel alive again. You're everything I thought I'd never find." Then, he pulled Jackson closer, kissed his lips, and stared into his eyes. "I love you, too."

Daimon kissed him again, Jackson kissed him back, and after a half-second gaze at one another, they started kissing fervently.

It didn't take very long for Jackson to become aroused; his body tensed up as the Alpha dragged his hands down to his waist, and the feeling of Daimon's tongue entwining with his own made him shiver in delight. He carefully moved his hand around to the back of Daimon's head and gripped a fistful of his hair, and when the Alpha eased his hand into Jackson's trousers and gripped his ass, he smiled excitedly and moved his face to nuzzle the Alpha's neck, taking a moment to catch his breath.

But then the door opened.

"Ehem…" came a man's voice.

Jackson sharply turned his head and set his eyes on Doctor Laurent, the blonde man who had been assisting Doctor Kowalski last night. He hastily—but carefully—climbed off Daimon and sat back in his seat, hiding his embarrassed face behind his can of soda as he took a sip.

Doctor Laurent sighed and walked over to Daimon's bed while staring at the clipboard in his hand, and when he got around to the side of the bed where the monitors were, he lowered his clipboard and looked at the Alpha. "How are you feeling?" he asked him.

"Fine," Daimon replied.

Laurent looked at each of the monitors. "You've been off the painkillers for a few hours now. No pain?"

"No."

"Good. Any headache, nausea, throbbing in your lower back?"

"No."

"All right," Laurent said, putting his clipboard on the table under the window. "I'm going to take your IV out. There's an epidural catheter in your back, so that might cause a little discomfort when I remove it."

Daimon nodded.

Jackson watched the doctor take the IV out of Daimon's arm. Then, he told the Alpha to roll onto his side, and once he did, Laurent slowly pulled a long, thin tube from Daimon's back. The Alpha grunted and grimaced, and Jackson felt a little sick when he saw that the tube was almost the entire length of Daimon's upper body. How the hell had Daimon been lying there all this time with that thing in his back?

"Are you all right?" Doctor Laurent asked Daimon.

"Fine," the Alpha grumbled.

"Okay, I'm just going to put something over the wound and then you can lay on your back again."

Daimon waited. The grimace didn't leave his face, though.

"Are you sure you're okay?" Jackson asked him quietly.

He nodded. "It just feels weird."

"Now that I've taken the catheter out, your body will finish healing. The discomfort will fade in around ten or fifteen minutes," Doctor Laurent explained as he put the catheter into the nearby medical waste bin. "Okay, Daimon. You can move now."

With a quiet grunt, the Alpha turned onto his back.

The doctor held up a bottle of green pills. "*These* are very important. Purifico-inficio, an antibiotic specifically for wolf walkers. You need to take one of these every twelve hours. They'll prevent an infection from developing. Ensure you finish the entire bottle. Do not miss a single dose," he said sternly, handing the bottle to Daimon.

Daimon seemed a little disgruntled with the fact that he had to take pills, but he didn't say anything. He took the bottle and put it on the bedside cabinet near Jackson.

"You can change out of your gown now, too. There are clean clothes in that cabinet," Laurent said, nodding to a cupboard at the foot of Daimon's bed. "I've been told you're heading out into the forest, so take it easy. If you need anything, Sebastien will be able to—"

"Communicate with this place, I got it," Daimon grumbled.

"All right. I'll leave you to it." Laurent picked up his clipboard and left the room, pulling the door shut behind him.

The moment the door shut, Daimon let out a deep, irritated groan.

"What's wrong?" Jackson asked as he put his soda can on the cabinet.

"This is the first time in my life I've had to take pills like some mundane human," he grumbled.

Jackson stood up so he could look down at him. "Well... at least you don't have to take that many," he said, taking the bottle. "There's only sixty in here. So that's only a month."

He sighed again and turned his head to look up at him.

"You know what? I'll keep them safe, and I'll make sure you take them when you need to, okay?" Jackson said with a smile. He was sure that Daimon might forget—maybe even purposely—and he didn't want him to get an infection, so he'd ensure he took them.

"Fine," the Alpha mumbled.

Jackson headed over to the cupboard and took some clean clothes out for Daimon. Then, he placed them on the bed beside him. "Here."

Daimon smiled slightly and took the clothes. "Thank you."

"Do you want me to help you? Or I can, like... stand over there and not look if you don't want me to," he mumbled shyly.

But the Alpha laughed quietly in amusement. "You've seen me naked enough times, Jackson. You don't have to turn away while I change."

Jackson shrugged as he watched Daimon get out of bed. "I know, I just... I don't know." He didn't know where he was going with that. Maybe he was still trying to get used to the fact that Daimon was comfortable being naked in front of people.

He sat on the bed and waited. Although Daimon said he didn't care, Jackson tried his best not to glance at him. But he couldn't help it. He could sit there and stare at the

Alpha's muscular body all day. However, seeing it was starting to arouse him again, so he *had* to look away. It was time to leave this place; there was no time for sex.

Instead, he shifted his thoughts to what was going to happen next. They were leaving; it was time to head to the lab, and Ethan was coming with them. Even though Daimon had asked him to drop it, he wasn't going to let his guard down and believe that the knife in Daimon's back was a coincidence. Someone did it, and he was going to find out who.

Chapter Thirteen

The Mission Begins

| Daimon |

Daimon was glad to see that his pack were fine. They shot a flurry of concerned questions, relieved greetings, and assuring sentences his way as they headed through the hospital halls. Lalo joined them, and everyone was just as glad to see that he was doing okay, too. Now, it was time to head back out into the forest and get the job done.

But no matter how much he tried to focus on the mission, he couldn't escape the worry and thought of the half of the pack who left with Nyssa and Caius. He'd never stop blaming himself; it wasn't safe out there, especially not for the kids, but there was nothing he could do. Wolf walker law prevented him from seeking them out and trying to convince Nyssa to change her mind. He rejected her claim, the once-united packs split, and there was no way to bring them back together again.

A part of him hoped that some of Nyssa's pack might leave and try to find their way back to *him*, but he also hoped that they *didn't*. A lone wolf wouldn't last long out there, not with all the hunters, cadejo, and the hostile pack. *Kane's* pack.

That was something else he needed to be cautious about. Kane sent several wolves to try and stop his pack from getting to Silverlake, and he was positive that Kane wouldn't let them get away with murdering his wolves. He looked at Julian, who was walking on Jackson's right side. "Will your old Alpha be looking for us?"

Julian gawped at him. "Uh…I mean—"

"Is he going to be a problem?"

"I can't say for certain. But…judging by what I know of him, it's likely that he'll send more wolves once he finds out you guys killed the last party. So…maybe."

Daimon snarled quietly to himself as the guards led them through a pair of double doors and into an elevator.

"Wouldn't he have lost our trail after we got picked up by the Venaticus, though?" Jackson questioned, looking at Daimon and then Julian.

"His trackers are *really* good," Julian said.

"Even if we disappeared into thin air and reappeared elsewhere, a good tracker would still be able to follow the scent," Daimon grumbled. He didn't want to have to deal with Kane or his pack; he just wanted to get to Greykin Valley, find the lab, and settle into a new home. But if hostile wolves showed up, the mission wasn't going to be so simple.

"We're like...days ahead of them, though," Julian said as the elevator started moving down. "Maybe more. And I've never seen Kane pursue something or someone *too* far outside his territory, so maybe everything will be fine," they said nervously.

"You don't sound too confident," Lalo said.

Julian glanced at him. "N-no, I am. I'm just...I've never been involved in a mission like this before."

"Just stick close to someone at all times," Tokala told them.

They nodded.

What if Nyssa's pack ran into Kane? What if they'd already run into him? There was no way for him to tell. He wasn't connected to any of them anymore.

Had he done the right thing? Was rejecting Nyssa and mating with Jackson selfish? Should he have put the packs before himself? He was miserable with Nyssa; he *hated* her for what she'd said and done to him and Alaric, but staying with her meant the packs stayed together, and the more numbers they had, the safer they'd be. If he were stronger, then maybe he would have chosen to stay miserable for the sake of his wolves.

The elevator dinged when it arrived, and once the doors opened, the guards led the way out into the loading bay.

Daimon immediately set his sights on Ethan. The cuffed, brown-haired man was standing between two guards, and when his eyes locked with Daimon's, he scowled in hostility, as did the Alpha. He couldn't believe he had to let this muto come along, but he didn't want to upset Jackson. He *just* got his friend back...and as much as Daimon loathed this guy, he'd try and deal with it for Jackson's sake.

But was letting a muto come along a mistake? He already had a bad feeling about Ethan—he had from the very start—but Jackson's happiness was more important to him than his own comfort. He'd not let his guard down, though...especially not after what Jackson suggested about the knife in his back. He didn't want to entertain the idea that someone stabbed him purposely, but...what if Ethan had somehow done it? He was going to watch this guy like a hawk.

"Ethan!" Jackson exclaimed happily as he left Daimon's side and ran over to the muto.

"Hey, Jack." He lifted his cuffed hands and looked at the guards. "You gonna get these off me or what?"

The guards remained silent.

However, those who led the pack down there stopped by a van similar to the one they'd taken out to get Ethan and turned to face them.

"Officer Huxley will be down momentarily," one of them said.

"Right, and is *he* gonna let me out of these things?" Ethan asked.

They didn't answer.

If he could have it his way, Daimon would keep the guy in cuffs, but he knew Jackson wouldn't agree to that.

"So, you're the infamous Ethan, huh?" Tokala asked curiously.

"And you are?" Ethan asked.

Tokala held out his hand. "Tokala. I'm Alpha Daimon's Zeta."

Ethan shook his hand as his cuffs rattled. "So, you've been talking about me, then?" he asked Jackson.

Jackson shrugged. "A little."

Before they could say anything else, the elevator opened again, and Sebastien made his way over. "All right, all right. Enough chit-chat. We're heading out. Let's get in the van," he said, moving past the pack and towards the van.

"Let's go," Daimon said as he took Jackson's hand and then headed for the van.

"Hey!" Ethan called.

"What?" Sebastien replied, glaring at him.

"Are you gonna get these things off me?" he exclaimed, holding up his cuffed hands.

"Oh, right. Uncuff him," Sebastien told the guards.

Daimon rolled his eyes and got into the van. As he sat down, Jackson sat beside him, and Tokala sat next to Jackson. Everyone else filed inside and took their seats, and once Ethan got in, he moved past everyone and squeezed in between Julian and Lalo so that he could sit opposite Jackson.

The Alpha scowled at him, and the muto scowled back.

"So, Greykin Valley, huh?" Tokala said, glancing around at everyone. "I've heard it's a pretty place."

"Probably not anymore," Dustu grumbled.

"Yeah," Wesley agreed. "The cadejo have probably ruined it."

"What if they haven't reached it yet, though?" Lance suggested.

As the pack continued talking about Greykin Valley, Daimon kept his eyes on Ethan. The longer he glared at him, the more he sunk into his anger. He was already sure that he and this guy were going to be at one another's throats, but if he had to constantly remind this muto that *he* was in charge, then he would. He might be Jackson's friend, but he wasn't *his* friend—he wasn't even a wolf walker.

"So how did you two meet?" Ethan suddenly asked.

Daimon snarled quietly.

"Well," Jackson said with a smile, "after I was—"

"Listen up," Sebastien interjected as the van started moving.

Everyone stared at Sebastien, who was leaning around the passenger seat up front.

"We're driving up to Kingslake Pass. It's a couple of hours away. From there, we'll be going on foot through the forest. Greykin Valley is roughly six to seven days away at wolf walker pace, but we'll say seven to account for stopping for those of you who can't remain in your wolf forms for more than twelve hours. Show of hands, who are you?"

Jackson, Julian, Lalo, Dustu, Brando, and Lance held their hands up.

Sebastien looked at Ethan. "What about you?"

"Nope. No limit here," he said smugly.

Daimon's scowl thickened. This guy was full of himself, wasn't he?

"Right," Sebastien said, looking at everyone again. "There's provisions and some equipment in your packs, but what we have won't last the week. We'll have to hunt at some point."

"What about when we get to Greykin Valley?" Jackson asked, glancing at Ethan. "Do we know the exact location of the lab?"

Before Ethan could speak, Sebastien said, "Heir Lucian extracted everything he could from your muto friend's brain. The lab's location is somewhere within a twenty-mile radius north of the valley entrance we'll reach on our set course." He pulled out a map and unfolded it. "Here," he said, holding out the map so everyone could see where he was pointing.

Daimon examined the map. Greykin Valley had four entrances; one through the space where the two mountain ranges met, two over the mountains on either side, and the fourth through a cave. He didn't like the look of any of it, and if there were wolf walkers, cadejo, or other Caeleste out there, these entrances looked like the perfect ambush points.

"No," the Alpha said firmly. "We don't know who or what is out there, and this narrow space is a perfect ambush spot. We'd have to walk single-file, and turning would be hard, let alone fighting. We'll head around to the left mountain path and get in that way."

Sebastien shrugged. "All right, you're the lead on this anyway. You gotta know Greykin better than anyone since you lived out here all your life, right?"

Daimon nodded.

"Okay, but that's gonna take an extra half-day," Ethan argued. "I'm undetectable, so why not send me through the passage first to see if anything's waiting to pounce?"

"We're going to the mountain path," Daimon said sternly. "We aren't going to be taking any risks. There are too few of us."

"Alpha Daimon's right," Tokala said. "We should stick to the open; that way, we can see what's coming."

Ethan scoffed. "Aren't we supposed to be trying to get to this place as soon as possible?"

"We are," Jackson interjected, shifting his gaze from Ethan to Daimon and back to Ethan again. "But Daimon's right. We have to be careful."

With a heavy sigh, Ethan shrugged and leaned his back against the wall. "Fine. Whatever."

Sebastien folded the map back up and stuffed it in his pocket. "Jackson, Heir Lucian told you I'd be teaching you what I can, right?"

Jackson nodded.

"The inimă is in your pack; you should put it on."

Daimon frowned and looked at Jackson, who looked just as confused.

"Put…it on?" Jackson asked unsurely.

"Yeah…on…around your neck," Sebastien mocked in a stupid voice.

Jackson pouted and reached into the crafted bags he could wear in his wolf form. He pulled the black, red crystal-encrusted amulet out and held it in his hands as he looked at Sebastien.

"Well?" Sebastien urged.

"What is it?" Ethan then asked.

"The old demon amulet I mentioned yesterday," Jackson told him.

"It's part of the Zenith's Numen ethos," Sebastien explained. "When he started evolving into a Demi-Numen, his body wasn't equipped to hold all the new ethos. He and Lord Caedis came up with a solution to store the ethos elsewhere. Quite a lot of it was stored in Vespira, the Zenith's dragon companion. The rest was stored in demon-crafted amulets, called inimă, which is True Speech for 'part of the soul'."

Ethan nodded slowly. "So…that thing is a part of the Zenith?"

"Yeah," the white-haired demon confirmed. "And it responds to Jackson because he's an asmodi demon, a species which was created by both the Zenith and Lord Caedis. So, he's already got a little of their ethos in him."

"Makes sense," Ethan said.

Everyone else nodded and mumbled in agreement.

Daimon wasn't as intrigued as everyone else, though. Old demon ethos was *dangerous*, and he didn't want Jackson to end up getting hurt by it, something that was likely to happen because he had no idea how to control or even use his demon ethos yet.

As Jackson lifted the amulet towards his neck, Daimon gently gripped his wrist and made him lower it. "Shouldn't he only wear it when he needs to use it?" he questioned, looking at Sebastien. "This thing could be dangerous. He hasn't even learned to control his demon ethos yet. If he loses control, the amulet's power could destroy him."

"Wait, really?" Jackson exclaimed worriedly.

"Dude, it's Jackson," Ethan scoffed, glaring at Daimon. "He'll be fine."

Daimon growled quietly. "You have no fucking idea what you're talking about."

Ethan scoffed. "As a matter of fact, I do. I've worked with demons before, and—"

"I hate to interrupt, but…once again, Alpha Daimon is right," Tokala said slowly. "Jackson needs to learn to control his own ethos before using that of someone or something else."

"And that's why I'm here," Sebastien said. "On top of keeping an eye on you and making sure you stay on task."

Jackson put the amulet back in the bag. "Yeah, I…I'm gonna wait until I've learned a little more about my own ethos."

"I'll teach you whenever we have a spare moment," Sebastien said as he turned to face the windshield. "All right, that's it. I'm gonna get a few hours of rest in. You guys should do the same."

Daimon sighed and leaned back. He could feel the muto's eyes on him, but he didn't give a shit. He was certain that Jackson's friend was going to be challenging his decisions at every turn, trying to talk over him, and attempting to prove that he was smarter, stronger, or better than he was. But that wasn't the case. He was just a muto. What was he compared to a Prime wolf walker?

He closed his eyes and tried to dismiss the territorial feeling which was quickly enthralling him. He *hated* that this muto had to come with them, and having one stranger around was enough—at least Sebastien was tolerable—but *two*? Daimon clenched his jaw and kept himself from sinking deeper into his feelings.

And then Jackson leaned his head on his shoulder. He opened his eyes to look down at him, and as Jackson moved his arm around him, he smiled discreetly and eased his arm around Jackson's shoulders.

He heard Ethan snarl, and when he glanced at him, he saw a jealous look on his face. The guy was trying to hide it by staring out of the van window, but Daimon could see it as clearly as the daylight outside. Evidently, Ethan hated that Jackson belonged to *him*. And that was going to be something else that he had to ensure Ethan understood, wasn't it?

This was going to be a *long* week.

Chapter Fourteen

⌇ ≼ ☽ ≽ ⌇

Kingslake Pass

| Jackson |

Jackson stirred when he felt the van slowing. He frowned and opened his eyes but squinted when he was hit by blinding white light.

"We're here," came Sebastien's voice.

With a quiet yawn, Jackson lifted his head from Daimon's chest and glanced around. Everyone was getting ready to head out, grabbing their bags and waking up those of the pack who were asleep.

"Hey," Daimon said quietly. "We're heading out."

Jackson nodded and sat up.

"Good nap?" Ethan asked with a smirk.

He shrugged in response. "I guess."

When the passenger door slammed shut, Jackson flinched and woke up a little more. Then, Daimon took hold of his hand, and once the van doors opened, the Alpha got up, and Jackson followed him through the back of the van and out onto the snowy road.

It was admittedly a relief to see all the snow and trees. He breathed in the crisp, fir-scented air, and let himself sink into the feeling of the outside world again. But as the pack grouped up around him and Daimon, his suspicion that one of them was a traitor quickly grasped him, forcing him to glance at each of them with a skeptical frown.

"All right," Sebastien called as he closed the van doors. "We're heading this way," he said, moving through the pack and towards the tree line. Then, he turned to face them. "It's gonna be your call whether we travel like this or in our other forms," he said to Daimon. "To get to Greykin Valley as swiftly as possible, I advise we switch forms every twelve hours after a little rest. Sound good?"

Everyone looked at Daimon—all except Ethan.

"That's fine," the Alpha responded.

"Right." Sebastien shifted into his kludde form. "I'll follow behind."

Ethan flinched and backed off a little. "Holy crap. What the hell is that thing?" he exclaimed, looking Sebastien up and down.

"I'm not a thing, I'm *kludde*," Sebastien corrected. "I can speak to and feed astral Caeleste. Ghosts, spectres, phantoms. All that."

"Oh, yeah," Ethan said with a shrug. "I thought your kind died out a long time ago."

"I'm the last one."

"Feels like I'm the last of my kind, too," Ethan mumbled.

Jackson remembered what Sebastien told him Heir Lucian found inside Ethan's mind: he wanted to get to the lab to see if there was anything that would help him find his parents. He almost let it slip that he knew by telling Ethan that he might uncover a thing or two. All he could do was hope for his friend in silence until he was ready to tell him.

"Let's get ready to go," Daimon announced.

On his order, everyone shifted into their wolf form.

When Jackson took his wolf form, he looked at Ethan, and while he watched his friend transform into a *huge* tiger which stood a little taller than him on all fours, his eyes widened. He wasn't expecting a muto to be *this* big, and he was astonished. How did he not remember that Ethan was a massive tiger? Something like that would be hard to forget, even with the perception filter in place.

"Ethan?" he asked, staring at the tiger. Could he even understand him?

"Yeah?" Ethan replied, turning his head to look at him.

Evidently, he *did* understand. "I like...*knew* you were a tiger, right?"

He scoffed amusedly. "Yeah. You made cat jokes at me all the time."

Jackson didn't remember that. The only comment he *did* remember making that might be aimed at Ethan being a tiger was when he said that Ethan could carry him on his back through Greykin to get to the lab.

"We're all set, chief," Tokala said.

As he glanced at the pack, Jackson saw that they all had their bags on. Rachel, who hadn't shifted yet, made her way over with *his* bags. She helped get them on him, and once they were secure, she shifted into her wolf form.

"Wait, so...can we as wolf walkers talk to other Caeleste in our wolf forms, but not other wolf walkers unless they're in the same pack?" Jackson questioned, looking at Daimon.

"We can talk to other lycans," Daimon told him as he started leading the way forward.

"Lycans?"

Ethan appeared at Jackson's other side. "Yeah, like wolf walkers, muto tigris, muto leo—"

"Leo?"

"Lions," Tokala called from behind them.

Jackson frowned curiously. There were lion shifters, too? "Just…how many animal shifters are there?"

"A fair few," Daimon answered before Ethan could speak. "But we aren't going to come across any of them out here."

Ethan scoffed. "Aren't we? I mean, *I'm* out here."

Daimon glared at him. "No one was talking to you."

"Actually, Jack—"

"Is it all just big cats?" Jackson interjected. He could already tell that Ethan didn't like Daimon, and Daimon didn't like him. The last thing he wanted right now was to be caught in the middle of their argument.

But neither of them answered him. They kept glaring at each other on either side of him.

"No," came Tokala's voice.

Jackson looked back at him and the rest of the pack.

"From what I know, the shifters classed as lycans are those who have no choice but to shift on either a certain phase of the moon or time of the month," the orange wolf explained.

"So, it's not just wolf walkers who have to shift on the full moon?"

Tokala shook his head. "Loup-garou, which are an ancient species of shifter; they look a lot like Alpha Daimon's Prime form. They're a lot stronger than wolf walkers, though. They were mistaken a lot for rogue Alphas a long time ago. It looks like they went extinct during the war, though."

"What about berserkers?" Julian asked as they walked to Tokala's right side. "They're classed as lycans, right?"

The Zeta wolf nodded. "They're…a different case. They're not forced to turn on the full moon, but the full moon makes them weaker. It's on the *hunter's* moon that they're forced to shift. That's the first full moon after the Harvest moon; it's a super-lunar event that falls between Decem and Undecim."

Fascinated, Jackson fell back so that he was no longer walking between Daimon and Ethan and was instead walking between Tokala and Julian.

"Sleuths," Tokala then said.

"What?" Jackson questioned.

The orange wolf laughed a little. "That's our next lycan. They look like huge mountain lions; maybe a little smaller than us. They have to shift each quarter moon."

"What about the tigers?" Jackson asked.

"All the muto lycans have to shift every new moon," Ethan said, walking beside Julian. "The new moon is all about new beginnings and setting clear intentions, acknowledging your growth since the previous new moon—"

"Every wolf walker knows that," Daimon grumbled from up ahead.

Ethan rolled his eyes. "Clearly, Jackson doesn't. Or are you forgetting that he was bitten by one of your dis—"

Daimon snarled and abruptly turned to face him—

"Hey!" Jackson interjected, swiftly putting himself between them as the pack came to a halt. Then, he frowned at Ethan. "What the hell?"

"What?" his friend exclaimed.

"Don't 'what' me," he said with a scoff. "Stop being rude."

Ethan frowned irritably and glanced at Daimon.

Jackson looked at the Alpha, who appeared just as aggravated.

"Whatever," Ethan muttered and backed off.

Then, Jackson turned to face Daimon. He didn't know what he wanted to say; he wanted to ask him to stop letting Ethan get to him, but a part of him felt as though that wasn't something he should say in front of the pack. So, he just stared expectantly at him.

After a few moments, Daimon sighed and started leading the way again.

Jackson wasn't sure how to explain what he felt. A part of him was upset that this was probably how things were going to be for the entire journey; Daimon and Ethan were going to constantly be at one another's throats, waiting for the chance to snap at one another. Why couldn't they just get along? Was it really the ancient feud between wolves and muto making them act this way? No one else seemed incredibly bothered about Ethan's presence…unless they were hiding it.

He sighed and followed behind Daimon with Tokala on his left and Julian on his right.

"So, uh…muto," Julian said awkwardly. "Yeah…."

"Shifting on the new moon for muto is compulsory, yes," Tokala said with a nod, glancing at Ethan, who was walking beside Julian again. "They use the night of the new moon to discover new skills through the increased strength they receive during that time."

"The new moon gives us a sort of boost," Ethan confirmed. "That was why I was always busy every new moon."

Jackson frowned at him. "I don't…remember." He looked ahead at Daimon. "Will I eventually remember everything? I mean I took the sensus stone off."

Daimon glanced back at him. "I'm not sure," he answered with a concerned tone in his voice.

"It depends on how strong Eric's ethos was," Ethan said. "It took me a while to figure out how to mess with it just to get you to remember wolf walkers. It was in pretty deep, and although the stone is gone, some of its effects are probably gonna remain.

We'd have to take you to a demon who specializes in removing the damage of a perception filter."

"Without a demon's help, it could take years, could take months," Sebastien called from the very back of the pack. "The next Herald might help, but I'd advise seeking out a demon. I'm sure Lord Caedis knows someone."

"Really?" Jackson asked. Would he actually get to recover his entire memory someday?

The kludde nodded. "It's probably gonna take a while, though, if what Ethan is saying is true."

Ethan nodded. "Eric was a first-class asshole, but he knew what he was doing when he put those filters on people. It was his biggest asset."

Jackson frowned and nodded slowly. "Right, I remember. Eric used perception filters and messed with the memories of clients and targets."

"Clients and targets?" Julian questioned.

"My stepdad worked for a mercenary business—well, I say worked for, but what I really mean is that he owned it. He was super proud. Maybe he was under the impression that I'd ask for a job someday. I bet my stepbrother's loving it," Jackson answered sourly.

Ethan scoffed. "Little Eddie is probably working in the mail room."

Jackson laughed amusedly.

"Eddie?" came Daimon's voice.

When he took his eyes off Ethan, Jackson saw that Daimon was looking back at him. "Oh, Edward Kingsly. My stepbrother. He was always up Eric's ass about everything."

The Alpha grunted in acknowledgement and faced ahead again.

"He actually got a letter from the Nosferatu at one point," Jackson said, looking back past the pack at Sebastien. "I think he was looking into my mother's death. The letter was talking about how the Nosferatu don't investigate *all* Caeleste deaths, but all HG-caused deaths are recorded. He told me that my mom died in a car crash, but… after kinda fumbling into the Caeleste world, I'm pretty sure that isn't the case."

"I never believed that crock of shit," Ethan grumbled. "Eric's a piece of shit liar."

Julian then shook their head and interrupted them, "Wait, so…your stepdad has a mercenary business?"

Jackson looked at them, as did Ethan. "Yeah."

"That's pretty cool."

"Not when he brought his work home," Jackson mumbled. "I could hear the screams from the basement coming through the vents."

"Dark," came Wesley's voice.

Clearly, *everyone* was listening to their conversation.

But then something hit Jackson now that they were on the subject of family. "Wait, Ethan?"

"Wassup?" his friend replied.

"You...said you're the last muto tigris, but...what about Holt? Isn't your uncle one, too?"

That was when Ethan's once confident, smirky expression became a sullen one. "I don't know."

"You don't...know?"

"Yeah. I mean, I asked him, but he always kinda dodged the subject. Either he wants to hide the fact he's Caeleste, or he's embarrassed to be part of a muto family when he didn't inherit the gene."

"That sounds like Holt, to be honest."

"Wait, so some muto don't become muto?" Alastor asked curiously.

Jackson was wondering that, too.

"When it's a case of one parent being Caeleste and the other being human," Daimon said, looking back at them, "there's always a chance that their child might not inherit the Caeleste genes."

"There have also been cases where the child grows a proselytus but doesn't have access to ethos," Tokala added.

Ethan nodded in agreement. "So, maybe Holt is one of those guys. Or maybe he's more of a prick than I originally thought and doesn't want me to know."

"Why hide it, though?" Jackson asked with a frown.

"I dunno. Some muto can be real private," the tiger answered. "Either that or—if he is muto—he's keeping it from everyone in fear that someone might let it slip and hunters will come after him for his fur."

"That makes sense," Julian said.

"I saw a muto panthera once," Lalo called.

Everyone looked at him.

The coffee and tawny-brown wolf continued, "Yeah. Five-foot-ish on all fours. Huge thing. It was hanging around in a tree when I was out hunting with some of the others."

"So...that's a panther, right?" Brando asked.

Lalo nodded.

"I heard about muto pardus," Enola said. "Leopard shifters."

"Do you personally know any other muto?" Jackson asked Ethan.

"Nope. I guess I know some other lycans, though, huh?" Ethan said with a smirk, looking at him.

Jackson smiled, but when he heard Daimon snarl, he frowned and set his eyes on the trees ahead. The falling snow was getting heavier.

"Enough talk," the Alpha said sternly. "A storm is coming. Stay close."

The pack moved nearer to one another and walked in pairs. Jackson left Tokala and Julian to walk together and joined Daimon up front; he looked back and saw Ethan contemplating whether he should join him or stay back, and as much as Jackson wanted to continue catching up with him, he was glad that he chose to stay back there. If he came up front again, it was likely he and Daimon would continue arguing.

"Are you okay?" he asked Daimon quietly.

Daimon glanced at him. "Yes. Why would I not be?"

"Your…surgery. And you seem agitated."

"I'm fine."

Jackson examined the Alpha's face. His expression was a mix of mad and upset. Something was clearly wrong, but what? Was he *that* upset with the fact that Ethan was tagging along? Or was he trying to hide that he was in pain? Maybe it was time for him to take his first antibiotic. "Should you take your medicine?" he asked the Alpha, keeping his voice hushed. He was sure that having to take medicine was something Daimon would rather keep hidden from his pack.

"No," he replied. "Later when we stop to rest."

"Okay."

They continued through the woods as the storm picked up, and eventually, the pack reached a part of the forest where the trees were huddled so closely together that the falling snow couldn't break through. Fog ensnared the area, though, and Jackson could barely see ten feet ahead of himself.

That was when he got a bad feeling. The feeling of eyes on him; the same feeling he always got before something terrible happened, the same warning that he got when he became sure that someone had tried to kill Daimon. It felt like something or someone was watching them, but he couldn't detect anything other than the pack with *any* of his senses. He cautiously looked left and right, squinting in an attempt to see through the fog. "Daimon, I have a bad feeling," he said quietly.

The Alpha looked at him. "About what?"

"Just…in general. It feels like someone's watching us."

Daimon pricked his ears and looked around as he kept leading the way. But it didn't look like he could sense anything, either. "Sebastien," he called with a grunt.

In the blink of an eye, the black, winged hound appeared at Daimon's side. "What?"

"Sweep the area. Jackson feels like we're being watched, but I can't detect anything."

Sebastien nodded and then disappeared.

Jackson frowned as he looked around. Why did he get these strange feelings? It was his instincts, right? Was he detecting something and not understanding what it was or how to deal with it? There was a lot left for him to learn, and these feelings were something he wanted to get to the bottom of. But who could he ask? Was it a wolf walker thing, or a demon thing?

He looked at Daimon again. "Why do I get these feelings?"

"I don't know," he replied. "I know that some demons have sharper senses than most others."

"He's right," Sebastien said, reappearing beside them. He looked at Daimon. "Nothing." Then, he set his glowing blue eyes on Jackson. "You're an asmodi demon, a species created by Lord Caedis. He possesses a unique ability to sense a lot of things no one else could. For example, Lord Caedis…predicted, I guess, that a wolf walker-demon hybrid would somehow be involved in all of this. And it turns out that he was right; he's always right with his…Numen…prophecy shit."

"Hold up, prophecy?" came Ethan's voice.

"Bad word choice," Sebastien admitted. "He…sees things. I don't know how to explain it, but since you're a Caederian demon—"

"Caederian?" Jackson questioned.

"The bloodline name," Sebastien said.

"Right."

"Anyway, since you're Caederian, you might maybe have something like that. Asmodi demons are similar to Lord Caedis' demon species; your need to feed on blood, for example. You can probably do a whole bunch of shit that he can do, actually. I'll keep that in mind while teaching you. But yeah, his…Sight. Maybe your senses are a whole lot more advanced than a wolf walker's—heck, they might even be better than mine with training."

Jackson glanced from Sebastien to Daimon. Could that be it? Was he getting these weird feelings because his senses were sharper than he thought? But…if that were true, then wouldn't Sebastien have just found whatever he thought was out there? He looked at the winged hound. "So…you didn't find anything out there, then?"

"Tell me more about the feeling you got," Sebastien requested.

With a perplexed frown, Jackson stared ahead through the fog. He considered trying to find out if his suspicion about the knife could be some sort of foresight, but he didn't want to risk exposing that he knew. So instead, he said, "It's like…eyes are on me. I can *feel* something watching. I got the same feeling the very first time I arrived here in Ascela, and that same night, there was something outside the door of the place where I was camping. The next day, there was that feeling again, and I got attacked by that cadejo. And every other time I've felt like this, something has happened."

Sebastien nodded slowly. "Any other specific sensations?"

He thought hard, trying to figure out the best way to explain it. "It's kind of like a fight or flight mode. Like I *know* something is coming, but since I'm not sure what, my body is like…telling me to decide whether I'm gonna stick around to find out or run before it happens."

"And do you feel fight or flight-y right now?"

"Not *yet*. Sometimes, that feeling comes a little after I feel the initial feeling."

Sebastien looked at Daimon, who looked just as cautious as he did. "Yeah, now I'm thinking we need to stop and figure out our next move."

Daimon nodded in agreement and came to a slow halt.

The pack stopped, too, and grouped up around their Alpha.

"What's going on?" Alastor asked.

"We might have a tail," Tokala said as he looked around cautiously.

Ethan stood beside Jackson. "You sure, Jack?"

"I don't…know," he answered honestly.

"Never ignore a demon's feeling, guys," Sebastien drawled as he scanned the fog with his eyes. "That's probably one of the worst mistakes someone can make."

Jackson saw the cautious frown on Daimon's face thicken.

"Could it be hunters?" Leon asked as he, too, looked around.

"The Venaticus are handling them," Sebastien answered.

"Okay, but is there even the slightest possibility that your Venaticus buddies aren't doing such a great job?" Ethan accused.

Sebastien didn't answer.

Jackson took that as a yes. *Could* it be hunters?

"Yeah, that…Caedis guy came and talked to me before taking me down to meet you guys," Ethan said. "He said he was gonna send you, Jack, but there wasn't time or something. He was asking for whatever I knew about Riker's hunters. Numbers, plans, all that."

"So…it *could* be hunters?" Lalo asked fearfully.

Jackson slowly shook his head. No, this didn't feel like hunters. If it was, then they'd be able to smell wolfsbane or gunpowder, right? And this feeling…. It was getting worse. His heart was starting to race, and his body was tensing up. Whatever was out there wasn't human. He could *feel* it; he just *knew* that it was Caeleste…or used to be.

And it was getting closer.

Chapter Fifteen

⇨ ≤ ☽ ≥ ⇦

Debts

| **Jackson** |

There was something circling them. Jackson heard its feet hitting the snow, and along with everyone else, he followed the sound with his eyes, turning his head and then his body when the footsteps moved behind them. He had no idea what it was, but it sounded *huge*.

It was edging nearer. Jackson moved so close to Daimon that their bodies met, and when he looked at the Alpha, he saw the same look on his face that he adorned whenever he was about to fight.

Daimon snarled and grunted, and in response, the pack swiftly stood back-to-back in a circle with Jackson, Julian, Ethan, and Sebastien in the centre. They were protecting them... and getting ready for a battle.

A battle with what? What was out there?

Jackson searched the fog, desperately looking for something that might give him an answer. As each tense second passed, his heart beat harder, and his instincts urged him to run. But he wasn't going anywhere. He wasn't a coward, and although the pack wanted to protect him, he was going to fight. With a determined scowl, he dug his claws into the snow and readied his maw. Whatever was coming... he'd help his packmates deal with it.

But then something lit up the murk. A shimmering gold light cut through the fog, and it started pulsing like it was sending a signal.

"What the hell is that?" Leon blurted.

Everyone stared at the light, and as it grew brighter, the smell of wisteria and honeysuckle filled the air, banishing the scent of the forest. Before anyone could say a word, a sudden gush of wind raced towards them, forcing the pack to brace and take a few steps back. The wind cleared the area around them of fog, and when the source of the light was revealed, each wolf reacted with their own gasp or breath of awe.

Jackson's eyes widened. His heart didn't stop racing, but his determination to fight faded into wonder. The beast wasn't a beast at all—at least…not the kind that would tear someone's head off with its teeth. No…what he was staring at was the same horned horse he saw Ethan shoving into a cage the other night.

The *unicorn*.

It looked like an elegant white horse, but it was nearly twice the size of one. The shimmering, curving blue horn protruding from its head pulsed gold every few seconds, keeping the fog from ensnaring the area again, and in the breeze that the beast created, its long, ice-blue hair floated gently. Its tail was long—twice as long as its body—and the same hair as its mane grew underneath.

"Woah," Julian breathed.

"Yeah, woah," Wesley concurred, nodding slowly.

"Back off slowly," Daimon ordered.

Jackson frowned. Why did they have to back off?

The twisting, blue marks on the unicorn's white coat began to pulse gold with its horn, and as its bright amber eyes jumped from wolf to wolf, the pack did as their Alpha ordered and backed off. But the unicorn snorted and whinnied, patting the ground with its front right hoof. It shook its head, and it slowly leaned forward, lowering its face towards the ground.

"Is it…bowing?" Enola questioned.

"What do we do, Alpha?" Ezhno asked.

Daimon's cautious frown started fading.

"Boss?" Wesley called from the far-right of the pack.

"Daimon?" Jackson whispered, glancing at the bowing unicorn.

The Alpha stepped forward. Everyone watched him stand before the beast, and he gradually bowed in response, lowering his head and leaning forward on his front left leg.

"No way," Sebastien muttered.

Jackson sharply turned his head and looked at him. "What?"

"Dude's got the unicorn's trust," the kludde answered.

Ethan rolled his eyes.

But Jackson didn't understand. "What?"

"That's the unicorn we freed from Riker's camp," Julian said, looking to Sebastien for confirmation.

Sebastien nodded. "It sure is."

Jackson set his eyes back on Daimon and the unicorn. What was it doing here? He watched it lift its head, and as it did, so did Daimon. The unicorn grunted and patted the snow with its hoof, and then it gracefully turned around and started walking away.

Daimon followed without hesitation.

"W-what do we do?" Leon questioned, looking around at everyone.

"We follow," Tokala said, and when he began following Daimon, so did the rest of the pack.

Ethan and Julian swiftly glued themselves to Jackson's sides, Julian on his left and Ethan on his right.

"Shouldn't the unicorn be making friends with you?" Julian asked Sebastien, who wasn't far behind. "You were the one who freed it and all those other Caeleste beasts."

"I mean…sure, but a unicorn's whole thing is about trust," the kludde replied. "Maybe it doesn't trust a creature that speaks to and feeds astrals."

"I don't get why it would trust *him*," Ethan grunted, glaring ahead at Daimon, who followed the unicorn down a hill.

Jackson frowned at him. "Why do you say that?"

The tiger scoffed. "He's not worthy of a unicorn's trust—he's not even worthy of *your* trust."

"What are you talking about?" Jackson exclaimed, staring at him in confusion as he and the pack headed down the hill.

Ethan set his eyes on Daimon again. "A guy like that…. He's hiding something."

Jackson rolled his eyes. "He's—"

"I mean, how long have you guys *actually* known each other? Eleven days or so, right?"

Just because he'd only known Daimon for eleven days didn't mean he didn't know him. They were *mated*. He felt like he'd known Daimon forever. He loved him….

He looked ahead and watched the Alpha follow the white unicorn. Now that he thought about it…he didn't really know that much about him, did he? He knew that Daimon's parents were awful to him, that he loved his brother, and that there was some sort of calling in his bloodline that caused their mates to be from completely different lands, but that was about it.

What did *Daimon's* dad do for work? What was his mother into other than enforcing Lupi Sequi Veteris in abusive, questionable ways? And Alaric, too: what was he like? What did Daimon do when he was younger and before he was Alpha?

He didn't want to let his not knowing get to him, though. It was a fact that he and Daimon had only known each other for eleven days, but that was just it. Eleven days weren't long enough to get to know everything, and he was sure that he'd learn more as each day passed. Daimon was very closed off and reclusive before, but now he was opening up to Jackson, and he was also confident that Daimon wouldn't hide anything from him, either.

Guilt then struck his heart. *He* was hiding something from Daimon, though.

"Alpha!" Rachel called in concern.

Jackson snapped out of his thoughts and quickly located Daimon. He was now running with the unicorn, and the pack hurriedly tried to keep up.

They ran through the murk and the snow, following their Alpha and the golden glow of the majestic white unicorn. It took them through a vast crater filled with snow, rock fragments, and scorched, bent trees. They trailed it up a hill, down an icy slope, and out of the forest and into a glade.

No one was questioning it anymore. Sebastien was just as silent as everyone else, too. Jackson was expecting him to at least mention the fact that they were off track, but he looked curious and just as eager as the pack to find out where the unicorn was taking them.

The unicorn stopped in the middle of the glade next to a *huge* pile of hollowed-out logs covered in moss and flower-sprouting vines. It almost looked like a nest or burrow.

For a brief moment, Daimon stared at the beast with a confused frown, but then his face lit up, and he hurried over to the logs.

"What's he doing?" Bly questioned as the pack stopped twenty feet from where the unicorn was waiting.

"I don't know," Lalo replied. "What if it's hunters?"

"In a pile of logs, Lalo? Really?" Wesley grunted.

"Your boyfriend's crazy, man," Ethan grumbled, watching with the pack as Daimon jumped to the other side of the logs and disappeared inside the pile.

Jackson didn't like that he couldn't see Daimon anymore. Worry struck him like a fist to his face, and his instincts urged him to chase after him. What was he doing? Where did he go? He shook his head and gave in; he burst forward, raced across the glade and past the unicorn, which watched him with a curious gaze. And when he reached the logs, he searched for the entrance Daimon must have disappeared into.

There. A triangular entrance to the left of the pile. He stood in front of the entrance and stared inside. "Daimon?" he breathed, staring at the white wolf.

Daimon was lying on his front; it looked like he was nuzzling something—no, *licking* something in front of him.

Jackson stepped to the side in an attempt to see what it was, and when he spotted a hint of white and silver fur, he frowned strangely. A flurry of feelings hit him: confusion, worry, dread, dismay, and angst. That was a wolf, and Daimon was licking it. "Daimon?" he asked again, his voice a little shaky.

The Alpha lifted his head and looked back at him.

Now, Jackson could see the silvery wolf a lot clearer, and all his feelings withered and contorted into shock. "Is…is that—"

"Remus," Daimon confirmed worriedly, looking down at the still, unconscious wolf.

There was blood all over the kid's fur. Several open wounds clung to his legs, face, and belly, and he was covered in mud and ice.

Jackson didn't understand. How was he here?

Daimon went back to licking the wolf's wounds.

"S-should I get Bly?" Jackson asked as he realized what was going on. Remus' body wasn't as warm as it should be; that could be the only reason ice was clinging to his fur. He was barely breathing, his wounds were *horrific*, and it looked like he was hanging on by a thread.

The Alpha didn't answer, and Jackson didn't expect him to. He was trying to help heal his son, and Jackson wanted to do whatever he could to help.

He hurried around the side of the burrow and called, "Bly!"

The reddish-brown wolf immediately hurried over, and everyone else promptly followed.

"What is it?" Bly asked when she approached him.

"Quick," he insisted, leading her around to the burrow's entrance.

Bly frowned as she neared the entrance, but then she gasped. "Alpha? Is that…oh, my God," she exclaimed, moving to Daimon's side.

Jackson backed off and watched as Daimon and Bly fussed over Remus. He heard the pack exclaiming and gasping in shock behind him; he heard Ethan's voice, too, but he didn't catch what he was saying. His attention was solely on Daimon and what was going on inside the burrow.

"W-we need to get him somewhere warm. We need herbs," Bly stammered, shaking her head. "We need to make a fire."

Daimon looked back at the pack. "Set up camp!" he ordered. "Start a fire, gather healing herbs, and find food."

The wolves scrambled into action. Jackson watched Lalo, Alastor, and Wesley race into the trees. Lance started sniffing around, and everyone else began gathering firewood.

"What can I do?" Julian asked desperately. "I wanna help."

"And me," Jackson said.

But Daimon didn't respond.

Jackson glanced over at the wolves currently building a fire. "Come on. We can help with that."

Julian, Ethan, and Sebastien followed him over to the fire. But Sebastien didn't go with them when they went into the woods to gather sticks. Jackson didn't care, though. He just wanted to do his part, and if Sebastien wanted to stand around and do nothing, then whatever.

"Who's Remus?" Ethan asked as he watched Jackson and Julian pick up a few branches in their mouths.

"Daimon's son—w-well…nephew. He raised him and his twin brother, Romulus, though, so he's pretty much their dad," Jackson explained.

Ethan frowned. "Wait, he has kids? How old is this guy, Jackson?"

He didn't know the answer to that. "I dunno," he grumbled.

"God, Jackson. He could be like…forty."

"He's not!"

"How do you know?" Ethan questioned.

"I just do! He doesn't look much older than me, so—"

"So? You just assume—"

"Why does it matter?" Jackson snapped irritably as he stopped walking and glared at him. "W-why does *any* of this matter? Why are you on my ass about this? Daimon hasn't done anything to you."

Ethan scoffed. "He might not have done anything to *me*, but he's done a lot of shit to you, and that's pretty much the same as doing shit to me."

Jackson's confusion thickened. "What the hell, Ethan?"

"He's got you wrapped up in all this wolf walker Venaticus bullshit, travelling halfway across the country to find something that might not even be there! Talking about mates and packs and shit. He's turned you into someone else!" Ethan shouted angrily.

"Daimon's done nothing but help me!" he argued, dropping the branches from his mouth. "He hasn't wrapped me up in anything! I came out here to find you, and here we are, I found you!"

"So why are we still here, huh?! Why are we travelling around with these dogs and—"

"Hey!" Jackson snapped. "Don't be so fucking rude!"

"Calm down! You see, this is what I mean!" Ethan exclaimed, glancing at Julian, who looked like they had no idea what to do. "Why are we out here, Jackson? Why aren't we heading home or figuring out how to get back there?"

"Because there's a whole world of shit happening out here, and *I* can do something to stop it!" Jackson growled. "I *care* about these people, okay? And I *love* Daimon. The cadejo have killed enough wolf walkers, and now people are dying, too. If we don't do something to stop this, then Lyca Corp. wins!"

Ethan growled in frustration.

But before he could speak, Jackson frowned in confoundment and said, "You were literally talking about getting to the bottom of all of this last night. What changed? Don't you wanna find out what Holt's been doing? Those shipping containers? El'Vorian Industries? Lyca Corp.?"

The tiger huffed and glared at him. "I'm not...I'm not talking about all of that. I...I just...." He sighed deeply and shook his head. "I'm just stressed out. I'm sorry. So much shit is going on, you're here with all these wolves, and I just...need a minute to process it all."

"I get that, okay? But that's no excuse to be horrible to Daimon. He hasn't done anything to you. All he's doing is looking out for everyone, and right now, his son needs our help. So can we stop standing around here and get this wood to the fire, please?" Jackson insisted, trying to settle his frustration. He wanted to defend Daimon with a whole lot more anger, but he had to control himself. Ethan was stressed out, and he didn't want to make that worse for him.

With a quiet sigh, the tiger nodded and grabbed a large log in his mouth. "All right."

As they headed towards the glade, Jackson glanced at Julian. They looked anxious, and they shot an unsure frown at Jackson, who was convinced that Julian was thinking the same thing that Daimon had earlier suggested: what if Ethan was the one who stabbed Daimon? Jackson didn't think that Ethan would do it, even if he wasn't tied up and unconscious…but…what if he did? What if Jackson was letting his relationship with Ethan get in the way of his hunt for whoever attempted to murder his mate?

He frowned and glanced at Ethan. He needed to ask him; he needed to find out. But not yet. He needed to get him alone.

They made their way to the collection of sticks and twigs that the pack had formed in the middle of an area bordered by tree trunks. Once they added their sticks to the pile, they went to go and fetch more, but the pile suddenly went up in blue flames.

"That should last a while," Sebastien said.

Concerned voices cut through the silence.

Jackson turned to face Daimon, and he watched as the Alpha and Bly carried Remus over on their backs.

Everyone moved out of the way and observed while Daimon lay his son in front of the fire and then backed off, leaving Bly to tend to his wounds.

"Lance," Bly called hastily.

The light brown Iota barged through the crowd with a mouthful of leaves and fragrant flowers. He placed them down on the rock in front of Bly, and once she morphed out of her wolf form, she immediately began pressing and crushing the plants with her hands. Once they were mashed up enough, she started spreading the paste onto Remus' wounds.

Jackson turned his attention to Daimon. The Alpha watched with a terrified look on his face; he was breathing deeply in what might be an attempt to contain his emotions, and all Jackson wanted to do was try to comfort him. But was that what he needed right now? He frowned despondently and made his way over to the Alpha, and when he stood beside him, he glanced at his worried face. "Daimon?"

"I don't know how long he's been out here," the Alpha said sullenly. "He's…frozen, beaten. I don't…I don't know what happened or how he got here. He's just…here. And…" he paused as he turned his head to look at him, "I can't help but fear that…he's here because there's no one else left."

Despite the fact that he hated Nyssa, Jackson wouldn't wish death upon her or anyone who left with her. He felt pain in his heart; it was mostly pain for Daimon, but it was still pain. "Maybe…maybe he got lost," he said, trying to reassure him. "Like…separated from the others and just sorta wandered around."

Daimon shook his head as he set his sights back on his son. "He couldn't get lost. I can't let myself think that Nyssa would allow that to happen." He glanced back at the unicorn. "And I don't know what to make of that, either."

Jackson looked over his shoulder at the unicorn, too. The creature snorted and retreated into its burrow. "Why would he end up in a unicorn's burrow?"

The Alpha sighed and sat down. "Unicorns repay their debts. Maybe it found him or maybe he came to it for help. We helped that unicorn get away from those hunters, and this must be its way of repaying us—more specifically, you."

"Me?"

"Unicorns are very intelligent. It must know that we're mated, so bringing my son to me has to be it repaying its debt. But...I don't know if the unicorn did this to him to get him to us, or if it found him like this. I won't know more until he wakes up." He scowled in dismay. "*If* he wakes up."

Jackson shook his head and moved a little closer to him. "He *will* wake up, Daimon. He's *your* son, and if you can fight like hell and wake up from a coma in less than a day, then I'm confident that he can, too."

The Alpha glanced at him and smiled weakly but quickly set his sights back on Remus while Bly tended to his wounds.

"He *will*," Jackson said firmly as he placed his paw over Daimon's.

Daimon took a deep breath and glanced at him again. "I think...I just need to be by myself for a while."

His words cut like a blade, but Jackson understood. He wasn't going to overthink or argue. "Okay. I'll just... be over there with Julian and Ethan," he mumbled, trying to hide his sadness.

The Alpha nodded.

Jackson left his side and headed over to Ethan and Julian. He sat down, stared at Bly and Remus, and did his best not to take what Daimon just said personally. Of course, he understood that Daimon needed to be alone with his thoughts, and if they spent every minute of every day stuck to one another, then they'd get bored of each other, wouldn't they? Some personal space was needed now and then, especially in a time like this.

"Is he okay?" Julian asked.

"Yeah, he's just worried," Jackson mumbled.

What if Daimon wanted to be alone because Jackson wasn't good enough at making him feel better? Did he suck at comforting him?

No, he was overthinking; he was doing the one thing he'd told himself he shouldn't do. So he took a deep breath and gazed at the fire. Daimon would come to him when he was ready. It was nothing personal. After all, there were times when Jackson felt like he needed to be alone, so it was only fair that he left Daimon alone when he asked for it.

Jackson glanced at Ethan, and then he looked at Julian, meeting their gaze. They were thinking the same thing, weren't they? "Ethan…" he started and glanced around the glade, making sure that no one was listening.

"What?" Ethan replied.

"I need to ask you something, and you need to be honest with me," Jackson said, watching Julian as they got up and stood in front of him and Ethan like they were keeping watch while shielding them.

Ethan frowned strangely. "Uh… okay?"

"Did you try to kill Daimon when the van crashed?" he asked quietly.

He scoffed confusedly. "What?"

"Did you stab him in the back?!" Jackson insisted, keeping his voice hushed. His anger was growing alongside his impatience.

Ethan shook his head. "Did I stab—w-what?"

"Shh!" Jackson snapped. "Just answer me: did you stab him?"

"No, I didn't," Ethan answered. "I was unconscious; I woke up in that damn interrogation room."

Jackson listened to Ethan's pulse, and like Julian's earlier, it didn't skip to indicate that his friend was lying. So he exhaled deeply, and relief shrouded his anger. But he couldn't feel entirely relaxed. If it wasn't Julian or Ethan… then the person who tried to murder Daimon was still among them.

"So?" Julian asked.

"He didn't do it," Jackson said, shaking his head.

"Someone tried to kill Daimon?" Ethan asked quietly. "Can't say I'm surprised."

"It's not funny, Ethan," Jackson whispered with a scowl. "Someone tried to murder him, and Daimon trusts *everyone* here. Julian and I are trying to find out who it was before they make another attempt."

Ethan's frown thickened. "Why isn't Daimon helping?"

Jackson huffed. "He doesn't believe it. Like I said, he trusts everyone."

The tiger glanced over Julian at the pack and then set his blue eyes on Jackson. "What about Sebastien?"

"He wasn't in the van at the time," Julian answered.

"Don't say anything to anyone," Jackson warned Ethan. "Just let me work this out, please. Don't start snooping or asking questions or whatever. I don't want whoever it was to know that I'm onto them."

Ethan looked hesitant. "You're asking me not to take part in an attempted murder investigation?"

"Yes."

With a deep, long sigh, Ethan said, "Fine. I dunno what use I'd be anyway being an outsider and all. But if you need help, you know where I am."

Jackson was surprised that he didn't put up a fight, but he was glad. And he was also glad that he could cross Ethan off the list of suspects.

Chapter Sixteen

⌒ ≪ ☽ ≫ ⌒

A Wolf in the Dark

| **Daimon** |

The night Nyssa left, Daimon was convinced he'd never see Remus or Romulus again. He was certain that he'd failed his brother, that he'd failed to protect the people Alaric pleaded him to. And although Nyssa and Romulus were still out there somewhere, Remus was right in front of him.

He couldn't feel relief, though. How could he? His son...*Alaric's* son was lying there frozen and covered in wounds. He had no idea what Remus had been through or how he'd got here, and it wasn't like he could ask the unicorn. They couldn't speak.

But...they *could* understand.

Daimon reluctantly took his eyes off his son and looked back at the unicorn's burrow. Maybe he could find out what happened; what if it could somehow tell him how it found his son and where Nyssa and Romulus and the rest of the separate pack were? Not knowing where they were and how they were doing had been eating him up since Nyssa left, and as much as he loathed her and Caius for doing this...he still cared. She was still Alaric's mate, and he owed it to his brother to ensure that no matter where she was, she was okay.

The Alpha got up and started making his way towards the burrow. He stood at the entrance and saw the unicorn lying on the ground; it stopped cleaning its hooves with the ethos from its horn and lifted its head to look at him.

"Thank you for saving my son," he said sincerely.

The unicorn grunted at him as it jerked its head in a nod-like motion.

Daimon slowly sat down. "Was it just him out there?"

It nodded again.

"There weren't any other wolf walkers?"

With a quiet grunt, the unicorn shook its head.

Daimon sighed and looked down at the snow, but he knew better than to take his eyes off something as elegant as a unicorn. He quickly lifted his head to resume eye contact. "Do you know what happened to him?"

The unicorn nodded, but then its horn started pulsing. It moved its head as close to him as it could and whinnied.

What did it want from him? "I don't... understand."

As it grunted, it brushed its long tail over its face.

"You... want me to... touch your face?"

The unicorn nodded.

He wasn't sure why—perhaps it was another test of trust. So, he got up and lifted his paw—

But the unicorn pulled its head away and snorted, shaking its head. It looked him up and down and shook its head again.

It didn't take Daimon long to understand. "In my human form?"

The unicorn nodded and leaned its head towards him again.

Daimon did as the beast asked and morphed out of his wolf form. Then, he moved closer, sat in front of the unicorn, and gently placed his hand on its face.

A flash of golden light suddenly stole his sight. His heart started racing, and when the gold faded, it left a haze in his eyes—like he was caught in a dream. He couldn't see the unicorn or the burrow; what lay before him was a murky forest, and in the light of the moon, the shadow of the unicorn cast onto the snow.

It was showing him a memory—*its* memory.

He watched as the beast moved through the woods, following a trail of blood and wolf prints. When it moved down into a ditch, it located Remus, who lay bleeding and panting. The unicorn looked around for whatever did this to Daimon's son, but there was nothing and no one, only Remus bloodied and beaten.

But the unicorn showed him the memory *again*.

And again.

And only when he saw it a fourth time did Daimon notice something. It was only for a brief moment, but he saw the flicker that came from a wolf walker's eyes in the presence of light. Somebody was out there, and considering they didn't come running out to claim Remus told Daimon that they might be the one who did this to his son.

As he was freed from the unicorn's memory, Daimon gritted his teeth and clenched his fists. "Did you see the wolf?"

It shook its head.

Daimon exhaled deeply and tried to compose himself. He was furious; he wanted to find the piece of shit who did this to his son—he wanted to hunt them down and tear them apart. But right now, he had to be there for Remus. He couldn't leave to feed his desire for vengeance and let his son wake up without him there.

"Thank you," he said once more to the unicorn. Then, he shifted back into his wolf form and left the burrow.

He made his way over to the shimmering blue fire. But on his way, he spotted Jackson sitting with Ethan. The muto scowled at him when they locked eyes, but Daimon didn't have the interest nor the energy to deal with him right now.

"Anything?" he asked Bly as he sat beside her.

"His wounds are healing," she said while soothing what was left of the herb paste into Remus' wounds. "His body temp is rising, and all the ice is gone."

Daimon stared sullenly at Remus' wounds. Now that he knew a wolf walker had done this, he felt even worse. Could it have been a desperate rogue looking for a meal? Or could it have been something much more dangerous, such as a member of Kane's pack?

He took his eyes off Remus and looked over at Julian. Could their ex-Alpha have Etas out there looking for *his* pack? They had, after all, killed the wolves Kane sent after them the first time, and if their places had been reversed—and if he had the numbers—Daimon would have sent wolves out to find those that killed his packmates, too. But was this going to be a problem? Was Kane's pack going to get in the way of their mission?

"Julian," he called.

The silvery-black wolf lifted their head from their paws and looked at him. "Y-yes, sir?"

"Come here."

Julian left Jackson and Ethan and made their way over to him. "Do you need something?"

"I need you to tell me about your old Alpha."

"What about him?"

"He'd want to kill us for killing his wolves, correct?"

"Uh…from what I saw when I was there…yeah."

"How far would he be willing to trail us?"

Julian thought to themselves for a moment. "Kane would track people for *weeks*, even outside his territory. He was never afraid of coming across other packs, either. Kane's…well, he's strong, sir."

Daimon frowned in confliction as he looked down at his son. "So, it's possible that he's still looking for us."

"Yeah. He probably knows that his plan to lead those hunters towards us didn't work. He's got eyes everywhere. They…" Julian paused and looked around, "could be watching us right now."

That worried Daimon because his son was so vulnerable, and Jackson wasn't yet trained properly to fight and defend himself. However, he couldn't let his concerns get to him. He focused his senses and scoured the area, but he couldn't sense anything. He wasn't going to take any risks, though. "Tokala, Leon, Brando, and Enola."

The four wolves stopped what they were doing and hurried over to him.

"I need the four of you to check the tree line. Be thorough."

They nodded and headed towards the trees.

Daimon then stood up and called, "Everyone be on high alert. Whoever did this to Remus might still be out there." He looked at Julian. "You can go."

With a nod, Julian got up and went back over to Jackson and Ethan.

But as Daimon sat down, he saw Jackson getting up. He knew that he probably had questions—some that everyone probably had—and although he still felt like he wanted to be left alone with his thoughts, maybe talking about the possibility that Kane's wolves might be out there would distract him from his dismay.

"Is everything okay?" Jackson asked quietly when he stopped beside him.

He glanced at him and sighed. "I talked to the unicorn."

Jackson frowned as he sat down. "Wait, they can talk?"

"No, *I* talked and it just…nodded. It showed me where it found Remus, though, and there was a wolf walker lurking in the trees. *Someone* did this to him."

"Who?" he asked worriedly. "I-I mean…well, I'm not actually sure what I mean," he mumbled with an embarrassed look on his face.

Daimon smiled slightly, but a frown stole his face when he said, "I don't know. I was thinking that it could've been a rogue, or maybe it was one of Kane's wolves. Julian told me that Kane might still be looking for us, and if his wolves found Nyssa and her pack, then…." He scowled sullenly and looked down at his paws. The last thing he wanted was to think about what might have happened to them, but how could he not? His son was lying right in front of him beaten and bruised.

Jackson moved a little closer to him. "Remus is gonna be fine, Daimon. Bly's got him. And…if Kane sends more wolves, we'll just stop them, too. We have Sebastien and Ethan this time, and—"

"We don't need some muto helping us," he interjected irritably.

Jackson frowned at him. "I was just saying that—"

Daimon sighed and shook his head as guilt began outweighing his annoyance. "I'm sorry, I didn't mean to snap at you."

"You're worried. It's okay," Jackson assured him. "If Kane really does have wolves out there looking for us, then…we'll be okay, right? We have *you*."

He was right. If Kane sent more wolves, he'd stop them. He wasn't going to let anything happen to the wolves he'd sworn to protect. "You should start training with Sebastien," he said, setting his eyes on Jackson. The sooner he knew how to use his demon ethos, the stronger the pack would be…and the less Daimon would worry about him.

Jackson frowned again. "What?"

"You need to start learning to use your demon ethos. The sooner you do that, the sooner you'll be able to fight and better defend yourself. We have no idea what might be waiting for us out there," he said, nodding at the forest. "I don't want to take any more risks. And if there's ever a time where I can't protect you, I…I'd never forgive myself if anything happened to you."

With a sullen frown, Jackson looked at the fire. He was quiet for a moment, but then he said, "What if I suck?"

Daimon raised an eyebrow in confusion. "What?"

"What if I suck at learning? I don't wanna make an idiot of myself."

"Jackson, first of all, no one here is going to think you're an idiot. Second, that's what learning is all about. You're going to mess up, you're not going to get the hang of something on the first try. And if Sebastien thinks otherwise, then perhaps he isn't the best person to be teaching you."

Jackson sighed and glanced at him. "I don't know, I just…I'm scared of losing control."

"Of your anger?"

He nodded but there was a conflicted look on his face.

"What is it?" Daimon asked.

Jackson shrugged. "What if…I hurt someone that I don't mean to hurt?"

Daimon didn't know everything about demons, but he had heard of a lot of cases where demons lost control of themselves and ended up lashing out and killing someone they didn't mean to. That was one of the main reasons a lot of demons ended up in trouble with the Venaticus. He didn't know what to say, though. There was a very real probability that Jackson might lose control a time or two while training. "I'm sure that Sebastien will know how to keep you from hurting anyone if that were to happen, but I'll also be here for you," he said quietly. "I don't know what I can do when it comes to demons, but…I'll try."

Jackson smiled a little as he looked at him. "Thanks, Daimon."

Daimon edged nearer to nuzzle the side of Jackson's face, but that was when he heard a pained cough, and Bly gasped in shock. The Alpha took his eyes off Jackson and looked down at his son, and as he watched him slowly open his eyes while he stifled his breaths, his heart started racing. "Remus?" he asked worriedly, moving closer to him.

Bly moved out of the way as Daimon lay in front of his son and watched him wake up.

After a few seconds of squinting and looking around, Remus stared at Daimon, and a despondent frown quickly stole his tired, confused expression. "Dad?" he asked, his voice shaky.

Daimon nodded and moved his paw over Remus'. "It's okay, Rem. I'm right here."

But Remus started sniffling and tried to get up. "I-I tried to—"

"Don't get up," Daimon told him, shaking his head. "You need to rest."

Although he stayed where he was, Remus didn't stop trying to explain himself. "I-I…*tried* to find you," he said, his voice breaking. "I didn't know where you were, and…I-I got…lost," he said shamefully.

Daimon shook his head again as he moved a little closer to him. "That's not your fault, Rem."

His son grunted and rested the side of his head on the ground again. He closed his eyes and exhaled painfully, gritting his teeth.

"What happened out there?" Daimon asked him.

Remus didn't immediately answer. He exhaled through his teeth and adorned an almost tormented look.

"Alpha, I think he should rest a little more and get some food in him before he tries remembering anything," Bly said.

As much as Daimon wanted to know what happened, and as desperately as he wanted to know whether Remus remembered who did this to him, he wasn't about to pressure his son or make him feel worse. All that mattered at the moment was ensuring that Remus recovered, and now that he was awake, he needed food. But there was no sign of Lalo, Alastor, and Wesley.

"Have Lalo and the others not come back yet?" the Alpha asked.

Bly glanced around. "Maybe they're tracking something."

"It's been over an hour," Daimon mumbled. He was starting to feel concerned. What if something happened to them out there?

"Should some of us go and look for them?" Jackson suddenly asked.

Daimon looked back at him. He was a little surprised that he hadn't gone back to Ethan by now. But in response, he sighed and pondered for a moment. He wasn't going to leave Remus, nor did he want to send Jackson out there. He'd usually send Tokala, but he was busy searching the tree line, and he didn't want to risk sending anyone else. If there *were* other wolves out there, then sending more of his wolves away would be exactly what they were waiting for.

He glanced at Sebastien and Ethan. As much as he might like to send Jackson's friend away, he wasn't going to be so cruel as to put his life at risk, nor did he want to give that muto a reason to act like he was hot shit. Although Sebastien would be a better asset here if a fight were to happen, *he* was the only other guy he was willing to send.

The Alpha set his eyes back on Jackson. "Go and tell Sebastien to track them."

Jackson nodded. "Do you want me to go with—"

"No. I want you here where I can see you," he said possessively. But he quickly added, "I need you here in case anything happens."

With another nod, Jackson headed over to Sebastien.

"Smooth, Dad," Remus suddenly snickered.

Daimon looked down at him and frowned. "What?"

Remus opened his eyes as he snickered again. "Nothing."

"No, what?" he insisted.

His son closed his eyes again and exhaled deeply. "Nothing, really."

He glanced at Bly and caught her smiling. What was so funny? He frowned in confusion and set his sights back on Remus.

Remus opened his eyes again, and when he saw Damion's face, he smirked amusedly. "You suck at wording things sometimes."

Daimon tried his best to keep himself from feeling embarrassed. He rolled his eyes and sat up. "No more talking. Rest. We'll have food at some point." He looked at Bly. "What did the Venaticus give you?"

"I checked everyone's bags, and most of the provisions were those Caeleste protein bars—the ones Sam brought to the packhouse before—as well as some other stuff. No meat, though," the Theta answered.

The thought of those protein bars made Daimon grimace.

"Wait," Remus uttered, lifting his head to look at them. "You…you *actually* met the Venaticus?"

Daimon gently pushed his son's head back down. "No more talking," he said sternly. "We'll update each other after you've eaten."

Remus nodded and closed his eyes.

"They taste like shit," Daimon grumbled, "but they'll be useful if we can't find anything to hunt."

Bly nodded and then shifted into her wolf form. "I'm going to go and find some more herbs."

"All right. Thank you."

She smiled and headed towards the trees, leaving him alone with Remus.

Daimon sighed and watched as Sebastien got up and raced into the woods, and when he shifted his sights to Jackson, Daimon caught Ethan glaring at him again. What the fuck was this guy's problem? Did he seriously think that sitting there scowling at him from across the glade was going to do anything? If he had a bone to pick, he'd better bring his sorry ass over.

But then the Alpha huffed irritably and stared at the fire. He didn't want to be the one to start a fight—in fact, there was a part of him that felt like he didn't want to get into it with Ethan *at all*. He knew if he started fighting Ethan, then Jackson would get upset and maybe even mad at him. Was that why Ethan was sticking to snarky comments and mutters under his breath? Was he also afraid of upsetting Jackson?

Daimon scowled irritably. There was more to it. There had to be. When Jackson told him about Ethan, there was a part of him that suspected that maybe there was something else going on. And after seeing the way Ethan was acting around Jackson—around *him*—he was almost sure that Ethan might want their friendship to be more than that.

Was he overthinking? Was he letting his hatred of muto and general dislike of Ethan make him jump to conclusions? Or was he right? Was *that* why Ethan was giving him dirty looks and making comments?

As much as he might like to call him out, he didn't have enough evidence yet. For now, he was going to have to control and keep himself from falling victim to his possessive, protective instincts. If he snapped at Ethan for what would appear as no reason to Jackson, then that would only damage his and Jackson's relationship. That wasn't something he was willing to let happen, and if he had to guess, he'd think—no, he was almost *certain*—that Ethan's scowls and comments were an attempt to make him do exactly that.

With an irritated snarl, he shifted his eyes to Remus. He needed to stop thinking about Ethan; he was getting frustrated, and that was the last thing anyone needed right now.

"How are you feeling, Rem?" Daimon asked.

"Just...tired and hungry," he mumbled.

"Lalo should—"

"I *thought* I heard you say Lalo," Remus interjected, opening his eyes again. "He's...alive?"

"Another story to tell when you're feeling better."

Remus smiled a little and closed his eyes. "Okay. But...Dad?"

"Mm-hmm?"

"I'm glad you're here."

Daimon smiled. "Me too." He couldn't explain how happy it made him to hear that. The last things his sons had said to him broke his heart. But he wasn't about to sit there and overthink that, either. There was no more room for overthinking. Half of his very small pack was out in the woods, and he had no idea where they were or what they were doing. All he could do was hope that Tokala's group were fine and that when Sebastien found Lalo's group, he found them safe and unharmed.

The Alpha lay down and watched the blue fire flicker. He felt as though it was a good sign that he nor Jackson had a bad feeling right now, but that could change at any moment.

And if it did, he was ready to fight whatever might come. He wasn't going to lose anyone else.

Chapter Seventeen

Silver Traps

| **Jackson** |

Things felt tense. There could be wolves watching from the trees, and Lalo's hunting party hadn't come back yet. Jackson didn't feel like something bad happened, and although he'd been told to trust his instincts, a part of him still worried that Lalo and the others were in trouble.

He sighed quietly and glanced across the camp at Daimon. The Alpha was talking to his son, who seemed to be recovering quickly. He was relieved by that, of course, but he knew that Daimon's sons didn't think highly of him, and once the kid was on his paws, Jackson was sure he was going to get more than dirty looks and snarky comments.

"What's going on around here?" Ethan asked, nudging Jackson's side with his paw.

Jackson turned his head to look at him. "What?"

"Sending wolves into the woods, making Sebastien go looking for those other wolves. I don't know, man. Something's up."

He might as well start from the beginning. "Well, there's this other wolf walker pack out there—"

"My old pack," Julian interjected.

Jackson nodded. "*Kane's* pack. We were staying in a ruin in their territory—we had no idea. He sent one of his Betas, Ellis, to warn us to give Julian back and leave, but Daimon didn't want to hand Julian over since the pack were awful to them and the other Omegas."

"They still follow the old ways," Julian said.

Ethan nodded slowly.

"So, we snuck out using a tunnel under the ruin," Jackson continued. "Kane's wolves followed, though, and we ended up getting into a fight. We...killed them all, and then we got taken by the Venaticus shortly after."

"Wait, I remember now. You were that pack Riker's hunters were trying to capture when the Venaticus showed up and made him point his own gun at his head," Ethan said with a frown. "So, you were there…and I didn't even realize."

Jackson shrugged. "You couldn't have known. You didn't know I was a wolf walker."

"Still, I feel like shit."

"Well, you shouldn't. I don't blame you."

Ethan didn't look convinced. "Yeah," he mumbled. "So, these Kane wolves are still on your trail?"

"They might be," Julian said before Jackson could answer. "Like I told Alpha Daimon, I've seen Kane track people for *weeks*. He's relentless."

"If that's the case, then…why hasn't he just sent a bunch of wolves into the glade to slaughter us?" Ethan asked.

He had a point. "Yeah. Aren't there like…seventy of them?" Jackson asked Julian.

They shook their head. "Even if he had a thousand wolves, Kane's always done things the same way. He takes his time; he watches and works out someone's weaknesses. One time, he sat in the same tree for *four* days watching another pack. That's four whole days without food or water—four whole days in his wolf form."

Ethan scoffed at them. "You almost sound envious of the guy."

Julian pouted. "I might hate him, but I'm not gonna lie and say I wasn't impressed by the shit I saw him do."

"I heard you tell Daimon he was strong," Jackson said curiously. "Like…*how* strong?"

An uncomfortable frown appeared on Julian's face. "He's not like any of us. He…gets in your head and makes you think and do things. He convinced an Omega to fight her own sister to the death. He convinced three Etas to walk into a ditch of cadejo and try to lead them out, but…that didn't end well."

Jackson found it hard to believe Kane could just convince people to do things that no sane person would do. "He just…tells them? Orders them."

Julian shook their head. "He doesn't need to order people to do stuff. He burrows into people's brains like a demon doing mind tricks."

"*Is* he a demon?" Ethan asked.

"No. He's one of those wolf walkers who always talks about keeping bloodlines pure and strong," Julian answered with a grimace. "If he even heard a rumour that someone wasn't from a pure line, he'd strip them of their rank and treat them worse than Omegas, and *that* was when he was in a good mood."

"And…what happens when he's in a bad mood?" Ethan asked.

Julian went a little pale. "Just killing someone would be a mercy in his eyes. He'd put them through the worst pain…and then he'd let them hang somewhere and starve, or…worse."

Jackson could see that this conversation was upsetting Julian. It was time to change the subject. "Daimon said I need to start training. I'm a little freaked out if I'm being honest."

"Training to use your demon ethos?" Julian asked.

He nodded.

"You'll be fine," Ethan said, lightly punching his shoulder. "You've always picked things up real fast. You remember when we were learning formatting shit when we were entry-level? You had that crap down in an hour; took me and some of the others *days*."

"This is different," Jackson said with a sigh. "Formatting is just typing and pressing buttons. This is like…fighting and using magic."

"Ethos," Ethan corrected. "Whole big difference between the two."

Jackson frowned at him. "Really?"

"Ethos is our energy, and we can convert it into whatever, you know? But then there are things like blood magic and such. So, I guess magic is a craft or skill, whereas ethos is ours," Ethan explained.

"Makes sense," Jackson mumbled.

Ethan nudged him again. "Don't worry, Jack. You'll be fine. I can't speak for Sebastien; I don't really know the guy. But if he's the one the Venaticus assigned to train you, then he's gotta be good."

"Not just the Venaticus, but Lord Caedis himself," Julian said with a smirk. "Have you heard that guy talk? All that…vhat's goving on avound 'ere," they mocked, sticking his teeth out a little.

Jackson couldn't help but laugh with Ethan and Julian. Lord Caedis' accent was hard to digest at first, but the more he heard him talk, the easier it became to understand him. "Even after watching his movies and stuff, I was still finding it hard to follow."

"Movies?" Julian asked. "He was in movies?"

"Holy fuck, yeah," Ethan realized. "I *thought* I recognized him."

"He's Ezra Wright," Jackson said, wagging his tail a little as excitement filled him. "I *loved* him in Nefastian Horror Story."

"Oh, shit, yeah!" Ethan exclaimed. "That one episode where the fucking uh…what is it? The wolf thing."

"The black dog," Jackson said. "When it gets into the house and he kills it with the goddamn lamp," he laughed.

Ethan laughed, too. "And didn't he do that one movie about the like…The Midnight Murders or something like that?"

"Oh, yeah," Jackson said.

"What's that?" Julian asked.

"He plays this sort of like paranormal detective and investigates paranormal murders and whatever, and there's a serial killer in the streets of old Ripperton. He spends like half the movie hunting the killer down just to find that it's actually his partner," Jackson explained.

"Wow..." Julian drawled, wagging their tail, too. "So we met a real-life actor?"

"And model," Jackson said with a nod.

"Damn," they said.

Ethan then laughed a little. "Did you ever see the presentation he did for Bianchi? It's like... over a hundred years ago, but damn."

Jackson shook his head. "No, I don't think I did."

"Guy's so fucking hot," Ethan muttered.

Julian giggled. "He *was* kinda cute... despite the like... intimidating scowls and the fact that he's a demon god."

Jackson smiled a little and nodded; he was enjoying talking to Ethan just like old times, and he was relieved that his friend was still pretty much the same. Now that he was thinking about Lord Caedis, though, a flurry of questions flooded in—things he didn't even think to ask while he was in the man's presence because he had so many other things to focus on. He looked at Ethan. "Lord Caedis and everyone I talked to at the Venaticus seemed to already know a lot about Lyca Corp. and what they've been doing. I never got the chance to ask, but... do you think they've been looking into the same stuff as us? Like the shipping containers and El'Vorian Industries."

Ethan frowned skeptically. "I mean, it would make sense."

Jackson pondered, "What if they know more than they let on? It kinda felt like they were holding back."

Julian chimed in, "This cadejo virus has been around for a long time. I guess... if we wanted all the answers, though, we could try asking Sebastien. He seems to know a lot about what's going on around the Venaticus and Nosferatu."

Jackson looked around, but there was still no sign of the winged hound. Was he still looking for Lalo, Alastor, and Wesley? He frowned and set his eyes back on Ethan. "What do *you* know about the Nosferatu?"

"Only what we looked into... but you don't remember any of that, do you?"

He shook his head.

"They're pretty much the Caeleste government. The Zenith and Lord Caedis sit at the very top of it all, but they have two CEOs and a council that handles everything for them; we call them the Caeleste Council. You and I also found out that the Nosferatu— three hundred or something years ago—used to be only a vampire organization. But then Caedis met Zenith, they did demon bonding mate things and started conquering the world. For the better, though," Ethan said matter-of-factly. "There was a time when this world was a whole lot worse than it is right now. Wars all over the place, gods trying to prove to one another that they had the bigger, stronger cult."

"Sheesh," Julian mumbled. "I'm glad I wasn't alive back then."

"Your almighty Fenrisúlfr was, though. He lived through it, didn't he?" But then Ethan frowned. "Well, he disappeared like…a hundred and fifty years ago or something, right?"

Julian and Jackson nodded.

"Hmm. Yeah, we didn't come across anything about him. You sure you don't remember any of this?" Ethan asked, staring at Jackson.

"No," he said with a pout. "I wish I did. Then I wouldn't have to sit around asking people questions all day."

Ethan sighed and shrugged. "Well, hey. At least you'll remember everything someday, right?"

"Right," he grumbled.

| **Sebastien** |

It was *too* quiet.

Sebastien followed the trail left by Lalo, Alastor, and Wesley through the thick woods and out into another glade. He couldn't sense any life force other than that of the three wolf walkers for miles, and when he focused on the trio, they didn't seem to be moving. That couldn't be because they were stalking something; if that were the case, he'd be able to sense whatever their prey was.

He picked up the pace, heading back into the forest. But as he approached the area where he could feel the wolves' auras, he slowed down and looked around cautiously. It took him a mere moment to locate the trio of brown wolves, and when he saw that they were standing on top of a fallen log—and struggling to keep their balance—Sebastien frowned strangely.

What the hell were they doing?

Sebastien went to move towards them—

"Wait, no!" Lalo shouted, spotting him.

He froze and stared at the trio as Alastor and Wesley set their eyes on him, too. "What the hell are you three doing?" he called confusedly.

Wesley raised a paw and pointed at the snow-covered ground. "There's traps hidden under there."

"Traps?"

"Like…bear traps, but silver," Alastor explained.

Sebastien glanced at the ground, searching for the traps. There must be at least one visible if the trio knew they were lying in wait. But he couldn't see a thing.

"Over there," Lalo said, nodding to Sebastien's left.

He looked over there, and *that* was when he saw it. The teeth of a silver bear trap were sticking a few inches out of the snow, shimmering brightly in the sunlight. He would have never seen that there. But these traps could only mean one of two things: A, there were hunters nearby who laid the traps and would come back to see if they'd caught any unsuspecting Caeleste or B, these traps had been left by hunters with the sole purpose of trapping Caeleste and ensuring they remained stuck there until they either bled to death, tore their trapped limb off to escape, or were picked off by some other predator.

Sebastien scowled and growled quietly. He *loathed* hunters. But there was no way for him to tell by traps alone whether this was done by the group the Venaticus said they'd deal with, or if it was another, different party. He'd try to work that out after getting Daimon's wolves to safety.

He set his eyes on the trio. "I'm gonna fly over there and bring you over here one by one. You gotta shift back, though. Sound good?"

They all nodded and shifted into their human forms.

Lalo, however, seemed to be the most nervous of them all. "Just get us the hell out of here, man," he pleaded, frantically searching for signs of more traps.

It made sense that he'd be this terrified. The guy was captured by hunters and locked in a cage. *Anyone* would be traumatized by that. But it was probably best to take Lalo last. If he brought him over there first, there was a chance the guy might bolt and get into trouble elsewhere. Sebastien *really* didn't want to deal with that, nor did he want to get yelled at by these guys' Alpha. He got yelled at enough by Heir Lucien and his uncles.

"All right, just keep calm," he said with a sigh as he stretched out his wings.

Sebastien flew over to the log and grabbed Alastor's shoulders with his front paws. He carried the man over to where he'd been standing, and once he placed him down, he swerved around and headed back to grab Wesley. But when he grabbed the brown-haired man, Lalo went a little pale.

"W-wait, can't you take me next?" he pleaded.

"I'll be right back. Literally two seconds," Sebastien assured him.

The man nodded and glanced at the ground.

Sebastien swiftly took Wesley over to Alastor, but when he placed the man down, Lalo's panicked voice got worse. As he turned to face Lalo, Sebastien frowned irritably and watched as the guy shuffled around on the log. "Calm down!" he called.

"Come and get me, man!" Lalo insisted.

"He's like…super freaked out by hunters now," Wesley said.

"Can't blame him," Alastor mumbled.

Sebastien rolled his eyes and hurried over to Lalo. "Dude, you're fine," he told him and gripped his shoulders.

"W-what if there's rope or snipers or—"

"There's no one else here," Sebastien assured him. "I can sense life force *miles* away, and there's nothing within five, all right?"

Lalo nodded as Sebastien carried him over to Wesley and Alastor, and when Sebastien placed the guy down, he immediately shifted into his wolf form. The other two shifted, too, and then they stared at Sebastien.

Evidently, they were waiting for him to tell them what to do next. But what *he* wanted to do was fly around and see if he could find the hunters responsible for placing those traps. Although it wouldn't take him long to travel five miles, there was no telling whether he'd actually find anything that far out. The hunters could be *days* away.

He also had to remember that he was with these wolf walkers to ensure they got their mission done. What kind of example would he be setting if he wandered off for hours? They were already off course thanks to Daimon chasing after that unicorn. He wasn't mad, though; the guy found his son, so Sebastien was trying to be patient. But if they didn't get back on track soon, he was going to have to say something.

With a quiet sigh, he dismissed the idea of searching for hunters and started leading the way back to the glade. "Come on. We better get back."

"What about food?" Wesley asked. "Remus needs to eat."

"I told you, there's nothing for miles," Sebastien said, glancing at him. "Those Caeleste protein bars are gonna have to do for now."

Wesley and Alastor grunted.

But Lalo was silent.

Sebastien set his sights on the light brown wolf, who was looking around cautiously and watching his every step. "I walked this exact way, man. We're fine."

The guy wasn't convinced, though. He kept frantically glancing left, right, and down at the ground.

"Lalo, chill," Wesley said.

Sebastien sighed and told him, "Look, I've dealt with a lot of hunters in my life, okay, and I know their habits. They don't place traps absolutely everywhere; they usually put a bunch of them in one area, places where Caeleste are likely to stop or walk through. That little area with the log was a prime location because a lot of Caeleste beasts would use that log as cover or a resting stop. They also leave their traps and move on fairly quickly. *Sometimes* they come back, sometimes they don't and just leave them there."

"Could it be those hunters Jackson's friend was with?" Wesley asked, looking at Sebastien.

"I don't know," he answered. "The Venaticus are supposed to be dealing with them. But I'll let your Alpha know when we get back. I don't think we should hang around this place." He should also contact Heir Lucian and ask for an update on Riker's hunters. But that was also something he'd have to do once they got back to the glade.

"I don't think Remus is gonna be able to travel," Alastor said.

"We'll figure something out," Sebastien mumbled. "We need to get back on track anyway."

"Alpha Daimon isn't gonna go for that," Wesley said with a nervous laugh.

"Well, he'll have to. I'm not just here to keep you on track; I have to keep you safe, and leaving this place is me doing just that," Sebastien said.

Alastor huffed and drawled, "Well...rather you than me."

Sebastien rolled his eyes again. He wasn't afraid of Daimon. He might be a Prime and descendant of Greymore, but he entered into an agreement with Lord Caedis, and it was Lord Caedis who made it Sebastien's responsibility to ensure these wolves got the job done. So, he was going to do whatever it took to get Daimon moving.

Chapter Eighteen

↬ ≼ ☽ ≽ ↫

Onwards

| **Daimon** |

R elief filled Daimon when he saw Sebastien come out of the woods with Lalo, Alastor, and Wesley. And almost at the same time, Tokala, Leon, Brando, and Enola returned from their perimeter search.

"What happened?" the Alpha asked as both groups stopped in front of him.

Sebastien and Tokala glanced at one another.

"You go first, man," Sebastien said.

Tokala set his eyes on Daimon. "We didn't find any wolves—we didn't find *anything* living—but we spotted a couple of cadejo. One of them had its leg stuck in a silver bear trap, and the other two were just walking around like they do when they're lurking."

Daimon frowned. "Silver traps?"

"We found those too, Alpha," Wesley said. "We don't know how many of them were there, but we saw one and didn't wanna take our chances."

Sebastien nodded and said, "I couldn't sense any life force for miles, so there's a chance that the hunters who left them there won't be coming back. However, there's also the possibility that they will, and since it's my job to keep you guys from doing shit that might get you killed and fuck up the mission, I'm advising you that we leave this glade and move on."

Daimon scowled at the black hound. He didn't like being told what to do, but his main priority was keeping Remus safe while he recovered, and if there was a risk that hunters might turn up, then he wasn't going to hang around. Remus wasn't ready to move, though. His wounds might be healing, but he was still weak, and if he was going to get his strength back, he needed to eat something. Evidently, they weren't going to find anything to hunt around here. So, what should he do: give Remus a little more time to recover or get two of his wolves to carry his son?

He looked down at Remus.

"I can carry him, it's no problem," Sebastien said, moving closer—

Daimon sharply turned his head and snarled at him. This guy needed to learn his place.

Sebastien backed off. "All right, damn."

"What should we do, chief?" Tokala asked.

That was when Remus opened his eyes and looked up at him. "Dad?"

"I'm here," he told him.

"W-we…we shouldn't stay here if hunters could come, right?"

"We don't know if they'll come or not, but we can't leave until you're able to—"

"I'm fine, Dad. I promise," Remus said as he started getting up.

Daimon shook his head and tried to make him stay down. "You—"

"I'm fine," he insisted, nudging his paw off him as he climbed to his feet. "We…we can go."

He worriedly stared at his son. Remus' legs were shaking, and his breaths were a little heavy. He clearly needed more time to rest, but…what if he chose to stay here and the hunters who placed those traps came back? But there was also the risk of leaving the glade and getting into danger out there, too. Tokala had seen cadejo; what if there were more?

"Uh, chief?" Tokala asked.

Daimon glanced at him. "What?"

"Should we put it to a vote?"

With a quiet sigh, Daimon nodded. He'd rather know what everyone else thought than go right ahead and make a choice.

Tokala called everyone over.

Daimon set his eyes on Ethan, who was following Jackson. "You're not part of the pack, so you're not part of this discussion," he said sternly.

Ethan scoffed as he glanced at Jackson. "Seriously? Part of your little pack or not, I'm a part of this *team*. Are you gonna send Sebastien away, too? Because last time I checked, he ain't a wolf either."

The Alpha snarled impatiently. "Sebastien's an asset. You're not."

"You don't even know that. You haven't seen me do shit—"

"Exactly. What are you even doing here?" Daimon growled.

The muto growled in response and went to move closer—

Jackson held his paw out, and both Tokala and Brando moved in front of Daimon protectively. The whole pack moved closer to defend Daimon if need be, but he didn't want defending. He wanted to teach Ethan a little respect, but he could see the worried look on Jackson's face, and as angry as he was, he wouldn't do something that would hurt his mate.

But Ethan scoffed as he eyed Daimon's wolves. "Too much of a coward to face me again, huh?"

Daimon snarled—

"Ethan, what the hell is going on with you?" Jackson exclaimed, moving in front of him so that they were face to face. "Calm the heck down."

"*Me*? What about—"

"Yes, you!" Jackson insisted, cutting him off. Then, he turned to face Daimon, who dismissed his wolves. "Shouldn't he be a part of whatever we need to talk about? We *are* all working together."

Daimon's anger increased when he saw a smug smirk stretch across Ethan's face. But he had to control himself. If this muto wasn't Jackson's friend, he'd probably have killed him by now. He wasn't going to keep letting everything slide, though. Sometime soon, that muto was going to do something that pushed him over the edge, and he was going to maim him, Jackson's friend or not.

There was no time for his emotions now, though. "The hunting party came across several silver bear traps," he started, looking around at everyone. "It's possible that the hunters who placed them might come back, and we can't risk being here when and if that happens. However," he said, glancing at Remus, who had chosen to sit rather than stand, "my son still needs time to recover—"

"I'm fine, Dad. I can—"

"Let me finish," Daimon said calmly.

Remus nodded.

"Remus still needs to recover, but the hunting party were unable to find anything." He looked at Sebastien. "You said you sensed nothing for miles."

"Five miles to be exact. That's how far my sensory ethos reaches. But yeah, nothing that's alive, at least," the winged hound said.

"Tokala also discovered some cadejo," Daimon said, looking at his Zeta.

Tokala glanced around at the pack as he said, "There were three of them. One was stuck in one of the silver traps mentioned."

Daimon continued, "We can't risk there being more cadejo out there, either. We might be able to fight off a few, but the truth is that we're not as strong as we were before. So, we have to choose between spending longer here so that Remus can recover or moving on now and carrying him."

The wolves adorned nervous, conflicted expressions as they looked at one another.

"What do *you* want to do, Daimon?" Jackson asked.

"I'm not sure," he answered honestly.

Bly then stepped out of the crowd. "In my medical opinion, I think that Remus needs to get some more rest. But…my personal opinion is that we should move. Cadejo or hunters, we can't risk a fight."

Daimon nodded at Tokala, who was staring at him, waiting for his approval to speak. Tokala asked everyone, "Who thinks moving on is the best course of action?"

"Do I get a vote?" Ethan asked as some of the pack raised their paws.

The Zeta looked at Daimon again.

Daimon ignored both of them, though. He focused on counting each raised paw, and ten of thirteen voted to leave, including Jackson.

"It looks like we're moving on," Sebastien said.

Ethan snarled angrily.

"Stop," Jackson muttered to him.

Daimon felt hesitant, but he wasn't going to ignore what his pack thought was best. He set his sights on Remus. "Are you sure you're okay to travel?"

Remus nodded. "I'll be fine. It sounds like the sooner we get out of here, the better."

"Offer's still on the table," Sebastien said.

Daimon ignored him, too. "Start packing up," he told the pack. "We'll move out in ten."

As the pack dispersed, Sebastien moved closer to Daimon. "I know they're not as good as a like…deer or whatever you guys usually eat, but those protein bars are better than nothing. They'll give your kid everything he needs to feel better."

The Alpha sighed quietly. Sebastien was right. Something was better than nothing, and if there was *anything* that would help his son feel even a tiny bit better, then he'd take it. "Fine."

"Hey, wait up," Sebastien called to Jackson.

Jackson stopped walking, and so did Ethan and Julian.

Sebastien shifted into his human form as he headed over to them. Once he reached Jackson, he reached into the left pack he was carrying and pulled out what looked like three candy bars, but Daimon knew they were actually the protein bars. Why would they pack them like that? Were they trying to convince people that they didn't taste like shit?

The white-haired demon made his way back over to Daimon and held the bars out to him. "Make sure he eats them."

"I got it," Remus said.

Daimon watched his son shift into his human form, and when he saw the healing wounds and dark bruises all over his dirt-covered skin, he felt dismay latch onto his heart. He must be in *agony*, and there wasn't anything he could do to help him.

Remus took the protein bars and eagerly unwrapped one of them. When he took a bite, he made a disgusted face and groaned. "Ugh, this tastes like…I don't even know. Mud?"

Sebastien smirked amusedly. "Hey, when you've had to eat about a thousand of them, you get used to it."

"I don't think I wanna get used to it," Remus mumbled.

With a smirk still on his face, Sebastien turned around and headed over to where Jackson, Julian, and Ethan were sitting.

Daimon exhaled deeply and turned to face his son. "I'm sorry there's nothing else to eat. We'll find something by tonight."

Remus shrugged as he finished the first bar. "It's fine. They might taste like mud, but this is the first thing I've had in days."

Days? He had so many questions… but was now the time to ask them? The last thing he wanted to do was pressure Remus, but there were things he *had* to know. "How's your mother?"

His son's expression quickly faded from relieved to something sullen. "A lot happened out there, Dad."

He sat down. "What happened?"

Remus finished chewing and swallowed with a grimace. "Things were bad right from the start. Some of the pack were even talking about trying to find their way back to you, but Mom wouldn't let them go."

Daimon waited for him to elaborate.

He took a deep breath. "She… well, she and Caius got in a fight with some other wolves. We thought they were from that other pack."

"Kane?"

"Yeah. They threatened us and said they were gonna take us to their Alpha. Mom made the call to attack them, and this huge fight broke out."

"Is that how this happened to you?" he asked as his anger returned.

"No. Mom made me and Rom leave with Miakoda and Kajika. We met up with Mom and the others a few hours later. Some of them were really hurt, though. Caius got his ear bit off and everything."

"What about your mother?"

"She was fine as far as I could tell. But after that, we were travelling without even stopping to rest. We ended up near this old log hut, and that was where Mom *finally* decided to let everyone rest. And then… I heard Tainn and Fala talking. They didn't trust Mom or Caius anymore because they were talking about tracking wherever that other pack were staying and seeing if they could take them on. But there were like seventy of them, right?"

Why would Nyssa be so stupid? Daimon knew that she was reckless and didn't thoroughly think things through sometimes, but this was a whole new level. "That's what Julian told us," he answered.

"Tainn tried to tell her that, but she wouldn't listen. And they got into a big fight. She hit Tainn *real* hard, and that made a lot of the others start questioning if they actually wanted to keep following her. *I* wanted to come and find you. I tried to tell her that you would let us all come back, but she yelled at me and said that you'd kill us for being traitors."

Daimon scoffed in astonishment. He didn't even know what to say to that.

"Romulus believed her, even after I tried to get him to believe me. I didn't want to stay there, and I knew that I was going to have to come and find you by myself to prove to them that you'd take us back. So…I left on my own. But it got dark, and I knew something was following me. I didn't know what it was, so I started running. I…" he paused and hid his tormented face. "I…*tried* to hide, but…they *pulled* me out of the log, and…."

Daimon frowned despondently and nuzzled his head. "You don't have to talk about it," he told him quietly. But he wanted to know who did this—he wanted specifics so that he could hunt them down and tear them apart. "Did…you get a look at them?"

Remus exhaled shakily and frowned as Daimon pulled away to look at him. "I…think one of them had half an ear." His frown became a scowl, and the look of torment in his eyes thickened. "I…I don't know, I—"

"It's okay, Remus," Daimon said as he moved his front leg around him and pulled him into his embrace. "You're safe now. I'm not going to let anything else happen to you."

His son dropped the second half-eaten protein bar and wrapped his arms around him as he began crying. "They were gonna kill me, Dad," he wept, tightening his arms around him.

Daimon scowled *furiously* as he glared at the tree line. His desire to destroy whoever did this to his son increased so much that he felt himself tremble. It was getting harder to control his emotions. But he huffed and tried to settle. "No one is going to hurt you, Rem."

Remus sniffled and loosened his grip a little. "I wish Rom came with me. He's still out there with Mom."

"Do you know where they are?" he asked, looking down at him. He wasn't connected to Nyssa anymore, so the only hope he had of finding her and Romulus was through Remus.

"I…I don't know, Dad."

He didn't want to push him, though. "It's okay."

"But…if we found them, you could convince them," his son said with a look of realization on his face. "Y-you can make them see that you'd welcome them back." But then he frowned. "You…would, right?"

Daimon frowned at him. "Of course I would, Remus. I don't have the faintest idea where your mother came up with the idea that I'd kill any of you."

Remus looked down at the snow and shrugged. "Maybe she was just scared of people leaving."

"Sounds like her," he grumbled.

"Chief," came Tokala's voice.

Daimon glanced at him.

"We're all ready to leave."

With a quiet sigh, Daimon nodded. "Finish that last bar," he told Remus.

His son wiped his tears away and opened the third protein bar. He didn't hesitate to shove the whole thing in his mouth, and as he chewed it loudly, he held his thumbs up at Daimon.

The Alpha smiled slightly and stood up. "All right, let's get moving."

"Where are we going?" Remus asked, his voice muffled by the food in his mouth.

It only just hit Daimon that he hadn't told Remus anything about what was going on. "That's a long story," he answered, leading the way to where the pack was waiting. "I'll tell you along the way."

Remus swallowed his food and shifted into his wolf form. "Okay."

"Stay on high alert," Daimon called as he passed the pack. "Watch the snow for traps and keep all your senses sharp."

The pack followed closely behind him and called their acknowledgements of his orders.

They weren't too far off course, and once they were back on track, he'd send someone forward to scout. There was a long journey ahead of them, but it would be getting dark in a few hours, so he had to make sure they found somewhere safe to rest. He wasn't taking any chances.

Chapter Nineteen

↤ ≼ ☽ ≽ ↦

That Ominous Feeling

| **Jackson** |

After an hour of trekking through the woods, everyone seemed to relax a little. Sebastien assured the pack that there weren't any human auras within five miles of them, and they hadn't come across any more silver traps, either. But Jackson wasn't going to let his guard down. Anything could happen at any moment. Sebastien couldn't sense cadejo, could he? There could be zombies out there and they wouldn't know unless they saw them.

He glanced at Daimon, who was leading the way with Remus and Sebastien. Then, he looked at Ethan, who was walking on his left. He didn't want to leave his friend to walk alone, but he knew that Daimon wasn't going to come anywhere near Ethan, and it made him feel upset that he had to choose between walking with his friend or walking with his mate.

Jackson sighed quietly and focused on the path ahead. Was it wishful thinking to hope that Ethan and Daimon might eventually learn to get along? Neither of them was going anywhere, but if he had to keep choosing between who he sat with and who he walked with, he felt as though his sadness might begin to turn into frustration.

But he didn't want to let himself get worked up. That was the last thing *anyone* needed right now. So, he exhaled quietly and tried to keep calm.

"Hey, Jack," Ethan whispered.

He looked at the tiger. "What?"

Ethan nodded in Sebastien's direction.

Jackson watched as the winged hound started falling back, leaving Daimon to lead on his own with Remus. He knew what Ethan was getting at, though. Earlier, they'd hypothesized that Sebastien might know more about all of this than he was letting on. Of course, Jackson wanted to know as much as Ethan did, but would Sebastien tell the truth?

He waited to see where Sebastien was going, and when the hound stopped beside him—but a few feet away—he frowned curiously and asked, "Uh… Sebastien?"

The hound glanced at him. "Yeah?"

"Do you…well, do the Venaticus and Nosferatu know about El'Vorian industries? Ethan and I were looking into it, and—"

"I found all these off-book shipments and saw unmarked vans delivering stuff to El'Vorian," Ethan interjected, "the pharmaceutical company we think is a front for Lyca Corp."

Sebastien nodded slowly. "Yeah, you guys gathered quite the little evidence package, didn't you?"

Ethan and Jackson frowned, and then both asked, "You were listening to us?"

The hound scoffed. "Duh. Why wouldn't we listen?"

Jackson pouted and Ethan snarled.

"But yes, the Nosferatu were investigating Lyca Corp. years before you two kids were. At the time, we didn't know why they were trying to create hybrids, but we did know that was what their goal was. They captured demons and wolf walkers from places the Nosferatu doesn't have much power—like Ascela—and shipped them to their facilities. That's what all those shipping containers and vans were carrying."

That made sense. "Facilities?" Jackson questioned.

"Horrible places," Sebastien grumbled. "They experiment on Caeleste."

"Experiment?" Julian questioned with a grimace.

"So, it's not just wolf walkers they were doing shit to, then?" Ethan asked before Jackson could.

"Nope," Sebastien answered as Daimon led them up a hill. "Thirty-two years ago, Lyca Corp wasn't even on our radar. The company was owned by a human, yet it specialized in lycanthropes. They created medicines for lycans, provided medical expertise, and trained doctors to better understand lycans. Hence the name Lyca Corp. But what we didn't know was that they had a sub-division, and in that division, they experimented on lycans. That was how they got all their answers."

That made Jackson feel sick. This *whole* time, Lyca Corp.—El'Vorian Industries—was torturing innocent people. How could people do that? How could they sleep at night after spending their day cutting and stabbing someone?

"They had to hide their shady business, right?" Ethan mumbled. "So, that's why they hid all those deliveries using El'Vorian."

"Seems that way, yeah," Sebastien mumbled.

"So…how *did* they get on the Nosferatu's radar?" Julian asked.

"That's where things get a little…personal. Not for me," Sebastien said, glancing at each of them. "But for my bosses. All three of them, actually. You've met Heir Lucian—"

"Did something happen to him?" Jackson asked with a frown.

"Not him, no. He has a cousin, and Lyca Corp. took him when he was a child, and both the Zenith and Lord Caedis have spent the past ten years trying to find him. But Lyca Corp. is tricky. They have so many locations, underground and hidden facilities, and they hide behind more than El'Vorian industries. Despite all their power and resources, the Zenith and Lord Caedis can't find him."

Jackson grew sicker. A *kid*? They took *a kid*. These people were disgusting, and he was beginning to understand that more and more as Sebastien continued. But how did this tie in to—

"How does that tie into you guys looking into the cadejo virus?" Ethan asked.

"I was just gonna ask that," Jackson said.

"Well, their kid is a super powerful demon baby. Of course, Lyca Corp. would do anything to get their hands on something like that to use in their experiments," the kludde said.

"The wolf walker-demon hybrid experiments?" Ethan asked.

Sebastien nodded. "Yeah. As for the cadejo virus, that's been around for like…a hundred and fifty-five years. That was when *I* first encountered it. I was sent to an estate in DeiganLupus to investigate a strange sickness killing townsfolk, and…there was something there. It looked like a huge black wolf. And months later was when the first cadejo started turning up. I wasn't kept in the loop—I don't know what happened for the next year or so—but when I was called back into the Nosferatu, they told me that black wolf was the result of Lyca Corp.'s experiments."

"The hybrid Lord Caedis is looking for?" Jackson asked.

"Yep," Sebastien confirmed. "Only we didn't know Lyca Corp. was involved until they took Lord Caedis and the Zenith's kid."

Ethan exhaled deeply. "What a fricken mess we've gotten ourselves into, huh, Jack?"

Jackson rolled his eyes. "As always." But as he glanced around, he locked his gaze with Tokala's. The orange wolf was staring at them—he'd obviously been listening—and when he saw Jackson had noticed, he frowned and looked away.

"Although it's only speculation that the hybrid we found in DeiganLupus is the cause of the virus. That's why we need to get to this lab and find out whatever else we can," Sebastien explained.

"What about the hybrid that Lord Caedis said Cyrus was trying to capture?" Jackson asked.

"That hybrid and his packmates are also on our radar. It's a lot to take in, but there are a lot of pieces to this puzzle. We're all hoping we'll know more once we find the lab," the hound said.

Jackson nodded slowly. That certainly *was* a lot to process, but at least Sebastien answered their questions and didn't evade them. This all made a little more sense now. What if that black wolf from DeiganLupus *was* the cause of the virus? Could they use it to create a cure? What about the wolves Cyrus failed to capture? He wanted to know *right now*, but just as Sebastien said, they had to get to the lab if they wanted solid answers.

He lingered on the fact, however, that Lord Caedis and the Zenith had a son, and that demons *that* powerful couldn't find him after Lyca Corp. took him. How powerful was that company? And if they were able to take on the Nosferatu, then what chance in hell did a wolf walker pack have against them? What if they got to the lab and there were hundreds of guards? What if they couldn't even get close to the lab because they had snipers and troops and whatever else set up all around Greykin Valley? No…Ethan said that some people saw the lab and it looked like it was attacked. If some hunters could get close enough to see it, then the pack would be fine, right?

He set his eyes on Daimon. Then, he glanced at Tokala, who he caught staring again. Why was he looking at them? Jackson wanted to know, so he left Ethan and Julian with Sebastien and headed over to the orange wolf.

"Is, uh…everything okay?" he asked when he reached Tokala.

The orange wolf chuckled. "Yeah, yeah. I was just listening in. Everyone was," he said, glancing back at the pack. "The more we know about what's going on, the better, right?"

Jackson nodded. "Yeah. I guess I'm just a little more worried now about what might be waiting for us when we get to Greykin Valley. If people like Lord Caedis and the Zenith couldn't get their son back from Lyca Corp., then what are *we* gonna do?"

"We'll figure it out. The chief always has a plan. Don't fret," Tokala said calmly.

Tokala was right. They had *miles* to go, and they hadn't even seen the place yet. There was no point in freaking out before they had a chance to see what they'd be dealing with. Daimon would figure out a plan, too. He *always* had a plan.

Jackson stared ahead at the Alpha again. He thought about how he could use his worry about Lyca Corp.'s power as an excuse to talk to him, but why would he need an excuse to talk to his mate? Ethan being here didn't change anything, so why did he feel like it did? It was because Ethan and Daimon hated each other. He didn't want to make one of them feel like he preferred the company of the other, but feeling like he had to be careful was beginning to stress him out. He wanted to go and walk with Daimon, but he was certain that Ethan would eventually join him, and *that* would irritate Daimon.

He sighed and shook his head. They were going to have to learn to get along, and Jackson wasn't going to let their hatred for one another get in the way. So, he left Tokala's side and caught up to Daimon. "Hey," he said when he reached the Alpha's side.

"Hey," Daimon mumbled.

"Is…everything okay?" Jackson asked unsurely.

"Fine," he replied, but he sounded irritated.

Jackson frowned and stared ahead as they approached the tree line. He didn't want to think about it, but he couldn't fight the thought that Daimon might be mad because he'd just been walking with Ethan for the last hour. He was afraid to flat-out ask him, but he had to bring it up eventually, and if he didn't do it now, he might *never* do it. So he asked, "Are you mad at me because I was walking with Ethan?"

The Alpha glanced at him and looked him up and down. "No." Then, he glared ahead.

"Well, you're mad about something. What's wrong?"

"Nothing."

"Daimon, I—"

"I said it's nothing," he snapped.

Jackson frowned in response. Evidently, he didn't want to talk to him right now, and Jackson didn't want to force it out of him. Making Daimon angrier was the last thing he wanted. So, he let it go. "Okay," he mumbled.

Remus then grunted quietly.

Daimon sharply turned his head to look at him. "Are you all right?"

"Yeah," Remus said, nodding. "How much further?"

The Alpha looked ahead. "Once we cross this tundra, we'll find a place to rest." He looked back at Tokala. "Tokala, I need you to scout ahead and find us a place to rest."

With a nod, the orange wolf turned left and hurried off, sticking to the tree line.

Daimon led the pack out of the forest and into a barren tundra. Puddles of ice were scattered here and there, and a few shrubs broke through the thick blanket of snow. The forest was visible on the other side—perhaps a mile or so away—and there wasn't a single sign of any other life.

Jackson didn't like the feeling this place gave him. As he crossed the wide, open field of ice, a harsh breeze raced by, and with it came trepidation. He could feel eyes on him. It was the same ominous feeling he got when he first arrived in Ascela; the same feeling he got just before something bad happened.

He wasn't going to sit on it. "Daimon, I…I'm getting that feeling again."

The Alpha looked at him and adorned a concerned frown. He started looking around, slowing his pace as he continued leading the way.

"What is it, Dad?" Remus asked worriedly.

Daimon looked back at Sebastien.

The hound—who had clearly been listening—shook his head. Could he not sense anything?

"Return to the trees," Daimon called, turning right.

The pack began murmuring to one another, searching around with confused, unsettled looks on their faces. They followed Daimon as he led the way back towards the trees, and as Lalo started panting out of fear, Rachel attempted to calm him.

Jackson looked around frantically, staring in the direction of the slightest sound. The ominous feeling grew heavier, burdening him with dread. He knew something was coming—he could feel it approaching like a storm on the horizon—and whatever it was, it was making his instincts go haywire.

And then he saw something.

A flicker of silver—the kind of flicker the scope of a sniper reflected in the sunlight.

Jackson tensed up and looked at Daimon. "There's somethi—"

His words were silenced by a deafening, *piercing* boom, and when Jackson felt something impale his back leg, the most excruciating pain he'd ever felt electrified through his body. He collapsed and *shrieked* in agony; he looked down at his leg and saw his blood oozing from a horrific wound, and when he looked for Daimon, he instead set his eyes on the crowd of silver-wearing men who burst out of the forest and began firing their weapons.

Hunters.

Chapter Twenty
The Woman in Silver

| Jackson |

Jackson's vision was blurring. Pain surged through his numbing body, and everything started spinning. He whined and groaned, unable to get up, unable to do anything to help the pack. All he could do was lay there, bleed, and watch his packmates fight.

Bullets rained in every direction.

The distorted voices of both the hunters and the pack echoed around inside Jackson's head. He watched the wolves collide with the men, snapping their jaws and snarling ferociously. Several horrified screams came before Ethan's monstrous growl, and Sebastien's blue flames swiftly lit up the battlefield.

But the pain in Jackson's leg worsened. He groaned and winced, and when he looked down at his wound, he saw that he was lying in a soggy puddle of blood and melting snow.

Something started *burning* through his veins. It was like fire eating him up from the inside, and it was the most excruciating thing he'd ever felt.

A hunter landed in the snow beside him. The man grunted and gripped the wolf bite on his left arm, but before he could try to get up, Ethan pounced onto the man and savagely tore his throat out.

"Jackson!" the tiger exclaimed worriedly, turning to face him.

Jackson stared up at him; his sabre-like fangs were covered in blood, as was his fur, and several cuts and wounds were scattered over his body.

As a circle of blue flames surrounded Jackson and Ethan, Sebastien descended and landed beside them. "Shift back," the winged hound told Jackson. "Now!"

But no matter how hard he tried, Jackson couldn't shift into his human form. He strained and groaned, but his ethos didn't respond.

Ethan examined his wound, and when he told Sebastien, "The bullet's silver," both the tiger and hound adorned anxious frowns.

"We gotta get him out of here," Sebastien said hastily.

The tiger nodded and began helping Sebastien move Jackson so that he was lying on his stomach.

What were they doing? What about the pack? What about Daimon? They were still fighting the hunters—he could *hear* the bullets and snarls and yells. He couldn't just leave!

Sebastien gripped the underneath of Jackson's front legs, and with several flaps of his wings, he began lifting him into the air.

Jackson didn't have the strength to try and pull free. When he attempted to tell Sebastien to stop, all that came out of his mouth was a wince. The hound pulled him higher, revealing the battlefield to Jackson's blurring vision. He could see Daimon in his Prime form defending three of his packmates as they tried to get to the trees, but there were *so many* hunters. So much gunfire, and so much blood in the snow.

He heard his racing heart; it started slowing, the pain surging through him grew weaker, and his limbs began to feel numb. It felt like his head was spinning. He wanted to close his eyes, but he had to fight and stay awake. He couldn't pass out now, not while Daimon and Ethan and his packmates were battling those men.

But Sebastien didn't turn back. The hound carried him away from the tundra, and just as Jackson saw the forest beneath him, his blood loss defeated him, and the world started fading away.

And the last thing he heard was a distorted yelp, and the sound of clanking metal.

Something ensnared him, and he started falling.

| **Daimon** |

With a ferocious roar, Daimon plunged his claws into the hunter's chest and ripped his heart out. He gripped the dead man's body before it could drop to the ground and launched it at the three incoming men. When they fell, Tokala and Brando pounced on them and tore them apart in seconds.

But there were so many more of them, and because of their silver armour, he couldn't tell if there were others incoming, or if those on the battlefield in front of him were all that were left.

"Are these Riker's guys?!" Brando called as he and Tokala backed away towards Daimon.

The Alpha looked around, but there was no sign of Riker. There were no jeeps or bikes, but that had to be because the hunters knew his pack would hear them coming miles away. He snarled and glanced around again—

"Sebastien's got Jack," Ethan called from across the battlefield.

Daimon set his eyes on the tiger and nodded. He might hate the guy, but killing these hunters and protecting his pack was more important than his feelings. He shifted his sights to Tokala and ordered him, "Take Remus and the others to the glade."

The orange wolf nodded and began helping his injured packmates get away.

Daimon burst forward and collided with the crowd of hunters. He avoided their silver armour and slashed each man and woman with his claws. He crushed their heads in his jaws, tore off their limbs, and smacked their precious rifles away before they could fire.

He was going to kill every single one of them.

"Chief!" came Tokala's panicked voice.

Dread shot through Daimon—it always did on the rare occasion that his Zeta sounded afraid—and when he turned to face what Tokala had seen, his eyes widened, and his dread evolved into fear.

Cadejo.

The smell of blood and the sound of fighting must have attracted them, and they were pouring out of the woods like moths to a flame.

"Undead!" the hunters started yelling.

"Retreat!" a woman called.

No. They weren't getting away. Cadejo or not, Daimon wasn't giving up yet. These hunters had followed them all the way here, and if he let them go, they'd *keep* following the pack.

"Get to the trees!" the Alpha called to his wolves, and then he turned to face the retreating hunters and raced towards them.

The hunters started firing at him, but he swerved right and used the tree line as cover. Splinters of bark exploded from the trees as the bullets hit them; in his Prime form, he was a much bigger target, so Daimon morphed into his normal wolf form and charged forward. And the moment he reached the hunters, he snatched the first man's arm with his teeth and swung him around, knocking several of the others onto the snow. He leapt back when the hunters recovered and fired again, and he burst in and out of the tree line, pouncing at a hunter each time.

But when he came out the third time and went for a man who'd tripped and fell, one of the others got a shot off on him. He felt the silver bullet pierce his back leg; it cut right through, and although it hurt like a bitch, his strength didn't fade. The bullet failed to wedge itself in his body.

He snarled and went for the man who shot him, and before the guy could scream, Daimon pinned him down and crushed his head in his jaw.

Horrific screams snatched Daimon's attention. He stopped chasing the remaining five hunters and watched as the cadejo began feasting on the fallen, injured hunters. What the hell was he looking at? Cadejo had no interest in humans; they craved the flesh and blood of wolf walkers…so why were they devouring humans?

He snarled in frustration and turned his head to watch the five hunters fleeing into the woods. He wanted to chase them—he wanted to tear them apart—but he wouldn't risk leaving his pack.

Daimon ran after his wolves, following their scent. Agonized screams and savage snarls echoed behind him, but no cadejo were on his trail.

Where was Jackson? He tried to locate him using their mated bond, but he couldn't feel him. Of course he couldn't. He'd been shot with silver, and evidently, Sebastien hadn't yet removed it.

He snarled angrily and sped up, but then he saw something shift through the snow. A silver shimmer and crimson. The grunt of a struggling woman came from the same direction, so Daimon raced over there and discovered an injured hunter. She immediately pulled her pistol from her belt and tried to fire at him, but he smacked the pathetic little weapon away and growled down at her.

"Get away from me, werewolf scum!" she yelled, but then she winced and gripped the bleeding wound on her waist.

She'd been bitten, but he couldn't tell whether it was the bite of one of his wolves or a cadejo.

Daimon wanted to kill her, but some of the hunters got away, and he wanted to know how many more of them there were, how they managed to find his pack, and why the Venaticus had failed to keep them off their trail.

He morphed into his Prime form and picked the struggling woman up. She protested and tried to break free, but he threw her over his shoulder and continued on his way to his pack. Her silver armour stung against his body, but there wasn't time to try and remove it. He wasn't going to risk being seen by a single cadejo.

As he ran, he concentrated again and tried to locate Jackson, but he *still* couldn't feel him, and he started to panic. Why hadn't Sebastien landed somewhere yet and pulled the bullet out of Jackson's leg? What the hell was taking him so long? He set his eyes on his pack, who were following Tokala through the forest. But Ethan wasn't with them. "Tokala," he called, catching up with the pack. "Where's the fucking tiger?"

His Zeta glanced at him. "He went to find Sebastien and Jackson, chief. Who's the woman?"

"Hunter," he grunted. "Is everyone all right?"

"A few cuts and wounds, but nothing serious," Tokala answered.

That made him feel a little relieved, but he wouldn't relax until he knew that Jackson was okay. "We need to find somewhere to rest and heal," he said, glancing back at his exhausted pack. And as the woman he was carrying kicked and writhed around, he added, "We'll find out what we're dealing with from her."

"How did the hunters find us, though?" Wesley called. "The Venaticus were supposed to be dealing with them."

"That's what I aim to find out," Daimon replied.

He attempted to connect to Jackson once again…and again…and again, but no matter how many minutes passed, he still couldn't find him. Something was wrong. There was no way it took this long for Sebastien to land somewhere safe and help Jackson. But he had to stay focused. Before anything else, he needed to get his pack to safety. So he took the lead, carrying the woman over his shoulder. She eventually stopped struggling, evidently succumbing to the bite, and since she wasn't seething or snarling, he felt it was safe to say that it was a wolf walker bite.

Daimon led his pack to the foot of a mountain, and not too far up the rocky path, he found a cave entrance. He headed inside and navigated the deep, narrow caverns; once he found an area large enough for everyone to rest, he put the woman down against the back wall and shifted into his human form. "Rope," he said, holding his hand out.

Ezhno, who also shifted into his human form, reached into his bag, took some rope out, and handed it to Daimon.

The Alpha tied the woman's wrists and ankles. Then, he slapped the side of her face to keep her from passing out and glared into her confused eyes. "Listen very carefully," he told her. "You're going to answer all of my questions, and if you tell me everything I want to know, you might just have time to get that bite cured."

She grunted and looked down at the bite on her waist.

"And if you *don't*," Daimon growled, "I'll let you turn, and then we'll leave you to fend for yourself."

A terrified look stole her frown. There was nothing a hunter feared more than becoming the very things they hunted. She understood what was at stake, and Daimon hoped that was enough to get her to talk.

"Are you part of Riker's group?" Daimon asked.

The woman nodded.

"Where is he?"

She didn't answer.

Daimon harshly gripped her wound and squeezed.

The woman cried painfully as she blurted, "He's with the Venaticus!"

"How did you find us?"

She grunted and exhaled deeply. "We've been tracking you since you left Silverlake. Riker stayed back with half the party to make it look like the Venaticus got all of us." She laughed and then grimaced. "Fucking demon scumbags. Always letting shit slip through their fingers."

Daimon snarled and looked back at his pack. Bly and Lance were seeing to everyone's wounds, and Tokala, Wesley, and Alastor were watching the tunnel.

"You'll all…pay for what you did," the woman uttered.

He set his eyes on her again. She was getting weaker. The bite was stealing her strength, and she would pass out at any moment. But not until he got what he needed. "How many more of you are there?"

She huffed and scowled. "Too many."

"Give me a number," he growled.

"A million," she sneered weakly.

Daimon gripped her wound again, making her scream. "Tell me."

"I don't know!" she yelled. "I-I don't…know how many of my friends you just killed. Those…fucking undead things. I don't…know. Please…just let me go."

"How many of you were there before the ambush?"

She groaned and rolled her head, breathing through her gritted teeth. "Forty-five!"

Daimon tried to remember how many hunters he'd seen die, but everything happened so fast that he couldn't. He didn't know how many more were out there, but one thing was certain: there *were* more of them, and his pack weren't safe yet.

"Please," the woman breathed weakly. "Don't…let me turn."

He snarled as he got up and walked away from her. She *deserved* it. She tried to kill his packmates; for all he knew, she could have been the one who shot Jackson. And upon the thought of him, Daimon tried to locate him, but *still*, he couldn't.

"What's the plan, chief?" Tokala asked as he walked at his side in his human form.

"I don't know," he replied. "I need to think. Tell everyone to get some rest."

Tokala nodded and left him alone.

Daimon went over to where Remus was resting and sat against the wall beside him. What *was* the plan? He wanted to go and find Jackson; his mate was out there somewhere with a silver bullet in his leg, and Daimon had no idea what might have happened. Had Sebastien managed to get him to safety? Did the hunters or cadejo slow him down?

The Alpha took a deep breath and tried to compose himself. He wasn't going to risk losing anyone else; he was inexplicably relieved that all his wolves managed to get away with only a few scrapes and cuts. But he had to get them far, *far* away from here. There were still hunters out there, not to mention all those cadejo that came to scavenge off what the battle left behind.

What he *didn't* see were variant cadejo, though. If those cadejo were just normal, undead wolf walkers, then things would be a little easier. They were still dangerous, but not as dangerous as prowlers or brutes. Daimon and his pack knew how to deal with ordinary cadejo.

Daimon exhaled deeply and looked around at his wolves. They needed time to rest, and as much as he hated to admit it, so did he. If he was going to find Jackson, he needed to be at full strength, and that was something that wouldn't happen unless he let his wounds heal. Sebastien was also with him, and although that guy was aggravating, he could handle himself, and Daimon knew he'd take care of Jackson in his absence. He had to; it was his job.

He grunted irritably and pulled his shirt off. Once he folded it up and put it on the ground, he laid on his back and rested his head on the shirt. For a few moments, he stared up at the cave ceiling and tried to connect to Jackson, but to no avail. So, he closed his eyes, tried to relax, and waited for his body to recover.

Chapter Twenty-One

⤳ ≼ ☽ ≽ ⤴

Sixteen Hunters

| **Jackson** |

Pain twinged in Jackson's leg. His body was numb, his senses were distorted, and through the ringing in his ears, he heard the faint voices of men and women.

Where was he?

He tried opening his eyes, but the bright whiteness of wherever he lay stung and sent pain through his head, forcing him to keep them shut. He could smell burning wood, cooking meat, and blood. And there was something else. Something that singed the insides of his nose and throat every time he inhaled.

Wolfsbane.

Dread shot through Jackson, and when he tensed up, his body hurt a whole lot more. He was sure that he knew where he was without even having to see it. The voices, the smell, and the fact that he was so weak that he couldn't even move a muscle. He was in a hunter camp, wasn't he?

Jackson attempted to open his eyes again, but the brightness hurt so much. He had to fight through it, though. So he grimaced and struggled, and after a few moments, the blinding light started clearing, and he could make out a few blurred figures and the glow of a burning fire.

He looked around for Sebastien; he remembered the hound being with him before he passed out, but there was no sign of him. But then he heard a familiar roar, followed by the sound of clanging metal. The hunters started whooping and laughing; Jackson searched for the source of their entertainment, and when he spotted a haze of orange, black, and white, he became almost certain that Ethan was there with him.

With a pained groan, he tried to move his limbs. Something dripped down his face, and as the feeling slowly returned to his body, it began to feel as though he lay in a puddle of something. Could it be blood?

"Hey, hey," came a man's voice. "Dog's coming around."

Jackson searched for the man, but a *crowd* of hunters quickly appeared in front of his cage and gawped at him like he was some sort of exhibit.

"I thought he was gonna die," a woman mumbled.

"What do we do with him now?" a man asked.

"What's left of his pack'll probably come looking. We'll take 'em out when they turn up," a gruff-sounding man said.

Jackson frowned in dismay. He knew that Daimon would come for him, and that was exactly what these people wanted. They were using him as bait, and they were going to try and kill his packmates. But Daimon wouldn't fall for it, would he? He was smart; he'd have to know that the hunters would try something like this, right?

He looked around frantically as the hunters surrounding him went back to what they were doing. It was only then that he realized he was in a cage, and the bars were shimmering silver in the sunlight. Was that why he felt so weak?

No. He'd been shot. He remembered that. But when he looked down at his leg—his *human* leg—he saw that it was bandaged. Albeit whoever patched him up did a crappy job, he was still glad that there wasn't a bullet wedged in his thigh anymore.

But he couldn't just lie around and do nothing. He had to get up. As hard as he tried, though, the most he could do was stiffly nudge his head a little, allowing him to see more of the camp. It *was* Ethan he'd heard, and he could see his friend locked up in a cage on the other side of the camp. There were several other cages, too, and in one... he could see the black, winged hound.

Sebastien.

He wasn't moving; silver chains constricted his body like snakes, burning his skin—it was *sizzling* and steaming—and blood sept down his body to join the puddle he lay in.

Jackson felt sick. How could these people sleep at night knowing they were *torturing* others? Just because Caeleste were different didn't mean they deserved this. Cages and chains... silver bullets and bear traps. It was disgusting. It was *atrocious*. And now, Jackson was beginning to understand more and more why every Caeleste he met expressed their hatred for hunters.

The men and women laughed and joked, sitting around their fire, burning wolfsbane while they ate their meat. Jackson had no idea what they were eating; he could see a corpse on a butcher table, but he was going to spare himself the horror of working out what it was.

He looked around his cage as best as his sore, frozen body would let him. To his relief, he wasn't lying in blood or piss; the reason he felt wet was because his clothes were drenched in his own sweat, which must be a result of his wound. His bags were gone, though, which meant the amulet was out of his reach. So the hope of using that to escape was shattered.

What if he connected with Daimon somehow? He knew that mated wolves could talk to one another from afar; he saw Daimon doing it with Nyssa—despite Daimon only being *claimed* by her—and Tokala had also told him about it. But how? He closed his eyes and concentrated on the fact that he and Daimon were mated—they were *connected*. However, all he found was emptiness. Nothing. He couldn't even feel his wolf. His ethos was silent. He felt…strange, like everything he'd worked for since coming to Ascela had been drained out of him.

It was the silver, wasn't it? The cage was keeping him from being able to do anything that required ethos, and when he realized that, what little hope he had left withered. What the hell was he supposed to do? He wasn't going to just lay around and wait to be rescued *again*. He was stronger now. But he couldn't use that new strength. Right now, he was no stronger than he was before he came out to Ascela.

The hunters started laughing again.

But then, with the sound of whipping fabric and heavy boots hitting the snow, the group sitting around the fire quietened down and all looked over at one of the tents.

Jackson looked over there, too, setting his eyes on a tall, dark-skinned man. He wore animal fur and clothes made of hide just like Riker, and a ghastly scar cut diagonally down his face from his right temple to his chin. He glared at the hunters with an irritated scowl, and everyone seemed to shiver a little.

"What the fuck are you all laughing at?" the man growled. "We lost *thirty* good people out there. Thirty!"

The hunters adorned shameful expressions and looked down at the ground. Some of them mumbled, "Sorry, Lieutenant Lewis."

"Those fucking dogs killed *our* friends, our *family*!" Lewis exclaimed as he started pacing around them like they were a bunch of schoolchildren being scolded. "We have no reason to be celebrating!" he yelled, slamming his hand against the bars of the cage Sebastien lay in. "We don't laugh, we don't cheer, we don't *drink*! Not until every single one of those fucking wolves' heads is on a pike!"

One of them nodded. "Yeah, pikes!"

"We know they're out there," the man who was clearly their leader continued. "We know they'll be coming for this piece of shit—" he kicked Jackson's cage, "—and when they do, we're going to make them wish they never fucked with Riker. Right?!"

Every hunter yelled, "Right!"

Lieutenant Lewis then glowered at Jackson, peering into his cage. "And *you*," he growled, gritting his teeth. "You're what's going to lead all those little packmates of yours right to us."

Jackson flinched when the man banged the cage with his fist. A shiver of trepidation shot through him, and as the man walked off, Jackson huffed shakily. Daimon *would* know this was a trap, right? His heart started racing as he attempted to move his body again. He wanted to see more of his surroundings. But his limbs ached and twinged every time he tried to move them. It was like he was chained to the cage's floor.

Why couldn't he move? Why couldn't he get up? He felt like such a useless idiot. First, he got shot and couldn't help the pack fight, and now he was trapped and being used as bait to draw out Daimon and his wolves. What next? Would he be stuck in this cage while his packmates fought for their lives again?

The lead hunter began barking orders. Jackson watched and listened as they started gathering silver bear traps and nets laced with wolfsbane. When he saw them loading a bunch of silver chains into a cannon on the back of a jeep, though, he frowned strangely. He glanced at Sebastien; the chains around him looked just like the ones the hunters were loading…. Was *that* how they'd got here? Had the hunters shot Sebastien out of the sky? That was the only thing that made sense. Jackson remembered falling before he passed out. He remembered the sound of metal and Sebastien yelping.

He looked over at Ethan. How did the hunters catch *him*? Muto couldn't be detected, right? Jackson didn't know how skilled of a hunter Ethan was, but he'd seen him handle himself in battle. He wasn't chained up or injured, either. So how the hell did he get in that cage?

Jackson gritted his teeth as pain shot from his leg and through his body. He rested his head back down and exhaled deeply, and then he set his eyes on the tiger again. "E-Ethan," he grunted.

Ethan stopped snarling and roaring and looked at Jackson—

"Shut the fuck up!" one of the hunters yelled as he hit Jackson's cage with his rifle.

Jackson flinched again and scowled up at the man, watching as he walked back over to join his friends, who were gathering ammo. Were they *all* heading out there to place traps? What was their plan? How were they going to use him? He didn't know any of the answers, and he didn't get any from looking around and watching, either. Were they going to take him out of the cage and tie him up somewhere? Or did they plan to lure Daimon's pack to their camp?

He listened to their quiet conversations, but no one said anything that helped him understand. It looked like they were gearing up for war, and every clink of their loading rifles sent angst coursing through Jackson's body. His heart beat faster, and his wound ached the more he tensed up. He had no idea what was about to happen, but what he *did* know was that there wasn't a thing he was going to be able to do to stop it.

| **Daimon** |

A flurry of grunts and voices woke Daimon from his sleep. He turned his head to locate the commotion and set his sights on Bly and Lance, who were trying to calm the bitten hunter down. But the woman thrashed violently and kept making lunges at them. Her body obviously wasn't handling the bite well.

Daimon didn't care, though. She was a hunter. Every ounce of pain she felt was deserved.

He closed his eyes and concentrated. Surely, Sebastien would have gotten Jackson to safety by now and removed the bullet. But he *still* couldn't feel his mate. His heart started racing, both anger and fear gripped him tightly, and all he wanted to do was shift and race outside so that he could start looking for him. But he had no idea where to go. Jackson's blood was tainted with silver the moment he was shot, so Daimon wouldn't be able to pick up his scent or a trail.

There was someone who he suspected might know, though.

Daimon hastily got up and stormed over to the hunter.

Remus called, "What are you doing, Dad?"

But he didn't respond. Bly and Lance moved out of his way, and when he snatched the woman's throat and pinned her against the wall, she shrieked weakly and tried to fight him off, but the bite had stolen all of her strength.

"Tell me where your friends are camped up," he growled.

She groaned and shook her head, trying to pull his hand off her throat.

The Alpha tightened his grip. "I have every reason to *slowly* pull you apart piece by piece—in fact, I *want to*," he warned her, leaning his face closer to hers. "I could skin you alive with my *bare hands* and watch you bleed out over the course of a few hours; now that you've got wolf walker venom rushing through you, it'll try to heal those wounds. But there's only so much it can heal. You'll hang on this wall, and when your body *finally* starts to give up, I'll dose you with *my* venom, and you know that will keep you alive *much* longer, and you'll suffer several more hours of the worst kind of pain imaginable."

The look of horror on her face thickened; she looked like she might cry. She trembled in his grip and stifled several breaths. And as she stiffly shook her head, she *begged*, "P-please…I don't…I don't know where they—"

"Wrong answer!" he yelled and abruptly gripped her healing bite. "Tell me where your fucking camp is or the next time, I'll use my claws."

She wailed and shook her head again, gritting her teeth. "I don't know!" she cried. "They move around!"

Daimon scowled at her. "But they'll tell you where they are, won't they?"

She frowned through her tears at him.

The Alpha looked at Bly. "Did you go through her bag?"

Bly opened her mouth to speak—

"Yes boss," came Alastor's voice.

Daimon looked at him. "Was there a radio or cell phone?"

"Uh…" Alastor mumbled, looking down into the bag. "I…uh…."

That was when Julian peered into the bag he was holding. They reached inside and pulled out a radio. "Right here."

The Alpha set his eyes on the woman again. "Here's what you're going to do: you'll radio your friends and tell them you barely made it out and had to find somewhere to hide. Now, you're ready to regroup. You'll ask them for their location, directions, and then you're going to lead us there."

She looked like she was about to argue, but Daimon squeezed her wound, making her grimace and whine.

"*Right?*" he growled impatiently.

The woman nodded. "Y-yes."

"No secret codes," Daimon added. "I know every single one of them, and if I hear *any* of the words slip out of your mouth, I'll tear your tongue out."

Her eyes widened a little.

Daimon held his hand out to Julian.

Julian handed him the radio as the rest of the pack moved closer.

"Don't try to test me, either," Daimon uttered as he held the radio to the side of her face. "You know what will happen."

Still with a terrified look on her face, she shook her head. "I w-won't."

Daimon kept his eyes locked with hers and pressed the radio's power button.

It beeped.

Then, he pressed the transmitter button and nodded once at her.

The woman shakily said, "T-this is Private Billy. D-do you read me? Over."

Daimon let go of the transmitter button.

Only static came through.

He pressed the transmitter again and scowled harder at the woman.

"R-repeat, this is Private—"

"*This is Second Lieutenant Lewis receiving. We read you, Billy. You still alive out there, huh?*" came a man's amused voice.

"Y-yeah, still kicking," she replied, trying to match his tone. "I-I had to find cover when those things attacked, sir. Took a nasty fall. But I'm good, sir. Is it safe to head back to camp? Over."

Lewis replied, "*That's a negative, Private. We've moved location since the ambush. You got your GPS? Over.*"

She nodded. "Yes, sir. Ready for coordinates. Over."

"We're currently at latitude 68.8, longitude -874.6. You're going to pass several narrow rivers along the way; follow the second farthest from the right to its end. Over."

Daimon ensured the transmitter wasn't live. "Ask him how many are left," he told her.

She frowned and grimaced. "C-copy that, sir. How many of us made it out of that shit storm? Over."

"Sixteen of us now, Billy, including you. It's good to hear your voice. Over."

So, there really had been forty-five hunters before the attack.

Billy replied, "And you, commander. I'll b-be there soon. Over and out."

Daimon pulled the radio away from her and switched it off. Then, he looked at Julian. "Do you know what a GPS is?"

"Uh..." they mumbled, digging around in the bag. They pulled out something that looked like a smaller radio but with a digital screen. "This, sir."

He handed them the radio back and took the GPS device. At first, he thought he might have to ask the woman how to use it, but there was one button to enter the latitude, and another to enter the longitude. He kept hold of her throat in his left hand and used his right to type the coordinates in. Then, when the device beeped and started showing him which way to go, he slipped it into his pocket and glared at the woman. "I'm going to leave you here with three of my wolves. If I don't come back with my mate, I'll be living up to my promise and skinning you with my hands."

She exhaled shakily and tried to scowl through her fearful expression. "T-they're there. They won't move again until dusk."

He didn't know how long he had. "Tokala," he called.

Tokala, who was still sitting over by the exit, looked at him.

"How many hours until dusk?"

The Zeta hurried off and disappeared through the cavern... and after a few moments, he came rushing back. "We've got about five hours, chief."

Daimon took the GPS out of his pocket. It said that the journey would take two hours on foot, but in their wolf forms, it would take less than half that. They had plenty of time. He put the device back in his pocket. "Gather up," he called as he let the woman fall from his grip, and as she hit the floor with a grunt, he turned to face his pack. "Lalo, Dustu, and Julian will be staying here to keep an eye on this hunter. Remus, you're staying here, too. The rest of us will make our way to this camp, rescue Jackson and Sebastien, and kill the rest of Riker's men."

His wolves nodded.

Remus looked a little disgruntled, but he didn't argue.

"Once we get a layout of their camp, we'll retreat and come up with a plan," Daimon said as he shifted into his wolf form and headed for the exit. "There are going to be traps; that much is certain. We're going to need to be extra vigilant."

"Are they the last of the hunters?" Brando asked. "She said that the Venaticus have Riker and a bunch of them, right?"

"There's no way to be certain," Daimon answered, leading the way through the tunnel. "But once that woman shifts, she'll have no choice but to tell me what I want to know."

"You're gonna let her turn?" Leon questioned. "But…she's one of *them*."

"Exactly," Daimon said, glancing back at his wolves. "She knows things we need to know—things that will come in handy if we have to face more hunters after this. She knows how they internally operate. She knows where they get their supplies, their wolfsbane, and their silver. We can share that information with the Nosferatu, and they'll be able to cut their supply lines off."

"Right, because the Nosferatu try to stop hunters," Tokala said with a nod. "Genius."

"We don't know how long she'll take to shift, though. It could be a few days or over a week. So we can focus on her later," Daimon said as he stepped out of the cave to a light flurry of snow. "Stay close."

"What about after we get the information out of her, Alpha?" Wesley asked him.

"That's a bridge to cross once we get there. But as of right now, I hope she's suffering," Daimon grumbled.

"Here, here," Rachel muttered. "Bitten by one of us or not, a hunter is always a hunter."

Several others mumbled in agreement.

Daimon tried connecting with Jackson one last time, but there was still nothing there. He was trying to keep his worry at bay by letting his anger creep in, but it wasn't enough anymore. He was terrified that something bad had happened. Maybe Jackson was bleeding out somewhere, unable to get the bullet out of his own wound. If he died…Daimon would have felt that like a stake through his heart. But knowing he was still suffering hurt just as much as that.

And he had to find him before the silver took Jackson from him forever.

Chapter Twenty-Two

⇄ ⩽ ☽ ⩾ ⇄

Inimă

| **Jackson** |

The hunters left in groups of four. They went with their weapons and traps; some were on foot, and others took the jeeps they'd loaded with chains. Jackson had no idea what their plans were, but he could assume that they were setting up a perimeter around this camp. They were going to use him for bait, right? And they hadn't moved him, so that was all that made sense.

Jackson still didn't feel great, but he felt better than earlier. He could move his body a little more now; he sat up, but the fact that he couldn't lean his back against the silver bars made it hard for him to stay up for long.

He waited until the last group of hunters left. Once their jeep departed, he sat up on his hands and knees and looked at the growling muto. "Ethan," he called, keeping his voice hushed. Lieutenant Lewis didn't leave with his men, and Jackson didn't want to wake him up and make him come out of his tent.

Ethan stopped glaring into the trees and stared across the camp at Jackson. "I'm gonna get us out of here," he told him.

"But...it's silver," Jackson replied. "Neither of us can break it, right?" He wasn't actually sure if silver was toxic to muto.

The tiger snarled quietly and shifted his sights to Sebastien. "We need him."

However, the winged hound hadn't said a word since Jackson woke up—the guy hadn't even moved. The silver chains binding him were still sizzling against his skin, and Jackson could swear he could now smell his burning flesh.

What were they going to do? They had to get out of there while the hunters were gone. Jackson wasn't going to let them use him as bait, but there wasn't much he could do against silver. He looked down at the floor; his ass wasn't burning, so maybe the floor of the cage was made of something else.

Jackson hastily glanced around, and when he spotted that one of the corners of whatever the floor was made of was bent upwards, he shuffled towards it and tried pulling it away. It hurt his body, but he couldn't let that slow him down. There was no telling how much time he had.

"What are you doing?" Ethan called.

"Trying...to...see," he grunted, tugging, "if I can...get out...through the floor—"

The material gave way and tore. Jackson fell back, his head hit the floor, and he groaned painfully. But there was no time to complain. He hurried back to the corner; however, what he saw made all his dismay come flooding back in. The floor beneath the material he lay on *was* silver.

He scowled sullenly and returned to sitting in the middle of his cage.

"What?" Ethan called.

"It's silver," he grumbled.

The tiger made an irritated sound and started looking around. "There has to be *something*."

"There's not," Jackson said despondently. "We're just gonna have to sit here like idiots." What was the point of lying to himself?

Ethan growled quietly as he paced around inside his cage. "The silver doesn't burn me like it does you guys, it just makes me as weak as a fucking human. Maybe I can...try busting the lock or—"

"It won't work, Ethan," Jackson muttered hopelessly. "Just face it. We're stuck here."

"What the hell's wrong with you, Jack?" Ethan asked, staring across the camp at him. "Usually, you'd be coming up with a hundred ideas of how to get us out of this place, but you're all...mopey and depressed."

Jackson rolled his eyes in frustration. "Well, what the fuck am I supposed to be coming up with, Ethan? Even if Sebastien wasn't chained up in there, he wouldn't be able to do anything. We're *all* weak against silver. There is literally *nothing* any of us can do but sit here and hope that Daimon figures out what the hunters are doing."

Ethan scoffed. "And how's he gonna work that out, huh? Does he have a third eye? Can he make little predictions or prophesies like Mr Billionaire Lord Caedis? And speaking of, where the hell is *he*? Where the hell are his Venaticus people? Because weren't *they* supposed to be dealing with all these fucking hunters so we could find this dumbass lab? Why isn't *he* out here looking for it? He's a fucking god; he can make shit out of nothing and teleport around the world. Why send us?!" he exclaimed, pacing again.

He only started ranting and pacing when he was anxious. Jackson knew Ethan understood just as well as he did that there was no way out of this.

"Lord Caedis is fighting a war, Ethan," he told him with a sigh. "And we're out here trying to help him. It's all connected. We're all he has to spare right now. But look at us." He gestured at his cage. "Some help, huh?"

Ethan huffed irritably. "Okay, well...why not teleport us to Greykin Valley? Why drop us off at the roadside and leave us to walk there?"

He had a point. If Lord Caedis could teleport people...well, *could* he? "I dunno if he can teleport others," he mumbled.

"Of course he can, dude. He can do whatever he wants. He could have just made a portal or whatever and dropped us in at the valley, but no! Here we goddamn are," he exclaimed, holding out a paw.

Jackson sighed and rested his arms on his legs. "It's not Lord Caedis' fault, Ethan. He did everything he co—"

"Did he, though?"

He frowned but tried his best not to lose his patience. Sometimes, he really *hated* when Ethan was like this. "Do you really think that if he *could* have teleported us, he wouldn't have? This hybrid-making stuff is linked to those Diabolus people, right? The Nosferatu are at war with them, so this is probably one of the most important operations they have going at the moment. I truly think they gave us everything they could spare. I mean...they even let me keep that demon amulet—the *Zenith's* amulet. That thing is a piece of his power."

"Yeah, all of that just makes me feel like they could have done more."

Jackson rolled his eyes. "Whatever, Ethan. I don't know what else I'm supposed to say."

"Oh, I don't know, maybe something about how that so-called Alpha of yours had no idea we were being followed by—"

"Hey, this has nothing to do with Daimon!" he interjected, scowling at him. "*None* of us could have known they were coming. They were wearing silver."

Ethan grumbled, "He should have had scouts or whatever behind us."

"In case you didn't notice, there are only fourteen of us left. Half of Daimon's pack is gone—*more* than half. Keeping everyone close together in case something happens is the best call," Jackson argued.

"How would you even know that? You've been one of them for what? Two weeks?"

Jackson scowled again. "Stop being such a dick."

"Stop defending everyone who could have helped us avoid this."

"You don't know what you're talking about," Jackson uttered.

"*You* don't know!" Ethan exclaimed. "You didn't even remember the Caeleste world existed until two weeks ago!"

Jackson went to snap back, but he didn't even know what he was going to say. Ethan was being a jerk, but he had several good points. What *did* Jackson know? He hadn't been a wolf walker long enough to comment on Daimon's orders or actions, nor did he know enough about the Caeleste world. Despite the perception filter being gone, he hadn't remembered much else. He didn't know anything about the Nosferatu-Diabolus war other than what he'd been told, and he had no idea what Lord Caedis was actually capable of.

He frowned sadly and looked at his lap. "This is all my fault," he mumbled.

"What?" Ethan called.

"You're right. I don't know what I'm doing or talking about. If I *did*, then maybe I wouldn't have gotten shot. And if I didn't get shot, then Sebastien wouldn't have had to carry me out of there, and you wouldn't have come after us when whatever happened."

"He was shot out of the sky, like a pigeon."

Jackson frowned and looked over at him to see that he looked just as amused as he sounded. "You think that's funny?"

Ethan sat down and smirked. "A little."

"Hey!" came Lieutenant Lewis' voice from inside the tent. "Shut the fuck up before I send you back to sleep!"

Jackson sharply turned his head to stare at the tent, expecting the guy to come out with his shotgun, but he didn't. The fact that he and Wilson had been able to say as much as they just had without interruption also made him think that Lewis was trying to get some sleep of his own. But before he could convince himself that could be an advantage for him and Ethan, he remembered that there was no way out of their cages.

He sighed and turned his attention to the trees. Maybe Daimon was out there somewhere thinking of a way to get him out. Perhaps the hunters who left to place their traps were already dead. But he hadn't heard anything. No growls or howls or gunshots.

Sebastien suddenly grunted.

Jackson gawped at the winged hound and watched as he came around.

Sebastien flinched and shuffled as the chains binding him clinked. He started panicking, trying to break free, and when he thrashed around and managed to turn to face Jackson, he stared at him in confusion.

"W-we're in a hunter camp," Jackson told him.

"And apparently there ain't no way out," Ethan called from his cage.

With a grunt and a grimace, Sebastien's shining blue eyes darted around the camp. "J-just... us?" he asked, his voice nothing more than a murmur.

Jackson nodded. "I don't know where everyone else is. But... these hunters said they were gonna use me as bait to catch them."

The hound snarled and tried to get up, but the chains kept him lying on his side. He even tried to pull his wings free, but it looked like they were so tightly bound to his sides that he'd surely break them if he tried too hard.

"So, I guess this means we're fucked, right?" Ethan asked, watching Sebastien, too. "I was hoping that when you woke up, you'd have some kludde trick to get out or use something you learned from Caedis or the Venaticus. Guess I was wrong."

Sebastien growled irritably. "Can you shut your mouth?" he exclaimed, glaring at him. "You talk so fucking much."

Ethan responded with an aggravated growl.

The ruffle of blankets came from inside the tent, and moments later, Lewis burst out with his shotgun and waved it around as he yelled, "I told you fucking freaks to shut the fuck up!" He kicked Sebastien's cage. "The next time I hear *any* of you, I'm skinning the fucking cat!"

Jackson's blood ran cold as he glanced at Ethan.

"Not a fucking peep!" Lewis shouted. Then, he turned around and stormed back into the tent.

"Asshole," Sebastien grumbled but then winced painfully. He shifted his sights to Jackson. "Don't…say anything. You're the only one of us he can hear. Just…listen…and nod or something, okay?"

Jackson frowned and nodded.

"Did you see that guy's back pocket?" Sebastien asked.

"See what?" Ethan questioned.

In response, Jackson shook his head.

"His right back pocket," Sebastien muttered, glancing at the tent. "He's got the inimă."

Jackson frowned harder. So what if Lewis had the inimă? He couldn't use it, not while in this silver cage.

"The Zenith…Zenith's ethos isn't negated by silver," Sebastien told him, struggling. "*You*…are asmodi, Jackson. You remember…what I said about how asmodi were created, right?"

He thought for a moment…and he *did* remember. Asmodi were created with both Lord Caedis and the Zenith's ethos.

"There's this…tiny little part…of you…" Sebastien breathed and paused, "…that isn't susceptible to silver. You gotta…you gotta find that part, man."

Jackson was still confused. Even if he did have some resistance to silver, wouldn't the weakness he got from being a wolf walker negate that?

"Yeah, he's right," Ethan said, nodding. "All being a wolf walker would do is like…make you just as susceptible as an ordinary Caeleste, but it wouldn't cancel out the resistance you get from having the Zenith's ethos."

Jackson had questions; he wanted to be sure, but he couldn't speak. What was Sebastien even trying to say?

The hound exhaled shakily as the chains continued sizzling against his skin. "You gotta…try connect to the inimă, Jackson," he told him, struggling to get his words out.

How the hell was he supposed to do that? He frowned and shook his head, hoping that they'd understand that he was confused.

Sebastien got it. "You have a connection to it. You gotta...." He exhaled weakly and closed his eyes, grimacing as his flesh sizzled.

The hound didn't say anything else.

"Sebastien?" Ethan called. "Hey, dude!"

Nothing.

Worry filled Jackson. He wanted to call Sebastien's name, but even if he could risk talking, he knew it wouldn't do any good.

"Jack," Ethan said.

He looked at the tiger.

"You know what to do, right?"

Jackson frowned anxiously as he set his eyes on the tent. No, he had *no* idea what he was supposed to do. But he had to figure it out. If there was a way for him to get himself, Ethan, and Sebastien out of the camp and away from the hunters before Daimon even had to come near, then he'd do his best.

Sebastien said he had a connection to the amulet, and he knew that was because he was an asmodi demon. His species was created using some of the Zenith's ethos, and the inimă *was* the Zenith's ethos. So, somehow, he had to be able to tap into it. After all, when he killed Kane's wolves a few days ago, he didn't even *think* about the inimă, yet it attached *itself* to him. Perhaps what Sebastien meant was that he needed to find out how to make it do that again.

He closed his eyes and concentrated. Maybe it was just like connecting to his *own* ethos. He remembered what Daimon taught him, but instead of reaching within himself, he reached towards the tent—he reached for the inimă. He knew where it was, and he knew what its power felt like, so he kept those things on his mind while he focused.

"Yo, Jack," Ethan called. "You doing it?"

He sighed as he stopped and opened his eyes. Then, he glanced at Ethan and nodded.

"All right," the tiger said.

Jackson closed his eyes again. "Come on," he whispered to himself, focusing on the inimă. He thought about the rush that consumed him when the amulet wrapped around his neck; he recalled the feeling of intense power that surged through his veins like fire. And all the blood. The tearing flesh, and the fact that in that moment, his rage and desire to kill the wolves who were trying to hurt his packmates had made him *stronger*. It all turned him into something he'd wished he was *all* the time. Someone who had no weaknesses, someone faster, and an asset to the pack.

The inimă woke up a side of him that had been dormant for *years*. It made him the creature he was born as—it made him more demon than wolf walker. Jackson wanted to feel that again. He wanted to feel his demon blood, his demon *ethos*. He found himself craving that powerful surge like his wolf craved the flesh of something living—the *blood* of someone else.

He scowled when he felt it.

When he salivated at the thought of blood.

Something stirred inside him. But it wasn't his wolf. It wasn't the beast that lived in his body. It was the *monster*.

The *demon*.

And it wanted to feed.

Jackson heard something hit the ground a small distance away.

He opened his eyes, and that was when he saw a shimmer of red. The inimă…it was on the floor inside the tent. Had it slipped from Lewis' pocket? Or was Jackson's attempt to connect to it working?

"Jack!" Ethan called excitedly.

He closed his eyes and concentrated. He focused on the feeling of bloodlust, the desire to get out of this cage, kill the people who wanted to harm his friends, and get back to Daimon.

But it was the blood that possessed most of his thoughts. He wanted to taste it again; he wanted to sink his teeth into whatever he could reach and feast. He was hungry—the creature inside him needed blood, and he was going to do whatever he needed to get it.

Something clanged against the silver bars.

Jackson opened his eyes. He'd been so lost in his thoughts that he hadn't even heard Ethan speaking, but as his friend's voice became louder, and the world came back to him, Jackson set his eyes on the inimă.

There it was, right outside his cage.

He scrambled towards the amulet and grabbed it, and the moment it touched his skin, he felt a rush of anticipation spiral through him. The pain in his leg withered, his body began to feel warmer, and as he raised the inimă to his neck, he exhaled deeply.

Whatever happened next…he was going to make sure he freed his friends, killed every last one of those hunters, and found Daimon.

Chapter Twenty-Three

Asmodi

| Jackson |

It was so much different than before. All Jackson felt when the amulet locked around his neck was rage and bloodlust so strong that it was like he'd been starved for *months*. He could feel his fangs yearning to sink into the throat of whoever was closest, and he was *so* angry. He'd been shot, locked away, and used as bait; he was tired of being so weak and useless. The inimă urged him to show everyone who and what he really was, and he didn't feel any hesitation.

Jackson felt the creature inside him wake from an eighteen-year-long sleep. It *hurt*, but he didn't care. The flesh on his back tore, his shoulder blades cracked, and as Jackson grimaced and gripped the material covering the cage floor, something burst from his back, sending a rain of blood splattering onto the inside of the cage and the snow surrounding it.

But it wasn't over yet. Jackson grunted as he looked over his shoulder, and when he saw a pair of wing-like bones attached to his back, he frowned in confusion. The inimă glowed brightly, and while Jackson's bloodlust and desire to kill increased, he watched the bones adorn black scaley skin and crimson membranes. The wings protruding from his back looked almost like those of a dragon, and they were so large that their carpal claws almost reached the cage roof.

His head started aching. The pain got worse with every second, and his bloodlust did nothing to help. He gritted his teeth and gripped the sides of his head with his hands as he yelled in agony; he heard his skull cracking, and he felt something sharp cut through his skin above his ears. Blood trickled down his face and onto the floor, and when Jackson pulled his bloody hands from his head and leaned onto them, he watched his nails morph and sharpen to look just like the black claws that he saw at the tips of Lord Caedis' fingers, but Jackson's didn't change colour.

Jackson's ears were ringing, his aching body trembled, and his heart was racing. The inimă kept pulsing, and the feeling of its warm, enticing ethos quickly relieved the pain.

The power gushed through his body like fire, and as Jackson's bloodlust returned, he lifted his head and set his eyes on the closest living thing.

"Jack?" Ethan asked. There was a desperate look on his face like he'd been trying to get Jackson's attention without success.

Although Jackson knew the huge tiger was his friend, it didn't make him feel any less eager to break free, get over to him, and drain every ounce of blood from his body.

But then he shifted his sights to the tent. He could hear Lewis grumbling to himself as he got up, and when he came out of his tent and saw Jackson, the man frowned in confusion.

"What the fuck is this?!" he yelled, cocking his shotgun.

Jackson wasn't going to let Lewis or Riker's hunters hurt Daimon's pack anymore. He focused on his desire to kill them, and as the inimă used his anger to increase his power, Jackson used his new wings to propel himself forward. The silver bars shattered like ice, and Jackson reached Lewis before he could even *think* to pull the trigger.

He didn't hesitate. Jackson savagely sunk his fangs into Lewis' neck, and the moment the man's blood touched his tongue, a feeling of utter delight surged through Jackson's body. He bit harder, forcing the grunting, gurgling man down onto his back. Jackson nailed the man's hands to the ground with his wing's carpal spikes, keeping him from attempting to fight him off, and then Jackson drank…and drank…and drank. He gulped Lewis' intoxicatingly sweet blood down as fast as he could, each mouthful pulling him deeper into the overwhelming power that the inimă gave him.

But once the man's body was drained, Jackson didn't feel satisfied. The monster *inside* him wasn't satisfied. He needed more. *It* needed more. He could feel it clawing under his skin—it wanted *out*, and Jackson wanted to give in.

He pulled his fangs from the man's neck, and as he folded his new wings against his back, he looked around the camp. There was a muto in a cage not far from him…and a demon hound in another. But neither of them appealed to his hunger. He needed *human* blood.

And he seemed to know exactly where to find it.

Jackson let his demon take control. He burst towards the trees and followed the scent of a nearby human. His vision started shifting, and as everything became different shades of blue, he set his eyes on the red silhouette of a man up ahead. Crimson waves pulsed from the guy's body in beat with his pulse, which echoed through Jackson's head. His new vision let him see the man's heart, his veins, and his nervous system, and it let him pick out the perfect place to strike before he even reached him.

He could see the human had a healing wound on his left shin; he sped up, used his wings to propel himself forward, and before the man had any idea he was coming, Jackson mercilessly plunged his right wing's carpal spike into the man's healing leg. The guy tried to yell, but Jackson slammed his hand over his mouth as he pinned him on his back, and then he sunk his fangs into his neck.

Jackson groaned in relief, downing the man's blood as fast as he could. But then he heard voices and heartbeats. He could smell more humans. The clink of chains, the groan of stretching springs, and the rumbling of an engine. He knew the rest of the hunters were nearby; they were setting their traps…and Jackson—no…the *demon* that the inimă set free from his body was going to kill them all.

| Daimon |

This was it. His pack were closing in. The hunters were up ahead, and before he could get to Jackson, Daimon had to make sure not one of them was left standing.

But as he was about to give Tokala's team the signal to move in, something raced through the trees a hundred yards ahead so quickly that it left a storm of kicked-up snow in its wake.

He crouched into the snow, and his pack did the same, taking cover.

"What the fuck was that?" Alastor panicked.

"Shh," Rachel hushed.

Daimon searched the trees from where he lay, but he couldn't see what ran past. He could smell blood, though. *A lot* of blood. And people were screaming. Something was snarling.

Gunfire.

What the hell was going on? Could it be Sebastien? Daimon concentrated…and that was when he realized that he could feel Jackson's aura. He wanted to get up and run to him. His instincts urged him to go, but he couldn't leave his wolves. They were in the midst of hunter territory; there could be traps anywhere. He wasn't going to run off and leave his wolves to fend for themselves or risk getting ensnared in silver.

"Alpha?" Brando asked quietly. "What are we doing?"

Daimon didn't know what was out there. It could be Sebastien, or it could be something else entirely. Whatever it was, though—if it was hostile—he didn't want to risk it getting to Jackson. He glanced at his pack. Half of them were on the other side of the hill getting ready to flank; what if they hadn't seen that thing? He scowled and tried to come up with a plan, but he had no idea what he was dealing with. "We have an unknown entity up ahead," he told his wolves. "Treat it as if it's hostile. Watch each other's backs. We're moving in."

Everyone nodded.

Daimon then lifted his head and let out a short, snappy howl, letting Tokala know that there was an unknown hostile nearby but to continue with the plan. Then, he got up and started leading his pack towards Jackson's aura.

But when he cautiously approached the place where he'd seen the entity race past, he stopped and stared at the carnage. Severed limbs, torn-out organs, and mangled corpses lay everywhere. The snow was red, the tree trunks were red, and the only footprints he found were those of the hunters. Could whatever had done this be Caeleste?

"Fucking hell," Wesley gagged. "I've seen some shit, man…but this is like…what the fuck, you know?"

"Shut up," Alastor muttered.

"I don't like this," Enola told Daimon. "Whatever did this could still be out here."

"We have to find Jackson," Daimon said, heading through the massacre.

His wolves followed, mirroring his movements as he prowled low to the ground and led the way up the hill.

Daimon kept all his senses alert. The gunfire died down, but the screams grew worse. And suddenly, something exploded, shaking the ground at the pack's paws. As everyone braced themselves, Daimon looked back at them and made sure each of them was okay.

"What the hell was that?!" Enola exclaimed.

"Do you think it's the Venaticus?" Alastor asked.

"Or maybe Sebastien?" Wesley suggested.

Daimon frowned cautiously and continued up the hill. "Keep moving," he instructed.

"What if it's a cadejo?" Brando questioned worriedly. "It could be some new variant we don't know about."

He had a point, but Daimon didn't want to stop. Jackson's aura was so close; all he had to do was get to the top of the hill. So he kept going. He led his pack closer and closer, and when he finally reached the top, he hurried to the edge and stared at what lay below.

Thick black smoke spewed through the treetops. Daimon followed it with his eyes to the hunter jeep, which was up in flames. More mutilated bodies lay scattered all over the glade, and in the centre was the creature responsible.

He knew he was looking at a demon. It had wings on its back and horns on its head. It feasted from the neck of the man in its grip, and there was something glowing on the front of its body. The demon had its back to him, so he couldn't see what it was, but the light was crimson…and it felt familiar.

Daimon focused harder on Jackson's aura, and when he realized that his mate was somewhere in that glade, terror surged through him. "No," he breathed. And then he let his instincts rule him.

The pack called anxiously to him, asking him what he was doing and where he was going. But he just ran. He ran and ran and ran, rushing down the hill, through the trees, and into the glade.

"Jackson!" he called, searching frantically for him as he burst into the opening.

The demon snarled as it let go of its victim and abruptly turned to face him.

Daimon stopped in his tracks. At first, he thought that he was going to have to fight the creature... but then he saw its face.

Jackson's face.

"Jackson?" he questioned in confusion.

Jackson slowly turned to face him as he stood up straight. Two springbok-like horns protruded from the sides of his head above his ears, and the wings on his back looked like those of a dragon. His eyes were as red as the amulet around his neck, and the claws which sat in place of his fingernails were covered in blood and fine pieces of torn flesh.

It was *him*. Jackson did this.

And Daimon didn't know how to react. He was glad to see that Jackson was okay, but... what happened to him? Why did he have horns and wings?

No... he knew the answer. Somehow, Jackson had discovered his demon form. That's what Daimon was looking at, and his mate had used it to slaughter what Daimon hoped was the remainder of the hunters.

A part of him felt almost *proud*. Jackson did all of this by himself. He didn't even need his or the pack's help and seeing and knowing that Jackson handled this banished all of Daimon's confusion and worry.

"Jackson?" he asked again.

But his mate didn't respond. A scowl clung to his bloody face, and the look in his eyes was like that of a starved beast. He didn't seem to recognize Daimon, and when he started prowling towards him, the Alpha cautiously backed off.

"Jackson?" he insisted. "It's me—it's Daimon."

Jackson didn't respond. He gritted his teeth, baring his fangs.

"Jack—"

He lunged at Daimon with a ferocious snarl, trying to grab him with his arms and then his wings when the Alpha managed to leap out of the way.

"Alpha!" the pack called worriedly.

Jackson swung around and lunged again, missing Daimon by mere inches. With a frustrated growl, Jackson then propelled himself forward using his wings, but he didn't aim for Daimon—he was heading for the pack.

Daimon snarled and burst into action, reaching Jackson before he could get to the retreating pack; he grasped Jackson's arm with his teeth and gently yanked him away, but Jackson swung his left wing around and slammed it into him, sending him tumbling across the snow with a grunt.

The Alpha hurried to his paws, but by the time he was up, Jackson had already reached the others. "Jackson!" he yelled, running after him as fast as he could.

Jackson grabbed Rachel, who'd jumped in Bly's way, but before he could hurt her, Daimon grabbed Jackson's arm again and pulled him away. This time, he pulled with enough force to make Jackson stumble and fall, and when his mate hit the snow, Daimon pounced on him and pinned him to the ground.

"Jackson!" he yelled in his face. "Wake up!"

"Back off," Tokala ordered the pack as he helped Rachel up.

"H-he could have killed me!" Rachel cried out in horror.

Jackson writhed and snarled beneath Daimon, trying to break free; he slammed his fists into his sides, trying to throw the Alpha off, but he held his ground. He knew what his mate was going through—a lot of demons lost control when they first discovered their forms, and he was going to do whatever he could to help Jackson find his way back to himself.

"Jackson!" Daimon shouted again.

With a struggled groan, Jackson still tried to pull free, but hesitation flickered across his face.

"You have to fight it," the Alpha told him. "Just like your wolf, your demon form is a part of you. Control it."

Jackson snarled and attempted to push Daimon away.

But he held firm. "Fight it!"

As he growled angrily, Jackson swiped at Daimon's face—

Daimon yelped as his mate's claws cut his muzzle, but he didn't let it distract him. He kept Jackson pinned down, watching him snarl and yell and struggle. "Fight it, Jackson," he said quietly.

Jackson growled again, but he closed his eyes and shook his head, and when he opened them, the crimson faded, and he stared up at Daimon with cerulean instead.

He was doing it. He was fighting it.

"Keep fighting it," Daimon told him. "You can do it."

Jackson closed his eyes again and grunted. "D-Daimon, I—"

"You can fight it!"

He nodded frantically, shivering, gritting his teeth. And when his trembling slowed, he stared up at Daimon again. "I-I... I'm sorry."

Daimon shook his head. "It's okay," he told him as he slowly loosened his grip.

Jackson frowned in confliction as he sat up, and then his eyes widened when he stared at the carnage. "I just... wanted them to stop hurting us."

The Alpha shifted into his human form and placed his hand on the side of Jackson's bloody face. He hastily pressed his lips against his and pulled him closer, holding him tightly. "I thought something happened to you," he told him, resting the side of his head against Jackson's. "I couldn't feel you anymore. I was terrified that the hunters…I thought I'd lost you," he uttered, trying to keep his composure. He could hear his pack murmuring behind him, and he was certain he might have to calm them down.

"What…happened to me?" Jackson asked worriedly. "I…I don't remember."

"You found your demon form," he said as he helped Jackson to his feet. "A lot of demons lose control when they first find it, just like wolf walkers. But you fought it. You're okay," he said, moving his arms around Jackson.

Jackson hugged him back. "I think…the hunters…they shot Sebastien down with a silver net gun or something. They had us in their camp—they were going to use me to lure you all in, and—"

"It's okay," Daimon interjected when he heard the distress in Jackson's voice. He leaned back so he could see his mate's face and stared into his eyes. "*You're* okay, and so are we," he said, glancing back at his pack.

They waited a small distance away, gawping at Jackson. Daimon knew he was going to have to convince most of them that Jackson wasn't a threat, but he'd save that worry for later.

He stared into Jackson's eyes again. "What happened? How did this happen to you?" he asked, looking him up and down, and he noticed that there was no wound in his leg from when he was shot. "Your leg?"

Jackson exhaled slowly as he shook his head and shrugged. "I…I was in the cage and…it was silver, so I couldn't do anything. But then Sebastien woke up and he told me that I could get the inimă to come to me, and it *did*. And then…this," he explained, looking over his shoulder at one of his wings. "It healed me, too."

"It helped you find your demon form?" Daimon asked.

"I…guess so. It was like…*this* was hidden inside me since I was a kid, and the inimă…brought it out of me?" he said, but he didn't sound so sure. Why would he? He only discovered he was a demon under two weeks ago.

Daimon caressed Jackson's cheek with his fingers. "I'm glad you're okay," he said softly, and then he pulled him into his embrace again. "I won't ever let anyone take you from me again."

"It wasn't your fault, Daimon," Jackson said, reciprocating his hug. "I should've seen it coming or moved instead of standing there like an idiot and—"

"Don't blame yourself," Daimon said sternly, leaning back to look at his face again. "If this is anyone's fault, it's the Venaticus'. They were supposed to be dealing with these fuckers," he growled, glancing at the slaughtered hunters.

That was when Jackson's eyes widened. "Sebastien—I left him back at the camp. And Ethan."

Daimon nodded and looked at his pack. "We'll get them." Then, he faced Jackson again. "Did you kill them all?"

"I…think so."

"Can you leave this form?" he asked, glancing at Jackson's wings.

"I'm…not sure." Jackson gripped the inimă with his hand and carefully pulled it from his neck. But his wings and horns didn't disappear. "Am I stuck like this?" he asked with distress in his voice.

"Uh…chief, if I may?" came Tokala's voice.

Daimon set his eyes on him. "What?"

Tokala gawped at Jackson. "It's…like shifting out of your wolf form. This demon form is a part of you, just like your wolf. You can leave this form the same way you leave your wolf's."

Jackson frowned unsurely and said, "O-okay…well…." He closed his eyes and concentrated, and after a few moments, his horns and wings crumbled into ash and disappeared, leaving him as his normal self. Then, he opened his eyes and hastily checked himself over. He looked over his shoulders, patted the sides of his head, and examined his hands. "I thought the claws were gonna be permanent like Lord Caedis," he mumbled with a pout.

Daimon smiled amusedly. "And you're disappointed?"

"No, actually. I'm glad," he said with a shrug.

The Alpha took his hand and started heading over to his pack with Tokala. "We'll head to the camp and grab those two, and then we're going to meet up with the rest of the pack and get back on course."

"Is everyone else okay?" Jackson asked worriedly.

"Everyone's fine," Daimon assured him. "What about Sebastien and Ethan?"

"Ethan's fine, but…Sebastien was all wrapped up in silver chains. I-I don't think he's doing so good. We need to get to him before—"

"We'll get to him," Daimon said with a nod, stopping by his pack.

"Do you want me to keep hold of that?" Tokala asked Jackson, nodding at the inimă. "You can put it in my pack."

Daimon shifted into his wolf form and said, "No, let Rachel hang onto it again until we get your gear back."

Jackson nodded, but when he approached Rachel, she backed off defensively.

"It's okay, Rachel," Daimon said calmly.

But Jackson looked a little pale. "Did I…hurt you?"

She scowled at him. "You grabbed me, and—"

"It wasn't his fault," Tokala insisted.

"I'm sorry," Jackson said shamefully. "I'd…never intentionally hurt any of you. You all…know that, right?"

Daimon glanced around at his pack; they looked unsure, but once Tokala said, "We all trust you, Jackson," everyone else started agreeing.

Rachel still looked skeptical, though. She watched Jackson closely as he put the inimă into her bag, and then she walked off, hiding behind Wesley and Alastor.

Jackson shifted into his wolf form.

"Let's go," Daimon said. "We don't know if all of the hunters are dead, so be cautious, move quietly, and watch for their traps."

Everyone nodded, and as Daimon led the way with Jackson at his side, the pack followed.

Chapter Twenty-Four
Lock and Key

| Jackson |

Although he was glad that he did something useful, Jackson couldn't help but feel conflicted about what he'd done. He slaughtered all those hunters like it was nothing; killing people wasn't something he should be proud of, so why did he feel accomplished?

He glanced at Daimon, and when he looked back at the rest of the pack, he caught a few of them quickly taking their eyes off him. It was to be expected, though. Of course they'd be wary of him. *He'd* be wary if he saw any of them sprout wings and horns all of a sudden, so he didn't blame them. And he'd grabbed Rachel. She looked both angry and scared, and he wanted to apologize to her again, but now probably wasn't the best time.

The power he felt running through him while in that form, though.... It was exhilarating and like he'd finally been set free. Was that how it was for all demons when they first found their demon form? He had so many questions, but the only person who could answer them was still locked up in the hunter camp, and so was his best friend.

However, there was *one* thing he was already sure of: he was going to learn to control this new power so that he could be more of an asset to the pack. He wasn't going to get shot or captured anymore; he was going to be just as useful as everyone else, and he'd prove that he wasn't weak.

Daimon slowed down. "I see it up ahead," he told everyone.

Jackson set his eyes on a tent visible through the trees a hundred feet or so in front of them. It was Lewis' tent. "This is it," he confirmed, looking at Daimon. He wanted to rush ahead and start helping get the cages open, but he wouldn't do so without Daimon's approval. The last thing he wanted was to race off on his own and set off a trap or start something that got others hurt.

The Alpha took a step forward but then immediately stopped. "Wait," he called.

Everyone stopped behind him.

"What is it?" Jackson asked.

Daimon nodded at the snow a few feet from them.

Jackson frowned and searched with his eyes, and when he spotted a shimmer of silver among the white, he understood. "A trap," he said, glancing at the Alpha.

"Tokala," Daimon said.

The orange wolf nodded and started foraging around in the snow. It took him a moment to find a rock, and once he gripped it in his jaw, he threw it towards the trap. The moment the rock hit one of the teeth, the silver bear trap snapped shut, making most of the pack gasp.

"Keep your eyes peeled," Daimon instructed, and then he began leading the way forward again.

Jackson nervously searched the ground as he walked, and after only taking a few steps, he spotted something else. He wasn't sure what it was, but it flickered just like the beartraps did in the sunlight, and he wasn't going to risk getting close. "Daimon," he said, and when the Alpha looked at him, he nodded in the direction he saw it.

The Alpha made the pack stop and lowered his head, searching the area Jackson pointed out. "I see it," he said.

Jackson watched the Alpha follow something with his eyes, and when it led them up the trunk of a tree, he saw what looked like a fishing line wrapped around a very small hook which had been hammered into the tree.

"That's a new one," Brando said.

"Alpha," Tokala said. He stepped forward and pointed his paw at four rocks placed in a perfect square shape. "There's a net under there. You trip the wire, the net grabs you, and you're left hanging in silver rope until the hunters come back."

Daimon snarled quietly. "We'll head around it. Come on."

Jackson walked on Daimon's side as he navigated the pack around the trees and towards the camp, and once they were out of the tree line, Jackson burst forward and hurried over to the cages. He wanted to run to Ethan first, but Sebastien was still ensnared in silver, and if they didn't get him out soon, he had no idea what might happen to him. "We gotta get him out first!" he insisted, watching as the pack hurried over.

"Jack!" Ethan called. "You're okay?"

Jackson looked over at him. "Yeah, we just gotta get Sebastien out first."

Ethan shook his head. "Yeah, yeah. All good."

"How did you get out of your cage?" Tokala asked, gawping at what remained of the cage that Jackson was locked inside.

"Uh...my demon form. I kinda just...burst out," Jackson answered, watching Daimon inspect Sebastien's cage.

The Alpha then stopped in front of Jackson. "Can you use your demon form again to break the other cages?"

Jackson glanced around at the pack. "I can try." He didn't want to let himself overthink it. His demon form helped *him* get out of a silver cage, so he had to be able to use it to help Sebastien and Ethan out, right? He turned to face Sebastien. "Oh, the inimă," he said, looking at Daimon.

"Can you not do it without the inimă?" Daimon questioned.

"You have the form now," Tokala said. "The initial discovery of a demon's true form is always the hardest, but once you get through that, it's just like shifting into your wolf form."

Jackson frowned unsurely. He didn't know how any of this demon stuff worked; would he have to use the inimă now that he'd used it to first find his demon form? Would Tokala know the answer to that? He glanced at the orange wolf, but then he saw the concerned look on Daimon's face. He could also see the unnerved pack. Was Daimon asking him to try without the inimă because he knew some of the wolves were unsettled by it? That made sense. The last thing Jackson wanted to do was scare anyone, so…he'd try.

He nodded and faced the cage again. Then, he left his wolf form and concentrated on the part of him that the inimă helped him discover. And there it was…. He didn't know how else to describe it other than by saying it felt like his wolf form was *sitting* inside him right next to his demon form…as though they were both switches inside his proselytus. They were, after all, two different ethos', right?

With a deep exhale, he focused on his demon ethos, and when he slipped into it the same way he did when shifting into his wolf, he felt his wings and horns appear on his body. His wings weighed on his back, and his horns made his head feel a little heavier, and to his relief, when he opened his eyes, he wasn't seeing in shades of blue, and the wolves around him weren't shimmering red. Whatever his vision became while he was hunting was something he'd ask Sebastien about later. Right now, he had to focus on getting the hound and Ethan out.

The inimă only empowered the ethos he already possessed, didn't it? So even without it, he still had resistance to silver; he wouldn't have been able to pull the amulet out of Lewis' tent if that wasn't the case. But then his eyes shifted to the padlock keeping the cage shut. The lock was silver, and he was certain that the key to it was, too. But if he could touch both the lock and key, then he could just unlock the door, right?

He looked around for Lewis' severed legs, and when he spotted them over by the fire, he hurried over and rummaged through his pockets.

"What are you doing?" Ethan asked.

"Jackson?" came Daimon's voice.

Jackson knew he found the keys when he felt something burn his hand. He took them from Lewis' pocket and stood up, turning to face Daimon. "I figured…if I can touch silver without it hurting me as much, then maybe I can open the cages," he said, looking at his hand. But the silver was burning into his skin; it felt like he was holding a piece of fresh-off-the-barbeque coal. He grimaced and pulled his sleeve down to cover his other hand. Then, he placed the keys over his sleeve.

"That's gonna work, right?" Ethan called.

"Only one way to find out," Jackson mumbled, heading over to Sebastien. He stared at the lock for a moment…but then eased the key inside.

It wouldn't turn.

"So…plan B?" Wesley asked.

Jackson frowned irritably and tried twisting the lock, but no matter how hard he tried, it wouldn't budge.

"I don't think it's gonna work, Jackson," Alastor said.

Sebastien groaned quietly.

Jackson stopped trying to break the lock and gawped at him. "Sebastien?"

The winged hound opened his eyes slightly, but the blue glow they emitted was gone.

"Is he awake?" Ethan asked. "Get him to tell you how to do the thing with the silver again."

"Sebastien," Jackson said, crouching in front of his face. "I should be able to open this lock, right?"

The hound glanced up at the padlock and then at the key in Jackson's hand. He exhaled deeply, and murmured, "Just…focus on your resistance."

Jackson frowned and tried to do as Sebastien said. He concentrated on the part of his demon ethos that was resistant to silver; when he felt it coursing through his body, he focused on the key…and turned it.

The lock clicked.

Several relieved mumbles came from the pack, and Jackson smiled victoriously as he pulled the cage door open.

"Quickly, get him out onto the snow," Daimon said.

Jackson gripped hold of the chains binding Sebastien, but as he did, he saw that they'd burned so deeply into the hound's flesh that it was almost like melted, bloody rubber. He could only imagine the pain Sebastien was in, and it made him feel even more desperate to free him. He started pulling, and although the chains still felt warm against his skin, they didn't singe his palms. He hastily dragged the hound out of the cage, and once he was out, Jackson began tugging on the chains, looking for a way to free Sebastien from them.

"There," Tokala said, pointing under Sebastien's wing.

Jackson found where Tokala pointed and gripped the end of what looked like a single chain rather than multiple. He started untangling it, frantically pulling, twisting, and turning the metal until it gave way and allowed him to yank the entire thing from around Sebastien. "Sebastien?" he asked eagerly as he chucked the huge chain into the cage.

The hound grunted in response. He didn't attempt to get up, though.

"Is he good?" Ethan called. "'Cause, uh…not to be insensitive, but I'd kinda like to get out of here."

Daimon rolled his eyes. "You'll get out when you get out."

"I wasn't talking to you," the tiger snarled.

The Alpha didn't respond to him. Instead, he looked down at Sebastien. "Can you shift back? We can carry you to where we're resting."

Sebastien nodded, and with a pained grimace, he returned to his human form.

While Daimon shifted into his Prime form, Jackson took the keys out of the lock and hurried over to Ethan's cage. Just as he did with Sebastien's lock, he concentrated and turned the key, and the moment the door unlocked, Ethan pounced out and exclaimed in relief, stretching his body.

"Let's go," Daimon called as he threw Sebastien over his shoulder. "If we move now, we should get back before dark. Rachel, grab Jackson and Sebastien's things from that tent."

Rachel nodded and went into Lewis' tent.

Jackson left his demon form and shifted into his wolf. He joined the others once Rachel had grabbed everything, and when Daimon began leading the way back, he followed beside him.

"I'll…contact the Venaticus when we get back," Sebastien grumbled, staring down at Jackson from Daimon's shoulder. "You got them all, right?"

"Yeah, I think so," Jackson said with a nod. "I mean…we didn't see any others on the way here."

"It was fricken awesome," Ethan said, catching up to run beside Jackson. "You just burst out of that cage like it was paper, man."

Jackson glanced at him and smiled as enthusiastically as he could. He still felt a little conflicted about how he'd killed all those people, but the fact that he'd saved his friends and done something useful kept him from sinking into the same guilt that almost consumed him after he killed Daniel, Elsu, and that other wolf.

He looked up at Sebastien. "Do you know what the Venaticus are gonna do to Riker and those of his hunters that they caught?"

"Hunters convicted of killing innocent Caeleste usually go to hunter-specific prisons, but they'll be kept in holding for a while so the investigators can look into everything they've done. If we didn't need your muto friend here with us, they'd be talking to him as a witness right now."

Ethan scoffed. "I've seen them do some real fucked up shit. I'd testify or whatever."

"Does Heir Lucian look into this stuff?" Jackson asked curiously.

"No. Lord Caedis has him chasing the lead you gave us on Ridge," the white-haired demon answered. "He took your blood, so if he really is raising an army against the

Nosferatu, Heir Lucian's gotta shut it down. They've already got enough on their plate with Lyca Corp. and the Diabolus."

A shiver ran down Jackson's spine at the mere thought of Ridge and what he was doing in that cave. The creatures he saw hanging from the ceiling.... He shook his head and focused on the forest up ahead. "When they catch him, he'll go to Daevor, right?"

"He sure will," Sebastien confirmed.

They *were* going to catch Ridge, right? Jackson already felt bad enough that the guy got away with his blood, which he intended to use to create a hybrid army to use against the Nosferatu. If Ridge succeeded, and the Nosferatu had yet another threat to deal with, Jackson was going to become so overwrought with guilt that he'd feel like he was drowning. The last thing he wanted was to be the reason this whole situation got worse; he didn't want to cause Lord Caedis any stress.

He sighed quietly. Heir Lucian could obviously handle himself. Ridge was going to get caught, and the only hybrids Jackson had to worry about were those he and Daimon's pack were out here searching for.

Chapter Twenty-Five

⇝ ≼ ☽ ≽ ⇜

Report

| Sebastien |

Sebastien grunted when Daimon put him down. He sat with his back against the cave wall and watched as the wolf walker pack settled and rested. His wounds were sore and throbbing, but they were slowly healing, and that brought him a little relief.

With a quiet sigh, he reached into his bag and pulled out a protein bar. It didn't look like the wolves were going hunting any time soon, so it was going to have to do. He took a bite and exhaled deeply through his nose. Seeing Jackson with Daimon made him miss Clementine more than he already did; he'd much rather be in bed being nursed by his mate than sitting in some damp cave waiting for his wounds to heal naturally.

Despite the fact that he needed to report to the Venaticus, there was something else he wanted to do first. After all, Heir Lucian or Lord Caedis weren't around to scold him, were they? He pulled his small rectangular mirror out of his bag and examined it for cracks. To his relief, it was undamaged, which meant he could still use it. He imbued his ethos into the rune on the back, and as the mirror flickered and faded to black, Sebastien waited patiently, taking another bite of his protein bar.

The mirror flickered again, and as the darkness cleared, it revealed the inside of his and Clementine's bedroom. The curtains were open, and the light of the city spilt in. Clementine was sitting on the edge of their bed in front of the mirror, and beside him were several books and pieces of paper. He'd been researching in bed again, and that brought a wide smile to Sebastien's face.

"Hey," Clementine said. "Where are you? It's kinda dark."

"Yeah, I..." he paused and glanced around. "We're resting in a cave."

"What happened to you? What's that on your face?" Clementine exclaimed worriedly as he leaned forward and touched the mirror.

Sebastien waved his hand dismissively. "It's nothing. I'm fine. We just had a run-in with some hunters. How's everything over there?"

"Well," Clementine said with a sigh, sitting cross-legged. "The Venaticus have closed all the gates and set up these quarantine points. No one goes in or out of Silverlake without being examined. This cadejo stuff is getting out of hand, isn't it?"

"Lord Caedis is trying to contain it as much as he can. There's really only so much he can do, right?" Sebastien mumbled.

"He's stopped worse things from happening," Clementine assured him.

He shrugged and leaned his head back against the wall. "I know, I just…I just—"

"I know," Clementine said softly. "None of this is your fault."

"But none of this would be happening if I hadn't—"

"Sebastien, if it wasn't you, it would have been someone else. That thing was going to find its way out of that tomb one way or another. Why else do you think Lord Caedis sent *you*?"

"Because I'm the only kludde left," he grumbled.

"No, because he trusted you. Anyone else might have tried to use that creature for their own purposes. If someone else got their hands on it, the whole situation might be a whole lot worse than it already is."

Sebastien shook his head and looked down at his lap.

"I mean, if it's anyone's fault, it's Lord Ca—"

"No," Sebastien said with a sigh, shaking his head. "Lord Caedis was just trying to keep it out of the hands of the Diabolus."

"And look where that's gotten us." Clementine then lowered his voice. "Do your new friends know?"

Sebastien glanced at the pack and scoffed. "These people aren't my friends, Clem. I'm just their babysitter. But no, they don't."

"Are you gonna tell them?"

He frowned at him. "Why would I tell them?"

Clementine shrugged.

"I mean…I told them that I first encountered the virus back then, but that was all they needed to know." He shuffled around uncomfortably. "Can we talk about something else?"

"Yeah," Clementine said with a nod. "I'm writing a new article about this quarantine stuff. I'm interviewing Yuri and Sinclair again."

Sebastien grunted. "I dunno which one of them is worse."

"Doctor Kowalski is kinda fascinating."

"And Sinclair's miles up his own ass," Sebastien muttered.

"They're both really smart guys, though. Which one of them do you think will come up with the cure or a vaccine?"

Sebastien smirked at him. "Are you interviewing me, babe?"

Clementine tapped his chin. "Maybe," he drawled.

"Well, Sinclair—sorry, Doctor Laurent—is really good in the Caeleste medical field. He's cured a bunch of stuff previously deemed terminal, so if he doesn't come up with it himself, I'm certain he'll be involved. As for Kowalski…he's a bit of a whack job, but Lord Caedis made him the Dean of Medicine at Ethospital, so that's gotta mean he's good, right?" Sebastien explained slowly.

With a nod, Clementine adorned a sterner expression. "On a more serious note, though…do you think they'll be able to find a way to stop this thing? If it spreads all over the world, the disease will be the least of the Nosferatu's problems. People are gonna use it as an excuse to cause trouble."

"I know," Sebastien said with a deep exhale. "Things are different now, though. The Nosferatu is everywhere." But then he groaned and dragged his hand over his face. "I gotta call them, order a clean-up."

"A clean-up?"

"Yeah. The hybrid, Jackson…he like…killed a bunch of hunters who were placing traps everywhere. Gotta get all that cleaned up."

Clementine nodded and mumbled, "So, I guess you gotta go?"

"For now, yeah. But I can call back when we stop someplace else. Probably tomorrow afternoon."

"Okay," he said. "Wait, can I see the muto?"

Sebastien smiled and looked around for Ethan. When he spotted the tiger over by the entrance with Julian, he turned the mirror around. Then, he turned it so he could see Clementine.

"He's like…huge!" Clementine exclaimed excitedly.

"Almost as big as a Prime wolf walker, yeah."

"You're so lucky."

"Not really. The guy's a bit of an asshole."

Clementine laughed and shook his head. "You say that about everyone you meet."

"Nah, I mean it this time. He's supposed to be best friends with Jackson, but I don't get it. Maybe that's why they work so well. One's rational, the other's irrational."

"That pretty much sums up our relationship."

Sebastien smirked at him. "I guess so."

Clementine smiled. "I'll let you go. I love you."

"I love you, too. Be careful out on the streets, okay?"

"Don't worry. I'm always careful," Clementine assured him.

Sebastien nodded. "All right. I'll talk to you later." Then, he tapped the rune on the back of his mirror. It faded to black, and after a few moments, became a normal mirror again.

He huffed as he rested his legs flat on the ground and placed his arms in his lap. But he wasn't about to let himself sink into his guilt. He knew that what happened in that village all those years ago wasn't his fault... well, everyone told him that it wasn't, but there was a part of him that would never let him forgive himself.

"Hey, Sebastien," came Jackson's voice.

Sebastien looked at the guy; just like everyone else but Ethan, he was in his human form. "What's up?" he called.

"You doing okay?" the kid asked.

"Yeah."

Jackson made his way over. "Did you call the Venaticus?"

He shook his head. "Nah, not yet. I'm about to, though."

"So... who were you talking to?" Jackson asked, sitting beside him. "Wait, that's a mirror. I thought it was a phone."

Sebastien lifted the mirror so Jackson could see it better. "It's, uh... an old form of demon communication and travel. Demons can talk through mirrors... kinda like how we can see each other through phones and shit, but this was like... hundreds and hundreds of years ago. The very first demons would get around through the sub-astral plane; they... evanesced. That's what it's called: evanescing. They figured if they could use mirrors like doorways, maybe they could use them like windows, so... we can see each other and talk through them."

Jackson's eyes were wide with awe. "Woah, that's pretty cool. I thought everyone just communicated with like... letters and owls and old ass telephones back then."

He smirked amusedly. "Well, yeah. There was that, too. Evanescing was a demon-only thing." He looked down at the mirror. "Anyways, I better call them up... get this out of the way."

"All right," Jackson said with a nod. "I'll leave you to do that. If you need anything, I'll just be over there with Daimon and Remus."

Sebastien grabbed Jackson's arm as he went to get up. "You came over here to ask me something, right? I'm pretty sure you didn't only come to ask who I was talking to—that was my mate, by the way."

Jackson's face went a little red. "Uh... well... I just had some questions about the demon... form stuff."

"Yeah, I thought you might. Let me get this Venaticus shit out of the way and rest a bit, and then we can talk."

"Okay," Jackson said with a smile. "Thank you."

"No probs."

Jackson then got up and went back over to Daimon and his son.

Sebastien sighed deeply and looked at the mirror. Putting it off wasn't going to help anyone, so he tapped the rune on the back, watched as the mirror faded to black... and waited. When the mirror flickered and a white room became visible on the other side, Sebastien exhaled again and prepared for the next few minutes.

An orange-haired uniformed man sat in front of the mirror and greeted him with a nod as he said, "Officer Huxley."

Sebastien nodded in response. "Officer Cabott."

"You're two hours late," Cabott grumbled.

"Yeah…" Sebastien drawled, dragging his hand down the back of his head. "There was a situation. It turns out that—"

"What kind of situation?" the man questioned, raising an eyebrow on his stiff, expressionless face.

Sebastien tried his best not to lose his composure. He *hated* being interrupted. "A hunter situation. The Venaticus brought in Riker and his men, but it turns out that there were some of them left out here. They tracked us down and—"

"Are you certain they were with Riker?"

"Yes, Cabott…" he said, deadpanning. "The Alpha wolf walker caught one of their soldiers; she confirmed it."

"Is the soldier still with you?"

Sebastien glanced at the unconscious woman, who was being guarded by Wesley and Alastor. "Yep. She's bit."

"Define bit," Cabott grunted.

"Wolf walker bit. She's tur—"

"Was she cured in time?"

Sebastien lost it. "Can you literally let me finish just *one* sentence?" he exclaimed, holding up his index finger.

The orange-haired man scowled.

"No, she was not cured. She's turning. I don't know what the wolves plan to do with her, but all of the other hunters are dead. I have the coordinates of their camp, and within a ten-mile radius, you'll find bodies and traps. It needs a clean-up team."

"Coordinates?"

"Latitude 68.8, longitude -874.6," Sebastien answered, glancing at the GPS device Daimon gave him.

Cabott wrote it down and then typed something on his computer. "You're further from Greykin Valley than you should be at this—"

"Did you literally not just hear me say that we got into a situation with some hunters?" he snapped irritably.

"I heard your explanation, but—"

"Don't but me, Cabott. I've been shot out of the fucking sky, chained up like some fucking medieval dragon, and to top it all off, I'm eating these fucking protein bars, which taste like shit, for your information," he yelled. "I don't have time to get Cabotted today, all right? Send the clean-up team, update Heir Lucian, and go be a prick elsewhere." He tapped the rune on the back of the mirror and stuffed it into his bag. Then, he dragged his hands over his face and huffed angrily.

He felt eyes on him.

Sebastien slowly pulled his hands away from his face and looked up. *Everyone* was staring at him. "What?" he called, flailing his arms.

The pack frowned at him and went back to whatever they were doing.

Sebastien sighed and rested his arms on his knees.

"Everything okay?" Jackson asked.

"Yup," he muttered.

Jackson sat beside him. "I know you said you wanted to rest…but it looked like things were getting pretty heated."

"It's just Cabott," he muttered, leaning his head back against the wall again.

"Who?"

"Cabott. He's the Silverlake Venaticus communications officer. He's a dick. We all call him Carrot 'cause he fucking looks like one."

Jackson snickered.

Sebastien sighed and glanced at him. "Everything okay with everyone?"

"Yeah, Daimon says we're gonna rest here for a few hours and then get back on track."

"All right. The Venaticus are sending out a team to clear all those hunter traps away, so at least no one's gonna have to worry about that anymore."

Jackson nodded. "So…Riker's hunters are dealt with, then?"

"Yeah. I don't think we're gonna have to worry about them anymore. Hopefully, now we can get to the valley without any other detours," Sebastien said.

"Okay, well…you sure you're good?"

"Yeah, I just need to get some rest."

Jackson stood up. "Okay, we'll talk later then, right?"

"Sure thing."

The kid then went back over to Daimon.

Sebastien watched him go. He knew Jackson was eager to get answers, and it *was* his job to teach Jackson all he could, but right now, his body was trying to heal, and to speed the process up, he needed to sleep. So, he lay on his side and used his bag as a pillow. Then, he closed his eyes and tried to relax.

But he couldn't fight the feeling that something else was going to happen. This mission was already a shit storm, and Sebastien was sure that this was just the beginning.

Chapter Twenty-Six

Back on Track

| Jackson |

Something tickled Jackson's cheek. He frowned and opened his eyes, and when he realized that Daimon was stroking his face with his fingers, he smiled up at him. He dragged his hand down from the Alpha's shoulder and moved his head from his chest and up to nuzzle his neck.

"Sorry," Daimon mumbled.

Jackson shook his head. "No, it's okay," he assured him quietly. "Did you get any sleep?"

"A little," the Alpha replied as he guided his hand down to Jackson's waist. Then, he eased it under his belt and lightly gripped Jackson's ass.

As much as Daimon's attention excited him, Jackson quickly grew nervous. He glanced around the cavern at the resting pack; knowing they'd all heard him and Daimon having sex in the shower at the Venaticus building was embarrassing enough, but if they *saw*, too… then Jackson was sure that he'd melt into a puddle of anxious, humiliated goop. He grasped Daimon's wrist before he could guide his hand around to his crotch. "They're gonna see."

"So?" Daimon muttered.

"So…you don't feel uncomfortable about that?" he asked with a frown.

"No."

Why *would* Daimon care if his pack saw? He was their Alpha; they'd know better than to stare, right? They always saw each other naked. But Jackson wasn't accustomed to how they did things. He wouldn't even *think* about bringing a date home when Ethan was around, so having sex ten feet from fourteen other people wasn't something he was going to do. He pulled Daimon's hand from his trousers. "Not right now," he mumbled.

Daimon returned his hand to Jackson's shoulder. "I'm sorry."

"It's fine, I just…I'm not used to being around so many people."

The Alpha hugged him tightly and kissed his head. "Once this is done, we'll have somewhere else to call home."

Jackson nodded but didn't say anything. Why did what Daimon said make him feel despondent? Was it because he wasn't entirely sure whether he wanted to live in Ascela or not? A part of him still wanted to go back to New Dawnward, but he knew that he couldn't. He was wrapped up in this mess. There was no telling what might happen to him and Ethan if they went back; Holt was involved, too…and Jackson needed to find out how deep all of this went. But he couldn't do that until they got to the lab out in Greykin Valley.

He couldn't ask Daimon to consider leaving Ascela for him. It wasn't safe anywhere else in the world for wolf walkers right now, was it? And Daimon and his pack had lived out here all their lives. Switching from snowy forests and an icy tundra to an urban environment wouldn't be easy for *anyone*.

With a quiet sigh, he glanced around again, and as he glanced at everyone's faces, the unease of knowing that one of them had tried to kill Daimon crept in. He needed to continue his hunt for the traitor, but as he looked around, not one of the wolves aggravated his senses, and it frustrated him. If his instincts could tell him that someone had tried to murder Daimon, then why couldn't they tell him *who*?

He frowned and sighed quietly, but then he remembered what Doctor Laurent said. Daimon needed to take his antibiotics every twelve hours, and Jackson was sure that it was time for his first one. He reached around inside his bag and pulled the bottle of green pills out. He stared at it for a moment, searching for side effects on the bottle, but all the information told him was that Daimon might feel sleepy or nauseous.

"Why are you looking at those?" Daimon suddenly asked.

Jackson glanced up at him. "Oh, uh…it's about time to take your first one, right?"

He grunted and looked away.

"Do you want some water or something to take it with?" Jackson asked as he opened the bottle and took one of the green pills out.

"No," the Alpha grumbled.

Jackson opened Daimon's clenched fist and placed the pill on his palm. "Take it."

"No," he replied stubbornly.

"Daimon…" Jackson said with a sigh. "You need to take them, or you could get an infection."

"I'm fine."

Jackson sat up and stared at the Alpha's face. He looked aggravated and uncomfortable. "What's wrong?" he asked quietly.

"Nothing."

Something was definitely up with him, but whatever it was, Jackson was convinced that he wasn't going to get it out of him. However, getting him to take his medicine was more important. Jackson looked around, and when he saw that the pack were either still asleep or talking quietly with one another, his hesitation to reciprocate Daimon's affection withered a little. He edged closer to Daimon's face. "If you take your medicine, I'll suck your dick," he offered quietly.

Daimon's glower faded slightly as he glanced at Jackson. "I want to fuck you," he replied, and he didn't bother keeping his voice hushed like Jackson.

Jackson was sure his face went a little red, but he did his best to keep his composure. "I mean…but…I don't want anyone to see. At least I can like…hide behind you to—"

"No one will see," he said, turning on his side to face Jackson.

He tried to determine how that would be possible since there was nowhere for them to hide away, but he couldn't ignore his growing anticipation. He *wanted* it…and if Daimon said no one would see, then he'd take his word for it. So, he mumbled, "Okay," and pushed Daimon's hand with the pill on it closer to the Alpha's face.

Daimon smirked and threw the pill into his mouth. Once he swallowed it, he moved his hand to the back of Jackson's head and kissed his lips.

Jackson kissed him back, and when Daimon hastily turned him around and pulled his back against his chest, Jackson smiled excitedly. He faced the cave wall with Daimon behind him so no one would see him; if anyone did so happen to look over at them, they'd probably know what was happening, but as long as Jackson didn't have to see them or be seen, he was fine with it.

As Daimon pulled his and Jackson's trousers down, he whispered seductively into Jackson's ear, "Don't make too much noise; you might wake everyone up."

The Alpha's hushed voice sent a shiver of aspiration down Jackson's spine. His body trembled as an intense heat quickly grew between his legs. His desire for Daimon's affection consumed him so quickly, and when the Alpha eased his dick into his pussy, he exhaled deeply and closed his eyes, trying his best to keep quiet. But the moment Daimon started thrusting into him, he sunk into the pleasure and groaned quietly.

Jackson gripped his shirt and breathed deeply, moving his left leg behind Daimon's legs. Any anxiety he had before was gone; the only thing he felt now was desperation for more. But just as he was about to let a pleasured sigh escape his breath, Daimon clamped his hand around his mouth.

"Shh," the Alpha murmured into Jackson's ear and then started gently rubbing his t-dick with his index finger.

With a desperate huff, Jackson held his eyes shut tightly. Daimon plunged his hard shaft deeper inside, making him grunt and scowl in struggle. He wanted to moan; it felt *so* good, and it was quickly intensifying, but all he could do was sigh and utter.

He struggled even more when he felt himself approaching his peak. "Daimon," he breathed, tensing up.

The Alpha thrusted harder, breathing heavily against the back of Jackson's neck.

Jackson shivered and grunted, his moans muffled against Daimon's hand, and as he climaxed, he whined as quietly as he could manage; his walls throbbed as waves of sheer delight electrified through him, and a content smile found its way to his face as the Alpha kissed the back of his head.

Daimon then pushed Jackson onto his front and eased his dick into his ass. He thrusted softly for a few moments, and Jackson hummed quietly as the discomfort quickly became pleasure, and that was when the Alpha began thrusting aggressively. He pinned both of Jackson's hands to the ground and nuzzled the back of his neck as he panted and groaned; Jackson could feel every hard inch, and he wanted to cry out as his body was pushed to its limits, but he didn't want to wake anyone.

So he held on, sighing and humming, and when the Alpha moaned into Jackson's hair, his dick convulsed inside him, filling him with his warm cum. Jackson responded with a delighted groan, and as Daimon exhaled and kissed the side of his face, he rested his head on the ground. But that was when he saw Ethan...*staring* right at him. There was a look of hostility on his face, and it looked like he was about to get up and storm over to him and Daimon.

The Alpha exhaled deeply as he pulled himself from Jackson and buttoned his trousers.

Jackson hastily did his trousers up and sat beside the Alpha. He tried not to glance over at Ethan, but he couldn't help but look to find out whether he was still staring or not.

He *wasn't*. Ethan returned to muttering with Julian.

With a quiet sigh, Jackson looked down at Daimon, who lay with his hands behind his head. "When are we heading out?"

"Maybe thirty minutes," the Alpha answered. "I have to check on the hunter before we leave."

"What are you gonna do with her?" Jackson questioned curiously as he glanced at the hunter Daimon had captured. The woman was shivering and sweating and lay on her side with Wesley and Alastor keeping watch over her.

"I was going to throw her out into the woods and leave her to the cadejo."

"But...you're not?"

"I didn't say that," he mumbled, gazing up at Jackson. "She's a hunter. She's the very thing that helped drive our kind to near extinction. Everything within me is telling me to make her suffer, but there's this tiny little part that's trying to convince me to give her a chance. I've said it many times before: there aren't many of us left and we need as many wolves as we can get. I don't know how loyal she is to her people; if I give her a chance and she finds a way to contact other hunters, then it would be my fault. I'm not sure I want to take that risk."

"But…wouldn't she *have* to be loyal to you as her Alpha? And can't you get Tokala to find out her intentions?" That made Jackson wonder about whoever attempted to kill Daimon. *Did* everyone have to remain loyal to him? Caius hadn't. And he also considered asking Tokala to help him find the traitor. The Zeta could determine someone's intentions, right?

The Alpha then frowned. "It sounds like you *want* her to stay."

Jackson shrugged. "I know what it's like to be in her place. Everything is changing for her; her whole world is being turned upside down, and if she makes the wrong choice, it could cost her her life. And…I know that she's a hunter, but she's just a private. Something I learned from my years of talking to people and finding what makes them tick is that when there's these huge power structures, the little guys like her can be easily swayed. They're not as important as the ranks above them. She might jump at the chance at a new life—one where she'd matter more."

"She begged me to not let her turn."

"Yeah, and there were a lot of things I know *I* wouldn't have done or agreed to if I hadn't become a wolf walker. Having this new power and responsibilities changes you. I just think you should talk to her before deciding what you're doing."

Daimon sighed heavily and nodded. "I'll need to ask for Wesley, Tokala, and Rachel's opinions first, though. The council might be small, but its vote still matters." He sat up and glanced around at his pack. "I'll get that done now."

"All right," Jackson said.

As the Alpha headed off to gather his council, Jackson set his sights on Ethan again. He watched his friend fiddle with his light-brown hair while he listened to whatever Julian was talking about. He knew his friend was mad; Ethan always twisted his hair around in his fingers when he was angry about something…but Jackson didn't understand *what* he could be mad about.

He got up and headed over there, and when he sat with them, both Ethan and Julian greeted him.

"Do you know when we're heading out?" Julian asked.

"Daimon said in about thirty minutes," Jackson answered, making himself comfortable. "He's just talking to his council about the hunter." Then, as his friends looked at the bitten hunter, Jackson located Sebastien. The hound was still sleeping, so he couldn't yet ask his questions.

Ethan leaned his back against the wall. "Julian and I were just talking about what we're gonna do once this is all over."

Jackson gazed curiously at them both.

Julian looked at him. "Do you think…Alpha Daimon would let me go and see if there's anyone still alive in my old village?"

He frowned unsurely. "Uh...well, I don't know. I mean...he's reasonable, so maybe."

Ethan scoffed. "I'm sure he'd come up with some excuse as to why you couldn't."

"We're not Daimon's prisoners," Jackson snapped irritably. "He'd want to make sure it's safe, sure, but he wouldn't flat-out deny Julian's request. Once we get this done...the Nosferatu might be able to put a stop to all this cadejo stuff."

"And if they don't?" his friend questioned.

Jackson didn't know what to say to that, but he was confident that whatever was hidden inside the lab would reveal what the Nosferatu needed to know in order to create a cure or vaccine. So in response to Ethan's question, he shrugged.

"I just hope everything is smooth sailing from now on," Julian said. "The hunters are dealt with, right? So all we have to worry about is cadejo."

Jackson glanced at Sebastien. "Yeah. I heard him talking and the Venaticus are sending out a bunch of people to clear up the traps." Then, he looked at Ethan. "What do *you* wanna do once this is over?"

"By once this is over, I hope you mean once we find out how Holt is involved," Ethan replied. "I wanna go back to New Dawnward, and the only way that's gonna happen is if we uncover what's going on over there."

He was right. If either of them ever wanted to go home, they needed to get to the bottom of Holt's involvement. "When do you think Holt started working for El'Vorian—for *Lyca Corp.*?"

Ethan exhaled and shrugged. "Who knows, man? If I had to guess, I'd say it was when he started restricting what people write about. Remember when Alice was looking into those murders?"

Jackson took a moment to recall. "Oh, the Caeleste ones? The guy was like...taking their teeth or something?"

"Yeah. Holt shut that shit down, so she went off on her own with it, and then poof...she wasn't a journalist anymore. Stuck working down at the convenience store on Lawton Street."

Julian frowned at them both. "So...they tore her whole career away from her because she was doing her job?"

"That's what happens when people and places are corrupt," Ethan told them. "Holt obviously has contacts and friends in high places. I mean, how else would he have been able to ship a bunch of us out here to die?"

Something then hit Jackson. "Ethan...where *did* you end up?"

"Huh?" his friend questioned.

"Like...in the shipping container. Where was it delivered?"

"Oh, I dunno. I got out of the thing before they could load it onto the truck. I got the hell out of there and found my way to the closest town."

Jackson pondered as he spoke, "Do you think they were sending you to Lyca Corp.?"

Ethan adorned a perplexed expression. "I mean…maybe."

"What about the others?" Julian asked. "There were a bunch of those journalists, right?"

That was a good question. "I found Thomas in Farrydare," Jackson told Ethan. "I have no idea where the others are, though."

"Those who were Caeleste were probably sent to Lyca Corp.," Ethan muttered. "Makes sense."

"Are you gonna try to find them?" Julian asked.

Jackson nodded. "I came out here to find all of them, so…yeah. But we have to get to that lab first. Maybe there'll be something there that tells me what happened to the others."

"Did Thomas wanna go back to New Dawnward?" Ethan asked.

"I don't know," Jackson answered. "After Daimon helped me get away from those demons, the authorities got everyone else out of the cave. I didn't actually stick around to see what Thomas was gonna do. I assume he's still in Farrydare."

Just then Jackson heard the hunter's strained voice. He looked over there, and when he saw Daimon crouched in front of her, he turned to face them and listened, and so did everyone else.

Daimon glared at her. "You have nowhere to go," he told her harshly. "No hunter will let you re-join their ranks. They'll lock you up, skin you alive, and toss your body out to be picked at by whatever's nearby. You won't survive out there, and because of the simple fact that you're now one of us, I'm going to offer you *one* chance," he said, holding up his index finger as she gawped at him. "You can come with us, or you can stay here."

The woman stared at him; it looked like she was thinking, and as sweat trickled down the sides of her face, she huffed weakly and looked away from him. "I'd rather be left to die than join…you," she grunted, shooting a look of disgust at Daimon.

"Suit yourself," the Alpha snarled. Then, he stood up and looked around at his pack. "We're heading out. Get your things."

As they were told, everyone grabbed their bags and shifted. Jackson headed over to where he'd been sleeping with Daimon and grabbed his bags, and when he shifted, Rachel cautiously approached to help him get them on.

Now was his chance. "Rachel, I'm really sorry for—"

"Forget it," she said as she attached his bags. "We're heading out." And then she walked off.

Jackson watched her help the other wolves. He felt guilty; he really *was* sorry, but she wouldn't let him speak. With a quiet sigh, he walked over to Daimon, who was waiting by the cavern exit with Remus.

"Just give her a little more time," Daimon said, nodding at Rachel. "She'll come around. She understands as well as we all do that it wasn't your fault or your intention."

"I hope so," he mumbled. "I didn't mean to grab or scare her." He trusted what Daimon said, though. If his packmates didn't trust him, then they'd be refusing to share the same cave as him, right?

"I know, and we *all* know. She's just always been a little slower to come around than everyone else."

With a nod and sigh, Jackson shifted his attention to the bitten hunter. "Are you really gonna leave her here?"

"She made her choice," the Alpha grumbled. "Trying to convince her would be a waste of time."

"But—"

"She isn't coming," Daimon interjected before Jackson could speak. "We need to move on."

Jackson frowned and looked at the woman again. A part of him wanted to try and convince her… but if she would rather die than go with the only people who could help her, then what could he say that might change her mind? Daimon's explanation of what would happen to her if she tried to make it alone clearly wasn't enough.

"We'll get back on course and then continue towards the valley," Daimon said as everyone joined him. "We'll travel for most of the night, and once dawn approaches, we'll find somewhere to rest."

Ethan—in his tiger form—stood beside Jackson. "So, it's safer to travel at night because the cadejo have shitty night vision, right?"

"Yeah," Jackson said with a nod.

"Let's go," Daimon called, and then he started leading the way out of the cave.

But as the pack left, Jackson took one last look at the woman. He hoped she might ask them to wait and that she'd changed her mind, but she just sat there… shivering and sweating. So, Jackson sighed and followed the pack.

Chapter Twenty-Seven

The River

| Jackson |

While the pack traversed the dark woods, Jackson tried to focus on the questions he needed to ask Sebastien. Now wasn't a good time, but once they found somewhere to rest, he wanted to pick his brain. There was so much he didn't know about his new demon form and the inimă; he wanted to learn to control it. It finally made him feel useful, and like he was finally beginning to understand who and what he was. Of course, there was a part of him that felt a little hesitant, but he wasn't going to let that stop him from utilizing it. He wanted to be helpful—*useful*.

"How are you feeling?" Daimon quietly asked Remus.

"I'm okay, Dad," his son replied.

"We're coming up on a river, chief," Alastor called.

Wesley sighed in relief. "Good, 'cause I'm about to die of thirst."

"How far are we from being back on course?" Ethan asked.

"A few more hours," Sebastien answered.

The pack followed the winged hound, whose wounds had healed very quickly. Vague scars clung to his skin where the silver chains had scathed him, but they were getting fainter with every passing hour.

Jackson had *so* many questions. Did demons heal faster than wolf walkers? Did being a demon mean his increased healing abilities were greater than both a demon's and a wolf walker's? When was he going to start craving blood again? What did being a demon give him? And could he learn to control both his demon form and the inimă? He didn't want to black out again and wake up surrounded by corpses, nor did he want to lose control like he did with his wolf. But he'd managed to come out of the bloodthirsty trance before, so he could do it again, right?

Ethan frowned at him, walking beside him. "What are you thinking so hard about?"

"Just my demon form," he answered. "I wanna learn to control it."

"And you will," his friend said confidently.

"You knew I was a demon, right?" Jackson asked him.

"Yeah."

"So...what do you know about demons? Or asmodi."

Wilson exhaled deeply. "Well, I did my research, but I'm pretty sure I don't know nearly as much as Sebastien. Demons are really strong and fast, some need blood, others need sex."

"He isn't an incubus," Julian said with a scoff. But then they frowned. "Are you?"

"I...don't think so," Jackson said unsurely.

"If asmodi *did* possess the Zenith's incubus abilities, your Alpha would probably be dead," came Sebastien's voice.

Daimon then snarled quietly. "Less talk, more walking."

But Jackson wanted to know what Sebastien meant. He left Daimon's side and walked closer to the hound. "What do you mean, he'd be dead?"

"Incubi drain the ethos and energy from those they have sex with; even so much as kissing drains the other person. It takes a long time for incubi to learn to control themselves and how much they take from another person, and since you're a baby demon, you wouldn't have had any idea what was happening. You'd have drained everything out of him," he said, nodding at Daimon, who rolled his eyes.

"Aren't incubi, like...super rare?" Alastor asked.

"*Super* rare," Wesley said with a nod.

"The Zenith was the very first one," Sebastien said matter-of-factly. "Then a few others popped up here and there. They're incredibly powerful, thus very dangerous, so the Nosferatu keeps tabs on them. There are currently only four of them including the Zenith."

Ethan mumbled, "Huh...so if they're super rare, why don't they just...have babies and make more?"

"Because an incubus is an incredibly rare occurrence. When a succubus has children, their daughters are always born as succubi, but if they have a son, he's just born as a normal Lilidian demon. But in the Zenith's case, he was born with powers similar to but much more advanced than those of a succubus. A succubus can kill someone by having sex with them, but an incubus can drain the life out of someone with a single touch," Sebastien explained.

Alastor laughed quietly. "Death by sex."

Wesley, Brando, and a few of the others giggled.

Tokala then cleared his throat loudly.

Everyone mumbled their apologies to Daimon and Tokala and continued forward in silence.

Jackson had more to ask, but they needed to be quiet, so he went back over to Daimon and walked with him. "Sorry, I just wanted to know more about demons."

"It's fine, but there will be plenty of time for talk later," the Alpha said.

With a nod, Jackson followed along quietly.

The pack navigated the thick, silent woods. Snow started falling, and the sound of flowing water soon filled the air.

But there was something else.

A chill ran down Jackson's spine when he figured out that what he thought was distorted, distant wind brushing through the trees was actually the muffled snarls of cadejo colliding with the loudly flowing water.

Everyone slowed as they approached the tree line, and Jackson was quickly consumed by dread once he spotted what waited fifty yards ahead.

On the other side of the river, at least thirty cadejo lurked. Most of them were standing in place, snarling, and twitching. The only cadejo that was moving was much taller and slimmer than the rest….

A prowler.

The rotten monster grunted and groaned as it prowled through the crowd. It sniffed the air and dragged its feet along the snow, looking around frantically.

"We can't risk getting too close to that thing," Julian whispered. "Their sense of smell isn't as good as ours, but it's way better than that of a normal cadejo."

Daimon nodded and started leading the pack to the right. "We'll follow the river from a distance and find another path across."

The pack hastily followed.

Jackson felt more and more uneasy with each step he took, though. The snarling, the smell, and knowing that there were more cadejo than they could handle just fifty yards away terrified him. The cadejo hadn't seen them, though, and they weren't going to. *That* was what Jackson needed to focus on. That… and that he now had his demon form. If something happened, he'd be able to do more this time.

Daimon led the pack further upstream and away from the cadejo, but just when the sound of snarls and growls began fading… the same noise echoed up ahead.

"Chief," Tokala said cautiously.

Jackson lifted his head so that he could see over the wolves ahead of him, and where the river bent, there was another crowd of cadejo on the other side. A prowler was with them, too, and there were more of them than there had been back down the way they'd come. Jackson spotted several once-human zombies, too. Two of them were wearing the same armour that the rest of Riker's hunters wore, and the other three looked like villagers, dressed in bloody, torn casual clothes.

"Do you think they're attracted to the sound of the river?" Remus suggested.

"Maybe," Daimon answered, continuing through the trees. "We'll keep travelling up. There has to be an area where we can cross."

"And if there isn't?" Ethan asked with a scoff. "We've only got so many hours of dark left."

Jackson watched Daimon scowl. He was evidently trying to keep himself from snapping at Ethan.

"We'll find a way across," the Alpha grumbled.

"How long does the river go on for?" Ethan asked.

No one answered. Did anyone even know?

Sebastien glanced back at the pack. "Several miles at least. If we find somewhere to take cover, I can try and find us a way around."

"You have a map?" Alastor asked.

"Not a physical one, no," the hound replied as the pack took cover behind some snow heaps. "Demons have very good memories. We remember everything... well, almost everything. I made sure to stare long enough at a map of Greykin before we came out here, but I can't concentrate while trying to avoid being detected by cadejo."

The pack started glancing around, and assuming that they were looking for a place to hide, Jackson searched, too.

"What about over there?" Dustu whispered. "Some logs."

Daimon nodded. "That'll do for now. Stay low and close to one another. Let's go."

In a tight huddle, the pack turned their backs on the river and headed towards the pile of logs. Once they reached it, everyone hurried to get behind them, and when they were all concealed, Sebastien closed his eyes and concentrated.

Jackson wondered: was learning to remember everything something *he* could do? He'd always had a good memory, but there were times when he took longer than usual to recall. Was that just how it was? He gawped at the winged hound, watching as his face went on a journey from focused, to confused, to a look of realization.

"Two miles from here, there's a waterfall," Sebastien said as he opened his eyes. "If the sound of the water *is* attracting the cadejo, then I'm sure there are gonna be *hundreds* of them up there. We need to cross within the next mile."

A flurry of concerned mumbles circled the pack.

"Can we go back?" Leon asked. "What if we head downstream and find the lake this river connects to? It won't be as noisy down there, right?"

Sebastien shook his head. "The lake is at least half a day away. We're already behind schedule. I think we should scout the next mile, and if we can't figure out a way across, then we can try heading down towards the lake."

Everyone looked at Daimon. A conflicted frown clung to the Alpha's face. The silence grew tenser with every passing second, but after a minute or so, Daimon seemed to decide what to do.

"Since you can fly," the Alpha said, setting his eyes on Sebastien, "you can create a distraction so we can cross. You can meet up with us later."

"I mean, sure… but there's no way to know whether these zombie wolves are gonna be interested in me. They want wolf walker flesh, right?" the hound mumbled.

"They were coming after you when we were rescuing Ethan," Julian said.

"Yeah," Lalo said with a nod.

Sebastien huffed deeply. "That's true, and their tastes seemed to have switched a lot lately. Wolf walkers, humans, me."

Daimon said, "So it's settled. Sebastien will draw the cadejo away from the water, we'll cross and meet up with him deeper in the woods. You can follow our scent, correct?"

The hound nodded. "All right. I guess I'll see you on the other side."

"Good luck," Julian said worriedly.

Sebastien grunted as he got up and then scurried off to the left.

Jackson shivered. He was getting a strange feeling about this, the same feeling he got moments before something terrible happened. "Daimon," he uttered, turning his head to stare at the Alpha.

"What?" Daimon asked as a concerned frown stole his vacant glare.

"Are you getting one of those feelings?" Julian asked.

"Should we tell him to come back?" Enola panicked.

"Sebastien's got this," Ethan said, trying to reassure everyone.

"Sebastien is a highly trained professional," Daimon said firmly. "He knows what he's doing, and above that, he can't be infected."

Jackson tried to settle his nerves, but his anxiety was getting harder to handle. What if it was just that, though? What if this feeling wasn't the kind he got moments before disaster, but was his own anxiety? He watched Sebastien disappear into the woods. Then, he shifted his sights to the cadejo. They hadn't seen him, and the prowler was still sniffing around as it had been before. Would it be naïve of him to try and tell himself that it was fine, though? Sebastien told him not to ignore these feelings, and he wasn't going to. "I think it's one of *those* feelings," he insisted.

Daimon stared in the direction Sebastien disappeared, and moments later, the darkness lit up with bright blue flames. "Everyone stay alert," he told his pack. "Stay together, watch your backs." Then, he looked at Jackson. "Tell me if your feeling gets worse and we'll retreat."

Jackson nodded nervously. "O-okay." He didn't know what his feeling was trying to tell him, but considering that it struck him when Sebastien left, he felt as though it might have something to do with the hound. But what?

"They're leaving," Wesley said.

"All of them," Alastor added.

"We'll wait for them to move further away," Daimon said. "We can't risk even one of them catching a glimpse of us."

The pack waited, eyeing the twitching, seething cadejo as they left the riverside and started shuffling towards the blue fire. They only walked at first, but when the prowler roared, the zombies sped up and raced into the trees.

"Okay, stay close," Daimon said, and as he led the way around the logs and towards the water, the pack and Ethan followed.

Jackson did his best to remain quiet, keeping his eyes fixed on the departing cadejo crowd. Maybe things were going to be fine. Perhaps it really was just his own anxiety making him feel like something bad was going to happen. The cadejo were leaving, the pack was just about to reach the river, and Sebastien hadn't yelped or started a fight with the zombies.

He exhaled deeply and quietly, encouraging his heart to slow as the pack started crossing the river. They used the rocks and pebbles protruding from the water to ensure they didn't make a sound, and Jackson followed every step that Daimon took. He didn't want to slip or mess up.

When his paws sunk into the snow on the other side of the river, Jackson became a little more relieved. He didn't take his eyes off the trees the cadejo disappeared into, though. The snarls and groans echoed through the woods, and the blue of Sebastien's flames was starting to fade.

Daimon picked up the pace once every wolf was across. They hurried towards the trees; Jackson could feel everyone's desperation to get out of the open. And when he followed the Alpha into the woods, Jackson let himself sigh in relief.

But angst struck his heart like a bullet. It electrified through him so quickly— *it* happened so fast that Jackson didn't have a chance to utter a word. No one did.

A ferocious, guttural roar cut through the silence, and before any wolf could even *gasp*, a prowler burst out of the darkness and crashed into them all.

Petrified screams filled the air.

Jackson felt something tightly grip his back leg, and then it pulled.

Everyone's voices collided with one another, and as Jackson was dragged through the snow, he was so stricken with fear that all he could do was stare at the rotten beast which was prying him from his packmates.

"Jackson!" Daimon yelled.

"Kill the fucking thing!" Ethan shouted.

Jackson winced fearfully but wouldn't let the terror control him. He grunted and snarled, trying to break free, struggling and yanking as the monster roared. It was pulling him back towards the river. "Daimon!" he shouted and writhed around. He tried to leave his wolf form so that he could adorn his demon form, but he *couldn't*. His ethos didn't respond—was the prowler the cause? Was it stopping him from shifting?

Someone suddenly clashed with the prowler. A wolf jumped at the beast and sunk its teeth into it, and when the monster was thrown aside, Jackson scurried to his paws and watched as Tokala pinned it down. Daimon rushed past Jackson and snatched the prowler's arm with his teeth before it could swipe the Zeta, and Alastor, Wesley, Brando, Enola, and Ezhno quickly joined the fight.

"Jack!" Ethan called. "He told us to back off—come on!"

Jackson wanted to help; he didn't want to retreat, but Wilson quickly appeared at his side and started tugging him away from the fight and to where the rest of the pack were taking cover, watching as their Alpha and his best fighters tackled the rotting beast.

"I literally have no idea why anyone would ignore your feeling after everything that's happened," Julian said, shaking their head.

"We're all anxious," Ethan exclaimed quietly.

Jackson shook his head, his heart racing. He had to do somethi—

Someone yelped.

Jackson watched Enola hit a tree and land on the ground with a thump. The prowler kicked Ezhno away. Daimon tried to hold it down by shifting into his Prime form, but the decaying creature managed to throw Brando away, leaving only Daimon, Tokala, Alastor, and Wesley to try and tear the monster's heart out.

"Rachel," he blurted and turned to face her. "I need the inimă!"

"W-what?" Julian stuttered. "Y-you can't go—"

"You could hurt the others," Rachel said, shaking her head.

Another yelp snatched everyone's attention, and when Jackson saw Wesley hit the ground and groan, he scowled and set his eyes on Rachel again.

"I can help!" Jackson shouted.

"Give it to him!" Ethan insisted.

"They need help!" Lalo snapped at Rachel.

Rachel frantically looked at each of them with a look of confliction in her eyes, but when Ethan grunted and pulled the bag on her side open, she didn't fight him.

The tiger quickly grabbed the amulet, and when he turned to face Jackson, the inimă shimmered and abruptly flew from Ethan's grip. It attached itself to Jackson, and the moment he felt its power surge through him, Jackson frowned in determination and raced towards the prowler.

But that was when blood sprayed onto the snow, and an agonized yelp cut through the snarls and growls.

The monster pulled its infectious teeth from the throat of one of the wolves... and Jackson gawped in horror.

Someone was bitten

Chapter Twenty-Eight

↤ ≼ ☽ ≽ ↦

Stop

| Jackson |

Panic shot through Jackson's body.

Everyone went still for a moment.

"Alastor!" Wesley shrieked, hurrying to his paws.

Jackson was stricken with so much horror that all he could do was stand there and watch Wesley try to pull his friend away from the prowler, but Alastor yelped and convulsed, writhing around in the snow as the monster's venom enthralled him.

"Tokala!" came Daimon's voice.

Taking his eyes off Alastor and Wesley, Jackson watched Daimon grab the prowler's arms and hold them behind its back. Then, Tokala pounced and went for the creature's heart, but the prowler roared and kicked its right leg up, smashing its bony foot into Tokala's face. It then pulled free from Daimon and swung around—

Jackson's fear was shattered by the desperate need to protect his mate. He didn't even think about it. He burst forward. "Stop!" he yelled as if it were a command, and when the inimă's power surged through his veins, he felt his strength peak. He smashed into the prowler, which stopped trying to grab Daimon, and when he pinned it to the ground, it stared at him in what looked like confusion for half a second. But then it started struggling, trying to break free.

However, Jackson was stronger. A crimson glow swiftly wrapped itself around his body, and when Jackson felt his jaw tremble with anticipation, he sunk his teeth into the prowler's throat. He bit so hard that he felt the monster's spine crack, and when the beast gurgled and lost control of its limbs, Jackson plunged his muzzle into its chest, gripped its rotting heart, and tore it out.

The taste of the cadejo's blood gave him no satisfaction, though. To Jackson's relief, however, the bloodlust which consumed him before didn't enthral him, and when he heard Wesley's mournful cries, the inimă's power faded, leaving Jackson with the heavy weight of fear, guilt, and dismay.

"Alastor," Wesley cried, shaking his head as he lay beside his panting, wheezing friend.

Everyone stood around them with their own looks of sorrow and grief. No one said a word, and when Jackson shifted his sights to Daimon, he saw the same expression on his face that appeared whenever the Alpha was blaming himself.

But this wasn't Daimon's fault. It was Jackson's. He should have reacted faster, he should have just taken the inimă from Rachel. But because he'd let her argue with him about handing it over, Alastor got bit.

"It's okay, it's okay," Wesley insisted quietly, and then he started licking Alastor's wound.

Bly's despondent frown thickened. "W-Wesley, I...that's not—"

"He's gonna be fine!" Wesley snapped, lifting his head to glare at her. Then, when he saw the same worried, sullen expressions on everyone else's faces, he scowled. "Why are you all standing there?! G-go and fetch some herbs or help me get him somewhere safe!"

"Wesley," Daimon said, stepping forward. "There's nothing we—"

"No!" he wailed, shaking his head. "Y-you said they could still be them for a while before turning, r-right?" he asked desperately, staring at Daimon. "M-maybe...maybe that gives us time to save him! What about grim root?" he suggested, gawping at Bly. "I-it can extract the venom, right? Right?!" he cried, trembling.

Remus started crying and hid his face in Daimon's fur.

Rachel wept, too, and turned her head away to try and mask her tears.

Seeing her cry...it aroused anger deep inside Jackson. Alastor was dying, turning into a monster, and if *she* had just given him that fucking amulet—he couldn't stop himself. "Why didn't you just give me the fucking inimă?!" he yelled as he got in her face. "I could've stopped it!"

"Woah, calm down," Julian insisted, trying to usher Jackson away from Rachel, who looked terrified.

"Get away from me!" Jackson shouted and shoved Julian away. He got into Rachel's face again. "I told you to give it to me!"

"Jack's right!" Ethan concurred, glaring at Rachel.

"I-I-I'm sorry," she stuttered, shaking her head.

"Jackson," Daimon said, using his paw to pull him away from Rachel.

"I told her to give it to me!" Jackson snapped at his mate. "I could...I could've stopped it!" he lamented as his eyes shifted to Alastor. "I...could've stopped it." He was shaking, both anger and despair battling for dominion inside him.

When Bly failed to continue trying to convince Wesley of the truth, Lance spoke up, "Wesley, there's nothing. I'm sorry." He was clearly trying his best to keep his composure, but the despair and tears were contagious. "The best thing we can do for him now is… free him before the virus takes him entirely."

Wesley groaned in anguish, staring down at Alastor, who was struggling to breathe.

"W-Wesley," Alastor uttered. "P-please."

"There has to be something!" Wesley begged, and when his sore, teary eyes locked onto Jackson, they widened. "Y-you can do something!"

Jackson's anger and sorrow was accompanied by confusion. "I-I—"

"Y-you were bitten by one and lived, right?!" Wesley insisted.

"Wesley…" Tokala said, limping closer. "We—"

"Please!" Wesley wailed at Jackson. "C-can't you give him demon blood? Can't you make him like you?"

Everyone started setting their sights on Jackson, even Daimon.

"W-Wesley," Alastor grunted. "P-please… it hurts."

"Jackson!" Wesley insisted. "Save him!"

"W-Wesley, I—"

"Just try," Ethan suddenly said, cutting Jackson off. "Some demons can make other demons."

Tokala nodded. "He's right."

"Then hurry!" Wesley begged.

Ethan ushered Jackson closer. "Come on."

Jackson had no idea what he was supposed to do, and after seeing the demons that Ridge had created, he felt hesitant. What if Alastor turned into one of those Neophytes? But if it would save his life… he had to try. He hurried to Alastor's side. He stared at Alastor's bite; the brown-furred Eta was shivering and grunting, and Jackson didn't know how long he had.

What turned a human into a vampire? Blood, right?

Jackson shifted into his human form and extended his demon claws from his fingernails. Then, he cut his hand and let the blood drip into Alastor's mouth.

Everyone edged nearer.

"Alastor?" Wesley murmured, patting his neck with his paw.

"Did it work?" Julian whispered.

"Alastor?" Daimon asked while Remus turned his head and pulled his face away from the Alpha's fur so that he could see what was going on.

Alastor's pained grunts faded, and his twitching body calmed.

Jackson's face lit up, and his heart started racing harder. *Did* it work? Was his blood saving Alastor?

"Alastor?" Wesley urged.

The brown-furred Eta flinched.

Everyone started murmuring his name with hope in their voices.

Even Jackson felt hopeful.

Was it *actually* going to—

Alastor convulsed and snarled.

Everyone but Jackson and Wesley backed off cautiously.

Wesley frowned and anxiously asked, "Alastor, can you hear—"

Alastor abruptly lunged at Wesley with his teeth bared.

"Wesley!" Dustu shrieked and pulled him away from Alastor before he could latch his jaws around him.

"Everyone get back!" Daimon yelled, pulling Remus and Jackson with him as he moved away from Alastor.

Everyone stared in horror as Alastor climbed to his paws; his eyes were crimson, he was snarling and twitching, and it looked like Jackson's blood had only made him turn faster. There was no emotion on his face, and black goop oozed from his maw.

"Alastor!" Wesley wept.

The cadejo's eyes darted from each wolf frantically…like it was deciding who to go for first. But when its gaze met Jackson's, a look of malice appeared on its face, and it charged towards him.

Mournful cries echoed from the pack, and in the blink of an eye, Daimon moved in front of Jackson, snatched the cadejo by its throat, and then plunged his other hand into its chest.

It was over.

Wesley dropped to the ground when Alastor's rotten corpse did, and as the pack cried with him, Wesley grieved for his friend.

Jackson pulled the inimă from around his neck. His heart sunk into his gut, and his throat tightened so much that it became hard to breathe. Why didn't it work? Why didn't his blood save Alastor?

"What the hell happened here?" came Sebastien's voice.

No one answered. They cried and whined for their fallen packmate.

"We need to move," Sebastien insisted, standing in front of Daimon, who was still holding Alastor's decaying heart in his wolfish hand. "Hello? The rest of those cadejo heard the commotion; they're gonna be on top of us any second!"

Daimon dropped the heart and morphed into his normal wolf form. The look of dismay which sat on his face disappeared, and he looked around at his wolves. "We need to leave—"

"We can't just leave him here!" Wesley wailed. "We have to bury him!"

"There's no time," Daimon said regretfully. "We can't risk losing anyone else."

"Please!" Wesley sobbed.

Jackson watched Daimon hesitate.

After a few seconds, though, the Alpha looked at Sebastien. "Can you carry Alastor's body?"

Sebastien huffed and said, "Yeah."

Daimon was obviously as sure as Jackson was that Wesley wouldn't leave without his friend's body. The hound swiftly got Alastor onto his back between his wings with the help of Rachel and Lalo, and then once Jackson put the inimă in his bag and shifted into his wolf form, the Alpha started leading the way.

There was no time to grieve their packmate fully, and the dismay ensnaring the pack grew thicker the further they ran. Wesley whimpered quietly as he ran beside Sebastien so that he could stay by his fallen friend, and every time a member of the pack glanced at him, they tried to hold back their tears.

Jackson hung back, following behind everyone else. He didn't understand. Ridge said that his blood could create hybrids, so why couldn't it save Alastor? Why couldn't it save his packmate from the virus?

"Uh…Jackson?" came Rachel's voice.

He glanced at the brown-furred council member.

She looked terrified, but guilt smothered her face. "I'm…I'm sorry," she said sadly. "I-I froze up, and…I just…I should have given you the inimă."

Jackson huffed as his frustration intensified. "Yeah, you should've," he muttered.

"I won't…I won't hesitate again, and—"

"It really doesn't matter anymore, does it?" Jackson interjected, letting his emotions control him. "Alastor's dead."

Rachel looked horribly ashamed, and instead of replying, she left Jackson's side and ran beside Dustu.

Jackson was glad that she left. He didn't want to talk to her. And he wasn't sorry for yelling at her, either. If she'd listened to him and given him the amulet, Alastor might still be alive.

―⧫―

As the night grew later, the Alpha led the pack deeper into the woods; they didn't stop running for a good thirty minutes, and once the sound of the river was no longer within earshot, Daimon slowed down. They continued walking in silence, though. Most of the pack kept their heads down; some glanced at one another like they were expecting someone to speak, but no one did.

It was silent…all the way through until dawn.

Once his paw was healed, and he was able to walk on his front leg again, Tokala went ahead with Brando to find a place to rest, and when he returned, *he* was the first one to break the quiet.

"There's an abandoned burrow, chief," the orange wolf told Daimon.

Daimon nodded and let Tokala lead the way.

They followed a frozen stream, passed a derelict hut, and navigated a narrow path down into a wide ditch. Daimon cautiously led them through the ice-edged entrance of what looked like an old bear burrow, and once everyone was inside, Leon, Brando, and Enola stood watch.

Sebastien carefully placed Alastor's body on the ground by the entrance, and Wesley immediately sat beside it and continued weeping.

Jackson sat by himself. He didn't want to see or be seen by anyone. But *of course*, Ethan and Julian joined him.

"Stop blaming yourself," Ethan said quietly. "It was worth a try."

"Yeah," Julian agreed.

"No," Jackson mumbled. "If I just…got to the prowler faster, then—"

"Dude, *everyone* was freaked out," Ethan exclaimed.

"Not Daimon. Not Wesley or Alastor. Tokala, Brando, Ezhno, or Enola," Jackson uttered.

"No one is blaming you," Tokala suddenly said.

They all looked at the orange wolf, who appeared behind Julian and Ethan.

"No one blames anyone but the cadejo," Tokala assured him, sitting down. "I've just had to tell Alpha Daimon the same thing. When these things happen…it's never anyone's fault."

"If I got the inimă faster, then maybe I could have stopped that thing from even biting Alastor in the first place," Jackson insisted. "I should've just…taken it instead of asking."

"Rachel was just being cautious. We all saw what the inimă can do, and she was afraid; you *did* grab her, Jackson," the Zeta explained.

"But it's his," Ethan argued. "Jackson knows how to use it; we've all seen him in action. She should've just given it to him."

Tokala looked hesitant…almost as if he agreed but didn't want to say it aloud. "We're going to bury Alastor soon," he said, diverting the subject. "We're going to make sure it's safe out there. We'll mourn him tonight before we leave."

They were obviously waiting for Jackson to reply, but when he didn't, Tokala nodded and walked off.

Ethan sighed quietly. "See? No one blames you, Jack."

"Whatever," Jackson muttered as he lay down and rested his head on his paws.

"And there's also the fact that you're totally new to this," Ethan added. "You didn't even know that you were a demon until like…what? A little over a week ago. How the hell were you supposed to know how to turn someone into one?"

"It doesn't matter," Jackson grumbled. "I should be learning how to do demon stuff, but I'm not—"

"You *are*," Julian told him. "You learned to use the amulet, you found your demon form, and you're gonna learn to control it all better, right? That's one of the reasons Sebastien is here."

Jackson shook his head and then moved his paw over his eyes. "I just...wanna be alone right now," he murmured.

"Are you sure that's a good idea?" Ethan questioned. "You know...you tend to overthink when you're by yourself."

"We can talk about something else," Julian offered.

But Jackson didn't want to change the subject. He didn't want to act like none of what happened didn't matter. "No," he replied. "Leave me alone...please."

They went quiet for a moment, and Jackson was sure that they were trying to figure out what to do.

Ethan sighed and said, "All right. We'll be over there if you need us."

Jackson listened to them get up and leave, and once he was alone, he curled up and lay with his back to the pack. He hadn't had the inimă long, nor had he had much time to learn about the things he could do as a demon. Maybe he should have fought against Lord Caedis' decision to have him train out in the field with Sebastien rather than at the Venaticus with Heir Lucian. Perhaps he should have argued that it wasn't a good idea for them to hurry into this. But...there they were...out in the field again while he had no idea what he was doing.

He turned his head and set his eyes on Wesley, who was still crying by Alastor's body. Why did his blood make Alastor turn faster? He didn't understand, and the more he thought about it, the more confused he felt.

And that wasn't the only thing he was confounded by. He told that prowler to stop...and it *did*. It understood him, it halted when he commanded it, and Jackson wondered...could he tell cadejo what to do? Would they listen to him? If he'd known that before now, he could have prevented what happened to Alastor. But the sad, discouraging truth was that *no one* knew what he was capable of as a hybrid. No one could tell him these things. He just had to figure it all out for himself.

Chapter Twenty-Nine

⌐ ≼ ☽ ≽ ⌐

Doctor's Orders

| **Daimon** |

Daimon dragged his hands over his face and stared at the ground. Someone else was dead because of *him*. He should have been more cautious—maybe he should have just found another way for them to get back on track instead of crossing that river. And the fact that he couldn't even handle that prowler by himself made him feel worse.

He looked around at everyone. For a moment, he wondered if one of them would follow in Caius' footsteps and challenge him.

"Well, you're right, chief," Tokala said, appearing beside him.

Daimon glanced up at the orange-haired man.

"Kid's blaming himself."

The Alpha set his eyes on Jackson. "This isn't his fault in any way whatsoever."

"Yeah…and it isn't yours, either."

He frowned and looked at his Zeta, who sat beside him.

"Permission to speak candidly, Alpha?"

Daimon nodded.

"I've known you a long time; we grew up together. You've confided in me a lot, and I know when you're overthinking. True, our friendship drifted a little as we went our separate paths in the pack, but I still know you," Tokala said quietly. "I saw you out there…after releasing Alastor."

The Alpha huffed and looked away. He wasn't about to pour his feelings out to one of his subordinates, especially when he had no idea what to do about any of it.

"It wasn't your fault; it wasn't Jackson's fault—it wasn't *anyone's* fault. No one blames anyone," Tokala said firmly.

Daimon turned his head to look at the Zeta again. It was true that he and Tokala were a lot closer back when they lived in the packhouse, and since leaving, they'd drifted. Daimon drifted from *everyone*…but that was just one of the many burdens of leadership, another being that he had the responsibility of making the right calls, and when he made a wrong one…the people who trusted him suffered.

He sighed deeply and rested his back against the wall. For a moment, he let himself seek the advice of someone who had once been his closest friend. "What if Alaric made a mistake?"

Tokala frowned at him. "What?"

"I couldn't keep everyone together. Nyssa's out there somewhere with Romulus because I chose Jackson over her—over my own brother's mate. And now Alastor is dead because I chose to cross that river. If Alaric were here, everyone would still be together—"

"I'm sorry, chief, but…there's no way you can know that. And I'll say this again because it's true: no one blames you for any of that. You had every right to choose Jackson; he's your mate, and Nyssa destroyed your bond when she decided to start sneaking around with Caius. Everyone understands," Tokala said sympathetically. "And I mean…chief, we're out here seeking something that might cure the cadejo virus, something none of us would have ever thought possible. We all knew the risks, but we all came with you anyway. You're our Alpha, we trust you, and wherever you go and whatever you choose, we're with you."

Daimon sighed again and stared at the burrow ceiling. "Ever since Nyssa left with half of the pack, I've just been feeling a lot unlike myself."

Tokala nodded as he rested his arm on his knee. "Of course you'd feel like that. Everything changed, like…immensely, chief. You lost Nyssa and your sons, you lost half the pack, and you found your mate. And then we were all evicted from the place we thought we'd call home. But you handled it all very well. And even *now*, what you're doing is for the better of all of us—hell, not just us, but *all* wolf walkers. The world, even. Alaric wasn't wrong when he made you our leader."

Did everyone really think that highly of him despite everything that happened to prove otherwise? Did no one think that they might have been better off with Nyssa? Wasn't there a single wolf that regretted leaving the safety of the Venaticus building?

"We've all got your back, chief," Tokala assured him. "And you know…I *am* here if you ever need to talk. I mean, it's sort of my job, right?" he asked with a smirk.

Daimon laughed quietly and dragged his hand over his head. "Thank you, Tokala."

The orange-haired man nodded and got up. Then, he walked off and joined Remus, who was sitting with Brando, Bly, and Lance.

Daimon huffed and exhaled deeply. Tokala was right; the pack trusted him, and he couldn't let them down. They were out here to find a way to stop the cadejo virus, and *that* was what he was going to do. Alastor didn't die in vain, either, and Daimon would make sure that everyone knew that. He took a deep breath and banished as much of his uncertainty as he could. They still had a long way to go, and Alastor needed to be buried. His pack deserved to mourn him properly. "Everyone," he said as he stood up.

They turned their heads and stared at him.

"Alastor deserves a proper burial, and I'm going to make it my personal mission to ensure that he and everyone else we have lost will not be forgotten. What we're out here doing is for the benefit of every wolf walker, and we'll fight on to ensure that no one else has to suffer the same fate as our packmate," the Alpha called sternly. "Alastor was a brave, resilient fighter, and without him, not one of us would be who we are today. But above that, he was a friend—he was family—and we will all carry his memory with us."

Everyone responded with their words of agreement.

Daimon looked at Sebastien, who was no longer in his hound form. "Will you carry Alastor outside so that we can bury him, please?"

Sebastien nodded and shifted, but when he tried to get Alastor's body on his back with the help of Tokala and Brando, Wesley snarled defensively at them.

"Leave him alone!" the Epsilon warned, glaring at the pack as they grouped behind Sebastien.

"We have to bury him, Wesley," Tokala said softly.

"No!" he shouted, standing protectively over his friend's body.

"Wesley..." Bly said, taking a step closer to him. "For him to join his ancestors, we need to give him a burial. Otherwise, he'll remain trapped in that body forever."

"Come on, Wesley," Rachel said as she cautiously approached.

Wesley frowned hesitantly, but when Rachel began escorting him away from Alastor's body, he didn't fight and let Tokala and Brando lift his friend's body onto Sebastien's back.

Daimon felt his heart aching when he watched Wesley whine while his friend was carried outside. He instinctually searched the burrow for Jackson, who he knew would comfort him.

His mate was still lying at the back of the burrow, hiding his face beneath his paws.

The Alpha frowned worriedly and headed over to him. "Jackson?"

Jackson didn't respond.

Daimon sat beside him and gently placed his hand on the tawny-brown wolf's head. "Listen to me," he said quietly. "What happened out there wasn't your fault, okay? No one—"

"It *was*, though," Jackson replied sullenly, his voice muffled beneath his paws. "I could have stopped it if I got the amulet faster."

"The prowler bit Alastor before you could have done anything. But what you *did* do was prevent it from killing anyone else," Daimon told him, massaging his head. "You saved us, okay? And I know Alastor wouldn't take back giving his life for everyone else's."

Jackson lifted his head and stared at Daimon with a look of anguish on his face. "If I moved faster than I did, if Rachel had just given me the damn inimă, then Alastor would still be here!" he insisted.

"Jackson," Daimon said firmly.

He folded his ears behind his head and looked away.

"You saved us, okay? You killed that prowler," the Alpha told him softly, trying to assure him. "If it weren't for you, then…maybe none of us would be here," he admitted.

Jackson frowned in confusion.

"I…don't know why—maybe it's because I'm still healing from my injury—but I couldn't stop that thing," Daimon mumbled. "If *I* hadn't needed help, then…." But he stopped, sighed, and shook his head. He couldn't let himself sink into doubt. "Jackson, believe me when I say that you're just as much of an asset to this pack as everyone else. Stop blaming yourself for things that are out of your control."

With a despondent pout, Jackson lowered his head. "Maybe I should have fought harder when Lord Caedis changed his mind about me training with Heir Lucian."

"Sebastien is supposed to be teaching you to use your demon ethos, isn't he?" Daimon asked with a frown.

"Yeah, and…I guess there just hasn't been time. And I keep thinking that if I knew how to do all this demon stuff, then maybe I could have done more. Maybe I can *do* more," he said, lifting his head to look at Daimon's face. "Maybe I could have killed that prowler without needing the inimă. Maybe I could have saved Alastor with my blood."

"Jackson, killing that prowler wasn't your responsibility. Stop being so hard on yourself."

He shrugged and hid his face again.

Daimon moved his hands to either side of Jackson's furred face and made him lift his head so that they were at eye level. Then, he gazed into his mate's eyes. "Nobody expects you to suddenly be this powerful, unstoppable force because you're a hybrid. All of this is still new to you, and everyone understands that. It's going to take time for you to learn to use and control your new power, both demon *and* wolf walker."

Jackson shrugged again and murmured, "I guess."

"This isn't all on your shoulders, okay?"

With a slight nod, he mumbled, "Okay."

"I'll talk to Sebastien about teaching you more frequently. Now that Riker's hunters are gone, there's one less threat for us to worry about. The cadejo are still out there, though—they always will be—so I'll ensure everyone is on watch while you learn."

Jackson nodded. "Thank you."

Daimon then exhaled and said, "We're going to bury and mourn Alastor. After that, I'll talk to Sebastien."

"Okay. And...thanks for...well, everything," he mumbled.

The Alpha smiled and stood up. "Come on."

Jackson shifted out of his wolf form as he stood up, and then he followed Daimon towards the burrow exit.

Daimon hoped that he'd convinced Jackson that none of this was his fault, and he also tried his best to remember what Tokala told *him*. His pack needed and trusted him, and he couldn't fall victim to his self-doubt right now. He had to be strong—he had to be their Alpha—and accept that Alastor's death wasn't his fault.

But he wouldn't forget how he couldn't face that prowler alone. His strength had failed him, and he needed to make sure it didn't happen again. He headed outside with his pack, and while they got to work digging a grave for Alastor, he told Jackson to wait where he was and then headed over to Sebastien.

"If you're gonna tell me to help them dig, I'm gonna pass," the hound said, glancing at him. "Sorry, I'm just not a digging holes kinda—"

"Can I speak with the surgeon who operated on me?" Daimon asked him.

"Uh...Sinclair?"

"Yes."

"Well...why?"

"There are things I need to ask him that I didn't have the chance to when we were still with the Venaticus," Daimon answered.

Sebastien frowned unsurely, but after a few moments, he sighed and said, "I don't see why not...unless he's busy."

"Check."

The hound nodded and got up. As Daimon followed, he headed back into the burrow, shifted into his human form, and pulled the mirror he'd been talking into before from his bag.

Daimon sat beside him and leaned against the wall, watching as Sebastien activated the mirror's rune, and after flickering, it revealed an office on the other side...like looking through a window.

Footsteps echoed through the mirror, and after a few moments, a uniformed woman appeared in front of it. "Yes, Officer Huxley?"

"Is Doctor Laurent available?" Sebastien asked her.

She started typing on her laptop. "Um...he's scheduled for surgery in thirty minutes. I think he's in the canteen."

"Can you put him on for me, please?"

"Of course. There *should* be a demon around him to connect him. One moment."

The mirror went black.

"What's happening?" Daimon asked.

"It's kinda like…when you phone a place and they put you on hold so they can transfer you. You know what I mean?"

Daimon frowned at him. "No."

Sebastien scoffed. "Yeah…why would you?"

The mirror flickered again, and this time, it revealed the blonde doctor sitting in what must be his office.

"Hello?" Sinclair asked.

Sebastien handed the mirror to Daimon. "He said he needs to talk to you."

"Oh, hey Daimon. How have you been doing?" the doctor asked.

The Alpha tried to figure out how to word his concern. He glanced over the small mirror to make sure that everyone was still outside and then shot an uncomfortable glare at Sebastien.

"I'll…be outside," the white-haired demon said; he got up and walked off.

Daimon sighed and looked at Sinclair, who was eating his salad while waiting for him to speak. "I've noticed that I haven't exactly…been myself since my injury. I struggled against an opponent that I once before defeated without so much difficulty."

"Well, you're still in the recovery process, so that's understandable. My advice would be to keep taking your medication and take it as easy as you can."

He shook his head in frustration. "How long am I going to feel like this? I lost one of my wolves today because I couldn't fight with my full strength. I can't let that happen again."

Sinclair calmly explained, "It varies from person to person, so I can't really guarantee a certain timeframe. But if you keep pushing yourself to your body's limits, that's not going to help."

Daimon dragged his free hand over his face. "I've seen wolves recover from far worse injuries than a knife in their back. Why—"

"It severed your nerves, Daimon. Even for a wolf walker, that's a serious injury—one that someone who isn't as strong as you might not have come back from," he told him firmly. "I know it's frustrating, but there isn't much else either of us can do. You need to take your antibiotics and avoid as much physical combat as possible, just until you finish the medication."

He was beginning to feel more angry than frustrated. "Why do I need antibiotics? The wound healed."

"Because you had foreign objects in your body. Wolf walkers might heal at an alarming rate, but your bodies aren't so great at fighting off everything else that comes with a wound like that while it's busy using all its energy to keep you alive. You're lucky it didn't leave a permanent scar."

Daimon huffed irritably.

"I'm sorry that I couldn't be of more help, but that's just the way it is, unfortunately. Do you have any other questions? I don't have much more time."

The Alpha grunted irritably and shook his head. He had his answer. All he could do was take his medicine and try to refrain from pushing himself. But how could he do that with the cadejo out there? His pack were bound to need him; was he supposed to just stand around and hope someone else could protect them for him?

No. He wasn't going to put them at risk. If he had to fight, then he would fight. And when he *could* rest…he'd rest. But he wouldn't actively avoid fights. He wasn't going to lose anyone else.

"Thanks for your time," he said to Sinclair.

"Take it easy," the doctor told him. "If you aren't feeling like your normal self once you've finished the antibiotics—and I haven't seen you before then—you can contact me again."

Daimon nodded and watched as Sinclair handed the mirror to the blonde woman. Then, the mirror faded black…and returned to showing his reflection moments later.

He huffed and rested his arms on his knees. But he wasn't going to sit around and overthink. There wasn't anything else he could do. Right now, he needed to be with his pack and mourn Alastor.

And once he had time to process everything, he'd figure out what to do next.

Chapter Thirty

Burial

| Jackson |

As Brando, Tokala, Ezhno, and Lalo lowered Alastor's body into the ground, Jackson tried his best to keep it together. His heart was aching with guilt, but he attempted to focus on what Daimon told him. This wasn't his fault...and no one blamed him. He took a deep breath and listened to the pack speak.

Everyone simultaneously said, "As we commit our fallen packmate to the ground, we plead to the Moon Goddess: take Alastor of the Ash Mountain Pack into the Eternal Night. Let him join his ancestors, let his ethos be returned to the world it was born from, and let him live on in your embrace." Then, they all began howling.

"Is this a like...born wolves-only thing?" Ethan whispered from beside Jackson.

Jackson, Ethan, Sebastien, and Julian were all sitting on the same log pile in their human forms, watching the burial.

"From what I know, there are several original wolf walker *tribes* out here," Sebastien said. "They're typically all born into the pack and come from the older bloodlines, so...yeah. They have different traditions and practices than other packs might, but like his ancestor, your Alpha is changing things up—for the better, I might add. I might not be a wolf walker, but I always hated seeing how Omegas were treated."

"Tell me about it," Julian grumbled.

The pack stopped howling. They shifted into their human forms and began taking the scissors from the small medical kits in each of their bags.

"What are they doing now?" Ethan questioned.

Jackson frowned curiously when he saw Daimon begin cutting his hair, and everyone else quickly did the same.

"I've seen Kane do this," Julian said quietly. "It's like...their hair is a physical manifestation of their spirit. Cutting it and stuff has a very strong meaning, and they bury it with their fallen loved ones."

That made Jackson's despondency grow. The fact that no one had hair longer than a few inches—even when he first arrived—proved that they were always losing their packmates. And now was evidently the first time in a while that they got to spend mourning. Every other time someone died, they had to run.

Once everyone finished cutting their hair, they placed it into Alastor's grave. Then, they backed off, giving Wesley space to approach his friend.

As Wesley placed his severed hair into the grave, he sniffled sullenly and scowled in dismay. "You were my best friend," he uttered, his voice breaking. "You were like a brother to me, and I'll never forget you and everything we did. I wouldn't be here without you, and now…now I don't really know what I'm supposed to do," he said with a painful laugh, lifting his teary face towards the sky. "I don't know what to do."

"It's okay, Wesley," Bly said softly, moving closer to him. "We're all here for you."

Wesley inhaled through his stuffy nose and wiped the tears from his face as he looked back down at Alastor. "I'm gonna miss you so much, man. I know we argued and didn't see eye to eye on everything, but at the end of every day, we could still laugh and make each other forget for a little while that we weren't in the middle of a shitstorm."

Everyone laughed with Wesley but fell silent when he did.

"I love you, man," Wesley said through his tears.

"May the Moon Goddess embrace him," Daimon said.

And the pack replied, "May the Moon Goddess embrace him."

The pack began returning the earth to Alastor's grave, burying him.

"Can we help?" Jackson asked, looking at Julian.

"I don't know," they answered. "When Kane buried people, the only ones he allowed to take part were those from his original pack…or tribe. Everyone else that he recruited or turned couldn't even be within a hundred feet of the ceremony."

Jackson wasn't going to intrude or do something to offend the pack, so he stayed where he was. He wanted to help, but if he wasn't supposed to, then he wouldn't.

"I feel so bad for Wesley," Julian mumbled. "Those two were super close, from what I could tell."

"Yeah," Jackson replied sadly.

"At least he has the pack, though…right?" Ethan said, looking at them both. "If I lost someone that close to me and I was all alone, I'd go crazy."

Sebastien grunted quietly. "Been in his position. It fucking sucks."

Jackson knew how it felt to lose someone he loved, and he wasn't about to let the memory of that pain consume him. "Do demons have burial traditions?" he asked Sebastien.

The white-haired man nodded. "Yeah, uh…a lot. Different kinds for different demons. Though the saddest is probably a mate burial."

"What happens?" Julian asked.

Sebastien took a deep breath. "Well, in most cases where a demon has lived with their mate for a long time, losing them is like losing a huge part of themselves. Demons have this like... internal instinct to search for their mate the moment they reach maturity, and they don't stop until they find them. *That's* when their real life begins. So... it's like dying, and they treat it as such. They'll kill themselves so that they can join their mate in whatever waits for demons after death."

"Sounds a little cultish," Ethan muttered.

"I think it's... romantic in a way," Julian said. "I mean... a part of them is literally dying when their mate dies. Living without them would be like living without half of their body and being, right?"

"Precisely," Sebastien said with a nod. "The only reason I didn't kill *my*self when my mate died was because I knew I could get him back. And I did."

Ethan turned to face him. "So, like... this whole whatever we want thing from Caedis is legit? He'll literally give us whatever the hell we want once we get this mission done with?"

Jackson felt both curious and skeptical. What could Ethan want that was only obtainable through a god?

"Yup," Sebastien confirmed. "I admit, I was a little suspicious at first; the guy pulled a bunch of loopholes from our contract, but that was mostly my fault for not reading it. He lived up to his end of the deal, so." He then adorned an intrigued expression. "Why? What are you thinking?"

"My parents," Ethan answered with a shrug. He dragged his hand through his light brown hair and mumbled, "They were taken from me. I don't know if they're dead or alive, but I know that El'Vorian took them. A part of me was hoping I'd find something out at this lab; that was part of the reason I was looking into this stuff in the first place."

Jackson felt awful about already knowing what Ethan was sharing, but he'd do his best to act like this was all new information. He moved his arm around his friend to try and comfort him.

"And if they're not at the lab?" Sebastien asked.

"Then maybe I can ask Caedis to find them or something."

"I was kinda thinking of asking for the same thing," Jackson mumbled. "I wanna know the truth about what happened to my parents."

"Yeah, I always thought it was bullshit about the car crash," Ethan said. "Why is it always a car crash? Like... even in the movies and shit the stepparents or guardians or whatever *always* say their parents died in a car crash when it was actually some huge conspiracy or something."

Sebastien laughed quietly. "You're not wrong. Maybe because it's easier to say they got drunk and lost control of a vehicle."

"Yeah, but what if they don't drink?" Julian questioned.

"I don't know," Ethan said with a sigh. "Blame it on some other drunk driver."

"You wanna know what the Nosferatu said happened to my family when they shut down Aldergrove Academy?" Sebastien asked everyone with an amused tone.

They all looked at him and waited.

"Gas leak."

"Gas leak?" Jackson scoffed.

"Come on, man," Ethan snickered.

Jackson then slapped his friend's arm. Sebastien might be smiling about it, but that could mean he was trying to hide his pain. That was his *family*.

"Nah, it's all right," Sebastien said to Jackson. "My family were a literal cult. Yeah, it sucks being the last of my kind, but I'd rather that than sit around knowing the rest of my kind are feeding teens to a hungry spirit."

Julian then asked, "So…they set the place on fire?"

"Only way to banish a phantom like that for good," the white-haired demon said with a nod. "I didn't even know it was possible until Lord Caedis proved me wrong. It was this super long, super draining ritual, but it was pretty cool to watch. Lord Caedis can do a whole bunch of cool shit, ain't gonna lie. Bringing back dead people isn't even the half of it."

"You're always talking about him, but what about the Zenith?" Julian asked quizzically. "He comes up in wolf walker stories sometimes—he's even in some of the old paintings and books with Caedis—but we haven't met him or seen him or anything."

Sebastien laughed nervously and scratched the side of his face. "Honestly, you should be glad that you got to the Venaticus when Lord Caedis was there. If the Zenith was there…well, let's just say things would have gone a whole different way."

"Why?" Ethan questioned.

"The Zenith is just less understanding…or tolerable of certain behaviour, I guess. A lot of people see Lord Caedis as the nicer one of the two," Sebastien explained, resting his arms on his knees.

Was this a good time for Jackson to ask his questions? They were already on the subject of the Zenith, Lord Caedis, and the Nosferatu. "So, when I was with Doctor Kowalski, he said that asmodi would like…need blood two or three times a week," he started, looking at Sebastien.

"Uh-huh," the white-haired demon mumbled.

"So…what happens if I don't get blood?"

Sebastien exhaled and shook his head. "Not pretty," he drawled. "If you don't feed, your body will kinda like…let instinct take over to keep you alive. And if you're starving because you're too weak or something, your body does this kind of last-stand thing. I've…seen it happen. A lot of demons have little ethos reserves for when they direly need it, such as if they're starving. That reserve will activate and give you a sort of burst of energy, enough to find something to feed on."

"Kinda like vampires?" Julian asked.

"Yeah, the older ones," Sebastien confirmed.

Ethan chuckled nervously. "Well, uh…we better make sure you get your blood, then."

"Can it be any blood?" Jackson asked.

Sebastien nodded. "As long as it's from something that's alive, yeah."

Jackson's next question came before he had time to process the answer to the first. "So…since I'm a wolf walker *and* a demon, does that mean I heal faster than both? I have a tolerance for silver because of the demon in me, right?"

"I don't think so, no," Sebastien said, tapping his chin. "Being a hybrid doesn't add one species' power on top of the other. Hell, in some cases, a hybrid can be weaker than the two species it's a part of."

"So…Jackson's weaker or what?" Ethan urged.

"From what I've seen, no. See, Lord Caedis and the Zenith designed asmodi demons to be without *their* flaws. Wolf walkers and vampires are deadly to one another—"

"Vampires?" Julian interjected.

"Yeah. Lord Caedis is the creator of vampires. Keep up," Sebastien muttered. "Uh…yeah, deadly. So, they made asmodi without that weakness. Therefore, you don't get any weaknesses from that combo. As for healing faster and stuff, that's where things get a little more scientific."

Jackson frowned curiously.

"Someone can't…increase their total ethos capacity," Sebastien started, glancing at each of them. "It's, uh…." He sighed frustratedly and groaned. "Clem is so much better at explaining this kinda shit." He held out his hands and said, "Okay, so, as a demon, let's say you have forty copias—that's the unit of measurement for ethos—and the average wolf walker has thirty. When you became a hybrid, your copias didn't jump to seventy. You still have forty demon copias, but you *also* have thirty wolf walker copias."

Ethan hummed curiously. "So, he's got *two* different types of ethos, and he…what? Can't use both at the same time?"

"Exactly," Sebastien said. "So, your healing abilities won't increase. Your body will automatically select which ethos to use to heal a wound. Demons can regenerate limbs, wolf walkers cannot. So, if you lost an arm or something, your *demon* ethos would kick in and heal it. What's also really cool is that demons heal a lot slower from wounds inflicted by other demons, but if *you* were beaten up by another demon, your wolf walker ethos could heal it like that," he said, clicking his fingers.

"Huh…pretty cool," Julian said.

"Well, if I plan on getting beaten up by demons, at least I know I'll heal," Jackson uttered. "How long is it gonna take me to learn to control my demon stuff?" he then asked. "Am I always gonna need the inimă?"

"The inimă is just a tool, Jackson," Sebastien told him. "You don't *need* it to use your demon ethos. And as for how long it's gonna take, I can't really say. Demon children usually begin learning to use their ethos once they're three, which is like…a year and a half in human years. Demons grow twice as fast when they're young. Once they're four or five, though, they start ageing like humans."

"So, what you're saying is that Jackson's fucked because he didn't learn when he was a toddler?" Ethan questioned.

Sebastien shrugged and answered, "Truthfully, it isn't going to be easy. The idea is to start learning when your proselytus grows beyond a form of protection. It's why demon babies grow faster; survival and all that. Their ethos essentially has a mind of its own for the first year and a half so that it can protect the baby, and once the ethos settles and becomes part of the demon, they can start learning to control and use it. *But* from what I've seen, you've been picking shit up real fast," he assured Jackson. "And the inimă is definitely going to help you learn quicker. Once you've got a grip on your own power, though, the inimă can go back to being a tool."

"Right," Jackson mumbled.

"Your Alpha said something about getting a few hours of training in before we leave," the white-haired demon then said. "Once the funeral is over, we can get started on a few basics, if you want. Fire, speed, and strength. That sorta thing."

"Fire?" Julian squealed. "That's so cool!"

"Just don't set the forest on fire, huh?" Ethan said with a smirk, nudging Jackson's arm.

Jackson smiled amusedly in response, but he was quickly becoming overwhelmed with excitement and relief. He was going to begin learning *soon*, and he was eager to get started. The quicker he learned to use his demon ethos, then the quicker he'd be more of an asset to the pack. He wanted to be able to prevent anyone else from getting hurt, and he'd do whatever he had to.

"It's gonna be tough, though," Sebastien said, patting Jackson's shoulder. "Might even hurt a little."

"That's fine," Jackson said confidently. "I'll do whatever it takes."

"Good," he replied. "Keep hold of that positive attitude. You're gonna need it." He got up and said, "I'm gonna go let Clem know I'm safe, and then we can get started."

"All right," Jackson said, watching him head into the burrow. Then, he set his eyes back on the pack and watched them as they continued burying Alastor.

Julian nudged Jackson's shoulder.

He glanced at them. "What?"

"Have you uh…got any more like…suspects?" they asked.

Jackson shook his head. He hadn't had much time to think about it, but even if he had, he wasn't sure whether he'd have any new suspicions, and a part of him was beginning to wonder if Daimon was right. What if there *wasn't* someone trying to kill him? What if that knife really had just impaled his back accidentally?

He didn't want to believe it. The feeling that someone had done it was *too* strong to dismiss. He needed to get to know the pack more; he needed to watch them, he needed to search for even the smallest signs that someone might have attempted to kill their Alpha. And sooner or later, he'd find out who did it.

Chapter Thirty-One

Fire

| **Jackson** |

Jackson stood twenty feet away from Sebastien, his heart racing in his chest. He was nervous enough that he was about to start learning to use fire ethos, but the fact that several packmates were watching made it worse.

"You gotta find it," Sebastien called. "Just like when you found your wolf and your demon. Search inside yourself. It's there."

With a deep breath, Jackson closed his eyes and concentrated. He had to find his fire ethos, so he reached inside, focusing on the idea of fire. The burning warmth, the bright flickering, and the ashy smell. And then he clenched his fist, trying to push his ethos into his palm.

Nothing.

He sighed and let his arms dangle at his sides. "What am I doing wrong?"

"It takes time, Jackson," Sebastien told him. "We don't know what fire type you possess. It'd be so much simpler if we did."

"Can we find out?" Ethan called.

"Only by knowing what types his parents had," the white-haired demon replied. "Do you remember anything about them? A colour or smell could narrow it down."

Jackson frowned, but everything about his parents was a blur. "I don't know, I…" he mumbled, but then something came to him. He *did* remember the night those masked men came into his nursery. Silver and crimson lights. "I remember silver and red flashes in the hall."

"Crimson flames come from Lord Caedis' bloodline," Sebastien said. "Demons usually inherit more of their father's abilities and traits than their mother's. So, there's a high chance you have crimson flames."

"Okay, so…do I think about red fire?" Jackson asked unsurely.

"No. You think about fire that burns something into nothing. Lord Caedis can create hellfire."

"Like *actual* hellfire?" Ethan asked.

"From hell?" Julian added.

Sebastien sighed. "That's literally why it's called hellfire."

"And what does the Zenith create?" Tokala called curiously.

"It purges," Sebastien said. "It can burn rock and metal, and it burns the literal life out of someone. Their life force and ethos; some people say he can burn someone's soul out."

"Damn…" Julian drawled.

"Could Jackson have both?" Remus suddenly asked.

Jackson looked over his shoulder to see both Remus and Daimon watching.

"No," Sebastien answered. "The only people who do are Lord Caedis' and the Zenith's children."

"*Children*?" Julian questioned. "They have more than one?"

"We're getting off track," the white-haired demon said. "Think about burning something until it's nothing, not even ash. Think of fire that burns until there's no trace of it. Red fire. It smells of sulphur, burning roses, and a kind of sweet ash."

Jackson closed his eyes. "Okay," he mumbled, attempting to concentrate. He connected with his ethos and focussed on the things Sebastien told him. And when he felt his hand warm up, he opened his eyes and gawped at the simmering red flames hovering an inch from his palm. Everyone who was watching gasped or cheered, and Jackson felt excitement and relief.

"Now concentrate," Sebastien instructed. "Keep it contained to your hand."

Jackson frowned and held his hand in front of him.

"Yeah, don't set us all on fire," Ethan laughed.

"Now," Sebastien drawled, "slowly close your hand and extinguish the fire. And remember, what you're thinking matters *a lot*."

As he was told, Jackson gradually clenched his fist while thinking about putting the flame out. And to his relief, when he clamped his fist shut, the fire vanished.

"Good," Sebastien said.

Jackson smiled and asked Sebastien, "Can I ask you something?"

"Sure."

"When I talked to Daimon, he said there are demons who choose to disregard the Zenith's laws. Are those traitor demons or something?"

Sebastien sighed and leaned against a tree. "Some demons want to return to the times when there was no Caeleste government. The Diabolus are one such group of people. Except they don't want it to be every demon for himself; the Diabolus want the control that the Zenith and Lord Caedis spent hundreds of years *earning*. The Diabolus want control of all demons to use them to assume control of *everyone*."

"The existence of the Diabolus dates back hundreds of years, though," Ethan called. "Have they been at war with the Nosferatu for *that* long?"

"On and off. At first, the Diabolus were a group that served Lucifer; their purpose was to find Lord Caedis and return him to his father. Now, their purpose is to try and take everything from the Nosferatu," the white-haired demon explained.

"But why?" Daimon asked. "Isn't there more to it than them simply wanting control over the Caeleste world?"

Sebastien replied, "We have theories. The Diabolus have been trying to find a way to resurrect their old God for centuries; they're convinced that they can pull him out of Lord Caedis' soul. All of this might be to cut down the Nosferatu's defences so that they can get to Lord Caedis. The wolf walker-demon hybrids would speed that process up, so it all kinda makes sense."

"Well, now it's kinda looking like we're out here to help save the entire Caeleste world," Julian mumbled.

"This is just one of many parts of doing that, yeah," Sebastien said. He set his sights on Jackson again. "Ready for step two?"

Jackson cleared his throat and said, "Yeah."

Just then, Enola, Ezhno, Lalo, and Lance walked over.

"We're ready to go hunt, chief," Lalo said.

"All right, be careful," the Alpha said.

Jackson watched the four of them head into the trees.

"Hey," Sebastien snapped, clicking his fingers.

"Sorry," Jackson said, looking at him.

"Now you're gonna try and throw the fire, kinda like how I do."

"Okay, so...throw it...like it's any other ball?"

"Exactly. Just make sure to tell your ethos what you want to do with it."

Jackson held out his palm. "Okay," he said and focused like before, and to his relief, a ball of red flames appeared above his palm. Although he'd already done it, it surprised him and brought a proud smile to his face. But he had far to go before he could let himself think that he was anywhere close to being like other demons.

He concentrated and slowly closed his fingers. But he stopped before his fingertips touched the fire.

"You can touch the flames, Jackson," Sebastien said. "A lot of demons are resistant to their own fire type as well as normal fire."

With a nervous frown, he stared at the spiralling red flames and edged his fingertips closer. He wasn't sure what he'd been expecting when he touched the fire, but it wasn't the strange, *cold* sensation that caressed his skin the moment it came into contact with it.

"What does it feel like?" Julian asked curiously.

Jackson replied, "Like...I'm dipping my fingers in cold water."

"But it's fire," Ethan said with a frown.

"That's ethos you're feeling," Sebastien revealed. "You're feeling the energy in what you've created. Every ethos type has its own unique feeling."

Jackson gripped the fireball in his hand and looked at Sebastien. "Okay, so…where do I throw it? Isn't it going to burn whatever it touches into nothing?"

"The fire will only burn what you tell it to. So, start with something small," the white-haired demon instructed.

Jackson exhaled deeply and stared at the fireball. "Okay," he whispered and started looking for something to throw it at.

"What about that?" Brando suggested, lifting his paw towards a large boulder.

"Too far away," Sebastien said. "And Jackson doesn't know how to make the fire stick to something, so we don't want to risk it bouncing off and hitting someone."

Everyone murmured worriedly.

"Should we head into the burrow?" Remus asked.

"No," Daimon said. "Wesley wanted to be alone. No one goes in until he comes out. What if he throws it in the snow?"

"I wouldn't advise setting fire to the ground until Jackson has a good understanding of how to control and contain it. Maybe if we find an isolated tree," Sebastien said, glancing around.

"That one?" Tokala suggested, pointing at a dead tree not far from the burrow entrance.

Sebastien asked Jackson, "You up for it?"

He was nervous about losing control, but if he let that feeling consume him, then he'd *definitely* screw up. "Yeah."

"All right," Sebastien said, heading to the dead tree.

Jackson followed him.

"So, remember what I said," Sebastien said as he backed away from it. "Think about what you want to do as you do it."

"Right. Got it," he said, glancing at his crimson fireball. Then, he glared at the tree, which was the *only* thing he wanted to burn. He didn't want to catch the snow or any surrounding trees on fire.

"You got this, Jack," Ethan called.

He didn't want to overthink. All he had to do was throw the fire and send the tree up in flames. So, he threw the fireball, and when it hit the tree, he thought about how he wanted the flames to engulf only a few inches of the trunk, and that's exactly what happened.

"Nice," Sebastien drawled. "You're picking things up faster than I thought you would."

Jackson smiled triumphantly. Maybe this wouldn't be so hard after all. He'd be learning to reduce things to nothing in no time.

"Uh, Jackson," Sebastien suddenly stammered.

The flames spread up and down the tree, swallowing the whole thing in moments.

"Uh-oh," Ethan said.

Jackson backed off; his heart started racing as panic gripped him tightly. He'd lost his focus, and now everything that could go wrong was going wrong.

"Put it out!" Julian called worriedly.

Sebastien rushed to Jackson's side and grasped his arm. "Hold out your hand and call the fire back. It's your ethos, you tell it what to do. Now!"

"U-uh, okay," he said, nodding frantically. He held his hand towards the flaming tree, concentrated, and thought about the flames coming back to him and re-joining his ethos. And thankfully, the crimson fire began withering, and what was left oozed off the tree and raced back to Jackson's palm, forming a ball again.

Relieved sighs and murmurs came from the spectating crowd.

"*That's* why you *always* need to make sure you stay focused," Sebastien told him, patting his shoulder. "Fire can be difficult to control sometimes. It takes even the strongest demons years to master it."

"Sorry," Jackson said, lowering his hand as he clenched his fist, extinguishing the fireball. Then, he set his eyes on the tree. The entire thing was black and thinner than before, and if he'd left it burning much longer, he was sure that it would have disappeared.

"Take a break," Sebastien said. "We'll get back to it in ten minutes or so." Then, he headed over to a log and sat down.

Jackson wasn't sure whether he wanted to go and sit with Daimon or Ethan and Julian. The Alpha was with his son, though, and Jackson didn't want to interfere or barge into the conversation it looked like they were having. So, he headed over to his friends.

"I was kinda worried that you were gonna blow something up there for a moment," Ethan said with a smirk as Jackson sat on the same log as him and Julian.

"It was super cool, though," Julian said. "Once you learn to control fire like a pro, those cadejo won't stand a chance."

"I'm not sure which type of fire I'd want if I was a demon," Ethan pondered. "Like... burning something to nothing is cool, but burning someone's *soul* out?"

"Allegedly," Julian said.

"Uh... hey guys," came Dustu's voice.

They all looked behind them and saw the brown-haired Omega standing there like a shy schoolkid.

Jackson knew that the guy wasn't much of a talker, and he'd been even quieter since Aiyana died. And that made him wonder... was Dustu a suspect? Could he have tried to kill Daimon for what happened to Aiyana? Jackson wasn't sure that the guy had it in him, but he couldn't afford to underestimate anyone right now. He *did* need to get to know him a little more, though. That way, he might be able to decide whether or not the Omega might be guilty. So he said, "Hey Dustu," with an encouraging smile. "You wanna join us?"

Dustu nodded and walked to the log. Then, he sat next to Jackson and adorned a look of awe. "All that fire stuff was pretty neat."

"What would *you* rather have?" Ethan asked Dustu, leaning past Jackson so that he could see him. "Caedis' fire, or the Zenith's fire?"

Dustu frowned. "Uh… well, being able to burn someone's ethos out sounds really useful. I mean… that could pretty much render your opponent useless."

"Yeah, but burning them into nothing in a few seconds means you get to avoid a fight altogether," Julian said.

"Aren't there other fire ethos types, too?" Dustu asked curiously. "I mean… like Sebastien's blue fire."

Ethan waved at Sebastien. "Hey, Seb. Come here."

Sebastien frowned in what looked like hostility. "First," he said sternly, making his way over, "don't ever call me Seb. Second, what?"

"Sorry," Ethan muttered.

"How many fire ethos types are there?" Julian asked.

When he reached them, Sebastien leaned against another tree. "If I knew that, I'd probably be an *actual* teacher teaching in some demon academy somewhere."

"There are demon academies?" Dustu questioned.

"Yeah. There's schools out there for demons, lycans, witches… and some even welcome all Caeleste at once," the white-haired demon said with a nod. "As far as *I* know, though, there are maybe around… twelve or more types. That's how many I've seen in my hundred and fifty years, anyways. Lord Caedis', the Zenith's, mine, and then a few others. Basic fire, which is the kinda fire anyone can make if they have the right tools. I've seen *black* flames; now *that* is a fire ethos to be envious of. It's Numen ethos and usually forms in the trail that a Numen leaves behind when they're in their Numen form. I've seen Lord Caedis use it the odd time or so. Dangerous stuff. Drained the guy."

"What does it do?" Jackson asked.

"I don't know the full extent of it, but I saw him use it to banish someone."

"Banish?" Ethan asked.

"Yeah. Lord Caedis has access to some other realm that only people with his blood can travel to. I heard him call it The Darkness one time."

Julian shivered. "Yeah, that gives me a creepy feeling."

"What other kinds?" Dustu asked—no, he *insisted*.

Everyone frowned at him.

"Why are you so interested?" Sebastien asked him.

The guy shrugged and looked down at his lap. "I'm just curious."

Jackson glanced at Sebastien and nodded his head towards Dustu, trying to get him to answer his question. This was the most Dustu had ever talked in one sitting and Jackson didn't want something to shatter the confidence it must have taken him to come over. That…and he didn't want to lose the opportunity to examine the Omega. As of right now, he *was* acting a little suspicious. Why was he so interested in demon fire? But then again…there was no relation between demon fire and the attempt on Daimon's life.

Sebastien huffed quietly. "All right, well…gold fire is often used by healers. Some demons can heal other demons with it."

"What about…purple?" Dustu asked, gawping at him.

"Purple?" Sebastien repeated with a frown.

Jackson's curiosity increased. Why was Dustu asking? And why did it look like Sebastien was confused? Did he not know of purple fire?

"I just saw some once," Dustu mumbled. It looked like he was getting uncomfortable.

"Is it demon fire?" Jackson asked Sebastien, urging him to answer.

"Yeah, it is. It's just one of the rarer ones," the white-haired demon confirmed.

"What is it?" Ethan questioned.

"Purple fire is cursing ethos," Sebastien answered with a frown. "You saw someone getting cursed?"

Dustu's face had gone a little pale. "I didn't know it was a curse."

Jackson's frown thickened. "What was a curse? What happened?"

The brown-haired Omega looked at him with a sullen expression. "It was a long time ago. I was just a kid."

"Wait, did *you* get cursed?" Julian asked, wide-eyed.

He shook his head. "No, it…it happened way before Alpha Daimon's pack found me. It was just me, my parents, and my two sisters. We were doing okay out in the woods on our own; this was back when the cadejo weren't around—or at least…not out here. It was during the Long Night."

"The what?" Jackson asked.

"Long Night," Julian repeated. "There's this part of Ascela where the sun sets on Undecim eighteenth and doesn't rise again until Primis twenty-third. Two whole months of darkness."

"Woah," Jackson mumbled.

"So, what happened?" Ethan urged.

"A lot of crazy stuff would happen out there during the Long Night," Dustu continued, his tone becoming despondent. "You'd see cult activity and even more hunters because they were convinced that rare, special Caeleste appeared during that time. Usually, wolf walkers would have found somewhere to wait the two months out, but my family didn't find a place in time. We were seen by this group of fanatics—"

"Wait," Jackson interjected. "Fanatics.... I heard a guy mention that when I first got to Ascela."

Dustu nodded. "They're these...estranged people who live in the mountains. A lot of people think they're cultists and the reason they look all...I don't know, weird and dirty is because they don't come out of their caves until the Long Night. They *hunt* during that time."

"Shit," Ethan mumbled.

"We were running," Dustu continued, "but lost each other. I found some logs and waited for my family, but I saw purple flashes. I didn't know what it was, but I heard my sisters screaming. I was scared of the fanatics, but I wanted to help, so I ran towards the light. When I got there, though...they...." He scowled in dismay. "They were dead. There was purple fire burning their fur."

"Oh, damn," Ethan said sadly. "I'm sorry, man."

"Yeah, sorry," Julian said.

"I never knew what happened or why, and even now that I know it was curse ethos, I still have no idea what happened. Why would someone curse my family?" Dustu asked them, confused.

"People curse others just because they can, sadly," Sebastien answered. "There're two reasons people learn to manipulate curse ethos: one is so they can hurt every person they judge as deserving, and the other is so they can own and control someone. I've seen a fair amount of curses and nothing will ever make me think that curse ethos isn't evil."

"It *is* evil," Julian said.

"My family didn't do anything wrong," Dustu sniffled.

Sebastien sighed quietly and sat next to him. Then, he placed his hand on the Omega's shoulder. "One thing about people who use curse ethos is that they themselves are cursed. That kind of dark ethos *consumes* the user; that's probably why those crazy mountain people are called fanatics, right? They probably *yearn* for suffering just like any other curse user, and your parents...well, you understand, right? They didn't have to have done anything wrong for these people to have hurt them."

Dustu wiped his nose with the back of his hand and nodded.

"But they're with the Moon Goddess now," Julian said, trying to assure Dustu. "They're safe and free."

"Yeah," Dustu sniffled, wiping his nose again.

"I don't mean to be rude," Sebastien then said, glancing at them all. "But we're not gonna run into these fanatics out here, are we?"

"No," came Daimon's voice. "From what we know of them, they stick closely to settlements. They steal clothing and food from people when they need it." Then, he looked at Tokala. "Go and find the hunting party. A storm is coming."

Tokala nodded and shifted into his wolf form.

Jackson watched the orange wolf race deeper into the woods. But the longer he stared…the tenser he felt. His heart beat a little faster, and when a familiar feeling of trepidation ensnared him, he frowned anxiously.

He wasn't going to dismiss another feeling.

With a desperate huff, he flew off the log and raced over to Daimon. "Something's wrong," he blurted.

Daimon stood up. "What?"

"I-I have a feeling—a *feeling* feeling. W-when you sent Tokala, it hit really fast," he explained as quickly as he could.

It looked as though Daimon wasn't taking the risk of questioning another feeling, either. "Brando, Dustu, stay with Remus. Go into the burrow and tell Wesley and Bly that we're going after the hunting party. Do not leave the burrow until we get back."

"Dad," Remus insisted, tugging on Daimon's shirt. "Let me come."

"No, it's too dangerous for you. Go with Dustu and Brando."

Remus sighed and nodded, and while he followed Dustu and Brando into the burrow, everyone else quickly grouped up around Daimon.

"Listen up," Daimon called. "We're going after the hunting party. We have no idea what's out there or what could be waiting, but don't let your guard down. Let's go!" he instructed and shifted into his wolf form.

Everyone quickly shifted, and when they started following Daimon into the woods, Jackson frowned anxiously. He didn't know what his feeling was trying to tell him, but what he *did* know was that something was very wrong. Had something happened to the hunting party? Was something *going* to happen to them? He hoped that whatever it was, they got there before anyone got hurt.

Chapter Thirty-Two

⌐ ⋞ ☽ ⋟ ⌐

Hounds

| Jackson |

Jackson's heart raced in his chest. A thousand horrible thoughts raced around inside his head, and he couldn't fight them. What if the hunting party were *dead*? What if cadejo got them? What if there were still more of Riker's hunters out here? He scowled worriedly, racing behind Daimon between Ethan and Julian as the pack hurried deeper into the woods. What if they didn't get there in time?

"How far are they?" Jackson asked.

Daimon didn't answer. The concerned look on his face thickened, and he sped up.

Something was wrong.

Something was *really* wrong.

And then Jackson caught it—that scent. The scent that everyone seemed to catch, adorning the same terrified expression as their Alpha.

Blood.

Jackson's chest tightened, and his legs started trembling. But he had to fight it. He had to keep himself composed. He did his best to shove aside his anxiety and followed Daimon as he navigated the way through the thick forest. But when they passed a boulder...Jackson's heart dropped into his stomach.

There was blood and fur everywhere.

Ezhno, Lalo, and Lance lay bloodied and wounded in their human forms, and Enola—the only one still in their wolf form—lay by a tree with huge chunks of her fur missing, and the snow around her was red with blood.

"What the hell happened here?" Julian exclaimed.

Lalo suddenly coughed.

"Lalo!" Tokala called, hurrying over to him with Rachel.

Leon transformed into his human form to roll Lance onto his back and then started carefully pressing snow into his wounds.

Daimon and Julian went over to Enola, and Jackson slowly followed Ethan to Ezhno.

But Jackson's feeling of trepidation started to feel like a compass in his head. It wasn't pulling him to Ezhno. He turned his head and set his eyes on Enola; he watched Daimon nudge and try to wake her, and when both he and Julian adorned horrified stares, it felt like a knife was plunged through Jackson's heart.

"Enola?" Daimon insisted, nudging her neck with his muzzle.

"They... they came out of nowhere," Lance breathed.

"Who?" Leon questioned.

"En... Enola?" Lalo called weakly.

Jackson gawped at the unresponsive Enforcer. There was something strange about her. The look on Daimon's face made Jackson think that Enola was dead—it looked like everyone was waiting for Daimon to say the words—but her body... there was something wrong with it.

"Chief?" Tokala asked sullenly, stepping forward. "Is... is she... ?"

Daimon shook his head, backing off. "I... I don't under—"

"Get away from her," Sebastien barked.

"Why didn't she leave her wolf form like the others?" Ethan questioned. "Don't *all* lycans turn back into their human forms when they're knocked unconscious?"

Jackson could feel something else. Alongside his angst and dismay, there was a *warning*. His instincts started screaming, urging him to move away from Enola. And her ethos... he could feel it... changing. Enola was changing.

He didn't understand why he felt like this, but he wasn't going to ignore it. Jackson raced past Ethan and reached Daimon. "S-something's wrong with her!"

"Get the hell away from her!" Sebastien insisted.

Enola twitched.

Jackson, Daimon, and Julian stepped back.

"Enola?" Julian asked.

Daimon started backing off. "Don't make any sudden movements," he warned them quietly.

"W-what's going on?" Julian stammered.

Enola's body convulsed.

"Was she bit?" Ethan called, keeping his voice hushed.

"N-no... cadejo," Lalo grunted, leaning on Tokala.

Enola's eyes shot open. A distorted snarl oozed through her bloody teeth, and there was something so terribly wrong with her aura. Jackson couldn't feel her ethos anymore—in fact, as far as he could tell, there was *nothing* familiar about her. Her dark grey fur slowly became black, and as she gradually rose to her paws, clumps of her fur fell off her body, revealing rotting, dark skin beneath it.

"W-what the hell is she?!" Julian panicked, shivering beside Jackson as they both continued backing off with Daimon.

With a savage growl, Enola turned her mangled body to face the pack, who all grouped up behind Daimon. She jerked her head and trembled as her body cracked and squelched. Her skin tore, and dark smoke began oozing through her wounds.

"That's a hellhound," Sebastien said cautiously.

"A what?!" Lalo shrieked.

Enola widened her jaw *way* beyond the capability of any wolf, letting out a deafening, demonic roar. The snow at her paws started melting, and her eyes became empty, black pits.

Jackson had never seen anything like it, and he somehow knew that what was inside her was *demon*. Her aura was dark…twisted—like something evil. Something…wrong. And his instincts *begged* him to turn tail and flee.

Enola burst forward faster than any wolf.

Daimon moved to attack as his pack panicked, but Sebastien sprung past him and collided with the hellhound before it could reach them.

Sebastien and Enola rolled across the snow, and when the kludde managed to pin the hellhound, he looked at Daimon and yelled, "Get everyone out of here!"

"Let's go!" Daimon ordered.

The pack immediately turned around and followed their Alpha, but Jackson stayed where he was. He watched as Sebastien wrestled with the beast that was once Enola; he dug the spike on his wing carpal into the hellhound's side, but the creature didn't react—like it didn't feel pain. It smacked its pack into the side of Sebastien's muzzle, staggering him, and then it escaped from his grasp.

"Jackson!" Daimon shouted, appearing at his side. "What the fuck are you doing?! Move!"

Jackson watched the hellhound sink its teeth into Sebastien's neck. He stared, fighting the emotions racing around inside him. He was too late to save Enola; what was the point in this ability to sense things if he couldn't stop them? What was the point if he couldn't save anyone?

No…he *could* save someone. He could save Sebastien.

"Jackson!" Daimon insisted, trying to pull him away by his scruff.

But Jackson fought him off, and before Daimon could speak, he ran towards the fighting hounds.

"Jackson?!" Daimon yelled.

Jackson shifted into his human form, skidded to a halt, and held out his hand. A sizzling ball of red flames appeared above his palm, and then he waited, watching as Sebastien pulled out of the hellhound's grip and swung his wing around. But Enola dodged and sprung forward; she sunk her teeth into Sebastien's leg and tugged.

Sebastien whined, but when he spotted Jackson, they locked sights for a moment. Then, the kludde grunted and yanked his leg from the hound's jaws—

Jackson seized his chance and threw the fireball at it. Sebastien used his wings to propel himself up and out of the way, and as the beast attempted to jump and catch him, Jackson's crimson fire hit its side. Jackson focused all of his energy into the flames, remembering everything Sebastien taught him, and as he commanded, the fire ensnared the hellhound.

The creature yelped and shrieked, rolling around in the snow to try and extinguish the flames, but Jackson kept it burning. He wasn't going to let it hurt anyone—*no one* else was going to die.

He raised his hand, increasing the strength of his flames, and in a matter of moments, the wailing beast went silent, and its body started dissolving in the fire.

And then it was gone. Not a single trace remained, not even ash. Just as Sebastien said it would, Jackson's fire reduced something into absolutely nothing.

But it took its toll. The moment his fire was extinguished, Jackson felt a heavy weight fall on his shoulders. He dropped to his knees, breathing unsteadily as his heart raced, increasing the painful feeling of a knife through it with every thump. It was unlike anything he'd felt before…like he was having some sort of heart attack.

"Jackson!" Daimon's voice echoed inside his head. The Alpha appeared at his side and left his wolf form; he moved his hand to the side of Jackson's face and lifted his head so that he could see his face. "Are you okay?"

"Jackson?" Sebastien shouted. In his human form, he kneeled beside Daimon and stared at Jackson. "Take deep, slow breaths."

"What's happening to him?" Daimon demanded.

"He's not used to using that much ethos," the white-haired demon said.

Jackson tried to do as Sebastien said. He attempted to slow his breathing, but it *hurt*.

"Lay him down," Sebastien instructed.

Daimon helped Jackson lay on his back, and that helped him with his breathing control. His body didn't hurt so much anymore, and he was quickly recovering.

Sebastien then dragged his hand over his face. "Who would do this? It couldn't be cadejo or hunters."

Daimon didn't answer. He stared down at Jackson, holding his hand firmly.

"Is everyone okay?" Jackson asked him worriedly.

The Alpha nodded. "Tokala's taking them back to the burrow."

He took a deep breath and closed his eyes. "What…why did that happen to Enola?" he asked, looking at them both.

Daimon's vacant expression gave way to a despondent frown. "I've only ever heard stories about hellhounds," he said slowly. "Ever since the cadejo virus, I guess…I almost forgot. We were all so used to losing people to the undead that we forgot there's an even worse fate waiting for us when we die."

Jackson frowned and waited. What was he talking about?

"It happens to every lycan," Daimon said as he took his eyes off Jackson. "When a lycan dies, if their head isn't severed, the ethos that remains in their bodies while they pass on attracts hungry spirits. They possess the body of the dead lycan and use it as a vessel to feast. Some say these spirits come from hell, and that's why they're called hellhounds."

That made Jackson feel sick. "Is…that why I got a strange feeling? Almost like…she was empty."

Sebastien nodded. "Those kinds of spirits sap away whatever might be left in the vessel they find."

Jackson shifted his sights to Daimon. "And…what happens to Enola?"

"She's gone," Daimon muttered. "Her body and soul were tainted; the Moon Goddess won't accept her."

Sebastien sighed quietly and said, "I'm sorry, guys."

Jackson didn't know what to say. Was it *his* fault? Could there have been a way to save her? He looked at Sebastien. "Did…I…was—"

"There was no way to save her, kid, if that's what you're trying to ask," the white-haired demon said. "Trust me, I know. I've seen Lord Caedis try to save lycans from this fate."

"At least she isn't suffering while her body is used for destruction," Daimon mumbled. He looked at Sebastien. "Are you good to search the area? I want to find out who or what the fuck did this," he growled.

Sebastien nodded. "I'm on it. I'll meet you back at the burrow."

Daimon helped Jackson to his feet as Sebastien shifted into his hound form and raced off.

"Are you okay?" Daimon asked.

Jackson nodded. "Yeah."

Just then, Ethan appeared in his tiger form. "I…came back to help. Where's Sebastien?"

"We don't need your help," Daimon snarled.

Ethan scowled. "You don't need to be a fucking prick about it."

Daimon clenched his fists—

"Don't," Jackson complained, looking at Daimon and then Ethan. He didn't have the energy to deal with this right now. He knew they didn't like each other, but were they really going to start fighting *now*? Enola was dead and they had no idea who was responsible. "Can we just…get back to the others? Maybe Lalo or Ezhno can tell us what happened."

The Alpha snarled at Ethan again, but he swiftly shifted, and so did Jackson.

"Let's go," Daimon said, and as they ran, the Alpha stuck closely to Jackson's side…almost like he was trying to keep Ethan away from him.

"What happened?" Ethan asked as he moved closer to Jackson, but Daimon growled at him, and the tiger responded with a snarl.

Jackson huffed irritably. "I had to use my fire to save Sebastien. He said that there was no way to save her."

Ethan frowned sympathetically. "Shit, I'm sor—"

"Don't act like you give a shit," Daimon snapped.

"Oh, my fucking God!" Ethan shouted. "Why are you such a—"

"Stop!" Jackson insisted, shooting angry glares at them both. "Enola just fucking died! What the hell is wrong with you two?!"

Daimon lost his scowl and focused on what was ahead, and Ethan backed down, too.

And then they ran in silence, heading for the burrow. Jackson had no idea who or what attacked the hunting party; his feeling didn't go so far as to tell him what to expect. But what if it was hunters? He thought they were through with them.

But…what if it was something worse? A new kind of cadejo or some other monster that lived out in the woods.

He frowned worriedly and tried to focus on getting back to the burrow. If there was something else out there hunting the pack…then what would Daimon choose to do: turn back to keep everyone who was left safe, or find whatever did this and destroy it?

Chapter Thirty-Three
Warning

| **Daimon** |

Daimon was going to find out who or what did this to Enola and he was going to kill it. With his *bare hands*, he'd tear Enola's killer apart. He was tired of losing people—he was tired of seeing his pack hurt. His pack needed him at full strength. Daimon needed to shove aside the worry that his injury was affecting him and do what needed to be done. Enola was the last wolf he'd lose.

He set his eyes on the burrow up ahead. Tokala was waiting outside, and when he reached it, the Alpha led the way inside.

The pack were waiting, sitting around Ezhno, Lalo, and Lance, who were all being seen to by Bly. Lance begged her to let him help, but she refused.

"Alpha," Lalo said the moment he saw Daimon. He tried to get up, but Bly made him stay down.

"Rest," Daimon told him, stopping beside Bly. He then watched Jackson and Ethan join Julian. Anger started boiling inside him. Why did that muto have to stick to *his* mate like a parasite? He scowled at Jackson's friend, who shot a hostile glare back at him.

"W-what... what happened with Enola?" Ezhno asked through his laboured breaths.

Daimon did his best to remain composed. "We couldn't do anything to save her," he explained. "But she's no longer suffering."

"We couldn't... do *anything*," Lalo lamented. "There were so many of them—they came from every direction."

"Who did?" Daimon questioned, taking a step closer to where Lalo lay.

Lalo's blue eyes were filled with fear. "Wolf walkers."

Daimon's anger turned into rage... but worry accompanied it. There was only one pack he could think of that would want to harm his wolves: Kane. A cold shiver ran down his spine, but he shoved his concern aside. He wouldn't sit by. He wouldn't run. No one else was going to die, and Daimon wouldn't let another thing hinder their progress. They were getting to that lab, and if he had to go through Kane to do it, then he would. He was a *Prime*. He was *built* for this.

"How many?" he asked Lalo.

Lalo frowned. "I…at least ten. Maybe more. They were so fast."

"I recognized one of them," Ezhno said. "That…dark brown wolf. Gold eyes."

Daimon clenched his fist.

"Ellis?" Julian called with trepidation in their voice.

Ezhno nodded.

"Oh…this is bad," Julian shuddered, shaking their head. "I-I knew he wouldn't just let us go. I knew he'd come—they found us!" they exclaimed, standing up. "W-we have to leave!"

Daimon went over to them. "Tell me every single thing you know about Kane, Ellis, and that pack," he demanded.

Julian frowned at him. "W-well, I-I don't know where you want me to start. I-I heard them say he's descended from a Crescent Alpha, and that's why he's so fucked up."

Tokala stood beside Daimon. "Chief, if this is Kane's pack…there are at least seventy of them. We have to think carefully about what our next move is."

Daimon glanced at him. He was right. The last thing they needed right now was for Daimon to let his anger consume him. Seventy wolves against his pack…plus Sebastien…and *him*…Ethan. An all-out war would be suicide, but if he could take them out a small group at a time….

"Dad?" Remus asked, tugging on Daimon's shirt. "What's going on? They said…Enola turned into a monster."

The Alpha sighed quietly and tried to collect his thoughts. He couldn't ponder battle plans right now. Enola was gone, and his pack were still grieving Alastor. There was a possibility that Kane's wolves already knew where they were staying…but if that were so, why hadn't they attacked?

He looked at Julian's petrified face. "Why didn't they just kill all my wolves? Why only Enola? Why haven't they found us and slaughtered us?"

Julian gulped and shivered. "Kane, he…he does things a certain way. He likes to torment people—*torture* them. Them killing Enola was a warning. Kane always kills one to let everyone else know that he's coming for them—he's coming for *us*. He either kills a pack all at once or he takes them out one but one…like some sort of game. I've seen him spend months killing off one wolf a day in larger packs."

Daimon growled quietly and moved away from Julian. He paced and pondered, doing his best to remain calm. They couldn't stay in the burrow; they needed somewhere else to rest. But was moving his pack right now the best move? What if that was what Kane was waiting for?

Sebastien was still out there searching the perimeter. He'd wait for the kludde to return… and then it was time to leave.

The Alpha turned to face his pack. "We can't stay here," he told them firmly. "If this really is Kane's pack, we can't risk him knowing that this is where we're staying. We need to find somewhere else to rest and grieve. We'll wait for Sebastien to return, and then we're heading out."

Nobody looked angry at him. They all nodded in agreement… even Wesley, who was sitting at the back of the cave with Dustu.

"Alpha," Brando said, and when Daimon looked at him, he continued. "What are we going to do? We can't fight Kane's pack; there's at least seventy of them, right?"

Julian nodded.

"Are we gonna circle back around… find another way to Greykin Valley?" Brando questioned.

Daimon shifted his sights to Julian and adorned an expectant expression.

"Uh…" Julian stuttered. "If… Kane has sent wolves out *this* far, then he isn't going to give up. He won't stop following no matter where we go."

"So the only option is to fight," Tokala said, glancing at Daimon.

"Fight?" Ethan scoffed. "Ten or whatever to seventy?"

Daimon snarled in his direction. "You don't take part in our debates," he scolded. "You're not part of my pack; you don't have a say."

Ethan scowled and stood up—

"He's right, Ethan," Jackson said, gripping Ethan's wrist. "When I wasn't part of the pack, I didn't get a say either. Just… sit down."

With an irritated huff, Ethan slumped back down beside Daimon's mate.

Daimon wanted to go for his throat *so* desperately… but he needed to fight the urge. There were far more important things to deal with.

"What are we gonna do, Dad?" Remus asked quietly.

The Alpha looked at his son. "We're not going to let them take anything or anyone else from us, Remus."

Although he appeared afraid, Remus nodded. "So… are we gonna hunt *them*?"

"I need time with my thoughts," Daimon answered, setting his eyes on his pack. "I'm sorry that we don't have time to properly grieve, but once we're somewhere safe, we'll mourn our fallen packmates."

Tokala glanced at the pack and then stared at Daimon. "We all understand, chief. We're with you, no matter what," he said, assuring him.

Everyone called their words of agreement.

Daimon then headed away from where his pack was gathered and sat with his back against the wall. He needed to work out what his next move was. He'd already decided that he wasn't going to flee this time. Kane took away the place he thought his pack could call home; he had Enola killed, and he was planning to kill the rest of them. But Daimon wasn't going to let that happen.

He had *hundreds* of years' worth of ancestral knowledge that he could dig through; his ancestors fought wars, taking on huge packs of lycans, demons, and monsters with numbers as little as five. And if *they* could do it, then so could he. He was a *Greyblood*—war was in his blood, and it was time to let that part of him free.

| Sebastien |

He found something. An aura a kilometre ahead. No…more than one. Sebastien concentrated, covering behind a mound of snow. He sensed twelve auras, all the same. Wolf walkers.

Could *they* be responsible for Enola's death? He needed to check it out, just in case. He knew how wolf walkers worked, and if the twelve wolves up ahead were a threat, then they would have to be dealt with. He couldn't afford to let anything else slow the mission down. He wanted to get back to Clementine as soon as possible.

Sebastien stretched his wings out and took off. He broke free of the trees and travelled just below the clouds, using them for cover. Following the twelve auras, he soared through the sky and reached their location in a matter of minutes. He descended silently, landed behind an old, abandoned horse carriage, and waited.

The twelve wolves were a hundred feet away. He peered through the cracked wood, eyeing each wolf closely. One was larger than the rest with almost-black fur and yellow eyes. The other eleven stared at him obediently as he spoke, and Sebastien focused on their voices.

"*Why can't we just kill them all?*" a brown and white wolf asked.

The big, dark wolf replied, "*Because we have our orders.*"

"*Do you think the one we killed turned?*" a grey wolf mumbled.

"*I heard it roar, Gale,*" the brown and white wolf muttered.

Sebastien scowled. Those wolves *were* responsible. But what should he do? They were a threat, and one of his jobs was to make sure that nothing hindered the mission.

He had to kill them.

Twelve wolf walkers against one kludde. The reckless part of him wanted to take the risk, but the smarter side of him knew it was stupid. There was also the fact that killing them all would leave him without answers. He wanted to know *why* they killed Enola and who gave them the order. The only way he'd get that information would be by capturing one of them.

Sebastien peered through the wood again, his sights shifting from each wolf. If he could capture that big one, then he'd probably be able to get the most information out of him. But how was he going to get their leader away from the others?

"*Come on,*" the dark wolf then said as he stood up. "*We're meeting up with the others.*"

Others? If there were more of them, Sebastien wouldn't stand a chance. He had to act now.

He watched the wolves follow their leader towards the thicker trees. It wasn't snowing, so Sebastien wouldn't have much cover, and once they reached the denser woods, flying wouldn't be an option.

It was now or never.

Sebastien stayed low to the ground and prowled in their direction. Like most wolf walkers, they travelled in a single-file line, which would make it easier for him.

He stretched his wings and propelled himself into the air, flew over to the travelling wolves, and swiftly swooped down and snatched the one at the back of the line. He dug his claws into its neck to keep it from making a sound, and as he lifted it above the trees, he broke its neck.

The others didn't notice.

Sebastien tossed the corpse as far as he could and then dived down again. He snatched the next wolf, and although no one noticed when he carried it away, one of the wolves reacted when Sebastien broke the second wolf's neck.

The golden-brown-furred wolf immediately turned around and looked up, like she knew exactly where Sebastien was. He must have killed an Epsilon, and the wolf who stared up at him could only be a Gamma.

"Ellis!" the female wolf shouted.

Every wolf saw him, and to his relief, there was nothing they could do from down there. But now that he was made, there wasn't much else *he* could do, either. He couldn't risk taking on ten of them. But he and the pack needed information.

Sebastien snarled and widened his jaws. He spat a ball of blue flames down at them, and as the fire broke into several smaller projectiles and hit the snow, the wolves started yelping and moving away from each other, trying to avoid the spreading flames.

He used their moment of panic and swooped down. With his claws, he grabbed the closest wolf and then raced back above the trees. The brown and white-furred beast writhed, snarled, and struggled in his grip, but it wasn't going anywhere. He'd make sure of that.

Sebastien raced through the sky as fast as he could, and once he was far enough away from the others, he dove down to the ground, dropped the wolf, and smacked its head with his paw before it could try to fight. The wolf fell unconscious, and once it shifted back into its human form, Sebastien picked the naked man up and began heading back towards the burrow.

He had no idea how many others there were or what their reason for killing Enola was, but these wolves were evidently a threat, and he was going to get the answers he needed from this guy, and then he'd do what was necessary in order to keep Daimon's pack alive and on course. They'd faced enough setbacks already, and Sebastien wasn't willing to leave Clementine alone in Silverlake any longer than he had to. There could be more and more infected humans gathering up outside the walls with every hour, and the mere thought of it horrified him.

But he had to concentrate. He couldn't give in to his fears. If something *did* happen in Silverlake, he trusted Heir Lucian and the Venaticus to get Clementine to safety as protocol stated, and he knew Clementine could handle himself…somewhat. No, what *he* needed to do was focus on the mission. Clementine was fine.

Wasn't he? Sebastien frowned as he flapped his wings and focused on the connection he had with Clementine through his imprint. From what he could tell, his mate was calm; he was probably studying or writing. Either way, he was fine, and Sebastien could let himself relax and focus on the mission.

But that fact could change at any moment, and if Clementine's aura suddenly became panicked and afraid…what was Sebastien going to do all the way out here?

Chapter Thirty-Four

⌁ ≼ ☽ ≽ ⌁

Declaration

| **Daimon** |

Seventy wolves against fourteen. Daimon didn't like those odds, and even with a muto and a kludde, his pack were at a disadvantage. But that was only if they faced Kane's pack all at once. If he could separate them and attack the hostiles in smaller groups, then they'd stand more of a chance. But he couldn't make any solid plans until he knew *exactly* what to expect.

He looked across the burrow at Julian. Would he be able to get all the information he needed from them? He dragged his hand through his hair and watched Jackson talk to Ethan. The last thing he wanted was to let his mate take part in something so dangerous, especially when he was so new to all of this. And Jackson wasn't prepared. He was only beginning to learn how to use his demon ethos, and there was no way that he was ready for a fight like the one that was brewing.

Daimon stood up, but before he could make his way over to Julian, the sound of something scraping across the ground snatched his attention. He turned to face the noise, and when he saw Sebastien dragging an unconscious, naked man into the burrow, he frowned strangely. But he saw a symbol *burned* into the man's upper left arm in the same place all wolf walkers had their pack marks. That was one of Kane's wolves.

"There were twelve of them heading north," Sebastien said once he dropped the man. Then, he shifted into his human form. "Whoever this guy works for was the one responsible for Enola's death."

Julian shot to their feet. "T-that's Kyle!" they exclaimed.

Daimon asked, "Who's Kyle?"

"One of Kane's Betas," they answered, moving closer.

Everyone gawped at the unconscious man.

"I killed one of the others, but the second one I grabbed must have been an Epsilon. Some other wolf reacted when I killed it," Sebastien said.

"Hecate was there?" Julian questioned.

"I didn't get any of their names—well, one was called Ellis," the white-haired demon answered.

Daimon scowled and clenched his fist. Ellis, the black wolf who came to tell him that his pack needed to vacate the old Nosferatu Consulate.

"*Ellis*, too?" Julian frowned in confusion.

"What?" Daimon asked, stepping closer to them. "What do you know?"

Julian looked at him. "W-well, it's just…Kane only sends his best team out to do things like herd cadejo or divert a pack he's targeting. No offence, but…killing wolves is an Eta job."

Daimon glanced at the unconscious man. He might have more answers than Julian. A Beta was much closer to an Alpha than an Omega was, and there was a chance that Kyle knew *exactly* what Kane was planning.

"Wake him up," Daimon told Sebastien.

"Yeah, uh…about that," Sebastien said, scratching the side of his face.

"What?" Daimon questioned. "You're a demon."

"Yeah, but not the kind that can just wake people up and send them to sleep." He crouched beside the unconscious man and started shaking him. "This is the best I got, man."

Daimon rolled his eyes and looked at Tokala. "Find something to tie him up with."

The orange-haired man nodded and went over to where the pack left their bags.

"Do you think he can tell us what Kane's planning?" Jackson asked Julian.

"I mean…maybe," they answered as Jackson and Ethan stood beside them. "Kyle and Ellis were always the closest to Kane; some of us thought they were even closer than Kane was to his Luna."

Daimon watched Rachel and Tokala tie Kyle up with some rope, and once the bindings were secure, the Alpha kicked the unconscious man's face. "Wake the fuck up, you piece of shit," he snarled, and when he kicked his face again, the guy grunted and jolted awake.

Kyle immediately tried to get up, but his ankles and hands were tied, so all he could do was writhe around. He tried using his enhanced strength to break free, but before he could, Daimon stomped down on the man's leg and snapped the bone. Kyle winced and grimaced, and when Daimon snatched his throat and pulled him up off his feet, the man glowered at him.

"I'll make this nice and simple for you," the Alpha growled as Kyle choked. "You answer my questions, I don't break any more bones. You *don't* answer them…well, we've got two hundred and five more to go," he warned, glancing at his broken leg.

Daimon then slammed the man's back on the ground and leaned into his purple face. He loosened his grip just enough for Kyle to take a few desperate breaths, and then he tightened it again.

"I'm not…telling…you shit!" Kyle growled.

The Alpha mercilessly slammed his free hand on Kyle's chest, and the sound of his breaking ribs echoed through the burrow. "Two hundred and two."

Kyle groaned and choked; he tried pulling Daimon's hand from around his throat, but his strength was laughable compared to the Alpha's.

"Tell me what your Alpha is planning," Daimon demanded.

"And don't lie," Sebastien warned. "I'll know."

The man laughed through his struggled breaths, but when he set his eyes on Julian, he scowled angrily. "Fucking traitor!"

Daimon punched his face, breaking his nose.

"Fuck!" Kyle spat.

As his pack moved out of the way, Daimon picked Kyle up and pinned him against the nearest wall. "Answer me!" he yelled.

"Fuck you!"

"Can I suggest something?" Sebastien then asked. "I mean, he's obviously not gonna say anything no matter how many bones you break, right?" He looked to Julian for confirmation.

They nodded and said, "He's probably had every bone in his body broken a thousand times."

Daimon snarled irritably and stared expectantly at Sebastien.

The white-haired demon looked at Jackson.

Jackson frowned in confusion and pointed to himself. "Me? What am *I* gonna do?"

"You can put those shiny new fangs of yours to use," Sebastien said, pulling him away from Ethan and Julian.

"W-why can't you just use yours?" Jackson protested.

"Because I'm a kludde; I don't have multi-purpose venom and rift travel and whatever. I do spirit stuff," he explained, escorting Jackson towards Daimon. "If Kyle here was a ghost or phantom or what have you, then maybe I could do more than carry him away from his pack."

Kyle struggled in Daimon's grip, and when Sebastien and Jackson reached him, the Alpha pinned the man on the ground again. He knew what Sebastien was getting at; demon venom was one of the most excruciating things someone could experience, and it might be what got Kyle to talk.

But Jackson frowned unsurely. "I-I don't really know what I'm doing."

"Come on, you got the hang of fire pretty quickly. Venom's a breeze. Just like with the fire, it's all about intention," Sebastien explained.

Jackson looked down at Daimon and Kyle. He seemed conflicted, and Daimon was sure it was because he was worried about messing up.

Kyle grunted and tried pulling free. "Get the fuck off me!"

Daimon hit the side of the man's face. "Shut up," he growled. Then, he looked up at Jackson. "Don't overthink it," he said, trying to assure him. "Just like Sebastien said, you've got the hang of things quickly. This will be no different."

Although his hesitant frown didn't fade, Jackson kneeled beside the grunting man.

"Just sink your fangs into his skin," Sebastien instructed. "While doing so, focus on what you want him to feel—that's pain, of course—and all we have to do is watch him squirm until he gives up and tells us what we want to know."

"And if he doesn't?" Ethan asked.

"Then Jackson bites him again," he answered.

Daimon snatched Kyle's wrist with his free hand and lifted it towards Jackson.

"Get off me! What the fuck is this shit?!" Kyle yelled.

"Do it," Daimon insisted.

Jackson took hold of Kyle's arm, glanced unsurely at the choking man's face, and then bit down, sinking his fangs into his skin.

Kyle screeched and convulsed, and as Daimon watched Jackson's black venom ooze into the man's veins, he felt Kyle's strength waning.

It was working.

After a few moments, Kyle went silent and still. He didn't move when Daimon let go, but he wasn't screaming, either.

"What did you do to him?" Tokala asked before Daimon could.

Jackson let go of the man's arm and wiped the blood from his lips. "I just...wanted him to stop fighting and answer your questions," he said with a worried frown, looking at Daimon.

"Huh...nice job, kid," Sebastien said, patting Jackson's back.

Julian then stepped forward. "I, uh...I think we should hurry this up. Kane might send his other Betas to find him."

Daimon didn't want to risk that happening. He glared down at Kyle's confused, dazed face. "Tell me what your Alpha is planning!"

Kyle's eyes darted from each pack member who stared at him. "I...what did you do to me?"

"What is your Alpha planning?!" Daimon yelled.

The man's eyes locked with his almost like he was compelled. "A-Alpha Kane," he said slowly. "The river...."

Daimon frowned. "The river?"

"Divert...here. I...." It was like he was trying to fight whatever Jackson did to him.

"Do it again," Daimon instructed, shifting his sights to Jackson.

Jackson nodded and grabbed the man's arm. He sunk his fangs into him, and his venom infected Kyle's veins.

The man tensed up and groaned. He shook his head, grimacing as the veins in his neck revealed themselves, stained black with demon venom.

"Tell me what your Alpha's plan is," Daimon growled, gripping Kyle's throat again.

With a pained grunt, Kyle wriggled around. "You killed...our packmates," he answered, his voice quiet and rough. "You...you didn't actually think you'd get away with it, did you?"

Daimon tightened his grasp.

Kyle choked and growled. "W-we used the undead to make you cross where we wanted you to cross!"

The pack glanced at one another with confused expressions.

"You put those cadejo by the river?" Tokala asked.

"Y-yes," Kyle answered. "We...needed you in this part of the woods. We...we were waiting. We had to leave a warning...Alpha Kane's warning; we had to let you know that he was coming for you."

Daimon scowled angrily. Kane wasn't only responsible for Enola's death, but Alastor's, too.

Wesley suddenly pulled his packmates out of the way so that he could see Kyle. "It was *you*?!" he growled, the first words he'd spoken since Alastor's burial. "He's dead because of you?!"

Tokala grabbed Wesley when he went for Kyle. "Calm down," the Zeta insisted, holding him back.

"He killed Alastor! You heard him! He led those cadejo to the river! It's his fault!" Wesley screamed, attempting to escape from Tokala.

Bly and Rachel tried to assist Tokala, but Wesley wouldn't yield.

Daimon shifted his attention back to Kyle. "What is he planning to do next?" he questioned through gritted teeth.

Kyle tried to fight the venom, but he said, "He's...going to make you *all* pay! He won't stop until you're *all* in the ground!"

"S-see! I told you!" Julian panicked. "He's gonna kill us all one by one—"

"And when *you two* are the last ones left," Kyle said, glaring at Daimon and then Jackson, "he'll make you watch as he kills your precious little mate!" he snapped, glowering at the Alpha. "He'll take everything from you; he'll make you wish that you never crossed into his territory."

Daimon's anger quickly evolved into fury, and with an enraged yell, he slammed his fist into Kyle's face. "The only one who's going to regret anything is your Alpha," he stated, watching as Kyle spat blood from his broken jaw.

The Alpha then stood up and wiped his bloody hands on his shirt.

"What are we going to do?" Remus asked as he moved closer to him.

Daimon glanced at Kyle and then set his sights on Wesley, who was still trying to escape Tokala, Bly, and Rachel. There was no further use for Kyle; they couldn't take him with them because he'd leave a scent trail that any one of Kane's wolves could follow. So, he nodded at Tokala and said, "Let him have him."

Tokala let go of Wesley, who burst forward, and as he jumped over the pack, he shifted into his wolf form and landed on Kyle.

Daimon and the pack stepped back and watched as Wesley mercilessly ripped the screaming man apart. He tore off his limbs and sliced huge chunks of flesh from his body, and when Kyle was moments from succumbing to blood loss—after he'd experienced the pain Wesley wanted him to—the Epsilon grasped the man's head in his jaws, twisted, turned, and yanked, and as blood sprayed over the burrow ground, Wesley pulled the man's head from his body.

And that was it. Kyle was dead, Wesley had his revenge, and Daimon had his answers.

"Damn," Ethan muttered as everyone watched Wesley back away from the corpse with blood dripping from his maw.

Daimon turned his back to everyone and tried to calm his rage. He clenched his fists so tight that he could feel his nails breaking the skin on his palms. *Kane* was responsible for the cadejo by the river. It was *he* who orchestrated Alastor's death, and it was he who killed Enola and left her to turn into a monster, stealing her right to return to the Moon Goddess. He planned to kill Daimon's pack one by one, and right now, they were exactly where Kane wanted them.

It was time to leave. They had to go back to that river and leave this part of the forest. He had no idea where Kane was, nor did he know where he might have wolves lying in wait. But what Daimon *did* know was that his pack weren't safe here. It made him even angrier that they had to backtrack and cause the mission to take longer, but the lives of his packmates were more important.

He turned to face them. "We need to leave this part of the woods. We'll head back to the river and find a way across. Then, we'll find a new path to continue towards Greykin Valley."

Everyone nodded obediently. No one spoke up, either—not even Sebastien.

"However, we now know that Kane isn't going to stop. He wants to kill every one of us, and there is no doubt in my mind that he'll follow us. We can't risk ourselves, nor can we risk the mission. So, we're going to fight. We stick together at all times, and when Kane's next group shows up, we'll be ready for them. We'll send *him* a message," the Alpha said firmly. "*We* are the Ash Mountain Pack; we don't die easy, and we don't let our packmates die for nothing!"

His pack called their firm agreements.

Ethan then stepped forward. "Can't we just get the Nosferatu or whoever to deal with these guys? Getting to the lab is—"

"You do not speak!" Daimon yelled at him. "This is wolf business only!"

Ethan scowled and went to argue—

"Don't," Jackson said, moving his arm in front of Ethan.

"This…this is what the beginning of a pack war looks like," Julian said with a haunted tone. "It's only gonna worse from here."

"They're right," Sebastien said with a sigh and a nod. "The Venaticus or Nosferatu can't get involved even if they had the manpower to spare. But we need to find a way to keep this from affecting the mission."

Daimon nodded and then said, "We're leaving". The sooner they left, the more space they'd put between them and their enemies. "Let's go."

He led the way out of the burrow and shifted into his wolf form. His pack followed, shifting as they pulled their bags on. And then they followed him back towards the river.

Battling Kane and making their way to Greykin Valley was going to be hard to do simultaneously. Kane was set up somewhere, and Daimon needed to find a place to operate out of, too—a place to wait for Kane's next group of wolves. And *that* was what he'd do—*that* was how he'd do it. He'd lay in wait just as they did and take them out. Then, he'd move on elsewhere and repeat the process, ensuring their progress towards the valley. Kane was likely to figure out his tactic eventually, but by then, Daimon would have a new approach to taking out his enemies.

Chapter Thirty-Five

⌐ ≤) ≥ ⌐

War Plans

| **Jackson** |

War? How were they going to win a war against a pack with over seventy wolves? Would Daimon's plan work? Jackson trusted him—of course he did. Daimon was the Alpha for a reason, but Jackson couldn't shake the feeling of trepidation which gripped him the moment he saw Kyle.

As he followed beside Daimon, he glanced behind him at the pack, who all looked as serious-faced as their Alpha. Ethan, on the other hand, had his eyes focused on Daimon, and he looked *furious*. Jackson understood why, though. Every time Ethan tried to speak up during a pack discussion, Daimon shut him down. But that was just how things worked, right? Outsiders weren't welcome to take part.

With a worried frown, Jackson shifted his sights to Daimon. "Daimon?" he asked quietly.

The Alpha glanced at him. "Hmm."

"What happens now? I mean…this is gonna be a pack war, right?"

"It already is," Daimon said firmly. "It was war the moment Kane lured us towards that prowler."

Jackson's frown thickened. "But…how will he know that you declared war?"

"He'll know when we kill his next group," the Alpha snarled.

With a slow nod, Jackson stared ahead. "But…wouldn't that make us Ucigaş? That's what a wolf walker is when they kill their own kind, right?"

"Not in certain cases, like war and justified revenge."

"Oh…okay." It didn't feel like Daimon was in much of a talking mood right now. He was concentrating and Jackson didn't want to disrupt his thoughts. So, he gradually fell back to where Ethan and Julian were.

The giant tiger looked at him. "Do we have any sort of solid plan or what?" he asked Jackson.

"We're going back across the river like Daimon said," Jackson answered. "And...I think we'll stop somewhere to discuss a plan."

Julian shook their head. "I know that Alpha Daimon is a Prime, but...I don't know if that's gonna be enough. Kane's smart and resourceful. He's killed at least *fifty* packs since I was recruited, and I've never seen anyone get a hit off on him, either." They then frowned and said, "Well, there was this one wolf a long time ago—the one who gave him the scars on his face."

"Scars?" Ethan questioned. "Don't all lycans heal eventually? No scars?"

"Well, yeah...but this wolf left scars. I don't know why, and no one really talks about it. It was like...ten years ago, so I've only heard rumours."

"I'm sure Daimon knows what he's doing," Jackson said confidently. But then again...there were things he still didn't know about his mate, and one of them was what Daimon was like before he met him. He became a Prime, he was an amazing fighter, and yet...Jackson didn't know the stories behind any of that. All he knew was that Daimon's brother, Alaric, died and passed leadership onto him.

But now probably wasn't the best time to ask Daimon to tell him stories. The Alpha declared war, and Jackson had no idea how they were supposed to fight it *and* get to Greykin Valley. But he was sure Daimon knew what he was doing.

"You're always defending him," Ethan mumbled.

Jackson frowned at him. "What?"

"Daimon. You're always protecting him and acting like everything he says goes. Just like you always used to defend those assholes you dated."

His frown became a scowl. "I don't wanna get into this again, Ethan. You and Daimon need to learn to get along—"

"I don't want to. He doesn't deserve you, Jack. I know an asshole when I see one, and I'm telling you, if he hasn't already, he's gonna make you feel like shit."

"You're wrong," Jackson argued.

"I'm not," he insisted, frustrated. "It's like he's trying to keep you away from me. We've barely spent any time together since you found me and it's 'cause you're always with *him*. Y-you're like...stuck to him like glue, just like you were to everyone who came before him."

Jackson scowled irritably. "All Daimon's ever done is try to protect me—and he's done a pretty good job of that. He's not like those fuckboys I used to date; he's my *mate*, Ethan, and until you can accept that, I'm done with this conversion." He sped up and cut through the pack to join Daimon again.

But he could feel his throat tightening. Why was Ethan being like this? Why couldn't he just accept the fact that he loved Daimon? Why did he have to be so hostile and take whatever chance he could to try and start an argument? If he kept at it, Jackson feared that very soon, Daimon wouldn't be able to hold back for his sake anymore. Jackson didn't want to see them fight, but he didn't know what to do.

He looked at Daimon. "What's the plan? Sorry if you're trying to think one over right now, I just…I'm worried about this whole war thing."

"We're going to cross the river and find someplace to hide. A cave, another burrow, or something that keeps us out of sight. Once we find that, we'll all come together and suggest ideas, but the main goal is to take out Kane's wolves and continue our journey towards Greykin Valley. We can't sacrifice mission time, so we're going to have to do both things at once," the Alpha explained.

"Kill them as we go?" Remus asked.

Daimon nodded.

"It's a good plan," Sebastien said from behind them.

"Agreed," Tokala concurred, walking beside Sebastien.

The Alpha then slowed down. "The river's up ahead. Everyone be on high alert. Watch for cadejo and hostile wolves."

Everyone went silent and followed the Alpha to the tree line. But when the river was in sight, there were no cadejo to be seen. Daimon stopped and looked around, and once everyone joined him, they all mumbled unsurely.

"I think…Kane must have led them back to the pit," Julian said as they and Ethan stood behind Jackson.

Daimon glanced at them and then glared ahead. "We can't take any chances. Stay close, keep your senses focused, and if you see even the *slightest* thing you think might be dangerous, you speak up. Understand?"

"Yes, Alpha," everyone said.

The Alpha stepped out of the trees and walked towards the flowing river. Jackson and Remus followed behind him, and the pack trailed them in a single-file line with Sebastien and Ethan at the rear.

A harsh breeze rushed past, carrying the scent of the forest, and as his fur floated in the wind, Daimon called, "We'll keep moving downwind. Kane's wolves won't be able to follow our scent, so we'll find somewhere to take cover before the winds shift."

"Do you want me to scout ahead?" Sebastien called.

"Go," Daimon agreed.

The winged hound took off and disappeared into the forest across the river.

When Jackson's paws touched the water, he looked down at the small fish swimming above the pebbles. He didn't sense danger, and it didn't look as though anyone else did, either.

The pack crossed the water without disruption, and once they moved into the woods, Daimon picked up the pace, following the river.

"We'll use the river to get us to the Great Lake," the Alpha called.

"The Great Lake?" Jackson questioned curiously.

"A lake which all paths connect to. From there, we'll follow the river that passes Greykin Valley."

"Why didn't we just head to the lake in the first place?" Ethan called from the back.

Daimon adorned an irritated expression.

"Because it's dangerous," Brando answered, looking at the muto. "There are a lot of stories about the Great Lake. Wolf walkers travel miles to bathe in its water; it's said that the Moon Goddess grants wishes and answers to those who drink it, and the wounds of those who swim inside are healed."

"I've heard that, too," Dustu said. "I thought I could go there and ask for my family back after what happened, but… even the Moon Goddess can't bring people back to life."

Ethan asked, "So why is it dangerous? It just sounds like some sort of shrine or temple."

"It's neutral ground," Daimon answered. "Any pack could be there, and if they have ill intentions, the moment we leave the Great Lake, that pack could come after us."

Tokala nodded and added, "There's also a story of a monster in the water. If someone breaks the laws of neutral ground, the beast comes out of the depths and drags them to an inescapable place."

"So… why don't we just drink the water and wish for Kane's pack to die?" Ethan asked, glancing at Julian, who looked like they were wondering the same thing.

"The Moon Goddess does no harm," Rachel answered as Daimon led the way up a hill. "When you ask Her for something, you ask for guidance, knowledge, and power. But wishes of death are never granted. Wolf walkers live by a code—even those of us who choose to turn our backs to Lupi Sequi Veteris—and if a wolf walker wishes another dead, they must do it by their own claws."

Just then, Sebastien abruptly appeared out of nowhere and walked beside Jackson, who flinched in startlement. "There are some old ruins two kilometres up ahead. The place is abandoned and looks like it has been for a while."

Daimon nodded. "Lead the way."

The hound walked in front of Daimon, and when he started running, so did everyone else.

Jackson tried to focus on the forest around him, but all he could think about was the Great Lake and the creature that resided inside it. The thought sent a cold shiver down his spine, and he couldn't help but wonder… what *was* the monster? Were the stories true? And if he drank the water, could he ask the lake for guidance or strength? Could he ask it to reveal to him who had attempted to murder Daimon?

Now wasn't the time to be thinking about that. He needed to concentrate. There weren't only cadejo to look out for anymore. He could get back to his investigation when the pack stopped to rest.

The wolves travelled quickly and silently, following Sebastien through the woods as a storm brewed overhead. Snow started falling, so Daimon ordered Sebastien to pick up the pace, and just when the storm transformed into a blizzard, they reached the crumbled brick walls of an old ruin.

Jackson couldn't make out what the ancient walls were once a part of, and there was no time to glance around and wonder, either. The snow fell *hard*, and the winds became spiteful. He hastily followed everyone down some icy stairs and into an old, empty wine cellar. Cobwebs were frozen to the ceiling, and several smashed bottles lay on the frosty floorboards.

"Move this," Tokala called.

Brando and Wesley helped the Zeta push a large shelf along the floor and towards the exit, but the wind was relentless and fought them from blocking the stairs. So Jackson hurried over before anyone else and pressed the weight of his body against the shelf, helping keep it up as the others pushed it forward.

"Lalo, Dustu, move that barrel," Daimon instructed as he shifted into his Prime form and grabbed a barrel.

Everyone worked together, stacking whatever they could find in front of the shelf to keep the wind from pushing it over, and once the barricade was steady, the pack backed off and waited to see if it would hold.

"How long do you think the storm's gonna last?" Leon asked.

"There's no way to tell," Daimon answered, looking around as he shifted into his normal wolf form. "This is good, though. We can rest here and come up with our first plan."

"I actually had an idea," Wesley said, sitting down. "Kane's going to send another group after us, right? So, we lead them into a trap."

"An ambush?" Dustu asked.

"Not necessarily. We don't know how many are coming."

Jackson watched everyone wait for Wesley to continue. It was like killing Kyle and partly avenging Alastor had given him back some of his strength, and he seemed *eager* to get this war started.

"Kane led us across that river; Kane left those cadejo waiting for us, and I say we use his tactics against him. We've got rope, so we set up traps. Sebastien can fly, so he can grab as many wolves who didn't get caught in the traps as he can, and then we let the cadejo kill the rest of them—we *lead* the cadejo to Kane's trapped wolves. That'll send a message," Wesley said firmly.

Everyone looked a little surprised by the fact that he had so much to say.

Daimon, on the other hand, looked *relieved*. "It's a good plan," he said with a nod. "How much rope do we have? Dustu, check."

Dustu shifted into his human form and started looking through everyone's bags. Then, once he was done, he looked at Daimon and said, "Seven."

"How long is each rope?" Daimon asked Sebastien.

"The Venaticus pack standard is ten meters," the hound answered.

"Good. We can make a few traps with that. But we're not killing all of them," Daimon said, glancing around at everyone. "I need one of them alive."

"To send back to Kane and tell him it's war, right?" Remus asked.

Daimon nodded. "Once the storm has passed, we'll head out and find a place to set up the traps."

While they began discussing what kind of traps they could create, Jackson looked over his shoulder. Ethan was curled up in his tiger form by the back wall. He couldn't see his friend's face, but he could tell that he was upset...and he was sure that he knew why, too.

Jackson was still annoyed about what Ethan said to him on the way here, but there was also a part of him that felt bad. Ethan was *right*. Ever since he found him, they hadn't spent very long together *at all* apart from the occasional conversation here and there. Ethan was his best friend and had been since he was a kid. Jackson knew how he pushed Ethan away every time he started dating someone new, but his friend always put up with it. He didn't want to do that to him again, though. Ethan deserved better, so Jackson was going to be a better friend.

He got up and walked over to where he lay. "You, uh...not listening in on the whole war plans thing?" he asked him.

"Why would I? It's not like I'm allowed to get a word in," Ethan grumbled.

Jackson sat down. "Look, I'm sorry I snapped at you and walked off."

Ethan sighed and sat up so that they could face each other. "No, *I'm* the one who should be saying sorry. I've been an ass."

"Well...kinda, yeah," he said with a quiet laugh. "But I know that I have, too. I know how I used to ignore you and blow you off whenever I was seeing someone, and I hate that I did that to you. And...I'm not asking you to be best friends with Daimon, I just want you to understand that this is different."

The tiger groaned—

"*And*...I know that I've gotta do better, too. I'm sorry I haven't given us much time, there's just a lot going on and I'm always so nervous or have no idea what I can do to help. I stick with Daimon because he makes me feel safe, not because he's trying to take me away from you. You're still my best friend, and I'm gonna make sure we get to hang out more, all right? Just...please stop almost getting into fights with him," he pleaded, glancing at Daimon.

Ethan sighed again. "It's hard not to when he keeps trying to order me around. I'm not one of his lackeys."

Jackson frowned and said, "He just tells you not to get involved in pack stuff, that's all. And I mean…I get it. All of this would probably be so much easier if you *were* a part of the pack."

"I'd rather be lost out in the tundra again than work for him," the tiger snarled.

"But at least you'd be able to take part in discussions."

"Not worth it."

Jackson's frown thickened. "Can…that even happen? Can other lycans join a wolf walker pack or can they only stick with their own people?"

"It can happen," Ethan grumbled. "But lycan mix-packs are frowned upon. They're seen as cowardly or tainted or whatever. And even if that wasn't the case, I still wouldn't join."

Jackson knew better than to argue. Ethan seemed pretty firm in his answer. So, he gave up and looked over at the barricaded door.

"Jack, look…" Ethan said with a relenting tone. "All of this is just…a lot to take in. Just a few months ago, wolf walkers were just stories, and now not only am I surrounded by them, but my best friend is one, too. And not only that but you're also *mated* to one. It's just…I'm trying, okay?"

He nodded. "I get it. It's been a lot for me too. And now we're going to war with this other pack while trying to reach the lab. We're all gonna need to stick together."

An aggravated glare danced across Ethan's face. But he huffed quietly, looked down at his paws, and shrugged. "I'll try. But sometimes, it feels like he's fishing for a fight."

"I'll talk to him too, okay? But…" he looked over at the pack, who were still discussing traps, "…not yet. We can just hang here for a bit."

Ethan nodded and lay on his side.

Jackson relaxed, too.

"Did you uh…figure anything out yet?" his friend asked quietly. "About the whole…knife thing."

"I don't know. I kinda think that Dustu might be a suspect; maybe he tried to kill Daimon because of what happened to Aiyana."

"What? Who?"

"Aiyana. She was another Omega. She got bitten by a prowler when we went on a hunting trip, and Daimon had to kill her."

Wilson nodded slowly. "Yeah, that's a motive all right. You gonna interrogate him?"

"Yeah. Not yet, though, I don't wanna risk anyone seeing."

"All right, well…if you need me, let me know."

Jackson nodded and then set his eyes on his packmates again. He didn't know how long the storm would last, nor did he know when the pack would be done. He didn't have much to give in terms of laying traps and coming up with war plans. If they needed him, he'd be there. But for now, he'd stay with Ethan. He didn't want his friend to think he didn't need him anymore or that he'd always choose Daimon. He just hoped the two would eventually find common ground and stop almost going for each other's throats.

Chapter Thirty-Six

Wait Out The Storm

| Jackson |

Daimon called for everyone's attention. Jackson and Ethan brought their reminiscing of old times to a halt and turned their heads to look at the Alpha. Everyone else gawped at him, waiting for him to tell them what he had to say.

"We may be fewer in numbers now," Daimon said, looking around at them. "But we remain strong even in the toughest of times. You have all proven not only your loyalty but also your strength—your *will*—and not one of us would be here without each other." He paused for a moment. "As Alpha, it is within my power to bestow ranks on each of you, and as we are now in a time of war, the time has come for me to do so. Wesley," he said, setting his eyes on the brown and white-furred Epsilon.

Wesley stood up and approached Daimon.

"You've proven yourself a great warrior," the Alpha told him. "And I trust that you will serve me well as my new Gamma."

Jackson saw Wesley's eyes widen, and the pack all adorned surprised but excited expressions. It was like most of them knew it was a long time coming, and Jackson agreed that Wesley deserved what he could only think to call a promotion. But what he didn't know was what a Gamma did.

He leaned over to Julian, who was sitting on his right. "Uh...what does a Gamma do?"

"Third in command," they answered quietly. "They act as a military leader and work alongside the Zeta or Beta and Alpha during battle or war plans. They also maintain order and give advice.. kinda like an elder."

Jackson nodded slowly and watched as Wesley bowed in front of Daimon. The Alpha then placed his paw on the wolf's head and closed his eyes.

"Under the witness of my pack and the Moon Goddess, I name you, Wesley Ayek-Blood, Gamma of the Ash Mountain Pack," Daimon said firmly.

Wesley stood up and turned to face the pack. Everyone bowed their heads, so Jackson quickly did the same, and when everyone else said it, he also said, "Gamma Wesley."

Daimon then looked around again as Wesley went and sat back down. "Brando, Ezhno, and Leon."

The three called wolves approached him.

"Time and time again you three have proved your strength, and I now bestow upon you the rank of Epsilon. Bow," Daimon said. Once they bowed, he placed his paw on their heads one by one and said their names, "Brando Marniq-Blood, Ezhno Serkoak-Blood, and Leon Ashevak-Blood. Under the witness of my pack and the Moon Goddess, I name you Epsilons of the Ash Mountain Pack." Then, he stepped back and said, "You will now link with your Gamma."

Wesley went over there and shifted into his human form. Brando, Ezhno, and Leon shifted back, too, and then held out their right hands. With the knife from his bag, Wesley cut their palms and then his own. He gripped the hand of each of them, and one by one, their eyes gleamed purple for a moment before returning to their usual colour.

The four wolves then went and sat together.

"Dustu Ansong-Blood," Daimon said.

With a startled whimper, the Omega wolf tensed up. "Y-yes, Alpha?"

"It's time for you to become Upsilon. Have you decided which role you wish to pursue?"

The light-brown-furred wolf looked down at the ground and adorned a look of pondering. But after a few tense moments, he slowly stood up and stared across the room at Daimon. "I-I…I think that in the absence of Etas, I'd like to put myself forward to be trained as one."

Daimon nodded. "Tokala, you'll train Dustu."

"Yes, chief," the Zeta said with a nod.

Dustu nervously headed over to sit with Tokala.

The Alpha then spoke to everyone, "Once the storm passes, we'll find somewhere to lay our traps, and then we'll wait for Kane's wolves to fall prey to them. We kill all but one; one must take our declaration to Kane."

Everyone called their agreements.

"Now rest and prepare yourselves for what is to come," Daimon instructed. "Leave your wolf forms."

The pack did as they were told and shifted into their human forms. Even Sebastien and Ethan complied.

"Do you know what *you* want to do?" Jackson asked Julian.

"No," they mumbled, sitting with their arms wrapped around their knees. "I guess I haven't really thought about it. Kane never really promoted Omegas, so none of us set goals."

Ethan sighed deeply as he sat with his back against the empty wine rack. "What are you…like, Alpha's…boyfriend?" he snickered.

Jackson rolled his eyes. "No, I'm a Cupitor. I seek stuff out…like I go to towns and stuff to get supplies."

"I guess I could be an Eta," Julian mumbled. "I could keep watch. But I haven't been in the pack long enough to become Upsilon yet, so."

"Outsiders don't get ranks in muto-tigris packs," Ethan revealed. "If you're bitten, that is. My kind are very selective of who we have in our packs. Even if you were born a muto-tigris but lost your pack, it's really hard to be accepted into another."

Jackson turned to face him. "That's…actually really sad, I'm sorry." He never thought about the fact that Ethan was always alone. He never saw his friend with anyone else. "Were you and Holt the only muto-tigris in New Dawnward?"

Ethan shrugged. "As far as I was aware, yeah. I have no idea where my sister went. Like my parents, she just up and vanished one day—except I know that my parents were actually taken by Lyca-Corp.," he mumbled.

"I kinda wish Edward would've gone missing," Jackson mumbled.

"Edward?" Julian asked with a frown.

"My stepbrother," Jackson told them. "If it wasn't my step*dad* making my life hell, it was my step*brother*."

Ethan scoffed. "Little snooty brat was so far up his dad's ass that he probably didn't even know what the sun looks like."

Jackson laughed amusedly.

"Do you remember when we were all at Cones and Things and you were getting the chocolate chip and little fucking Eddie wanted it, too?" Ethan asked him. "He went crying to his dad so he could cut the line," he said, looking at Julian while Jackson shook his head, snickering. "So, Jackson and I stuffed some gummies into the dispenser hole, and when Eddie tried squeezing the ice cream out, it wouldn't budge. So he pulled the lever harder and harder until the gummies gave way and there was chocolate ice cream *everywhere*."

The three of them laughed together.

Jackson then frowned and said, "I kinda wonder what he's doing now, though. Do you really think he's working for Eric's merc company?"

Ethan sighed and scratched the side of his face. "I don't see that loser shooting guns and killing people. So, if he *is* working there, like I said, he's probably in the mailroom or serving people in the cafeteria."

"Did you have any other siblings?" Julian asked curiously.

"No," Jackson answered, glancing at them. "Well, Ethan's always been like a brother, so...does that count?" he asked with a smile, but when he looked at Ethan, a sullen look appeared on his friend's face.

But Ethan exhaled deeply and quickly laughed to dismiss his frown. "Yeah, good times."

Jackson leaned closer to him and quietly asked, "Are you okay?"

"What? Yeah, no. I'm just not really looking forward to fighting some wolf walker pack war while trying to get to this lab, but we gotta do what we gotta do, right?" he answered with a sigh.

Now that he was thinking about it, Jackson hadn't seen Ethan fight much. He'd seen him kill hunters and avoid cadejo, but he hadn't seen his friend fight wolf walkers. Could he be worried about *that*? Did he not know how to fight a wolf? He edged nearer so that no one would hear. "Have you...ever fought wolf walkers bef—"

"Yeah," he snapped defensively. "I kicked your precious boyfriend's ass, didn't I?"

"Woah..." Jackson scoffed, frowning.

Ethan huffed. "I'm sorry. I'm just on edge. Yeah, I've had my fair share of wolf walkers since ending up in Ascela, but the way Julian and that wolf Sebastien captured talk about this other pack.... It's kinda unnerving."

"I agree," Jackson said, leaning against the wine rack beside Ethan. "But...I've seen these guys fight," he said confidently, looking around at everyone. "And Daimon has his Prime form, we have Sebastien, and then me...if I don't fuck up."

"What the hell you talking about? You ain't gonna fuck up, Jack. I mean look at all the cool shit you've done already. You made fire, you broke silver bars, and you literally destroyed your opponents with that amulet thing. Even without it you kick ass."

Jackson smiled at him and looked down at his lap. "Thanks."

"I mean it." He moved and sat facing Jackson. "I heard rumours among your packmates, too. You slaughtered some of Kane's wolves already, right?"

"I don't...feel particularly proud about that."

"Why not? They're the enemy. They tried to kill *you*, and they tried to kill your packmates. I bet you could kill every single one of the wolves we're waiting around for in half a minute like you did that first time," he said with a smirk, nudging Jackson's leg.

With a quiet exhale, Jackson shrugged. "I just...I don't know. There's a part of me that *wants* to kill—it *enjoys* it—and I'm afraid that if I give in and kill too much, that part of me might...I don't know, grow. I don't wanna turn into some bloodthirsty killer. I *already* need to drink blood two or three times a week or whatever; what if I drink too much? I don't know anything about this stuff."

"I don't think you can drink too much," Ethan said. "I'm not some demon expert, but I've heard and seen things. I think drinking too much is only a problem for vampires. They turn into these like...fiends or whatever. Their brain gets all hooked and all it thinks about is blood. There's no coming back from it, apparently. *Demons*, though, it's drinking too *little* that'll get you."

Jackson nodded. "Yeah, I was told about that."

Ethan adorned an intrigued expression. "Have you made any sort of plan...you know, to get blood?"

"Uh...well...I guess not. I've been getting it from the hunters we killed and stuff. I haven't really thought about where I'm gonna get it from now." He glanced over at Sebastien, who was sitting by himself in the far-left corner. "I guess I'd have to ask him what sort of blood I need."

"Hey, Sebastien!" Ethan called.

Jackson frowned at him. "What are you doing?"

"Asking him. Hey, Seb—"

"Stop," Jackson insisted, shoving him lightly. "I don't want everyone hearing."

"What?" Sebastien asked, appearing in front of them.

Jackson flinched a little and looked up at him. How did he move so quickly and silently?

"Well?" the white-haired demon asked impatiently.

"Jackson has a question," Ethan said.

"I'm waiting."

"It's...sort of private," Jackson mumbled.

Sebastien sighed and crouched in front of them. "What?"

Jackson shuffled around nervously and glanced at Julian, who didn't seem to be listening. "Well...I was just wondering since there aren't any hunters around anymore...um...where I get blood from, you know? I don't know what kind I need; does it have to be human or...?"

The white-haired demon rested his chin on his hand. "Well, I don't know. Asmodi demons usually get sick from drinking wolf walker blood, but you've killed wolf walkers and evidently consumed their blood and you're perfectly fine. You didn't feel sick after, did you?"

"Uh...no, I—"

"So, if you ask him nicely, your mate might act as your personal blood bank. That's usually how mated demons get their blood, anyway. On the other hand, I know some demons have their preferences. Some prefer a certain kind of demon blood, and others get ridiculously high drinking specific lycan blood."

Jackson glanced at Daimon, who was sitting and talking to his son. He felt bad having to ask him for blood; surely, losing his blood would weaken the Alpha, and Jackson didn't want to be responsible for that. But he also didn't want to *not* ask Daimon. For all he knew, the Alpha might actually *want* to give him what he needed, and he didn't want to piss him off or upset him by asking someone else.

"I'll ask him," he said quietly.

Sebastien stood up. "Is that it?"

He nodded.

The white-haired demon left and went back to where he was sitting.

"You think he'll agree?" Ethan mumbled.

"I don't know, maybe," Jackson said. "He's talking to Remus right now, too, so I don't wanna go over there and interrupt. I'll wait until a better time."

Ethan then went a little red-faced. "I don't know...if...you know, if he says no," he stammered, clearly trying to decide how to word whatever he was going to say. "I mean...*I* wouldn't mind. We've been close since forever, so it wouldn't be weird or anything."

For some reason, his offer made Jackson feel a little flustered. "Oh, well...I mean...thanks." He stopped himself from saying he didn't know whether Daimon would be okay with it or not; he knew that would upset Ethan.

"No probs," Ethan said with a shrug.

They went silent. Jackson didn't know what to say; he was distracted by his growing curiosity. What would Ethan's blood taste like? What would *Daimon's* taste like? It wasn't something he would've thought he'd be thinking about. The blood he tasted before was fine; it was *adequate*...like stale crackers in the back of the cupboard when there was no food and he was starving. But what if he didn't have to always have stale-cracker-tasting blood? What if Daimon's tasted *so* much better?

He sighed and looked at the barricade keeping the storm out of the cellar. "How much longer do you think the storm's gonna go on for?"

Ethan didn't answer.

"Maybe another hour," Julian said. "At least I hope so. Sometimes, these storms go on for *days* in the winter."

"It's Spring," Ethan said.

"I know, I'm just saying," Julian muttered.

Jackson glanced at them both. "Well, we've clearly got at least another hour to kill. Anyone got any ideas?"

They looked at each other unsurely.

Julian then shrugged. "I could tell you guys more about my village—the place I was at before I was bitten. Some crazy stuff used to happen."

"Go for it," Ethan said.

As Julian began telling their story, Jackson did his best to concentrate and listen. However, he couldn't stop thinking about blood—*Daimon's* blood. He wanted to try it, but he was too nervous to ask. Even if he wasn't with his son, Jackson felt he'd be too anxious to bring it up.

But he had to ask soon. He didn't want to find out what happened if he didn't get blood. Would he lose control of himself and end up attacking someone…again, or would it be like before when he could do nothing while his wolf tore his own packmate apart?

Chapter Thirty-Seven
Fangs and Blood

| Daimon |

The storm was calming. Daimon listened to the settling wind and watched the barricade slowly begin to fall still. It wouldn't be much longer now until it was time to go outside and lay the traps.

He was confident that he made the right choice making Wesley his new Gamma, and he knew that Brando, Ezhno, and Leon would serve the pack well as Wesley's Epsilons. Even if it wasn't wartime, he felt he would have still made those choices.

"Dad?" Remus asked.

Daimon looked at his son, who was sitting beside him.

"Do you…think we'll ever see the others again?"

With a quiet sigh, Daimon leaned his back against the wall. "I don't know, if I'm being honest. There's a part of me that *wants* to find and help them despite what happened, but I also know that Nyssa and Caius won't accept any help I offer."

Remus shuffled around and looked a little uncomfortable.

Daimon frowned at him. "What is it?"

"I just…miss Rom."

"I do, too."

"Can't we just…go and look for them?" he asked, turning to face him. "Mom and Caius might not accept your help, but I know others *will*, especially after Mom hit Tainn. I feel like we'd all stand a better chance against Kane if we had even half of the other half of the pack."

Daimon dragged his hand over his face. "I have no way of finding them, Remus. I wish I did. The best we can do is take out as many of Kane's wolves as we can to ensure the others are safe out there. If we cross paths with them someday, I'll do whatever I can to try and convince as many of them to come back as possible."

Remus looked down at the floor and nodded sadly.

The Alpha placed his hand on his son's shoulder. "If we don't find them by the time we're finished with this mission, I'll ask the Venaticus for help locating them, I promise."

His face lit up as he looked at Daimon. "Really?"

He nodded. "Caedis said that we can have whatever we want in return for our help, so as well as someplace for us to set up a new packhouse, I'll ask them to find your mother and the others."

Remus threw his arms around him and hugged him tightly. "Thanks, Dad."

Daimon smiled slightly but placed his hands on both of Remus' shoulders. "Listen, when I take the pack out to set up traps, I want you to stay here with Jackson."

He frowned. "But…wouldn't it be better to have Jackson out there helping you fight those guys? I've seen what he can do, and—"

"I need to keep you both safe," Daimon said protectively.

Remus looked over at Jackson. "Is he gonna agree to that, though?"

Daimon sighed deeply. "I don't know. I need to talk to him about it."

"Do you want me to go get him? I know you don't like his friend, so…I don't mind."

The Alpha nodded. "Sure. Thank you."

He watched his son get up and head over to Jackson, who was talking to Ethan and Julian. When Remus interrupted them and told Jackson that Daimon wanted to talk to him, the Alpha saw Ethan shoot him a hostile glare. He did his best to keep himself composed, though; he needed to remain focused.

When Jackson got up and headed over, Remus went and sat with Tokala and Dustu.

"Uh…hey," Jackson said nervously.

Daimon reached up and took his hand. He pulled him down, making him sit beside him, and then leaned his face closer to Jackson's. He kissed his lips, smiled at him, and then leaned his back against the wall again, keeping his eyes on his mate's flustered face. "I need to ask you to do something that I know you're not going to like."

Jackson adorned a sullen expression. "You're gonna ask me to stay here, aren't you?"

He nodded.

"Daimon, I—"

"I just want to protect you, Jackson. We don't know what kind of wolves Kane is sending and we don't know what they're capable of. We've lost too many wolves lately, and I can't stand the *thought* of you getting hurt," he insisted softly, squeezing Jackson's hand.

Jackson shook his head. "I'll be okay, Daimon. I promise. I'm kinda more confident now, you know? Sebastien's taught me how to use fire, and I'm sure that could be really helpful, right?"

The Alpha sighed deeply and frowned in confliction. On one hand, Jackson's new abilities could be *very* useful, but on the other, Daimon was worried about him. He was *always* worried about him. "I don't know," he mumbled. "Anything could happen."

"We'll *all* be okay," Jackson insisted.

He sighed and shrugged. Although he was very confident in his wolves, it didn't outweigh his concern for Jackson.

"Um…Daimon," he then said.

Daimon looked at him.

"There's…actually something I need to ask *you*."

"What?" he asked curiously.

Jackson twiddled his fingers together. "Well…I was talking to Sebastien, and 'cause I'm an asmodi demon, I'm gonna need blood like two or three times a week, right?"

He nodded. "Mm-hmm."

"And…I've been fine so far because…well, you know…I killed people and stuff. But there aren't any hunters anymore and Sebastien says I need to find somewhere to get it…or some*one*."

"And you want to ask if *I'll* be that someone."

Jackson nodded. "I-I mean, like…I'll ask Sebastien how to do it without hurting you or anything before we try—i-if you even want to, that is."

Daimon smiled and ran his fingers through Jackson's hair. He found it cute when Jackson became flustered and nervous like this. And he didn't even need to think about what he asked. "Of course I will," he said, pulling him closer. When Jackson rested his head on his chest, the Alpha fiddled with his hair. "All I want to do is take care of you. If you need blood, then I'll give you blood."

"Thank you," Jackson said as he moved his arm around him.

"When do you want it?"

"Uh…well…I don't know."

Daimon didn't need to see his face to know that he was flustered again. "Doesn't it make you stronger?" he asked. "I know some demons drink blood before a fight so that their strength and ethos will be at their peak."

"I mean…I guess so, yeah. But I don't wanna take it from you before we go out there and fight Kane's wolves. I don't wanna weaken you."

"I'll be fine," the Alpha said, caressing his head. He also wasn't going to deny the fact that he was a little curious about what it felt like. He'd heard stories about a demon's bite—especially their venom—and he felt just as eager to feel Jackson's fangs in his neck as he felt to have sex with him before they were mated. In fact, he was *so* eager that he didn't want to have to wait for Sebastien to tell Jackson what he already knew.

Daimon took Jackson's hand again and got up. He led him behind a tall barrel—he knew Jackson would probably want privacy—and then made his mate straddle his lap as he sat with his back against the wall.

Jackson frowned nervously. "Y-you mean…right here?"

The Alpha nodded.

"But…what if I do it wrong?"

"You won't. I trust you," he assured him.

His anxious look didn't fade much, but Jackson nodded and quietly said, "O-okay."

Daimon moved his hand to the back of Jackson's head and pulled his face closer to his own. He kissed his lips in an attempt to help settle his mate's nerves, and to his relief, Jackson kissed back, and his tense body started to relax.

With each kiss, Daimon felt his anticipation increasing. His heart beat a little faster, and his desire to feel Jackson's bite quickly clashed with his growing arousal. He wanted to start taking his clothes off, but he had to resist and remain focused. This wasn't about sex; it was about giving *Jackson* what he needed.

After one final kiss, Daimon tilted his head to the side and gently guided Jackson's face towards his exposed neck. He closed his eyes and waited, his heart racing, and his desperation becoming unbearable. Would it feel as amazing as he'd heard, or would it hurt like hell? Either way, he wanted to give Jackson what he needed, and knowing that he was doing so made him feel content.

But then Jackson shakily whispered, "Are you sure?"

Daimon lightly gripped a fistful of Jackson's hair. "I'm sure," he replied.

Jackson nodded and then nuzzled Daimon's neck.

The Alpha tensed up and exhaled deeply, and when he felt Jackson slowly widen his jaw, he tried his best to prepare for whatever he was about to experience.

And then Jackson's fangs pierced through his skin.

Daimon flinched as the pain of his breaking skin struck him, but after a brief moment of discomfort, he felt Jackson's venom ooze into his veins, and it sent a surge of euphoria through his body. He tightened his grip on Jackson's hair and let out a quiet, pleasured groan, and he dragged his hands to his mate's waist.

Jackson moaned quietly through his desperate gulps, and when he moved his hand to the back of Daimon's head and grasped his hair, he slowly pulled his fangs from his neck and let out a pleased sigh.

Daimon smiled at him and dragged his thumb over Jackson's bottom lip, wiping his blood from it. Then, Jackson licked the blood from his thumb and smiled contently as he rested his forehead against Daimon's.

"How is it?" Daimon asked with a smirk.

"It's…hard to explain, it's just…really good," he said, gazing into the Alpha's eyes.

The Alpha smiled and stroked the side of Jackson's face. "You can have it whenever you want."

Jackson went to speak—

"But—" Daimon interjected, leaning into Jackson's ear— "I should warn you that biting me made me very hard, and if everyone wasn't in this room right now, I'd be fucking you."

He felt Jackson tense up, and when he gripped and squeezed his mate's ass, Jackson exhaled shakily and looked away to hide his flustered face.

Daimon grinned as he pulled Jackson forward so that his arousal was digging into his leg. "Do you want me to fuck you?" he whispered, guiding his hands into Jackson's trousers. He then gripped his ass again as Jackson nuzzled his neck.

"I want it," Jackson breathed, moving his hand under Daimon's shirt. He started guiding his fingers over the Alpha's abs.

"If you promise not to make a sound, I could slide my dick inside you right now," he murmured, tightening his grip as a rush of anticipation spiralled through him.

Jackson groaned quietly in frustration. "Fuck me," he pleaded.

Daimon laughed lightly and stroked his hands up Jackson's back. "You're going to have to wait," he told him.

His mate huffed and pouted, pulling his hands out of his shirt.

The Alpha gently gripped his jaw and pulled his face closer to his. "Be a good little demon and help me kill Kane's wolves, and then I'll fuck you so hard that you'll cum more than once for me."

Excitement flickered across Jackson's reddening face, but a frown quickly stole his shy expression. "So…you want me to help and not stay here?"

Daimon sighed quietly as he dragged his thumb over Jackson's cheek. "I'm not going to lie and say I'm not worried about something happening to you, but I've seen that you can handle yourself. Sebastien is actually doing a good job teaching you, and your new abilities will help us ensure victory in this war. So, yes, I'm saying that you can help, but I need you to promise me that you'll be careful—no recklessness…no risks," he said firmly.

Jackson nodded. "I promise. I just want to be helpful."

The Alpha kissed his lips and told him, "You *are* helpful in more ways than you know, Jackson."

He smiled shyly in response. "I love you."

"I love you, too," Daimon said, wrapping his arms around him. As much as he might like to sit there and hold him for a while, though, Daimon knew that it was time to get to work. They needed to get the traps down before dark, which he could see through the cracks in the barricade wouldn't be long. "We need to get outside and start working on the traps," he said to Jackson.

He sat up and nodded. "Okay." Then, he stood up and helped Daimon to his feet. "I, uh…I've never set traps or anything before, so someone's gonna have to teach me."

Daimon smiled at him. "Don't worry. You can keep watch with Dustu." The Alpha then stepped out from behind the barrel and looked around at his pack. "It's time to get to work," he announced.

Everyone started getting up.

"Are we heading straight to the lake after we kill them?" Jackson asked, following him towards the barricade.

"Everyone's going to need to rest after the fight, but we can't stay here because the messenger could lead Kane right to us. We'll head towards the lake but find somewhere to rest along the way," the Alpha said to everyone.

"I could scout ahead again," Sebastien offered as Daimon began taking down the shelves and boxes blocking the door.

The Alpha nodded and tossed a box aside. Once the doorway was clear, he turned to face his pack. "When the traps are ready, Julian, Dustu, and Remus will head back here and wait. The rest of us will take up our ambush positions."

"Understood," the pack said simultaneously.

Daimon led the way outside. The snow was knee-deep, perfect for setting traps. He didn't know how many wolves Kane was sending, but he knew his pack were ready for anything.

Chapter Thirty-Eight

The Ambush

| Jackson |

As the night grew later and the moon climbed higher into the clear sky, the pack lay in wait.

Jackson hid in the brush with Brando, Rachel, and Ethan. Across the way from them, Wesley hid with Ezhno and Lance. Daimon, Lalo, and Leon were fifty feet to the right, and Tokala, Bly, and Sebastien lay fifty feet to the left. Everyone was ready.

It was silent. The thick bed of snow absorbed every sound for miles, and although it made Jackson a little uneasy, he was sure that it was a good thing. If Kane's approaching wolves couldn't hear them, it gave them another advantage. As for detecting the incoming hostiles, the pack had Daimon's senses to rely on.

The feeling of euphoria Jackson got when he drank Daimon's blood was almost gone, but the spike in his ethos remained. He felt almost *eager* to clash with his enemies. However, he had to contain himself. Kane's wolves weren't there yet.

He focused on what he could see through the leaves. To his relief, he didn't have a bad feeling about this. But he'd not let his guard down. Anything could happen at any moment.

And that was when Jackson heard the snow crunch.

He tensed up and frantically searched for what made the sound.

There they were. A group of six...eight...*twelve* dark-furred, scarred wolves. Jackson waited to see if more would appear from behind the rocks, but that seemed to be it. They were led by a rather beefy-looking grey wolf with a clawed-out right eye and scars all over his face, and they were all snarling quietly as if they were talking, but Jackson couldn't understand any of them.

His eyes shifted to the snow where the traps lay hidden. The wolves were getting closer...and with each step they took, Jackson's heart beat a little faster. Any moment now he'd be bursting out of cover and fighting to the death with Kane's wolves. But he was ready. Daimon trusted him to be an asset, and that was exactly what he was going to be.

"Will you stop?!" a muffled, foggy voice suddenly growled.

Jackson frowned and looked at Brando, Rachel, and Ethan, but the three of them were watching the approaching wolves like hawks.

He slowly turned his head to face Kane's group again.

"All I'm saying…" another distorted voice said, but it cut out for a few seconds, and when Jackson heard it again, they said, "…We just all come and…." It cut out again.

Jackson's frown thickened. *Someone* was talking…but who?

There was no time for him to find out. The one-eyed wolf stepped into one of the hidden traps, and as the rope ensnared his front left paw and pulled him fifteen feet up off the ground, his packmates started panicking.

"Now!" Daimon yelled.

On the Alpha's call, Jackson and the pack burst out of cover and charged towards the enemy. In the commotion, three of Kane's wolves triggered more of the traps and were pulled up off their paws and dangled from the branches the ropes were looped around.

The packs clashed. With four wolves writhing and snarling in the air, Daimon's group had the advantage. Jackson watched as everyone fought, growling and slashing and biting. Blood sprayed onto the snow, and when two of Kane's wolves fell lifeless, Jackson rushed in and found Ethan.

When Ethan smacked his opponent's face with his huge paw, Jackson lunged forward and snapped his jaws around the brown wolf's back leg. The beast yelped and tried kicking him off, but Ethan took advantage of it being distracted and clamped his teeth around its neck. And with a roar and a tug, the giant tiger twisted and pulled the wolf's head from its body.

"Thanks," Ethan said.

Jackson nodded and turned to face the battle.

"You go help Lalo, I'll help Bly," the muto said.

"Okay," Jackson said and then hurried over to Lalo.

The blonde wolf Lalo was facing grabbed the Kappa's muzzle with his teeth, but before he could bite down hard enough to do some real damage, Jackson crashed into him and sent the hostile wolf tumbling across the snow. The wolf rolled over one of the traps, and when he was pulled up to join his four dangling packmates, he whined and tried to break free.

Lalo panted and said, "Thanks, man."

"Jackson!" came Sebastien's voice.

Jackson turned his head and set his eyes on the winged hound. But then the branch that the rope holding the buff, one-eyed wolf was wrapped around snapped, and the beast hit the ground. The wolf immediately went for Sebastien, who snarled and charged at the wolf.

As he ran, the hound called, "Use your fire before the ropes break!"

"Keep one of them alive!" then came Daimon's voice.

Jackson looked at the Alpha, who had just torn the head off his opponent. Then, he scurried through the fight and took cover behind a nearby tree. He left his wolf form and held his hand towards the dangling wolves, but then somebody yelped painfully, and when Jackson saw Bly pinned down by one of Kane's wolves, he tensed up and aimed his hand towards the enemy.

But Daimon quickly raced to help her, so Jackson turned his attention back to the four dangling wolves. He focused and created a ball of crimson fire in his hand, and then he threw it at one of them. The wolf went up in flames; it wailed and whined, burning into nothing in no time. Jackson ensnared two others, leaving just one hanging and panicking as his friends disappeared before his eyes.

Jackson stood there, glancing at the fighting packs and making sure that the wolf Daimon asked him to keep alive didn't escape. His packmates took down the remainder of Kane's wolves in a few minutes, and when the last wolf's head was removed, Daimon let out a howl of victory. The pack joined in, and the sound sent a chill down Jackson's spine.

They won. The plan worked.

It wasn't entirely over yet, though.

"Get him down," Daimon said, nodding at the dangling, panicking wolf.

Sebastien spat blue flames at the rope, and when it withered, the wolf fell and landed on the snow with a thump. The wolf hurried to its paws and tried to flee, but Daimon's wolves quickly surrounded him, blocking any chance he had at getting away.

Daimon pounced and pinned the wolf down. "You're going to listen to me *very* carefully," he growled.

With a terrified whine, the wolf tried to break free, but its attempts were useless.

"Your Alpha picked the *wrong* pack to fuck with," Daimon snarled, baring his teeth as he moved his maw into the wolf's line of sight. "You run back to him and tell him that I'm going to kill every single one of his wolves, and when he's all alone, I'll tear him apart one piece at a time until he's *begging* that I kill him, too. And you tell him…this is war, and he isn't going to win. We're the last pack he will ever try to destroy."

The wolf whined and writhed, still attempting to get away.

Daimon then savagely tore the wolf's left ear off with his teeth, grabbed it by its scruff as it wailed painfully, and then tossed it across the snow. The moment it hit the ground, it hurried to its paws and fled as quickly as it could.

"How long do you think it'll take him to get back to his pack?" Tokala asked Daimon.

"Long enough that we'll be far away from here," the Alpha answered. "Well done, everyone," he then said as he headed back towards the cellar. "There will be time for proper celebration once we find somewhere safe. Is everyone okay to travel?"

The pack called their confirmations.

Tokala appeared at Jackson's side. "You've picked up the fire ethos pretty quickly, huh?" he said with a smirk.

Jackson smiled slightly. "Yeah, I guess so," he replied, but then he grimaced when a strange nauseous feeling struck him. He felt like he might throw up…but after a few moments passed, the sickly feeling faded.

"You okay?" Tokala asked in concern.

He nodded. "Yeah, I'm good."

"You know, with the inimă, your fire could probably kill someone in less than a second."

"Oh…well, I didn't really think of using it," Jackson replied.

"You're keeping it close, though, right? Just in case?" the orange wolf asked.

Jackson nodded and patted the bags he was carrying over his shoulder now that he was no longer in his wolf form.

"Good," Tokala said. "Don't hesitate to use it if you think it's necessary. It's yours to use."

"I know, I just…I guess I'm a little worried about losing control. I think I want to wait until I have better control over my demon ethos before I start using it again. I mean…unless I *need* to use it…say if another cadejo or something came. I don't know," he said with a sigh.

"Trust your judgement," the Zeta told him.

Jackson smiled again. "I will."

Ethan then joined him, and Tokala walked off to join Daimon.

"I guess it's really started now, then," the tiger said.

"I guess so," Jackson agreed.

The pack stopped outside the cellar and waited while Wesley headed inside to grab Julian, Dustu, and Remus.

Jackson frowned and turned to face Ethan. "Something weird happened just before the fight."

Ethan frowned. "Something weird how?"

"I don't know. I thought I heard someone speaking. But when I looked at you guys…well, I don't think it was either of you."

"What did you hear?"

"Uh…someone said, 'Will you stop?', and then I heard someone else say something like…'All I'm saying is', but I couldn't hear the rest of it. It was like…fading in and out."

The tiger's frown thickened. "One of Kane's wolves was talking about how they should just *all* come out here looking for us rather than sending a little group, and then their leader told him to stop."

Jackson felt confused. "What...so...I was hearing *them*?"

"I don't know, man. Wolf walkers can only understand their pack members or something, right? Only Alphas, Betas, and Zetas or something can understand all wolves," Ethan drawled. Then, he set his eyes on Sebastien. "Hey, Sebastien."

The winged hound made his way over. "What?"

"Tell him," Ethan urged.

"Tell me what?" Sebastien questioned.

Jackson scratched the back of his head. "Well...I think I was catching some conversation between those Kane wolves. But...that's impossible, right? I'm just a Cupitor."

Sebastien sat down. "Well, there's this little thing called True Speech, which only the oldest demons know how to use. I was taught by Lord Caedis—well...more like he kinda stuffed the knowledge into my brain—but those with the blood of someone who possesses True Speech will also inherit the ability. Since you're asmodi, it would make sense that you'd possess it."

"Okay, so what is it?" Ethan asked.

"The ability to understand and communicate with all Caeleste, save for the Aegis," Sebastien answered.

Could that be why he understood cadejo? Could that be why that prowler stopped when he told it to...because it could understand him, too?

"How does he like...improve the ability?" Wilson asked.

"He doesn't," Sebastien said, standing up. "True Speech isn't a right, it's a gift. It'll decide itself whether or not Jackson is worthy."

"Let's go," Daimon suddenly called. "Jackson, shift."

With a nervous nod, Jackson shifted into his wolf form.

"Here, let me help," Ethan said, helping him make sure his bags were secure.

"Thanks," Jackson said, and then he hurried to catch up with Sebastien. "What do you mean it'll decide if I'm worthy?"

"I mean exactly what I said," Sebastien replied, following the pack through the woods. "It isn't a part of you unless it chooses to be."

"Okay...and how do I prove my worth? How did you prove yours?" he asked curiously.

Sebastien sighed quietly. "Through my loyalty to Lord Caedis."

Jackson frowned and pondered. That made sense since asmodi demons were created by Lord Caedis and the Zenith. But how could he prove his loyalty? The only thing he could think of was getting the job done. "Okay," he answered. Then, he left Sebastien's side and headed to the front to join Daimon. "Hey," he said nervously.

"Is everything okay?" the Alpha asked, glancing at him.

"Yeah, I was just asking Sebastien some demon stuff."

"Anything we need to be worried about?"

"No, he was telling me about something called True Speech."

Daimon frowned at him. But he didn't say anything. Concern flickered across his face as he quickly stared ahead again, and it looked like he was on edge.

And then came that feeling. Jackson tensed up as a shiver of trepidation crept down his spine.

Something was coming.

Jackson looked around fearfully, trying to locate what it was. Could it be Kane's wolves? Or was it something else?

"Stay alert," Daimon called, keeping his voice hushed.

"What is it?" Remus whispered.

"I don't know," the Alpha replied. "Keep low."

Everyone crouched and followed him through the thick trees.

But with every step they took, Jackson's fear grew. They were getting closer to whatever his instincts were trying to warn him about. "I-I think we should go a different way," he said, looking at Daimon.

The Alpha didn't even question him. "All right," he said, turning right.

That didn't make Jackson feel any better, though.

It was *following* them. *Something* was following them.

He looked left and right, searching for a glimpse of what it was, but there was nothing but endless white and empty silence. He looked back at Sebastien when Daimon did, but the hound shook his head, telling them that he couldn't sense anything.

Cadejo. It *had* to be cadejo, right?

"D-Daimon, I—"

A horrific, gurgling screech cut through the silence, echoing behind.

"What the hell was that?" Dustu panicked, stopping in his tracks.

The rest of the pack slowly came to a halt and stared back the way they'd come.

"Some kind of Caeleste beast?" Wesley suggested

"That didn't sound like any beast I know," Tokala replied warily.

"Keep moving," Daimon called.

Something rushed through the trees a hundred feet away.

The pack backed off and huddled closer as confused, unnerved looks appeared on their faces.

Jackson froze and stared; he didn't get a good look at it, but it moved *so* fast that he already knew it was dangerous.

And then it appeared again, darting from behind one tree to another.

He saw it this time, and he wished he hadn't.

"Human?" Lalo questioned. "Hunter?"

"Too fast to be human," Sebastien said, "and I can't feel an aura."

"Vampire?" Lance muttered as everyone took a defensive formation.

"I'd feel it," the hound answered.

The creature moved again, getting closer with every reveal of its human-like, lanky body.

And then came the smell.

That rotting, putrid stench.

"Cadejo," Jackson breathed.

Chapter Thirty-Nine

⤝ ⋞ ☽ ⋟ ⤞

Metamorphosis

| Jackson |

The creature had no face.

Each time it peered out from behind the tree it hadn't moved from, Jackson saw just a little more of it.

Its human-like body was at least seven feet tall with lanky arms and grey, slimy-looking skin. The only orifice on its face was a gnarly, rounded mouth which stretched from its chin to where its nose would meet between its eyes if it were actually human, and inside were several rows of razor-sharp teeth.

When it leaned its body out from behind the tree again, the creature let out a shrill, rhythmic wail... but it almost seemed curious. It didn't attack, nor did it roar or growl as if it thought the pack was a threat. The thing just... stood there.

Jackson's feeling of unease lingered. It clawed at him, urging him to flee. He was horrified—he had no idea what that thing was or what its intentions were—but he needed to fight his fear. He'd not freeze up, nor would he let anyone else suffer. He swallowed the spit which pooled in his mouth and looked at Daimon. "W-we need to get the hell away from that thing," he whispered.

But... no one moved. No one *spoke*.

Jackson set his eyes on the monster, and when it backed behind the tree, he looked at his packmates. "Guys?" he asked worriedly. "We need to move!"

Still, no one moved or said anything. It was like... they were frozen with fear. But they didn't look afraid; they looked... mesmerized. *Entranced*. And when Jackson stared closely at Daimon's face, he noticed that his iris' had swirling black patterns inside.

It looked as though *everyone* had it—even Ethan... and Sebastien.

"Ethan?!" he insisted quietly, moving in front of the tiger.

What the hell was going on?

Was that creature doing it to them?

Jackson turned to face it again and watched it peer out at him. It made another sound... clicking quietly as the teeth in its mouth slowly twisted around. He didn't know what it was waiting for, but Jackson wasn't going to wait and find out. He had to do something... but what? How was he supposed to snap everyone out of it?

He stood in front of Daimon and nudged him with his paw. "Daimon? Daimon?!" He then shoved his side, and the Alpha stumbled, but he didn't snap out of his trance.

The creature suddenly chirped... and several chirps replied, echoing through the trees.

There were more of them, and they were coming.

Jackson's heart started racing as he rushed and stood in front of each of his packmates and tried to wake them up, but it was useless, and when he looked back at the creature... it wasn't leaning out from behind that tree anymore.

He frantically searched for any sign of it, but then distorted chirps started echoing from every direction, and Jackson began to feel so overwhelmed with fear and confusion that all he could do was stand there and stare at the place where he'd last seen the monster.

Footsteps crunched in the snow beside him.

Jackson turned to face the sound, but then it came from behind him.

He swung around, his breaths stifled, and his body stiff.

The creature's clicks came from behind a rock, but when Jackson looked over there, the snow to his left crunched—

With a shrill wail, the monster burst out from behind a tree and charged towards the frozen pack.

There was no time for Jackson to hesitate. He shoved aside his fear and charged forward, and before the creature could grab Brando, Jackson snatched its extended arm with his jaws and yanked as hard as he could. He managed to pull the creature away from his packmate, and as it screeched, he used all the strength he had to sharply turn his body and launch the monster away.

The creature tumbled across the snow, letting out muffled wails as it did, and when it hit a tree, it fell still and whined quietly where it lay.

"Daimon!" Jackson insisted, trying to wake the Alpha from his trance once again.

But then someone grunted.

Jackson searched the faces of his packmates, and when he saw a struggled scowl on *Tokala*, a slither of hope raced through him.

"Tokala?" he panted, leaping over to him. He stared into the Zeta's purple eyes—there was no sign of the blackness which had ensnared everyone else's.

"J-Jackson," he grunted through gritted teeth. "K-k... kill it."

The creature screeched, and a flurry of chirps replied. He didn't know how many more were coming, but they were getting closer. There was no time for him to ask Tokala why he had to kill it.

When Jackson turned to face the monster, it had already pulled itself to its feet. And then it charged.

He wasn't going to let it hurt anyone.

Jackson scowled and raced towards it, ready to tear it apart. But that was when he saw something move in the corner of his eye. He looked over there, seeing another creature... and another... and another. They appeared one by one, getting closer, heading straight for his packmates.

He wasn't looking where he was going.

Jackson crashed into the creature, and as it wrapped its arms around him, he grunted and snarled.

And then he felt its sharp, jagged teeth pierce his skin.

Jackson yelped as pain surged through his body. The monster slammed him on the ground, and then it tried to head for his pack. But he wasn't going to give up. He lunged forward and gripped the creature's ankle with his jaws, but holding back just one wasn't going to save his pack. The others were closing in... and everyone was still frozen.

He pulled the creature back and climbed to his paws. He managed to pin the monster down, and then he savagely tore at its chest with his teeth until he gripped its heart. Jackson tore it out, and the creature went silent.

It wasn't over, though. He lifted his head as the heart hit the snow.

There were at least seven more... and they were mere feet from his pack. What was he supposed to do? There were too many of them for him alone and there was no way he would be fast enough to tackle even *one*!

But he *wasn't* alone.

He felt something pulse inside him, and a strange warmth soaked into his right side. From his right bag, crimson fog crept out; it swiftly ensnared his body, and when he felt the inimă wrap around his neck, burning, enthralling demon ethos electrified through him.

Jackson gave in to it the same way he did before. All he could think about was protecting his packmates—

The ground shook

The monsters stumbled and gripped the trees to steady themselves.

And as the inimă sent forks of crimson light through the snow, a flurry of shimmering red-black crystals burst up from the ground and formed a protective barricade around the pack.

Now... it was time to kill.

With a ferocious snarl, Jackson burst forward. He reached the first creature in seconds and pounced at it. He sunk his teeth into its throat and tore its head off, and when its body hit the ground, he turned to face the crystal barricade. The other monsters were trying to reach through the gaps between the crystals, shrieking and wailing.

Jackson raced towards them. He grabbed the arm of one of them and tossed the creature away, and then he lunged at another and plunged his maw into its chest like a hot knife through butter. Once he tore its heart out, he fixed his eyes on his next target, which was trying to climb the barricade.

He snatched the creature's leg and slammed it onto the ground, and before it could try to get up, Jackson mercilessly tore its heart out. Then, he sprung from creature to creature, tearing them apart as quickly as he could. And when there was only one left, it stopped trying to get past the barricade and turned to face him.

Jackson snarled and glowered at it. The demon power inside him urged him to charge and destroy it, but he held back. There was a small part of him that wanted to wait…so he did. He watched it slowly move forward, clicking and chirping. It tilted its head and swayed its arms—was it trying to communicate? If it was, Jackson didn't under—

"*You…*" a snake-like voice breathed, echoing around inside Jackson's head. "*You… here.*"

Jackson stepped back, and the raging demon ethos retreated ever so slightly, giving him room to contemplate.

"*You're… the one,*" the voice drawled as the creature stopped moving.

Jackson frowned and breathed, "W-what?"

The creature suddenly groaned and jerked its body. "*H… help…*" it choked, dragging itself towards him. "*Help… m-me….*"

He didn't know what to do, but his instincts were telling him to kill it—the power of the inimă was telling him to kill it. *Tokala* had told him to kill the monster, and maybe if he did, then his pack would be free from whatever trance they were trapped in. That was all Jackson wanted right now.

So he lunged and the monster and pinned it on its back. The voice was gone; the creature shrieked and wailed and tried to fight him off, but Jackson savagely tore its grey, slimy body apart in a matter of seconds.

And finally… it was over.

Jackson stepped away from the corpse and exhaled deeply. Relief flooded through him when he heard his packmates' confused voices from inside the crystal barricade. But he couldn't remove the inimă until he freed them.

He focused on the barricade and the fact that he wanted it to release his pack, and to his relief, crimson light forked along the ground towards the crystals, and then they slowly sunk back into the earth they'd come from.

"Jackson!" a flurry of voices called.

Everyone started running towards him, and when he saw Daimon and Ethan, Jackson found himself conflicted about who he wanted to run to first. But by the time he decided that it was Daimon, they'd all crowded around him and asked him what happened.

He shook his head. "I-I don't know, you guys were just…frozen. It was like you were in a trance."

"I feel sick," Julian complained with a grimace.

"What the hell are these things?" Wesley snarled, looking down at the corpse of the creature Jackson just killed.

"Jackson," Sebastien then said.

He looked at the hound.

"You gotta let it know that you don't need it anymore—it's done its job," he said, nodding to the inimă.

Jackson glanced down at the amulet around his neck and nodded. He took another deep breath and tried to relax, letting the inimă know that he no longer needed its help. He felt the demon ethos inside him begin to wither, and the red fog that sept from his fur quickly returned to the shimmering crystal.

And then the inimă fell from his neck and hit the snow.

"Are you okay?" Daimon asked worriedly as he moved closer and nuzzled the side of Jackson's face.

"Y-yeah, I'm okay."

"You're bleeding," Ethan exclaimed.

Jackson glanced at him. "It's fine, I'm okay," he assured him.

Daimon then picked the inimă up with his teeth and put it back in Jackson's right bag. "Thank you," he whispered and caressed his neck with his head.

The Alpha's affection made him smile, and as he rested his head on Daimon's, he was able to relax the rest of his body.

"Uh…guys," Lalo called.

They all turned to face him.

"This one's got a tattoo," the Kappa said.

Everyone moved closer. On the upper arm of one of the dead creatures was a rose tattoo with the name Charlotte beneath it.

"Was…this thing human?" Brando questioned.

Jackson tensed up and watched Sebastien examine the body further.

"I think…what we're looking at is some sort of…metamorphosis. Maybe this is some kind of final form," Sebastien said with dread in his voice, glancing at the wolves.

"Like…*this* is what those human infected turn into?" Ethan asked.

Sebastien nodded. "It looks like it." He shook his head and shifted into his human form. "I need to call this in. The sooner the Venaticus know, the better."

"We don't have time," Daimon said sternly. "We've already lost too much being trapped here by these things."

The white-haired demon grunted and reached into his bag. He pulled out a small device and hastily stuffed it inside the corpse.

"What are you doing?" Tokala questioned.

"Tracking device," Sebastien answered, wiping his hands on his trousers. "They'll send a team out to come and grab it." He shifted back into his hound form.

Daimon then moved past him and called, "Come on. We need to move."

"Don't have to tell me twice," Ezhno said, hurrying after him.

The pack quickly followed the Alpha away from the corpses and deeper into the woods.

"W-what if there's more of them?" Remus asked, walking beside Daimon.

"Then Jackson can deal with them, right?" Ethan said before the Alpha could answer.

Daimon glanced back at him and scowled. "We're going to keep moving and avoid contact with *anything* until we find somewhere safe."

"Does that mean there's variants of infected humans now?" Julian asked.

"It looks that way," Rachel answered.

Jackson then looked at Sebastien, who was awfully quiet. He expected the hound to be talking about the possibilities of human infected variants, but he followed in silence with a *haunted* look on his face. It looked like he was *terrified*.

"Sebastien?" he asked quietly. "Are you okay?"

The hound glanced at him. "Yeah. How did you create those crystals?" he asked, obviously avoiding Jackson's question.

Jackson wouldn't press him, though. "I don't know, I just…did."

"That was Luciferium; I only know two demons who can summon it, and they're Lord Caedis and the Zenith. You also used demon ethos in your wolf form, which shouldn't be possible."

"It's because of the inimă, right?" Julian suggested from beside Sebastien. "I-I mean…he did it before when Kane's wolves attacked us."

Sebastien adorned a skeptical expression. "It would appear so."

"You say that like something's wrong," Ethan said, walking beside Jackson.

The hound shook his head. "No, there's just never been a case of someone using one of the Zenith's inimăs before, so no one really knows what to expect. I'm learning shit as you are about it," he said, nodding at Jackson.

"What *are* those crystals?" Julian asked.

"They come from somewhere else, a place we've all just come to call Lord Caedis' Realm. Maybe Hell, if you will," Sebastien explained.

Jackson frowned strangely. He could summon crystals from *Hell*?

"Come on," Daimon then called, picking up the pace.

Jackson wasn't sure what he was most concerned about: variant infected humans…or the fact that Sebastien didn't know what he might be capable of with the inimă. What if he did something *bad*? What if he broke something or hurt someone? What if he was messing with things he shouldn't be messing with? He was still struggling to remember what he knew about the Caeleste world, and the last thing he wanted to do was meddle in things that weren't to be meddled with. What if he set a bunch of Hell demons free? What if he opened a portal to Hell and plunged the world into darkness?

He shook his head. Was he overreacting? He'd seen his fair share of apocalypse movies…so maybe he was worrying a little too much about fiction.

But what if he wasn't? The power inside the inimă was *literally* part of a god. He didn't know what to expect. All he'd done so far, though, was *help* his friends. He hadn't torn holes in the fabric of reality or set huge, demonic beasts free, had he? He *had* grabbed Rachel, but she seemed to have forgiven him, just as Daimon said she would.

He took a deep breath and focused on following the pack. There could be more of those faceless creatures out there, and if he had to kill more, he would.

What did that monster mean when it told him that he was the one, though? He'd heard similar things from cadejo; they always called the word here when they were close to Jackson. What if it was connected? Why did it ask him to help it? He didn't know, and there wasn't any way for him *to* know. It wasn't like he could strike up a conversation with a cadejo, was it?

…Unless he could.

Chapter Forty

Evolving Danger

| **Daimon** |

So much was going on. Faceless, undead humans, a war with Kane's pack, and Jackson summoning crystals from Hell. Daimon wasn't sure which thing concerned him the most.

He led his pack through the woods, focusing all of his senses, moving as fast as he could without tiring his wolves out. He was glad that he was able to fight Kane's wolves without stumbling, but he couldn't ignore the ache in his back. He couldn't remember when he took his last antibiotic, but he was sure that Jackson did. When he looked back to where his mate was, though, he saw him walking with and talking to Ethan, and that made Daimon feel irritated.

With a quiet snarl, he tried focusing on getting his pack somewhere safe to spend a few hours of the night. He was sure that they were tired from the fight, and they probably also wanted time to process what they'd seen. Daimon was admittedly a little unsettled knowing that the cadejo virus was now evolving in humans and that some of them seemed to have the ability to paralyze people, and he didn't know what else to expect.

He looked back at Tokala. "Take Dustu and scout ahead. Find us somewhere to spend a few hours."

The Zeta nodded and hurried off with Dustu.

"Dad?" Remus then asked.

"Mm-hmm."

"Do you… do you think that… there are more infected human variants like there are cadejo variants?"

"I don't know, Remus," Daimon answered, leading the pack up a hill. "But after what we just saw, I think we better assume that there are."

"How did it make us freeze like that?" his son questioned.

"I don't know that either. I think the only way we'll get answers is when the Venaticus pick up the body Sebastien tagged."

Remus nodded. "I just...I'm scared."

Daimon looked at him and frowned worriedly.

His son continued, "If there's a variant that can do something like *that*, then...what else could be out there, you know?"

"Unless it wasn't an infected human," came Sebastien's voice.

The Alpha shifted his sights to the hound and saw a haunted look on his face. "What?"

Sebastien glanced at him. "If the virus has evolved and spread to humans, then it's only a matter of time until it evolves to infect other Caeleste."

"I don't like the sound of this shit," Ethan called.

"Even demons?" Jackson asked.

The hound shook his head. "I don't know. I was bitten not long ago, and I haven't turned, so maybe it hasn't evolved that far yet. But it's only a matter of time in my opinion."

Remus stared at Sebastien. "So...that thing could have been...what? An infected elf or something?"

"No, I don't know any elf species who can make a bunch of lycans and a demon freeze on the spot like that," the hound answered.

"Fae," Wesley suggested. "I, uh...there were a lot of fae stories in my family. I heard a few when I was a kid. Something about...a kind of fae which can paralyze someone with this low-frequency sound."

"That thing didn't look fae," Rachel mumbled.

"Have you ever seen one?" Wesley questioned defensively.

"No...but I've heard they have wings," she replied.

"Not all fae have wings," the Gamma said matter-of-factly.

Daimon sighed and said, "Fae are extremely powerful, so if the virus has evolved to infect them, then there's no telling what else might fall victim to it." He looked at Sebastien. "I suggest you be as cautious as the rest of us when fighting cadejo from now on. And you," he said, glancing back at Ethan.

The tiger scoffed. "When have I not been cautious?"

"Come on," Jackson interjected before Daimon could answer. "Stop."

"W-what if we come across like...infected vertora or something?" Julian asked fearfully. "I mean...a zombie *dragon*?"

"Yeah...I'm getting more freaked out by the second," Lalo uttered.

"Dad?" Remus asked shakily. "What if we *do* come across other infected Caeleste? W-what are *we* supposed to do against a vertora? I-I'm not sure if this mission is a good idea anymore."

"The mission is all that matters," Sebastien said sternly. "We've made it this far, and we're gonna keep going. We *have* to because it's not only the Venaticus and wolf walkers relying on us—it's *everyone*. It's *my* mate, and it's the entirety of Ascela. And God forbid this virus spreads overseas, because if it does, it'll be the entire *world* relying on us getting to that lab and getting what the Nosferatu need to create a cure."

Daimon was worried for his son and his pack, but Sebastien was right. There were too many people relying on them getting to that lab for him to turn back. He was doing this for the people he loved above all else, and nothing was going to stop him, not Kane, and not infected Caeleste. He had to keep going.

He glanced back at his worried pack. "Listen," he called. "I know things are getting scarier by the day, but we have to keep going. There's too much riding on us; if we don't get to this lab, the entire Caeleste world could suffer. Now more than ever, we must look out for and protect each other. We must be strong, we must be wary, and we must not let the dangers wear us down."

His words improved the looks on his wolves' faces. He felt the tense atmosphere lift a little, and as he led the way, the uneasy chatter faded.

Tokala and Dustu returned ten minutes later.

"Chief, we found an abandoned hut not too far away," Tokala said.

Dustu added, "We scoured the area and didn't find any cadejo or hostiles."

The Alpha nodded. "Good. Lead the way."

Then, as Tokala and Dustu turned left, Daimon and his pack followed.

| Sebastien |

The place that Tokala and Dustu found looked as though it once belonged to a hunter. An old, rusted car sat in the open garage, and the hut itself had boarded windows and half a door. It appeared as if it had been abandoned long ago, so at least they didn't have to worry about anyone coming home.

Sebastien followed the wolves inside and sat in the far-right corner away from the pack. He needed time by himself to think; he didn't want to call Clementine before he knew what he was going to say.

He shifted into his human form and dragged his hands over his face. Calling the Venaticus was probably more important if he wanted to remain professional, but he couldn't stop worrying about Clementine. Knowing that the virus was evolving and infecting humans and other Caeleste *terrified* him; Silverlake City was already a risky place to live but now it was just plain *dangerous*, and he wanted to get Clementine out of there before anything happened.

As he reached into his bag, he glanced around at the pack, who had all shifted into their human forms. Jackson seemed busy talking to Ethan and Julian, so he didn't have to worry about him coming over and hammering him with questions. He pulled out his mirror and activated the rune on the back.

The mirror faded to black... but a few moments passed, and his mate didn't answer.

Sebastien's heart started racing as angst consumed him. Why wasn't he answering? Surely, he'd be home at this time, right? He frowned and nervously tapped his fingers on the back of the mirror, trying his best to remain composed. But as the seconds ticked by, his worry increased, and he felt he was just moments away from losing it—

The mirror flickered, and his bedroom appeared on the other side. To his relief, Clementine sat on the edge of the bed in front of the mirror. But he looked... sick.

"Clem?" he panicked, pulling the mirror closer so that he could examine Clementine's condition.

Clementine shook his head and waved his hand as he used the other to wipe his nose. "I'm fine, Seb."

"You don't look fine!" he exclaimed.

"It's just a cold. I've been spending too much time in the park. And I know, I know," he said with a sigh. "I should wrap up better."

"Are you sure it's a cold? Did you see a doctor? It could—"

"Calm down, Sebastien," Clementine said with an assuring tone. "I went to the pharmacy and got something to help. I'm fine."

He wasn't convinced. "Please go to a doctor," he pleaded.

Clementine then frowned at him. "What's wrong? You look like you've... well, I'd say seen a ghost, but you see more of those than most," he said with a smirk.

Sebastien shook his head. "I'm not in the mood for jokes, Clem. I've just seen some fucked up shit... and I think things are getting a whole lot worse out here."

"Fucked up how?"

"This... thing," he said, scowling anxiously. "Some sort of infected Caeleste. One of the wolves here thinks it was fae because it did this thing."

"What did it do?" Clementine asked, shuffling closer to the mirror.

"It... froze us," he drawled. "Paralyzed, maybe. None of us could move a muscle, and if it wasn't for Jackson, I don't think I'd still be here."

Clementine's concerned expression thickened. "It didn't affect Jackson?"

"No. I don't know why; I haven't really had the chance to ask or hypothesize. I've been too worried about you."

"Why?" he asked with a quiet, amused scoff. "I'm fine, Seb. You gotta stop worrying and focus on—"

"I need you to do something for me," he interjected.

Clementine adorned an unsure look. "What?"

"I need you to leave Silverlake. Just...pack up some things, ask Heir Lucian to get you a flight on one of their jets, and go and stay with Mavis in Eimwood."

His mate scoffed again and frowned in confliction. "Sebastien, I...I can't just pack up and go. I've got cases—people who are relying on me."

"Clementine, I'm serious. Please. The city is too close to all of this, and I can't focus on what I'm doing out here knowing you're in the middle of it. This virus is evolving *too* fast. It could breach Silverlake's walls at any moment, and I'd rather you be far, *far* away from it all. Eimwood is the safest place in all of Aegisguard, so just...*please* go," he begged despondently.

Clementine didn't answer right away. He wiped his nose, glanced around the room, and adorned a pondering gaze. When he looked at Sebastien, he sighed and said, "If it was *that* bad, wouldn't Lucian and Lord Caedis have packed up and shipped out?"

"How do you know they're not planning to?" Sebastien challenged.

"I saw Lucian a few hours ago. He looked pretty settled."

"And Lord Caedis?"

"No one ever sees him outside of that building. But if Lucian is here, he's here, right? He's gotta babysit that guy so he doesn't blow up a building." He then took a sip of what looked like hot chocolate and continued, "Look, at the first sign of danger, I'll get out of here."

Sebastien's heart was still ensnared by fear. "We can't risk there not being time for you to get out. I've seen cities overrun in a matter of hours; people get violent and lose their minds, they turn on each other, and it becomes nearly impossible for people to escape when they don't have the means to."

"If it comes to that, I'll get to the Venaticus."

"Go *now*," he insisted, pulling the mirror closer. "Just...trust me, please? I have this awful fucking feeling that something is coming, and I need to know that you're safe."

Clementine sighed heavily and took another few moments to think. "All right," he said.

The relief that filled Sebastien was inexplicable. "Thank you," he breathed, letting his anxiety leave his body upon his deep breath. "You're gonna have to call Mavis and let her know you're coming; there's no way for me to contact her from out here."

"Yeah, I'll call her as soon as we're done."

Something about Clementine's despondent tone unsettled Sebastien. "I don't mean to be so adamant, I just...you're the most important thing in the world to me, Clem. If I lost you again, I don't know what I'd do."

Clementine shook his head. "It's okay. I'm going to have to put in for a transfer at the agency...but I'm sure there's a lot of work in Eimwood."

"The city where the Nosferatu's government began?" he said with a smirk. "You'll have a whole bunch of shit to choose from, I'm sure."

He smiled in response. "Yeah."

Sebastien then sighed longingly. "I wish I could hold you," he mumbled sullenly. "And kiss you...and other things," he flirted.

Clementine tried to hide his flustered face behind his mug as he took a sip from it. "How much longer until you're done out there?"

"Originally, it was supposed to take around a week to get to Greykin Valley, but...we've had a few setbacks. We're on course, though. I'm hoping we'll only be a day or two behind schedule."

"And you're coming straight back once you get what you need from that lab, right?"

He nodded. "I'll be coming straight to Eimwood."

Clementine smiled. "Okay. Be safe out there."

"I will, babe. And see a doctor in Eimwood, please?"

He nodded. "Okay. I love you. I'll call you when I land in Eimwood."

"Thank you, and I love you, too." Then, when the mirror faded to black, Sebastien sighed and lowered it into his lap. He missed Clementine so much, and he wished he could be there to protect him, but knowing that he was moving to Eimwood made him feel a whole lot better. That city was the most fortified, safest place in the world. Even if the virus crossed the seas, there was no way it would penetrate the wards protecting the city where the Nosferatu's main place of operations was—the place where Lord Caedis and the Zenith themselves lived.

With a deep, shaky breath, he put the mirror back into his bag and closed his eyes. His tense body relaxed, and his heartbeat steadied. It was going to be fine...Clementine was going to be *fine*.

But what if something happened while Clementine was getting ready to leave?

Sebastien tensed up again. There'd be no way for him to know if Silverlake was suddenly breached, and he wouldn't know if Clementine made it to Eimwood safely until he landed...which could be *hours*.

He buried his face in his hands and tried to calm down. But no matter how many times he told himself that Clementine would be okay, he couldn't let go of his fear.

Letting his trepidation rule him, Sebastien took the mirror from his bag again and tapped the rune on the back which would connect him to Heir Lucian.

But it wasn't Heir Lucian who answered when the mirror faded to reveal his office. Instead, the kid's assistant answered, "Officer Huxley, sir?"

Sebastien sighed and asked her, "Where's Heir Lucian?"

"He's in a conference room with his uncles, sir."

He knew better than to intrude on such a situation. "Fine. I need four soldiers sent to my apartment to escort Clementine to the building. I also need a jet ready to take him to Eimwood. Clear it with either Lord Caedis or Heir Lucian and tell them it's to move Clementine. They'll understand."

The woman nodded. "Yes, sir."

"Pronto," he said firmly.

"R-right away, sir." She then put the mirror down without severing the connection.

Sebastien tapped the rune on the back, severing it himself. Then, as he returned the mirror to his bag once more, he let out another deep, heavy sigh. *Now* he felt a little less afraid. Knowing that there would be trained, armed soldiers escorting Clementine helped him relax. All he had to do now was wait to hear that Clementine had landed.

Would four soldiers be enough?

His anxiety returned. Should he have sent more? Maybe five or six. Should he have asked a whole platoon?

No... he was overreacting.

Was he?

He groaned quietly as he dragged his hands over his face. "It's gonna be fine," he whispered to himself. "He's gonna be fine."

"Who?" someone asked.

Sebastien flinched in startle and lifted his head. Wesley was staring down at him. In response, he waved his hand dismissively and said, "Nothing. I'm just talking to myself."

"Yeah, I kinda figured that."

He sighed. "Do you want something?"

The Gamma crouched in front of him. "I'm honestly quite sure that thing was fae," he started, keeping his voice hushed. "I don't wanna freak anyone out, but... should you contact the Venaticus about it? They're picking the corpse up, right? Can they fast-track results?"

"Probably. With the virus evolving, the more we know—and the sooner we know it—the better."

"I... haven't told anyone this—it's kinda a family secret, I suppose—but there's... a fae chorus in Ascela."

Sebastien frowned. "Chorus?"

"A chorus refers to a group or family of fae," he explained. "But if they're in trouble, I... think we need to help them—*I* need to help them."

His frown thickened, and he sat up straight as his curiosity was piqued. "Why?"

Wesley looked cautious. "I... I've got fae blood," he drawled, whispering.

Sebastien was admittedly surprised. "Huh... well I would have never guessed, honestly."

The guy shrugged. "Yeah, I'm not some half-and-half like Jackson. I've just got the blood. I never learned to do anything with it."

"And... you're whispering about it because...?"

"Let's just say wolf walkers and fae don't have a great history. My bloodline was the only exception because one of my ancestors' mates was a fae woman."

"What kind of fae are we talking about? The chorus here in Ascela," Sebastien questioned.

Wesley shuffled around. "The dangerous kind."

He sighed heavily. "Great. I'll contact the Venaticus before we leave; gotta give them a little time to retrieve the body and study it."

"Okay." Wesley stood up. "And, uh... I'd appreciate it if you didn't say anything."

"Don't worry," he assured him.

With a nod, the Gamma walked off and joined his Epsilons.

Sebastien closed his eyes and took a few deep breaths. If there was anything that he knew about fae, it was that they always steered very clear of human settlements. So, they were *definitely* far from Silverlake, which meant they couldn't be a threat... yet. Clementine would be far away before infected fae reached the walls.

At least he hoped so.

He leaned his head back against the wall and tried to keep himself from sinking into panic again. But he knew he'd not be able to feel completely settled until he knew that Clementine was in Eimwood.

And all he could do was wait and hope that he'd told him to leave soon enough.

Chapter Forty-One

⌐ ≼ ☽ ≽ ⌐

A Missing Piece

| Jackson |

Jackson must have been sitting around for hours thinking. The night grew later, and the pack started finding places inside the abandoned hut to sleep. But he wasn't ready to sleep yet. He was too busy pondering. So much was going on and he couldn't help but feel a little overwhelmed. He was using power that Sebastien didn't understand, and he wondered if he should have fought harder to have Heir Lucian train him. Surely, Lord Caedis' own nephew would know more about the inimă.

True Speech was rolling around inside his head, too. He wanted to be able to learn to use it; then he could talk to and understand other wolf walkers. It was true that he probably didn't necessarily need the skill while in a pack with an Alpha and Zeta who could talk to other wolf walkers, but what if there was ever a time when Daimon and Tokala weren't around?

He sighed and glanced at Ethan, who found an old blanket and was curled up inside it over by the empty fireplace. Julian wasn't far from him, and everyone else was huddled close together against the back wall.

One thing he didn't yet understand, though, was how he could hear cadejo. It wasn't True Speech, was it? Because if it was, then Sebastien would be able to hear and talk to them, but Jackson hadn't seen the hound doing so. So why could he hear them? Was it because he was a hybrid? That had to be it. It was the only thing that made sense.

"Are you okay?" came Daimon's voice, snapping Jackson out of his thoughts.

He looked up at the Alpha, who was standing beside him. "Yeah."

Daimon crouched so that he was at eye level with him. "Are you sure? You've got that look on your face—the one you make when you're overthinking," he said with a smirk, but there was concern in his quiet voice.

Jackson sighed and shrugged. "Yeah, I'm just thinking about True Speech and those weird creatures."

The Alpha nodded. "It's been a long, strange day." He leaned closer so that his face was mere inches from Jackson's. "But we made a little deal before the fight, remember?" he whispered seductively. "And now that everyone's asleep, I think it's time for *us* to get some rest, too."

As he tensed up, Jackson stared into the Alpha's eyes. He *did* remember their deal, and all his thoughts swiftly faded, leaving him with a feeling of growing anticipation. He nodded in response, and when Daimon took his hand, he got up and followed him to the door beside the old kitchenette.

Daimon led him into the only other room inside the hut, and when he closed the door behind them, Jackson set his eyes on the bed under the window. The mattress looked a bit torn, and there was only one pillow, but he didn't care.

The heat of Daimon's presence behind him sent a shiver down Jackson's spine. When the Alpha's lips brushed the back of his neck, a jolt of pleasure coursed through him, making his breath hitch. Slowly, agonizingly slowly, Daimon's hands traced down Jackson's body, each touch igniting a fire beneath his skin. Jackson tilted his head to the side, a silent invitation, and Daimon responded, his warm breath caressing Jackson's neck before his lips followed, nuzzling the sensitive skin with a possessive tenderness.

Jackson's pulse quickened as Daimon's hands slipped lower, fingers teasing at the edge of his trousers. The anticipation was almost too much, his body aching for more as Daimon finally slid his hands inside, the sensation sending a wave of heat that left Jackson trembling with desire. And when the Alpha's fingers gently caressed Jackson's t-dick, he leaned his body back against Daimon and hummed quietly in delight.

He reached back and gripped the side of Daimon's ass, and when he squeezed it, the Alpha smiled against his neck. Daimon then turned Jackson around and pulled him closer. He started kissing his lips, and as Jackson kissed back, the Alpha slowly guided him back towards the bed. When they reached it, Jackson gradually fell on it and shuffled up towards the pillow, where he rested his head. Daimon leaned over him, and as their tongues desperately entwined, Jackson's heart started racing.

He started feeling eager, and as he pulled the Alpha's shirt off, Jackson took the pause in their kissing to catch his breath. Then, once they began kissing frantically again, he stroked his fingers over Daimon's muscular body. With his free hand, he gripped the Alpha's hair, pulling his face closer and his tongue deeper into his mouth. Daimon aggressively pushed as much of his body against Jackson's as he could, and when Jackson felt the Alpha's hard dick press against his inner thigh, his eagerness became anxious desperation.

Jackson turned his head to the side and breathed, "Fuck me."

Daimon started kissing Jackson's neck again, and while he did, he pulled off his own and Jackson's trousers. He hastily urged Jackson to roll onto his front. Jackson complied, gripping the pillow as he tried to relax, but his anticipation was making that hard.

The Alpha slowly eased his shaft into Jackson's hot, wet pussy and gripped his wrists. Jackson groaned quietly as pleasure shivered through him, intensifying as he felt each inch gradually bury itself inside him, and when Daimon kissed his shoulder, he shivered and sighed in anticipation.

Daimon didn't drag things out. He pulled back and started thrusting, breathing against Jackson's neck, and in response, Jackson moaned quietly in contentment. He relaxed his body, giving in to the Alpha's assertive movements, and as his heart raced in his chest, Jackson struggled to keep himself as quiet as he'd like. He didn't want everyone to hear... but it wouldn't be the first time, would it? It seemed almost normal to everyone else.

However, he couldn't ponder much longer. As pleasure raced through him, all he could think about was Daimon and how he loved that he made him feel so powerless beneath him. He moaned and breathed heavier as the Alpha thrusted harder, enthralling him in sheer delight as he approached his peak. Jackson tightened his grip on the pillow, gritting his teeth in struggle as he became overwhelmed. But as he was about to climax, Daimon pulled his dick from his pussy and rolled him over onto his back. Jackson whined in confusion; however, the Alpha quickly slid back inside him, and that was when Jackson climaxed. He moaned contently as Daimon's shaft moved deeper inside him, and then he started thrusting again and kissing Jackson's lips as he did.

Jackson felt overstimulated at first. He'd just climaxed, and his body was trembling and sensitive. But he didn't want Daimon to stop. He pulled him closer, and as the Alpha nuzzled his neck, he dragged his body over Jackson's, moving a little faster. Jackson wrapped his legs around Daimon's waist, pulling him closer; the pleasure quickly returned, and when he started kissing Daimon again, the Alpha hummed contently into his mouth.

It didn't take long for the Alpha's long, hard dick to bring Jackson closer to another orgasm, but when he heard Daimon's moans growing more frantic, he tensed up and desperately breathed, "Don't cum in me."

Daimon groaned and nuzzled Jackson's neck for a moment, and then he pulled his dick from his pussy. He moaned loudly, his hot cum dripping onto Jackson's stomach, and then he growled pleasurably and playfully bit Jackson's neck.

"Fuck," Jackson breathed as he slowly unwrapped his trembling legs from around Daimon's waist. "I'm close," he told him.

The Alpha smiled and slowly descended Jackson's trembling body. When he reached his legs, he gripped his thighs in either hand and pulled them apart. With a seductive smirk, Daimon dragged his warm tongue over Jackson's t-dick, which sense tingling, enthralling pleasure spiralling through him.

Jackson let out a desperate groan, leaning his head back, and when Daimon swirled his tongue around and gently bit his t-dick, he fidgeted in the Alpha's grip and moaned quietly in content. Daimon started sucking, twirling his tongue around it, tightening his grip on Jackson's legs. Jackson winced and moaned, grasping a fistful of Daimon's hair, and as he climaxed, he pulled Daimon closer and whined loudly.

Daimon dragged his tongue up Jackson's t-dick and crawled back up to him, and when their eyes met, the Alpha smirked at him. "I told you I'd make you cum more than once."

He pouted embarrassedly and glanced around for something to clean up with.

"Wait there," Daimon said as he stood up.

Jackson did as he was told and tried to hide that he was staring at the Alpha's naked body while he walked over to a closet with only one door. Daimon snatched an old shirt from inside, walked back over to the bed, and used it to clean them both. Then, he lay beside Jackson and pulled the blanket over them.

With a quiet, satisfied sigh, Jackson rolled onto his side and rested his head on Daimon's chest. "Who do you think lived here before?" he asked quietly as Daimon moved his arm around him.

"It's usually hunters who live out in the middle of the forest," he answered.

Jackson frowned. "Why, though? I mean…there's all sorts of dangerous stuff out here. Wouldn't it make sense for Caeleste killers to live *away* from the Caeleste?"

"You'd think so, but hunters' places are usually surrounded by traps or dogs. Thankfully, this place seems like it was abandoned so long ago that there aren't any traps left to trigger."

"I guess so," Jackson mumbled. "Why do they even…hunt us?"

Daimon sighed deeply. "A number of reasons. Old grudges, old wars, the fact that a lot of Caeleste are valuable to people like alchemists and mages. A lot of medicines are made with things taken from Caeleste, and the Caeleste isn't always willing. That's where hunters make most of their money."

Jackson frowned uncomfortably. "Isn't that illegal?"

"Yes, but there are places that ignore the law, and that's where hunters come in."

His frown thickened. "You don't think that the Nosferatu are like that, do you?"

"I don't know. But it would be rather dystopian if the Caeleste government broke its own rules, wouldn't it?"

Jackson leaned on his arm so that he could see Daimon's face. "I don't know. There's just so much I still don't know. I've been waiting for all my memories to come back, but it's taking forever."

Daimon moved his hand to the side of Jackson's face. "They'll come back. You just need to wait."

"Yeah, but…how much longer?"

The Alpha then frowned as he dragged his palm down from Jackson's face to his shoulder. "What are you hoping to remember?"

He shrugged. "Anything. Everything. I worked with Ethan for years, and I wanna remember all of the Caeleste stuff. I want to remember what I knew about the Nosferatu and Lyca Corp. and demons and dragons and vampires and everything else," he said as his frustration grew.

"What if you didn't know much?" Daimon suggested. "There *are* Caeleste who tune the world out nowadays."

He shook his head. "I don't feel like I'd tune it out."

"Well, is there a way to trigger your memories?"

"I don't know. I guess maybe I could ask Ethan to tell me more about the stuff we did together."

Daimon looked a little disgruntled but quickly dismissed his expression and said, "If you think it will help."

"I *hope* it does," he said with a sigh, laying back down. "I still have this kinda like…I don't know. It feels like there's still a part of me that's missing, you know?"

The Alpha nodded. "I know how that feels."

Now that he was thinking about it, Jackson really *did* feel like there was a pit inside him. Something *was* missing, and his memories were the only thing that made sense. Sure, he'd *always* felt like he had all these missing pieces, and most of them had been returned to him now that he'd found his true self, Daimon, and the Caeleste world, but there was still a hole, and the longer he spent waiting for the rest of his memories to return, the worse he felt.

"Don't worry about it too much," Daimon told him as he fiddled with his hair. "You'll get them back."

"Yeah," he murmured, letting himself sink deeper. He didn't feel very hopeful; if they *would* come back, then wouldn't it have happened already? It had been a while now since the perception filter was removed.

Daimon kissed him and said, "We'll figure something out tomorrow, okay? Let's get some sleep."

Jackson nodded and tried to make himself comfortable as Daimon pulled the rest of the cover over them. *Would* they work something out? Would he ever recover *everything* the perception filter took from him? Or would he feel like there was a hole inside him forever?

Chapter Forty-Two

⊷ ≼ ☽ ≽ ⊶

Exes

| Jackson |

The sun was rising outside, and Jackson lay beside Daimon unable to fall back asleep. He must have only gotten a few hours. Ever since last night, he hadn't been able to stop thinking about the fact that something was still missing from him.

He glanced at Daimon, who was still sleeping. No matter how many times he told himself that the Alpha was right—that he'd eventually get all of his memories back—he couldn't settle. He couldn't stop worrying that something would go wrong and he'd stay feeling lost and as though there was a hole in his chest.

With a quiet sigh, he rolled onto his side and gazed at Daimon. A part of him wanted to wake him up so that they could talk and he didn't have to lay there alone in silence, but so much was going on lately, and he knew that Daimon needed his sleep.

Jackson rolled onto his back and stared at the cracked, frozen ceiling. But then a strange, disorientating nausea struck him. He frowned and shuffled back onto his side, but the sickly feeling didn't relent. It got worse.

He groaned and sat up; he took several deep breaths, hoping that the nausea would pass. But his stomach started churning, and his throat felt sore. He was going to throw up.

With a quiet gag, Jackson held his hand over his mouth and moved to the end of the bed; however, before he could get up and rush to find somewhere to vomit, he heard rustling outside. As he turned his attention to it and peered out the window, the sickly feeling faded. He was admittedly afraid that he might see cadejo or hunters, but he couldn't smell rotting flesh, nor could he hear humans.

It took him a moment to locate what made the sound, and when he set his eyes on the white and brown-striped tiger crouched in the snow, Jackson calmed down. What was Ethan doing out there, though? He watched him prowl through the snow towards the tree line, and when he spotted a brown hare eating the berries from a bush, he assumed that his friend must be hunting.

He watched through the window as Ethan slowly moved through the snow, and when he pounced, the rabbit fled into the woods before he could try to grab it with his teeth.

"Fuck," Ethan grumbled.

Amused, Jackson smirked slightly. Then, he looked at Daimon again. He didn't want to be alone, and he didn't want to wake the Alpha up. *Ethan* was awake, so maybe he could go and hang out with him for a little while.

He carefully got out of bed, and to his relief, getting up didn't make him feel worse; he still felt nauseous, but he was confident that he wouldn't throw up. He left the room as quietly as possible, and he didn't wake any of the pack as he crept past and over their sleeping bodies towards the door.

When he got outside, he made his way around to the back of the hut. But Ethan was nowhere to be seen. Jackson frowned and looked around; he noticed paw tracks in the snow leading into the woods, so he followed them. However, the further he got from the hut, the more hesitant he started feeling. He glanced over his shoulder, and as he realized that he could no longer see the building, he unsurely called, "Uh…Ethan?" looking around as he moved deeper into the woods.

Something rustled through the brush.

Jackson stopped walking and sharply turned his head towards the sound. But he couldn't see anything.

A twig snapped behind him.

He swung around again, "E-Ethan?" he questioned nervously. He focused his senses and tried to locate what he was hearing, but he couldn't feel an aura or anything.

And then came a low, rumbling growl.

Jackson prepared to shift, but before he had the chance, a blur of orange and white burst out of the bushes and crashed into him. He shrieked and went to adorn his demon form, but when he realized that he wasn't being torn apart, he frowned and stared at what had him pinned to the ground.

"Boo," Ethan said with a grin, his sharp teeth glistening in the early morning sunlight.

Jackson scowled and pouted. "You're not funny," he grumbled, trying to push the tiger away.

Ethan laughed as he backed off and let Jackson stand up. "I was just testing you. With you being a hybrid and all, I was curious as to whether you could detect me."

As he wiped the snow from his trousers, Jackson rolled his eyes. "And you *had* to pounce on me to determine that?"

"No," he said with a shrug. "I just thought it'd be funny."

"Well, it wasn't."

Still laughing, Ethan shook his head and sat down.

"What are you doing out here anyway?" Jackson questioned.

"Hunting. I got hungry and didn't feel like waiting for everyone else to wake up."

"Yeah, well. You suck," Jackson sneered. "I saw you miss the hare."

Ethan scoffed. "Hey, I'm not used to all this snow. I'm supposed to be out in rainforests."

Jackson leaned against a tree as a curious frown made its way to his face. "I don't know if you ever told me—and I don't remember anyway—but why did you move to New Dawnward? If you're meant to be out in rainforests and all that, then shouldn't you be in Samayō-Akuma or Samjang or something?"

The tiger sighed sullenly. "Yeah, I told you this one. But since you don't remember—perception filters and all—I'll tell you again."

As much as he *wanted* to know, he could see that Ethan was upset. "You don't have to talk about it. It's—"

"No, it's cool. When I was a kid—before I met you—we *were* in Samjang. I know there are a few scattered families of muto-tigris; some are in Dor-Sanguis and others in Lǎohǔ Zhī Dì. But my family fled from Samjang when hunters started closing in on where we were hiding. My parents, my sister and I were the only ones who got away. We knew New Dawnward was safe because the Nosferatu have a big influence over there. And it *was* safe until we started digging into the wolf walker business," he explained.

Jackson frowned sympathetically. "Wow…I'm sorry. And I'm sorry that I don't remember. I'm trying to…it's just…I don't know what to do. I talked to Daimon last night and—"

"Yeah, we all heard you *talking*," Ethan muttered bitterly.

He refrained from snapping and continued, "And I said that maybe asking you to tell me more about the stuff we did together could help."

Ethan's sour expression ran away from his face. "Sounds like a plan. Well…I could tell you about Keith."

Jackson frowned. "I remember Keith."

"Yeah, but do you remember that he was an energy vampire?"

His frown thickened. "Uh…no." Of course he wouldn't remember that. The perception filter probably made him think that *all* of his exes and one-night stands were human.

Ethan chuckled and shook his head. "You gotta remember *always* feeling tired around the guy, right?"

He tried to recall the two weeks he spent dating Keith. "Um…I mean yeah. I thought I was sick or something."

"And you ran to the ER asking for scans and everything," he laughed.

Jackson scowled in embarrassment. "I was worried, okay!"

"You were scouring the internet for answers and were convinced you had the most rarest of sicknesses, Jack," Ethan laughed.

He rolled his eyes again. "Whatever."

"I remember what happened when the doctor said that you were being fed on by an energy vampire, though."

"What happened? All I remember is...uh...he gave me something. A pill?"

"He gave you vitamins," the tiger snickered. "Specially made for people who live with energy vampires."

Jackson sighed deeply. "Why did I break up with him again?"

"Oh, he broke up with you...maybe because I told him to."

"What?" Jackson exclaimed. "I actually liked that guy."

"Yeah, but at the rate he was draining you, you'd have been a corpse in a few more days. He *had* to go," Ethan insisted.

Jackson looked down at the snow as he felt his sadness growing. "Yeah...I remember how he used to talk and talk and talk, and I'd get tired pretty fast."

Ethan then shifted out of his tiger form. "I might as well conserve my energy for when we get moving."

But Jackson didn't respond. The memories of Keith were all coming back: the places they went, the conversations they had, and the things Jackson felt for him. He was one of the few guys he dated who he actually developed real feelings for. But it would have never worked out, especially if he was draining his energy whenever they were together.

Why...did he feel so depressed? He'd found his mate; why was he moping over ex-boyfriends?

"What about Ben? Do you remember him?" Ethan asked as he walked over and leaned against the same tree.

Jackson glanced over his shoulder at him. "Yeah, the coffee shop guy." He huffed and glared down at the snow. "Let me guess: some kinda soul-sucking lizard person?"

"Close," Ethan said with a smirk. "Dude was a geomi."

"I literally have no idea what that is."

"A spider guy," Ethan told him.

Jackson grimaced. "What?"

"I found you both all wrapped up in webs one morning. It was kinda gross."

"Yeah, I...I think I'm gonna be sick," Jackson said, feeling his nauseousness growing.

"I dunno what it was, to be honest. You always attracted all these crazy guys who all wanted to suck something from you."

"Gross," he groaned.

"And not just sexually—"

"I get it, Ethan. God." He exhaled and crossed his arms. "He wrote his number on my coffee cup."

"Yeah, and you called him that same night. Next morning…webs everywhere," Ethan said with a sigh.

"I remember it differently. I was tangled up in my blankets or something," Jackson said, trying to recall the moment. "I despise the thing, but I gotta admit that the perception filter did a pretty good job at covering shit up."

Ethan stood in front of Jackson and leaned his hand against the tree beside Jackson's head. "All right, what about Shaun?"

Jackson grunted. "How could I forget that asshole? Not only did he fetishize me, but he stole my phone and wallet…*and* my laptop."

"That's valefar demons for ya, Jack. Kinda like how an incubus feeds off sexual energy or whatever, valefar feed off the thrill of stealing shit from people and breaking trust and all that."

"How long did he get? I forgot."

"Two years. When they arrested him for stealing your stuff, they got him on several other counts of theft, too," Ethan answered. "Dude's probably still inside."

Jackson nodded and shrugged. "I think he was the worst guy I dated."

Ethan scoffed.

"What?" Jackson questioned…waiting for him to say Dai—

"Cory," Ethan said, taking his hand off the tree. "That guy was the biggest prick you'd *ever* brought home, and that's saying something because Harley, James, and Brandon were fucking assholes, too."

Jackson thought to himself for a moment. "I didn't think Cory was *that* bad."

"That's 'cause you couldn't see it. You were too in love with that guy. The fancy hair, the rich-boy car, the expensive dates. And don't get me started on the gifts—"

"Just because he had money doesn't mean he was an asshole," Jackson said with a pout.

"You couldn't see what he was doing to you," Ethan said as he scratched the side of his face. "You stopped clubbing, you stopped hanging out with me, and you even spent less and less time working. I had to suck up to Holt to stop him from firing you."

Jackson wanted to argue…but now that he was thinking about it, Ethan was right. "Yeah…and he was?"

"Vampire."

"Of course,"

Ethan snickered amusedly. "Sorry, it's just kinda funny now that you're not forgetting all this stuff."

Jackson sighed sullenly and shrugged. "Yeah, I guess." But he still felt that hole in his heart. For some reason, remembering all the people he'd been with made him feel sadder. Back then, he'd been through so many guys searching for the right one...and that was Daimon, wasn't it?

"Hey, you all right?" Ethan asked, placing his hand on Jackson's shoulder. "I'm sorry if I upset you, man. I didn't—"

"No, it's not you. I just...I don't know. Maybe I'll remember everything someday."

Ethan moved closer, keeping his hand on Jackson. "What's up? You can tell me."

He shrugged again and shook his head as he sunk a little deeper into dismay. "It's like...there's something missing from me, you know? I think it's my altered memories, but...what if it isn't? Yeah, I remember some stuff now, but it's not *that* which made me feel something. It was when you were talking about Keith. I really liked that guy...and then there were all the other guys, and I know that I was going through them like dominos, and I think it was because I was trying to find 'the one'," he muttered, rolling his eyes.

"Well...Sebastien did say something about how demons have this instinct to search for their mate. Maybe sleeping with all those guys was you trying to find your mate," Ethan said with a shrug.

"But I've *found* him," Jackson insisted. "It's Daimon."

Ethan looked away from him with a pondering expression on his face. "Well," he drawled, slowly turning his head to look at him again. "You're a hybrid...you're two Caeleste who find mates. I mean...maybe...."

Jackson knew what he was getting at. "I...might have two?"

"I mean...maybe," he said, dragging his hand over the back of his neck. "What if Daimon's your wolf walker mate, and your demon mate is still out there somewhere?"

He thought about it...he thought *hard* about it. Could that be it? Was that the thing making him feel like there was this huge part of him that was missing? And was that why when he looked at Daimon when he felt this emptiness, the Alpha only made him feel so much better?

Jackson slowly sunk down to the ground and sat against the tree. "I don't know," he mumbled despondently. "I love Daimon—I love him *so* much," he said, shaking his head.

"But you can love more than one person, right?" Ethan suggested.

"I don't know," he uttered sullenly. "I just...I don't know!" he insisted, becoming frustrated.

Ethan frowned in confliction. "Well...I don't know everything about demons, but Sebastien has a human mate, right? So...maybe...I guess Daimon could also be your demon mate."

Could he? Jackson glanced in the direction of the hut and pondered. "There's imprinting for demons, right?"

"Yeah," Wilson answered.

"So...maybe that's what it is. Maybe I need to imprint on Daimon," he said, and the more he thought about it, his sadness started withering. "I should ask Sebastien how to do it."

Ethan looked down at the snow. "Yeah, he might know."

Jackson frowned at him. "What?"

"Nothing, I'm just...sorry if I upset you, is all."

"You didn't upset me, it's cool," Jackson assured him. "You actually helped, so thanks."

"Yeah, no worries," Ethan said, but he still sounded sad. Was it because he *hated* Daimon?

Jackson didn't want to have another conversation about that. He knew that Ethan didn't like his mate, and Daimon didn't like his best friend. He was pretty sure that things would stay that way; they might learn to tolerate one another, but that was probably as far as things would go.

"I think we should get back," Ethan then said. "I think I heard a couple of your wolf friends waking up."

When he concentrated his senses in the direction of the hut, Jackson heard a few muffled voices. "Yeah, you're right. We're heading to the lake today. I'm kinda curious about the monster they were saying lives in the water," he said as he followed Ethan through the woods.

"You actually think there's something in there?" his friend asked with an amused smile.

"Well...yeah. I feel like I'm inclined to believe a lot of things. I mean I barely know or remember anything about the Caeleste world; I'm still learning."

Ethan nodded slowly. "What do you think it is?"

"What do *you* think it is?"

"I dunno. Some sort of crocodile or water monster. Maybe a snake or eel or something weird like that."

"I mean...if it comes out to stop people from breaking the neutral ground laws, it's gotta be something big and powerful, right?" Jackson assumed as they reached the tree line.

Wilson replied, "Maybe it's a dragon."

"A sea dragon," Jackson concurred. "Is it weird that—" The nausea hit him like a bullet, and Jackson turned and vomited into the snow with a painful groan.

"Shit, Jack," Ethan exclaimed and placed his hand on his back. "Are you all right?"

Jackson winced and grimaced, and when he went to take a deep breath, he vomited *again*. "Fuck," he groaned.

"Should I go get someone?" Wilson asked.

He waited…and took a deep breath, and the nausea slowly withered. "No," he breathed, shaking his head. "I'm good."

"Good? Jack, you just threw up all over the place!"

"I'm fine," he insisted, slowly standing up straight. He didn't want to be babied, but he *was* starting to worry. This was the second time he'd thrown up since they got back from extracting Wilson, and he was afraid that something was wrong. Was it demon-related? Wolf walker-related? Or cadejo-bite related? What if his body was finally succumbing to the many zombie bites that he'd received? He didn't want to panic himself, nor did he want to worry Ethan. So he took a deep breath and said, "Anyway…uh…yeah. Is it weird that I wanna see a dragon? I always thought they were fairy tales and from movies."

Ethan frowned unsurely but started leading the way again. "I haven't seen one, and I want to, so you're not weird. But are you sure that you're—"

"I'm *fine*," he assured him.

"Oh, there you are," Tokala suddenly called. The orange wolf hurried over to them as they stopped walking. "Where were you?"

"Just out huntin'," Ethan answered before Jackson could. "We were tryna catch breakfast for everyone, but all I found were hares."

Tokala looked a little skeptical but nodded and said, "Yeah, hares are hard to catch sometimes. We're just waiting for everyone else to wake up and then we'll head out. We'll hunt on the way to the lake."

"Is Daimon awake?" Jackson asked. He didn't want to walk in there and find Daimon waiting for him; he'd probably be mad that he left him to go and hang out with Ethan. He understood why, though. Daimon was just trying to protect him.

Tokala shook his head. "Not yet."

"What about Sebastien?"

The orange wolf adorned a conflicted expression. "He *is*…but he's a little snappy. I think he's waiting for his mate to call."

As worried as he was, Jackson didn't want to bother him. "Okay, thanks." Then, he started heading for the hut.

"I'm gonna stay out here," Ethan said as he followed Tokala away from Jackson.

"Oh…okay," Jackson replied. He then headed inside, and as he crossed the room, he glanced at Sebastien. He looked *paranoid*, trembling while he held onto his mirror as if it were his most prized possession. Had something happened? Jackson wanted to ask, but he also wanted to make sure that Daimon woke up with him beside him. He also didn't want to get snapped at.

He quietly pushed the bedroom door open, slinked inside, and closed it behind him. To his relief, Daimon was still asleep. He made his way over to the bed and climbed in; he shuffled closer to the Alpha, and when he rested his head on his chest, Daimon stirred and rolled onto his side. He wrapped his arms around Jackson, pulling him closer, and *finally*, Jackson felt totally content.

Maybe he was right. What if Daimon *was* his demon mate, too? What if the emptiness he felt was because he hadn't yet imprinted on him? He wanted to find out, and once Sebastien was in a calmer mood, he'd ask.

"Where did you go?" Daimon suddenly asked, his voice a murmur.

Jackson wouldn't lie. "I couldn't sleep. I saw Ethan hunting, so I went out there to help."

"Mm," the Alpha muttered. "Did you catch anything?"

"No."

The Alpha grunted and started grinding his crotch against Jackson's.

Jackson quickly became aroused, heat throbbing between his legs, and as he felt Daimon's hard dick rubbing against his thigh, he couldn't help but give in.

"Can I fuck you again?" Daimon murmured as he nuzzled Jackson's hair.

"Yes," Jackson immediately answered.

The thought of being enthralled by Daimon's affection increased his contentedness, and all he wanted to feel right now was the happiness and relief that his mate brought him.

Chapter Forty-Three

⌒ ≼ ☽ ≽ ⌒

Waiting on Fate

| Jackson |

Could Daimon be his demon mate? The question stuck with Jackson since they left the hut, and all he could think about was asking Sebastien about demon imprints. He wanted to know how to do it, and then maybe he'd stop feeling like a part of him was missing.

But his conversation with Ethan clung to him, too. He thought about all the guys he dated before he found Daimon, and although some were decent, most of them were assholes—he was even surer of that now that he knew they were energy vampires or weird spider people. They just wanted to use him, and he finally found someone who loved him for who he was rather than what he could give them.

He looked at the white wolf while he led the pack and smiled a little. He loved Daimon so much; he *had* to be the answer to Jackson's current dismay the same way he was to everything that came before. Daimon saved his life and introduced him to a world he would have never known existed. He was kind, gentle, and understanding. He was everything Jackson could need and want in a man.

Jackson looked behind him and located Sebastien, who was trailing behind. The winged hound still looked like he was panicking, and when Jackson focused, he could hear Sebastien's racing heart.

But then his eyes shifted to Ethan. Talking about his exes helped him remember a few things, and he wanted to talk more…but he also wanted to stay with Daimon.

He looked at the Alpha while he pondered, and then he asked, "Did you…have any exes?"

Daimon glanced at him and frowned. "Why are you asking?"

"I'm just curious."

"I went on a few dates with a few different women, but I never found what I was looking for, and I didn't know what it was until I found you."

Jackson smiled again. "I felt that way for a long time; I was kinda searching, I guess, for the right one. For *you*."

"Did you ever think that your right one would be thousands of miles away from home?" the Alpha asked curiously, but there was also a smirk on his face.

He thought about it for a moment. "It crossed my mind a few times. One time, I even considered taking a vacation somewhere just so I could see if I could find someone who wasn't a snooty or selfish city boy."

"Why didn't you take the vacation?"

"Work," Jackson said with a sigh. "Ethan and I were close to having all the evidence we needed to expose an illegal gambling operation. I had to use my savings to play the game and record their conversations about laundering and smuggling."

Daimon laughed quietly and shook his head. "You make me wonder more and more each day why you didn't just become a detective."

"I don't know," he mumbled as Daimon led the pack towards a river. "Maybe after all this stuff is over. I'm sure there's a lot of room for people willing to try and solve mysteries out here, huh? Although now that I remember everything, things would probably be so much simpler in New Dawnward."

The Alpha's amused expression faded. "You're going back to Nefastus after this?" he asked, glaring ahead.

Jackson could see the sadness on Daimon's face, and it made him feel guilty. "Well, I don't know," he answered truthfully. "I haven't decided. But one thing I know for sure is that I wanna be where you are."

"I won't be leaving Ascela," the Alpha said firmly. "This is my birthplace and home, and that of my family, too."

"Would you not even consider it if it was safe?" Jackson asked with a frown.

Daimon glanced at him as he said, "No. The snow and mountains and forest are all I know; even if I wanted to migrate to an urban area, the only place I'd consider would have to be out here."

Jackson understood. It upset him to think that Daimon would never want to see New Dawnward, but if his family had been in Ascela all their lives, it made sense. Daimon probably felt the same anxiety about being in a totally different place as *he* did. He'd been thinking more about New Dawnward lately—especially since finding Ethan—and although there was a part of him that wanted to go back once all of this was over, the part of him that wanted to stay with Daimon was stronger.

Would that change, though? Would his homesickness outweigh his desire to stay with the man he loved?

No. He didn't want to think about it.

He looked at Daimon, and when he saw the Alpha's conflicted expression, he tried his best to think of a way to change the subject. "What was your old packhouse like?" he asked curiously.

Daimon looked saddened. "It was a large manor in the middle of one of Greykin's larger forests. It was gifted to my family by the Zenith and Lord Caedis when wolf walkers had to flee out here. It had a lot of murals and art on the walls or in frames. The master bedroom where my brother slept had a terrace which looked over the valley; we'd just stand out there a lot of the time watching the forest."

Jackson smiled sadly. "It sounds really pretty."

"What was it like where you lived?" Daimon asked him.

His sadness thickened. "Well...I lived in a lot of places. The apartment with my parents, then my stepdad's place, and then I had my own apartment before Ethan and I became roommates to save on rent costs. The apartments weren't much, but Eric's house was huge. There were too many rooms for me to remember, and from what I *do* recall, a lot of them were empty or unused guest rooms. The place felt like this huge lonely, empty maze when no one was home. And when they were...well, when *Eric* was, it felt like a massive prison, and I was always sneaking around like some escaped convict."

Daimon frowned at him.

Jackson shrugged and tried to keep the dismay of his past from ensnaring him, and when he remembered that Daimon didn't really know much about it, he felt worse. He could see that the Alpha wanted more information—maybe he was curious or wanted to understand—and although Jackson didn't want to keep things from him, talking about this stuff always hurt and upset him.

He attempted to sigh away his despondency and stared ahead as Daimon led the pack deeper into the woods. "I...never really knew why before, but it makes sense now," he said, realizing that recalling his childhood was bringing back memories the perception filter had warped. "Eric always treated me like this disgusting little outsider, and like I wasn't good enough for his money or whatever. He never wanted to be seen around me, so I was never invited to the fancy parties or was made to stay in my room when he had guests over. I thought it was because I was just his wife's kid, but...it was because I was a demon."

"Wouldn't he have felt the same way about your mother if that were the case?" Daimon questioned.

"I don't know. I guess because she was an adult, she could control herself or hide what she was. But I was just this brat kid who couldn't keep his temper in check," he mumbled sullenly. "And of course, my stepbrother made it worse. Edward and his snooty little friends pushed me around and called me a whole bunch of things, and then when I snapped back, they all went crying to Eric, and *I* was the one who got beat for it."

Daimon frowned sympathetically. "I'm sorry you had to deal with that. My mother was similar; some of the other pups teased me, and although Alaric stood up for me, my mother saw it as a weakness. My father told me that if someone hit me, I should hit back harder. And my mother told me that if I didn't grow up, I'd remain—and I quote—an Omega bitch for the rest of my life."

Jackson's sadness transformed into anger. "Wow," he mumbled. "She sounds like a delight. N-no offence," he said, looking at Daimon.

The Alpha laughed quietly and adorned a relaxed expression. "My mother was an atrocious woman. I miss her, of course, but that doesn't mean I forgive her for the shit she put my brother and me through."

"It's kinda like…the other way around with us," Jackson said amusedly. "Your dad tried to help…kinda, and my dad was an asshole. Your mom was an asshole, and my mom tried to help…also kinda. I mean…I know she meant well. I think that she was just being careful—you know, treading on thin lines. Eric was this big mercenary guy who hunted and captured Caeleste for a living, and he loved my mom, so he was keeping her safe. But she had to be careful 'cause Eric loved *her*, not me. She was the only thing keeping him from sending me off to some Caeleste boarding school."

When Daimon looked at him again, there was a confused and sorrowful look on his face.

But it wasn't despair that Jackson felt. He was *surprised*. "I think I just remembered a bunch of other stuff," he said, wide-eyed. "I knew Eric was this mercenary company guy, and now I know what he did specifically." As much as it upset him, it really did seem like talking about his past would help him uncover everything that the perception filter masked. However, his frown returned. "But…I saw the Nosferatu sigil on some of his letters. Why would a guy who hunts Caeleste for a living be actively communicating with the Caeleste government?"

Daimon sighed deeply. "That would be a question for Sebastien."

Jackson looked back at the hound again, but he still looked tormented. "I don't know…he looks like he's going through something right now."

His eyes then locked with Wesley. He wanted to look away, but it seemed like the Gamma had something to say. So, he adorned an expectant expression.

Wesley moved closer so that he was walking *right* behind him and Daimon. "I heard him talking in his little mirror. He asked his mate to leave Silverlake and seemed pretty adamant about him contacting him once he got to wherever he was going."

"Oh…yeah, no wonder he looks like he's freaking out. Aeroplanes are freaky," Jackson mumbled, keeping his voice hushed.

But Wesley shook his head. "No, it was more like he was afraid that his mate wouldn't even get out of the city. I think seeing that infected fae spooked him and made him think Silverlake wasn't safe."

"That makes even more sense," Jackson said with a sigh. "Maybe I should leave him alone."

"Or talking to him and distracting him could help," the Gamma suggested.

"Or it will annoy him," Daimon said.

"Yeah...I don't know which will happen 'cause I don't know him all that well," Jackson mumbled.

"No harm in trying," Wesley said.

Daimon nodded. "We're going to stop by that ravine, so you can try talking to him while we rest."

Jackson set his eyes on the narrow ravine up ahead and took a deep breath. The thought of getting yelled at by some huge, winged demon hound made him nervous, but Sebastien was meant to be teaching him, right?

He stayed beside Daimon until they reached the narrow passage, and when the pack started resting, he made his way over to Sebastien. As he glanced around, he saw both Ethan and Julian move to follow him, but Wesley quickly let them know not to.

Sebastien shifted into his human form the moment the pack stopped and sat on a rock with his back to everyone. He was clasping his mirror in his hands, nervously tapping his feet on the ground. And it looked like he was trembling.

"Uh...Sebastien?" Jackson asked unsurely.

The white-haired demon sighed quietly and looked over his shoulder at him. "What?"

"I uh...had something to ask. I'm sorta remembering some stuff, and when I was thinking about my stepdad, it kinda confused me how he'd like...." He huffed and scratched the side of his face, trying to collect his thoughts. "My stepdad had this mercenary business where he hunted Caeleste. But I saw him communicating with the Nosferatu, and it's just a little confusing why a guy who hunts and even kills Caeleste is getting away with it."

Sebastien sighed again and turned to face him. "The Venaticus isn't the only law enforcement division within the Nosferatu. For example, while the Venaticus hunts troublesome demons, we have the Strigoi, which hunts troublesome vampires. Then we also have grey areas; some targets turn out to be in cities where our divisions don't have authority or headquarters, so we have third-party operations, like the one your stepdad runs. Bounty hunters, in a sense. Their practice bypasses laws that the Nosferatu can't, so we use them to find and bring in off-limits targets."

"What about the killing and torturing? I could hear all kinds of stuff coming out of the basement," Jackson muttered, cringing.

"Some targets are wanted dead," Sebastien said with a shrug. "Others have information, and there are sometimes targets who both have information and are wanted dead." He glanced down at his mirror. "Is that all? I'm kinda busy."

"Well... there was another thing," he drawled.

Sebastien waved his hand, inviting him to speak.

"It's about demon imprints. I was talking to Ethan a little about it and like... I wanna know how to imprint on Daimon."

"You... want to know *how* to do it?"

"Yeah. I just... have this feeling like something is missing, and I love Daimon, so I know it's him I need to imprint on. I think the feeling will disappear once I do it," he explained anxiously.

"Uh-huh..." Sebastien droned with a confused expression on his face. "See, kid... here's the thing," he said, leaning back against the tree beside the rock, slouching. "Demons aren't like lycans. We don't find our fated mate and get to choose whether we reject them or imprint on them. When we find our mate, it just happens. It can happen at first glance, or it can happen weeks, months, or even years after we've found them. We don't get to slap our imprint on them and call it a day," he said rather aggressively.

Jackson frowned at him. "So... I just have to wait?"

"Yep."

He looked down at the snow as he felt his despondency returning.

"Daimon might not even be your demon mate," Sebastien added. "You're a hybrid of two—"

"Yeah, Ethan already said that," he interjected. "But I *know* it's Daimon. It has to be."

Sebastien shrugged. "It could be anyone, kid."

Jackson wasn't going to argue about it. It *was* Daimon, and all he could do was wait for his imprint to happen. But how long would it take? He didn't want to have to feel like a part of him was missing for another day, let alone weeks or months. But there wasn't anything he could do, was there? He just had to try and be patient about it.

"Right," he mumbled to Sebastien. "Thanks."

The white-haired demon then turned his back to him and the pack and stared down at his mirror again.

"There's... just one more thing," Jackson said.

Sebastien sighed irritably and turned to face him again. "What?"

"Well... I was just wondering if... well, I don't know," he said with a huff. "I've been feeling kinda sick lately, and I'm worried that maybe it's the cadejo bites or something."

"If the cadejo bites were affecting you, you'd be doing more than feeling sick, kid."

"I threw up like twice."

Sebastien looked a little confused. "Why?"

"I don't know, that's why I'm asking you."

"Demons don't get sick like that. The only time they throw up is if they drank bad blood or injected poison. You haven't eaten anything poisonous, have you?"

Jackson scoffed. "No. I *did* have Daimon's blood, but I didn't feel sick from it."

Sebastien seemed like he was thinking. He looked Jackson up and down, and then he waved him closer. When Jackson moved nearer, the white-haired demon placed his hand on his chest.

"What are you doing?" Jackson questioned.

"Trying to find out what's wrong with you," he muttered, closing his eyes.

Jackson waited patiently, growing nervous that it *was* the cadejo bites.

But after a few moments, Sebastien let go. "You seem fine to me. Maybe it's just your body getting used to blood and whatever. The awakening of people's demon ethos is sometimes a lot harder for some than it is for others."

With a nod, Jackson sighed in relief. "Okay. Thank you."

"Mm," Sebastien murmured, turning his back on him again.

Jackson then headed back over to Daimon, but although he was relieved that he wasn't succumbing to the cadejo bites, his heart felt heavy, and his head even more so. All he could think about was the pain inflicted by the feeling of emptiness, and his heart hurt knowing that he was going to have to wait for his demon imprint to happen on its own.

But a part of him was horrified that Sebastien and Ethan might be right. What if Daimon *wasn't* his demon mate? What if there was someone else out there who he hadn't even met yet? The thought scared him, and it made him panic about how Daimon would react if there was someone else. Jackson didn't want there to be someone else, and surely that desire was enough evidence that it *was* Daimon.

It *had* to be him... didn't it?

Chapter Forty-Four

⌒ ≼ ☽ ≽ ⌒

The Great Lake

| Jackson |

As the pack approached the tree line, the smell of pine and lavender was accompanied by a strong floral scent. Jackson couldn't determine what it was, but it was sweet and earthy. He tried to focus on it; maybe attempting to work out what it was would distract him from his thoughts, but it was useless.

He couldn't stop thinking about what Sebastien told him. How long was he going to have to wait? How long was he going to have to suffer from the tormenting feeling of having a piece missing from him?

With a sullen frown, he stared ahead, but when he spotted the *huge* lake at the foot of a mountain range, his dismay withered, leaving him awe-struck. A huge, *purple* iceberg-like structure protruded from the centre of the lake, and it looked like golden wisps were slithering around inside. The whole area was smothered by a magenta glow, and the water around the structure which wasn't frozen was still and silent.

"Woah…" Julian drawled from behind Jackson.

"I never thought I'd see it," Brando said.

Tokala caught up to Daimon. "Hey, chief. I think I should scout the perimeter with Dustu, just in case."

The Alpha nodded as he stopped at the tree line. "Go."

"What the hell is that thing?" Ethan questioned, lifting his huge striped paw to point at the purple structure.

"That's natural ethos," Brando said as everyone stared at it. "It's mostly found in Avalmoor and in much smaller forms."

Jackson frowned. "So…natural power?"

"Pretty much," the Epsilon confirmed. "Though it can't be used by many. I've heard that some mages can harness it or even create a similar phenomenon, but if one of us was to try and draw the ethos from that thing, it'd probably make us lose our minds."

"Yeah...now it's not so pretty," Julian mumbled.

Remus adorned a worried frown as he looked at Daimon. "Uh...Dad, are we gonna be safe here? I don't know it just...feels a little scary walking into the place that basically connects *all* of Greykin's paths."

"Don't worry, Remus," Daimon assured him. "If Tokala and Dustu find anything, we'll deal with it."

His son nodded in response.

"Let's go," the Alpha said and then stepped out onto the ice.

"Buckle up," Lance said ominously. "Abandon all ill-intent ye who enter here."

"Oh, stop," Rachel mumbled as everyone started following Daimon.

"What would happen if someone with bad intentions or secrets or something walked into this place?" Lalo asked.

Wesley glanced back at him. "Then the lake would expose them."

Jackson frowned and wondered, would the lake expose whoever tried to kill Daimon? Would it show who had ill intent towards their Alpha?

"Have you ever seen it happen?" Ethan questioned.

"I've heard stories," the Gamma replied.

Jackson saw that Sebastien hadn't left the tree line. "Sebastien?" he called. "What's wrong?"

Everyone stopped and turned to face the hound.

"Are you okay?" Julian asked in concern.

Sebastien looked down at the ice and then at the pack. "Yeah...for the sake of everyone's and my own sanity, I'm just gonna wait here. There's a lot of shit I know, and I don't wanna risk blurting it out because of some magical lake."

Daimon frowned skeptically. "The murk only forces us to expose dark, destructive secrets which could affect and hurt those close to us. If you're hiding something—"

"It's literally none of your business," Sebastien snapped. "I'll join your Zeta and his protégé and look around for trouble."

The Alpha growled at him and stood protectively in front of Jackson. "Either step onto the fucking ice, or I'll be forced to halt this mission until I know what you're hiding."

Sebastien growled in return. "Don't threaten me, wolf."

"Why won't you step on the ice?" Ethan demanded, also moving closer to Jackson. "You know something, don't you? You and those Venaticus assholes are hiding shit."

"And I bet you it has to do with Jackson," Julian said slowly. "Right?"

"Make your mind up," Daimon warned him.

Sebastien scowled in hostility and looked like he was about to pounce.

Daimon looked like he was getting ready, too.

Jackson moved in front of Daimon and Ethan and frowned at Sebastien. "Look, whatever it is, just tell us. I know you haven't been with us all that long, but... you've been helping, so the least we can do is give you the benefit of the doubt, right?" he said, glancing at everyone.

A few of the wolves nodded in agreement.

Sebastien shook his head and looked in the direction Tokala and Dustu went.

"Sebastien?" Jackson insisted.

The hound sighed heavily and glared at them all. It looked like he was going to speak... but after a hesitant grunt, he slowly lifted his front paw and placed it down on the ice. Then, he took another step... and another, and once he reached the pack, a confused frown appeared on his face.

"So..." Ethan drawled. "What's supposed to happen?"

Daimon huffed irritably. "Clearly nothing."

"Or he has nothing to hide," Julian suggested.

"Then why did he hesitate?" Remus questioned.

"Let's just get a move on," Sebastien complained, moving past them all.

Jackson frowned cautiously and caught up to the hound. "Why *did* you hesitate?"

"Because I know a lot of fucked up shit, all right? I've done my fair share of heinous crap, and I've seen shit that would give you nightmares for years. I didn't want to have to relive any of it."

His cautious frown became a sympathetic one. "I'm sorry."

"*I* thought you were gonna blurt out something about the Venaticus doing experiments on Jackson if we didn't find anything at the lab," Julian muttered, following beside Jackson.

"Yeah, well, if that were the case, it wouldn't happen," Ethan said firmly.

"And there'd be a dead kludde on the ice," Daimon growled, barging past Ethan so that he could walk beside Jackson.

"Hey, fucking watch it!" Ethan snarled.

Daimon snapped back, "Know your fucking place."

The tiger grunted. "Oh, I'm starting to want you to make me."

"Don't test me, you muto piece of—"

"Stop!" Jackson insisted, glaring at them both as they approached the part of the lake which wasn't frozen. "Please, can we just... try to get along?"

Both Daimon and Ethan growled quietly.

Jackson adorned a hopeless stare. He was almost certain that his mate and best friend would never see eye to eye. They'd always be at one another's throats, no matter how much he asked them to try and at least tolerate each other. And it upset him. Would they go too far someday? Would they make him choose between them?

"Which way do we go, Dad?" Remus asked as they stopped by the still water.

"We'll take a minute to rest until Tokala returns with the perimeter information," the Alpha responded.

Jackson watched the pack disperse. While some rested and talked, others started trailing the water's edge, gawping into the water. Were they looking for the monster the stories said lived in the depths? He was curious, too, and although he wanted to go and join Julian and Ethan in their search, he also wanted to stay with Daimon. He looked at the Alpha, who was staring into the water while talking to Remus. But then he morphed into his Prime form, and using his man-like hands, he carefully climbed into the water and floated with only his head above the surface.

"What are you doing?" Jackson asked, moving closer.

But the Alpha didn't answer. He closed his eyes, tilting his head towards the sky.

"He wants to heal his injury," Remus answered, looking at Jackson. "He said it was still hurting and…maybe stopping him from performing properly."

Jackson frowned and watched Daimon bathe in the lake. Why hadn't he said anything about it to him? Was he…embarrassed? "I didn't know," he mumbled sadly. "Daimon?" he called.

He didn't respond.

"I think…he just needs to float there for a while," Remus said, glancing at Jackson.

The last thing Jackson wanted to do was disturb him, so he headed over to Ethan and Julian. "What are you doing?" he asked, joining them by the water's edge.

"Looking for the monster," Julian mumbled, gawping into the depths.

"Yeah, I'm starting to think it was just a story," Ethan said defeatedly as he sat down.

Jackson stood beside the tiger. "Maybe it's not. Maybe we just gotta look harder. I mean…there's a lot of water," he said, glancing around. "Most of it's frozen."

"Hmm," Ethan mumbled.

While he watched Julian search for the apparent creature, Jackson thought about what he heard the pack saying about the water. Brando mentioned that those who drink the water could be granted answers and wishes, and he wondered…what if he drank some and asked it to help him imprint on Daimon sooner? He stared down at the lake, pondering and hesitating. What if…Ethan and Sebastien were right, and the water told him that his demon mate was someone else? He didn't want to hear that. He'd rather sit around waiting for his imprint to appear on Daimon than know that there was someone else out there waiting for him.

So what if he asked it to help him find whoever stabbed Daimon? He glanced around at the pack, but nothing was happening to any of them, and for a moment, he asked himself whether Daimon was right. What if it *was* an accident?

But his instincts….

"You all right, Jack?" Ethan asked quietly. "You're making that overthinking face."

Jackson sighed and looked at him. "Do you...do you really think that my demon mate is someone else? I can't stop thinking about it. It *has* to be Daimon, but both you *and* Sebastien suggested it might not be, and I don't know what to do with that information."

Ethan shook his head and said, "Don't overthink it. I mean it's not like you can do anything to speed fate up, right?"

"I guess so," he lamented. "I just hate this feeling."

The tiger frowned sympathetically, but a devious smile quickly chased his sorrow away. "Hey, you wanna take a sip?"

"Huh?"

"The water. Should we take a sip?"

Jackson looked at Ethan and then at the lake. If Ethan was going to do it too, he might as well. Maybe it'd help, or maybe it'd push him deeper into the depressive pit that was tightening its grip around him. "Do you really think it works?" he mumbled as he followed Ethan closer to the water.

"Only one way to find out, right?" he said with a grin.

As Ethan edged his face closer to the water, so did Jackson. His heart started racing, and anxiety quickly ensnared him. He was afraid...but he was also curious, and his curiosity and desperation to defeat the empty feeling inside him was winning. So, when Ethan took a few sips, so did Jackson.

The moment the ice-cold water touched his tongue, a shiver ran through his tense body. It was the best water he'd tasted since getting to Ascela—it was actually probably the best water he'd *ever* had.

But then he saw something. A slither of striking white moved through the depths.

Jackson pulled his muzzle from the lake and stepped back. "What the hell was that? Did you see that?" he exclaimed, looking at Ethan.

Ethan didn't answer. The muto stood there with a dumbfounded look on his face—no, it looked as though he'd seen a ghost.

"Ethan?" he asked, moving closer. "Hello?"

He snapped out of it and frowned at him. "What?"

"What's wrong?"

"Uh...nothing, I just...I don't know," he mumbled, looking at the water.

"Did you see it, too?" Jackson asked.

"Uh...yeah, I...I don't know what it was," he said unsurely, glancing at Jackson.

Jackson stared at the lake and gradually moved closer, searching for the white gleam below.

But then it hit him.

He started feeling lightheaded, and his heart thumped rapidly in his chest. All his thoughts of the creature in the lake vanished and were replaced by something else. A voice? No...a message. It told him that his demon mate was *here*, and they always had been.

It *was* Daimon, wasn't it? Relief filled so fast that he couldn't help but smile brightly. But when would the imprint happen?

Another message came to him, and it told him that nobody on the ice had ill intent; nobody among him tried to kill Daimon.

So...Daimon was right. That knife had just impaled him by chance.

No. The water made him question that. Was it telling him that someone *had* stabbed Daimon but they weren't among them...or that there was no would-be-murderer? He didn't know. The water didn't clear it up for him. Was he right to still question Dustu?

He wanted to be absolutely sure, so he went to dip his muzzle into the water again; however, that was when he saw the white shadow zoom around in the lake again.

"You saw it too, right?!" came Julian's excited voice. "Tell me you saw it!"

Jackson looked at them and nodded. "Yeah...I did."

"What do you think it is? What if it's a mermaid?!" they squealed, fidgeting around the spot and wagging their tail beside Jackson and Ethan. "Or a siren!"

Ethan broke his silence with a sigh. "It's probably just a bunch of fish grouped together."

Julian frowned at him. "Wow...what's got you so glum all of a sudden?"

The muto rolled his eyes. "How long do we have to sit around here?"

Jackson looked over at Daimon, who was climbing out of the lake. "Probably not much longer."

Julian stared intensely into the lake again. "What if it's a whale? A sky whale!" They looked at Jackson and Ethan. "I remember a story I heard when I was a kid about the skyfish. I've never seen them, though."

"There's not enough moisture in the air here for them, and it's too cold," Ethan muttered. "I've seen a few skyfish in New Dawnward, though." He looked at Jackson. "You remember, right? We were out getting pizza at like midnight or something and it started raining, and there were these tiny little tetra-looking skyfish swimming around a lamppost."

Jackson thought about it...and he *did* remember. "Yeah...and then that bass-looking one came along and scared them all away."

Ethan laughed a little. "Yeah, good times. Getting pizza at midnight, sitting on a park bench eating bagels for lunch. But now we're out here," he said resentfully, glowering at the lake. "I miss the fuck out of pizza and soda, man."

"I miss pizza, too," Jackson mumbled.

"I tried it once," Julian said. "The base was super flowery, though."

"Ugh, Marone's Pizza on Fritz Street," Ethan said with a groan, salivating. "The fucking wings from that place were amazing."

Jackson salivated, too. "The Golden Dragon place just down the road; their butter chicken is to *die* for."

Ethan groaned again.

"Wow, you guys really had it good, huh?" Julian mumbled sadly. "The only time I got to eat something other than hares and venison was when my dad would take me into the town with him to pick up his mail. They had this like…homemade meals place, and it was owned by this old couple who cooked a bunch of different stuff every week. My fave was the salmon risotto."

"That sounds so good right now," Jackson said.

"Let's go," came Daimon's voice.

Jackson took his eyes off his friends and looked over at the Alpha, who was heading towards the narrow stream which stretched out into the lake from between a narrow gulley. Tokala was standing there with Dustu.

As the pack began following Daimon, Jackson got up and headed over there with Ethan and Julian. He felt relieved knowing that his demon mate was there with him, but how long would he have to wait until the imprint happened? The water didn't tell him that part, but what it *did* tell him was enough to settle his nerves.

He needed to interrogate Dustu. When would he get him alone, though? He'd jump at the first chance he got.

"We're setting up our next ambush a few miles past the gulley," Daimon called, looking back at his pack. "Sebastien, once we find somewhere, I need you to locate Kane's next hunting party and get back to us with how far out they are."

The hound mumbled, "Yeah, whatever."

Jackson shoved aside all his thoughts of demon mates and the knife and focused on his senses. He needed to be aware; he needed to be ready. Anything could happen, and he couldn't become distracted. He'd figure out getting Dustu alone later.

Chapter Forty-Five

Final Warning

| **Daimon** |

Daimon tried to focus on the fact that his body felt a whole lot better after bathing in the lake, but he couldn't stop *seething*. Jackson was spending more and more time with Ethan, and whenever he looked at the muto, Daimon saw a look in his eyes that made him want to pounce. He was certain that Ethan wanted his mate for himself, and Daimon wasn't going to let it happen.

He glanced back at them while he led the way towards a glade. Jackson was talking about his stepdad, and Ethan was staring at him with that longing look in his eyes. And every time Jackson said something, Ethan had to butt in and make it about something *he* did with Jackson however many years ago.

The Alpha clenched his jaw and scowled ahead as the snow started falling.

"Do you think Kane will send more wolves this time, chief?" Tokala asked, walking beside him.

"It's possible," he replied, glancing at him. "Sebastien should return with a number soon, and then we can plan before we reach our ambush point."

"What if we found some cadejo?" Lance suggested.

"I, uh... don't think that would work," Julian called. "Kane's used to dealing with them."

"And it's too dangerous," Wesley uttered. "After that infected fae, we have no idea what else might be out here."

Daimon couldn't formulate a solid plan until he knew how many wolves he was dealing with. However, he *could* throw out ideas and ask for them from his pack. "Whether Kane sends ten wolves or twenty, we're equipped to deal with it. Not only do we have me and Sebastien, but we also have Jackson. His demon ethos is probably our biggest asset right now," he said, glancing at his mate, who looked a little flustered in response to his compliment. "But if anyone has any ideas, you can share them."

Remus stuttered, "What about... well... I don't know."

"What about what?" Bly asked with an encouraging tone.

"Well..." Remus drawled. "I was thinking about what happened to Brando back when we were at that castle ruin."

"Oh, the mine?" Brando called.

"Yeah," Remus said with a nod. "What if we find a cave and collapse the entrance? That way, we don't even have to kill anyone. I mean...they'll probably starve to death eventually, actually...."

"Good," Wesley snarled. "They all deserve a slow, painful death for what they did to Alastor and Enola."

"Or we could lead them into a cave and Jackson fills the place with fire," Ethan called.

The rage buried inside Daimon began to surface as he snarled and sharply turned his head to look back at him. "How many fucking times do I have to tell you to keep your fucking nose out of my pack's business?!" he yelled, stopping and turning to face him.

As the pack came to an unsure halt, Ethan scoffed and shoved past Lalo so that he could see Daimon. Lalo stumbled and complained, and everyone else quickly backed away.

"If I have something to say, I'm gonna fucking say it," Ethan snapped back.

Jackson stepped in front of Ethan and frowned disapprovingly. "Can we please not do this here?"

"If not here, then where?!" Ethan snarled at him.

And *that* made Daimon even angrier.

"I'm *sick* of this controlling, possessive piece of shit talking to me like I'm a stupid child!" Ethan growled, taking his eyes off Jackson to scowl at Daimon. "You might be able to treat everyone else like a bitch, but I'm *done* sitting down and taking your bullshit!"

Daimon didn't reply. The moment the muto charged towards him, he burst forward. They collided and snarled, snapping their jaws and swiping their claws. Daimon didn't care—all he wanted to do was teach this asshole a lesson—so he didn't hold back. He clamped his jaws around the tiger's leg the moment he got the chance, and when Ethan wailed as his teeth tore his flesh, Daimon used all his strength to launch the muto through the air.

When Ethan's body hit a tree, the sound of his breaking ribs made Jackson adorn a horrified frown, and it caused Daimon to stop and hesitate for a moment.

But Ethan climbed to his paws, snarled furiously, and raced towards him.

"Stop!" Jackson insisted.

The muto clashed with Daimon, who used his strength to shove him away. He didn't want to keep fighting; he didn't want to make it worse. Jackson didn't want this, so

Daimon didn't want it. But Ethan kept coming back; the tiger managed to smack Daimon's muzzle, so Daimon hit back, and the force made Ethan stumble to the side.

"I said stop!" Jackson shouted, rushing over. "You guys are wasting your time with—"

Ethan harshly kicked Jackson away with his back leg before he could get between them, and then he pounced at Daimon.

Daimon watched Jackson tumble across the snow-covered ground; he wanted to run to him, but before he could snap out of it, Ethan sunk his teeth into the Alpha's neck.

With a painful wince, Daimon flinched and tried to throw him off, but no matter how hard he yanked or slammed his paws into the tiger, he wouldn't let go.

"Get the fuck off me!" he yelled.

Ethan *laughed* through his clamped teeth, pulling harder and harder and harder—

Daimon snarled furiously, watching Julian try to help Jackson up. Knowing his mate was hurt was enough to horrify him, but the fact that Ethan was responsible made him angry enough to *kill* him. But that wasn't an option.

However, he'd still put him in his place.

The Alpha roared in frustration, and without hesitation, he morphed into his Prime form. As his body transformed, Ethan lost his grip, and Daimon immediately snatched the tiger's neck, picked him up, and pinned him against the closest tree.

"Listen to me, you piece of shit," he growled glaring into Ethan's eyes as he squirmed around, trying to escape. "The next time you so much as *touch* my mate, I'll rip every fucking limb off your body, and when you're this pathetic, legless freak, I'll leave you out in the snow to bleed out—or maybe I'll draw some cadejo over and watch them tear the flesh from your bones."

Ethan snarled and struggled. "You ain't got the fucking balls."

"Don't I?" he tested, leaning his face closer to his. "Jackson is *mine*, and whether you like it or not, it's going to be that way for as long as we live. This is the *last* time I'm going to warn you: know your fucking place, and if you step even an inch over the line, you know what's coming."

The tiger scoffed at him.

"Do you understand?"

He growled—

Daimon tightened his grip, digging his claws into his flesh. "Do you fucking understand?"

With a struggled grunt, the tiger choked, "Yes."

The Alpha let go of him and stepped back. He watched him for a moment, ensuring that he wasn't going to pounce once he turned his back, and then he hurried over to Jackson, returning to his normal wolf form.

His mate was sitting between the pack, who were all standing around him.

"Jackson?" he asked worriedly, moving through the crowd.

When he set his eyes on his mate, pain and guilt struck his racing heart. Ethan's kick had hit Jackson's face, and a ghastly cut spread across his muzzle. Blood trickled down onto the snow, and there were tears in Jackson's blue eyes.

Daimon frowned sullenly. "I'm sorry," he said, moving closer to him.

To his relief, Jackson didn't push him away. Daimon nuzzled his neck and pulled him closer, holding him as he cried quietly.

"It's okay," the Alpha told him.

"I said stop," Jackson murmured, his voice muffled in Daimon's fur.

"I know," Daimon replied despondently. "I'm sorry. I won't let that happen again."

Bly stepped out of the crowd. "I should really put something on that," she said, nodding at Jackson's wound.

"Jack?" came Ethan's shaky voice.

Daimon snarled angrily and carefully let go of Jackson. Then, he stood protectively in front of his mate as he lay down on the snow behind him. "Get the fuck away from him," he warned, ready to attack.

Ethan glared at him for a moment, but when he looked down at Jackson, the anger left his eyes. "I'm sorry," he said and then glanced around at everyone. "I just...lost control for a second."

Tokala scoffed at him. "For a second? You could have killed someone. What the hell was that?"

"Did you even ever learn to control yourself in your tiger form?" Wesley questioned, moving closer to Daimon in order to defend him and Jackson if need be.

Ethan started stuttering. "I did, I just...I just...I'm sorry!"

"Sorry isn't gonna cut it!" Julian suddenly blurted. "You hurt Jackson! You're supposed to be his friend!"

"I think you'd be better off elsewhere," Lance snarled.

The *entire* pack moved closer, forming a protective circle around Jackson.

But that was when Jackson spoke up. "Guys, it's okay," he mumbled, slowly climbing to his paws. He moved out from behind Daimon but stayed close to him. Then, he glared at Ethan. "I told you to stop. I *asked* you yesterday to stop this."

"I'm sorry, Jack," the tiger said shamefully. "I couldn't...stop."

Jackson shook his head. "You shouldn't have attacked him in the first place!" he exclaimed. "I don't know how many times I need to ask you or tell you or try to get you to understand. I'm Daimon's mate, and I love him the way he is. I don't need you to act like my mom and try to save me from him!"

Ethan scoffed and frowned in confusion. "He's...I..." but he didn't snap back. He lost his frown and looked away. "I'm sorry."

"So you keep saying," Jackson muttered.

"Chief, what do we do?" Tokala asked quietly. "We can't risk something like this happening again. If he can't fully control his tiger form, none of us are safe."

"I can control it!" Ethan shouted. "I'm just sick and tired of being treated like a child! I'm here to help, so let me fucking help!"

"Calm down," Jackson growled but then winced and lifted his paw to the slowly healing cut on his muzzle.

Daimon wanted to side with Tokala. He wanted Ethan gone... but the decision was ultimately Jackson's. He loved Jackson, and he cared about him, how he felt, and what he thought. He wasn't just going to banish his friend if he didn't want the same thing. The Alpha carefully licked Jackson's muzzle to try and soothe his wound a little, and then he quietly asked him, "What do you want to do? It's your choice."

Jackson glanced at him and looked down at the snow. A pondering expression appeared on his face, and after a few moments, he set his sights on Daimon and shifted his gaze to Ethan. "Ethan, you're my best friend, okay? But I've asked you I don't know how many times to try and get along with Daimon. He's not going anywhere, and I don't want you to go anywhere, either. But if something like this happens again... I...."

"You what?" Ethan asked with a frown.

He shook his head. "Just don't let it happen again."

Ethan didn't argue. "It won't." He shot a glare at Daimon.

The Alpha snarled quietly and turned to face Jackson. "Are you okay?" he asked him, keeping his voice hushed. "Do you need to find somewhere to rest?"

"No," he mumbled. "It's just a small cut. We should move, right? We don't want Kane's wolves catching up."

Daimon nodded and looked around at his pack. "Come on," he said before moving forward. He walked past Ethan, who he heard snarl quietly, but he did his best to ignore it.

As Daimon led the way, he stuck closely to Jackson. He was going to do everything in his power to keep Ethan away from him. He didn't care if it made him look like an asshole; that muto hurt his mate, and he was certain he'd do it again. Ethan evidently didn't know how to control himself, and that made Daimon feel an even stronger urge to keep him away from Jackson.

From this moment forward, as far as he was concerned, Ethan was his enemy; he couldn't leave him alone with Jackson, and he was going to keep a very close, very *watchful* eye on him. And the moment he so much as *looked* at Jackson in a way that seemed like he might attack, Daimon wouldn't hesitate to put him down.

Chapter Forty-Six
Bloody Glade

| Jackson |

Melancholy constricted Jackson like a starved serpent. Although the wound on his muzzle had healed, those inside his heart hadn't. He'd asked Ethan *too* many times to try and get along with Daimon, and it just wasn't happening.

He didn't want to have to choose between his mate and his best friend, but with the way things were going, it was starting to look as if he was going to have no choice. They could have killed each other if someone didn't step in, and Jackson was afraid that if they started fighting again, he might not be able to stop them next time.

And his heart ached when he thought about the fact that he almost let himself tell Ethan that if it happened again, he should go back to the Venaticus. He didn't want that, but... he didn't know what to do. Ethan kept butting into pack conversation despite being told that he had no place doing so, and while Jackson understood how frustrating that must be for him, there *were* rules among lycans, right? Ethan knew that better than he did, yet he was still breaking them.

However, Ethan was travelling with them, so surely he should be allowed a say? *Sebastien* was—but then again, Sebastien wasn't a lycan.

He was starting to feel frustrated. Why couldn't Daimon and Ethan just get along?

While the pack followed behind him and Daimon, Jackson glanced back at Ethan. The tiger was walking at the very end of the line, hanging his head in shame, and a sorrowful frown clung to his striped face. Jackson felt bad for him—of course he did. Ethan was his best friend, and he knew how much he preferred being included; being pushed aside like this was probably upsetting him, and even more so since he couldn't join Jackson in any discussion he was having with the pack.

"Are you okay?" Daimon asked quietly.

Jackson took his eyes off the muto and looked at the Alpha. "Yeah."

"How's your muzzle?"

"It's fine."

Daimon nodded and faced ahead.

Everyone seemed tense right now. Jackson could feel it in the air, and he could see it on every wolf's face.

"When do you think Sebastien will be back?" Remus asked Daimon.

"I don't know," the Alpha answered.

"Do you want me to go and look for him?" Tokala called from behind them. "It's been over an hour."

"We'll give him until we reach a place for the ambush," Daimon replied.

Tokala nodded.

"What's the plan this time?" Wesley asked as he moved past Tokala and walked behind Daimon. "I'd be up for an all-out brawl; tear those fuckers apart."

"There aren't enough of us for that," Daimon replied, glancing back at him. "We have to be cautious and smart. We'll use all our resources."

"Resources meaning Jackson and Sebastien, right?" the Gamma questioned.

Daimon looked a little hesitant to agree.

But Jackson didn't mind it. He knew that his demon powers were a valuable resource to the pack. So, he looked at Wesley and said, "I'll do whatever I can."

"Wouldn't it be cool if we all had these like…unique abilities?" Julian said almost excitedly, wagging their tail a little.

Lalo frowned at them. "What are you talking about?"

"I don't know," they mumbled, shut down.

"You mean like how some vampires have their own unique abilities?" Brando asked Julian.

They nodded. "Yeah…like Jackson can make fire, it'd be cool if one of us could create ice or paralyze people like that infected fae did."

"Wolf walkers have always had abilities unique to their bloodlines and rankings within a pack; what you're talking about sounds almost like the very thing that started all this shit in the first place," Wesley muttered.

"Experimentation," Ezhno said hauntedly.

"You ever hear about the Howler?" Brando asked, looking around at everyone as they moved through the forest.

"The what?" Julian questioned.

Jackson frowned curiously, glancing back at Brando every few moments so he didn't walk into a tree or trip on anything.

"The Howler," Brando repeated. "It was maybe…two years ago, stories of this wolf walker with a deafening howl started spreading around the forest. Cleo and Maab told a few of us about it once."

Everyone looked clueless.

"Lalo, you were literally sitting right next to her," Brando complained.

Lalo shrugged and mumbled, "Sorry, I probably wasn't paying attention."

"What's the Howler?" Julian asked impatiently.

"An all-white Luna who wanders the forest every full moon," Brando answered. "The stories said her howl can deafen her enemies."

"That doesn't really sound like some wolf walker superpower," Lance muttered. "Just sounds like someone with a loud howl."

"How many wolves do you know who can make someone deaf from howling, huh?" Brando challenged, glaring at Lance.

Lance scoffed and went to snap back, but Bly growled disapprovingly, and he held his tongue.

"So, is it just a story?" Jackson asked.

"I don't know," Brando said with a sigh. "Could be. But after everything we've seen showing up around here, wolf walkers with powers wouldn't surprise me."

"Enough," Daimon then called. "I see a glade up ahead. We'll be taking formation G. Jackson, you're with me. Dustu, take Remus and hide in the brush. We'll take our positions and wait for Sebastien."

The pack all simultaneously called, "Yes, Alpha."

As Dustu and Remus broke off, Daimon picked up the pace towards the glade. When they emerged from the trees, everyone moved away in pairs to different areas of the open space. Jackson stuck with Daimon, and when the Alpha stopped in the tree line on the other side of the glade, Jackson watched him burrow himself into the snow. So, he did the same, keeping only his head above the surface.

"Are you sure you're okay?" Daimon asked quietly.

Jackson looked over at him. "Yeah, I'm fine."

He nodded and looked out at the glade.

Although he didn't want to let silence consume them, Jackson didn't know what more to say. Should he ask about Sebastien? Should he ask Daimon if *he* was okay?

Where was Ethan?

Jackson glanced around, but he couldn't see the muto—he couldn't see anyone, for a matter of fact. But that was because they'd all taken their positions. Had *Ethan* taken cover somewhere?

"Did you hear the story of Filtiarn?" Daimon asked.

As he looked at the Alpha again, he frowned curiously. "No."

"It's a popular story among lycans," he started. "Some believe that there lives a two-faced wolf in the forest of Dor-Sanguis."

Jackson's curiosity grew, and he appreciated the fact that Daimon was trying to create conversation. Like him, it seemed as though the Alpha didn't want to let the fight with Ethan make things difficult and awkward for everyone.

The Alpha quietly explained, "A few hundred years ago, Deltas could evolve into Amaroks; huge, blue-furred creatures which looked a lot like my Prime form. They had no humanity left, nothing worth saving. They were mindless killers. But one Amarok, thought to have once been a Crescent King, had moments where he'd snap out of the Amarok's insanity. He was at war with himself, fighting for control of his own body. The stories say that he fought *so* hard that the Amarok's body grew another head; the Crescent King couldn't win back his mind, so he created himself a new one."

Jackson's frown thickened. "So...the Crescent King's consciousness was alive in this new head, and the Amarok's was in the other?"

Daimon nodded. "Correct. But they both wanted control of the body. Once again, they fought for ownership, but they grew tired, and the Amarok proposed a deal. If the Crescent King would allow the beast its rampage at night, the King could control the body during daylight. It was said that an Amarok's venom was so potent that it killed anyone bitten in moments. But the King didn't want to let it kill thousands of innocent people, and whenever the Amarok's head bit someone, the King would bite at the same time. His venom would dilute the Amarok's, and it was a painful process for the victims, but the combination would turn them into wolf walkers in moments."

"So they just created a bunch of new wolf walkers together?"

"That's why they named him Filtiarn; it means Lord of the Wolves. Over time, the Amarok and the King became one consciousness, although both heads still remained. The stories say Filtiarn now prowls the lands at night in search of humans to turn into wolf walkers."

Jackson pondered as he looked out at the glade again. "Is it a *true* story?"

Daimon laughed quietly. "If it were, I don't think wolf walkers would be as few in numbers as we are. But perhaps he was real hundreds of years ago when our kind flourished."

"Do you think the Howler is real?" Jackson asked.

The Alpha glanced at him. "Maybe. Like Brando said, after everything we've seen, *anything* could be out there. My point in sharing this story, though, is the fact that Julian said Kane might be descended from a Crescent King. All Crescent wolves are prone to extreme violence and horrific warpaths, and a lot of wolves believe that Filtiarn is the cause. Everything we've heard about Kane is starting to add up, and if he *is* of Crescent blood, he has just as much ancestral knowledge as I do."

Jackson was starting to feel a whole lot more unnerved. "What...does that mean for us?"

"He won't stop his hunt until we're all dead, but that will be his downfall. He'll keep sending wolves, and we'll keep killing them until his numbers have fallen so drastically that he'll have no defences left to hide behind. He'll have to face us himself, and I'll tear him apart."

Something shuffled behind them.

They both sharply turned their heads, and Jackson's heart started racing.

But it was only Sebastien. The hound had just landed, and as he folded his wings against his sides, he exhaled quietly. "Fifteen wolves just over a mile out. Their security was tight as fuck this time. I hope whatever you're planning can account for that."

"Elaborate," Daimon grunted.

As he crouched into the snow, Sebastien said, "They've got that Gamma with them—the one Julian told us about. Ellis, the Beta from before, and several tough-looking fighters. I didn't get their ranks, but if the Gamma's there, I'm sure there are Epsilons."

Ellis *and* a Gamma? Jackson was starting to worry. Were they prepared for this? He looked at Daimon, who had a conflicted look on his face. Was he worried, too? He *was*, wasn't he? What were they going to do? Were they going to run?

"Look, if you guys can deal with the rest, I can take on the Gamma," Sebastien said. "She looks tough, so if I can draw her away from her packmates, we'll both have an easier time dealing with them."

Daimon nodded in agreement and then looked at Jackson. "You're going to stick close to me at *all* times. What do you want to use? Demon ethos or the inimă?"

Jackson didn't know. He hadn't trained with the inimă yet, and the last thing he wanted was to lose control again—he didn't want to risk turning on his packmates. But if he was in his human form so that he could use his hellfire, he'd be a lot more vulnerable, right? If only he'd learned to use his wings.

However, he *was* confident with his fire ethos. After all, he'd successfully used it to destroy that hellhound...as guilty as he felt knowing that it was once Enola. And if a wolf charged at him, he could just throw a fireball at it, couldn't he? Or...if it came to it, he had his fangs and claws. He'd never been a great fighter, but he'd do whatever he could when he had to.

He set his eyes back on Daimon and said, "I'll use my fire ethos."

"All right," the Alpha said.

"All we do now is wait," Sebastien muttered.

Jackson watched the tree line across the glade, searching for the slightest sign of movement. A mile wasn't far for wolf walkers, which meant Kane's wolves could turn up at any moment. But he was ready; he held his own against the first group of hostiles, and he was going to do just as fine this time.

He took a deep but quiet breath, trying to relax.

"You good?" Sebastien asked, keeping his voice hushed.

Jackson glanced back at him. "Yeah, just...a little nervous, I guess."

"Don't be. You got this."

"He's right," Daimon said. "Don't overthink it. Just focus on taking out the enemy. They have nothing on your demon ethos."

With a nod, Jackson set his eyes on the tree line again.

Daimon pricked his ears up.

Jackson sharply turned his head to look at him, and when he saw the Alpha's eyes darting from tree to tree on the other side of the glade, he did the same. Could he hear them? Were they coming?

"Jackson," Daimon murmured. "The moment I charge and take my Prime form, leave your wolf form and start firing."

"O-okay," he said anxiously.

"I've got the Gamma, remember," Sebastien muttered.

Daimon nodded. "There," he whispered.

Jackson looked to where the Alpha was staring, and when he saw the group of hostile wolves cautiously prowl out of the tree line, his heart started racing. Fifteen *huge* wolves; they were bigger than the last group, and they all looked like they'd been through hundreds of fights. Some had torn ears, missing pieces of fur with scars below, and the golden-furred wolf walking beside Ellis was missing a few inches off the end of her tail.

Those wolves were evidently Kane's fighters. But Daimon didn't look unnerved. The Alpha looked confident and determined, so Jackson did his best to follow Daimon's lead and attempted to settle his anxiety. He waited, shifting his sights from Daimon to the prowling hostiles.

He waited…

And waited…

The wolves edged nearer, Jackson's heart beat faster, and the falling snow grew thicker.

And then the wolves came to an abrupt halt, turning to face Tokala, who pounced out of the brush to their right.

Daimon burst out from his cover the moment they turned their heads. He morphed into his Prime form as he ran, and Jackson left his wolf form as he hurried after him.

At the same time, the pack emerged from their hiding spots, charging towards the hostile pack, who quickly prepared to fight. And when Jackson saw Ethan among them, relief broke through his anxiety.

But it was time to fight.

The moment Sebastien collided with the golden wolf and tumbled across the snow with her, Daimon clashed with Ellis, who lunged at him. Ethan and Julian worked together, Tokala took two on at once, and so did Wesley.

In a matter of seconds, the silence was filled with roars, snarls, and yelps. Blood splashed onto the snow, and fog was created from all the white being kicked up into the air.

Jackson created his first fireball and launched it at a wolf who Lalo and Leon kicked across the snow. Before it could climb to its feet, Jackson's crimson fire engulfed its body, and it started rolling around shrieking as it was quickly burned down into nothing.

Then, as Daimon slammed his fist into Ellis' face, Jackson went to throw flames at the black wolf, but he recovered too quickly, and his fire hit the snow. Before he could panic, though, Brando shoved his opponent back, making him stumble into the fire, which quickly latched onto the wolf's body like a swarm of ticks out of the long grass.

A bright blue light snatched Jackson's attention, and when he turned to face it, he saw Sebastien struggling against the golden wolf. It had its jaws around his neck, and he was trying his hardest to escape. He knew that Daimon wanted him to stay close, but he wasn't going to leave Sebastien to struggle alone.

Jackson left Daimon's side and rushed to where Sebastien had managed to lead the golden wolf. But as Jackson came to a sliding halt and held his hand out, he couldn't get a shot. Sebastien was flapping his wings around, trying to impale the wolf with his carpal spikes, but she kept avoiding each of his attempts, and his blood was spraying all over the frozen ground.

With a growl of frustration, Jackson stepped left and right, up and down, trying to find the perfect moment to strike, but he saw the golden wolf's blue eyes lock with his— she knew what he was trying to do. She was *purposely* making it difficult for him to—

A wolf smashed into Jackson, throwing him off his feet. He tumbled along the snow, his heart racing as panic ensnared him. And when he came to a halt, he tried to get up, but a light grey wolf pinned him down before he could. It snapped its jaws at him, trying to go for his throat; he held it back as best as he could with his hands, gripping its muzzle and its neck, but it was thrashing back and forth so much that Jackson kept losing his grasp and snatching it again just in time to save himself.

As desperation quickly enthralled him, he turned his head to the left, hoping to see that someone was coming to help, but everyone was fighting. Daimon was still battling Ellis, Sebastien was struggling against the Gamma, and the pack were busy brawling.

Jackson strained and grunted; he tried to kick the wolf, but his feeble attempts did nothing but piss it off. Should he use the inimă? It was the only way he could think of getting out of this. His strength was waning, and the wolf wasn't letting up. Its jaws were getting closer and closer and—

"Jack!" came Ethan's voice, and with a blur of orange and white, the wolf was thrown off Jackson.

Jackson scurried to his knees and watched as Etan clashed with the grey wolf after they both stopped rolling across the snow. The wolf tried swiping at him with its claws and lunging with its teeth, but Ethan dodged and smacked the beast's head, sending it to the ground again.

As he watched Ethan tear the stunned wolf apart, Jackson climbed to his feet. Ethan ripped the wolf's head from its body, and then he turned to face Jackson, blood dripping from his maw.

"Are you okay?" the muto asked, hurrying over to him.

Jackson nodded but hastily turned to face Sebastien. "We need—"

"Use your demon form," Ethan urged. "Come on!"

He didn't want to let himself hesitate. Sebastien needed his help. So Jackson focused and summoned his wings and horns, and as he felt his demon ethos surge through him, he scowled and immediately sprinted faster than any wolf over to Sebastien and the golden Gamma.

Jackson collided with the hound and the wolf, sending them crashing along the ground and away from each other. Using his wings to help him turn in the blink of an eye, Jackson held out his clawed hand, created a ball of red flames, and then launched it at the golden wolf before she could climb to her feet.

But the Gamma kicked herself along the snow and away from the projectile. She snarled furiously and started running towards Jackson; he stood ready, claws bared, and wings folded. His heart was racing, but he ignored his worry that he might lose control. All that mattered right now was doing what he could to help his packmates and friends.

The moment the Gamma jumped at him, he reached forward and grabbed her by the underneath of her front legs. She yelped when he pulled her over his head and threw her across the glade, and that was when Sebastien reappeared and pinned her down, stabbing his wing carpal spikes through her sides.

Jackson swung around and quickly observed the rest of the battle. Daimon had Ellis pinned, and the rest of the pack had either killed or subjugated the others.

It looked like it was over.

Ethan hurried over and joined Jackson. "Are you okay?"

Jackson looked down at his clawed hands. Although he could feel the demon ethos raging through his veins, he didn't feel like he was slowly approaching a point he couldn't return from. Unlike before, he was still himself. He didn't black out and murder forty hunters, and he'd managed to help instead of get in the way.

He nodded slowly and glanced at the tiger. "Y-yeah…I'm okay."

Ethan opened his mouth to speak, but a piercing howl cut through the trees, snatching the attention of every wolf on the battlefield.

And then came that feeling. That ominous, chilling feeling that something was coming. Jackson's instincts warned him, and he knew that he had to warn Daimon. But wolves flooded out of the tree line before he could take a step.

Hundreds of wolves.

Chapter Forty-Seven

⌐ ≪ ☽ ≫ ⌐

Kane Ardelean-Blood

| **Jackson** |

Ellis started laughing as Daimon backed away and tried to run to Jackson, but the swarm of wolves hit the glade like a tsunami. Jackson and Ethan were surrounded by twenty hostiles before they could attempt to move, and when a wave of at least fifty enemies hit Daimon, the Alpha tried to fight them off, but they quickly overpowered him.

They overpowered *everyone*. There were at least thirty wolves to one, and Daimon's pack didn't stand a chance.

"Daimon!" Jackson called as panic gripped him in a tight, cold fist. "Dai—"

The wolves clamped their jaws around Jackson's arms, legs, and wings, pinning him down on his back the same way they pinned Daimon. Several wolves latched onto Ethan, stopping him from swiping and kicking.

Jackson had to use the inimă—it was the only way he could get out of this. But he could feel the wolves' venom spreading through his body, weakening him, making him feel disorientated and like the world around him was spinning. He couldn't focus; he couldn't summon the inimă, and he couldn't even feel his ethos. What were they doing to him?

But then he saw him.

A wolf as black as an abyss. His eyes were as *white* as the snow, and the steel, jewel-encrusted bracers on both of his upper front legs shimmered brightly in the white of the snow. He prowled through the ocean of wolves, his eyes fixed on Daimon, who growled and snapped his jaws, trying to escape from under the wolves keeping him down.

Something of an amused cackle came from the black wolf, and the closer he got, the louder his voice became in Jackson's head. And this time, he heard more than pieces of sentences.

"So, *you're* the piece of shit who's been killing my wolves?" the black wolf questioned, stopping in front of Daimon.

His wolves? Was that…Kane?

The black wolf's face possessed ghastly scars; three slash marks which were clearly inflicted by claws cut from the top of his head and around to the right side of his face, barely missing his eye. It went down to his neck and ended on his right shoulder.

Daimon snarled in response. He was still trying to get free, but it was no use, was it?

Jackson began struggling to take full breaths. What the hell were they going to do?

The inimă—

"And *that* must be your half-breed mate, correct?" Kane asked with a grunt, looking over at Jackson.

"J-Jackson," Ethan grunted.

Jackson struggled to break eye contact with Kane, but once he did, he looked at Ethan.

"D-do something!" the tiger growled.

But then Kane started moving towards Jackson. "I see you," he said with a challenging tone. "And I see that look in your eyes, boy. If you so much as *try* anything, your entire pack dies."

Fear flooded through Jackson as his blood ran cold.

When Kane reached him, he moved his very human-looking front leg towards him and revealed a paw which looked almost like Daimon's Prime form. He gripped Jackson's chin and lifted his head so that he'd look up at him, and a smirk crept across the black wolf's scarred face.

"Aren't you a pretty little thing?" he drawled.

Jackson wanted to pull his head away, but he was terrified that if he did anything at all, Kane would hurt his friends.

However, Kane quickly lost interest in him and prowled away. "You little fuckers really thought you'd get away with all of this, didn't you?!" he called angrily as he moved around the bloody battlefield. "You filthy mix-pack scum!" he yelled furiously, stomping his front paws down into the snow. Then, he hurried over to Daimon and glared into his eyes, his face just inches from his. "I'm going to make you regret every single drop of blood you've spilt from my pack. I'm going to make you *suffer* for every life you took."

Daimon snarled in response and tried to snap his jaws at him, but Kane backed off and laughed loudly.

That was when Ellis limped towards his Alpha. "Alpha Kane, sir," he said meekly.

Kane set his eyes on him and scowled. "After *years* of training, you couldn't even fight this sorry excuse for a fucking wolf?!" he yelled, his voice getting louder with each word.

Ellis bowed his head in shame. "I—"

The black wolf didn't give him a chance to reply. Kane harshly slammed his front paw against the side of Ellis' face, and the Beta stumbled and almost fell. Then, Kane swung around. His white eyes shot from each of Daimon's pack members, and when he locked sights with Jackson again, a cold chill ran through his body.

What was going to happen now?

Kane snarled and glanced around the glade. "Knock 'em out. Let's move," he called.

Jackson watched in horror as Kane's wolves started harshly swiping over and over at his packmates' faces until they passed out, and their wolf bodies morphed back into their human ones.

And then they started hitting him and Ethan. Each smash of their paws sent pain gushing through Jackson's body; he attempted fighting when he saw Ethan struggling, but it was no use. The moment he saw the tiger weaken beside him, he could feel himself slipping away. He tried to hold on, watching as Kane's wolves dragged his packmates away, following Kane into the woods. But there was nothing he could do.

The world started fading away from him, swirling and blurring. And the last thing he saw before his eyes rolled to the back of his head was the greying sky above him.

| Daimon |

The moment he jolted awake, Daimon shot to his feet and tried to shift into his Prime form, but his ethos didn't respond, and as the adrenaline which abruptly hit him started fading like a flame without oxygen, dread filled his racing heart.

He stood in the centre of a small cavern, and at his feet lay his unconscious pack. Dead ahead, silver bars shimmered in the moonlight, and hundreds of voices, scents, and heartbeats enthralled his senses.

And something *burned* around his neck.

Daimon moved his hands up to his neck, and when he gripped the cold, metal collar wrapped around it, his palms burned. He grunted in response, and when he stared down at his singed hands, he noticed a flicker of silver to his right. The Alpha turned his head, setting his eyes on Wesley; a silver collar hung around his neck, and the neck of every single one of his packmates—even Jackson, Sebastien, and Ethan had one.

He rushed to Jackson, who like everyone else was in his human form. Daimon kneeled beside him and gently shook him. "Jackson?" he asked desperately. He eyed the dried blood on the side of his face, and an unhealed cut on his left temple. The silver collar around his neck had burned his skin, which was red and sore—parts were even bleeding.

When Daimon gently moved Jackson's hair away from his wound, his mate murmured and started to come around.

"Chief?" came Tokala's strained voice.

Someone else grunted.

"What…where the hell?" Wesley growled.

"Dad?" Remus called in confusion.

Daimon looked at his son, who was waking and sitting up with the rest of the pack. He wanted to go to him, but he didn't want to leave Jackson.

"What…Daimon?" Jackson groaned. "Where…where are we?" he asked as panic smothered his face, and he frantically looked around.

Before Daimon could give Jackson his best guess, Julian shrieked from the other side of the cavern. Everyone sharply turned their heads to look at them; they were pale and terrified, shaking their head as they backed up against the wall.

"No," they uttered and started hyperventilating. "No, no, no!"

Despite their own confusion, everyone tried to ask Julian what was wrong, but they didn't reply. They stared in horror, shaking their head as tears trickled down their face.

Someone appeared on the other side of the bars.

Daimon set his eyes on the tall, scruffy man who wore only a pair of torn trousers. The guy peered into the cavern and then hurried off before Daimon had a chance to question him.

"Julian?!" Ethan insisted, his voice bellowing over everyone else's. "What the fuck is it?!"

Julian stammered and stuttered. "T-t-the pit—the pit!" they cried.

"The pit?" Lalo questioned. "What's the pit?"

"You're in it," came a deep, smug voice.

As Daimon helped Jackson sit up, he turned his attention to the bars again, and that was where Kane was standing. Now in his human form, he waited on the other side of the silver bars with a grin on his scarred face, and three other men behind him.

Daimon snarled defensively as he moved his arms around Jackson and pulled him as close to himself as he could. He glared at Kane, and when they locked sights, the black-haired man laughed amusedly.

"It's still *so* fucking funny how you imbeciles thought you could win," Kane said, shaking his head as the men behind him snickered. "You should've stayed behind those city walls."

Although he wanted to yell, Daimon knew that there was no use—and it was probably exactly what Kane was hoping for. He knew that there was no way out of this cage. Silver bars, silver collars, and *hundreds* of wolves on the other side; his pack wouldn't stand a chance. No, what he needed to do was wait, observe, and plan. He had to stay calm, and he had to keep himself from slipping over the edge into hopelessness.

His pack weren't going to die here.

"Where are the rest of you?" Kane then demanded with a much sterner tone.

Daimon wordlessly scowled at him.

Kane snarled and moved closer to the bars. "This can go either of two ways, asshole. Tell me where they are…or I start killing your mutts," he warned.

"I don't know where the fuck they are," Daimon snapped as he felt Jackson tense up in his grip.

"Wrong answer," Kane growled.

The three men pulled shotguns from behind them, and as they cocked them, they moved towards the bars.

Daimon's heart started beating a little faster as he yelled, "I don't know where they are!"

"Shoot the little one," Kane muttered.

The three men aimed at Remus—

Everyone quickly moved in front of his son, and as Daimon moved closer, he protectively pulled Jackson with him.

But then Kane started laughing. "Look at these guys!" he cheered as if he was having the time of his life.

Daimon scowled harder, his heart racing, his hands shaking. He wanted to lunge at him and grab him through the bars—he wanted to tear what was left of his face off—but he had to control himself. The men at his sides had guns, and he along with his pack were powerless with the silver collars around their necks. Now wasn't the time to attack.

Kane's laughter died down, and as he scowled at the defensive pack, he uttered, "Let them stew for a bit. I need to go fuck my wife." Then, he turned around and left, and his three men slowly followed after shooting hostile glares at Daimon.

Everyone's panicked questions slammed against Daimon's eardrums, but all he could do was stare and try to work out what he was going to do. No one had their bags, so there was no telling where the inimă was; the fact that they'd left Jackson in the same cage as everyone else was evidence enough that Kane had no idea what he or the inimă was, and Daimon could use that to his advantage.

Sebastien was sitting in the far back corner with a haunted look on his face, and he was bound by a silver collar, too. The guy looked like he'd cracked, so he might not be much use.

"Chief?" Tokala asked desperately, crouching in front of him. "What do we do?"

Julian's wails got louder and louder, and it was starting to piss Daimon off. He couldn't think with all the noise.

"Daimon?" Jackson asked as he pulled free from his protective grip and stared into his eyes. "W-what the hell do we do?"

Daimon took a deep breath and glanced around the cavern again. He climbed to his feet and moved closer to the bars; he was expecting to find a camp outside, but instead, his eyes were met with what looked like an arena. Tall, clawed-up walls stood twenty feet from the ground, and as far up as he could see were rows and rows of platforms and ledges carved into the sides of the huge crater they were locked up in the bottom of. What the hell was this place?

He scowled and turned to face Julian. While his pack moved closer to the bars to peer outside, Daimon stormed over to Julian and pulled them to their feet. "What the hell is this place?!" he demanded.

With tears streaming down their terrified face, Julian stuttered, "T-the arena—"

"You've already said that. What's the arena?"

"T-the…where…Kane executes people," they cried. "E-everyone watches—t-they place bets!" they screeched. "W-we're all gonna die down here!"

Daimon let go of them and turned to face his pack, who were gawping at him.

"It's some sort of pit," Bly said.

"It doesn't look like there's a way up," Dustu said shakily.

"What do we do, Dad?" Remus asked, moving closer to him.

Daimon placed his hand on Remus' shoulder and pulled him nearer. Then, his eyes shifted between each of his packmates before he turned to face Julian again. "Tell me everything you know about this place."

Julian looked up at him, sniffling and crying. "T-there's no—"

"What do you know?!"

As Julian flinched and whimpered, Jackson moved past Daimon and crouched in front of them.

"Julian?" Jackson asked softly. "We're not gonna die, okay? Just tell us what you know so we can work out how to get out of here."

"You can't!" Julian insisted. "We're all gonna die!"

But that was when Sebastien shoved Jackson aside, snatched Julian's collar, and pulled them to their feet. "Tell us what the fuck you know about this place or I'm gonna kill you right fucking here!" he yelled.

"Sebastien, what the hell?!" Jackson complained, but before he could try to pull the white-haired demon away from Julian, Daimon gently grabbed his arm and pulled him away.

They needed answers, and if Sebastien could get them, then Daimon would let him.

"Talk!" Sebastien shouted.

Julian whimpered and closed their eyes. "Th-this is where Kane takes everyone he captures! He takes them out one by one, and he slaughters them!"

"You said people place bets: why? Against who?" Sebastien asked.

With a terrified gulp, Julian glanced at the silver bars. "The creature."

"Creature?" Jackson questioned before anyone else could.

Julian nodded frantically. "He-he'll make us face it one at a time until there's no one left."

"What is it?" Sebastien insisted impatiently.

"I-I don't know," Julian insisted. "A big... wolf."

Daimon snarled angrily and turned to face the bars again. "How did Kane walk out of here?"

"There's... there's a pathway," Julian answered. "A tunnel. But there's bars on that, too."

Sebastien let go of Julian and stood beside Daimon. "So, what do we do?"

Daimon looked at Jackson. "Can you call the inimă and break the bars like you broke out of that hunter cage?"

Jackson looked anxious but nodded. "I-I think. I can try. But I don't know where it is."

"But you can sense it, right?" the Alpha asked.

"You can; it's a part of you now," Sebastien said.

His mate's anxious look thickened. "I-I can try," he repeated.

"You got this," Ethan said to Jackson. "You did it before, and you can do it again."

"Okay, but what happens once the bars are down?" Sebastien asked. "There were easily over a hundred wolves in that glade. There could be a whole lot more waiting for us out there, too," he said, waving his arm towards the bars.

He was right. Once they were out of the cage, they had to deal with Kane's pack. But they'd only managed to get the better of Daimon and his wolves before because they weren't expecting them. *This* time, Daimon knew what to expect. "We've got you, Jackson, and my Prime form. The three of us can do most of the crowd clearing, and we make a break for the trees."

"It's not gonna work!" Julian insisted, shouting.

They all turned to face them.

"We're not leaving this cage unless it's to go out there and fight the creature! He has too many wolves and a lot of resources—where do you think he got these collars from?!" they exclaimed, gripping the collar around their neck as they shot to their feet. "He's got snipers, traps, guards who've been trained since they were little kids. Even if we had *ten* Jacksons, there's no way out!"

Daimon hutted irritably and took his eyes off everyone. There *was* a way out, he just needed time to think. If Jackson could break silver bars, then he had to be able to break the collars around everyone's necks. And if he couldn't—if the strength it took to break the bars was too dangerous to use too close to someone—then they'd fight their way to wherever the key to the collars was.

He needed time to think. But how long did they have before Kane came back? He looked at Julian and asked, "How long until Kane comes back down here?"

Julian shook their head and sunk back down onto the ground. "I don't know," they mumbled. "Usually, he lets the creature out for after-dinner entertainment."

"And when's dinner?"

"I don't know," Julian answered. "It depends how long it takes them to catch something."

"Well... if they were out there capturing us all day, then maybe they haven't had time to go hunting yet," Wesley suggested.

So, he had time to think.

"What are you thinking?" Sebastien asked.

"I need time to come up with a plan. While I do that, I need you to see if you can help Jackson locate the inimă," Daimon answered.

The white-haired demon nodded. "All right. Jackson, let's get to work."

As Sebastien headed over to the wall with Jackson, Daimon looked at everyone else. "Get ready for a fight. It's likely we'll be in our human forms once we're out of here, so we'll wait until they send guards; if Jackson can't pull the inimă down here, we'll overpower the guards and take their weapons."

Everyone nodded and said, "Yes, Alpha."

Daimon headed over to the back wall and sat down. He rested his arms on his knees, glared at the arena outside the bars, and started thinking. This wasn't going to be the place he died—it wouldn't be the place where *any* of his pack died. He was done losing his people, and he was going to do whatever it took to get them all out alive.

Chapter Forty-Eight

⌒ ≼ ☽ ≽ ⌒

The Arena

| **Jackson** |

As hard as he tried, Jackson couldn't find the inimă.

With a frustrated sigh, he opened his eyes and shook his head before looking at Sebastien. "I can't find it. All I feel is this like... invisible barricade. Maybe it's too far away."

Sebastien, whose frustrated expression was worsening with every failed attempt, gritted his teeth and grunted, "Keep trying. You did it before, you can do it again."

It wasn't working; he'd been trying since Kane left, and that must have been well over an hour ago. But he couldn't give up. If Daimon's escape plan was going to work, they *needed* the inimă. He knew that the Alpha had a backup plan, but Jackson liked the sound of the one where they had his demon ethos at their disposal much better, and he was sure that everyone else felt the same.

He closed his eyes and focused, trying to connect with the amulet the same way he had back when he was stuck in that hunter cage. He connected with his demon ethos—the silver collar around his neck made it a struggle, but he managed—and then he tried even harder than he did last time.

But Jackson hit that invisible wall again. It was like all his senses just suddenly shorted out, leaving him feeling winded. He grunted and exhaled as he opened his eyes, and when he looked at Sebastien, he shook his head.

"God fucking damn it!" the white-haired demon exclaimed.

"I'm sorry," Jackson insisted as he started feeling guilty.

"I told you," Julian then said. "We're not getting out of here."

"Stop it," Tokala told them. "You're upsetting everyone."

Jackson dragged his hands over his face and exhaled deeply. He glanced at Daimon, who was sitting with Remus. There was a pondering look on his face; was he trying to think of other ways for them to get out of there? Wesley and his Epsilons were watching the arena outside the bars, and everyone else sat with haunted looks on their faces... even

Ethan. Jackson wanted to go to his friend, but he couldn't waste a single moment. He *had* to find the inimă.

He closed his eyes and concentrated again, connecting with his demon ethos. But his attempts were starting to make his head hurt. He didn't care, though. He wouldn't stop; his pack were relying on him. So he frowned and tried as hard as he could to reach beyond the invisible wall that he kept hitting. The pain in his head got worse and made him grimace, but he didn't care—

The wall suddenly started giving way, but the sound of scraping metal, cocking guns, and grunting voices forced Jackson out of his focus before he had a chance to reach beyond it.

"Grab one of 'em," one of the *ten* men standing outside the barred cavern said as another guy slowly pulled open a door-like section of the bars.

Daimon's pack burst into action, leaving Jackson with a confused, nervous look on his face as he jumped to his feet. He watched the Epsilons grab the two men who walked in, and Wesley grabbed the guy who opened the door. They snatched their weapons as they shoved the men away, and then aimed at the guys outside the bars, but in the commotion, one of the men outside managed to grab Bly and had her pulled against the bars with a gun to her head.

"Put the fucking guns down or she gets it," the man growled.

Bly grimaced and grunted painfully as the silver burned the back of her head. "Don't," she insisted.

Jackson's heart started racing. He looked at Daimon, who stood between his armed packmates with a conflicted look on his face.

"Drop them!" one of the other men yelled as he pointed his weapon at Daimon.

"Chief?" Tokala asked quietly.

For a moment, it looked almost as if Daimon was considering sacrificing Bly so that the plan could go ahead. Would he really do that? Would he let one of his wolves die so that everyone else could *maybe* get away? Jackson wasn't sure, but when the Alpha's conflicted frown faded, he felt relieved.

"Put them down," Daimon growled.

Although his pack looked hesitant and confused, they dropped the weapons and backed off. The guns' original owners cautiously grabbed the rifles and then hurried out of the cage while Daimon's pack snarled at them.

"Let her go," Daimon demanded, glaring at the man who was holding Bly.

"Well, that depends," came Ellis' voice.

Jackson watched Kane's Beta strut out from the left and stand in front of the bars as the armed men made space for him.

"Are you going to give Alpha Kane what he wants?" the Beta asked.

Daimon snarled in response. "I don't know where they are!" he insisted angrily.

"It's true!" Bly said but then winced as the man pressed the muzzle of his gun harder against her head.

"One more chance," Ellis threatened.

"Just tell them!" Julian urged.

"How can we tell them something we don't know?!" Lalo growled at Julian.

Sebastien glared at Jackson from the corner of his eye. "If you Alpha's holding back, you better get him to give up. We need to get the hell out of here—"

"Shut the fuck up!" one of the guards yelled, aiming his weapon at Sebastien.

"Clock's ticking, Daimon," Ellis said impatiently.

"I said I don't fucking know where—"

"Bring her out," the Beta grumbled to the guard holding Bly.

Bly started fighting and panicking as the three guards inside the cage grabbed her.

Daimon went to move towards her, as did everyone else, but the other guards aimed their weapons at them.

"Don't move a fucking muscle," Ellis warned them. "I don't *want* to shoot anyone tonight, but I will if you don't all behave."

"Where are you taking her?!" Lance demanded—

Ezhno grabbed him by his shirt before he could try to lunge at the guards, who dragged Bly kicking and screaming out of the cage.

"If you lay one fucking hand on her," Daimon snarled.

Ellis laughed as one of the guards pulled the bars to seal the cage. "You'll what? *You're* in there…and *I'm* out here. Doesn't look like you'll be doing anything…" he started backing off, "…but watch."

Everyone rushed to the bars, and Jackson watched them laugh and throw Bly onto the dusty ground. Julian's dismayed whimpers grew louder, and when Jackson saw all the wolves and people filling up the space which overlooked the arena, dread struck him like a fist. It was happening, wasn't it? Julian told them that Kane would slaughter them one by one…and Bly was all alone out there.

"Bly!" Lance called in terror as he reached out through the bars.

Bly tried to get up, but the guards kicked her and laughed.

"Stop!" Lance shrieked.

"Dad, what do we do?!" Remus panicked.

Everyone stared at Daimon for orders, but it didn't look like he had any. He looked like he was trying to think, but all of the commotion coming from the growing, cheering crowd might be making that hard for him.

"Daimon?" Jackson asked, staring at him.

The Alpha snapped out of it and glanced at Jackson. "Can you break the bars without the inimă? Can he do it?" he asked, shifting his sights from Jackson to Sebastien.

Sebastien shook his head. "He's just as useless as we are right now."

"But he *could*?" Ethan interjected, standing behind them all. "I-I mean you practically said you guys barely know anything about what Jackson could be capable of, so maybe he doesn't even need the amulet to do shit, right?"

Jackson was starting to feel a whole lot more nervous.

"Maybe, I don't know," Sebastien said frustratedly.

Daimon moved past his son and Tokala and gripped Jackson's shoulder. "Can you do it?"

"I-I don't know," he stuttered. "I—"

"Try," Sebastien insisted. "Ethan's right; we don't know what you could be capable of."

One of the guards grunted, snatching everyone's attention.

Jackson trembled as he watched a guard unlock Bly's silver collar with a key while his skin *melted* against the metal. All three guards then kicked her again, and as she grunted painfully and spat blood onto the dusty ground, the guards hurried off and disappeared beyond what the bars would let the pack see.

"Bly!" Lance called again.

"Jackson," Daimon said firmly.

As nervous as he was—and as pressured as he was starting to feel—Jackson nodded. "O-okay." He backed away from the bars, and once everyone else moved, he held out his hand…and focused on his demon ethos.

But nothing happened—he couldn't even feel something *trying* to happen. His demon ethos was as silent as his wolf walker ethos. He had to keep trying, though. He scowled, gritted his teeth, and focused *harder*.

Bly tried to run over to the cage that they were locked in, but someone from above fired their rifle at her feet, making her stumble back as Jackson and the pack flinched.

He tried to concentrate; he could hear Sebastien and Daimon questioning Julian behind him, trying to get them to explain what the hell was going on, but Julian just kept insisting that there was nothing anyone could do now.

Not if Jackson could help it. He *strained*, trying to *force* his ethos to respond. He grunted when pain spiralled through his chest, but he didn't care.

"Come on, Jack," Ethan encouraged from beside him.

The pain started worsening, and he tried his best to bear it. He could feel something…was it his ethos?

However, the cheering outside died down, and Bly stood frozen as she stared at the pack from across the arena.

And there was something else. *Roaring*…growling, and clanging metal. Whooping and wary voices.

The ground shook lightly, causing the dust to pounce up, and then a loud, metallic banging drowned out everything else.

"It's coming," Julian said eerily.

Jackson kept trying, but when he saw the arena wall opening up dead ahead, he slowly lowered his hand as confusion struck him, and the pack moved closer to the bars.

The wall opened to reveal pitch darkness, but the strange roars and growls were coming from inside.

"What the hell is that?" Ethan uttered.

"What's in there?!" Daimon demanded, looking at Julian.

"Bly!" Lance called.

And when a low, maniacal growl came from the opening, *everyone* started calling her name.

Jackson wanted to keep attempting to summon his demon ethos, but dread quickly snatched away any focus he might be able to grasp; a pair of glowing red eyes cut through the darkness…and they climbed higher…and higher…and when their owner made its way out of the murk and into the light of the arena, Jackson's heart sunk into his gut.

The beast was *massive*—at least twice the size of Daimon's Prime form. Its fur was navy blue, and it looked like a wolf…but it was built like some kind of beefy, wingless gargoyle.

Fearful, anxious murmurs came from the pack, and Bly immediately took her wolf form. But she was calling for help; she was *terrified*.

"W-what the hell is that?" Jackson stammered, watching as the beast prowled out of its cage, each stomp sending a wave of angst through his stiff body.

"That's an Amarok," Tokala drawled.

Lance gritted his teeth and grabbed the bars. "Bly!" he cried, ignoring his burning skin. "Get the hell out of there!" He then pulled his hands from the metal and looked at Daimon. "We have to help her!"

But Daimon looked just as horrified as everyone else. He *did* look at Jackson as if he was urging him to keep trying to use his demon ethos; however, he didn't speak.

Jackson raised his hand and tried again, scowling as the pain returned. He watched the beast stretch its limbs, and Bly raced to the left wall and tried to jump up. When she failed to reach the top and landed on the ground with a thump, the observing crowd laughed, and the Amarok let out a deafening howl.

The beast charged towards Bly.

Everyone started calling out to her as the crowd cheered and whooped.

Jackson tried his best to call on his demon ethos, but he couldn't. It wouldn't listen, and the pain got worse until it felt like someone stabbed his side, forcing him to grunt and stumble.

"Jack?!" Ethan panicked, grabbing hold of him before he fell.

But he didn't want to stop. He pulled out of Ethan's grip and continued, holding his hand out towards the bars, grunting, straining, putting all his strength into it. And when the pain returned, he growled in frustration and smashed his fist against the silver, but it burned his skin, and he swore his knuckles broke, making him yelp painfully.

And that was when he saw Bly running from the Amarok across the arena with tears in her eyes. It reached her before she could swerve, and when it clamped its huge jaws around her body, Lance's desperate calls turned into agonized wails. The pack tried to tell her to fight, but as her blood spewed onto the ground, one by one, they went silent, and the pain in Jackson's hand was nothing compared to that in his chest.

Why couldn't he do it? Why didn't it work? He'd done it before; why couldn't he do it again?

"Bly," Lance sobbed as he fell onto his knees.

"Who the fuck does this?!" Wesley yelled furiously.

Jackson watched the pack sink into despair, and as Daimon turned around and walked away, he wanted to follow. However, not only did his own guilt and dismay keep him where he was, but so did the fact that Remus was following him with tears trickling down his petrified face. And... it was his fault, wasn't it? He should have tried harder. He could have blown those bars off, the pack could have escaped and helped Bly, and... and....

He sunk onto his knees, too. No. No matter how hard he tried, his demon ethos wasn't going to respond. Just like his wolf walker ethos, it was powerless against silver. And *he* was powerless without the inimă.

What were they supposed to do now? They couldn't break the bars, and trying to overpower the guards was useless, wasn't it? The silver collars took away all their wolf strength; they were as useless and powerless as humans.

Daimon would come up with another plan, right?

Jackson glanced at the Alpha, but he was sitting with his back against the wall and a hopeless stare on his face. He... hadn't given up, had he? There *had* to be something they could do.

"Jack?" Ethan's voice broke through his thoughts.

He looked up at him.

"Are you okay?"

With a despondent frown, Jackson nodded and glanced out at the arena, but when he saw the Amarok devouring Bly, he shut his eyes tight and turned his head away.

Ethan helped him to his feet and took him over to where he'd been sitting with Sebastien. They sat down, and to Jackson's relief, Ethan didn't try to convince him that everything was going to be okay... because it wasn't. *Nothing* was going to be okay. Kane was a sick psychopath; he planned to send them out there one by one to get torn apart by that creature until Daimon coughed up information he didn't have.

Jackson tried to muster the strength to attempt to come up with a plan, but his despair made it impossible. And anything he thought of had probably already been considered by Daimon.

"We gotta do *something*!" Sebastien insisted as he looked around at everyone.

No one said anything, though. They all sat with their heads hung, some crying, others silent.

Sebastien went over to Daimon. "Hello? Are you just going to fucking sit there and give up?! You're Thomas fucking Greymore's relative; you guys don't just give up!" he exclaimed. But when Daimon showed no signs of reaction, the demon stormed over to Wesley. "And you? Can't you do something? You've got fucking fae blood!"

Jackson frowned at the revelation, as did a few of the others, but still, no one said a word.

The white-haired demon growled in frustration. "So you're all just gonna sit around here and wait to fucking die?!"

"Will you shut the fuck up?!" Tokala suddenly snapped.

Jackson gawped in surprise. He'd never expect that from the Zeta.

The orange-haired man stood up and gestured to the mourning pack with his arms. "Read the fucking room. It might be easy for *your* kind to just brush off the death of one another like nothing, but we actually give a shit!"

Sebastien snarled and stormed towards him. He grabbed Tokala's collar, and Tokala grabbed his wrists. "What the fuck did you just say to me?"

"You heard me."

"Enough," Daimon called defeatedly.

Tokala growled at Sebastien but then pulled away and went back to where he was sitting.

"You're all weak," Sebastien exclaimed, but there was dismay in his breaking voice. "You're all... you're all just... fuck!" he yelled and then stormed over to the bars, where he slumped down and sat with his back to everyone.

Jackson understood his frustration. He'd have no way to make sure Clementine was safe now, would he? He was probably fighting the urge to cry... just like Jackson was.

He looked over at Daimon, but the Alpha didn't have a look of pondering on his face. He wasn't trying to work out how to get away, was he?

And... there was no way out. They really *were* all going to die here, weren't they?

Chapter Forty-Nine

⌐ ≼ ☽ ≽ ⌐

The Last Option

| Daimon |

The silence grew heavier with despair and grief as the hours passed. Kane's pack had left the arena, the monster was returned to its cage, and no one said a word since Sebastien's outburst. The sun rose, snow was falling, and some of Daimon's packmates had let sleep take them.

But not Daimon. He sat there…staring from the back of the cage at the bloody ground where Bly had been torn apart. It was *his* fault. He should have known that Kane would do something like that—that he'd turn up after his hunting party to capture him and his pack. He should have been ready for it, and because he wasn't, Bly was dead, and the rest of his pack was soon to follow.

There was no way out, was there? Jackson couldn't find the inimă, nor could he break the silver without it. His pack couldn't overpower the guards—there were too many of them. And even if they *did* get out of the cage, there was an Amarok a hundred meters across from them. They couldn't deal with that monster, wolf forms or not.

"Dad?" Remus asked sleepily.

He glanced down at his son, who lay on the ground beside him.

"What are we gonna do?"

Daimon exhaled deeply and rested his head against the wall. "I don't know, son." The Alpha then looked over at Jackson, who was sitting close to Ethan with a look of dismay on his face; he was blaming himself, wasn't he? He looked at Remus. "I'll just be over there with Jackson."

Remus nodded.

Daimon got up and went to his mate. He sat beside him, moved his arm around his shoulders, and pulled him into his embrace. "It's not your fault, Jackson," he told him quietly. "I don't blame you, nor does anyone else."

Jackson moved his arms around him and held him tightly. "I couldn't do it," he mumbled sadly, burying his face in Daimon's shirt. "I should've tried harder."

The Alpha sighed and nuzzled Jackson's head. He didn't have enough emotional energy to try and convince Jackson that it wasn't his fault; he felt exhausted and overwhelmed with guilt. He'd spent hours trying to figure out how to get his pack out of Kane's territory, but there was *nothing* anyone could do.

However, sitting around and waiting to die wasn't an option, either—it couldn't be. If he gave in, his ancestors would be ashamed of him, and he wouldn't soil his bloodline's name with a defeat so humiliating. This wasn't the first time he'd been captured by hunters—or people using silver was a better way to put it. However, that was when his pack was much larger, and they weren't all in the same cage as him.

He huffed in frustration and leaned his head against the wall.

Jackson looked up at him. "What?"

Daimon slowly shook his head. "I can't let my pack die here. I can't let *you* die here," he said as he stared sullenly into his mate's eyes. "But I can't come up with a way to get everyone out safely."

"But you'll figure something out, right?" Jackson asked him.

"I don't know," he admitted shamefully as he looked down at the ground.

Jackson slipped his hand into Daimon's, and when Daimon looked at him, his mate's despondent frown grew thicker. "I can try to connect to the inimă again. Maybe—"

"Julian said Kane has a whole lot of hunter equipment, and these bars and collars are evidence enough of that. Wherever they have the inimă, it's likely that they've stored it someplace they *know* you can't access it."

"But they don't know...what I am, do they?"

"I don't know. They saw you in your demon form, not your wolf one. But you're *my* mate, and you *do* smell like a wolf walker. They found the amulet on you, and I'm sure it took Kane no time at all to piece everything together."

Jackson sighed hopelessly. "So...we're all just...gonna sit around and wait for them to do to the rest of us what they did to Bly?" he asked sadly, and the anxiety in his voice was as clear as it was in his eyes.

Daimon huffed and looked away again. He wasn't just going to lie down and die. There had to be *something*. He needed to weigh *all* of his options...not just those which got *all* his pack out alive. He hated that he had to consider it, but it was his job as their Alpha to save as many of them as he could in a situation like this. But knowing that more of his already tiny pack would be lost made him feel dreadful. He had to be strong, though...for Jackson, for his son, and for his pack. It was time to start thinking about sacrifice.

He glanced around at his grieving pack, but as his eyes shifted between them, his despair grew heavier. He didn't know that Wesley had fae blood, and if it weren't for the silver collars, then the pack might just have another incredible asset. And it frustrated him that there *were* demons and fae who were resistant to silver, but evidently, nobody here was such a species.

Daimon set his eyes back on Jackson. "I don't know what to do," he admitted quietly. "All I can think is just...charging at the guards and fighting as much as we can, but I don't want to sacrifice anyone."

"I have an idea," Ethan suddenly said.

Anger slithered through Daimon's dismay-ensnared body and formed a scowl on his face as he turned his head to glare at Jackson's brown-haired friend. "What did—"

"Wait, please," Jackson insisted quietly. "What is it?" he asked, looking at Ethan.

Ethan shuffled closer. "There's no way we can take this pack on by ourselves, especially not with that Amarok out there. We need help, and there's only one way we're gonna get it."

Daimon waited, glaring at him.

"If we can get Jackson out—and only Jackson—then he can go and get help. We can all create a distraction, take out the guards, cover Jackson. The second he gets the amulet, he gets the fuck out of here—you know what, no. He doesn't even need the amulet." He looked at Jackson. "You can just get the hell out of this place and go back to Silverlake. Get Lucian or Caedis or anyone."

The pack started moving nearer.

"That could work," Sebastien said, appearing beside Daimon. He crouched and looked at him, Jackson, and Ethan. "Jackson gets back to the Venaticus, and they'll send a whole damn Vârcolac army out here to kill or arrest all these fuckers."

"What's Vârcolac?" Remus asked.

"The Nosferatu division that deals with wolf walker and other lycan-related crimes," Sebastien answered.

"Kill them? I thought wolf walkers were endangered," Ethan scoffed.

"I-it doesn't matter what the Venaticus do; what matters is that they get us out here, right?" Wesley said.

Daimon hated to admit that this muto had a point...but he was right. And it was very close to what he was pondering. His pack were going to be putting their lives at risk to get Jackson out; however, it was the only plan which might work. And he trusted his mate to get back to the Venaticus swiftly.

But he was reluctant to let his mate go. He loved Jackson so much, and the thought of him being alone out there terrified him. What if something happened? What if he never made it to Silverlake?

He scowled in confliction and tightened his grip on Jackson's hand. His possessive, protective instincts urged him to hold him close and never let him out of his sight; he wanted to protect him, but maybe...the best way to protect him was to get him the hell out of there. Daimon knew too well how Alphas treated another Alpha's mate... and he didn't want to see that happen to Jackson. It would haunt him forever.

Getting Jackson out of this place was the *only* way to save him from that.

The Alpha let out a deep, heavy sigh. "All right," he grunted. "This is the only option we have at this point. I'll do everything in my power to get you all out of here alive, but there's a chance some of you might not make it. If any of you object, I won't hold it against you. But getting Jackson out of here to go and get help is the only plan which might work."

Nobody objected; they all looked afraid, but Daimon trusted them to do what was necessary.

"We're with you, chief," Tokala said firmly.

Daimon looked at his mate. "Jackson?"

Although he had a nervous look on his face, he nodded. "So... you guys distract Kane's wolves, and I just... run?"

"Yeah," Ethan said before Daimon could. "You just fucking leg it. Get as far away from here as you can and get to the Venaticus."

He nodded again and went a little pale.

"You should feed first," Sebastien said. "Lord Caedis' species of demon can drink blood not only to regenerate ethos but to also increase their strength. I'd assume the same applies to you."

Jackson anxiously replied, "Okay."

"When do we do it?" Rachel asked.

Daimon glanced at Julian, who was huddled up in the corner. "When they next come to take one of us. Julian said they throw someone in the arena every evening, so *that's* when it happens."

Wesley nodded. "We'll be ready."

All they had to do now was wait. Daimon was anxious—of course he was. He didn't want to lose another member of his pack, but this was the only option they had. He'd do everything in his power to ensure not one of his wolves was killed, though. He'd protect them with his life, and he'd ensure that Jackson got out... because if he didn't, this place might very well be where they all died.

| **Jackson** |

The hours raced by faster than Jackson could comprehend. As the sun slowly set, his heart pounded quickly. He was terrified and worried that he might fuck up; one wrong move would blow the entire plan, and everyone would die because of *him*.

He took a deep, shaky breath and glanced at Daimon, who turned his head to look at him. No. He had this. He wasn't some weak, powerless little rogue anymore. He was a demon, he was a wolf walker, he was a *hybrid*. He'd get out, and he'd get help. Everyone was relying on him, and he'd not let them down.

"Are you doing okay?" the Alpha asked quietly.

Jackson nodded. "Yeah."

Daimon placed his hand on the side of his face. "You'll do just fine." He kissed his lips. "I love you."

His words calmed his racing heart a little. "I love you, too." But he knew that Daimon was saying that because he was just as aware as everyone else that he might die doing this. *Everyone* might die... and Jackson's escape would be for nothing.

He glanced around at everyone. They were all going to get hurt at the very least... *for him*, and for a moment, he let himself wonder... "Why... why me?"

Daimon exhaled deeply and ran his fingers through Jackson's hair. "Several reasons, Jackson. I can't lose you, and neither can wolf walkers as a whole. You could be the answer—the way the Nosferatu find a cure. And because you're the only one who can make it out there with those new cadejo variants. That infected fae ignored you; if I go and come across one, I'll be totally helpless." He pulled him closer. "We all believe in you. You're going to get out of here, you're going to make it to Silverlake, and you're going to come back here and help the rest of us. None of that works without *you*."

Jackson sighed deeply. What if he got caught? What if he came across some sort of new cadejo variant that he couldn't fight? Or what if there was some other pack out there and *they* caught him?

"Hey, don't overthink," Daimon told him. "You've got this."

With a nod, he dismissed as much of his nervousness as he could and then smiled weakly at the Alpha. He hated feeling confident and nervous at the same time; it was the strangest sensation. But Daimon was right. He could do this.

"It'll be dark soon. Do you want blood now?" the Alpha asked him.

As fluster shot through him, Jackson nodded.

Daimon pulled his shirt collar away from his neck, revealing the faint, healing wound where Jackson had bitten him the other night. Half of it was hidden beneath the silver collar; Daimon's skin behind it was sore, and it made Jackson feel guilty and hesitant. He didn't want to cause him any more pain.

"Go on," Daimon said. "It's okay."

Jackson shuffled a little closer to him. He moved his left hand over Daimon's right shoulder and then edged his face nearer to the Alpha's neck. His worry faded when the sound of Daimon's beating heart filled his ears; the scent of his blood quickly enticed him, and his fangs *begged* him to bite.

But he *still* felt hesitant. "I don't wanna hurt you," he said sullenly.

"It's all right," Daimon said softly as he placed his hand on the back of Jackson's head and pulled his face closer to his skin. "Take what you need."

Jackson exhaled deeply... and the longer he waited, the louder the hungry demon inside him became. He wanted to bite; he wanted to taste Daimon's sweet, tantalizing blood again. And he gave in. He widened his jaw but kept himself from being savage; he bit down on Daimon's neck *slowly*, and when he heard Daimon groan pleasurably in response to his venom, anticipation spiralled through Jackson's tensing body.

However, now wasn't the time to become aroused. He needed to drink the blood, and then he needed to prepare himself for what he was about to do. It unnerved him, but he had to be strong. He took a few gulps of Daimon's blood—he didn't want to take too much. As he swallowed it, he hummed in delight and tightened his grip on the Alpha's shoulder. And once he was done, he pulled his fangs from his neck and dragged his tongue over the wound.

Daimon let out a long exhale and looked at him. "How do you feel?"

"I'm okay," he said confidently.

"Do you feel any stronger?"

Jackson frowned and pondered. He *did* feel something. Before, the silver collar made it hard for him to connect with his ethos, but now... he could feel it. It might only be a slither, but it was there. He nodded and replied, "I think so. I feel... my ethos—just a little."

"Do you need more blood?" he asked with a frown.

But that was when Jackson noticed the feeling growing. With each passing second, he felt more and more of his ethos reconnect with him as if it was waking from a slumber. It was working.

He shook his head. "It's getting... bigger."

For the *first* time since they arrived, Jackson saw hope flicker through Daimon's honey-brown eyes. Then, the Alpha kissed his lips and quietly said, "You're going to be fine, okay? I believe in you."

Jackson smiled at him, and when the Alpha kissed his lips again, he guided his hand to the back of his head and gripped a fistful of his hair. He didn't want to leave him and the pack behind; why couldn't Daimon come with him? What if this was the last time he saw Daimon? What if he didn't get to Silverlake in time? What if by the time he got back... everyone was dead?

"Daimon, I—"

"Don't overthink, Jackson," the Alpha said firmly. "Just focus on what you have to do, and I'll take care of the rest, okay?"

There was a part of him that wanted to beg Daimon to go with him…but he knew that it wasn't possible. So, he sighed sadly and nodded. "I'll come back with help…I'll get back here before Kane can hurt anyone else," he said as his voice started breaking.

Daimon caressed the side of his face. "I know you will." He wrapped his arms around Jackson and pulled him into a tight hug. "Just…please come back to me."

Jackson scowled despondently as he held Daimon. "I will."

Chapter Fifty

⌐ ≪ ☽ ≫ ⌐

Don't Look Back

| **Jackson** |

The guards would be arriving any time now. Jackson stared at the bars, dreading the moment they turned up. He was going to have to run faster than he'd ever run, and he was going to have to fight the urge to turn back and help his packmates.

He glanced around at everyone. They were ready; the dedication in their eyes was enough to amp Jackson up. *He* was ready, too. But when he set his eyes on Ethan, a frown stole his anxious stare. His friend was sitting in the corner with a conflicted—no, that was an *anguished* scowl on his face. Why?

"Jackson," came Tokala's voice.

Jackson took his eyes off his friend and looked at the orange-haired man. "Yeah?"

The Zeta crouched beside him and placed his hand on his shoulder. "You doing okay?"

He nodded. "Yeah, I'm just... a little nervous."

"Don't be. You've got this. And remember, just keep running. No matter what, don't turn back."

Jackson nodded again as his heart raced in his chest. He was anxious, he was worried, and he was *terrified*, but he wouldn't let it stop him.

Tokala got up and went over to Daimon, who was telling everyone where they should be and what they should do. Jackson thought he'd listen in case he couldn't immediately flee, but that was when Ethan appeared beside him.

"Jack, can I talk to you for a sec?" the muto asked.

Looking up at him, Jackson said, "Uh... yeah. What's wrong?"

Ethan sighed deeply as he sat beside him. He glanced at Jackson's face, looked at the pack, and huffed hesitantly.

"What?" Jackson questioned worriedly. He knew that face; Ethan was panicking, and he didn't blame him. They could all die in the next few minutes.

The muto then looked at him and said, "I'm just...gonna say something, and I need you to listen, okay?"

He frowned and nodded slowly. "Okay..." he drawled.

"This might be the last time we see each other; you could die, I could die—hell, we could both die. And...while I was trapped out here, I spent the first few weeks really thinking about all the shit I wish I'd said or done, and...one of those things was telling you how I...how I really feel about you, Jack."

Jackson's racing heart beat a little faster, and his anxiety's focus shifted from the plan to what Ethan was about to say.

"I *always* hated seeing you bring all these guys home, and it wasn't just because I was protective of you." Ethan huffed and looked down at the ground. "I fucking love you, okay?" he uttered, his voice breaking. "I always have, and I never knew how to tell you, and I took too fucking long to do it because now you're out here mated to some Alpha, and here I am...too late," he said sullenly as he lifted his head and looked at Jackson's face again.

He didn't know what to say. He didn't know what to *think*. Ethan's confession left him both confused and startled, but it felt almost as if a part of him always knew that Ethan loved him. They'd been together since they were kids; they knew so much about each other, and the only time they'd been separated was when Ethan was kidnapped and sent to Ascela.

Ethan frowned in distress. "Say something...please?"

Jackson snapped out of his thoughts and looked away. His heart beat harder, angst filled his chest, and he began to feel overwhelmed. Did *he* love Ethan? No...he loved Daimon. Of course, he loved Ethan like a brother, but not in the way Ethan was suggesting.

Or...did he?

He looked at Ethan and frowned. "I—"

A loud clang came from the silver bars, making Jackson flinch, and his heart skip a beat. He sharply turned his head to look over there, as did everyone else, and when he saw six of Kane's men—one of which was Ellis—he tensed up and shivered, slowly climbing to his feet.

Ethan snatched Jackson's hand, and when Jackson looked at him, he desperately said, "You gotta make it. Don't stop...for anything."

Jackson nodded, and when he turned his head and set his eyes on the guards again, he felt like he was going to be sick. *Not this again.*

"You ready to tell us where the rest of your pack is?" Ellis asked Daimon.

The Alpha, who stood in front of his grouped-up pack, snarled and scowled at the black-haired man. "I don't know where the fuck they are."

Ellis scoffed and glanced at the other guards. "Take the other bitch."

Rachel shuddered and hid behind Wesley.

The guards cocked their guns while one of them started unlocking the cage.

Jackson clenched his fists, his nails digging into his palms as he tried to prepare himself.

The bars unlocked, and the guards pointed their guns at the pack.

The first guard stepped into the cage, and the others cautiously followed. And once Ellis stepped in, Daimon's glower turned into a determined scowl.

It all happened so fast.

Daimon lunged at Ellis and grabbed his throat.

Tokala, Wesley, Brando, Ezhno, and Leon grabbed the other guards.

And Sebastien *shoved* Jackson. "Go!" he yelled.

Jackson ran for it. He bolted out of the cage, and when he heard gunfire and snarls, he wanted to look back. But he knew that he had to keep going. He veered left once he was out and set his eyes on a pathway which led up the side of the arena; the edges were gated off with silver bars, but a door was open, so he sprinted towards it.

Wolf howls and frantic voices filled the air.

More of Kane's men were coming.

But that was when Daimon appeared at his side and said, "Keep going. We've got you." He cocked his rifle and ran ahead.

Jackson's racing heart beat faster with every step, but knowing that Daimon and the pack were with him gave him hope.

When they reached the top of the sloped path, Jackson spotted a doorway, where several wolves flowed out from. Panic gripped him tightly, but he didn't freeze. His packmates raced ahead with Daimon, firing at the wolves, clearing a path for him. And Jackson wasn't going to waste it.

While his packmates fought Kane's men, Jackson hurried into the doorway and followed the narrow passage. He eventually saw light, and when he emerged, he found himself in a camp. There were at least twenty men gearing up a few meters ahead, so he dived behind a tent and waited.

"Come on!" someone yelled.

"Don't let them get away!" another man shouted.

Jackson sat there, his body trembling, his breaths stifled; he watched the armed group rush down into the passage, followed by several snarling wolves. There were so many of them. If he could find the inimă, then maybe he could help. It had to be around here somewhere. It.... No. He couldn't deviate. Daimon and his pack gave him this chance to run so that he could come back with help. He didn't want to waste it by attempting to save everyone *now*.

As much as he didn't want to leave, as much as it hurt knowing that he was leaving behind the man he loved and the man who was like a brother to him, he *had* to go.

He looked over his shoulder, and *far* across what looked like a very old, snow-covered ruin was the tree line. He had to get to the forest. But what about the silver collar around his neck? Should he try to find the key so that he could take it off? If he could take on his wolf or demon form, he'd be able to get to the Venaticus so much faster.

No. He couldn't risk searching for a key.

What about the inimă? If he could locate it—even call it to him—then once he was far from here, he'd use it to break the collar. However, he didn't want to sit there for too long. So he closed his eyes and concentrated as best he could, but the nearby gunfire, snarling wolves, and yelling voices were keeping him from being able to dismiss his angst for even a moment. What if Daimon was hurt? What if Ethan was hurt? Or...worse.

He couldn't think about it. He had to find the inimă.

But he heard footsteps.

Voices.

Someone was coming.

His heart beat so fast that he felt it might burst out of his chest.

He couldn't stay here.

He had to get to the trees.

Jackson watched from behind the tent as *Kane* approached the passage. But then he stopped and frowned skeptically. Jackson leaned back, holding his eyes shut, terrified that he might have been seen.

But no one grabbed him...and the footsteps faded into the tunnel.

He wanted to let out a sigh of relief, but he wouldn't risk making a single sound. Had the collar around his neck prevented Kane from detecting him? Silver obscured Caeleste senses, right?

There wasn't time to think about it. He was just glad that he hadn't been caught.

His body felt stiff, but he peered around the tent, searching for wolves or guards. No one was there. He got up...and he ran. He ran and ran and ran, keeping his eyes on the trees, focusing on his mission. Everyone was relying on *him*, and he wasn't going to fail them.

He crossed the camp, climbed over the eroded, icy wall, and sprinted through the ruins of a temple. Once he leapt over the final crumbled wall, he reached the tree line. He wanted to stop and look back; maybe someone else had made it out and would follow to help him. But he knew no one was coming. They'd stayed back so he could escape. And no matter how much it hurt him to leave them behind, staying or trying to be a hero would get someone if not everyone killed.

Jackson had to get back to Silverlake, and he'd not rest until he did.

But someone saw him.

A bony, beaten brown wolf skidded to a halt when he did, kicking snow towards each other as their sights locked. The wolf looked just as petrified as Jackson felt. It shivered and gawped at him like a deer in headlights, panting…and then it glanced around frantically, but it didn't howl or whimper. It looked…conflicted.

Jackson didn't know how to tell a Beta from an Omega, but if he had to guess—keeping Julian's stories of Kane's pack in mind—he'd say that he was looking at a poor, mistreated Omega. It didn't seem to want to attack; maybe it was too afraid or waiting for backup to come. And Jackson didn't want to hurt it, but…he couldn't let it stop him. He *had* to go. He had to do whatever was necessary to get to Silverlake.

But…the Omega started backing off. It looked around again—no one else was coming. And then it stared into the forest, set its hazel eyes back on Jackson, and then gestured towards the woods with its head.

Was it letting him go?

He wasn't going to ask. Jackson darted into the woods, running as fast as his aching legs would carry him. But the further away he got, the heavier his heart felt. He didn't know what happened to the pack once he left that tunnel. He didn't know what happened to Daimon or Ethan. They could be hurt. They could be…. No. He didn't want to think about it. He had to run. He had to focus.

It was all down to him now.

Chapter Fifty-One
Wait

| **Daimon** |

Kane's *fifth* punch to his face made Daimon's ears ring. He spat blood to the cell floor and groaned irritably, and when Kane gripped his jaw and forced him to look up at him, Daimon snarled angrily. He wasn't going to break.

"Tell me where that little fucker went!" Kane yelled furiously.

Daimon growled at him and pulled his face from his grip. He glanced at his pack, who—like him—were beaten and wounded from their fight; they all had their arms held behind their backs by one of Kane's guards, and seeing their bloody, bruised faces made his guilt grow with every strained breath he took.

The right side of Lalo's face was so badly beaten that he was struggling to remain conscious. Sebastien had a profusely bleeding gunshot wound in his shoulder, and Remus stared at his father with such fear in his eyes that it made Daimon want to cave. But he couldn't. They had to protect Jackson.

"Tell me!" Kane shouted and hit Daimon's face again.

As pain shot through his head and spiralled down his body, Daimon grunted and slowly turned his head to look up at him again. He glared at Kane's aggravated face, and the longer he remained silent, the angrier Kane visibly became.

But Kane then laughed and backed off. "That one," he said, pointing to someone behind Daimon.

Rachel started screaming and fighting as she was dragged towards the bars.

Kane snatched a fistful of Daimon's hair and glared down into his eyes. "Either tell me where that pathetic wolf went, or this bitch becomes our latest source of entertainment."

Daimon's guilty, worried eyes locked with Rachel's. She looked horrified, but she shook her head.

"Don't tell him!" she cried.

"Shut up!" the man holding her growled and slammed her down onto the ground.

Daimon didn't want to let anyone get any more hurt than they already were, and he didn't want anyone to die. But if he told Kane where Jackson was heading, he'd no doubt send out hunting parties and find his mate before he got close to Silverlake.

But he couldn't let Rachel die.

He thought as fast as his racing mind would let him, and then he shook his head to disguise a quiet, deep exhale. "Farrydare," he lied, keeping himself as calm as he could.

Kane's scowl thickened—he was listening to Daimon's heartbeat, wasn't he? "Why Farrydare?" he demanded, failing to detect that he wasn't telling the truth.

"Because he knows someone there," Daimon growled.

"Who? Is that where the rest of your pack are holed up?"

"Yes. Let her go."

As he glanced at Rachel, Kane snickered and adorned an amused smirk. "Take her."

Panic shot through Daimon. "What?"

"No!" Rachel shrieked.

Daimon tried to get up—he attempted lunging at the guard who was dragging her out of the cage—but Kane snatched his throat, and the men who weren't holding his pack pointed their rifles at everyone.

"I told you what you wanted to know!" Daimon growled.

Kane didn't respond. He kept hold of Daimon's throat, and once his guard had dragged Rachel a small distance from the cage, he glared down at Daimon. "You've killed a lot of my wolves, and I'm going to make you pay for every single one of them."

His guards let go of the pack and filed out of the cell, and once they were all outside, Kane harshly threw Daimon back. The Alpha collided with his pack, but he immediately climbed to his feet and charged towards Kane, but the man backed outside and pulled the bars shut with his bare hand. The silver melted his skin, but he didn't flinch or wince.

When Daimon reached the bars, he stopped an inch from them and scowled at Kane. But he didn't know what to say. He was *furious*, and when he saw them dragging Rachel to the centre of the arena while it filled up with Kane's cheering, hollering pack, guilt and dismay shoved all his anger aside.

"Wait!" he pleaded.

But it was useless. Kane started walking away, and even if he did listen, Daimon didn't have anything to bargain with. He was completely powerless; he couldn't stop it, and he couldn't save Rachel, just like he couldn't save Bly or Enola or Alastor. There was *nothing* he could do but sit around and wait for help to come... and the longer that took, the more of his packmates he'd have to see dragged out there and torn apart.

His pack moved closer to the bars and started crying Rachel's name. But *everyone* knew that there was nothing they could do. The guards removed Rachel's collar and beat her so that she wouldn't try to kill them, and once they left the arena, the massive door on the other side started opening, and the Amarok inside roared ferociously.

Daimon's racing heart hurt with every beat, and his body started feeling heavy. He turned his head away when Rachel shifted and tried to run from the beast; he didn't want to see another of his wolves getting torn apart.

"G-guys, we need help!" Julian called.

No one but Daimon turned to look at them. He tried to drown out the noise of Rachel and the Amarok, setting his eyes on Julian, who was on their knees beside Sebastien. The white-haired demon lay on his back, paler than Daimon had ever seen him, and Julian was holding their hands over Sebastien's gunshot wound with a terrified look on their face.

"I-I don't know what to do! He's bleeding too much!" Julian cried.

Ethan left the corner he'd been festering in since the guards left and kneeled beside Julian. He moved their hands to check the wound, and as blood burst out as if it were a breach in a pipe, Ethan grunted and slammed his hands over it. "If we don't close this wound, he's gonna fucking die," the muto exclaimed, looking at Daimon.

Daimon clenched his jaw as Rachel's screams and the horrified cries of his pack echoed around him. He tried to maintain his composure, but he could feel himself approaching a limit he didn't know he had. He closed his eyes and exhaled deeply, trying to block it all out. But his thoughts were racing as fast as his heart. How many more of his pack was he going to have to watch die? Was he ever going to see Jackson again? Was his fifteen-year-old son going to die here in some pit?

His pack started calling his name. He felt their eyes on him, and someone put their hand on his shoulder. The noise was pushing him closer and closer... but he couldn't let it win. He couldn't give in. Jackson was free, and he'd come back with help. All he and his pack could do was wait. But how long would it take? How many more were going to die before help arrived?

"Chief?" came Tokala's worried voice.

Daimon snapped out of it and opened his eyes. Most of his pack was trying to help Sebastien, and Tokala was standing in front of him with his hand on his shoulder. Remus was beside him, staring up at him with tears in his eyes, and when Daimon looked down at him, Remus gripped his wrist and frowned despondently.

The Alpha shook his head. "We can't do anything," he uttered, holding back his dismay. "Jackson's out, so all we can do is wait for him to come back with help."

"Is Sebastien gonna die?" Remus asked worriedly as he took his eyes off Daimon and looked over at the pack, who were trying to help the white-haired demon.

He wouldn't let anyone else die—not if he could help it. The Alpha hurried over to the pack, and when he reached them, he kneeled beside Sebastien. "Lance, you know what to do, right?" he asked the Iota; without Bly, Lance was their only healer.

"I-I... I don't... without Bly, I'm just... I'm not—"

"Pull yourself together!" Daimon snapped.

Lance gawped at him.

"You're an Iota for a reason. Save his life," he ordered, nodding at Sebastien, who looked like he was moments from passing out.

Although he looked terrified, Lance nodded. "O-okay...uh...okay." He glanced around at everyone. "I need thread and something I can use as a needle. He's a demon, so it doesn't need to be sterile, right?"

Ethan nodded. "I think that's true, yeah. Demons can't get sick or infections or anything, right?"

"Sebastien?" Daimon asked, looking at his pale face. "You're not going to get an infection, are you?"

Sebastien weakly shook his head.

"All right," Daimon said as he took his shirt off. He tore it a little, and once he found a loose thread, he started gently pulling it from the fabric.

"What about a needle?" Tokala asked, looking around.

"Y-you gotta get the bullet out, too," Julian said.

"Not until I know I can close the wound," Lance replied.

"Everyone look around for something," Daimon instructed.

The pack started searching the cage for something Lance could use as a needle. But it didn't seem like anyone could find anything.

"This is gonna sound a little insane, but what about his nails?" Wilson suggested as he lifted Sebastien's hand to display his claws. "Cut one in half...long and sharp enough, right?"

Several of the pack cringed.

"It could work," Lance said with a nod. "It's not like we have any other options."

"You're just gonna rip his nail off?" Dustu exclaimed.

"It's either his nail or his life, dude," Brando said.

Daimon nodded in agreement. "Do it."

Lance gripped one of Sebastien's claw-like nails while Ethan held his hand straight. "This is gonna suck," he told the white-haired demon.

But Sebastien didn't protest. He rolled his eyes and groaned quietly.

With no time to waste, Lance ripped Sebastien's nail off; he snapped it in half, wrapped the thread Daimon had given him around its end, and then looked at Sebastien. "I gotta get the bullet out, okay?"

He grunted and nodded.

Lance pushed his fingers into Sebastien's wound and started fishing around for the bullet, and once he removed it, the wound started bleeding a whole lot faster. And Lance started panicking.

"Oh, God...okay," Lance breathed, his hands shaking as he edged the makeshift needle closer. "There's so much blood, I...I can't see, I—"

"You got this," Ethan said as he placed his hand on Lance's shoulder.

"Bly wouldn't have chosen you as an Iota if she thought otherwise," Daimon added.

Lance took a deep breath and nodded. "Okay," he mumbled and eased the makeshift needle through Sebastien's skin.

Daimon watched him work, and once Lance sewed the wound shut, he tore what was left of Daimon's shirt and used it to wrap around Sebastien's shoulder. "Is he going to be all right?" the Alpha asked.

With a deep sigh, Lance sat with his legs crossed. "I think so. But he's lost a lot of blood. I don't know if he needs more or what."

Sebastien shook his head. "No," he uttered weakly. "I just…need rest."

"Give him some space," Tokala said as he backed off.

Everyone else moved away.

Daimon stood up, too, and let out a heavy sigh.

"How long is it gonna take for Jackson to get…*there*?" Lalo asked quietly.

"I don't know," Daimon replied. "But he *will* make it."

"I hope so," Ezhno said sadly. "Bly and Rachel deserve burials."

The Alpha turned to face the arena as the weight of his despair and sorrow returned. He'd lost two wolves in the space of twenty-four hours, and it made him feel so useless and powerless. He couldn't do anything to save them—he couldn't even try to help. And Kane was going to keep doing it; he was going to come back and make another of his wolves face that Amarok…and Daimon was going to have to stand there and watch.

He scowled angrily as he clenched his fists. What if *he* faced the beast? What if he could kill it? No…that was stupid. That Amarok was not only nearly twice the size of his Prime form, but it was also going to be a lot stronger, and he might not be able to beat it.

But what if he could? If he killed Kane's strongest asset—if he killed this barbaric pack's source of entertainment—then he wouldn't have to watch any more of his packmates get torn apart.

Tokala stood beside him and quietly asked, "What are you thinking, chief?"

"I'm thinking that if I face the Amarok next, I could kill it and save the rest of you—"

"Forgive my interruption, but you can't do that. You can't take that risk."

Daimon frowned and turned his head to look at him.

"We all need you, chief. If we lose you, everyone will fall apart; they'll give up, and if that happens, then…well, that would truly be the end of us."

"My ancestors have faced worse. I come from a line of wolves who have fought demons and vampires and armies of humans—humans who manifested divine beings. An Amarok is nothing next to that," Daimon said firmly.

Tokala nodded and said, "That may be so, chief, but as your Zeta, I can't let you take the risk. Jackson will make it. He'll come back, and we'll get out of here."

Daimon huffed irritably and glared out at the arena again. "I can't just stand around and let that psycho put any more of you out there to get torn apart by that thing!" he exclaimed quietly.

"There's nothing else any of us can do," Wesley then said as he stood on Daimon's other side. "We can't try another escape; there's too many of them. Waiting for Jackson was the plan, and it should still be the plan, chief."

The Alpha shook his head. But he knew that his advisers were right. All he could do was wait.

Chapter Fifty-Two

Patrol

| Jackson |

How long had it been since he'd escaped? There was no way for Jackson to tell. He wandered through the dark woods in search of something that looked familiar, but he had no idea where he was.

He tried to focus on his mission, but how could he? He didn't know if anyone was still alive back there. Kane could have killed Daimon, Ethan, and the entire pack for helping him escape. The man he loved could be dead…and so could his best friend.

Everything Ethan said to him before he ran started repeating inside his head. He told Jackson that he loved him, and Jackson didn't know how to feel about it. However, it helped him make sense of why Ethan hated Daimon so much; if Ethan really did love him, then of course he'd despise the man who had his heart. That was why he had such a short fuse around the Alpha, wasn't it?

Was…*that* why Ethan had tried convincing him that he might have a demon mate as well as a wolf walker one? Did he think that *he* was his demon mate? Or was he hoping for it? Jackson wasn't sure, but he *was* sure that Daimon was his demon mate. He had to be. *He* was the one who Jackson loved, and he didn't have room for anyone else. He didn't *want* anyone else. Ethan was his best friend—he was like his brother—and that was all it would ever be.

Right?

He scowled as he dragged his shins through the snow. If Ethan *was* still alive, Jackson worried about their friendship. Now that he knew how Ethan felt, he was concerned that it might ruin their relationship. That was how these things always went, right? Two close friends, one confessed their love, and because the other didn't feel the same, they grew further and further apart until they were strangers. Jackson didn't want that to happen. He didn't want to lose Ethan.

But what if he'd already lost him? What if he'd already lost Daimon?

Jackson's scowl thickened as dismay ensnared his aching heart. But he couldn't let it slow him down. He had to keep going. Everyone could still be alive, and they were depending on him. He wasn't going to let them down.

A twig snapped behind him.

As panic shot through his entire body, Jackson darted for cover behind a tree and held his hand over his mouth to silence his breathing.

The snow crunched as it would when someone walked on it, and several quiet whispers came from Jackson's left.

Jackson peered around from behind the tree and set his eyes on a group of four wolves. They were staring down at the snow as they moved closer, their eyes reflecting the moonlight in the darkness, and when Jackson saw his own footprints, dread struck him like a bullet. How could he have been so careless?

He looked around, but there was nowhere for him to run. Wherever he went, he'd leave footprints, and he was no match for four wolves, especially not while he had silver around his neck restricting him from using any ethos.

What was he supposed to do? He couldn't get caught; if those wolves found him, it would all be over.

"This way...I think," came a distorted voice.

Jackson frowned strangely.

"There's tracks all over the place, man," came another swirling voice.

He frowned harder. It was like before when he caught pieces of conversation among Kane's wolves; True Speech was letting him hear what those wolves were saying, wasn't it?

"Why are we even out here looking for one stupid Omega?"

"I dunno, man."

"What's an Omega gonna do?" the wolf laughed.

"Can you just shut up and concentrate?" a female voice exclaimed. "You two follow that trail, and we'll follow this one."

"This guy's got a silver collar, though," someone protested. "He's not in his wolf form, so why are we following wolf tracks?"

Jackson frowned in confusion. Wolf tracks? He looked down and searched the snow around him, and the moment he spotted a collection of pawprints twenty feet away leading up a hill, his angst ensnared him a little tighter. How did he not see them before? Were there other wolves out here? Or... cadejo? He tensed up as his legs trembled stiffly.

"Could be corpses," the woman said. "Keep your wits about you."

"Seriously, Selena? I ain't following these wolf tracks. We should stick together—"

The woman growled and then said, "Alpha Kane put *me* in charge of this hunt for a reason. So either fucking listen to me or I'll make sure you face the consequences when we get back."

The guy grunted. "Whatever."

Jackson peeked around the tree and watched the group split up. Two walked off in a different direction, and two were heading straight for him.

What the hell was he supposed to do? They were going to find him—there was nowhere he could go! He panicked; his heart raced in his chest, and his eyes darted around, looking for an escape.

He could hear them getting closer.

He could practically feel their breath against his skin—

"Hey, boss," one of them called. "Check this shit out."

The wolves turned around. They walked away from him… further and further….

"What is it?" Selena asked.

"I dunno," one of them answered.

Jackson exhaled deeply and quietly before leaning around the tree. He tried to see what they were looking at; they were standing on top of a pile of logs staring down at something.

"You think he's down there?" the darker wolf asked.

The light-brown one snorted. "Saves us a lot of work."

"No," Selena snarled. "We have to confirm it. Alpha Kane will want proof that he's dead."

Dead? What the hell were they looking at? What could make them think that he was dead?

"I'm not going down there," the darker wolf said.

"You're such a pussy, Mark."

Mark growled at him. "You fucking go down there, then!"

Selena then grunted angrily. "I swear to God, if you two don't shut the fuck up, I'll throw you both down there!"

The grey wolf—who had been silent until now—nodded her head and said, "If we head down this way, we can get close enough without actually having to go near them."

"Lia's right," Selena said. "Let's go."

Mark snarled, and the dark wolf rolled his eyes, but they followed the others as they disappeared behind the logs.

Now was Jackson's chance.

He hurried away from the tree as fast as he could, rushing through the woods. He didn't stop to look back; he just ran and ran and ran. And when the snow started falling, he spotted a river through the trees up ahead. All the rivers led to the Great Lake, right? *That* was where he needed to go.

Jackson made his way to the flowing water and crossed to the other side—there was more cover over there. Then, he followed it downstream, using the trees to keep himself hidden in case Kane's wolves wandered closer.

He trekked through the forest, navigated his way down a hill when the river became a waterfall, and stuck to the tree line when the water cut through a glade. The moon was climbing higher, and the forest was getting darker. A shiver of trepidation ran down Jackson's spine when the sounds of forest critters went silent, and that feeling of eyes on him that he hated so much gripped him tighter and tighter with each step he took.

Were Kane's wolves still on his trail? Or had something worse picked up his scent?

He wrapped his arms around himself and tried to move a little faster, but his legs were starting to feel like weights. Hours must have passed, and he was finally feeling the strain of it all. He needed to rest.

With a quiet huff, he looked around for somewhere close by where he could take ten or fifteen minutes, and the best his tired eyes could find was a dead, hollowed-out tree.

Jackson checked over his shoulder as he headed for the tree. He couldn't see anything following him—in fact, he could barely see anything at all. The silver collar was affecting all of his senses, and in the darkening night, his eyes weren't able to provide him with his ability to see clearly. It was like he was human again.

He crawled into the tree, and when he leaned his back against it, he let out a quiet, relieved sigh. The collar was even negating the endurance he got from being both a demon and a wolf walker. He shouldn't be feeling as tired as he was right now, especially not after he'd just had Daimon's blood, and it made him wonder if he'd even make it to Silverlake.

Jackson scowled and leaned his head back, and as he glared up at the starry sky through the hole at the top of the tree trunk, he tried his best to keep himself calm. But his heart was racing, and his throat was starting to tighten. Maybe he *should* have tried to find the inimă; if he had the amulet, he might have been able to break off his silver collar, and then he could *fly* to Silverlake in his demon form. But he *hadn't* stopped for it, and there he was…powerless, weak, and the pack's last hope.

Why *him*? Why was all of this happening to *him*? A month ago, he was nothing more than an ordinary journalist with a shitty stepdad who was trying to wipe away any record that he'd ever had anything to do with him, a stuck-up stepbrother who got anything he wanted, and a best friend whom he'd known since he was a kid—a best friend who'd *always* been there for him. A best friend who stuck with him through all the court cases, the fake accusations, and the visits from Eric's lawyers. A best friend who Jackson couldn't even admit he probably loved, too.

He dragged his hands over his face and sighed frustratedly; he couldn't let all of that consume him now. Everyone was relying on him—*Ethan* was relying on him—and he wasn't going to let anyone down. They'd put their lives in his hands, and he wouldn't fail them.

As the snow started falling harder, he sighed away as much of his fatigue as he could and crawled out of the tree—

"You hear that?" came a voice.

Jackson tensed up as panic shot through his body. He pushed his back against the tree and listened… and when he heard footsteps in the snow, he started trembling.

"Yeah, this way," came Selena's voice.

It was Kane's patrol.

He gritted his teeth as his eyes frantically shot around the forest in front of him. All he could think was *shit, shit-shit-shit*—what the hell was he supposed to do? There was nowhere to hide, no way for him to go that wouldn't get him spotted.

"Check over there," Selena ordered.

Jackson could hear them on his left and right. They were getting closer. He had nowhere to go, so he quietly crawled back inside the tree and stared out through the small cracks in the trunk.

Two of the wolves prowled past, sniffing both the air and snow as they looked around cautiously.

He moved his head away from the crack and held his hands over his mouth while his heart thumped in his chest. All he had to do was wait until they moved on. He listened to their footsteps, trying his best to stay calm.

"You hear that?" one of the wolves asked—it sounded like he was only a few feet from the tree.

"What?" the other wolf asked.

The wolves started sniffing… and they were getting closer.

They wouldn't be able to find him… right? The silver collar obscured their senses, not just his—why else would Kane have walked straight past him back at the arena?

Jackson glanced through the crack, and to his relief, the two wolves were walking away. He looked up at the stars, listening as their footsteps faded further and further away. And when he could no longer hear them, he let himself relax—

The jaws of a wolf snatched his leg before he took his next breath, and as he was yanked from the tree, his yell was stifled when his head hit the ground.

"Found you," Selena said with a grin as she stood over him.

Jackson tried to get up, but Selena pressed both her front paws down on his chest and glared into his eyes. He stared in horror, his heart racing so fast that he felt like it was seconds from exploding, and his fear and terror constricted him like a starved serpent.

"You really thought you were gonna get away, huh?" one of the wolves snarled as he and the other two grouped up around Selena.

"I say we just kill him and take his body back in parts—"

"No one asked you!" his comrade snapped.

"Shut up!" Selena shouted, turning her head to look at them. Then, she scowled down at Jackson. "Where were you going, huh? To meet the rest of your little pack?"

Jackson was so overwhelmed that he couldn't even think. What was he supposed to do? He had no ethos, no way to fight them—

"Answer me, runt!" Selena demanded.

"He can't understand us, duh," one of the others mocked.

Selena snarled angrily but morphed into a dark-haired woman. She grabbed Jackson by his shirt, pulled him to his feet, and slammed his back against a tree. "Where the fuck were you going?!"

"I-I—" he stuttered, but that was when the pain in his leg melted through his suffocating fear. He grunted and looked down at his bleeding shin, which was quickly painting the snow beneath him crimson.

"Tear his legs off!" one of the wolves barked.

Selena snatched Jackson's jaw with her free hand. "I swear to God, if you don't tell me where you were going in the next five seconds, I'm going to start ripping pieces of you off!"

Jackson shivered but he didn't want to let his fear rule him. He snatched Selena's wrists; however, he didn't have the strength he'd need to pull her off. The woman snarled angrily and grabbed his right arm.

"Five… four—"

His eyes widened as he stammered, "I-I wasn't—I—"

"Uh, boss," one of the wolves called cautiously.

Selena kept counting, "Three, two—"

"Selena!" another wolf shouted.

She growled angrily and sharply turned her head to look at them. "What?!"

As the wolves turned their heads towards the trees to Jackson's right, he slowly looked over there, too. And what he saw was a whole lot worse than Kane's patrol.

Shimmering red eyes lit up the darkness, and harrowing, distorted snarls cut through the quiet. The gut-wrenching stench of rotting flesh filled Jackson's nostrils, and he felt like he might be sick—that was if his fear-induced nausea didn't make him throw up first.

Selena's eyes widened in what might be fear as she let go of Jackson, and he dropped to the ground with a thud. He scurried away from her as she and the wolves turned to face the incoming cadejo, and when he climbed to his feet and darted into the woods, Jackson looked back over his shoulder. There was a whole pack of them.

He ran as fast as his trembling legs would let him, the sound of the undead clashing with Kane's wolves sending anxious, terrified shivers through him. But he kept running, sure that the cadejo would be coming after him once they'd torn through them.

However, pain started pulsing through his shin; he was bleeding all over the snow, leaving a trail for the cadejo to follow.

"Fuck," he breathed and skidded to a halt.

Jackson took cover behind a tree. He hastily ripped off a piece of his shirt and tied it around his wound. Then, he checked back the way he'd come, but there was no sign of the corpse wolves, so he kept going. He had no idea how far he was from the river, but he didn't have time to try and retrace his steps. He had to keep going; he'd find the water once he was sure that it was safe.

But then he heard it.

Savage, distorted snarling.

The cadejo were coming.

Chapter Fifty-Three

⇌ ≼ ☽ ≽ ⇌

Friend or Foe?

| **Jackson** |

Jackson couldn't run anymore. His legs felt numb, and his body was screaming for rest. He could still hear the cadejo—they couldn't be too far behind—and he needed to find somewhere to hide. That infected fae might have ignored him, but he wasn't taking any chances with those wolves.

He desperately looked around for somewhere to take cover, but there was nothing but trees, dead bushes, and logs too small for him to crawl into or hide behind. There had to be *somewhere*; maybe he wasn't looking hard enough.

The cadejo were getting closer. Their snarls scraped at Jackson's ears, forcing him to sink deeper into his desperation. What the hell was he supposed to do? Where was he supposed to go? What about that hollow tree over there? No, he wouldn't fit. That pile of logs? That could work. He veered right and hurried over there, and once he reached them, he frantically searched for a way inside. But the logs were piled on top of each other and had a leather strap around them. Evidently, someone had been cutting down trees.

With a frustrated huff, he hid behind them and lay on his back. He used his arms to shovel snow over himself, and when he was sure that he was covered, he held his hand over his mouth... and waited.

The cadejo got nearer... and nearer, and after a few seconds, footsteps echoed all around him. The creatures snarled and gurgled—they were searching the area. Did they know he was there?

"*Here...*" came a harrowingly familiar voice.

"*He's... here.*"

"*Search... find... here.*"

Jackson's heart raced faster. His instincts tried convincing him to make a run for it, but the cadejo were all around him. He wouldn't stand a chance. The moment he revealed himself, they'd all pounce on him, and he'd be dead in seconds.

"*Find him,*" a deeper voice commanded. "*Search the area.*"

That voice was a lot less distorted than the others; it wasn't ensnared with struggle and torment. It wasn't flat or stiff or accompanied by gurgles and snarls. And it made Jackson feel terrified—more than he already was. It gripped him like the maw of a beast, and as it clamped down harder, it let him know that he wasn't going to make it.

"*He's... near,*" a distorted voice called.

"*Find... find!*" another hummed.

The cadejo got nearer. Their footsteps crunched in the snow all around him, and when Jackson heard the paws of one of them press down in the frost just inches from where he lay, he held his eyes shut and tried his best to hold back his fear. But it was building up inside him so fast that tears started escaping from his eyes.

"*Smell... blood,*" a voice echoed.

They could smell his wound. They were going to find him, weren't they?

Maybe he should just make a run for it. Maybe he'd make it. No... that was stupid. He wouldn't make it. There were too many of them, and what was he going to do without his ethos? What—

A skeletal hand snatched his throat and pulled him out of the snow. He yelled in terror as he was pinned against the logs, and when his eyes met those of a ghastly, decaying *prowler*, he froze up, and not a sound came out of his dropped jaw.

"*Kill—*"

"W-wait!" Jackson shrieked. "I-I..." he frowned and gawped at the beast. It... wasn't killing him. The rotten wolves around it stared up at him, and the prowler waited with its jaws wide, its atrocious breath burning Jackson's face.

It... was waiting. *Was* it waiting?

He swallowed the saliva which pooled in his mouth and glanced around at the undead pack. "Uh... I... put... me down?"

The prowler did as he asked. It let go of him, closed its jaws, and took a few steps back while Jackson stood there with his back against the logs.

He trembled and clenched his fists, his heart racing, his wound throbbing. It *was* listening to him. They *could* understand him, couldn't they? With a nervous frown, he set his eyes on the prowler again. "W-what... w-why are you not killing me?"

The prowler tilted its head slightly. "*Said... not to kill.*"

"R-right... I did say that," he uttered unsurely. "B-but... why are you listening to me?"

For a moment, the creature seemed to ponder. It glanced at its pack of undead wolves, and then replied, "*Higher... lifeform.*"

Jackson frowned. "What?"

"*You... are a higher lifeform.*"

Higher lifeform? His frown thickened. "Like... Betas and Alphas?"

"*No,*" the prowler snarled angrily.

As he tensed up, Jackson held his hands out. "O-okay, sorry."

"*Harmonic... variant.*"

Harmonic variant? He was getting more confused with every word this thing said. "I don't...I don't understand any of this," he said, looking around at all the cadejo again. Despite the fact that they were frozen, he was terrified that they might snap at any moment. He wanted to get away, but he feared that if he tried to walk off, he might upset them...or worse.

The prowler stiffly tilted its neck, and when it cracked, the creature let out a low, rumbling growl. "*You are... more than we,*" it said, looking around at the other corpses. "*We are... imperfect. You are... perfect.*"

Jackson stared into the creature's red eyes. It started making sense—at least he thought so. Imperfect...perfect. It was referring to the fact that he was a hybrid, wasn't it? It wasn't long revealed that the cadejo were made using demon blood, so in a way, they were imperfect hybrids, right?

He asked the prowler, "Imperfect...hybrids? You were made using demon blood, right?"

"*Yes...*" the prowler drawled, its voice like a snake.

What if he could get valuable information from this prowler? What if it could tell him things they might not even find at the lab?

The lab.... No, he couldn't waste time. He had to get to Silverlake, he had to get the Venaticus, and he had to take them back to Kane's territory to help Daimon and Ethan and the pack.

"*The Master... wants you,*" the prowler then said.

Jackson's fear rapidly increased. "W-what?"

"*Must... take you to Master,*" it said. But it didn't move closer.

"Uh...n-no thanks," Jackson said nervously. "I, uh...I have to go somewhere and—"

"*No,*" the prowler snarled. "*Master wants you.*"

Jackson glanced at the cadejo again and shuddered in fear. It seemed like they were waiting for him to agree; if the prowler was going to take him, it would have just grabbed him, right? He exhaled deeply and tried to fight through his anxiety and trepidation. "Uh...well...what if...you let me go *now*, and we can go to your Master when I'm done?"

"*No,*" the prowler growled.

He started trembling, and his wound throbbed painfully. "W-well...I don't want to go to your Master," he told the prowler as firmly as he could manage, his voice shaky. "A-and...I want *you* to...to go." Why couldn't he get a hold of himself? Before the prowler could reply, he scowled and sternly said, "Go back the way you came. And… and kill any wolves you see." They'd keep Kane's patrols off his trail, right?

The prowler growled and titled its head, shifting its crimson eyes from each of the rotting wolves crowded around it. *"Yes…"* it drawled.

Jackson stood there stumped as the prowler started leading the cadejo away. It prowled back the way it came, and the pack of undead wolves followed.

For a moment, he couldn't fathom what just happened. But it *did* happen. The cadejo *understood* him. They listened… and they did as he asked. That prowler called him a higher lifeform—a *perfect* hybrid. And now it all made sense. That was why that infected fae ignored him. That was why he'd survived so many encounters with the cadejo—sure, some had bitten him, but they never killed him… he felt almost as if they purposely didn't kill him. And that was why he could hear them. They were—in a way—like him, weren't they?

But then the fear returned. Their *Master* wanted him. Who was their Master? Why did they want him? He frowned as he watched the corpses disappear into the darkness of the forest. Did the cadejo answer to someone? Did they have Alphas? Leaders? Were they all out here for a purpose, or were they really just wandering around aimlessly? He didn't know the answer, but he suspected that the former might be true. But who, and most importantly *what* was their Master?

Jackson didn't want to stick around in case they came back. He had no idea where he was, but if he kept walking, he was sure that he'd find another river. So he turned around and hurried off into the woods.

His leg was hurting. He knew that he needed to stop and get some rest, but not yet. He had to keep going.

He ran.

He walked.

He limped.

And he struggled. He wasn't certain how long he'd been moving, but his body was starting to feel numb with fatigue, and there was still no sign of a river or anything that looked familiar. Jackson had no idea where he was… but he couldn't keep it up for much longer. If he didn't rest, he might not be able to make it to Silverlake at all.

So he caved. He spotted a burrow up ahead and limped towards it.

When he reached it, he cautiously looked around for anything that might live inside, but there were no animals or tracks, so he assumed it must be safe. He headed inside, and to his relief, it was empty. And when he got to the back wall, he slumped down and let out a long, breathy sigh.

And as his heavy eyes closed, he gave in and let his fatigue take him.

Pain shot through Jackson's leg.

He flinched when he felt something tug on his shin.

And then he heard voices.

As fear shot through him, he jolted awake. He immediately tried to scurry away, but he was met by the green eyes of a silver wolf. He tried to dart the other way, but another silver wolf glared at him with its blue eyes, blocking his way. And when he looked straight ahead, he gawped at the orange-haired wolf tending to his wounded leg.

"T-Tokala?" he stuttered.

The wolf lifted its head to look at him, but its eyes weren't purple; they were gold.

Jackson then looked down at his leg. The orange wolf had its paw over his bite wound, and a golden aura was pulsing around it. "W-what are you doing? Who are you?" he asked desperately as he looked around and spotted several other wolves near the burrow entrance.

The silver wolves looked at the orange one.

"We'll get the doctor to look at him when we get back," the orange wolf told his packmates.

"Doctor?" Jackson questioned.

That was when the three of them shifted their sights to him and frowned strangely.

"You can understand us?" one of the silver wolves asked.

Jackson looked at him. "Uh…yeah."

"True Speech?" the other one questioned.

"Uh…yeah," Jackson replied, but it didn't look like he was asking him.

"Are you surprised?" the orange wolf muttered as he took his paw off Jackson's leg.

And it was healed. The wound was gone as if it had never been there.

"We can't get that collar off," the orange wolf said as he looked at Jackson's confused face. "We'll take you back to our packhouse; one of the mages might be able to help."

"Mages?" Jackson breathed. "W-what…who are you?"

The orange wolf nodded at the silver wolf on Jackson's right. "That's Amos, and that's his twin brother, Elias," he said, nodding at the other. "And I'm Raphael. We saw you stumbling through the woods a few hours ago. Where did you come from, and why do you have this?" he asked, flicking the silver collar around his neck.

Jackson's eyes shifted from each wolf in front of him. He didn't know who they were or what they wanted—other than their plan to take him back to their packhouse—but he was certain that they weren't Kane's wolves. If they were, they'd be binding and beating him to find out what they wanted to know, right?

He used his hands to sit up straight and frowned nervously. "I, uh…I escaped from another pack. Kane—"

The silver wolves snarled in disgust.

"Escaped?" Raphael questioned with a look of doubt on his face. "You?" He looked Jackson up and down.

"Yeah. He captured my pack—w-we're on a mission, and—"

Raphael frowned skeptically. "A mission?"

He nodded slowly as he saw the other wolves turn their heads to look in their direction. "F-for... for the Venaticus. We're looking for a lab that might help them fight the cadejo virus."

"The hybrids?" Amos asked Raphael.

Jackson looked up at him. "Y-yeah. They said something about other hybrids."

"Boss," one of the wolves by the entrance called.

Raphael looked back at him. "What?"

"Undead a mile out. We need to move," the blonde wolf said.

The orange wolf set his eyes back on Jackson. "You're coming with us. Get up."

Jackson got up, and to his surprise, his leg didn't even ache. It really *was* like he'd never been hurt. "Why are you taking me with you?" he asked. But then his face lit up a little. "D-do you work for the Venaticus?" He hadn't forgotten what he'd learned about the wolf walkers and their involvement with the Nosferatu.

"No," Raphael answered. "But we answer to the Zenith and Lord Caedis. I suspect you already know who they are."

"Y-yeah—w-well I've only met Lord Caedis," he answered as he followed the wolves out of the burrow. But then he stopped. "Wait, I can't go. I need to get back to Silverlake. I need to get help. My pack—"

Amos shoved him forward. "Move."

"You'll get your help," Raphael told him. "But first, we need to get out of these woods and back to the packhouse. It's much closer than Silverlake."

Jackson felt conflicted. He didn't know if he could trust these wolves, but they *did* know Lord Caedis, and they *had* helped him. And if they were going to help—and were much closer than the Venaticus—then he should jump at the chance, right? The sooner he brought help, the better. But what was going to happen once he got back to their packhouse? What if their Alpha didn't want to help him?

If these wolves answered to Lord Caedis, though... then Jackson should give them the benefit of the doubt. So he followed in silence as the wolves led the way through the woods, and he hoped that they were the answer that Daimon and the pack had entrusted him to find.

Chapter Fifty-Four

Reiner Manor

| Jackson |

These wolves were different. They didn't move like a pack; they moved like a *unit*, and they used military words and commands that Jackson didn't entirely understand. Every time they spotted cadejo, they navigated around them without a sound, guiding Jackson as he followed the two silver wolves. They knew what they were doing, and the hope that they'd be able to help him save Daimon, Ethan, and the pack was increasing.

He could see the tree line. The early morning sunlight barely cut through the thickening fog, but as they got closer, Jackson made out tall, black iron gates connected to stone walls.

"Stay close," one of the silver wolves said; it was hard to tell them apart.

Jackson nodded and trailed behind them as Raphael led the pack out of the woods and towards the iron gates. There was about twenty feet of open space between the walls and the trees, and because Jackson couldn't see very far beyond the murk, he could only assume that the forest surrounded whatever lay beyond.

The sound of creaking rock snatched Jackson's attention. As the pack stopped in front of the locked gates, he looked around for the source of the scraping, and when he set his eyes on one of the stone gargoyles sitting on either side of the gates, a shiver of trepidation danced down his spine. It was looking *right* at him. The statue had eyes as black as night, and they were staring into his soul. He hesitantly looked away and glanced at the other statue, which was also glaring at him.

"Sentries," one of the silver wolves said to Jackson.

After a few moments of shifting their black eyes from all the wolves, the stone gargoyles returned to their static poses, and the iron gates clicked and creaked open.

As the wolves headed inside, Jackson followed them past the gates and along a wide path between two small marble walls. He spotted several hedges and trees different to those the forests were made up of, as well as a fountain; the frozen water glistened and reflected the sunlight, and the snow shimmered like stars in a white sky. A certain serenity hung over the place, and it was quiet in a way that made Jackson feel relaxed instead of anxious.

He stared ahead at the silhouette of a *huge* house, and when he was close enough that the fog didn't obscure his view, his eyes widened a little in awe. He'd seen his fair share of luxury homes, mansions, and manors, but he'd never seen something as majestic as this.

The mansion looked like something out of a history book; its dark bricks and tall arched windows gave the place a gothic feel, and the several castle-like towers had high, sharp-tipped roofs, which cast long shadows across the grounds. The ten-foot-tall front double doors were black and decorated with gold metal swirls, and an empty brazier stood on either side. Stone gargoyles much like those back at the gates sat here and there on the walls surrounding the large balconies and patios above, and the building was so huge that it stretched far beyond what the fog allowed his eyes to see.

Once they reached the front doors, everyone stopped, and the wolves shifted into their human forms. Jackson glanced at each of them; the two silver wolves became tall, broad, silver-haired men who looked *exactly* the same, but one of them had a star-like shape around the pupil of his right eye. Raphael was a little shorter than the twins, and his orange hair was jaw-length and tousled. The rest of the pack looked like normal people, save for the woman with a scar over her eye and the man with a tattoo of a new moon on his left wrist.

Raphael pushed the right door open and led the way into the house. Most of the pack broke off and disappeared down the left corridor; the twins and Raphael continued straight forward and walked through a doorway under the grand staircase. They emerged into a large lounge, where a few people were sitting chatting or staring at phones and laptops. And above the burning fireplace was a *huge* gold-framed family portrait, and one of the men in it was Lord Caedis, who—like all of the men in the picture—was wearing a dovetail coat with a poet shirt and a jabot; they *all* looked like they were out of a history book.

There were *a lot* of paintings and photos lined along the walls of the hallway Jackson followed Raphael into. Several were either of Lord Caedis or had him in them with another man and some children, and Jackson started to wonder whether this was or used to be his home.

"Um... if you don't mind me asking, what is this place?" Jackson asked, looking over his shoulder at the twins.

"Reiner Manor," one of the twins answered.

And the other said, "Caedis and his husband used it as a family home during the first human-Caeleste world war to keep their kids away from it all."

"Human-Caeleste world war?" Jackson questioned.

"Yeah, hard to imagine, right?" the twin with the star in his eye said with a scoff. "Once upon a time, the humans got so sick of how insignificant they are that they started a world war."

"That wasn't the reason," Raphael called irritably as he turned right into another open lounge, but there wasn't anyone sitting on the black leather couches, the dark red curtains were drawn, and the fireplace was empty.

The twins went silent as they shot irritated looks at each other, and Jackson could have sworn he heard one of them mutter, "Nerd."

"What's with the star in your eye?" Jackson then asked.

"Sectoral heterochromia," the twin in question answered. "It's how everyone knows I'm Amos and he's Elias," he said, nudging his brother's arm with his elbow.

"That and how annoying you are," Elias grumbled.

Raphael stopped outside a pair of oak double doors, which he knocked on and then waited.

"Is Maleki even still here?" Amos muttered to his brother.

"No idea," Elias replied.

"Come," came a voice from behind the doors.

Raphael opened the doors and led the way inside.

Jackson glanced around the huge, bright office for a moment; like the halls, there were pictures and paintings all over the white walls and the mahogany panelling. Sunlight shone in through the three huge arched windows on the back wall, and a balcony wrapped around the left and right walls and above the door, providing access to many book-stuffed shelves. A crystal chandelier hung from the rib-vaulted ceiling, and the fireplace on the left wall was burning brightly.

But his attention swiftly shifted to the two people by the desk at the end of the room. The man sitting in the chair had a concerned look on his stubbly face; his black hair was combed and parted in the middle, falling to his jawline, and a cigarette was burning in the ashtray beside his coffee cup. The brunette woman standing beside the man had a tired look on her face, and sadness lingered in her green eyes.

"Oh, Elder Idina," Amos said nervously as he and his brother waited by the doors while Raphael escorted Jackson closer to the desk. "S-sorry, we didn't realize you were here."

"Oh, don't mind me," Elder Idina said as she looked over at them.

"Is this the guy?" the man asked as he picked up his cigarette and drew a light breath while nodding at Jackson.

Raphael stopped in front of the desk and nodded.

Jackson stood beside the orange-haired man; he was nervous, and the smell of tobacco was making him feel a little uncomfortable. Eric smoked a lot, and the stench forced the memory of his stepfather to the front of his mind.

Elder Idina patted the man's head and said, "I'll leave you to it." She walked around from behind the desk, and as she passed Raphael, she quietly said, "Be good, Raphael." And when she passed the twins, they both bowed their heads respectfully to her.

Although he was curious, Jackson was sure that there'd be time to ask all his questions, but that time wasn't now. His first priority was helping Daimon and the others.

"Leave us," the black-haired man called across the office.

Amos and Elias nodded and swiftly left the room, pulling the door shut behind them.

"Sit," the man said, gesturing to the armchairs in front of his desk.

As Raphael sat in one, Jackson sat in the other.

After taking another puff of his cigarette, the man leaned back in his seat and said, "Fill me in."

"We followed him from the border of Kane's territory," Raphael started.

Jackson frowned at him. He'd been following him that *whole* time?

"A hunting party was in pursuit, but the cadejo took care of them. That's when we saw him talking to them," the orange-haired man said as he slowly turned his head to look at Jackson.

The black-haired man finished his cigarette and put it out in the ashtray. He then rested his arms on his desk and stared skeptically at Jackson. His eyes looked him up and down, and it seemed like he was pondering…but what?

"He commanded them," Raphael said. "He told them to leave, and they left."

With a deep sigh, the man leaned back in his seat again. "You're the hybrid Alucard sent to find the Lyca Corp. lab, correct?"

Jackson drawled a little, "Uh…y-yeah."

"I'm Cyrus Greyson," he revealed.

Cyrus Greyson? The same Cyrus Greyson Sebastien talked about? The guy who captured another hybrid that the Nosferatu suspected might be the one they were looking for? Jackson shook his head and sat up straight. "I, uh…think I've heard about you."

"I'd be concerned if you hadn't given the mission you've been tasked with," Cyrus said and took a sip of his coffee. "Alucard sent over all the information he had on you and your group shortly after you left Silverlake. And no, he didn't ask us to get involved, if that's what you're wondering; we monitor Kane's borders to ensure our own safety, and one of my guys happened to see a pack of wolves with descriptions similar to yours being hauled down into their arena yesterday."

Jackson had a mountain of questions, but there wasn't time. "I was trying to get back to Silverlake to ask the Venaticus for help. Kane's gonna kill them all if I don't get back there soon enough," he said anxiously.

Cyrus leaned back in his seat. "Well, you're three days from Silverlake if you were to go on foot—as a wolf, that is, which reminds me," he said and shifted his sights to Raphael. "Go and get Maleki. He's with Aysel and Tarkik down in the lab."

"Who?" Jackson asked.

"Members of the hybrid pack we were tasked with finding."

"Hybrid *pack*?" he questioned, but then he remembered what Sebastien said. "Oh... the hybrids that Lord Caedis thinks were created in the lab we're looking for?"

Cyrus nodded and said, "Alucard did say that you guys only got the information essential to your mission; you'll learn the finer details when necessary." He looked at Raphael again. "Go."

With a nod, Raphael got up and left the office.

"Uh... who's Maleki?" Jackson asked.

"Maleki is our cheerful temporary resident vampire," Cyrus answered with a sarcastic tone. "Unfortunately, he's the only person amongst our ranks with a resistance to silver. He'll remove that collar for you."

"Oh... thank you. But, uh... are you... well, *will* you help my pack?" he asked desperately. "I-I don't know how long they have, and—"

"I've already got my Gamma assembling a strike team," Cyrus interjected. "Kane's pack is huge and very resourceful, though, so it's going to take a little time for us to work out our angle of attack."

"I wanna help," he insisted. "I-I *can* help. Once this collar's off, I can use fire and—"

"You can help by sharing whatever you've learned about Kane and his territory," he said, resting his arms on the desk.

Jackson frowned. "I want to help fight."

"That's not my call, kid. I've been told to keep you alive at all costs and sending you into battle would be the complete opposite."

His frown thickened as he shook his head. "No, let me help!" he insisted. He wanted to be there; he wanted to make sure that Daimon and Ethan and the pack got out okay. He wanted to be there so that he could watch their backs and defend them.

Cyrus sighed deeply. "My wolves are perfectly capable. We've faced Kane several times before, and I'm sure that if you've seen the guy, that ugly-as-fuck scar on his face is evidence enough."

Jackson remembered Julian saying that a wolf gave Kane a permanent scar ten years ago, and he'd seen it with his own eyes. "Were *you* the one who did that to him?"

"I was. Could've killed him, but like my old man, I have a tendency to offer mercy to my enemies. Kane was just a nobody with dreams too far out of his reach back then, but because I let him go, he's built an army," he said with a melancholy tone. "I've lost a lot of good wolves to him. But he's been too busy growing his numbers to protect himself from hunters and cadejo and such that he hasn't looked our way in a good year or so. We'll have the element of surprise."

As much as he wanted to join the fight, Jackson was admittedly starting to feel more confident as he learned about Cyrus and his pack. These guys were obviously experienced, they knew what they were doing—the wolves who escorted him to this manor were proof of that—and since this was the same Cyrus who Sebastien had talked about, he felt as if he should give the guy a little credit. And if the only way he could be of use was to tell him what he knew about Kane, then he'd give him every detail possible.

"Do you know about the Amarok?" Jackson asked.

"We sure do. Kane picked that thing up five years ago when he raided a hunter camp. Amaroks are too far gone even for someone like me to control, so if they let that thing loose, we're going to have to kill it," he said, but it looked like he was speaking aloud as he thought, tapping his chin as his eyes drifted.

"They have guns," Jackson told him.

"They do, and some of them are loaded with silver," he said, setting his sights back on Jackson.

And then he remembered— "The inimă."

Cyrus nodded slowly. "The demon amulet. Kane has it?"

"I don't think he knows what it is, but he took all of our stuff, and I wasn't able to get it back."

"Yeah, that's a top priority. We can't let that fall into the wrong hands. Do you know where he put it?"

"N-no, but I can find it," he said eagerly. Maybe he would get to join the battle after all.

Cyrus sighed hesitantly and tapped his fingers on his desk. He then muttered, "*Veni foras.*"

Jackson flinched in startlement when a cloud of orange smoke appeared out of nowhere in front of Cyrus, and when the smoke withered, a strange bat-cat-like creature floated down onto the desk. It looked like a bipedal hairless cat with wings, and its eyes were *huge*.

"Go to Alucard," Cyrus told it. "I need you to ask him whether I should let Jackson accompany the rescue team or not. The inimă is somewhere in Kane's camp, and we won't have any hope of finding it without Jackson, who said he can locate it."

The creature replied with a few chirps and then disappeared in a puff of orange smoke.

"What was that thing?" Jackson asked.

"An izuret," Cyrus replied and took a few gulps of his coffee. "Little demon messengers; much faster than a text message."

Just then, the door to Cyrus' office opened, and Raphael walked in with a very sleek, regal-looking man with long, platinum hair and tall, pointed ears much like Lord Caedis', only much longer.

"Ah, Maleki," Cyrus called pleasantly.

"Count Makeli, Greyson," Maleki corrected irritably.

Jackson couldn't help but stare at the man when he stood beside the armchair Raphael had been sitting in. His skin had a golden tint to it, and his eyes were as red as blood. His eyebrows and even his eyelashes were platinum—he almost looked like snow. His silk robes were white, and the long, sharp claws at his fingertips were ashen, too. Was *this* what vampires looked like?

Cyrus laughed and crossed his arms, leaning back in his seat. "Wake up on the wrong side of the coffin?"

Maleki gritted his teeth angrily. "What do you want?" he snapped.

"Take that off him, would you?" Cyrus said, nodding at Jackson.

When Maleki's red eyes locked with his, Jackson smiled awkwardly.

"You brought me all the way up here to take a collar off?" Maleki questioned.

Cyrus then sighed impatiently. "Just take the fucking thing off, man. We've got shit to do."

With an aggravated snarl, Maleki shoved past Raphael—who stumbled aside and tutted—and gripped either side of the silver collar around Jackson's neck. He pulled with a grunt, and the metal snapped in two like a twig. Then, Maleki tossed both pieces onto Cyrus' desk. "Next time you need something, don't make me come up here. I've got my own assignments, and none of them involve—"

"Yeah, yeah, yeah," Cyrus said as he waved his hand dismissively. "I don't care what you got going on in vampire land, Maleki—or is it elf land?"

Maleki rolled his eyes. He then turned around, and although he was clearly in a mood, he rather gracefully headed to the door and left the office.

"Love that guy," Cyrus chortled.

"I don't know what Strămoş Luca saw in him," Raphael muttered as he sat in the armchair. "Millions of elves out there and he chooses *him*."

"Hey, you gotta give him a little credit. Everything we know about the Holy Grail is thanks to that guy."

"But at what cost?"

Jackson's attention was immediately snatched from rescuing the pack and trying to figure out what Strămoş meant to the Holy Grail. "The Holy Grail?" he asked. "C can... can you tell me about them?"

They both looked at him and frowned.

"Some other time, kid," Cyrus said as the izuret returned in a puff of orange smoke.

The creature started chirping and squeaking, and Cyrus seemed to understand it.

"All right," Cyrus said and waved his hand in dismissal.

With one final chirp, the izuret departed again.

Cyrus looked at Jackson. "Alucard's agreed to let you join us—"

Jackson sighed in relief.

"—But you're to stick with Raphael at all times."

Raphael groaned. "Is he *seriously* putting me on babysitting duty?"

"I think this is his old grampy way of telling you that he trusts you to take care of the precious cargo," Cyrus teased.

With a roll of his eyes, Raphael slouched in his seat and then looked at Jackson. "You better know what you're doing."

Jackson frowned at him but confidently said, "Yeah, I do."

Cyrus finished his coffee and exhaled loudly. "Let's not waste any more time. Let's go." Then, he got up and headed for the door.

Jackson eagerly followed behind Raphael. It was happening. These people were going to help get Daimon and the others out of Kane's territory, and *he* was going to help.

Chapter Fifty-Five

Bloodlines

| Jackson |

When Cyrus and Raphael led him into the war room, Jackson stopped by the doors and stared around in awe. There were at least thirty people standing and talking loudly around the huge table in the middle of the room; the shelves on the left and right walls were packed with weapons and devices, and several computer screens were attached to the back wall with one woman sitting between them all. It looked like a government facility.

"Settle down," Cyrus called as he approached the table.

"This way," Raphael muttered to Jackson.

With a nod, Jackson followed him to the left and around the table to where Amos and Elias were standing. Raphael stood beside Amos, and Jackson stood between him and a very rugged-looking man, who grunted and stared skeptically at him from the corner of his eye.

"All right, word is in from the bosses," Cyrus said as he placed his hands on the table and leaned on them. "We're taking this one with us so he can locate Zalith's amulet," he said, nodding at Jackson.

Everyone glanced at Jackson.

"The mission is to extract all the targets," Cyrus said as he waved his hand towards the centre of the table, where *files* of each of Jackson's packmates lay, all with headshots and information about them. "Sebastien's with them, too."

But when Jackson saw Alastor, Enola, and Bly, his heart sunk into his stomach. "Um…" he mumbled sadly.

"What?" Cyrus questioned.

"Those…those three aren't…well…they're not…with us anymore," he said guiltily.

"Which three?" Raphael asked.

Jackson shuffled around uncomfortably. "Alastor, Enola, and Bly."

Cyrus waved his hand dismissively.

The woman closest to the files quickly pulled away those Jackson had mentioned.

"All right," Cyrus said. "*These* are who we're looking for. Sebastien *is* a high priority."

"What about the muto?" Amos asked.

Cyrus shook his head. "Turns out that Lucian went behind his uncles' backs and decided to read the guy's mind, so the location of the lab is now common knowledge."

"Fucking Lucian," Raphael muttered.

"Is that jealousy, Raphael?" Amos asked as he nudged his arm.

Raphael snarled at him.

"Enough," Cyrus called.

Jackson was interested to know more about these people and how they knew Heir Lucian and Lord Caedis, but now wasn't the time.

"Raphael, it's your team's job to protect Jackson while he locates the amulet," Cyrus said. "Amos, your team will strike from the west, and Elias, your team will strike from the north. My team will strike from the south, and Landon, you're coming in from the east. Amos and Elias, you're crowd control. Landon, you're taking out the beefier hostiles, and my team and I are getting the targets out. Understood?"

Everyone murmured and nodded in agreement.

"What about the Amarok?" Raphael questioned as he crossed his arms. "If I'm babysitting, I can't help you with it, and Zanthé's in Dor-Sanguis trying to reason with the Eclipse Redbloods."

Jackson frowned strangely. Was he talking about the same Redbloods that Tokala mentioned?

"Lucky for me, it looks like there's another from your line waiting for us," Cyrus said as he tapped Tokala's file. "Any way to tell if he's Eclipse?"

"No," Raphael muttered and sighed. "Did he ever tell you?" he asked Jackson.

"Uh…" Jackson drawled. "I don't… I don't know what you mean."

"Someone clue him in while ya'll get ready," Cyrus said with a wave of his hand.

"Oh, oh, I got it," Amos announced.

When Raphael rolled his eyes and turned around, Jackson went to follow him, but he didn't know whether he should stay with Amos. However, Amos placed his arm around Jackson's shoulders and escorted him towards the orange-haired man, who was making his way to a locker loaded with weapons and ammo.

"A few hundred years back, who *you* know as Caedis and the Zenith had some babies, kay?" the silver-haired man said.

"Uh…okay," Jackson said with a frown.

"One of those babies was Raphael's dad, Zacaeus. Now Zacaeus grew up with Alpha Cyrus and his siblings, and he fell in love with Cyrus' sister, Lydia, and he decided to marry her. *They* had Zephyr and Zanthé, who's Raphael's sister—o-oh, and Raphael is Zephyr, we just all call him by his middle name 'cause he prefers it."

Jackson's frown thickened as he stopped by the weapons locker. "So…your first name is Zephyr?" he asked Raphael.

He grunted in response as he loaded a rifle.

"And Cyrus…is your uncle?"

Raphael grunted again.

Amos continued, "Anyways, so Zacaeus' kids are these sort of…hybrids, in a way, but not like you. Hybrids can't be born, but because Zacaeus is the son of a Numen, his kids *did* gain some demon stuff, like their ability to heal real fast and the fact that some demons stop ageing sometime around their late twenties or mid-thirties," Amos explained.

"Get to the point," Elias muttered.

Amos tutted at him. "Anyway, so that was where the Redblood wolf walker line started. Somewhere down the line, some of the wolves got the idea that they were superior to both demons and wolves. Of course, not everyone shared their view, so the Redbloods ended up breaking off into two factions. The Eclipse Redbloods call themselves that because they turned to dark ethos in their search for what they called improvement, but they were actually messing around with some really dark shit."

"And…the others?" Jackson asked.

"Well," Amos said and gestured to Raphael. "They work with us."

Jackson nodded slowly. "Well…Tokala hasn't ever mentioned dark power or Eclipse wolves or anything. He *did* tell me this story about how Redbloods used to hold this sort of tournament a long time ago, and that if he wasn't out here with us, he might have been made to take part as the prize or something," he explained, trying to recall the entire story.

"Redblood Trials," Raphael said as he slammed the locker shut. "Eclipse tradition."

"But Tokala said he left all his line's traditions behind," Jackson said as he watched Raphael strap on a holster with a colt inside. "He said that his mother disagreed with what they were doing or something, so she left to find her mate."

Raphael frowned at him. "I did hear about one wolf breaking off from the rest. He ever tell you her name?"

"Uh…no, sorry," Jackson said, shaking his head. "He has purple eyes, though. I don't know if that helps."

"It doesn't," Raphael said as he moved aside so that someone else could get into the weapons locker. "All that tells me is that he's an Epsilon."

"He's a Zeta," Jackson corrected.

Raphael stopped counting his rounds and looked at Jackson. "A Zeta?"

He nodded.

"All right," Cyrus then called loudly. "Let's move out."

Everyone started filing out of the room, and when Raphael and the twins started walking, Jackson followed, keeping close to the orange-haired man.

"Fetch Maleki," Cyrus' voice echoed from the front of the crowd as he led them from the war room and through the *massive* house.

"When we get there, don't try to be a hero," Raphael muttered.

Jackson looked at him. "I'm not reckless, don't worry. I've been training with Sebastien to—"

"Training or not, your job is to find the inimă, and that's it," he said sternly. "You leave the fighting and rescuing to everyone else."

"But what if they need my help?" Jackson asked desperately.

Raphael scoffed amusedly. "Trust me, they won't."

"Well, forgive me if I don't just take your word for it," Jackson muttered.

The orange-haired man shot him and aggravated scowl.

"S-sorry," Jackson stuttered as he followed the crowd outside. "I just…this is my pack, my *friends*, and…one of them is my mate. We've all been through so much already, and we've lost *too* many people, too. I just wanna help."

"While I understand your motives, we have orders from the top to keep you out of harm's way."

"I'll be fine," Jackson grumbled.

"And Strămoş Luca believes otherwise," Raphael replied as he stopped in the courtyard.

Jackson stopped, too. The fog had cleared, revealing the vast manor gardens. The ground was covered in a bed of snow, and there were a few dead fruit trees and hedges here and there. He could see more gargoyle sentries sitting on the surrounding walls, and a few wolves were prowling the grounds, too.

He then looked at Raphael. "What does Strămoş mean?"

The man glanced at him as he answered, "It's ancestor in Dor-Sanguian; one side of my family originates from there. We use Strămoş whenever we talk about any relative older than our parents. Strămoş Luca is who you know as Lord Caedis or Alucard, and Strămoş Zalith is the Zenith. You'll hear a lot of names and titles being thrown around this place, so you best remember everything *fast* if you want to keep up."

Jackson nodded slowly. "Okay…so tell me."

Raphael glanced around at everyone. "Maleki's going to take his sweet ass time, so I guess," he said with a shrug. "Elder Idina is Alpha Cyrus' mother and Fenrisúlfr's mate and wife, and an Apex demon. Since you're both a demon and a wolf, I don't know which title you should be using for her; it's best to ask Alpha Cyrus. Fenrisúlfr is Greymore, a God to some, a friend to others. We *always* refer to him as Fenrisúlfr."

"Okay... and I just call all of you guys by your names, right? I'm not a part of your pack, so I don't have to use ranks, do I?"

"Correct."

Jackson then spotted Maleki. "What's his deal?" he mumbled, glancing at Raphael.

"He hates wolves, and he hates working with us even more. Strămoş Luca posted him out here to help us when the cadejo started showing up. Being an elf gives him immunity to silver, so he's one of Strămoş Luca's most valuable subordinates; it's why he acts so high and mighty all the time."

"Guy's used to being pampered and eating rich people food back in DeiganLupus," Amos muttered.

"And getting his feet kissed," Elias added.

Raphael rolled his eyes.

Jackson watched as Maleki—the very angry, very flamboyant elf-vampire—strutted through the crowd towards Cyrus. He frowned and looked at Raphael again. "Cyrus said something about him knowing stuff about the Holy Grail."

"He was Strămoş Luca's inside man for a long time back when the Holy Grail had just surfaced. The information he gathered saved millions of Caeleste lives," Raphael said as he, too, watched the elf-vampire tell Cyrus just how much he'd rather not be accompanying them on their mission.

"At least he doesn't boast about it," Amos muttered.

"Yeah, he just boasts about everything else," his brother said.

Cyrus then clapped his hands loudly. "All right, everyone. Time to shift. Let's get a move on."

Everyone swiftly shifted into their wolf form, so Jackson did the same. And then he set his eyes on Cyrus, who was the only pure white wolf among them; he looked very much like Daimon, which made sense since they were related, right?

Right?

Jackson frowned as he followed Raphael when the pack started heading for the gates. He remembered Sebastien saying something about the Grey bloodline, but he couldn't recall *exactly* what. So, he looked at Raphael and asked, "So, Cyrus and Daimon are related, right?"

However, Amos answered instead, "Distantly. It's likely they don't know each other; Alpha's like... three hundred and sixty years old or something crazy like that."

Jackson's eyes widened as he stared at the silver wolf in confusion. "What?" But then he remembered what he was told about Idina and Fenrisúlfr. Idina was a demon, which meant her children—Cyrus and his siblings—were the 'sort of hybrids' that Amos mentioned. "Oh, never mind, I got it. He stopped ageing like demons do, right?"

Amos nodded as they passed the gates and headed into the forest. "And three hundred years is a lot of space for a lot of new Grey babies," he said with a wink.

Raphael rolled his eyes again.

And then the pack picked up the pace. It seemed like the time for questions was over. It was time to run.

Chapter Fifty-Six

Liberation

| **Daimon** |

Daimon didn't know how much longer he could listen to his pack grieving. He didn't know what time it was, and he didn't know how long Jackson had been gone; he couldn't feel him through their imprints, and there was a part of him that feared Kane's wolves might capture him. No matter how hard he tried to remain strong for both himself and his pack, his dismay was eating away at him, and he was convinced that he'd crack any moment.

But if he gave in, his pack would crumble, too. He had to enforce the hope that Jackson would make it to Silverlake, and he had to do whatever it took to keep his pack calm.

Kane was coming, though. He could hear the deranged Alpha's voice, and he knew that he was going to throw another one of his wolves out into the arena to be slaughtered by the Amarok.

When Kane and his cronies stood in front of the silver bars, Daimon's pack retreated to the back of the cave, and he stood defensively in front of them. Although he knew that there wouldn't be anything he could do to stop Kane, he'd still stand in his way and protect his pack with his life.

"Your little whore killed my wolves," Kane revealed as he scowled at Daimon.

"Jackson?" Dustu questioned quietly.

"Did he get the inimă?" Lalo whispered.

Kane continued, "And what's strange is that he didn't seem to be heading in the direction of Farrydare." He smirked and moved closer to the bars as he glared in at Daimon. "I think someone's been telling lies."

Daimon scowled and snarled quietly.

With an irritated grunt, Kane waved his hand towards the bars, and one of his men unlocked the cage. "Either tell me the truth," he said as he stepped inside. "Or I'll take *two* of you this time."

As Kane's men stepped into the cage and fondled their pathetic weapons, Daimon ushered his son behind him with everyone else. He wouldn't reveal where Jackson was really headed; he'd fooled Kane's lie test before, and he was confident that he could do it again. But if he gave them another location, Kane might suspect that he was able to keep his heartbeat steady, and he'd kill two of his wolves. He needed to think of something else.

"Well?" Kane growled, moving closer.

"He was going to Farrydare," Daimon insisted.

"He probably got fucking lost," Lance suggested angrily. "He always was a little brainless."

"Watch your fucking mouth," Ethan snapped and grabbed Lance's neck.

"Get the fuck off him," Daimon warned as he shoved the muto away from his packmate. He knew that Lance was backing his lie, and the last thing he needed was Ethan fucking it up.

Kane and his men laughed amusedly.

"You're just gonna let him talk shit?!" Ethan exclaimed as Wesley grabbed his arms and pulled him back before he could lunge at Daimon.

"Calm the fuck down, dude," Sebastien complained from the corner he hadn't left since Jackson's escape.

"Take the kid," Kane said.

Daimon immediately grabbed Remus and pulled him behind him. "I told you where he's going!" he insisted and crashed his fist into the face of the man who tried to snatch his son.

The other men cocked their weapons and pointed them at the pack as the guy Daimon just hit scrambled to his feet.

Kane moved a little closer. "I don't believe you," he said with a sing-song voice. "See, Farrydare's *that* way," he said, pointing to his left. "But my guys—before they got slaughtered—reported that your little man-slut was going *that* way," he growled, pointing to the right. He then abruptly snatched Daimon by his silver collar, and despite the metal burning his skin, he pulled him closer so that their faces were inches apart. "If there's anything I hate more than a fucking fairy," he spat, looking him up and down, "it's a fucking fairy who *lies* to my face!" He smashed his forehead into Daimon's face and shoved him back.

Daimon grunted painfully when he collided with his pack, who grabbed him and kept him from hitting the floor.

"Come 'ere," Kane snarled as he grabbed Remus.

Daimon tried to get up, but his head was spinning, and Kane's men moved closer with their guns, blocking any of them from trying to get to his son, who screamed and tried to fight as Kane dragged him towards the bars.

"Get the fuck off him!" Daimon yelled over his shouting, panicking pack. He forced himself to his feet, shoved two of the men out of the way, and lunged at Kane, but the guy let go of Remus and slammed his fist into Daimon's face, sending him to the ground.

But when his face hit the stone, the arena *shook*, and a blinding flash of crimson light lit up the darkness outside.

Jackson?

"What the fuck was that?!" Kane exclaimed as he threw Remus to the ground beside Daimon.

Daimon grabbed his crying son and pulled him closer. "It's okay," he whispered.

"Are we under attack?" one of Kane's guys questioned as they all followed their Alpha out of the cage.

"Is it Jackson?" Julian whispered.

Daimon helped his son up and re-joined his pack. They all watched as the night sky lit up with crimson and silver light, and the sound of gunshots, snarling wolves, and *ethos attacks* filled the tense quiet. *Was* it Jackson? Had he got to the Venaticus?

"Shit!" Kane shrieked angrily. "Lock the fucking cage." He morphed into his wolf form and rushed off.

"What the fuck's going on up there?" one of the guards muttered as he started locking the bars.

"Doesn't sound like hunters," one of them replied. "Hurry the fuck up."

"I'm fucking trying, man. This shit's burning my—"

A trio of dark-furred wolves pounced out of the dark and grabbed Kane's guys; they tore them apart before they had the chance to shift.

Daimon defensively held his arms out, standing in front of his pack. But when he saw a huge bipedal white wolf which looked a lot like he did in his Prime form, he was quickly overwhelmed with confusion—even more so when a platinum-haired elf moved through the crowd of wolves and pulled the silver bars out of the stone wall like they were paper.

"Who the fuck are you?" Wesley questioned.

"You gotta be fucking kidding me," Sebastien uttered.

With a confounded frown, Daimon looked back at the white-haired demon and watched him approach the elf.

"Where the hell did *you* come from?" the demon asked the elf.

"Your little hybrid got picked up by Raphael," the elf replied as he pulled Sebastien's silver collar off.

Sebastien rubbed his neck and turned to face the pack. "They're cool. Better than the Venaticus, if I'm being honest."

"Where's Jackson?" Ethan demanded before Daimon could.

"Topside with Raphael," the elf replied as he moved towards Daimon.

"Who the fuck's Raphael?" the muto questioned.

Daimon smacked the elf's hands away before he could grab his collar. "Who are you people?"

The huge white wolf answered, "Cyrus Greyson. Alucard said he mentioned me."

Cyrus Greyson: one of Daimon's relatives. But he didn't look as old as he was supposed to be.

"One of my wolves found your boy out in the wilds. We're here to help," Cyrus told them as his blue eyes shifted from each of Daimon's packmates. "This is Maleki, elf-vampire. He's our silver-breaking guy. We gotta get you lot the hell out of here."

Daimon relented and let Maleki break his silver collar, and the moment it was off his body, he could feel his strength returning, and although his desperation to get to Jackson was intensifying, his desire to tear Kane apart was stronger.

He morphed into his Prime form—

"Where do you think you're going?" Cyrus questioned as he grabbed his arm before he could storm off.

"To kill that sick fucking—"

"No, no killing. My job is to get you the hell out of this place. We can talk killing when we get back to—"

"I'm not going to give him the chance to get away!" Daimon snarled, pulling his arm free.

But Cyrus grabbed him again. "Look, I want that piece of shit dead just as much as you, but there's a time and a place. Right now, my guys are up there giving us a window to get as far away from this place as possible, and I won't be losing our window. We ain't prepped for war, all right? This is a grab-and-go."

Daimon scowled and tried to pull his arm free again. He wasn't going to give up his chance to slaughter Kane for killing his packmates and almost killing his son. He wanted to make him pay—he wanted to tear him to pieces and feed him to that Amarok himself. But when he looked at his pack and watched as Maleki pulled their collars off, he hesitated. Not only did he want to make sure that what was left of his pack made it to safety, but he also wanted to get back to Jackson, who was up there right now with Cyrus' wolves. He didn't want to do something out of anger which put his wolves or the man he loved in any more danger.

"We're gonna have to deal with him anyway," Cyrus assured him. "You'll get your revenge."

With an aggravated huff, he pulled his arm from Cyrus' grip and turned to face his pack.

"Sebastien, go find Raphael and help Jackson find the amulet," Cyrus instructed.

Sebastien nodded and morphed into his hound form. Then, he took off and flew out of the arena.

"Where's the Amarok?" Cyrus asked Daimon.

The Alpha pointed towards the huge stone wall keeping the Amarok contained.

Cyrus then pointed at Tokala, who rubbed his sore neck. "You, Redblood. I need you with me in case they let that thing out."

Tokala frowned. "What?"

"Why him?" Ethan questioned.

"Because *my* Redblood's occupied," Cyrus answered as he waved his arm, urging them all to leave the cage now that their collars were off. "Come on, move it."

Everyone hurried out of the cave.

"I don't know what being a Redblood has to do with this," Tokala exclaimed as Cyrus grabbed his arm.

Daimon was wondering that, too. "I'll help with the Amarok—"

"No offence, but you're too far down the bloodline to stand a chance," Cyrus dismissed. "Go with my wolves and get your pack out of here."

Tokala then pulled his arm free and stopped walking. "I honestly won't be more useful than the chief," he insisted.

A loud explosion shook the ground, and a flash of crimson light cut through the dark again.

"He mustn't be like Raphael," one of Cyrus' wolves muttered.

Cyrus then sighed. "Whatever. If the Amarok's let out, I'll get Raphael on it. Now come on!" he insisted, ushering them all up the slope. "Let's get the fuck out of here."

"What about Jackson?" Daimon questioned as he hurried up the slope with his pack.

"He'll be right behind us once he finds the amulet," Cyrus answered.

"I'm not leaving without him," the Alpha denied.

"Neither am I," Ethan called.

"Jackson's fine," Cyrus insisted. "Nobody's hanging around, nobody's breaking off, and nobody's fucking up my plan. I'll drag you out if I have to."

Daimon didn't want to leave until he knew that Jackson was safe. The closer to the arena's exit he got, the louder the sound of the battle was, and the stronger the scent of blood grew. He didn't have to see to know he was about to head into a warzone and knowing that his mate was somewhere in the middle of it made him panic. Cyrus didn't honestly expect him to leave Jackson behind, did he?

He scowled determinedly; if he had to sneak off, he would.

Cyrus and his wolves led the way up towards the surface, and when they emerged from the arena tunnel Daimon's suspicion was confirmed. There were wolves *everywhere*, snarling and tearing and roaring and slashing. There were men and women firing rifles, and a massive explosion of crimson ethos came from the middle of the battlefield. Sebastien's blue flames were flying through the air, and Maleki sent a devastating blast of silver power towards three of Kane's wolves when they charged towards the pack.

"Let's go!" Cyrus called, veering left.

Before Daimon could bolt, *Ethan* burst towards the battle in his tiger form.

"Are you fucking kidding me?!" Cyrus exclaimed. "Go after him!"

Three of Cyrus' wolves chased after the muto.

Daimon took his chance. He rushed in the opposite direction, and now that he wasn't bound in silver, he could feel Jackson nearby. So he followed his mate's scent, ignoring Cyrus' yells. He didn't care about what he was sent here to do. *He* wanted to get to Jackson, and he wasn't going to let anything stop him.

The Alpha cut his way through the battle, destroying every wolf in his path that he saw with Kane's mark. He couldn't stop himself from searching the destruction for Kane on his way to his mate, but there was no sign of him. Had he run like a coward?

He couldn't let his desire for revenge consume him; he had to find Jackson. And once he found him, he'd hunt down Kane and make him wish he'd never laid his hands on his pack.

Chapter Fifty-Seven

⌒ ≤ ☽ ≥ ⌒

Hunt for the Inimă

| Jackson |

Amidst the battle, Jackson fought alongside Raphael and his team.

Kane's wolves were like cockroaches; they crawled out of every cave and hole in the ruin walls, and for every wolf who died, three more appeared to replace them. But Raphael was unlike anything Jackson had ever seen. He was so strong that he sent a wolf flying a hundred yards into the forest when his paw collided with its face, and the tree that its body clashed with snapped like a twig and fell to the ground.

But that wasn't even the most impressive thing Jackson saw him do. When a sniper started shooting at them from a stone tower, Raphael morphed out of his wolf form, pulled his rifle from his back, and returned fire. He killed the sniper with his second shot, and then he shifted back into his wolf form and re-joined his team, who were still battling with Kane's wolves.

"How far?" Raphael called as he tore the head off his grey-furred opponent.

"I-I don't know," Jackson replied as he stumbled back when one of Raphael's wolves raced past him and clashed with the man who was about to fire his shotgun at him. "Maybe...uh...." He looked around frantically, but the battle was making it hard for him to concentrate on the inimă's ethos signal. And the fact that he was worried about *his* pack didn't help, either. "Do you know if Cyrus got Daimon and the others out yet?" he asked desperately.

Raphael snarled as he pulled his leg from the jaws of the wolf who just jumped him. "You do your job," he said and slammed his free paw down on the wolf's head, making him yelp painfully, "and Alpha Cyrus will do his." He executed the wolf, tearing its head off with his teeth. "Find the amulet!"

Jackson nodded and tried to focus.

"Cover!" Raphael demanded.

Several of his team immediately hurried over to Jackson and surrounded him defensively.

He wouldn't waste what time they could give him. He crouched into the snow and closed his eyes, and then he used his ethos to scour the battlefield for the inimă. But there was so much noise, so many conflicting auras; he couldn't let any of it distract him, though. He scowled and concentrated harder…and although it was weak, he could feel the amulet calling out to him.

"That way," he said as he jumped to his feet.

One of the wolves protecting him relayed the message to Raphael, who then commanded his team to follow. Jackson's protectors ushered him to the front of the moving line, and once he was beside Raphael, the orange wolf picked up the pace.

Jackson held onto the inimă's aura. The closer he got to it, the stronger it felt, and there was something else…anticipation? He didn't want to think too much about it, though. He had to find it.

"Still this way?" Raphael asked.

Jackson responded with a nod, but when they reached a mound of ice-covered bricks, the signal led him to the right a little, so he followed it, and Raphael stuck close to him.

The aura navigated him through the battle, where several of Raphael's wolves broke off to hold the hostiles back. And then it took him under a stone bridge, down a hill and into a pit where at least fifty dead wolves and people lay, and then he reached the only part of the ruin that still looked somewhat whole. There was a steel door and barred windows, and the mark of Kane's pack was painted with blood on the bricks between two empty flagpoles.

Jackson stopped ten feet from the door, and when Raphael stopped beside him, he glanced unsurely at the orange wolf.

"You think he's holed up in there?" one of the remaining wolves asked.

"Coward," Raphael snarled.

Jackson didn't have to ask. He knew that they were talking about Kane. He hadn't seen that deranged, black-furred wolf on the battlefield, nor had there been any mention of him until now. And it would make sense that he'd be inside; *of course* the Alpha wouldn't sleep in a tent with the rest of his pack; he certainly seemed like the kind of guy who took the best of everything for himself.

"What's the call?" another wolf asked.

Raphael asked Jackson, "Is it inside?"

"I think," Jackson replied, setting his eyes on the steel door. He could feel the inimă reaching for him. He felt it *pleading*. He felt it…yearning. But he didn't know why, and he could only assume that Kane might be doing something to it. "W-what if he's trying to use it?"

The orange wolf shook his head as he slowly backed away from the building. "Only Strămoş' Luca and Zalith can use it, and evidently asmodi demons. It'll do ugly things to anyone else who tries to."

"Ghastly," one of the wolves agreed.

Once the group reached and took cover behind a shattered wall, Raphael turned to face them. "We wait here until Alpha Cyrus can send reinforcements. We don't know what's waiting on the other side of that door, and being the coward that he is, I'm sure Kane has his best fighters in there with him to protect his sorry ass."

The wolves snarled and snickered.

But a huge shadow of a winged beast suddenly swooped over them. Jackson looked up with everyone else and set his eyes on Sebastien. The winged hound glided down and joined them behind the wall.

Sebastien looked confused. "Cyrus sent me over to help find the amulet. What the hell are you doing this far from the fight?"

Raphael gestured towards the building with his head. "It's in there, and we think Kane is, too."

The kludde nodded and muttered, "All right. Raphael, you and I will take Kane. The rest of you can deal with whatever he's got waiting on the other side of that door."

"What about the Amarok?" Raphael questioned.

"As far as I know, it's still in its cage," Sebastien answered.

That relieved Jackson. The last thing they needed was that creature rampaging through the battleground.

"What about Daimon and Ethan?" Jackson asked anxiously.

"Fine. Cyrus is getting them away from the territory as we speak," the hound told him.

But for some reason, his reply didn't make Jackson feel any less worried about his mate and best friend. Why did he feel like something was wrong? Could something have happened in the time it took Sebastien to get from the pack to them?

"You good, kid?" Raphael asked him.

Jackson snapped out of it and gawped at the orange wolf. "Y-yeah."

"Shouldn't we wait for Alpha Cyrus, sir?" one of the wolves asked. "We all know how strong Kane is, coward or not."

Raphael looked conflicted but said, "No. He's busy getting the targets to safety. We'll be…" but he dragged his words and went silent as he set his eyes on something behind them.

Jackson frowned and looked over his shoulder, and when he saw *Ethan* rushing towards them, both relief and angst filled his heart. What the hell was he doing here? He was glad to see that he was okay, but… why wasn't he with Cyrus and the pack?

"What the fuck do you think you're doing?!" Sebastien snarled as he confronted the arriving tiger.

"Get the hell out of my face!" Ethan snapped back.

"Is it really so fucking hard for you to follow *one simple* order?!" the hound barked.

"Hey!" Raphael then called.

Although he was seething with anger, Sebastien took his eyes off Ethan and looked at Raphael.

Ethan looked at the orange wolf, too, but quickly shifted his sights to Jackson. "I couldn't just leave," he insisted. "Not when you're out here risking your life."

"Where are Cyrus and the others?" Raphael questioned.

"He probably left with the others already," Ethan answered.

"Probably?" one of the wolves scoffed.

But Raphael then snarled impatiently. "We don't have time for this. *All* of you, listen the fuck up."

Everyone stared obediently at him.

Ethan moved past Sebastien and joined Jackson. "Are you okay?" he whispered.

Jackson nodded. "Yeah. You?"

"Yeah."

Raphael spoke loudly, "We don't know how many wolves are on the other side of that door, so we're going to have to be smart about—" he paused and adorned a look of disbelief. "Are you fucking kidding me?!"

They all turned their heads again, and when Jackson saw *Daimon* rushing towards them, relief gripped him so tight that he stifled a breath.

"Should we just call the entire pack over here?" Raphael asked sarcastically.

Jackson stepped forward; he wanted to run to Daimon, but Ethan stepped in front of him and snarled irritably at the Alpha when he tried to get close.

"Could you seriously not just leave him alone for *five* minutes?! Why do you always have to be here?!" the tiger exclaimed.

Daimon growled angrily and went to lunge at him, but Sebastien and two of Raphael's wolves quickly stepped in front of Ethan, blocking the Alpha's path.

"We don't have time for whatever drama's going on between you two," the orange wolf grunted. "Save your shit for later. We've got work to do."

Although he clearly wasn't happy about it, Daimon huffed and nodded.

Ethan scoffed and returned to Jackson's side.

Daimon stood on Jackson's other side. "Are you okay?" he asked him quietly. "How did you find these wolves?"

Jackson couldn't wipe the smile off his face. He was so happy to see both of them, but especially Daimon. If he wasn't in the middle of a crowd of wolves and about to receive orders, he'd shift into his human form and wrap his arms around his mate, but he'd have to save the affection for later. "I'm fine," he answered with a nod. "And... well, I was running from some of Kane's guys, and then—"

"There'll be time to catch up later," Raphael interjected. "Everyone listen up."

Everyone stared at him.

"Sebastien, you'll breach the door," the orange wolf instructed. "You," he said, pointing his paw at Daimon, "you'll charge in with me and deal with whatever we're hit with first. Rianna—" he shifted his sights to the golden-brown wolf to Sebastien's right, "—you'll lead everyone in after and back Daimon and me up. And you—" he looked at Ethan, "—your job is to watch Jackson's back at *all* times. You make sure he gets in and out without a scratch."

Ethan seemed smug about it. "You got it."

Daimon snarled angrily but didn't say anything.

"And Jackson," Raphael said. "You don't come through to the next room until you hear me say clear. Got it?"

Jackson nodded confidently.

"And when we find Kane?" one of the wolves asked.

"*If* we find that coward inside, Daimon, Sebastien, and I are the only ones who will be able to deal with him at least until Jackson has the inimă," Raphael answered.

"Three against one?" Ethan questioned confusedly. "Why not just kill him? I'm sure you can handle it."

"Kane Ardelean-Blood comes from an ancient wolf walker bloodline. He's extremely powerful, and only someone from a bloodline as old as his stands a chance of defeating him. Alpha Cyrus has not only his bloodline but also his demon blood to his advantage," the orange wolf explained.

Ethan still looked confounded. "Isn't he from the same bloodline?" he asked with a scowl, glancing at Daimon.

"I'm a Greyblood," Daimon told Raphael.

"Yes, but Ardelean-Bloods are descended from Ada, the very first wolf walker, who was created by an Aegis," Raphael said, shaking his head.

"What's an Aegis?" Ethan asked.

"A Dragon God," Sebastien answered.

"Well, damn," the tiger muttered.

Raphael then sighed deeply. "Is everyone ready? The sooner we get in there, the sooner we can get back to base."

They all nodded.

The orange wolf then turned around. "Let's go. Everyone, get into position."

Jackson followed him, but he had a bad feeling that it was going to get messy fast. However, he knew that Raphael could handle himself, and so could Sebastien, Daimon, and Ethan. No... he had nothing to worry about. He was with the best group possible right now, wasn't he? Whoever or whatever was waiting inside that building didn't stand a chance.

Chapter Fifty-Eight

Butcher

| Jackson |

Sebastien prepared to breach the steel door. The winged hound prowled towards it; Daimon and Raphael lay in wait ten feet to the right, and everyone else grouped up behind them.

"Hey, don't worry," Ethan whispered to Jackson. "I've got your back."

Jackson smiled in response. He trusted Ethan, Daimon, and the others to get him through, but he was still nervous. Kane had already killed four of their packmates; that wolf was insane, and Jackson didn't know what to expect. He wouldn't let his guard down, though. He was ready for anything.

Sebastien glanced at Raphael, and the orange wolf nodded. The hound dragged out a guttural snarl; teal smoke began seeping through his teeth, and his glowing blue eyes shined brighter. It looked like he was charging his fire. The snow around him started melting, and a mirage surrounded his body. And then he abruptly opened his mouth and fired a blinding blue ball of flames at the door.

The moment the fire collided with the steel, it sizzled and burned away like ice in a furnace. Several panicked voices and loud coughs came from inside as the room filled with teal and black smoke, and before the metal had melted entirely to the ground, Raphael and Daimon charged into the building.

Jackson listened to the snarls, growls, and yelling voices coming from inside; he watched Sebastien hurry in with Rianna and the rest of the wolves, and when it was time for him and Ethan to head in, he hurried with the tiger at his side and stepped over the pool of melted metal.

Raphael and Daimon had already led the pack deeper inside, leaving multiple mangled, headless corpses all over the foyer. The brick walls were painted with blood, and every rifle was still stowed inside the crate sitting in the left corner. Kane's people evidently hadn't had time to grab their weapons.

"Come on," Ethan said as he walked towards the hallway which led deeper into the building.

Jackson went with him. The sound of battle echoed behind them *and* up ahead, but he knew that he was supposed to be focusing on finding the inimă, so he did his best to ignore the noise and concentrate on the amulet's aura.

"I'm glad you're okay," Ethan said as he walked beside Jackson. "A part of me thought I might not see you again. But I kinda also knew that I would, I mean…you're you. You always find a way to get shit done, right?" he said with a quiet laugh.

"I was worried that I took too long," Jackson replied as he stopped at the end of the hallway and looked down the left and right corridors. "I think…this way," he said as he turned to the right.

Ethan nodded and followed behind him. "Who are these new people?" he asked. "I mean…other than what we all already know from the Venaticus."

"Uh…" Jackson drawled as he felt the inimă's aura get slightly stronger once he approached a flight of stairs that led down. "The orange wolf is a Redblood like Tokala, but he's also related to Lord Caedis and the Zenith. And their Alpha, Cyrus, is as well."

"And the elf?"

"Some vampire guy who helped Lord Caedis gather information on the Holy Grail. I tried to find out what they knew, but we were in a rush." He stopped at the top of the stairs and glanced at the tiger. "The signal's coming from down there."

"So, the Holy Grail really was involved?" Ethan questioned as he headed down.

Jackson frowned when he remembered that he hadn't told Ethan the finer details about what he'd learned as the perception filter wore off. "I've been remembering stuff, and something that I kept seeing was the night my dad died. There were these…robed men with crossbows and shit. Some research led me to finding out that they're part of some cult called the Holy Grail, and that they're actually tied up in a lot of bad shit the Nosferatu has been investigating. I think Eric was looking into it, too—I found a letter on his desk when I was a kid. I was kinda hoping that Cyrus and his people might be able to tell me something that could help me work out what really happened to my parents, but I didn't get anything, really. Either way, though, I'm gonna find out. It was part of the deal I made with Lord Caedis. We find the lab, we all each get any one thing we want."

Ethan nodded slowly; it looked like he was trying to process it. But then he stared ahead. "I still can't believe they really tried the classic 'died in a car crash' move. You'd think if you're trying to cover something up, you'd come up with something more creative. Like…she was married to the head of a mercenary business, so she could have easily been targeted by rivals or people connected to someone Eric's pissed off, locked up, or killed."

Jackson was starting to lose focus again. He didn't want to think about his mother's death—not in this context. All he wanted was the truth.

"Sorry, I'm being insensitive," Ethan said. "I'll shut up."

"This way," Jackson mumbled once they reached the bottom of the stairs and emerged in a long, damp passage.

"What the hell is this place, man?" the tiger grumbled.

"Looks like a dungeon maybe…or storage," he suggested.

Something moved up ahead.

Jackson halted. "What the hell was that?" he breathed, startled.

Ethan, who froze beside him, shook his head. "I dunno. I don't…" he paused and sniffed the air, "…smell anything."

Dust fell from the ceiling when something heavy hit the floor above. Muffled snarling and growling echoed through the wood, and the smell of blood quickly followed.

"They're fighting above us," Ethan said as he stared up. "Do you think they found Kane yet?"

"I don't know," Jackson said and started slowly moving forward again. "Let's just find the inimă and get the heck out of here."

The tiger nodded and followed beside him. But then he stopped and said, "Wait…."

"What?"

"I smell…humans."

"Humans?"

Ethan nodded and headed to the left, the opposite way of the inimă.

Jackson didn't want to let his friend wander off by himself, so he caught up with him. "We need to find the amulet," he urged him.

But Ethan didn't reply. He kept on the trail of the scent he'd caught, and he didn't stop until they reached a wall of steel bars.

It smelled like something died—no, it smelled like *a lot* of things died down there. The windowless room was pitch black, but Jackson could make out the bloody, bruised, and frostbitten faces of at least twenty people on the other side of the bars, and some of them were missing limbs and huge chunks of their flesh.

Jackson felt sick. He grimaced as his eyes shifted from each man and woman; not one of them looked healthy or had every limb on their body. "What the fuck?" he breathed.

"Kane's farming humans," Ethan said with revolt in his voice. "This shit's illegal."

"What?"

Ethan glanced at him and then stared in at the humans. "Eating humans is illegal for all Caeleste but farming them is like…death-sentence-level illegal." The tiger then frowned and hurried to the other end of the cage as he said, "Janet?"

Janet? Jackson followed him, and when he located the woman whom Ethan was gawping at, he frowned in both disbelief and guilt. Most of her face was frostbitten, and she only had a few clumps of blonde hair left on her head. Her right arm was missing, and so was her left leg. And he couldn't detect any sign of life coming from her.

That was Janet Ulkman, one of the journalists he'd initially come to search for. And she was dead.

Jackson felt so heavy with guilt that he had to sit down. He was supposed to be looking for the rest of them, but he'd become so side-tracked by this new world and everything he'd managed to get caught up in that he hadn't really spared the missing journalists another thought.

One of the humans reached his icy, bloody arm towards the bars. "Help…us…" he groaned, his voice weak and croaky.

"What do we do?" Jackson asked Ethan. "We can't just leave them here."

Ethan went to speak, but then those who were still alive on the other side of the bars adorned horrified looks and backed up against the wall.

Jackson tensed up. That awful feeling of trepidation consumed him, and he felt a cold chill run down his spine.

They weren't alone down here.

Jackson and Ethan turned their backs to the cage and faced the empty cellar. Jackson couldn't find anything no matter how frantically he searched the gloom with his eyes, and it didn't seem like Ethan could see anything, either.

But he could feel eyes on him, and his instincts began telling him that it was time to run.

And then he saw something. A shadow peeked out from behind one of the brick pillars ten meters from where they were standing, but he didn't get a good enough look to see who or what it was. The clink of metal came from the same direction, but there was no way to tell what it was.

"We should get the hell out of here," Ethan said warily.

Jackson nodded in agreement, but before either of them could take another step, the shadow that he saw disappear behind the pillar shuffled around, and a low, rumbling growl echoed through the tense silence.

"Who's there?!" Ethan demanded.

The people behind them started whimpering, and Jackson could swear he heard one of them say, "Butcher."

Another growl came from a few meters ahead, but this time, Jackson could hear a voice.

"Who…are you?" Her voice was guttural and breathy, and she sounded injured.

Jackson didn't know what to say. "Uh…I…well—"

"Show yourself!" Ethan called impatiently. He sounded nervous, though.

The voice drawled, "You're...not Kane."

The fact that she didn't refer to him as Alpha Kane made Jackson sure that it wasn't a wolf behind that pillar—at least not a wolf who was part of Kane's pack.

"Come out!" the tiger insisted.

Jackson then frowned at him. "I-I don't think we should be—"

The figure behind the pillar shuffled again. A rumbling exhale accompanied the sound of wet footsteps against the icy, soggy ground, and metal scraped against it. As Jackson watched the wolf-shaped figure creep out of the shadows, his instincts forced him to make a decision between fight or flight.

However, the closer the figure moved, the more of her he was able to make out...and when he saw her face, his worry started to wither.

Her fur was icy blue with patches of white and grey, and her face was a lot softer-shaped than a wolf's. Her ears were shorter, too, and her tail was thick and bushy like that of a fox. Silver shackles were bound to her back ankles, and snaking chains connected them to the back wall. She stopped ten feet in front of them and shifted her dark brown eyes between Jackson and Ethan. She was unlike any wolf he'd seen before.

A look of hope then gleamed in her eyes. "Have you come for me?"

Jackson and Ethan glanced at each other with confused frowns.

"Did my mother send you?" she questioned eagerly.

"No one sent us," Jackson answered. Now, he was curious. "What are you doing down here?"

She adorned a disappointed expression and huffed sadly.

But Ethan seemed to be getting agitated. "We need to keep moving."

"What are you here for?" she asked them skeptically, but when a loud thump hit the floor above them and several snarls echoed through the floorboards, she backed off defensively and snarled at them.

Jackson didn't want to fight her. She didn't seem to want to attack; she would have lunged at them right from the start instead of approaching them if she was hostile, right? "W-we're...w-well, Kane kidnapped my pack, and we're breaking them out," he explained.

"Pack...battle?" she questioned, tilting her head to the side.

"Yeah," Jackson said with a nod.

"Jackson, come on," Ethan insisted.

The tiger went to head for the stairs, but the ice-blue wolf stepped in his way.

"You take me," she demanded.

Ethan snarled at her, but she didn't move and returned an irritated growl.

Jackson's curiosity was accompanied by confusion. "Take...you?"

She nodded, taking her eyes off the tiger. "Kane keep me down here to make meat. Kane is...ashamed."

Ethan scoffed. "He ought to be. Butchering humans is fucked up."

"Ashamed of Lumi," she said sadly, lowering her head.

"Lumi?" Jackson questioned.

She raised her paw and gestured to herself. "Lumi."

Jackson wanted to know why Kane was ashamed of her, but there wasn't time to stand around asking questions. He needed to find the inimă. But he didn't know if he could turn his back on someone asking for help, someone who had evidently been mistreated by Kane. But to set her free, he needed the amulet.

He didn't know how well she was going to take it, but he said to her, "We'll take you with us, but I can't break those chains without what we came here for."

Lumi looked confused.

"Something that Kane took from me," Jackson continued. "Just…wait here, okay? We've gotta come back this way to get out, anyway, so we'll come back for you."

She frowned in distress. "You won't come back," she said anxiously. "Mother left Lumi. Everyone leaves."

"Come on, man," Ethan insisted.

Jackson tutted irritably at his friend and then moved a little closer to the fox-wolf. "Lumi, I promise, okay? I can't break the silver without my amulet. That's the only reason we can't take you right now, but the amulet is nearby; we were on our way to get it when we saw the people in there," he said and glanced back at the humans in the cage. "Just give me ten minutes," he insisted, hoping that she'd believe him.

Lumi looked reluctant at first, but after a few seconds of shifting her sights between Jackson and Ethan, she backed down and nodded. "Don't forget about Lumi."

"We won't," he assured her, and then he looked at Ethan. "Let's go."

Jackson rushed towards the door they'd initially been heading to as Ethan followed. He regretted that he couldn't free Lumi now, but once he had the inimă, he could break her chains and get her the hell out of this place.

But he had to find it first, and he had no idea if he and Ethan were going to come face to face with danger on the way.

Chapter Fifty-Nine

The Missing, The Found

| **Daimon** |

There was blood and fur everywhere. What was once a large hall had become a battlefield, and everyone was tearing each other apart.

Daimon used his pent-up anger to his advantage. He used it alongside his brute strength to tear the wolf in his grip in half vertically, and when he dropped the mutilated corpse, he set his eyes on two of Kane's marked, scarred wolves heading for one of Raphael's team. The honey-brown wolf was struggling against his opponent, and Daimon was the only one close enough to get to her in time.

The Alpha burst into action. He raced through the fight, using his massive hand-like paws to smack away any hostile who tried to stop him, and the moment he reached his honey-brown ally, he grabbed the wolf that she was fighting by its neck and yanked it away from her. Daimon tore the creature's head off before it could try to fight back, and then he swung around and grabbed an incoming wolf's throat as it lunged at him. He broke its neck and ripped its head off, and then he looked down at his ally to ensure that she was okay before he left.

"Thank you," she breathed, staring up at him.

Daimon nodded, and then he turned around and joined the skirmish closest to him. But while he slashed and tore and bit, his worry for Jackson held him in a tight grasp. He focused on his imprint for a moment, and from what he could tell, his mate wasn't afraid or in danger, but that could change at any moment, and if it did, Daimon wouldn't be there to help him.

He couldn't let his worry distract him, though. Jackson would find the inimă; Daimon was confident that his mate knew what he was doing, even if Ethan didn't—and he didn't trust that muto *at all*. What *he* had to do was take down Kane's army and make sure that Jackson's path was clear and safe. So he kept fighting, and once the hall was clear, he followed Raphael and Sebastien's lead deeper into the building.

There was still no sign of Kane, though.

When the pack reached the end of the wide corridor, Raphael came to a halt. He looked down the left turn, and then the right.

"Which way?" one of the wolves asked.

Raphael appeared to be concentrating, but whatever sense he was tapping into, it wasn't one Daimon knew. The orange wolf didn't rotate his ears or sniff the air, he just stared... almost as if he was trying to peer through the walls.

"This way," Raphael said as he turned left and continued leading.

"What are we dealing with?" Sebastien questioned as he moved past Daimon and walked beside the orange wolf.

"Sixteen wolves on the ground and three guys with rifles on the balcony in the top right corner," he answered.

"How do you know?" Daimon asked. Not only did he want to make sure that Raphael's assessment was accurate, but he was also curious about *how* he made it. He'd seen this orange wolf do things *no* wolf walker should be capable of, and a part of him felt cautious. Could he really trust this guy and his packmates?

Sebastien glanced back at Daimon and said, "Heir Zephyr has very accurate ethos sensory abilities. It's similar to sonar; he can see ethos patterns through surfaces so long as there aren't any negating metals in the room."

Heir? "Are you related to Lucian?" Daimon asked Raphael.

"Unfortunately," he replied.

"Someone will get you caught up when we get back to Reiner Manor," Sebastien said dismissively. "Get ready."

Daimon shifted his attention back to the mission. It was time to fight again.

Sebastien blew the double doors at the end of the corridor open with his fire, and Raphael led the charge inside. Daimon went for the closest wolf, and while he tore it apart, he watched Raphael dive for cover, shifting into his human form as he did, and then he pulled his rifle from his back and started shooting at the riflemen above them before they could fire at his wolves.

With a determined snarl, Daimon stormed through the battle and executed every hostile he came across. He assisted Raphael's packmates, and he helped Sebastien when a wolf clamped its jaws around his wing carpal.

Once Raphael took out the riflemen, Kane's wolves started retreating. Sebastien led the chase after them, and Daimon hurried to be at the hound's side.

The fleeing wolves raced down the hallway and out through the patio into a snow-covered courtyard. But when the hostiles jumped up onto and leapt from bench to bench and flowerpot to flowerpot, Daimon frowned skeptically.

He was too late piecing it together, though.

Raphael's wolves raced across the snowy ground, and in a matter of seconds, six of them had their paws ensnared in silver bear traps. They shrieked and howled, and Daimon came to a halt—

"Keep going!" Raphael called from the back.

"Come on," Sebastien then instructed, and like Kane's wolves, he used the benches and flowerpots to get across the courtyard along with those of his allies who hadn't been trapped.

Daimon didn't need to be told twice; he was sure that Raphael knew what he was doing. So the Alpha used the benches to cross, following the rest of the pack as they chased after Kane's wolves.

He wanted to find Kane. He wanted to make him feel every ounce of pain he'd inflicted on Daimon's pack. He'd make him *suffer* tenfold for every second his wolves had suffered. He'd made Kane regret killing his packmates, and he'd make him regret every foul, twisted word that ever came out of his mouth.

Where the fuck was that coward? Hiding away while his army tried to fight off their attackers. Disgusting, filthy little bitch, a disgrace to all wolf walker kind. Daimon had a million reasons to want to tear him apart, and he'd use as many as he could until there was nothing but pulp left of Kane's corpse.

| Jackson |

Jackson and Ethan raced down the narrow passage and away from the cellar where Lumi waited for them to return. They followed the corridor left, and then right, and when they raced up a creaking staircase, they emerged in a gloomy, cobweb-filled storage room.

Everyone's things were there. His packmates' bags, Sebastien's mirror and radio, and the ring Jackson had given Daimon. There were crates filled with other people's belongings, old phones and even some laptops, rusted weapons, torn clothes—there was even a Balaur Blană fur-trimmed coat.

"The hell is all this stuff?" Ethan questioned, looking around.

"I think it's what belonged to all the people Kane's killed," Jackson said with a grimace.

The tiger rummaged through a chest with his paw, and when a pair of goggles hit the floor, Jackson remembered that he found Ethan's designer glasses in Farrydare.

"I found your glasses when I was looking for you," he said as he searched through the items for the amulet—the aura was the strongest it had been since getting inside the building, so it *had* to be around here somewhere.

Ethan glanced at him. "You did, huh?"

"Do you even need them? I mean…you *can* see, right?"

The tiger shrugged as he looked around, too. "It was more of a blend-in kinda situation. Lycans have amazing vision, so wearing glasses meant people were less likely to suspect me of being one. I didn't wanna get snatched by El'Vorian or something."

"Makes sense," Jackson mumbled as he used his paw to push the designer coat away so that he could see what was beneath it.

More clothes.

"Are you sure it's in here?" Ethan asked.

"I can feel it," Jackson said confidently. He turned around and hurried over to the pile of crates and chests on the other side of the small room. "It's…here…*somewhere*," he said frustratedly as he rummaged through more clothes and equipment. But no matter how many things he moved aside, he couldn't find the amulet. Could it be in a room above or beneath him? What about a room on the other side of the wall? He frowned and looked around desperately.

But then Ethan said, "Jack."

Jackson sharply turned his head and set his eyes on the tiger, who gestured into one of the chests with his head, and he hurried over to him.

And there it was. Sitting on top of an old fur was the inimă. The crimson crystal shimmered excitedly as Jackson stared at it, and it urged him to pick it up and claim it once again.

He didn't delay. Jackson used his paw to scoop the amulet up, and as he brought it closer to his face, he felt the warmth and darkness of its ethos greet him like an old friend. But it wasn't time to wear it yet. He didn't want to risk the power consuming him, so he'd only use it when and where he needed to.

Jackson looked around, and when he finally found his bags—looking inside to make sure that his things were still in there—he said, "Help me put this on."

With a nod, Ethan shifted out of his tiger form. His human hands allowed him to easily attach the bags to Jackson's wolf body, and once it was secure, he went to shift back.

"Wait," Jackson said. "Grab Sebastien's mirror and radio, and that ring," he instructed.

Ethan hastily put everything Jackson asked for into the bags, as well as the inimă, which Jackson handed to him. He then shifted into his tiger form and started leading the way back.

"We'll help Lumi, and then we'll find the others," Jackson said as he raced down the stairs behind Ethan.

"You really trust her?" Ethan questioned.

Jackson frowned and said, "You *don't*? She's locked up down there, Ethan. Kane's ashamed of her."

"It could be a trick."

"I doubt it, but if it is, we can defend ourselves," he assured him. But he didn't believe that Lumi had a single hostile intention. She was just someone else scorned by Kane's cruelty, someone who didn't deserve to suffer beneath his wrath. Jackson wouldn't leave her to rot in a dungeon. "Come on," he said as he rushed past Ethan to lead the way, and he picked up the pace. "The sooner we free her, the sooner we can help the others with the fight."

"You think they've killed Kane already?" Ethan asked.

"I don't know. I hope so, but I also have a feeling that he's still hiding like a coward," he muttered.

They approached the door to the cellar where Lumi was confined. When they stepped into the room, the fox-wolf—who had curled up by the cage—jumped to her paws and gawped at them.

"You come back?" she called, surprised.

"I told you we would," Jackson said, rushing over to her. He then reached into his bag with his muzzle, gripped the inimă with his teeth, and pulled it out. He closed his eyes and concentrated on the amulet's aura, and then he dropped it from his maw.

But the inimă didn't hit the ground. The black metal twisted and morphed as red mist surrounded it, and it quickly attached itself around Jackson's neck. He felt the rush of power gush through his body, filling him with a familiar bloodlust. He did his best to resist giving in, though. Killing wasn't what he needed it for right now.

Jackson snatched hold of the chain connected to Lumi's shackles with his teeth; he tugged and snarled, biting down a little harder into the metal. He felt it tear like wet wood, and after a few more pulls, the silver broke, and Lumi was free.

But before Jackson could drop the chain from his teeth, the fox-wolf pounced at him—

"Jack!" Ethan panicked.

"You save Lumi!" she cried happily, and Jackson realized that she wasn't attacking him…she was *hugging* him. She had her paws around him as best she could, and she nuzzled the side of his face.

He laughed nervously, a little flustered by being pinned on his back. "I-it's okay," he told her. "But we really gotta get moving. My pack need our help."

Lumi held on for a few more seconds, but then she let go and backed off. "Lumi help."

"We didn't just come back here to let you out for you to get yourself killed," Ethan denied. "You can run into the forest and—"

"We don't even know where Cyrus went," Jackson interjected.

Lumi's eyes widened. "Cyrus? Greyson Cyrus?"

Jackson frowned at her. "You know him?"

She nodded. "Cyrus and Kane enemies. Fought a lot years ago. Kane always talk about getting him back for leaving scars on his face, but he never find Cyrus. Too scared of Cyrus allies. Reiner-Blood…scary."

His frown thickened. "Reiner-Blood?"

"Come on," Ethan insisted.

As curious as Jackson felt, Ethan was right. They were wasting time. He used his paw to pull the inimă off, and once he slipped it back into his bag, he turned around and started leading the way. "Come on."

But Lumi didn't budge. "What about…them?" she asked, looking back at the people inside the cage.

Ethan grunted irritably. "They're just gonna slow us down. They're all dead or dying, anyway."

Jackson felt hesitant, though. He didn't want to leave people who needed help behind. But…Ethan was right about that, too. Every single person on the other side of those bars wouldn't make it, and if he was going to help the pack like he originally intended, he needed to get to them as fast as he could.

He looked at Lumi. "I can get one of our allies to send people down here to try and help them," he told her. "But *we* have to go *now*!"

She looked back over her shoulder at the cage again; she looked reluctant, but she caught up to Jackson and Ethan and followed them.

There wasn't a moment to waste.

Chapter Sixty

Cat and Mouse

| Daimon |

The chase led Daimon out through the back of the building and towards the battlefield. He didn't know if Kane was still inside or if he was attempting to flee his territory entirely, but Daimon didn't plan to stop until he found him.

He watched as Sebastien used his wings to propel himself into the sky, and then the hound dived back down and crashed into one of Kane's retreating wolves. Everyone else stopped around Sebastien, letting the rest of their enemies get away.

"Where the fuck is Kane?!" Sebastien growled into the wolf's ear.

"Get off me!" the wolf yelled back while he tried breaking free, but the hound was clearly a lot stronger than he was.

Sebastien harshly stabbed the spike of his left wing carpel into the wolf's side. "Tell me where Kane is!"

The wolf shrieked painfully and writhed around beneath him. "He's going for the Amarok!"

Dread filled Daimon's racing heart, shoving aside his anger and hatred. If that thing got out, it would kill hundreds—it might even kill everyone. And when he looked around at his new allies, it was written all over their faces that they knew the same thing.

Sebastien snarled frustratedly and stabbed both his carpel spikes into the wolf's neck, ending its life. Once he severed the head from the body, preventing the dead wolf from resurrecting as a hellhound, he turned to face Daimon and the others. "We can't let him free that thing. Cyrus is leading the targets away, and Heir Zephyr's back in the building healing your comrades. *We* are going to have to deal with it until Cyrus or Heir Zephyr can join us."

Although everyone looked nervous, they nodded. And when Sebastien hurriedly led the way back towards the battlefield, they followed.

Daimon thought as he ran. Wasn't that cadejo pit nearby? He remembered Julian talking about Kane leading undead into that place they found back when they were staying at the old Nosferatu Consulate ruin, so it couldn't be far from here. He looked around, taking in what he could see of the forest and mountains in the distance through the frost-filled air. If they could lead the Amarok to that pit, the cadejo would surely devour it down to its bones.

"Sebastien," he said, looking at the hound as he ran beside him in his Prime form. "I have an idea."

"Talk," the hound invited.

"There's a canyon filled with an entire fucking ocean of cadejo not far from here. If we lead the Amarok to it, then—"

"We dump it inside and let the corpses eat it. Good idea," Sebastien agreed. "Everyone, listen up," he called to the group.

While the hound shared the plan, Daimon took a moment to focus on Jackson through their imprints. To his relief, he could feel Jackson's determination—he had the inimă, and he wasn't far behind.

But then dread filled him again. Jackson didn't know the plan.

"Jackson's coming," Daimon told Sebastien.

"Good. We could use the inimă to help us guide that creature away from the battle."

Daimon looked over his shoulder, hoping to see his mate running towards him, but savage snarls closed in around his group, and he had no choice but to focus ahead. A gathering of Kane's wolves broke off from the battle and collided with him and his allies, but with him and Sebastien, they made quick work of their enemies.

And then he heard Jackson's voice call his name.

The Alpha looked behind as he dropped the mangled corpse of the wolf he'd just mauled, and he set his eyes on his mate, who came running over a pile of rubble, his tawny-brown fur spotless of blood. Ethan came running over next, but there was someone with them who Daimon didn't recognize. His protective instincts warned him that the ice-blue wolf might be a threat, but then Raphael rushed over the rubble behind them with his once-injured allies in tow, now fully healed and moving as if they hadn't just had their paws ensnared in silver bear traps.

Daimon ensured Kane's wolves were dead; Sebastien and the others were recovering, watching as their orange-furred ally raced towards them.

With a relieved sigh, Daimon wrapped his huge arms around his mate the moment he reached and pounced up to hug him. "Are you okay?" he murmured worriedly into Jackson's fur, nuzzling his neck.

"I'm fine," Jackson replied and pulled free. He dropped down onto all fours and gestured at the strange-looking ice-blue wolf beside him. "This is Lumi. We found her locked up in some dungeon."

Lumi gawped up at Daimon. "Greyson," she drawled, awed.

Daimon frowned. "No... Greyblood."

She adorned a confused expression and shifted her gaze to Jackson.

"This is Daimon," Jackson told her. "I don't know where Cyrus is."

"You got the inimă?" Sebastien asked, appearing beside Daimon.

Jackson nodded in response. "I grabbed your mirror and radio, too."

"Thanks." Sebastien then rushed to Raphael's side and told him the plan to lure the Amarok to the cadejo pit.

"You lead beast away?" Lumi questioned fearfully. "Too strong."

Before Jackson could reply, though, Raphael started barking orders. "Rianna, I want you to take your group and this civilian and head back to the woods to meet up with Alpha Cyrus. Daimon, Jackson, and Ethan, you three are coming with Sebastien and me to lure the Amarok to the pit."

But Daimon felt hesitant. He didn't want Jackson near that creature. He wanted to tell his mate to leave with Rianna; however, he knew that they needed the inimă to help them fight the monster in the arena. He scowled in confliction and watched as Rianna left with Lumi and the other wolves, but he was going to have to try and fight his protective instincts.

"Keep up and listen," Raphael said as he started hurriedly leading the way towards the arena. "Amaroks listen to no one. They're controlled by their bloodlust, and all they want to do is kill. To get its attention if we don't already have it, we have to piss it off. It'll target the strongest of us or the one it deems the biggest threat. Whoever the Amarok locks onto, it's your job to lead that thing towards the pit. The rest of us will stay close by, and if the Amarok shifts its attention elsewhere, we all work together to ensure it focuses on one of us again." He looked back at Daimon. "How far is the pit?"

The Alpha glanced at the trees again. "From here, roughly five klicks east."

Raphael nodded. "Every kilometre, we switch out so that we each get a break from running for our lives. Once we reach the pit, we work together to overpower it and push it in. Understand?"

They all nodded.

Ethan, however, glanced at everyone as he said, "I dunno about you guys, but that thing was faster than anything I've seen. How the hell are we supposed to lead it away if we can't run faster than it?"

"We can injure its legs," Sebastien suggested.

"Jackson, can you use the inimă to break one of the Amarok's legs if we keep it distracted?" Raphael asked.

Before Jackson could speak, though, Daimon snarled defensively, following Raphael down the passage which led into the arena. "I'm not going to let you make him risk his life like that. *I'll* do it."

"No offence, big guy, but we need a lot more force than what you're capable of creating," the orange wolf replied.

"It's fine," Jackson assured Daimon. "I can do it."

"No," the Alpha refused. "I—"

"Look, we've all been tasked with keeping Jackson alive," Raphael interjected with an irritated tone. "I wouldn't make him do something that would put his life at risk. So long as we do our job—which, trust me, Sebastien and I can do without you two—Jackson will be fine."

Daimon scowled at the orange wolf as he followed him down the side of the arena. But he didn't have time to hate him or wonder why he was such an asshole. Kane was up in the observing area of the arena, and he was tugging on a large lever above the place in the wall that opened to release the Amarok.

And the wall was lifting.

"He's opening the cage!" Jackson exclaimed worriedly.

"If the thing isn't out yet, maybe we can keep it contained," Raphael said to Sebastien.

Sebastien burst into action. The hound propelled himself up with his wings and raced towards Kane, and Raphael picked up the pace, hurrying down the path with Daimon, Jackson, and Ethan.

Daimon watched the hound crash into Kane and pull him away from the lever, but he'd managed to open the wall a few feet, and the creature inside was roaring and howling, and the loud crashes that came from inside suggested that the beast was trying to force it open the rest of the way.

But Kane was somehow stronger than a demon hound. Sebastien yelped painfully, and the black wolf threw him into the arena. His body hit the floor, and before Raphael could reach him—sprinting ahead of the others—Kane gripped the lever and pulled.

A deafening roar filled the air. Daimon came to a halt and grabbed Jackson. Ethan stopped, too, and Raphael quickly grabbed Sebastien's wing with his teeth and dragged him back towards them.

Daimon watched as the *huge*, monstrous Amarok emerged from its gloomy cage. It prowled on all fours out into the arena, and when it stood up on its hind legs to stretch its gargantuan body, it yawned savagely.

And then Daimon shifted his sights to Kane. The black wolf observed from above with a smug grin on his face, and when the Amarok dropped to all fours, Kane turned tail and ran. *Fucking coward.*

"Uh…okay," Ethan drawled nervously. "We're really doing this?"

"Stay behind me," Daimon told Jackson.

"You good?" Raphael asked Sebastien as he helped him to his feet.

The hound grunted and nodded.

"You know the plan," the orange wolf said, glancing at Daimon, Jackson, and Ethan. They nodded.

Daimon watched the Amarok eye them all up, scanning each of them to determine who might be the biggest threat. Daimon didn't want to let Jackson move from his side; he wanted to stick close and protect him, but if they didn't deal with that monster, it could very well assist in the total extinction of wolf walkers. And he trusted Jackson; he'd seen what his mate could do, and he had to shove his protective instincts aside and do what was necessary of him.

The Amarok widened its huge jaws and let out a devastating roar. And then it charged, rushing towards them all.

"Jackson, go," Raphael grunted.

With a nod, Jackson left Daimon's side and raced off to the left.

To Daimon's relief, the monster didn't lock its eyes on his mate; it kept coming for the rest of them.

It was time to get to work.

The monster lunged at the four of them; Raphael and Sebastien dodged to the right, and Daimon and Ethan veered left. With a savage snarl, the Amarok went for Daimon—probably because he stood taller than the others—and it tried to grab him with its monstrous hands. But the Alpha avoided its grasp and backed off. He caught sight of Jackson far behind the creature; he was putting the inimă on.

"Avoid its hands," Sebastien called when Ethan barely managed to dodge the Amarok's swipe.

But the Amarok seemed fixated on the tiger all of a sudden. It lunged for him again, and Ethan stumbled back—

A burst of Sebastien's blue flames hit the monster, which immediately snatched its attention. It sharply turned its body and went for the hound, but Sebastien propelled himself back with his wings.

And then it went for Daimon again.

With an irritated snarl, the Alpha dodged the Amarok's swipe and then slammed his furred fist into the beast's face, making it take a few steps back as it shook its head and growled frustratedly.

A flicker of crimson caught Daimon's attention, and as he stepped back to avoid the Amarok's jaws, he spotted Jackson. His tawny-brown-furred mate was surrounded by wisps of red smoke, and his eyes were glowing as red as the jewel inside the inimă—and he burst towards the creature faster than anything Daimon had seen.

Jackson crashed into the Amarok's leg, using his entire body as a battering ram. The force sent the beast flying forward, and when it hit the ground with a loud thump, it tumbled for a few seconds before coming to a halt. The creature looked startled, but it slowly climbed to its hands and knees—

It yelped painfully and looked down at its left hind leg. The bone was sticking out through its skin, blood pouring onto the snow.

"Fuck," Ethan drawled.

"Nice," Sebastien said as the group backed off.

Jackson huffed and snarled, and the wisps of crimson smoke surrounding his body started to wither. But he didn't take the inimă off, and Daimon worried that he might lose control again.

The Amarok climbed to its feet despite its injury, and it focused its eyes on Jackson.

"Back off slowly," Raphael ordered. "Keep away from Jackson."

Daimon didn't want to abide by that second command, but he had to resist his urge to protect his mate. He backed off to the creature's right with Ethan, watching as the beast shook its body and snarled almost challengingly.

"Jackson…you're leading it first," the orange wolf said.

Jackson didn't argue.

Daimon *wanted* to insist that he did it instead, but there wasn't time. The monster was already charging at Jackson, and his mate turned around and darted for the pathway that led up the arena.

"Come on!" Raphael called as he chased after the Amarok.

With a determined huff, Daimon dropped to all fours and ran with them. He wanted to be closer; he wanted to be near so that he could jump in the way if that thing caught up to Jackson, but the last thing he wanted to do was cause the plan to fail—he didn't want to be the reason that thing went on a rampage and wiped out hundreds of wolves. He had to be patient. He had to trust Jackson—and he did…he just couldn't stop worrying about him.

He hurried up the path, keeping his eyes on Jackson, who raced a hundred feet ahead. "When do we switch out?" he called to Raphael. He remembered what the orange wolf said, but he wanted to be sure.

"Every kilometre," he replied.

"I'll switch out first," Daimon insisted.

"Fine by me," Ethan muttered.

"All right," Raphael agreed.

That made Daimon feel a little less terrified; however, they had a kilometre to go before he could take his mate's place, and in that much time, *anything* could happen.

Chapter Sixty-One

⌐ ≼ ☽ ≽ ⌐

To The Pit

| **Jackson** |

It was chasing him. Jackson could hear its thumping, pounding paws and its heavy, snarling breaths. It wanted his blood, and if he didn't keep running as fast as his legs could carry him, it would grab him and toss him around like a ragdoll. He'd seen what that thing could do; he wouldn't stand a chance, inimă or not.

He raced through the forest, getting further and further away from the battle. He didn't really know where he was going; he just headed in the direction he'd seen Daimon point out. The cadejo pit was around here somewhere…right?

The Amarok's deafening roars cut through the tense silence, shaking the snow from the trees, and unsettling the frost lingering in the air. The ground beneath Jackson's paws was vibrating, whimpering every time the beast's massive paws slammed down on it. Even the forest felt afraid.

But he kept going. He *had* to keep going.

He ran deeper and deeper into the woods, and when he looked over his shoulder, he set his eyes on the Amarok. It had its glowing red eyes fixed on him, and despite the bone sticking out of its leg, it was doing well keeping up with him.

And then his sights shifted to Daimon, Ethan, Sebastien, and Raphael, who followed not too far behind the beast. Knowing that they were back there gave him a little more confidence, but he had a horrible feeling that something was going to happen.

Jackson glared ahead, frantically searching the darkness for signs of cadejo or any other threat. He leapt over fallen trees, dodged an old, frozen and rusted car, and kept heading forward.

But then a blur of rushing white to his left snatched his attention, and he glanced over there to find Daimon running in his Prime form thirty feet away. Was it time to switch places already?

He stared ahead again, focusing on the forest. The last thing he wanted was to lose his footing or crash into something. He glanced to his left every few moments, noticing that Daimon was getting closer, and soon enough, the Alpha was running right beside him.

"Are you okay?" Daimon asked him.

Jackson nodded, panting. "Y-yeah."

"Raphael said you've got to break off slowly; head to the left and join them," he instructed.

Would that work? Wouldn't the Amarok just follow him? "What if it follows me?" he asked worriedly.

"The inimă," Daimon said hesitantly. "You need to give it to me."

Jackson frowned strangely. "What?"

"He said that thing is after the inimă's aura, so when you hand it to me, the Amarok will stay on me. But he insisted that you have to want to give it to me," he explained.

His frown thickened, but he trusted Daimon, and he was sure that Raphael knew what he was talking about. So, as he ran, he reached into the bag he'd put the amulet in, and then he handed it to his mate.

But he felt something strange. A feeling of loss; a feeling that he'd had something or someone torn away from him. And he felt the inimă's pull. It pleaded that he took it back, almost *shrieking* at him the longer he left it in Daimon's grip. He *couldn't* take it, though. Daimon needed it to lure the Amarok, so he disregarded the amulet's cry and looked up at the Alpha, ready to break off.

"Slowly," Daimon repeated with worry in his voice. "Don't dart away."

Jackson didn't want to move away from Daimon—what if the Amarok didn't care about the inimă? What if it wanted *him*? He frowned and looked back at it, but he noticed that the creature had actually shifted its gleaming red eyes to Daimon. Maybe it really *was* locked onto the amulet's aura.

He took a deep breath and fought against his fear. Glancing back at the beast, he slowly moved a few feet to Daimon's left, and the Amarok's gaze didn't flicker. It wasn't interested in him anymore, and although that made him feel relieved, he was also horrified that something might happen to his mate. He still had a terrible feeling that *something* was going to happen, but it didn't feel as intense as all the other instinctual warnings he had. He didn't want to ignore it, though.

When he reached the others, he ran beside Ethan.

"You okay, Jack?" the tiger asked him.

He nodded and looked at Sebastien. "I'm getting a weird feeling."

The hound frowned. "What kind of weird?"

"Feeling?" Raphael questioned.

Sebastien glanced at him and said, "Asmodi demon, Lord Caedis."

A look of dread struck the orange wolf's face, the *first* anxious look Jackson had seen on him. "What is it?"

Jackson tensed up. "W-well...it feels like...I don't know, like something bad is gonna happen."

"When? Where?" Raphael questioned.

"I-I don't know," Jackson answered. "I just...feel it."

"He hasn't entirely mastered the ability yet," Sebastien told Raphael.

Jackson frowned in both confusion and curiosity. "Wait, if you're related to Lord Caedis, wouldn't you have the same ability?"

"No. We don't have enough demon blood for something that powerful," the orange wolf answered. "Heads up!" he then warned.

When Jackson looked ahead and shifted his sights to Daimon, he saw a vast frozen lake on the other side of the tree line. He didn't remember crossing this place when they'd stumbled on the cadejo pit, but then again, they *were* coming at it from Kane's side of the area this time.

Daimon led the Amarok out onto the ice.

Jackson tensed up again. What if something was going to happen on the ice? Was the Amarok too heavy? Would it crack the surface and send itself and Daimon tumbling in? Or would another creature come out of the dark and send the man he loved plunging into the depths?

No, it wasn't the ice; he became sure of that when his paws touched it. So what was it? Why was he convinced that disaster was creeping up on them?

Daimon continued across the frozen water, and when they got back into the woods, it was time for him to switch with Raphael. Jackson watched the orange wolf veer to Daimon's side, and once the Alpha handed him the inimă, he left Raphael and raced to Jackson's side.

"Guess I'll go next," Ethan suggested.

"No," Daimon said. "You'll take the last run; the tunnel we found to get down closer to the pit was narrow, so your agility will help you avoid the Amarok's attacks."

Ethan looked horrified, and Jackson felt anxious.

"Tunnel?" the tiger questioned. "Why not just take it to the edge and shove it?"

"We don't know how safe the edges of that canyon are. One wrong move and the entire ground beneath our feet could crumble," Daimon replied irritably.

"Hate to say it, but he's right," Sebastien said. "There's a way for us to push it into the pit though, right?" he asked, looking at the Alpha.

Daimon nodded.

"There's a sort of ledge," Jackson said.

"Great," Ethan grunted.

"You'll be fine," Jackson said, trying to assure him. He didn't like seeing his friend so nervous, and he wanted to help, but like Daimon said, the tunnel was too narrow for the two of them. However, he trusted that Ethan knew what he was doing; he'd seen the tiger in action, and he *knew* that he could do this.

They kept racing through the woods, and eventually, Sebastien switched out with Raphael. The cold, pine-fragrant air soon shifted, thick with the pungent smell of death and rotting flesh. The silence was stolen by anguished snarls and crying, distorted howls, and a horrible, terrible feeling of pain and suffering stole the atmosphere.

The pit was close.

"Get ready," Raphael told Ethan.

Ethan huffed and nodded; he was clearly trying to put on a brave face, but he was terrified.

Jackson ran closer to him. "Just keep running and don't look back."

"When you get down to the ledge, veer out of the way," Raphael said. "That thing is too big to match your agility, and it'll charge right over the edge."

The tiger huffed again. "All right… veer out of the way."

"You've got this," Jackson said.

"Yeah…" he drawled.

Jackson then shifted his sights to the Amarok. Despite its wound and the five-kilometre run, the creature didn't look anything close to tired. It snarled and roared, chasing after Sebastien, who held the inimă between his teeth. Through the tree line, he could see flat ground… and the drop that led into the pit of an undead tsunami.

"Where's the entrance?" Raphael questioned.

"Half a mile that way," Daimon said, waving his paw to the right."

The orange wolf nodded. "All right, time to switch out."

Ethan took a deep breath. "Are you guys following?"

"Sebastien will watch you from the air and swoop down if you need help. The rest of us will wait here," Raphael answered.

"You're all just leaving me?" the tiger exclaimed.

"Can't we go with him?" Jackson asked worriedly. "What if something happens?"

"Sebastien will be there," Raphael said firmly. "The last thing we need is to be down in that tunnel if that Amarok decides to turn around when it sees all those cadejo."

Ethan snarled frustratedly. "He's got a point," he admitted. He grunted irritably and sighed. "All right… all right, let's do this shit."

"Be careful," Jackson pleaded.

The tiger scoffed at him. "Don't worry, man. I got this, right?"

He nodded despite the anxious look on his face. "Yeah."

Ethan shot him a smirk, and then he started moving towards Sebastien.

Jackson watched his every step. When he and the others reached the tree line, they stopped running, but Sebastien and Ethan kept going. The hound passed the inimă to the tiger, they switched places, and Sebastien took off into the sky, leaving Ethan running from the Amarok.

The tiger ran close to the tree line, and when he headed back into the woods towards the cave entrance which led into the pit, the Amarok followed. Ethan got further and further away, and in a matter of minutes, he was out of sight.

"He'll be fine," Daimon said as he left his Prime form and stood in his normal wolf form beside Jackson. "Don't worry."

Jackson turned his head and looked at him. "What if something happens?"

Daimon nuzzled his neck. "Sebastien's covering him, remember?"

He sighed quietly and pressed his muzzle into Daimon's fur. It brought him a little comfort, but his anxiety didn't ease up.

"Come on," Raphael said. "We'll find somewhere to watch the edge from."

Jackson and Daimon followed him around the canyon edges. The sea of corpses seemed larger this time, *louder*. There were more prowlers attempting to climb up the sides to get out, and Jackson spotted a *huddle* of brutes. And…something else. He tensed up, and dread gushed through him as he came to a halt. There…standing on top of a boulder as if it were king, was a creature with no face. Its human-like body had lanky arms and grey, slimy-looking skin, and the only orifice on its face was a gnarly, rounded mouth which stretched from its chin to where its nose would meet between its eyes.

He didn't know what to call it. An infected fae? An evolved infected? *Were* all of those things fae?

"Jackson," Daimon called.

He took his eyes off the creature and looked at Daimon and Raphael.

"What is it?" Raphael questioned.

Jackson shifted his sights to the grey-skinned creature again. "I-its…one of them."

Daimon moved closer, and when he spotted it, he snarled quietly.

Raphael looked confused. "A siren."

Both Jackson and Daimon frowned at him.

"What?" Jackson asked.

"That thing…with no face. It's a siren," the orange wolf revealed. "Sebastien reported a sighting not long ago to HQ, and they've been called sirens. They emit low frequency sounds capable of paralyzing most Caeleste."

Jackson felt horrified. "So…they *are* infected fae?"

"They are," the orange wolf confirmed. "And they're probably one of the most if not *the* most dangerous variant we've discovered."

"W-we should call this off; we need to bring Ethan back!" Jackson insisted. "That thing could paralyze him, and the Amarok will—"

"We need to get rid of the Amarok," Daimon interjected. "We've got about ten minutes before Ethan gets down there, so we need to find a way to get that siren away from that ledge," he said as he pointed his paw towards the ledge that Ethan would soon emerge on.

Raphael nodded in agreement. "Come on," he said as he continued hastily leading the way around the edge. "We'll get it to the other side."

Jackson anxiously followed. Was ten minutes really enough time to get that thing a safe distance from where Ethan would be? He didn't know, but he'd do whatever he had to to ensure that his friend would be safe. But that siren...that *thing*...it horrified him. It *terrified* him. Knowing that the virus was evolving and spreading to other Caeleste was scary enough, but seeing an infected *fae* and what it could do made him feel more afraid than he might have ever been in his life—especially since his best friend was going to be getting close to it. That siren they faced on their way through the woods managed to freeze Jackson's entire pack without any effort at all, leaving him to save them. He didn't want to be put in that position again... but if he was, he wouldn't let fear rule him. There wasn't time for that. Ethan needed him, and nothing—not even a siren—would stop him.

Chapter Sixty-Two
Siren

| Jackson |

What was the plan? Jackson stared at Raphael, watching him while he stood a few feet from him and Daimon with a pondering look on his face. His eyes shifted every couple of seconds...like he was reading some sort of invisible book—maybe he was going over several plans or ideas or what he knew in his head.

Jackson then turned his attention to the siren. The faceless creature was still standing on the rock, its lanky body twitching and convulsing. It didn't look like the strange creature had spotted him, Daimon, and Raphael, but he didn't want to make any sudden movements and alert it of their presence.

"They react to sound," Raphael said quietly. "There's a good chance it can't hear us over the undead, so it's going to take something loud to draw its attention."

"Such as?" Daimon questioned, glancing around.

"If the three of us howl, the siren should be able to tell the difference between our call and the noises those cadejo are making."

Jackson felt a little embarrassed. "I uh...I don't know...how to howl." There were *a lot* of things that he didn't know how to do. He didn't know how to use his connection to Daimon to talk to him from a distance—he didn't know how to connect to him *at all*. He didn't know as much as he'd like to about scents or sounds or ethos, he didn't know how to track as well as he'd seen the others do, and he didn't know the full extent of what being a wolf walker meant.

Raphael frowned strangely at him.

"He hasn't had time to learn everything," Daimon said. "We've been too busy for lessons; he only knows what he needed to know at the time."

"Well, we don't have time for wolf walker school now," the orange wolf muttered irritably. "Once we have the siren's attention, it'll attempt to get within range so that it can paralyze us. Jackson, since you're the only one immune to its ability, you're going to have to lead it as far away from that ledge as possible. I'm hoping that it's going to be confused as to why you haven't frozen. Either that...or it's going to attempt to get up here to kill us."

Jackson knew how dangerous those things were; he hoped he'd never have to see one ever again...but there it was...and he was going to have to swallow his fear if they were going to help Ethan.

But Daimon confidently said, "He saved my entire pack from a group of those things. We'll be fine."

However, something suddenly hit Jackson, and it made him frown in confusion. "Wait...*you* aren't immune?" he asked Raphael.

The orange wolf looked at him. "Why would I be?"

"Well...I just...thought that *I* was immune because I'm a hybrid. Aren't you also some kinda...hybrid? You've got wolf walker and demon blood, right?"

"We don't use that term; we're not half-wolf walker, half-demon; we're wolf walkers with demon blood. And as for being immune, we haven't exactly exposed ourselves to cadejo to find out, and I don't plan to, either."

Jackson had a million questions, but now wasn't the time to ask them. Ethan would be getting down to that ledge soon, and he had to make sure that Siren was nowhere it could hurt him. "Okay, so...you guys howl, and then I protect you or lure the thing away if it isn't far enough already?"

Raphael nodded.

With a deep exhale, Jackson did his best to grasp a calm composure. "Okay...okay." He could do this. It wasn't like he had to go down there and face it, was it? All he had to do was ensure that he kept its attention. That wouldn't be so hard, would it?

"Are you ready?" Daimon asked him.

"Yeah, I'm good," he said with a nod.

"All right," Raphael mumbled. "Daimon?"

The Alpha nodded.

Jackson stepped back and watched them move closer to the edge of the cliff. And when they lifted their heads towards the moon and howled, a shiver ran down his spine. He'd only heard Daimon's howl a few times, and whenever he did, he always felt a strange sort of anticipation, like he was ready to face whatever might follow. And he *was* ready.

He set his sights on the siren. The faceless creature turned its head in Daimon and Raphael's direction, and a lot of the cadejo looked up, too. The entire ocean of undead turned around and started flowing towards the bottom of the cliff that they stood on, and the siren started moving, too. It climbed down off the rock, but it struggled to slip through the tight crowd...so it started climbing and walking on top of the cadejo as if they were the ground itself. And the snarling corpses didn't react, either; they let the siren walk on their backs, and it made its way towards the cliff.

"It's coming," Jackson told them cautiously.

Raphael stopped howling to glance at the siren. "Get ready," he told Daimon, and then he continued his howl.

Jackson kept his eyes on the siren, watching as it prowled closer and closer. He could hear it chittering as it tilted its head and moved its strange body, and the nearer it got, the faster Jackson's heart raced.

"It's halfway here," he told them, glancing at Raphael and Daimon.

And then it started moving faster.

"And...now it's speeding up," he said anxiously.

The creature sprinted over the corpses, snarling and panting—but then it stopped. It halted as if the cold had frozen its bones...and Daimon and Raphael went silent.

Jackson shivered worriedly when he looked at them both and saw the swirling black patterns in their iris', the same ones he'd seen when they first came into contact with a siren. They were stuck in its trance, and now it was down to him to deal with it.

He stood on the edge of the cliff, trying to calculate whether or not it was far away enough from the ledge that Ethan would soon be on. It was only roughly thirty meters away from Raphael and Daimon, including the vertical drop...and the ledge was at least *double* that distance away. So...Ethan would be fine, right?

But their howls didn't only attract the corpses in the pit.

The brush rustled behind Jackson.

He frantically turned to face the noise, tensing up, his heart racing. He could see something moving around in the gloom, and what it was, it was *big*.

Jackson stepped back and stood defensively by Daimon and Raphael. Maybe if whatever was stalking him saw that there were three of them, it wouldn't attack. But if it was a cadejo—and he had a horrible feeling that it might be—then it wouldn't care how many of them there were, would it? It would just want blood.

He held his ground anyway, staring into the woods. The snow crunched quietly, and a low growl echoed from the dark. He could feel eyes on him, and he knew that it was watching him...but what was strange was that his feeling of danger wasn't focused on whatever was beyond the trees. He felt afraid, sure...but his instincts weren't trying to convince him that something terrible was about to happen once the watcher pounced out of the trees.

In fact, whatever was stalking him didn't make him feel threatened. So he shakily asked, "H-hello? Is someone there?"

There was no answer.

Jackson frowned unsurely and glanced over his shoulder. The siren was still frozen where he'd last seen it, and there was no sign of Ethan or—

"Salvator..." came a low, raspy voice.

He sharply turned his head and stared back into the trees. He didn't know what the word meant, but it did something to him—it snatched his attention as if it were the most important word in the world to him, but he didn't know why. "Hello?" he asked again.

"You're...the one," the voice echoed.

Déjà vu struck him. That voice sounded familiar, and what it was saying did, too. The prowler that spoke to him when he was escaping Kane's patrol, the one which told him that he was a higher lifeform—a *perfect* hybrid. The prowler which told him that it was tasked to take him to its Master. Had it come back for him? Was it...was it going to take him to its Master?

No...no, it didn't feel like that. He felt...he didn't know how to describe it. Whoever was hiding in the shadows wasn't there to take him away—he seemed to know that. But what *did* it want? What did it mean? What was it talking about?

He swallowed the saliva which pooled in his mouth. "I'm...what? Who are you?"

The twigs snapped—whoever it was, they were getting closer. "Salvator," they called again.

But then Raphael grunted, and Daimon followed with a snarl.

Jackson turned to face them, and that was when he noticed the siren racing back across the ocean of cadejo. His heart started pounding as dread consumed him, but utter horror snatched him tight when he saw Ethan running along the narrow path in the side of the canyon, heading towards the ledge as the Amarok chased after him.

"Ethan!" he panicked, shoving past Daimon and Raphael, who were recovering.

"What the hell's going on?!" Raphael snapped.

"I-I saw something, and then...I-I—we have to get its attention back!" he insisted, glancing back at them. "It's going straight for him!"

"Fucking hell," Raphael growled, and then he howled again.

Daimon howled, too, but no matter how much noise either of them made, the siren didn't turn around.

And Ethan didn't notice it. The tiger kept running, getting closer and closer to the ledge, and the faceless creature was almost in range of him.

Jackson had to do something. He had to warn Ethan; he had to stop that creature from reaching him! So he immediately burst into action, darting to the right. He ignored Daimon and Raphael as they called his name; he hurriedly made his way around the edge of the canyon, racing as fast as his legs would carry him.

"Ethan!" he shouted as loudly as he could.

But the tiger didn't hear him. He kept leading the Amarok.

And the Siren was closing in.

"Ethan!" he yelled again, panting as his heart raced so fast that it felt like it might explode. If he knew how to use his wings, he'd take on his demon form and fly down there, but he had no idea. He wanted to use his fire, but he didn't know if he had the range or if he'd even land the shot. If only he had the inimă!

He kept running and running and running—he *had* to get close enough—

"Stop!" he yelled. "Get away from him!"

Some of the cadejo near the edge closest to Jackson stopped what they were doing, but the siren didn't hear his command.

"Stop!" he shouted again, running, trying to get close enough that the faceless creature would hear and do as he told it to. "Stop—"

Raphael came out of nowhere and pounced on him. The orange wolf pinned him down before he could attempt to wriggle away, and he snarled into his ear, "I fucking said stop!"

"Get off me!" Jackson growled, trying to overpower him, but Raphael was *so* much stronger. "He needs our help! He can't see it!"

"Get off him!" Daimon then growled and grabbed Raphael's sides, but the orange wolf bucked like a rabbit and kicked the Alpha back thirty feet.

And then he growled to Jackson, "I can't risk losing you; you're the only chance any of us have!"

Jackson struggled and snarled, trying to break free, but he knew it was useless.

And even if he did get free… he'd run out of time.

Ethan was frozen. The siren had him.

"You have to do something!" he pleaded to Raphael. "You… I… Ethan!"

The Amarok crashed into the motionless tiger, and although the siren froze the monster's body, too, the force of the collision sent them both tumbling across the rock…

and over the cliff.

Chapter Sixty-Three

⌝ ≼ ☽ ≽ ⌜

Blood and Stripes

| **Jackson** |

Jackson's heart shattered into a million pieces. He stared at the ledge, and he watched as the tsunami of cadejo swarmed the place where Ethan fell. He tried telling himself that it wasn't real; he tried to fight off the shock and dismay, but he saw it with his own eyes. His friend was gone.

"Ethan..." he breathed as his throat swelled and tears formed in his eyes.

He heard Daimon yell, and Raphael was torn off his back. Their arguing voices and savage snarls echoed around Jackson, but all he could hear was his racing heart and the sounds coming from the cadejo pit. The ripping. The tearing. The groaning. He scowled in despair, letting his tears fall, and the longer he lay there staring at the place he last saw his friend, the more it hurt.

Why? How? Ethan couldn't be gone. He'd spent so long trying to find him—he'd nearly died several times—and he only had him back for a few days... and now he was gone again, and this time... Jackson wouldn't be able to recover him.

But *anger* quickly began creeping through the cracks in his suffocating despair. It evolved into rage, and when he took his eyes off the pit and set them on Raphael, who was getting ready to pounce at Daimon, every ounce of fury that Jackson felt focused on him.

It was *his* fault! If he'd just let him run to Ethan's aid, this wouldn't have happened!

Jackson didn't hold back. He lunged at the orange wolf and sunk his teeth into his back leg.

Raphael yelped painfully and then snarled when he tried to yank his leg free, but Jackson wouldn't let go.

"Get the fuck off me!" the orange wolf growled.

"This is all your fault!" Jackson replied angrily as tears streamed down his face, and his voice muffled because he still had Raphael's leg in his maw. "He's dead because of you!"

He bit harder…and harder…and hard—

A loud snap was followed by Raphael's pained shriek; Jackson felt the bone snap under his teeth, and as the orange wolf's blood seeped into his mouth, his anger and rage were accompanied by bloodlust. This blood tasted unlike anything he'd had before; it blessed him with euphoria, and it urged him to take more. So he bit harder—

"Jackson!" came Daimon's voice.

But not even that could make him stop.

"Get him the hell off me!" Raphael demanded, yanking his leg.

Daimon grabbed Jackson's sides with his huge, furred hands and tried to pull him away from Raphael, but Jackson snarled in hostility as he gulped down the delicious, intoxicating blood.

"Jackson!" the Alpha insisted again.

"I swear to fuck, if you don't get this brat off me in the next five seconds, I'll break every goddamn bone in his body!" Raphael yelled.

The Alpha tugged harder.

He was starting to piss Jackson off. The rage consumed him, and he didn't even try to control it. What was the point?

But then Sebastien landed twenty feet away and raced over. "Oh, my fucking God," he growled, and when he reached Jackson, he helped Daimon, and together, they managed to pull him off Raphael.

The orange wolf snarled angrily and swung around, and he immediately went for Jackson, but Daimon stood defensively in front of him, and Sebastien pinned Jackson down with his wings.

"Do you have any fucking idea what you've just done?!" the hound exclaimed to Jackson.

"Get off!" Jackson roared. "He killed Ethan! It's all his fault!"

"It wasn't my fucking fault! I saved you from being a fucking brainless moron and dooming the entire wolf walker race to death!" the orange wolf yelled back.

"You just attacked a fucking Reiner-Blood!" Sebastien shouted with both anger and panic in his voice. "Do you even know what kind of a shit storm you've brought on yourself?"

Daimon looked back at them. "What are you talking about?"

Jackson didn't care. "Get off!" he yelled. He wasn't finished with Raphael yet.

Sebastien shifted his sights to Raphael. "You're not gonna report this…are you?"

Raphael scoffed and backed off.

"He's just a kid!" Sebastien insisted.

"Let me fucking go!" Jackson screamed.

Sebastien then snarled and thwacked his head with his paw. "Calm the hell down; I'm trying to save your ass!"

"What the hell are you talking about?!" Daimon demanded.

"Your little mate just attacked demon royalty," Sebastien snarled. "The last guy who did even less than you did was fucking executed."

"What?!" Daimon exclaimed.

"Oh, calm the fuck down," Raphael sneered. "He isn't getting executed; he's the fucking miracle wolf or some shit, right? They'll probably just send Lucian to smack him about."

Daimon snarled protectively. "If that white-haired shit comes anywhere near—"

"What? You'll hurt him?" Raphael scoffed. "Yeah, okay."

The Alpha growled angrily.

Jackson squirmed around and tried to escape while they argued—but then he saw something. He stared into the pit, watching as what looked like a lump of fur and flesh moved through the ocean of corpses, which were busy devouring the Amarok. He had no idea what it was, but it was huge. Maybe it was a brute. Maybe it was some other kind of variant. Whatever. It was stuck down there.

He scowled and kept trying to break free, but then the mound of fur *jumped*. He watched it latch onto the cliff face, and the creature's fur and flesh melted away, revealing white, orange, and black...stripes.

"Ethan?" he breathed.

The tiger was climbing up the cliff, using his huge claws like ice axes.

Relief hit Jackson so hard that he choked. "Look!" he insisted, but they were too busy arguing. He scowled and attempted to pull free. "Get off!"

Sebastien paid no attention to him.

Jackson grunted angrily, and at the top of his voice, he yelled, "Will you shut the fuck up?!"

The three of them stopped and looked down at him.

"It's Ethan!" he told them, pointing his paw in the tiger's direction.

Sebastien scoffed. "Of course he's still alive." He then took off and raced towards the climbing muto.

Free at last, Jackson eagerly sprinted towards the tiger, too. He panted and gasped as he ran, his heart still aching, but this time with relief. He didn't know how Ethan survived—it didn't matter; what mattered was that he was alive, and Jackson had to help him up the cliff.

"Ethan!" he called desperately.

The tiger kept climbing, now halfway up. He grunted and snarled, but he didn't give up despite the blood dripping from his paws.

Sebastien reached him; he hovered behind the tiger, grabbed his body with his front and back legs, and then pulled him off the cliff face. He carried him to safety, landing ten feet from the tree line, and when he dropped the tiger, Ethan collapsed.

Jackson hurried over to him. "Ethan!" he exclaimed.

But before he could reach him, Sebastien seemed to notice something, and he held out his wing to prevent Jackson from getting any closer.

"W-what?!" Jackson exclaimed.

Raphael and Daimon quickly joined them.

Jackson crouched so that he could see under Sebastien's wing, and that was when he saw it. A gaping, bleeding wound on Ethan's side. He shook his head in disbelief, his throat tightening and his heart breaking once again. "N-no…" he breathed.

Why was this happening? Why would the world let him think that his friend was okay only to shove in his face that he wasn't? Why would it let him see Ethan climbing to safety only to reveal that he was dead anyway? He scowled despondently and gritted his teeth; he could feel his rage returning, clawing its way to the surface—

"R-relax, man," came Ethan's breathy, tired voice. "It's just…the fucking Amarok. I'm good."

And then relief banished Jackson's growing rage. He tried to get past Sebastien—

"How are you sure?" the hound questioned, keeping Jackson back.

Ethan groaned irritably. "The fucking…thing bit me on the way down. It landed on top of me…and I just…snuck away while those things were too busy eating it. I used one of the dead cadejo to hide."

That was what Jackson saw falling off Ethan's back when he jumped up onto the cliff face. "Like camouflage?"

"Exactly," the muto mumbled.

"Not gonna lie, it's a good idea," Raphael admitted.

Sebastien folded his wings against his sides, letting Jackson through.

The moment he got to Ethan, he threw his paws around him and buried his face in his fur. "I thought you were dead," he lamented, sadness breaking through his relief. For the few minutes he thought he was dead, he felt as if he had nothing. He thought he lost his best friend, the one person who'd stuck around through all the shit his life had to offer, the one person who he trusted more than anyone else. He didn't know what he'd do without him.

"Where's the inimă?" Daimon questioned irritably.

Ethan exhaled deeply and lifted one of his huge paws. "Don't worry, man. I got it."

Jackson backed off a little and looked down at him. "Can't you heal him?" he asked Raphael.

The limping orange wolf scoffed. "Even if I wanted to, no. I can only heal wolf walkers."

With a roll of his eyes, Jackson looked back down at Ethan. But then he shifted his sights to Raphael once more. "How far away is the manor?" He looked at Sebastien. "Can you carry him?"

"That's the only way getting back doesn't take seven years," the orange wolf muttered.

Jackson asked Ethan, "Can you shift back?"

Ethan nodded. "Yeah." He shifted out of his tiger form with a pained grunt, and then he gripped the wound on his side with both his hands. "Hurts like a bitch."

"Don't worry, there're doctors back at the manor," Sebastien said as he got Ethan onto his back and held him between his wings.

Jackson picked up the inimă and put it into his bag.

"Now let's get the hell out of here before something else happens," Raphael muttered, shoving past Jackson to lead the way.

Jackson was too relieved by Ethan's survival to care about Raphael's shove. He hurriedly followed behind Sebastien, keeping his eyes peeled for danger. He felt so suddenly protective of his friend, and he'd do whatever he had to to make sure that he made it back to the estate safely. He'd already almost lost him once today; he didn't want to have to face that again.

But as he followed Raphael and Sebastien with Daimon at his side, he was struck by that unsettling feeling of eyes on him… again. A cold shiver ran down his spine, and he tensed up when he recalled the moment someone hiding in the dark called him Salvator. He didn't know who they were, nor did he know why they said that he was the one, but he had a horrible feeling about it, and he knew that he should tell someone. He had *a lot* to tell the people around him, and there would likely be time once they got back to base.

Before anything, though, he wanted to make sure that Ethan was going to be okay. That wound looked serious. But he trusted these people; they helped him and saved the lives of his pack, and he was certain that they'd save Ethan, too. They *had* to. If he lost him…. No, he didn't want to think about it anymore. He *hadn't* lost him. Ethan was fine. He was alive. He was breathing. He just needed a little help to recover. That was all. He'd be okay. He *had* to be okay.

"Hey," came Daimon's voice.

Jackson snapped out of his thoughts and looked to his right, where Daimon was walking in his normal wolf form.

"Are you okay?" the Alpha asked.

He frowned a little. "Yeah, I'm just worried about Ethan."

"It looked like you lost control back there," he said with a concerned tone. "You attacked—"

"I know," he interjected, shaking his head. "I… I didn't mean to, I just… I thought Ethan was dead. If Raphael just let me try to help him, then maybe he wouldn't have fallen in the first place."

"What would you have done?" the Alpha asked with a frown. "You wouldn't have reached him in time, Jackson. Raphael stopped you because you might have gotten yourself hurt... or worse."

Jackson huffed irritably and glared ahead. "It wasn't like I was just gonna dive into the pit."

"No?"

He scowled and glanced at him. "Why do you say it like that?"

"Because there was nothing else you *could* do, Jackson."

"I could have used my demon form; I could've swooped down there and grabbed him, and—"

"But you don't know how to fly yet," Daimon said.

He was getting more and more irritated by the second. With an annoyed snarl, he shook his head. "I don't wanna talk about it anymore. Ethan's fine and that's what I wanna focus on."

Daimon didn't argue with him. "All right."

Jackson was relieved that the conversation was over. It didn't matter what he could and couldn't have done. Ethan made it out.

A few minutes later, though, Daimon said, "I saw those cadejo stop when you told them to."

Jackson glanced at him.

"The ones by the cliff face. The prowler that killed Alastor stopped when you told it to, too," the Alpha continued, sounding both skeptical and hopeful. "They understand you, and you understand them, right?"

He wasn't sure whether Daimon was asking because he was worried or because he was hoping that they had yet another advantage against the undead. And Jackson wasn't going to lie. "Yeah. I came across a prowler before Raphael found me, and... we talked."

"About what?"

"Well... I don't know, really. It told me that I was a higher lifeform, and I think that's why they listen to me. And... it mentioned a Master. I think that maybe there's someone or something commanding them."

Daimon looked like he was thinking. "Why didn't you tell me this before?"

Jackson sighed deeply. "Because the pack were already suspicious that I was turning into a cadejo; if I told everyone that I could hear them talking, they'd only believe that I was turning more. To be honest, I thought that maybe I *was* turning, but... I think I understand them because I have demon blood—because... in a way, I'm like them."

"When did you first hear them?"

"Back at the ruin—actually... maybe before that when you first started teaching me to use my hearing. As for me talking to them, though, my first... conversation, I guess, was before Raphael found me."

The Alpha nodded slowly. "We'll likely be discussing this with everyone once we get back to base, but this is very important, Jackson. It could help us immensely with our mission."

"I know," he said and sighed. He felt a little silly keeping it a secret for as long as he had, especially from Daimon. "I'm sorry I didn't tell you sooner."

Daimon shook his head. "I understand why you wouldn't. It's okay."

Jackson smiled and nodded, and as they fell silent, they continued following Raphael through the woods.

Chapter Sixty-Four

A Long-Awaited Call

| Sebastien |

There was a whole shitstorm to report. Kane was still alive out there somewhere, they'd liberated Lumi, Kane was farming humans, and Jackson attacked Raphael, a crime which usually resulted in death or time in Daevor. But before all that... Sebastien needed to see if Clementine was okay.

When they got back to Reiner Manor, Sebastien took his mirror out of Jackson's bag and left Raphael to lead him, Ethan, and Daimon to wherever Cyrus was debriefing everyone. He headed upstairs and navigated the long, winding halls until he found an empty bedroom; once inside, he closed and locked the door, and then he slumped down on the barren mattress.

His heart raced in his chest as anxiety enthralled him tightly. A part of him was too afraid to make contact in case he heard something that he wasn't ready to hear. But if he didn't reach out... he might never know if his mate was okay. So he tapped the small rune on the back of the mirror and watched it fade to black.

He waited....

And waited....

And just as he was about to let his worry consume him, the mirror flashed and lightened up, revealing a gloomy bedroom lit by a single lamp.

"Clem?" he immediately asked.

Clementine moved what must be a small hand mirror up until his face was entirely visible. He smiled and said, "Hey."

"Are you okay? Did something happen?"

"Calm down, Sebastien," he drawled tiredly. "I tried calling when I landed, but you didn't answer. I assumed you were busy with something out there."

He exhaled deeply and tried his best to relax. After taking a few seconds to examine Clementine's surroundings, he realized that his mate was actually in a hotel room. The white and gold-patterned walls were familiar to him, as were the silk sheets and the

Balaur Blană bathrobe hanging on the wall to his right. He was staying at the Underground Royal, one of the safest places anyone could be right now.

"Sorry," Sebastien said with a sigh. "I was a bit caught up, yeah." He didn't want to tell him that he'd been a prisoner for the past few days and just had to fight a wolf walker turf war. Clementine had a lot on his plate right now.

"Everything okay? Where are you?"

"Uh...well, I'm at the Ascela manor."

Clementine frowned strangely. "Reiner Manor?"

"Yeah. We bumped into Cyrus and his guys along the way." He shuffled back and leaned his shoulder against the wall. "So, how's the Underground looking these days? Been a while since I was there."

With a shrug and a sigh, Clementine laid down and held the mirror above him so that Sebastien could still see his face. "Different than it was the last time I was here. There's skyscrapers...and cars instead of horses and carriages. Oh, and they have a Deiganish restaurant down on Holland Street, so I was thinking I'd order dinner from there or something."

Sebastien smiled fondly. "Are you comfortable? They better not have stuck you in economy."

He laughed a little and shook his head. "First class, baby."

The kludde laughed with him.

"I might've gotten the penthouse, but I heard that Zoe and Zerenity were up there."

"Even if they weren't, you'd still be in first class. The Reiners keep those penthouses empty in case they ever need them."

"Well, I can dream, I suppose."

Sebastien nodded and exhaled deeply. "Jackson attacked Heir Zephyr."

Clementine frowned. "Uh-oh. What happened?"

He huffed and shrugged. "It was stupid. We were leading an Amarok into a pit of cadejo and Jackson's stupid friend fell in."

"Ethan?"

"Yeah, but he's all right. Jackson thought he was dead and blamed Heir Zephyr, so he broke his leg."

"Uh..." he drawled. "That's.... Did Raphael tell Alucard or Zalith yet?"

"He's probably doing it right now," he grumbled.

Clementine looked worried. "Well...they wouldn't sentence him or anything, right? Isn't he supposed to be the answer to all this cadejo stuff?"

He scratched the side of his face. "Yeah, but I don't know. The bosses take this shit really seriously. If it was just a punch then maybe he'd get away with doing some time, but he broke his leg, blood and everything."

"Blood...yeah, he's kinda fucked, then. Didn't that guy who broke Zacaeus' nose get like thirty years in Daevor?"

"Tch, yeah," Sebastien muttered. "If he'd just broken his leg then he might've been fine, but he drew blood." He knew that he was going to have to fill out a report on this; the last thing he wanted was to play a part in damning someone who might just be the key to stopping the cadejo virus, but there were demon laws, and he had to abide by them.

After a few moments of silence, Clementine sighed quietly. "When are you going to join me here?"

Despondency banished Sebastien's aggravation. "I don't know. I'm stuck here until we find this lab up in Greykin Valley, and after that, well...I haven't been given any other assignments, so maybe Lord Caedis will let me take some time off."

"You should probably ask him ahead of time; for all you know, he could be planning your next big adventure this very moment," he laughed.

Sebastien rolled his eyes. "Remind me to never sell my soul again."

Clementine frowned but still had an amused smirk on his face. "Well, I mean...you can't. You only have one."

"*Had*," he mumbled. "But I don't regret it," he said, replacing his frown with a smile as he gazed at Clementine's beautiful face.

"I don't know, it kinda sounds like you do," Clementine teased.

He scoffed at him and smirked. "You're lucky you're nine hundred miles away right now or I'd be making you eat those words of yours," he threatened with a sultry tone.

"I'd love to see you try."

Sebastien smiled and then exhaled through his nose. "I'm glad you're okay. I was worried something happened with the plane or when you landed. I wish I could just...hold you."

"I'm glad you're okay, too," Clementine said quietly. "I miss you already. I wish you could just...portal over here for a sec and then go back. No one would know."

"They'd know," he said disappointedly. "They've got people monitoring the mirror realm *and* the phasing space. If I enter either of those places without permission, I'll get my ass handed to me."

Clementine pouted and scowled. "Your contract sucks, Sebastien."

"You're telling me? I feel so stupid every time I think about the fact that I never read it properly."

"Yeah, that was pretty dumb."

"Hey, I saved your life."

Clementine chuckled. "I know, and I'm grateful. And at least Alucard isn't a total dick. He could be treating you like a slave, but he isn't."

He exhaled a long breath and relaxed his shoulders. "I guess I *do* have it better than most of the others."

"And you get paid, too."

"I guess," he grumbled. "I just hate the fact that I can't choose to take a sick day or take some PTO. When I'm needed, I got no choice."

Clementine shrugged and said, "Yeah, but…you *do* get time off. Maybe you could ask for some?"

"Well, I'm sure I'll be seeing Lord Caedis real soon if Heir Zephyr decides to press charges against Jackson, so I'll ask him if I can take some time off after this mission. If I don't see him, I'll send a message. That's if I don't get scolded for letting Jackson do as much damage as he did."

"Why would you get scolded? Did you *let* it happen?"

Sebastien shook his head. "No…I wasn't around; I was on overwatch duty. When I got there, he was already latched onto Heir Zephyr like some kinda tick."

Clementine sighed and said, "Well, it wasn't your fault. Just make sure you tell the investigator where you were and what you were doing before you got there. Don't let them twist this on you."

"I know, I know," he breathed, lying down.

"Are you okay, Sebastien?"

He nodded. "I'm fine, babe."

"You sure? It looks like you've got a lot going on in your head."

Sebastien chuckled a little. "Yeah, you never miss a thing, do you?"

Clementine shrugged. "When you've been around someone for over a hundred years, you tend to get to know what all the little micro-expressions on their face mean."

With a dragged-out sigh, Sebastien stroked his hand over his face. "Promise me you won't freak out." He could ask, but he knew that his mate would lose his shit either way.

"I can't promise you that," he said as a worried expression struck his face. "What's going on?"

He groaned and rested his free arm beside him. "You remember Kane?"

"The Alpha wolf walker that Cyrus had dealings with?"

"Yeah, him—"

"Don't tell me you're involved in that, Sebastien," he complained with a tone of disbelief. "You're supposed to be finding that lab."

"We *are*," he insisted. "But we got wrapped up in some Kane shit on the way. Daimon's pack had a run in with them before the Venaticus picked them up; they killed some of Kane's wolves and now Kane wants revenge or something—you know, wolf walker law shit. He lured us all into a trap using cadejo, locked us up in some fucked up arena place, killed some of Daimon's pack with an *Amarok*, and then we managed to get Jackson out. The kid somehow bumped into Cyrus, who came and rescued us all. But

Kane got away, and I feel like it ain't gonna be safe to head back out there until we deal with him. He wants Daimon's head, and he isn't gonna stop until he's killed all of them."

Clementine's frown grew thicker.

Sebastien continued, "Cyrus is gonna be holding a meeting after debriefing, so I'm sure I'll find out then what the plan is. It *is* likely that we're going to have to deal with this situation first, though."

"You guys just keep running into trouble, don't you?"

"Feels kinda normal nowadays. But if I'm being honest, being out here is better than being on the front lines. I'll fight wolf walkers over demons any day."

"Being *here* would be better than either of those options," Clementine said with a pout.

"Eh, I dunno. Being around the royals is a pain. If those kids in the penthouse haven't caused any drama yet, I'd be surprised."

Clementine laughed a little. "Well, there *was* something about how the pool wasn't warm enough for them."

"Of course," Sebastien said with a sigh. "I shouldn't really be bad-mouthing them; they haven't done anything to me—well... Heir Lucian is a pain in the fucking ass, but the others are okay I guess."

"I know someone else who's a pain in the ass," Clementine said with a smirk.

Sebastien scoffed and shook his head. "You're really asking for it, aren't you?"

Clementine shrugged and smiled. "Maybe. How long do you have until the meeting?"

"Uh..." he drawled as he glanced at the clock. "I don't know, to be honest. Maybe a few hours. Everyone's gotta be debriefed."

"So... you have time for phone sex?" Clementine asked with a smirk.

"More like mirror sex," he laughed. "I'm sure we can make it work."

"Okay," Clementine said as he shuffled back in his bed and rested against the headboard. And then he started unbuckling his belt.

Sebastien smirked as he watched, and once Clementine pulled his belt off, he unbuckled *his* belt, too. "I'd much rather be in that bed with you right now," he said as he unbuttoned his jeans.

"Just imagine you are," Clementine said quietly and reached into his trousers.

Sebastien moved his hand into his trousers, too.

"Close your eyes," Clementine told him.

He closed his eyes.

"Imagine it's my tongue stroking the tip of your dick."

Sebastien let out a quiet groan as he dragged his thumb over his tip—

A loud, thumping knock came at the door.

"Fucking hell," Sebastien exclaimed as he pulled his hand out of his trousers and looked over at it. "What?!"

"Finally, God," came Amos' voice. "The boss needs you for debriefing."

"What's going on?" Clementine asked.

Sebastien sighed and mumbled, "One sec." Then he glared at the door again. "He literally doesn't need me," he insisted. "He can get the same story from everyone else who was there."

"Yeah, but…he said something about that kid attacking Raphael."

He groaned angrily. "Of course he fucking reported it."

"He reported Jackson?" Clementine asked worriedly.

"Looks like it," he muttered, glancing at his mate in the mirror. "I'm sorry, babe, I'm gonna have to go and get this shit over with."

Although he looked disappointed, Clementine nodded and said, "Okay. Just remember what I said and don't let them pin anything on you. It wasn't your fault."

Sebastien smiled at him. "I'll be okay. I love you, and I'll call you as soon as I'm free, okay?"

"Mm-hmm. I love you too."

"Okay, talk later."

"Bye," he said with a sad smile.

"Bye." Sebastien disconnected the mirror, which faded to black, and then back to a normal reflective surface. He sighed—

Amos knocked again. "Sorry dude, but—"

"I'm fucking coming, god damn," he complained as he climbed to his feet. He stormed to the door, unlocked it, and pulled it open. "Can I literally not get like twenty minutes of fucking privacy up in this place?"

"Sorry, man," Amos said with a frown. "I'm just following orders."

"Whatever. Let's just fucking get this over with."

Chapter Sixty-Five

There Are Laws

| **Jackson** |

It was quiet. No one in the war room spoke a word or moved a muscle; several people shot wary looks around the place, but not a single person dared to even breathe too loudly.

Cyrus looked so furious that anyone might think his head was going to explode. He had his arms crossed, and his eyes were fixed on Jackson, who tried to hide behind Daimon and between his huddled packmates.

But Jackson knew that there'd be no hiding once the investigator arrived. Who would come, though? When he debriefed him, Cyrus told him that a family representative would come to decide his fate, and he hoped to God that it wouldn't be Heir Lucian.

The stories that Cyrus practically spat at him echoed around inside his head, though. Demons went to Daevor just for so much punching a royal, and breaking a bone? Cyrus made sure he understood that was much worse than a punch.

He trembled fearfully, twiddling his fingers together as he stared at the door. They wouldn't send him to Daevor, would they? He didn't mean it—well, no...he *did*. He wanted Raphael to pay for letting Ethan die, but he never intended to kill him...did he? With a nervous frown, he shifted his eyes from the door and glanced around the room. So many of Cyrus' people were looking at him as if he was about to be escorted to the electric chair.

Was he? Was someone coming to end his life?

Jackson's heart started racing, and it almost burst out of his chest when he heard footsteps approaching the door.

This was it, wasn't it? Whoever was coming was coming to tell him whether he'd live or die for what he did. But how was that fair? He didn't even know there were laws! If he'd known it was illegal to attack someone like Raphael, then he never would have done it!

Daimon reached back and grabbed his hand.

But it didn't calm him down. If anything, knowing that his mate was worried panicked him even more. He tightened his grip on Daimon's hand with every echoing step, his heart racing faster. He stifled a breath when the door handle turned, and when it opened—

Sebastien?

Jackson let out a relieved huff—

But then Heir Lucian followed in behind him.

Jackson's heart raced so fast that he felt like he might start hyperventilating, and his instincts urged him to dive out the nearest window and make a break for it.

"You've got to be fucking kidding me," Raphael muttered as he stood up straight beside the locker he'd been leaning on.

Heir Lucian smiled across the room at him as he headed towards the table. "I heard you got beat up," he said mockingly.

Raphael snarled at him.

With an amused chuckle, Heir Lucian reached the table and stood beside Cyrus. "Where is he?" he asked with a sterner tone; his piercing blue eyes searched around the room.

Jackson hid behind Daimon, trembling, stifling his breaths. The last time Heir Lucian stormed into a room, he dragged Jackson across the floor and almost killed him in front of his pack, and obviously knowing that, his packmates moved a little closer to him, all with the same protective expression on their faces.

Heir Lucian set his sights on Daimon. "Move."

Daimon scowled in hostility. "No."

"Suit yourself," Heir Lucian said with a shrug.

He then waved his hand, and Daimon was flung off his feet and to the left. The pack looked as horrified and startled as Jackson felt, and when their Alpha hit the wall and landed on the floor with a thump, half of them went to help him, and Tokala and Wesley went to charge at Heir Lucian. But several of Cyrus' men grabbed *all* of Jackson's packmates before they could move and said the same thing: "I wouldn't if I were you."

Daimon climbed to his feet with a frustrated, furious growl and also went to charge at Heir Lucian, but Amos, Elias, and Landon grabbed him.

And then Jackson felt an invisible, giant fist wrap around his body. He stifled a grunt as his breath was stolen from him, and when he looked at Heir Lucian, he saw the kid holding his hand out with his fist clenched shut. *He* was doing it.

Fear shot through Jackson like a bullet as his packmates struggled and tried to escape, and Daimon yelled furiously, but there was nothing anyone could do. Jackson was yanked forward so hard that he fell back, and when his head hit the floor, he grunted painfully.

It didn't end there.

The invisible fist grasped his leg and dragged him along the floor and around the table, and when he was at Heir Lucian's feet, he came to a halt, and he stared up at him in horror.

"Is this really necessary?" Cyrus muttered.

Heir Lucian ignored him and crouched beside Jackson.

Jackson trembled and tried to move, but his body was frozen—and not because of his fear. "I-I-I didn't mean to hurt him, I—"

Wordlessly, Heir Lucian pressed his index finger against Jackson's shoulder—

Horrific pain suddenly shot through Jackson's right leg. He shrieked and writhed around as the pain intensified; it felt like his bone had snapped and cut out through his flesh, but there was no blood, there was no break, there was just *pain*.

"Get the fuck off him!" Daimon yelled.

"You can't do this!" Tokala shouted.

"What the fuck is wrong with you people?!" Wesley exclaimed.

Jackson whined and cried, and now that he could finally move, he reached down and gripped his leg to find no wound, and the pain was getting worse with each passing second. What the hell had Heir Lucian done to him?

"All right, that's enough," Cyrus insisted irritably.

Heir Lucian rolled his eyes and crouched beside Jackson again. This time, when he touched his shoulder, the agony withered, leaving Jackson trembling and breathing raggedly.

"Listen," Heir Lucian said sternly, scowling at Jackson's terrified face. "Demons have rules. The only reason you're not on your way to Daevor right now is because you were never made aware of them. If you *ever* attack a royal again, you'll be lucky if it gets you a few years in hell. You don't *ever* address any one of us without using our title, and if we tell you to do something, you fucking do it without a moment's hesitation. Understand?"

Jackson nodded, still gripping his leg; pain was lingering in it, but it wasn't nearly as intense. But his fear was growing by the second. He *hated* Heir Lucian, and he was terrified of him. He didn't want to do or say anything that might make him hurt him again.

"You have an hour," Heir Lucian said, and then he touched Jackson's shoulder again.

The pain came back. It felt like his leg broke again, like it snapped in two, and searing, horrifying agony burned through his body. He shrieked and yelled out; he could hear Daimon and his packmates shouting again, but Heir Lucian ignored them, stood up, and left the room, leaving Jackson to suffer.

As soon as the door shut, Daimon and his pack came rushing over; Jackson could hear their worried voices, but he couldn't make out what they were saying—not until Daimon placed his hands on either side of his face and made him look up at him.

"Jackson?" he insisted worriedly.

With an agonized grunt, Jackson shakily said, "It-it feels like my leg is broken."

"What the fuck did he do to him?!" Daimon yelled at Cyrus.

"Do something to help him!" Tokala insisted.

But Cyrus just stood there and shook his head. "It's demon curse ethos, man. I can't undo that shit."

"It's payback," Raphael called. "He's fortunate he isn't behind bars."

Daimon snarled furiously and went to lunge at him, but Tokala and Wesley grabbed his arms to keep him from doing so.

"Everyone, just calm down," Cyrus demanded, and then he looked at Daimon. "It's just an hour. The kid could've made him suffer for longer, so count yourselves lucky."

"Lucky?!" Jackson exclaimed painfully. "It feels like my leg is being torn off!"

"Okay, but it's still intact, so…" Cyrus said with a shrug.

Daimon went for him, but his Zeta and Gamma held him back.

Cyrus looked over at Amos and Elias. "Take him up to one of the spare rooms." He set his eyes on Jackson. "Sleep it off."

"Sleep it off?!" Jackson cried angrily. "How the hell am I supposed to sleep this off?!"

"Can't one of your doctors help?!" Lalo exclaimed, and then he shifted his sights to Lance. "Can't *you* do something?"

Lance looked like a deer in headlights. "I-I…I don't—"

"Come on," came Sebastien's voice.

Jackson didn't want to move, but he couldn't fight when Sebastien helped him to his feet, or when the kludde and Daimon moved his arms over their shoulders and assisted him towards the door.

"This is fucked up," Wesley uttered as they left the war room. "Can he seriously just do this shit?!"

"Yeah, he can," Sebastien answered. "Just like your ancient wolf walker laws, demons have laws, too—and we take them very seriously, especially when it comes to the royals. And honestly, you got off lightly, Jackson. If Lord Caedis and the Zenith didn't need you to help find a cure for this virus, you'd be in Daevor with an actual broken leg."

"I'm going to fucking kill him," Daimon growled.

"Good luck with that," Sebastien said as they started heading up a flight of stairs. "Heir Lucian might be an eighteen-year-old kid, but he's got the strength of all of you combined times fifty."

Daimon snarled frustratedly.

Jackson grunted with every step. His leg felt like it was on fire, and it wasn't getting any better. He felt weaker with each painful throb, and after a few moments, he couldn't move anymore. Daimon picked him up and carried him in his arms, and when they got into a gloomy room, the Alpha gently placed him down on a bed.

The blankets were soft and graced him as he lay down; the agony didn't subside, but at least he felt a little comfort.

"Come on, give him some space," Sebastien said.

As Daimon helped Jackson rest his head on the pillows, he watched the white-haired demon escort his worried packmates out of the room.

Daimon huffed angrily when Sebastien closed the door, leaving the two of them alone. "I hate that fucking Lucian," he snarled, sitting beside him.

Jackson grimaced and panted, trying to cope with the pain.

"I fucking hate demons. Their laws are just as bad as Lupi Sequi Veteris."

"A-agreed," Jackson muttered.

The Alpha then frowned despondently and moved Jackson's hair away from his eyes. "I'm sorry I couldn't stop him."

Jackson took a deep, shaky breath. "It's okay," he said quietly. "It's…fucked up, yeah…but I'd rather th-this than go to demon prison."

Daimon snarled again. "And Raphael's a little fucking bitch for reporting you."

"Y-yeah…I didn't…I didn't take him for one of those…snitchy, kiss-ass trust fund baby types—like Edward," he grumbled.

"It's probably safe to assume that they're all like that," Daimon growled.

Jackson took a deep breath and tried to relax. As Daimon lay beside him, he rested his head on the Alpha's chest. "I don't wanna see any of them ever again," he mumbled. "I don't wanna see *any* demons. Their laws sound crazy."

Daimon carefully moved his arm around him. "I won't let anyone hurt you again."

That didn't really bring Jackson as much comfort as he'd like. Daimon was powerless when it came to Heir Lucian; that kid tossed him across the room like he was nothing. But he *trusted* his mate, and he *did* feel safe with him. He just wanted to lay there with him and forget everything that just happened.

However, he wanted to go and see Ethan. His friend was down in the medical wing getting his Amarok bite treated, and Jackson promised he'd visit once he was done with Cyrus' meeting—which hadn't even happened yet. But now he was stuck in bed with a leg that felt like it was broken, and judging by what Heir Lucian said, it would be an hour until he was pain-free.

"I hate it here," he lamented as his throat started tightening. "I just wanna…be somewhere else." He wanted to say that he wanted to go home to New Dawnward, but he knew that would upset Daimon. "These people and this place and this mission…it's kinda overwhelming."

Daimon kissed his head. "We'll get it done with," he said firmly. "And once it's over, we'll have a place of our own again away from all this shit."

"Do you really think it'll all be over once we get to the lab and find whatever the Nosferatu needs?" he asked worriedly. "What if Lord Caedis ropes me into doing something else?"

"I won't let him. You agreed to help find the lab, and that's all. I won't let him use you," he said protectively.

Jackson closed his eyes and exhaled deeply. "What if we don't find the lab? Or what if we get there and it's destroyed or gone or something?"

"We'll find it, and if it is gone, we *still* reached the agreed location."

He frowned as guilt started to consume him. "I want to help; I wanna do whatever I can to find a cure for this virus, but I don't…I don't wanna end up like Sebastien. I don't wanna be some errand boy for Lord Caedis."

"You *won't*. Sebastien's deal was different to yours, okay? Once we get to this place, you're free," Daimon said firmly.

"I hope so," he mumbled sadly.

Chapter Sixty-Six

Talk of Ancestors

| Jackson |

The pain lasted *exactly* an hour. Jackson writhed and fidgeted beside Daimon, trying his best to cope with it. The comfort of the bed did nothing to help, and neither did his mate's embrace. Everything that usually helped soothe his discomfort was useless, and he suspected that whatever Heir Lucian did to him was the reason.

He didn't want to be around these people anymore—no...he liked the wolves, but the *demons*? He didn't want to be a demon. He didn't want to be a part of demon society. He wanted *nothing* to do with them. But did he even have a choice? Did he get to decide whether or not he wanted to be part of a society that let higher ranks *torture* someone? He pouted and buried his face into Daimon's shirt. Wolf walkers were the same, weren't they? At least they were supposed to be. He remembered what Julian told him about packs and how they treat Omegas, and that was pretty much how Heir Lucian had treated *him*, wasn't it? Heir Lucian was the Alpha...and he was just the lowly Omega.

And *Raphael*. Jackson hadn't taken him for a whiny snitch, but he was wrong. But he didn't exactly blame him; if *he* was part of a royal bloodline, he might end up using his status in the same way. If he'd had bloodline armour back when Nyssa and Caius and everyone else were bullying him, maybe he could have avoided everything that happened. But then again...he *wasn't* a whiny bitch, and if those things hadn't happened, then he might not be where he was now; he might not be Daimon's mate, and he might not be taking part in a mission that would save not only wolf walkers but probably the entire Caeleste world.

He was just glad that Ethan didn't have to see him get dragged across that floor and treated like a worthless insect. Yeah, it was embarrassing, and he hated that Daimon and the pack witnessed it, but for some reason, he felt as if his best friend seeing it would have been a whole lot worse. Not only would it make him look weak and stupid, but Ethan would have likely tried going for Heir Lucian, too, and unlike Daimon, *he* wasn't as strong and would have definitely had a bone or two broken if he was thrown against a wall.

And he hadn't forgotten about what Ethan said to him before he escaped Kane's arena, either.

"Are you feeling better?" Daimon suddenly asked.

Jackson snapped out of his thoughts and exhaled deeply. The pain was finally withering, but it still felt like his leg was on fire. "Not really, but it's fading."

Daimon huffed and muttered, "If that white-haired piece of shit wasn't some demon heir, I'd tear him apart."

"Yeah, well, karma will get him someday," Jackson mumbled, although he wasn't entirely sure that was true. As much as he hated to admit it, Heir Lucian had some sort of demon right to do what he did. "I just…wanna get out of here. We need to get to the lab."

"I'd leave right now if we could," Daimon mumbled. "But Cyrus said he's holding a meeting later regarding our mission, and we've all got to be there. As much as I want to get this over with, Kane is still out there, and we can't risk running into him again. I assume this meeting will tell us what the plan is and how we deal with this shit."

Jackson sighed heavily. "This pack is like…super strong, though. They have vampires and demons and wolf demons—why can't *they* deal with Kane while we get to the lab?"

"I guess we'll find out."

With a deep sigh, Jackson rolled onto his back and stared up at the ceiling…which was painted with murals. He frowned curiously and eyed the hand-painted artwork of dragons, wolves, and humanoid Caeleste; it reminded him of the paintings he saw in that ice cave when he first travelled with Daimon's pack, only the images above him had much more detail. Feather-winged men and women, and some with dragon-like wings, too. And in the very centre was a huge white dragon with an almost-white-blue furred mane. It was like something out of the Book of Lore—something someone might find in a Lethidian church.

"Why are there Lethidian paintings in some other god's house?" he asked, glancing at Daimon, who was also staring up at the art.

"It's Caederian," the Alpha told him. "That dragon is Vespira, a vessel for the Zenith's power."

His frown thickened. "How do you know th—oh, ancestral knowledge, right?"

He smiled slightly. "I don't know how my ancestors worked so closely with demons."

Jackson leaned up on his arm so that he could see Daimon's face. "Sebastien said that Fenrisúlfr is your ancestor—Greymore. I guess we've all been so busy and overwhelmed with multiple shitstorms that we haven't really…well, thought about any of it. And Wesley has fae blood, Tokala's bloodline is super powerful and half of them are cultists, and some crazy demons killed Dustu's family." He frowned and shook his head. "Sirens, Lumi, I can talk to cadejo, and God knows what else."

Daimon huffed and chuckled. "I think we need a long pack meeting."

"I suppose we could find out more at this meeting with Cyrus. These guys seem to know *a lot* about Redbloods and Greymore and Kane. Maybe we'll get some answers."

"All this time, I never really knew where my ancestral knowledge came from. I had my mother and father, and their parents, and their parents' parents, but after that, it's all a big blur. No names, no faces, just knowledge. I guess I know now, though. And nobody knows what happened to Greymore—or Fenrisúlfr—so maybe the fact that his soul isn't with the rest of my ancestors means he's still out there," Daimon explained slowly.

"That…kinda makes sense. Do you think the Nosferatu know? Lord Caedis? The Zenith?"

"I don't know, but I'm sure we'll get an answer to that soon, too. I plan to get as much as I can from Cyrus; he's supposed to be one of my relatives, and he's hanging out here with demon heirs, so he has to know a lot more than I do."

Jackson rested his head on Daimon's chest. "I hope he can give you the answers you're looking for, and the rest of us. They know about the Holy Grail, too. I know I was gonna ask Lord Caedis to tell me everything he knows about them as part of the deal we made, but if Cyrus can tell me, then maybe I can ask Lord Caedis for something else."

"Like?" Daimon asked with an intrigued tone.

"I don't know. He can…he can bring people back from the dead, right? Like he did for Sebastien. Maybe…I can ask him to bring my mom back," he said sullenly. "Or my dad, who I never got to know. Or both of them."

"Bringing people back from the dead sounds like it has a hefty price, Jackson," Daimon said sincerely. "Sebastien's bound to serve Caedis for eternity; you're *not* going to make that sacrifice."

He shook his head. "No, I don't want that. But he did say that I could have *anything* in exchange. Surely that counts."

"I don't know," the Alpha grumbled.

"I guess I could ask when the time comes. But then if I ask, he could twist things, right? Like the devil always does in movies and shit. I don't wanna make some stupid mistake and end up mopping the halls of hell or something."

Daimon stifled a laugh. "What? I don't think he'd turn you into a janitor."

"You never know. Sebastien's basically an errand boy."

"Well, Sebastien didn't read the terms properly."

"I guess," Jackson mumbled and shifted his attention back to his leg. Although he wasn't in utter agony anymore, he still felt uncomfortable. It was like his body was trying to heal a non-existent wound. But it *was* healing…somehow, and he felt better. When he glanced up at Daimon, he said, "I want to go and see how Ethan's doing. That wound looked…nasty, and I wanna make sure he's doing okay." He hadn't heard anything about his friend since Heir Lucian's backwards punishment, and he needed to see if he was okay.

Daimon sighed but said, "All right. I'll come with—"

"No, I…think I should see him alone. You guys don't exactly get on, and I don't want you to start arguing or anything while he's trying to heal."

"I don't trust him. He attacked you, Jackson," he insisted with a concerned frown.

"I know, but…" he paused and huffed. "I'm not gonna make excuses for him, to be honest. Yeah, he lost control of himself. But he's not riled up right now or even in his tiger form. He's probably sedated or something, too. I mean it'd hurt like hell to have that kinda wound operated on while you're conscious."

"Then I'll stand outside the ro—"

"I know you wanna protect me, Daimon, but I'll be fine." He felt bad turning him down, but he just wanted to have *one* conversation with Ethan that didn't evolve into an argument between him and Daimon. "I won't be long, either. Did Cyrus say what time he's having the meeting?"

"No," he grumbled. "But I'm sure he'll gather everyone up when it's time."

"Well…while I'm checking on Ethan, maybe you can find Cyrus and ask him about Fenrisúlfr?" he suggested.

"I suppose," Daimon replied, but he didn't sound too happy.

Jackson sat up and looked down at him. "I'll be *fine*, Daimon. I promise. I just need to see if he's okay."

Daimon stared up at him; the expression on his face journeyed from irritated to concerned and stopped at hesitant. But he relented and placed his hand on the side of Jackson's face. "Okay, but if I get any sense that you're in danger, I won't hesitate to come down there."

He smiled at him. "I'm not gonna be in danger." He leaned closer and kissed Daimon's lips. "I love you."

The Alpha smiled and ran his fingers through Jackson's hair. "I love you, too."

Jackson then concentrated on his leg again, and to his relief, the pain was pretty much gone. "Do you wanna meet back here when we're both done if Cyrus hasn't called for the meeting yet?"

Daimon nodded and sat up. "I should go and check on the pack, too."

He pouted and looked down at his lap. "Do you think…do you think they all see me differently because of how stupid and useless Heir Lucian made me look?" he asked sullenly.

The Alpha frowned and shook his head. "There wasn't anything you could have done, Jackson, and they know that. I'm sure that they all hate Lucian as much as we do."

"It was embarrassing," he grumbled. "I'm supposed to be this hybrid, and I couldn't even *try* to defend myself."

"It wasn't your fault, Jackson. These demons and wolves are from bloodlines older than even *mine*, and just like with wolf walkers, a demon's bloodline gives them power that others don't have. Even if you could have tried, there wouldn't have been much you could do except make it worse. And I fucking hate admitting it, but it's true. As much as I want to claw both Lucian and Raphael's eyes out, the only thing any of us can do right now is avoid them," Daimon said firmly.

Jackson nodded and looked over at the door to try and hide his embarrassed face. "Hopefully Heir Lucian's gone back to Silverlake. I don't ever wanna see him again."

"I'm sure he's run back to Caedis to write his little report."

"Yeah," he mumbled. He sighed quietly and glanced at Daimon. "Well, my leg feels better, so I'm gonna go see Ethan now. I'll see you back here later?"

Daimon nodded, and when Jackson got up, so did he. "Do you want me to see if Cyrus will tell me anything about the Holy Grail?"

Jackson shrugged as he headed towards the door. "Sure, thank you."

When Jackson pulled the door open, Daimon gently gripped his arm and turned him to face him. He kissed his lips and then his forehead before saying, "Just be careful, okay?"

"I'll be okay," he insisted. "See you in a little."

The Alpha nodded again and then turned around. He headed down the left hallway, leaving Jackson alone.

It was then that Jackson realized he had no idea how to get to the medical wing or hospital or whatever it was called. He pulled the bedroom door shut behind him and stared down the right hallway. He could hear voices coming from that way, so maybe he could find someone who would point him in the right direction.

He just hoped that he wouldn't see Raphael. *That* was the last thing he needed.

Chapter Sixty-Seven

Greymore, Greyson, Greyblood, Greykin

| Daimon |

Everyone seemed okay. Each of Daimon's packmates had been patched up, clothed, and fed. Tokala was sitting on the couch by the window with Remus, Julian, and Lalo; they each had a burger in their hands from some fast-food place, and when Daimon looked around, he saw that *everyone* had something. Where the hell did they get that from out here?

He got his answer when he spotted Sebastien sitting on his own by the fireplace. The white-haired demon had a vacant stare on his face while he watched the dancing flames, sipping loudly through his straw. Several empty fast-food bags lay at his feet, as did multiple wrappers.

"Oh, Dad!" Remus called excitedly. "Sebastien got us dinner from some place called Slappy's."

Daimon frowned as he crossed the lounge towards him. "What?"

"It's a fast-food chain," Sebastien called. "Heir Lucian was heading over there, so I thought I'd grab something for everyone. The guys here have been living off pizza and shit, anyway. No one cooks."

"Here," Remus said when Daimon reached him; he offered him a burger and some fries from the bag sitting between him and Tokala.

"Thanks," Daimon said as he took them from him and sat on the arm of the couch.

"Where's Jackson?" Tokala asked with a concerned tone.

"He went to see Ethan," the Alpha replied as he unwrapped the burger.

Wesley grunted irritably as he swallowed his food. "That fucking demon kid, I swear."

"Yeah, that's pretty much the gist of everyone's reaction to him," Sebastien said with a sigh.

"He shouldn't be allowed to get away with it," Lalo exclaimed.

"Jackson didn't even do anything to him," Julian agreed.

"I don't wanna get into this again," Sebastien said with a sigh. "It's demon stuff, okay? Heir Lucian had every right to do what he did. Now can we move on? It's done with."

"You wouldn't be saying that if it was you," Ezhno accused.

"I've already spent my free pass, so if *I* chewed up Heir Zephyr's leg, I'd be in Daevor," the white-haired demon said.

"You hurt one of them?" Dustu questioned.

Sebastien finished his drink and dropped the cup into one of the bags at his feet. "Yeah. I punched Heir Lucian a couple years ago."

A chorus of curious and amused laughter circled the room.

"*You* punched *him*?" Remus asked with a smile.

"I was babysitting him for Lord Caedis and he did some whack-ass shit—I mean, are we surprised?—and he wouldn't back the fuck down, so I broke his nose," Sebastien explained as he crouched and took another drink from one of the bags.

"I'm surprised you're still alive," Lalo mumbled.

"Oh, he wanted to kill me, but Lord Caedis let me off with a warning."

Daimon took a bite of his burger, and to his surprise, it was actually quite good. He waited for a break in the conversation, and then he asked, "Where's Cyrus? I need to talk to him."

Sebastien shifted his sights to him. "Uh... I think he's in his office with Apex Idina. Just like... go out that door, turn left and walk across the hall and under the stairs. Follow that hallway to the end. Door on the left."

Daimon ate a few of his fries and then handed them to his son. "I'll be back in a little," he told him.

Remus nodded. "Okay, I'll just be here with Tokala."

As he took another bite of his burger, Daimon got up and left the lounge. He navigated the house following Sebastien's instructions, and when he reached the door to what he presumed was Cyrus' office, he knocked.

"Yeah?" came Cyrus' voice.

Daimon pushed the door open, and when he stepped inside, he set his eyes on Cyrus. The black-haired man was sitting behind his desk, and a brown-haired woman—who he assumed must be Idina—was standing beside him.

"Oh, Daimon," Cyrus said as he put his phone down. "We're not ready for the meeting yet if that's what you're here for."

"No, that's not why I'm here," he told him, standing in the doorway. "I have questions... about my bloodline."

The woman patted Cyrus' head and said, "I'll just be upstairs."

Cyrus smiled up at her. "Get some rest," he told her.

She nodded and then headed towards the door.

Once she passed him and left the room, Daimon closed the door behind him and walked to Cyrus' desk. He watched the man pull out a cigarette from his pocket, and as he lit it with his lighter, he gestured to one of the empty leather armchairs in front of him.

Daimon sat in the right one and waited.

Cyrus put his lighter down and drew a light breath from his cigarette. When he exhaled, he blew the smoke to the side so that it didn't hit Daimon's face. "So, what do you wanna know?"

"Everything."

He chuckled and took another breath of his cigarette. "Everything is a lot, man. We got the time—we're waiting on Lucian to hear back from Alucard—but I need you to give me some sorta like…" he paused and drew another breath… "starting point, you know?"

Where *did* he want to start? "Fenrisúlfr is my ancestor, as he is yours, but I don't have demon blood like you or Raphael."

"Mm," he murmured as he leaned back in his seat. "That'll be the whole…weakening every generation thing. My father, Greymore, otherwise known as Fenrisúlfr, had kids with my mother, who's a demon. My siblings and I were born these sort of…wolf walkers with demon blood. Hybrids technically aren't possible and can't be created the way we were because the ethos doesn't mix; the stronger ethos would annihilate the weaker ethos, and whatever remains would die. But Fenrisúlfr isn't like other wolf walkers—*wasn't*. He was crafted by a cult to be a weapon, some proper cultist shit. Somehow, whatever those people did to him made it so his ethos bonded with my mother's."

Daimon nodded slowly.

"But again, hybrids aren't technically possible, so we're not demon wolf walkers, we just have demon blood because of my mother. Like demons, we don't age once we reach our late twenties or early thirties, and we also heal a lot faster. I don't know which one of my siblings you're related to, but there've been *a lot* of generations since we were born. My mother's blood weakened every generation because most of my siblings went on to mate with and marry wolf walkers, and it eventually got to a point where the demon blood was eradicated entirely."

That made sense. "And Raphael?"

Cyrus drew a *deep* breath from his cigarette and sighed when he exhaled. "Yeah, him. My sister, Lydia, married and had kids with Zacaeus, Alucard and Zalith's son. Alucard's ethos is stronger than Zalith's, though, so it's the dominant ethos in every one of his descendants. That's why they all have orange hair; it's like…a lighter shade than his because these kids only have a fraction of his power, you know?"

"So, the Redblood line was born from Alucard and Zalith—the Zenith?"

"Yup," he said and finished his cigarette. "So, Zacaeus obviously has hella ethos 'cause his parents are gods, and his and Lydia's kids have access to that power through blood or some shit. That's why Raphael's so powerful—and don't even get me started on his sister. Anyway, yeah... that's pretty much the gist of it."

Daimon pondered for a moment. Did this mean that *Tokala* had access to power that he didn't even realize was there? "So, my Zeta, Tokala, should have access to that power, too? He's a Redblood."

"Yeah..." Cyrus drawled. "We had a brief talk about him. Jackson tells me that his mother or someone left behind the Redblood way to join your pack. If his mother left before he was born, then there's a high chance that she never told him what he was capable of. When power like that isn't honed from a young age, it's likely gonna just... fall asleep, I guess, and it's real hard to wake it up."

If Tokala had access to the power Daimon had seen Raphael display, then their chances of getting through the mountains and to Greykin Valley would be a whole lot higher. "Could he learn to use it?"

"The best person to ask about that is Raphael. But the same generational weakening applies, I believe, just at a much slower rate since Alucard's ethos is a lot stronger than my parents'."

"Is Raphael still here?"

"I think he's with Lucian listening to Alucard's orders. I'd wait to see him if I were you."

Daimon nodded and shifted his attention back to his own bloodline. "I have the names of quite a few of my ancestors. If I told you, could you help me find out which of your siblings I'm related to?" If he had more family out there, he wanted to know.

Cyrus scratched the side of his face. "Uh..." he drawled. "I mean maybe, but my mom knows more than I do. I can get her to come back down here."

"I don't want to impose—"

"Nah, it's fine. I'll just shoot her a text," he said as he grabbed his phone. He typed on it for a few moments, and then he put it back down. "It wasn't too long ago that we all came out to Ascela, so it shouldn't be too hard narrowing it down."

Daimon nodded and waited, but before silence could fall between them, he said, "You've been in this part of Greykin longer than us. What else is out there? We didn't start seeing variant cadejo until we crossed the mountains."

Cyrus' nonchalant expression faded, and a conflicted frown sat in its place. "I reckon that's something we ought to cover in the meeting. The cadejo have increased in numbers very rapidly over the past week, and we don't know why. Alucard suggested that it might have something to do with Jackson being over here, and most of his council seem to agree."

"But you don't?" Daimon questioned.

"I don't know. It makes sense. I mean, Jackson's a hybrid. He could be the very thing that stops the virus, and maybe those smarter cadejo know that, so they're over here to try and stop him or something, but I can't help but feel like there's more to it," he said as he tapped his fingers on the desk. "Raphael and his team saw your little Jackson talking to and commanding cadejo; I want to hear more about that when we convene."

Just then, the door to Cyrus' office opened, and Idina walked in carrying what looked like a photo album. "I haven't been able to update it recently," she said as she made her way towards the desk.

"That's all right," Cyrus told her. "He has the names of some of his ancestors, so we should be able to make a connection."

Idina smiled at Daimon as she placed the photo album on the desk in front of Cyrus. "Who do you remember?" she asked.

Daimon took a moment to recall who and what he could. "My mother, Audrey West, and my father, Nanook Greyblood. My father's father, Siqiniq Greyblood, and my father's mother, Lenora Heartford."

Idina and Cyrus looked through the book, but they didn't find anything.

So, Daimon continued. "My great grandfather, Amaruq Greyblood, and my great grandmother, Alasie Geela-Blood."

They both shook their heads.

"Great great grandfather, Siku Silana-Blood. Great great grandmother, Koko Greyblood."

Idina's face lit up. "Oh, right here," she said as she pointed to the page she just flipped to. "Koko," she said as she turned the book and pushed it across the table to Daimon.

Daimon pulled the book closer and stared at the blurry photograph of a native Ascelan woman. Her hair was as black as his, and she had several feathers and ceremonial beads in it. The man at her side must be Siku, and they had their toddler son standing between them.

Cyrus reached across the desk and flipped through a few pages, revealing a hand-drawn family tree. He traced his finger up until he reached a line of six men and women, one of which was him, and another man was off to the side. But his finger hovered over a woman named Eden, who married and had children with an Ascelan native man, Ikiaq Kolaut-Blood.

"Oh, Ikiaq is so sweet," Idina said. "I'm glad he and Eden met."

"Are Eden and Ikiaq still around?" Daimon asked.

"Eden's my sister, so yeah," Cyrus confirmed. "Our whole demon agelessness didn't get passed on to our kids, so sadly, none of them are around anymore. But my siblings and their mates are; those who get imprinted on by an ageless demon stop ageing, too—you know…fate and all that."

Idina frowned despondently. "It's quite sad, really. I don't like to think about it much."

"I'm sorry for your loss," Daimon said to her.

"Thank you," she said sadly. "Eden is busy searching Greykin for survivors right now, but she's due back here next month if you want to meet her."

Daimon nodded and said, "I'd like to. But I don't know where I'll be in a month." He then realized that he was still holding his half-eaten burger. He didn't know whether he wanted to finish it or not.

"Yeah, a lot of crazy shit happening," Cyrus said with a sigh. "And shit just keeps getting crazier."

"How's Jackson doing?" Idina asked. "I heard about what happened with Raphael and Lucian."

"He seems better now," Daimon answered. "He went to see Ethan."

"I heard about him, too," the woman said sympathetically. "You and your friends have been through so much."

Daimon wanted to make it clear that Ethan wasn't his friend, but he didn't want to be rude, especially not to someone who'd only been kind and helpful, so he held his tongue and nodded. "We've been through a lot before; we'll bounce back."

Idina smiled and said, "I'm sure you will."

"I think we should have a talk with your Redblood friend," Cyrus then said. "If we don't cover it in the meeting, I'll get Raphael to join us after."

Daimon nodded. "All right."

Cyrus then looked up at Idina. "Do you know if Raphael and Lucian are done with Alucard yet?"

"I think they're still talking. I can check if you'd like."

He nodded and then set his sights on Daimon. "Do you have any other questions?"

Daimon thought about it for a few moments, but he felt as if he had most of the answers he was looking for. He *was* a descendant of Fenrisúlfr, but he was so far down the line that he didn't possess demon blood. He *did* have living relatives, and Tokala...he might just be as valuable as Jackson.

The Alpha shook his head. "No. Thank you for talking with me."

"No probs. You can head back to the lounge where all your pals are eating. I'll send someone to fetch you once we're ready to begin the meeting."

With another nod, Daimon stood up. "It was nice meeting you," he said to Idina.

"And you," she replied with a smile.

He then turned around and left the office. As he navigated the huge house, he finished his burger and tossed its wrapper in a trashcan. He wanted to go and find Jackson, but he didn't want to invade his space or privacy when he insisted on being alone. So, he dismissed that wish and instead focused on finding his way back to his pack. For now, he'd rest; a lot of talking, questions, and answers were due very soon, and he wanted to make sure that he had the energy to say everything that needed to be said.

Chapter Sixty-Eight
Lines

| Jackson |

When Jackson emerged into the huge entrance hall, he glanced around at everyone. Cyrus' people were sitting on the grand staircase, the couches between it, and even on the white fur rugs beside the archways which led into other rooms. Some of them didn't look like wolf walkers, though; three men and two women standing by the archway on the right wore much more expensive-looking clothes rather than the ripped, ragged attire Jackson saw Cyrus' pack wearing. One of the women and two of the men had eyes as red as blood, and it made him wonder whether they were vampires or demons or some other race he didn't yet know about… or remember.

He sighed and tried to choose someone to approach, but to his relief, he spotted Amos and Elias making their way downstairs. He waited for them to reach the bottom, and then he walked over to them. "Uh, hey guys," he said.

The brothers stopped walking and both said, "What's up, Jackson?"

"Could you tell me how to get to the medical…place, please? I wanna go and see how Ethan's doing."

Amos stuffed his hands in his pockets. "Well, we're actually headed down there right now. I guess you can tag along," he said as he glanced at Elias.

Elias shrugged. "Yeah, suppose so. Just don't touch anything or look at anyone or talk to anyone."

Jackson frowned strangely but nodded in agreement. "Okay.…"

"This way," Amos said as he and his brother walked towards the doorway under the stairs.

They stopped outside the mahogany double doors and pressed a button beside them. A few moments later, they opened, revealing that they were actually elevator doors. Jackson stepped inside when the twins did, and he stood beside Amos, who he felt was the less intimidating of the two, and watched the doors shut.

"How's your leg?" Amos asked him.

Jackson glanced up at the guy and shrugged. "Fine now, I guess."

"Lucian's a prat," Elias grumbled.

"Couldn't agree more," Amos said.

Although Jackson wanted to voice his opinion of that kid, he wouldn't risk it getting back to him, not after what happened an hour ago. So, he kept his mouth shut and waited as the elevator took him deeper into the ground.

But that was when he started feeling sick again. The nausea hit him like a bullet, and it made him grimace and grunt.

"You all right?" Amos asked.

He nodded and cleared his throat. "Y-yeah, just…not a fan of elevators." He took several deep, quiet breaths, hoping that the nausea would pass, but it didn't. It got worse with each passing moment.

"Yo, you sure you're okay?" Elias questioned. "You look pale as fuck."

Jackson closed his eyes and shook his head. "I'm good." He felt like he was going to throw up, but when the elevator came to a creaking, squealing halt, the doors strained open, and they revealed a long, white hallway with a black carpet covering the floor, and several glass doors and windows on either wall. Jackson huffed and followed the twins, peering through each window as he followed them forward, trying to distract himself; in some, there were labs with doctors and scientists hard at work, and in others were offices and storage rooms.

"Uh…so, what exactly goes on down here?" Jackson asked Amos. He was getting an uneasy feeling, recalling the conversations he'd had with Daimon about being experimented on. This place certainly had the vibe of a facility that conducted the sort of tests he'd been petrified of.

"Depends," Amos said with a shrug. "We've got doctors helping out those of us who got hurt in the Kane fight, as well as taking care of some of our packmates who still haven't recovered from past shit we've been involved in. Sometimes, we get sent high-profile Nosferatu workers; this place is in the middle of nowhere, and believe it or not, probably one of the safer bases. Ain't no one coming to raid us; we're so deep in the mountains that you'd have to be crazy to try and get past all those undead, especially the variants."

"Speaking of variants," Elias muttered as he stopped in front of one of the windows.

Jackson stood beside him and Amos and stared into the laboratory. An infected human corpse was sprawled out on the table, tied down with silver chains, and several doctors were leaning over it and prodding it with scalpels and strange devices that he didn't have the knowledge to name. "What are they doing?" he questioned.

"I dunno," Amos said with a sigh. "Science stuff."

"They're trying to narrow down how the infection spreads," Elias muttered. "To find a cure, you gotta learn everything about the way these things work."

"All right, Mr Genius," Amos mocked. "You should've gone to science school or whatever."

His brother rolled his eyes and continued down the long, white hallway. "Come on. The hospital ward's this way."

"Why are they still trying to find a cure this way if they're sure that what they need is at the lab we're heading to?" Jackson asked, walking beside Amos.

"Well, I suppose just in case it isn't. And the more you know, the better, always," he said matter-of-factly. "For all we know, whatever you find in Greykin Valley might only help with one variant. We thought this virus affected only cadejo—"

"It did affect only cadejo," Elias said as they turned right at the end of the hallway and went through a pair of double doors. "It only started infecting other Caeleste very recently."

Amos frowned. "But what about those undead animals that Seba—"

"They weren't Caeleste."

Jackson frowned, too. "Wait, Sebastien found undead animals?"

"Uh…" Amos drawled.

"Forget it," Elias said warily, looking back over his shoulder at him.

Jackson was sure that Amos had just let slip something he shouldn't have. He knew better than to question them further; he stared ahead and followed the brothers into what looked like a hospital waiting area.

Elias led them to the front desk, where a nurse was slouched back in his seat reading something on his phone. "Where's the muto kid?"

The nurse looked up at him. "Which one?"

Which one? Jackson's frown returned.

"The muto tigris," Amos answered.

With a quiet sigh, the nurse put his phone down and rolled on his chair over to the computer. He typed and clicked for a few moments, and then he said, "Room twenty-four C."

Elias turned to face Jackson. "C's that way," he said, pointing to a pair of double doors with 'C Wing' written above them. "Amos and I are needed in A Wing. If we're not here when you're done, just head back upstairs."

Jackson nodded. "Okay. Where are you guys—"

"Later," Elias said and dragged his brother along with him.

"Okay… bye," Jackson said with a frown.

With a quiet sigh, Jackson turned around and headed towards the doors to C Wing. When he went through them, he emerged into what looked like any standard hospital hallway lined with doors to patient rooms. Doctors and nurses were floating about doing this or that, carrying sheets, food, and medicine. Everyone seemed busy, but to his relief, he wouldn't have to ask where Ethan was. Room 24 was right ahead of him.

He headed for the door, but he still felt sick, and it was starting to worsen again. He huffed quietly in an attempt to deal with it, and once he reached the door, he pushed it open and stepped into the room. Ethan was sprawled out in the hospital bed with bandages wrapped around his waist and torso. An IV was connected to his left arm, and the monitors were beeping steadily, which was a huge relief.

"Oh, hey Jack," Ethan said as he put down the soda can he'd been sipping from. "I didn't think they'd let you see me. Whenever I asked about guests, the nurses were all super dismissive."

Jackson let the door shut behind him and made his way towards the bed. "Are you doing okay? I was worried—"

"Worried about *me*?" He scoffed amusedly. "Can't get rid of me that easily. Apparently, I'm healing up just fine," he said with a cocky smile.

"Well, I'm glad to see you're normal," Jackson said with a quiet laugh as he sat on the edge of the bed. "Honestly, though...are you really okay? The Amarok and that pit. That siren."

Ethan leaned back and relaxed. "I mean...I'm still pretty freaked out. I hoped we wouldn't have to see those faceless freaks again."

"Yeah, I feel that," he said with a huff. "I'm kinda hoping these guys here know more than we do about the variants; it seems like the closer we get to the valley, the more variants pop up. Prowlers, brutes, sirens, and not forgetting the infected humans, too. I'm kinda panicking about what else we're gonna come across."

"Yeah...you're not alone. When they were operating on me—which they did while I was awake for some weird reason—they were asking me all these questions about like...coming into contact with cadejo blood or like...bites and scratches and stuff. One of them even asked me if breathed the same air as like...what did he say..." he paused and frowned as if he was trying to recall a lost memory. "Uh...something about black fog."

"I didn't see any black fog," Jackson said skeptically. "I mean that alone is enough to tell us that they know something we don't."

Ethan nodded in agreement. "You think they'll explain? I mean *we're* the ones heading to the lab; surely they want us to be ready, right? And like...why not tell us before we left Silverlake? It's all a little sus if you ask me."

"That's what I've been thinking," Jackson mumbled, still trying to fight the nausea. "Sebastien didn't even know what that siren was back when we first came across it, and he's supposed to be Lord Caedis' errand boy or something, so if even *he* doesn't know stuff, there's no telling how much we really don't understand. And then on the way here, Amos said something about Sebastien finding infected animals or something, and since this virus is affecting humans now, maybe it's like...evolving into something that's eventually gonna affect *everyone*."

With a haunted expression on his face, Ethan sipped from his soda. "This is fucked, man. How the hell did we get pulled into this?"

Jackson shrugged. "Price of being an illegal hybrid, I suppose."

Ethan put his drink down and sighed deeply. "Any word on when this meeting is happening? I don't know how long I'm supposed to stay down here."

"Didn't anyone tell you?"

"No. No one's even come in here since the nurse delivered my dinner, so I guess I'm supposed to just sit around and wait."

"Do you want me to go and ask?"

Ethan shuffled around a little and said, "I actually kinda wanted to talk about something, and I guess now is just as good a time as any."

Jackson frowned worriedly. "What?"

His friend sighed deeply and looked away as a conflicted expression appeared on his face. "You remember what I said before we broke you out of the arena, right?"

He *did* remember, and now that Ethan's words were rolling around inside his skull again, he tensed up and tried to work out whether he felt uncomfortable or eager for an explanation. "Yeah, I remember," he answered.

Ethan glanced at him. "Well...what do you think?"

"What do you mean, what do I think? I—"

"I didn't just...say it because I was afraid of dying and whatever, I said it because it needed saying, and I already waited too long," Ethan interjected, and he sounded upset. "For all those years, I just kept telling myself that it was never a good time, and by the time I felt ready to tell you, you were already seeing someone else. I didn't wanna be the guy who poured his heart out when you're already with someone, but I just...I couldn't leave it any longer, Jack, especially *now*."

Jackson's heart beat a little faster as confliction gripped him tightly. He didn't want to lose Ethan; he didn't want them to grow apart because he didn't feel the same. He was convinced that Ethan thought he was his demon mate, but Jackson didn't feel the same pull to his friend as he did to Daimon. *Daimon* was his demon mate, he was sure of it. He had to be. Jackson loved him, and he was the only one he wanted to be with.

But he was terrified of losing his best friend. He *did* love Ethan, just not in the way that Ethan loved *him*. He *couldn't* love him like that.

Could he?

Did he?

The more he thought about it, the thicker his confliction grew, and the more confused he felt. What if Ethan was right? What if he *was* his demon mate? What if demons didn't feel the pull of fate that wolf walkers did? What if...what if this confusion and fear and desperation to understand was some sort of sign that maybe Ethan *was* supposed to be more than his best friend?

No….

But what if…?

No.

He frowned in distress and looked away from Ethan. "This is all just…too much right now," he managed to reply. "I don't fully understand any of this demon stuff, but what I *do* know is that I love Daimon, Ethan, and—"

"So? You can love more than one person, Jackson."

"Not like that," he denied, shaking his head as he set his eyes on him again. "I don't…*want* to love more than one person like that."

Ethan scoffed in offence. "Right, I get it—"

"That's not what I meant," Jackson said frustratedly. "I don't…know what's going on, okay? I don't know if I have two mates or one, and there isn't even anyone I can ask because I'm the only one like me."

With a deep, despondent sigh, Ethan sat up and leaned closer to him. "Maybe it isn't up to someone else to tell you. Maybe you need to work it out for yourself, Jack. After all, you're the only one who would know, right?"

Jackson stared at him. "I don't know," he said unsurely. "I feel so many confusing things at once, and I don't—"

Ethan abruptly kissed Jackson's lips, silencing him.

Utterly startled, Jackson stared wide-eyed at him. His mind went blank, and his heart *raced*.

"How did *that* make you feel?" Ethan questioned.

Jackson didn't know the answer to that. He was so shocked that he couldn't even think.

Ethan didn't give him time to try and understand, though. He edged his face closer to Jackson's once again, and he kissed his lips—

But Jackson turned his head away. "No," he said shakily as his heart raced in his chest. "I don't…love you like that, Eth—"

"You *do*," Ethan insisted as he gripped Jackson's jaw and turned his head so that he'd look at his face. "You *have* to, Jack. We've been friends for so long—we're practically already a thing, I mean we *live* together, for God's sa—"

"That doesn't mean I love you, Ethan," Jackson said as he pulled his jaw from his grip and backed off a little. "You're my best friend. Please don't ruin that."

"*Ruin* it?" he scoffed as a scowl appeared on his face. "*You're* the one who's ruining it! You've known me for fucking years, Jack, and you're gonna choose some guy you've known for like two weeks over me?!" he exclaimed.

Jackson scowled, too. "I'm not having this conversation again. I told you how I feel about Daimon, and that's that."

Ethan huffed and looked away, but then he exhaled deeply and adorned a despondent frown as he set his eyes on Jackson again. "You're everything to me, Jack. You've always kept me going, even when I was shipped out here to die. You came *all* the way here to find me, you risked your life for me, and you're gonna tell me that means nothing?"

"Of course it doesn't mean nothing, Ethan. Like I've said a million times, you're my *best* friend—you're like a brother to me—and the only person who stuck with me through all that bullshit with Eric and Eddie."

He shuffled closer as his face grew sadder. "*Exactly*. I was the one who was always there for you no matter what. But I want more than sitting on the sidelines watching some other guy get your full attention. I want more than hearty handshakes and quick, loose little hugs, Jackson, okay? I want…I want…*this*—"

Ethan gripped Jackson's collar and pulled him closer, and when his lips met Ethan's, Jackson went to pull away, but he saw the tears trickling down his friend's face, and it made him feel awful. So he didn't fight him off, but he didn't kiss back, either. He didn't know *what* to do.

But then Ethan moved closer; he kissed Jackson's lips again, and he dragged one of his hands down his body—

"No, Ethan," Jackson refused and pulled away from him. He got off the bed and frowned at his friend. "I—"

"Please," Ethan pleaded as he grabbed Jackson's wrist and tried to pull him closer. "Just…*once*."

Jackson yanked his arm free as guilt, dismay, and discomfort enthralled him. "I said no, Ethan. I don't want you like that, and it isn't going to happen," he said firmly.

Ethan glared at him as if he'd insulted his entire bloodline. But his anger quickly turned to tears, and he rolled over and lay with his back facing Jackson. "Just go," he muttered sadly.

He might usually stay and try to comfort him, but what just happened made Jackson feel so confused and uncomfortable that leaving was probably the best thing for them both right now.

Without another word, he left Ethan's room and headed for the double doors. He started breathing hard; it felt like his chest was being crushed, and his breaths became shorter as he struggled to take each one. He didn't know what was going to happen now. Ethan wanted more, but Jackson didn't, and…he didn't even know what Ethan was trying to do. No…he didn't want to think about it. Why would he do something like that? That didn't seem like Ethan at all….

Jackson exhaled deeply and shook his head, but now that he was up and walking again, the nausea returned, making him grimace. He didn't want to stop and wait for it to pass, though; he just wanted to get back to Daimon.

Before he reached the doors, though, something moved in the corner of his eye, snatching his attention. He stopped walking, staring into the patient room on his right. A smiling couple were staring at a screen while a nurse monitored their baby's heartbeat, and at first, it made Jackson smile, but then it made his blood run cold.

He backed away from the room as his heart started racing, and he frantically searched for a supply room. Once he spotted one by the doors, he walked towards it and glanced around, making sure that no one saw him. Then, he slipped inside and began desperately searching for what he needed.

As he scoured each shelf piled with syringes, thermometers, medication, and bandages, his heart raced faster. And when he found a container of pregnancy tests, he hesitantly grabbed a few and stuffed them into his pocket. He then left the supply room and rushed into the restroom, where he locked himself inside one of the cubicles and slumped down on the toilet. He closed his eyes, placed his head in his hands, and breathed deeply, trying to calm his thumping heart. He didn't want to let the panic consume him in case he was wrong… but he had to be sure.

He took the pregnancy tests out of his pocket, unwrapped them all, and pulled his trousers down. While his heart continued racing, he held each of them between his legs and peed on them, and then he sat there… staring at them, dreading whether he'd seen one or two lines.

He waited…

And waited…

Each test only showed him one line, though.

His racing heart started slowing, and his tense body relaxed—

But then one by one, a second line appeared on each test, and Jackson's heart sunk into his stomach.

He wasn't nauseous and throwing up because of some demon or hybrid thing. He was nauseous and throwing up because he was pregnant.

Chapter Sixty-Nine

⌐ ≪ ☽ ≽ ⌐

Conference Hall

| **Jackson** |

Jackson stared at himself in the mirror as he washed his hands. His heart was racing, his legs were trembling, and he felt so overwhelmed with confliction and the dismay of dysphoria that all he could do was stand there and gaze. He didn't know what he was going to do. He didn't really know how he felt. And he knew that he should tell Daimon, but...how? When? What if Daimon didn't want the same thing as him? What *did* he even want?

He scowled frustratedly and switched the water off, and as he dried his hands, he tried to work out the answers. He tried to work out how it even happened. But he couldn't concentrate. It was like his thoughts hit a brick wall.

And when the bathroom door opened, he flinched, snapping out of it. He watched in the mirror as a nurse headed over to the stalls. With a quiet sigh, Jackson finished drying his hands and left the restroom.

He left C Wing and went into the waiting room; the confliction and dysphoria were creeping back in, making him quietly stifle every few breaths. There was no sign of Elias and Amos, and he wasn't going to wait around. He wanted to see Daimon—he *needed* to see Daimon. And he needed to *tell* Daimon. He had too many secrets locked away and everything that just happened wasn't something he could add to the list. He didn't want Daimon to find out what happened with Ethan from someone else somehow, nor did he want to let his mate discover on his own what Jackson had just found out, and...he needed someone to make him feel something other than what he was currently feeling. Only Daimon could do that.

As he left the elevator and headed through the house, Jackson's racing heart didn't calm down. His discomfort and confusion had been completely devoured by worry and angst, and he was afraid of what Daimon might think or do once he told him what happened. A part of him wondered if he should even tell his mate or if he should tell him about his discovery first, but he didn't want to risk him hearing it from Ethan. *That* would make things a whole lot worse than they already might be. No, he had to tell Daimon himself.

He navigated his way back to the room he'd rested in and followed the hallway the way Daimon had gone when they parted ways. Familiar voices echoed from ahead, and when he emerged into a lounge, he looked around at all of his packmates, as well as Sebastien, who was standing by the fireplace with a Slappy's drink in hand. Where the hell did they get Slappy's out here?

"Oh, hey Jackson," Julian called.

Everyone set their eyes on him, but *he* focused his sights on Daimon. The Alpha was sitting on one of the couches with his son and Tokala, and when he saw Jackson coming, he got up and made his way towards him.

But a concerned frown quickly stole Daimon's look of relief. "What's wrong?" he immediately asked, standing in front of Jackson.

Jackson glanced around at everyone. "Can we, uh... can we go somewhere private? I need to talk to you."

"Did something happen?" he asked worriedly.

He huffed and gripped Daimon's hand. "Can we just go somewhere?"

Daimon nodded and turned around—

"All right, listen up," came Raphael's voice.

Jackson tensed up even more and sharply turned his head to look at the orange-haired guy, who was standing in the doorway with a vacant stare on his face.

"I'll be taking you to the conference hall," Raphael announced. "When you get inside, you sit down where you're told, and you don't speak, nor do you touch anything. You're going to be seeing several new faces sitting at the front of the room; if one of them happens to ask you a question, you stand up and answer. Got it?" he asked, shifting his sights to Jackson.

Everyone nodded.

"Walk single file and don't wander off; the last thing we need is one of you getting lost," the orange-haired man said with a grunt.

"Lost?" Dustu murmured.

"Let's go," Raphael called and started leading the way down the hall.

Jackson waited for a few others to go before him, and as he followed behind Tokala, he held tightly onto Daimon's hand. He was going to have to wait to talk to his mate, and as much as that aggravated him, it also gave him a little relief. At least he'd have more time to work out how to tell him that Ethan had kissed him... and that he was pregnant.

Raphael led them through to the house's entrance hall, and not only was it empty— save for the armed guards—but there was also a circular hole in the marble floor; its edge was glowing gold, and a narrow staircase led down below.

Jackson's anxiety was overshadowed by awe when he followed the stairs down into a *massive* hall. Huge stone pillars at least thirty feet tall connected the ceiling and the ground beneath them, and the massive area was lit by bright, golden fires. The further down they got, the more statues of people and creatures alike were carved into the walls, and the louder the distant crowd of conversation became.

"What the heck is this place?" Remus asked Daimon.

"I don't know," the Alpha replied.

"A Nosferatu stronghold," Sebastien answered, looking back at them. "The kind of place where Caeleste leaders come to discuss the type of shit that's going on in Ascela."

"I thought we just needed to discuss what to do about Kane?" Jackson questioned.

"Yeah, well, there's more to this than Kane," the white-haired demon mumbled and faced ahead again.

What more could they need to discuss right now that required using this kind of place and the presence of Caeletse leaders?

Once they reached the bottom of the stairs, Raphael led them through the colossal stone double doors just ten feet ahead. Inside was a huge, dome-shaped cavern-like room, and there were several rows of seats lined around the walls—it reminded Jackson of Kane's arena.

In the centre of the room was a round table. He immediately noticed Lord Caedis, and sitting on his left was Heir Lucian. The man on his right, however, didn't look familiar, but his aura was just as terrifying as Lord Caedis'. His hair was black, and so were his eyes, but when the light hit them, they shimmered red. He wore dark, elegant clothes just as expensive as Lord Caedis, too—the kind of brands that sold blazers which cost more than Jackson would ever see in his life—so he had to be important, especially if he was sitting *next* to someone like Lord Caedis.

Both the dark-haired man and Lord Caedis then looked at him as he followed his packmates up to a row of seats. His blood ran cold, and he tensed up so much that he felt as if he might freeze on the spot if Daimon wasn't holding his hand so tightly, but even his mate's protective presence couldn't help him shake the intimidation.

And then that man, Lord Caedis, and Heir Lucian muttered to each other. Jackson couldn't hear them over the noise coming from what must be over a hundred people in the room, but he could see their lips moving, and it looked like they were saying his name.

"Sit," Raphael muttered.

Jackson immediately sat in the seat he was standing in front of, as did everyone else.

"Be quiet," the orange-haired man muttered and then headed down the stairs towards the table. He sat beside Heir Lucian, who scowled irritably, and then Cyrus sat beside Raphael.

The room filled up fast; people came in through smaller doorways between each wall of seats, and soon enough, there were probably three hundred or more people staring down at those around the table. Maleki, the elf-vampire, sat beside Cyrus, and two dark-skinned men joined the table, too; one man had orange eyes and a buzzcut, and the other had green eyes and short black hair. Only one of them dressed expensively, though. And the last people to join the table were Idina and three other women who looked a lot like her.

Jackson shifted his eyes to the wall of seats at the back of the room between two large pillars decorated with the carvings of animals and creatures he couldn't name. Every man and woman sitting there looked important; some of them had inhuman features, and one woman even had a pair of dragonfly-like wings. He assumed that *they* were all the Caeleste leaders.

All of the doors started closing on their own, and armed men and women much like those Jackson saw at the entrance up in the house stood around the room. Once the doors shut, everyone's voices died down until it was utterly silent, and the atmosphere was so tense that Jackson felt like he might start suffocating.

Lord Caedis stood up, and everyone set their eyes on him. "Council President Xerxes is currently on business elsevhere, so ve'll be leading zhis meeting in 'is place," he started, glancing at the black-haired man beside him. "You all know vhy you've been called 'ere. Zhe cadejo virus is evolving, and is likely zhat is no long just volf valkers who are in danger of being invected." He pulled a small remote from his pocket, and when he clicked it, a hologram screen appeared in the centre of the room above the table. "Shown 'ere are several variants our operatives 'ave come across in zhe Greykin Mountains," he said as images of prowlers, brutes, and sirens were shown alongside images of infected humans. "Zhe most concerning study so var being zhese sirens," he said as the screens displayed several images of the faceless creatures.

Alarmed murmurs circled the room.

"What are they?" an elf woman called from the wall of leaders.

"Invected vae," Lord Caedis answered.

"Fae?" several voices exclaimed.

"If this virus can infect one of the most resilient species out there, what chance do the rest of us stand?" a panicked man called.

Lord Caedis slid the remote across the table to Doctor Sinclair Laurent, who Jackson hadn't even noticed next to all the rich, intimidating people sitting around it. As Lord Caedis sat down, Sinclair stood up.

"We've tested the virus against the blood of every Caeleste species," Sinclair started as the screens displayed images of cells, some looking a lot worse than others. "So far, the virus has only shown signs of infecting the blood of wolf walkers, humans, and a very specific species of fae." He clicked the remote, and the screens displayed images of very regal-looking men and women with light blue skin and yellow eyes. "The Ascela Chorus—"

"There *is* no Ascela Chorus," the dragonfly-winged woman exclaimed.

"Actually, there is," Sinclair said matter-of-factly. "They're a very private family, so it isn't surprising that a Fae Queen such as yourself isn't aware."

The woman scoffed.

"Although we know *of* them, we don't know much about them. However, it turns out that one of the wolves we've got heading out to Greykin Valley so happens to possess the blood of this particular chorus." Sinclair pointed up towards Jackson's pack.

Everyone quickly diverted their eyes to Wesley, who looked horrified.

"Wesley Ayek-Blood," Sinclair said. "In order for us to find out exactly why this particular kind of fae has been affected, we need to find them. The last contact the Nosferatu had with them was over fifty years ago; they went radio silent and we haven't been able to locate them. Anything you can tell us would be greatly appreciated."

Wesley looked at Daimon, who nodded. He then stood up and said, "I only know what my ancestors did."

"Share," Sinclair invited.

"They lived up in Greykin Loch, and whenever things got bad, they'd head to an underground forest, which they called Sanctuary."

Sinclair shifted his sights to Lord Caedis and the man sitting beside him.

"And how does one find Sanctuary?" the black-haired man asked.

Wesley looked conflicted, like he was reluctant to answer. But he quickly came to a decision and said, "An entrance under the lake. An old archway."

The man then nodded at Sinclair.

Wesley sat down when Sebastien told him to.

"Have you found out why it's suddenly affecting humans like this?" a woman called from the leader wall. "It used to make them sick and kill them. Why is it now turning them?"

"We don't know," Sinclair answered, looking up at her. "But the sample of the virus we gathered a hundred and fifty years ago is *very* different to that which we've been gathering today. And we also don't know if it's evolving on its own or if someone is giving it a helping hand."

"That someone being Lyca Corp. and the Diabolus?" a man questioned.

Maleki then stood up. "Recent intelligence suggests that the Holy Grail might also be involved. They've been spotted in Greykin."

Jackson tensed up. The Holy Grail? The *same* Holy Grail who killed his parents and kidnapped Ethan's? But then he frowned and looked around the hall. Where *was* Ethan?

"Why would the Holy Grail have a hand in modifying a virus that kills the very species they insist they represent?" an elf called.

And then Lord Caedis stood up, and both Maleki and Sinclair sat down. "'As been common knowledge vor a long time zhat zhe 'oly Grail aren't 'ere to protect 'umanity. Zhey serve zheir valse God and zheir own ideations. Vor all ve know, zhey could very vell vant to vipe out every living ving to vestart Aegisguard zhe same vay Levoldus tried to do centuries ago."

The room went silent again, and the tense atmosphere returned.

Lord Caedis returned to his seat.

Sinclair stood up. "We hope that reconnecting with the Ascelan fae will help us understand the virus' evolution a little more. That's all we have until we find them and our wolf walker allies find the Lyca Corp. lab up in Greykin Valley." He sat back down, and the hologram screens disappeared.

Jackson wasn't sure how to feel about this. He knew how important it was to get to the lab, but being reminded of just how many lives were at stake intensified his guilt. There he was worried about dysphoria, losing a friend, and what the man he loved might think because that friend kissed him, meanwhile, people were suffering, dying, and living in fear of being turned into an undead monster.

They *had* to get there...no matter what.

"On zhe subject of zhe lab," Lord Caedis said and looked at Cyrus. "Ve'll get zhis out of zhe vay bevore moving on."

With a nod, Cyrus stood up. "All right, so getting to this lab is still at the top of the important list," he started, resting his hands on the table. "But Kane Ardelean is gonna get in the way. We raided his territory, freed his prisoners, and took someone who might be important to him. He's going to be looking for revenge, and he'll likely start with trying to recapture or kill the pack we've tasked with finding the lab."

"So we have to remove Kane from the equation entirely," Raphael said.

Lord Caedis nodded slowly and remained in his seat. "Volf valkers are endangered, so zhe less of zhem you kill, zhe better. Zhe best vay to deal vith zhis vould be vor you to challenge 'im, no?"

"Yeah," Cyrus confirmed, "but finding him will be hard. He hides behind his numbers."

"Have you spoken to the wolf you rescued from that dungeon?" the black-haired man asked.

"Not yet. I wanted to wait for approval before we started interrogating," Cyrus answered.

"Do it," the man said. "Find out what she knows about him and the way he operates."

Cyrus nodded. "All right. And Daimon's pack?"

"They stay put until Kane is dealt with."

"Got it." Cyrus then stood up straight. "Jackson," he called.

Jackson tensed up. He stared down at Cyrus, and as everyone's eyes hit him, he felt his heart race faster in his chest.

"Stand up," Sebastien snapped quietly.

Jackson shot to his feet and tried to hide his trembling hands behind his back.

Cyrus frowned slightly. "My wolves spoke in their reports of you *talking* to cadejo; you told them to leave, and they left."

Several murmurs and whispers echoed through the hall.

"We need to know more about that," Cyrus continued. "What were they saying to you? Did you learn anything that might help us?"

Jackson's entire body trembled. "Uh...it...well—"

"Speak up," Raphael called.

He raised his voice a little, gasping onto his confidence as tightly as recent events would allow him. "T-they said something about...their Master."

"Master?" the black-haired man questioned.

Jackson nodded. "They said that...well, the *prowler* kept saying that *the* Master wanted me...and that it had to take me...but not yet."

"Can you control them?" a woman from the leader wall asked.

"I...I think so," he replied. "When the prowler initially pulled me out of the snow I was hiding under, I told it to wait because it sounded like it wanted to kill me, and it waited. And after it was done telling me about how it had to take me to the Master, I told it to leave and kill Kane's wolves—the ones following me—and...it did," he explained.

More murmurs and whispers travelled around the room.

"You were standing there for a while, though," Cyrus said over the other voices. "What else were you talking about?"

Jackson recalled the memory. "Well...it said that...it listened to me because I'm a higher lifeform or something. And that it itself was imperfect...and that *I* was perfect—a harmonic variant. After that was when it started talking about its Master wanting me. They also confirmed that they were made with demon blood if that's any help."

Everyone around the table started muttering quietly. The concerned expressions on their faces made Jackson feel a whole lot more uneasy than he already did, and he wasn't sure what to make of it.

"The cadejo have a leader?" someone questioned worriedly over the crowd.

"Someone's been pulling the strings this whole time?" someone else called.

"Can Lyca Corp. actually control these things?" a woman asked in a panic.

Lord Caedis then stood up, and everyone went quiet. He said, "Ve've suspected vor a vhile zhat somevone vas pulling strings. 'As been very odd zhat cadejo 'ave been appearing in very convenient places, and Jackson 'as convirmed zhat zhese creatures answer to somevone. Ve'll be pulling vhat vesources ve can vrom ozzer operations so zhat ve can try and vind zhis Master."

"Resources from where?" a man protested. "All of our specialists and armies are strapped as thin as possible right now."

"No one has to worry about it," the black-haired man beside Lord Caedis answered. "We'll handle it on our end."

"Zhe only ving all of you should be doing vight now is keeping your people safe and vatching your perimeters. As var as ve are avare, zhe virus 'asn't levt Ascela, but if zhat changes, ve need to know."

"Why are we even still here?" an elf exclaimed as he stood up. "We should just head beyond the glaciers and leave these undead things to starve and eventually turn on Lyca Corp.! Why are we even still talking about this?!"

Beyond the glaciers? Jackson glanced at Sebastien, but the white-haired demon shook his head with a wary look on his face.

"The land is underdeveloped and in many cases not suitable for living to any standard or comfort that the average person needs," the black-haired man said.

"Who is that guy?" Julian asked. *Finally* someone did.

"Zalith," Sebastien replied. "Otherwise known as the Zenith."

Jackson frowned. *That* was the Zenith? *That* was Lord Caedis' mate?

"So make it suitable!" the elf insisted.

Zalith frowned irritably and said, "Well, when you have the money to fund a few continents' worth of development, plus what it costs to relocate billions of people *and* provide them with healthcare manufacturing and necessities, we'd love to get started."

The elf scoffed and slumped down in his seat.

And then Lord Caedis said, "Ve're not just going to abandon Aegisguard. As ve 'ave said, zhe virus is still contained to Ascela. Zhe moment ve 'ave vhat ve need to create a cure, zhis vill all be over."

After a few seconds, the murmurs and whispers died down again.

But despite Sebastien's expression, Jackson's curiosity hadn't waned. Beyond the glaciers: what did that mean? And what continents were they talking about? As far as Jackson was aware, every continent was habitable.

Zalith looked at Cyrus and said, "Take the pack and deal with the Kane situation. Zephyr, go with him."

Cyrus and Raphael got up, and as they made their way towards the huge double doors, Sebastien stood up, too.

"Come on, that's us," the white-haired demon said.

On his word, the pack stood up and started following him down the stairs.

Jackson focused on the crowd, though. They started asking for more reasons as to why they couldn't leave Aegisguard and start anew. He had questions—of course he did—but there were already so many things that he needed answering that his curiosity about continents beyond some glaciers would have to wait.

Chapter Seventy

A Few Hours' Rest

| Jackson |

Cyrus explained his war plans to everyone, and Lumi, the fox-wolf Jackson and Ethan had rescued—who now appeared as a small, shy girl with long, icy hair and dark blue eyes—told him why each approach wouldn't work. So Cyrus quickly came up with another plan one after the other, evidently hoping that Lumi would eventually tell him that he was on the right track.

However, every word either of them said went in one of Jackson's ears and out the other. He couldn't concentrate; all he could think about was what happened in the medical wing. Usually, he might be stuck pondering over what he learned in the conference hall; he'd be thinking about the evolving virus, the Zenith, whatever beyond the glaciers meant, and the leaders that he saw inside, but no... his mind was trapped reliving the moment his best friend kissed him... and the moment every single test strip told him that he was pregnant.

He hadn't had a chance to tell Daimon, and he wasn't sure when he'd get one. It was 4 a.m. already, and after this meeting, it seemed like everyone would be heading off to get some rest before the fight. Maybe *then* he'd get to tell his mate what happened.

Cyrus then sighed loudly and said, "Guy's clearly gotten a lot smarter since the last time we faced each other."

Lumi wriggled around in her chair and nodded in agreement.

"Okay, so we take Maleki," Raphael said as he leaned on Lumi's chair.

"Nah," Cyrus said, shaking his head. "If we show up with anything but wolves in our midst, he has every right to turn down my challenge." He looked down at the map on the table and shifted his eyes from each of the pins Lumi had marked Kane's hiding places with. "Numbers are gonna help us in most situations, but if he's in this narrow gully formation, he could attack from any angle and have the advantage."

Daimon then asked, "How do we find which place he's at without alerting him?"

Cyrus tapped his chin while he pondered, and then he looked at Raphael. "You think Alucard will let us use some of those bird things?"

"The căutător," Raphael muttered irritably. "And I don't know. I'll ask him after he's done in the conference hall."

"What's a căutător?" Lalo asked.

Cyrus answered, "They're these little demon things that Alucard created. There's these crow-looking ones that act like little drones and scour miles of territory in minutes."

"And if we can't use them?" Elias asked.

"We'll figure something else out," Cyrus answered. "All right, we can't really come up with much of an attack plan until we know where Kane is, so just take the next few hours to get some rest. I'll send someone to get you all when it's time to get ready. There's a bunch of spare rooms on the second floor, so go take your pick."

As Cyrus left the room with Raphael and Lumi, everyone else started mumbling and heading for the door.

Jackson was relieved that he'd be able to get some more rest, but he wasn't sure that he'd get any. He had to tell Daimon…and now was probably the only chance he'd get. He followed the pack out and up to the second floor, and once he and Daimon picked out a room, his heart started racing. He felt anxious and hesitant; however, he wasn't going to convince himself that it was better left unsaid until later.

Daimon pulled the curtains shut and slumped down on the bed with a deep sigh. He then looked at Jackson—who was still standing by the door—and frowned strangely. "What's wrong?" he asked.

He twiddled his fingers together and tried to fight his anxiety, but it was getting harder to breathe, and all he could say was, "I…need to tell you something."

The Alpha sat up. "Tell me what?" He sounded worried.

Jackson exhaled heavily and crossed his arms. "When I went to see Ethan, I…well…something happened."

Daimon's frown thickened. "What happened?"

His heart raced so fast that he felt as if it might break free from his chest. He tried to pull the words together, but he couldn't. Maybe he should have brought one of the tests with him and just given that to Daimon. But his mate would have questions, and he didn't have the answers. Maybe he should talk to a doctor first. Maybe he should just wait until after the mission. Telling Daimon could distract him from the objective, and that was the last thing he wanted to do.

"Jackson?" the Alpha questioned.

He exhaled deeply and instead shifted his thoughts to what happened with Ethan. His fear that Daimon was moments from charging out of the room with murder in his eyes urged him to either find the perfect words—words which would keep Daimon from losing it—or just lie. No... not lie. Tell him something else. But he wasn't sure that Daimon would believe him.

No, he didn't want to avoid it.

Jackson sighed. "I... well...." He paused and made his way towards Daimon. He sat beside his mate, and as he looked down at his lap, he let out another deep exhale. "Just promise me that you won't get mad—w-well... you're gonna get mad, so just... please don't go on a rampage."

Daimon scoffed confusedly. "What are you talking about?"

Jackson looked at his confounded face. "Ethan... kissed me."

The confusion immediately faded from Daimon's face, and a dangerous, *infuriated* look warped it—

He grabbed Daimon's wrist. "Please don't—"

Daimon snarled angrily and stood up, but Jackson tugged him back before he could try to head for the door.

"It meant nothing, okay?" Jackson insisted. "And I made sure that he knows that."

He pulled his arm free and stormed towards the door. "I'm going to kill that fucking—"

"Daimon!" he insisted as he hurried after him and grabbed his arm again.

The Alpha stopped and looked at him with a furious huff.

"He's just... confused or something. We all went through a whole lot of shit when we were in Kane's arena—he thought that we were gonna die. And I guess it just... I don't know! Just please don't hurt him," he pleaded.

But Daimon wasn't convinced. "That piece of shit has been taunting me since day one," he snarled, glaring at Jackson. "And now he thinks that he can *touch* you?! I have every fucking right to rip his insides out and make him swallow them!"

Jackson grimaced at the thought of it and shook his head. "I'm mad at him too, okay?" he said, trying to pull Daimon away from the door. "I don't know why he thought it was okay or what would happen, but you can't hurt him. He's still my friend, and—"

"He clearly wants more than that," he growled.

"Well, he's not going to get it," Jackson said firmly. "And I made sure that he gets that. Maybe... maybe it had something to do with all the meds he's on from his surgery or something—maybe he got confused."

Daimon scoffed again, but he was calming down—at least Jackson hoped he was.

Jackson exhaled and slowly pulled the Alpha back towards the bed. "Maybe now that I've told him exactly how I feel, he won't be so weird and rude around you," he said as he sat down and pulled Daimon with him.

The Alpha slumped beside him with an angry huff. He scowled aimlessly for a few moments, but then he shook his head and snarled. "No, he needs to be taught a fucking less—"

Before Daimon could get up, Jackson pushed him down on his back and straddled his lap. "Please," he implored. "Just...let it go."

Daimon glared up at him. "Let it go? How the hell am I supposed to let something like this go?"

Jackson pondered for a moment, but he didn't really have an answer. However, he *did* know how to take Daimon's mind off it. If he could distract him, then maybe he'd calm down enough for them to have a proper conversation about it. He shrugged and dragged his hand down the Alpha's chest and to his waist. "I don't know," he answered. "Maybe I can take your mind off it?"

Daimon huffed and turned his head to the left, but when Jackson gripped the bulge in the Alpha's trousers, his mate tensed up, and the irritated scowl on his face lifted a tiny bit.

Jackson smiled deviously as he stroked Daimon's dick. "Maybe I can remind you that I'm all yours," he said quietly.

The Alpha looked conflicted; however, with each stroke of Jackson's hand, the fury on his face lessened. He frowned, he grunted, and he exhaled angrily, but then he growled frustratedly and abruptly grabbed Jackson's shoulders. He rolled over with him and pinned Jackson on his back, and after an aggressive huff, he started kissing him.

Jackson tensed up as anticipation spiralled through him. He felt a little guilty using sex to distract him, but he wanted it, and he wanted to make sure that Daimon understood that he was his and only his. He returned each of the Alpha's kisses, and when their tongues entwined, he moved his hand into Daimon's trousers and grasped his dick.

An eager growl carried upon Daimon's breath as he stopped kissing him and nuzzled his neck. Jackson hastily pulled the Alpha's trousers off, and they quickly undressed one another. They started kissing again; Jackson moved one leg over Daimon's back and caressed his shaft with one hand, and with the other, he gripped a fistful of his mate's hair. Desperation enthralled him when Daimon's fingers met his t-dick, and as his mate skilfully rubbed his arousal, Jackson sunk into the delight, and everything he was worried about faded away.

But Daimon was clearly battling with his patience. Just a few moments later, the Alpha pressed the tip of his dick against Jackson's pussy, and Jackson used his legs to pull Daimon closer, urging him to slip inside. Daimon complied; he slowly moved his shaft into Jackson's body, and they both moaned quietly in content.

"You're so fucking tight," Daimon breathed as he pinned Jackson's arms above his head, and then he slowly pulled back.

Jackson exhaled deeply and smiled—

Daimon abruptly thrusted deep into him, making him exclaim pleasurably. The Alpha laughed quietly in response and then started thrusting, nuzzling Jackson's neck as he hummed contently.

Jackson tightened his grip on Daimon's hair and moaned in relief and satisfaction as the pleasure spiralled through his tense body. *This* was *exactly* what he needed; a break from his overwhelming emotions, a break from all the worry and despair and confliction.

The Alpha sped up. His thrusts became more aggressive with each plunge, and Jackson couldn't help but cry out in sheer delight. And then Daimon tightened his grip and growled against Jackson's neck, "You're mine."

Jackson's heart raced in his chest. He wrapped his legs around Daimon's waist and whined contently, "Yes!"

Daimon lightly clamped his jaw down on Jackson's shoulder and thrusted harder and faster. Jackson moaned and whined as the pleasure quickly became too much for him to handle. He could feel himself approaching his peak—

"Say it," Daimon demanded and gently bit Jackson's ear.

He panted and tried to find his voice, and with a moan upon his breath, he replied, "I'm yours."

The Alpha snarled and bit Jackson's neck. "You're *mine*," he growled possessively.

"I'm... y—fuck, fuck!" he cried as his body reached its limit. He whined feverishly as he climaxed, his walls tightening around Daimon's hard dick.

Daimon kept thrusting, moaning against Jackson's neck. "Where do you want it?" he breathed.

Jackson asked himself if there was any point in telling Daimon to pull out; it wasn't like he could get him twice as pregnant, right? "Inside," he murmured. Maybe Daimon would take it as a hint or a sign and Jackson wouldn't have to work out how to tell him.

"You're sure?" his mate asked with a desperate groan.

He nodded.

Daimon moaned as he sped up, thrusting deep and hard, and when the Alpha pushed deep into Jackson one last time, he whined in relief, and Jackson felt his dick throbbing inside him. An overwhelming feeling of satisfaction consumed him as he felt his mate's cum ooze into him, and he couldn't help but hum contently. For a moment, the pleasure and satisfaction banished his confliction again.

The Alpha exhaled deeply against Jackson's neck as he slowly pulled his dick out, and then he lifted his head to look down at him. The Alpha smiled, and Jackson smiled back, and when Daimon kissed his lips, Jackson relaxed his legs and ran his fingers through his mate's hair.

"I love you," Jackson said quietly.

"I love you, too," Daimon replied and kissed his lips again.

When the Alpha lay beside him, Jackson rested his head on Daimon's chest, and after a deep, relieved sigh, he closed his eyes and relaxed. He wanted to hold on to this feeling of serenity; even if it was just for a few minutes, he wanted to continue ignoring his worries.

But as the silent minutes passed by, Jackson's euphoria faded, and Ethan crept back into his head. He didn't want to think about it.

"How long do you think this Kane stuff is gonna take?" he asked Daimon.

The Alpha exhaled deeply. "I don't know. It could be over in a day, or it could take a week. I wanted to suggest leaving Cyrus to deal with it and clear a path for us, but I don't want to risk that plan not working. This'll probably be over faster with us helping, and Cyrus definitely has the numbers to face Kane's pack, but I don't know Cyrus well enough to feel confident that he can beat Kane."

"He's got demon stuff or something, too, right?" Jackson asked.

"He does, and he confirmed that Fenrisúlfr is both our ancestor, but I'm so far down the line that the demon blood was eventually bred out of us Greybloods. But if he's anywhere near as powerful as Raphael, then maybe he will stand a chance."

Jackson wasn't surprised to hear that Fenrisúlfr was Daimon's ancestor; after the name Greymore was thrown around so much, and everything he heard while at the Venaticus building, it was pretty much as clear as day, but Daimon had confirmation now, and he was glad for him. "So, is Greymore where you're getting all your ancestral knowledge from?"

"I still don't know. But we talked about Tokala, too. He might be able to access the Redblood ethos, and if he can, then our chances of getting through the mountains would be a whole lot better. I need to talk to him and Raphael, but I don't know when I'll have the time. Maybe before the meeting," the Alpha mumbled.

"Yeah, I mean…Raph—Heir Zephyr…I don't really have the words," Jackson fumbled. "He can heal people, he's crazy strong; if Tokala could do that kinda stuff, then…yeah, we'll be a whole lot safer out there."

Daimon sighed and tightened his embrace around him. "We can work it all out later. Let's just get some rest while we can."

Jackson nodded in agreement. He didn't want to think right now; he just wanted to lay there, rest, and enjoy Daimon's embrace. But it wouldn't last forever. In a few hours, they'd be planning their attack on Kane, and Ethan would also likely be out of the hospital.… He didn't know how he felt about that. He wasn't ready to face him, nor was he ready for the shitstorm that was going to erupt when the muto and Daimon came face to face.

Chapter Seventy-One

The Redblood Line

| Daimon |

Daimon couldn't sleep. He lay awake as the hours passed by; all he could think about was how much he wanted to rip Ethan apart. He seethed and scowled, trying to resist the urge to get up because Jackson asked him not to act on his anger and possessive, protective instincts... but how could he just fucking lay there and do *nothing* after that filthy, pathetic little muto *kissed* his mate?

He gritted his teeth and clenched his jaw. No matter how much he tried to focus on the fact that Jackson and his feelings mattered more to him than his own, he couldn't stop thinking about all the ways he wanted to make Ethan suffer. He wanted to rip his tongue out so he couldn't say another word to Jackson; he wanted to break every bone in his hands so that he couldn't touch Jackson, and he wanted to gouge his eyes out and shove them down his throat so that he couldn't so much as lay eyes on his mate, and only when he was on the very urge of bleeding out would he end his miserable life.

With a conflicted scowl, he looked down at Jackson, who was sleeping silently beside him with his head on his chest. He didn't want to do something that would hurt and upset the man he loved... but he couldn't just lay there knowing that someone else had touched and kissed his mate. He couldn't ignore the growing desire to do what he had every right to do.

He tried and tried and tried to ignore it... but when the clock struck eight, he gave in. He couldn't fight it—he didn't *want* to. Ethan deserved what Daimon was about to give him, and not only because he kissed his mate, not long ago, Ethan also *hurt* Jackson— he lashed out—and Daimon wouldn't let anything like that happen again. He'd not leave someone in his midst who wanted Jackson, someone who evidently didn't give a shit that Jackson was mated.

Daimon got out of bed. He looked back at Jackson as he got dressed and before he left the room, but any hesitation he had withered away. He was doing this *for* Jackson. The sooner Ethan was gone, the sooner things would be better for *everyone*. And it wasn't like they needed him; Lucian had already extracted the lab's location from Ethan's mind, and even if he didn't have *exact* coordinates, Daimon was capable of finding the place once they reached the general area.

He navigated the halls of the still, silent mansion. It seemed like everyone was asleep, so getting to Ethan would hopefully be easier.

When he reached the main hall, he made his way to the elevator and pressed the button. He waited for it to arrive, watching as the dial above the doors slowly shifted from number to number. But he quickly became impatient. His anger and frustration grew with each passing second, and his hands ached to get around Ethan's neck. He was going to make him wish he'd never so much as *thought* he'd have Jackson.

The elevator arrived, and the doors slid open—

"There you are," came Raphael's voice.

Daimon sharply turned his head and set his eyes on the orange-haired man. "What?" he snapped confusedly.

"Cyrus said you and your little Redblood friend had questions, and since I'm waiting for Strămoş Luca to finish doing whatever he's doing, I thought I'd get it out of the way." He stopped beside Daimon and glanced at the elevator. "Going somewhere?"

The Alpha glared into the elevator; he tensed up as his anger and desperation to protect Jackson urged him forward. He wanted to do it—he *had* to do it—

"Hello?" Raphael drawled, waving his hand in Daimon's face.

Daimon snarled irritably. His anger shifted towards Raphael, but it was just as well. Despite his instincts, his right, and his emotions, he knew that if he did this…Jackson might not forgive him. As much as he wanted to make Ethan pay…he shouldn't. So he sighed and stepped away from the elevator. "Has Cyrus found out where Kane is yet?"

"Nope. The căutător are still out searching."

"So what are you waiting on Alucard for?"

Raphael got defensive. "That's my business."

The Alpha scoffed, and when the elevator doors shut, he sighed and turned to face Raphael. "Tokala's upstairs in one of the rooms."

"Actually he's in one of the lounges. Elias caught him snooping around in the winter study—a place no one is supposed to go," Raphael said as he crossed his arms. "Said he was looking for information about the Greyblood line…for you."

Daimon frowned strangely. But he wasn't completely surprised that Tokala would want to help him. "Is Lucian going to break his leg, too?" he asked with a snarl.

Raphael scoffed. "That's for you to decide. This way." He turned around and started walking back the way he'd come.

Daimon followed him through the corridor and past Cyrus' office. When they reached a lounge—which was deserted apart from Tokala, who was sitting on the couch in front of the fireplace—Raphael invited Daimon to sit next to his Zeta and slumped down in the armchair.

"So?" Raphael mumbled impatiently. "Talk."

The Alpha sat down.

Tokala cleared his throat and said, "I really was just looking for information on Alpha Daimon's bloodline."

"That's not what we're here for," Raphael muttered. "Your Alpha wants to know about *our* bloodline."

The Zeta frowned confusedly. "Oh... okay."

Daimon turned to face him. "Did your mother ever teach or tell you about the power that comes with your bloodline?"

Tokala scratched the side of his face and shook his head. "No. To be honest, I didn't even know the wolves in my line could do the kinds of things you do," he said, glancing at Raphael.

"Cyrus already told you that if our power isn't practised and mastered before a certain age, it can become very stubborn and hard to wake up," Raphael said to Daimon. He shifted his sights to Tokala. "So, if you want to tap into it, it's going to be near impossible, and it'll take more time than we have here for me to teach you."

"Well... I've managed all my life without it," Tokala said, glancing at Daimon. "And if we don't have time, I won't make us stick around so—"

"It could be an incredible asset," Daimon interjected. "And with the increasing cadejo threat, we could do with as many upper hands as we can get."

But to Daimon's confusion, Tokala looked hesitant.

"You're also quite far down the line," Raphael said. "Our blood doesn't weaken as fast as the Greyblood line did, but you're going to have a much smaller number of ethos copias, which will limit what you're capable of."

"So it's possible that I'm not even capable of anything at all," Tokala mumbled. "Right?"

"No," Raphael disagreed. "Like I said, our line is stronger. Strămoș Luca is a Numen, and Numen blood is the strongest kind you'll find in any of the worlds. It doesn't weaken easily, and it doesn't dilute when mixed with the blood of other Caeleste, either. You could be the hundredth generation and you'd still have enough of Strămoș Luca's ethos to use the abilities our line can access."

Tokala looked increasingly uncomfortable, and it only just hit Daimon *why*. He knew that Tokala and his mother distanced themselves from the clan of Redbloods they were related to, and talking about it like this must be upsetting him. But Daimon wanted what was best for his pack, and as a Zeta, Tokala should want the same.

He *was* curious about one thing, though. "Do the Eclipse Redbloods have access to different abilities?" he asked Raphael.

"In terms of Strămoș Luca's ethos, no. But they've been involved in so much cultish and dark shit over the years that we don't really know what they've gained access to now. My sister is trying to reason with them and get them to talk to Strămoș Luca, but the last we heard, it's not going so well, and they've somehow managed to find a way to see through her cloaking ethos, which should be impossible," he explained with a pondering tone.

Tokala then sighed deeply. "Look, I don't want to be rude, but my mother left that life behind for a reason. If I start using the ethos that she tried to spare me from, then I'd be making all of her sacrifices for nothing."

Daimon hadn't considered that. From the stories he heard, he knew that Tokala's mother went through a great ordeal to escape from the Redbloods, and he didn't want to order Tokala to make all of that meaningless. But it *wouldn't* be meaningless, would it? Tokala would be using that power to help people instead of feeding his own ego and climbing his way to some sort of superior pinnacle like the Crescent Redbloods seemed to be doing. Still, he wouldn't demand it... but he *did* expect Tokala to come to this conclusion himself.

Raphael's pondering expression returned. "Did she ever tell you about the Eclipse Redbloods?"

Tokala shrugged uncomfortably. "A little."

"Such as?"

He huffed and leaned back. "The Redblood Trials, and the reason they went off on their own in the first place. I didn't even know this Alucard Numen was connected to my line."

Raphael sighed irritably and said, "Well, if you decide that you want to learn, I can tell and teach you what I can before you guys go off to find the lab."

Tokala shook his head. "I don't."

"Think about it," Daimon said firmly.

The Zeta frowned strangely at him. "I'm not going to change my mind, chief. I'm sorry."

Daimon sighed quietly and set his eyes on him again. "Your mother wanted to spare you from the cult and dark ethos; if you were to use your Redblood power for something like ensuring that we got to the lab where the answers to a cure to the cadejo virus could be, she wouldn't feel betrayed, Tokala. You'd be saving not only us but the rest of the Caeleste out here."

Tokala sighed and shook his head. "I understand what you're saying, but I just... can't."

"I don't blame you," Raphael muttered. "But Daimon's right. You guys need all the help you can get out there. Even without the cadejo prowling around, the mountains are a dangerous place."

The Zeta's discomfort was quickly accompanied by frustration. "We've got Jackson," he insisted.

"But Jackson is just a hybrid—"

"An asmodi demon," Tokala cut Raphael off. "He's got access to *two* Numen's ethos."

"It's not the same," Raphael said, crossing his arms. "Blood is stronger than ethos. Jackson's Caederian ethos is like a pinhead next to a fucking moon. He can punch someone through a wall, *you* could probably punch someone through several buildings."

But Tokala wasn't at all tempted. He shook his head again. "I don't want it, okay? I'm sorry." He got up and left the room.

Daimon let him go.

"So much for that," Raphael mumbled. "Aren't you gonna go after him?"

"I'm not going to force him to do something he doesn't want to," Daimon said with a roll of his eyes. "I'll give him time to see if he changes his mind, and if he doesn't, we'll manage."

"At least you have Sebastien to count on."

"Hmm," he mumbled. "What *is* Alucard planning to do with Tokala's Eclipse relatives?"

Raphael sighed deeply and stared into the fireplace. "Well, they're his descendants, so he wants to try and come to some sort of agreement with them; offer them sanctuary, help them find what they're looking for, that sort of thing. But they're getting dangerously close to both Strămoş Luca's and Strămoş Zalith's limit. They're using forbidden spells and ethos, they've murdered countless Caeleste and humans, and my Strămoş' are worried that they might soon forge alliances with the Diabolus."

"And that's a huge problem because…?"

"Because the Diabolus are another cult of crazy fucking psychos who use dark and dangerous ethos. They've been trying for centuries to resurrect Lucifer, and if they get a hold of a Redblood close enough to Strămoş Luca, they might just be able to do it. We can't have that."

Daimon had heard stories about Lucifer; that long-dead Numen was Alucard's father, and to become a full Numen, Alucard had killed Lucifer and absorbed his power, so bringing Lucifer back probably involved *killing* Alucard, and Daimon didn't want that to happen because then the Nosferatu would be weaker and the chances of finding a cure would drastically drop. But it wasn't like there was anything that *he* could do to help.

"Anyway, you just focus on getting to the lab after we're finished with this Kane business," Raphael said as he sat up straight. "Is there anything else or can I go?"

He didn't have any burning questions to ask. All he could think about was how he hoped Tokala would change his mind…and how he still wanted to tear Ethan apart. He shifted his sights to Raphael and shook his head. "That's it. But if Tokala agrees, how long will it take for you to teach him enough so that he doesn't lose control of his power?"

"It varies from person to person. I don't know what abilities he has, nor do I know how well he'll handle it. But if he wants to learn, I'll do what I can with whatever time we get."

Daimon nodded and said, "Thanks. I appreciate it."

Raphael nodded and stood up. "I don't think it's going to be much longer until we're ready to talk about a plan, so get as much rest as you can." He then left the room.

The Alpha sighed deeply and glanced around. But he didn't want to sit there too long and let the silence encourage his anger, so he got up and started making his way back to the room where he'd left Jackson. He hadn't gotten *any* sleep yet, and he knew that if he didn't at least try to get some rest before it was time to head out, he might not be able to focus as much as he needed to. He needed to be alert and ready out there; he wasn't going to let any more of his packmates get hurt… or worse.

Chapter Seventy-Two
⌐ ≤ ☽ ≥ ⌐
Demon Name

| **Jackson** |

A voice murmured to Jackson.

"Salvator..." it drawled, sounding like a snake. "You're... the one."

Jackson didn't know where he was, and he couldn't find whoever was speaking. There was darkness in every direction, and he felt almost as if he was floating around... maybe he was sinking in an ocean, but as the voice called to him, a horrible sense of unease grasped him.

"Salvator..." it called again, closer this time.

He looked around, searching for them.

The darkness suddenly shifted.

As the pitch black twisted around and lit up with purple and red, Jackson was tugged down so fast that he didn't have a chance to try and find something to hang onto. It pulled him down, further and further and further—

He hit the floor with a grunt, and as he scrambled to his feet, the world formed around him; dark shadows spewed down from above like ink dripping in water and morphed into four black walls, old oak furniture and closed, draping curtains. The gloomy place smelled damp and dusty, and several loud bells rang in the distance. Church bells?

"Salvator," the voice said once more, but this time, it was much clearer... and right behind him.

Jackson swung around and set his eyes on the man standing behind an altar, upon which lay candles, animal skulls, dried herbs, and bottles of glowing liquids. The man's vestments were purple and harrowingly familiar, as was the silver rosary around his neck. Deep violet eyes glowed behind his silver mask, which, along with his hood, shrouded his entire face. And the stench of wolfsbane grew stronger the longer Jackson stood there staring at him.

This man was of the Holy Grail; he looked just like the ones Jackson saw in his memory of the night his father died.

Fear struck him so hard that he stifled a breath and stumbled as he backed off. He tried to work out where and when he was, but this didn't feel like a memory. He couldn't smell the air when he remembered things, and he couldn't freely walk around, either— he couldn't back off... which he kept doing when the man raised a hand and lit another black candle with a wave of his palm.

"I've been searching for you for a long time," the masked man said as he crossed his arms, hiding his hands in his long sleeves.

Jackson's heart raced in his chest. His instincts were telling him that he needed to get as far away from this place as possible, but when he looked around, there wasn't a single door in sight, and that made him panic.

"There's no way out this time," the man taunted him. "No one to protect you, no mercenary to hide you."

He was talking about his parents and Eric, wasn't he? Jackson scowled at the masked man, and when his back hit the wall and he realized that he couldn't back off anymore, his panic was accompanied by desperation. Was he going to have to fight?

The man started creeping out from behind the altar. "You belong to us—to me," he claimed, reaching his hand towards Jackson as he approached him. "No one will stop us this time, not now that we know where you are—"

"Who the hell are you?!" Jackson blurted.

With a snide laugh, the man stopped ten feet in front of him and extended a bony finger, pointing at Jackson. "You know."

He didn't know. He'd never seen this man before... unless....

"I could have had you," he said as he buried his hand in his robes again. "I could have... grabbed you."

Jackson tensed up and stifled another breath. Was this the man who was calling 'Salvator' out of the darkness by the cadejo pit? "W-what do you want?" he asked shakily.

The man laughed. "You, creature. I want you." He burst forward and snatched Jackson's collar, and he glared into his soul with his bright purple eyes as Jackson panicked and tried to escape, but the man was so much stronger than he was. "You're the key to everything!" he growled, lifting Jackson up off his feet. "And we won't lose you again—"

"Jackson!" came Daimon's panicked voice.

Jackson opened his eyes, finding himself in the bedroom in Reiner Manor surrounded by *everyone*.

And standing over him was *Lord Caedis*. He took his clawed hand off Jackson's head and stepped back to where Raphael and Sebastien were standing.

The pack looked horrified, and Daimon pulled Jackson into a tight hug before he had a chance to ask what the hell was going on. A flurry of concerned questions came from his packmates, but it was what Lord Caedis, Sebastien, and Raphael were mumbling which had Jackson's attention.

"Is it bad?" Raphael asked.

"Zhey vere trying to pull 'im into a soul prison. Zhey knew 'is zemon name, vhich gives zhem a lot more power over 'im," Lord Caedis replied.

"How did they find his demon name?" Sebastien questioned.

"I zon't know," Lord Caedis replied. "But ve can't visk zhem getting 'im like zhat again."

"Jackson?" Daimon asked worriedly.

Jackson shook his head and pulled out of Daimon's hug so that he could see his mate's face.

The Alpha frowned. "Are you okay?"

He exhaled deeply and nodded.

"What the hell was that?" Julian asked as if they and nobody else had understood what Lord Caedis was just talking to Raphael and Sebastien about.

Before anyone could answer, though, Jackson set his eyes on Lord Caedis and asked him, "What's a demon name?"

"Every demon has one," Raphael answered.

"Demon names are our true names," Sebastien added. "And our other names—mine, for example: Sebastien—are the names we go by in this world, names that other Caeleste use for us."

"Like Alucard," Cyrus said, nodding at Lord Caedis. "Caedis is his demon name."

Sebastien continued, "Our demon names are only used in official cases…say you were going to Daevor or something…or addressing someone of higher ranking, like Lord Caedis."

"So…Lucian's demon name is Lucian?" Julian muttered.

Raphael scoffed. "No, he just prefers to be difficult. It makes him feel special."

Jackson was still confused. "What the hell was going on? Where was I?"

This time, Lord Caedis answered, "Zhe 'oly Grail vere trying to lure you into a soul prison; zhey vould trap your aura and later vecover your body, vhich is much easier zhan capturing you vhile you're conscious. Zhey vere using a very dark ethos vhich vequires zhem to know your zemon name—Salvator. I zon't know vhere zhey vound out, but now zhat zhey know, ve're going to 'ave to take even 'igher precautions to ensure zhis mission is a success and zhat zhe 'oly Grail zon't get zheir 'ands on you."

"Why do they want him?" Tokala asked before Jackson or Daimon could.

"Why would any of our enemies want him?" Raphael scoffed. "He's a *created* hybrid; he might be the key to curing and stopping the cadejo virus altogether. Can you imagine what the Diabolus or Lyca Corp. could do if they had him?"

Lord Caedis sighed deeply. "I broke zhe link in time, but I can't babysit you in case zhis 'appens again." He looked at Raphael. "You're going vith zhem to zhe lab. You're zhe only ozzer available person who can counter zhat sort of ethos."

Raphael looked like he was going to complain, but he held his tongue and crossed his arms. "Yeah, fine."

Jackson shuffled around uncomfortably, and when Daimon held and squeezed his hand, he glanced and smiled at the Alpha as best he could. But he was still anxious. The Holy Grail were trying to get a hold of him, too? What if *they* were who that prowler was talking about? "Could the Holy Grail be the Master that the prowler was referring to?"

"We haven't made any solid connections between the cadejo and the Holy Grail," Cyrus answered. "We only have suspicions."

"Vor now, ve 'ave to treat zhis like a separate vhreat," Lord Caedis mumbled and reached into his pocket. He pulled out his phone and then glanced at Raphael before he turned around and walked out of the room, presumably to answer whoever was calling.

Raphael huffed and set his eyes on Jackson. "What did you see? Who was there with you?"

Jackson shrugged and looked down at his lap. "I don't know...I think maybe it was an old church or something. And there was just one man. I didn't see his face or anything, but his hands kinda looked like...well, bones."

"Is he going to be okay?" Daimon asked, looking over his shoulder at Raphael.

"I don't know," the orange-haired man answered.

"This *would* have to happen now," Cyrus said with a long exhale. "We're all strapped for both people *and* resources, and the Holy Grail decide to make their move now; it's a little *too* coincidental."

Jackson had heard this kind of talk before—it was common among the people he chose to interview and investigate. Cyrus was suggesting that there was an informant among them, wasn't he? That made Jackson feel even worse. Was it someone in the house? Someone back at the Venaticus?

Raphael seemed to understand what Cyrus was saying. "Yeah, well, it's not like I can do shit about it. I'm on babysitting duty...as per usual."

Sebastien smirked amusedly. "Seems to be your best quality."

"Fuck off."

Daimon then snarled irritably. "Is Jackson going to be safe?" he demanded.

"Look, he'll be fine," Cyrus answered as he placed his hand on Raphael's shoulder just as the guy was about to snap back. "Alucard pulled him out of that place, and Raphael can do the same if it happens again."

The Alpha huffed and moved his arm around Jackson; he pulled him closer and nuzzled his head.

Jackson didn't know how to feel. The very people who killed his parents were after him, and they knew his demon name. Salvator? He hadn't even known it until now.

"Look, I don't mean to dismiss all of this freaky demon shit, but we're ready to plan our attack. We've got Kane's location," Cyrus said.

As confused and unsettled as he was about the Holy Grail, Jackson was glad to hear that. The sooner they dealt with Kane, the sooner they could get to the lab... and maybe all of this would be over.

"Are we just... going to ignore that Jackson was almost like... fucking soul snatched or whatever the hell Alucard just said?!" Julian panicked.

Dustu then spoke up, "I-I for one don't really want to get messed up in demon stuff."

"We're technically already messed up in it," Wesley mumbled. "We were caught up in it the day we all accepted Jackson. I mean... look around. We're standing in a Demon Lord's house."

"He's right," Brando said. "It's not new. Yeah, it's scary, but the cadejo came from demon blood, right? This whole situation revolves around demons."

Daimon looked at Raphael. "Are you certain that Jackson's going to be okay? I'm not willing to leave this place and Alucard if he's the only one who can guarantee Jackson's safety."

Raphael almost looked offended. "How many times do we need to say it? Strămoș Luca wouldn't have put me on babysitting duty if I wasn't capable of breaking someone out of a curse."

"Then why didn't you just do it?" the Alpha questioned. "Why go and get Alucard?"

"Because I didn't know what we were dealing with at first. I can break curses, but I can't tell which is which."

"He knows now, though," Sebastien assured Daimon. "Everything will be fine."

Although he didn't look entirely convinced, Daimon sighed and looked at Jackson. "Are you okay to walk?"

Jackson nodded. "Yeah, I'm okay."

Daimon stood up and said, "All right, let's go and get this Kane shit dealt with."

"This way," Cyrus said as he, Raphael, and Sebastien headed for the door.

Once Daimon nodded, letting everyone know that it was okay to follow them out, the pack walked towards the door, too.

Daimon waited for Jackson to get up and walked beside him.

Jackson felt... weird, for the lack of a better word. So much was going on that he was starting to feel overwhelmed again. The lab, Kane, Ethan, the fact that he was pregnant and didn't know what to do about it, and now the Holy Grail. He *did* feel a little better knowing that Raphael would be able to help him if he was pulled into another... dream?

Vision? He didn't know what to call it. All he knew was that he had yet another thing to deal with. Would this ever be over? Would he ever get a break from all the people who seemed to want him?

Chapter Seventy-Three

⇨ ≼ ☽ ≽ ⇦

Wolf's Rite

| Jackson |

Everyone filed into the war room. Jackson stood beside Daimon, who leaned against the wall, and the pack waited on his right. Raphael was across the room with Sebastien and Lumi, and Cyrus was standing in front of the table with his hands resting on it, staring at the map.

Jackson felt nervous; they were about to head out to face Kane in what was supposed to be a final battle that would end in Kane's surrender and the addition of his pack to Cyrus'. But when *Ethan* was escorted into the room by one of Cyrus' men, his dread skyrocketed. He felt Daimon tense up and heard him growl quietly under his breath, and he watched as the Alpha's hostile glare locked with Ethan's frustrated glower.

They eyed each other closely as Ethan was led across the room towards the pack; it didn't take long for Daimon's wolves to pick up on their Alpha's anger, and they *all* watched Ethan closely and glared cautiously when he stopped and stood a few feet away from them.

Jackson shuffled around uncomfortably. After what happened between him and Ethan, he didn't feel ready to face him. But he could feel Ethan's eyes on him, and the longer he stood there trying to fight the urge to glance over there to see if he'd looked away yet, the more unsettled he felt. And he could also *feel* the anger seething from Daimon's body; he knew that his mate wanted to beat the shit out of Ethan for kissing him—he knew that Daimon wanted to *kill* him—and he sorely hoped that the Alpha would stick to his word and refrain from doing so.

"Listen up," Cyrus bellowed through the packed room. There must be at least a hundred people inside. "Alucard's căutător located Kane and his pack fifteen klicks from here. They're set up in an abandoned mining town—"

"The tunnels," Lumi said worriedly.

"You know this place?" Raphael asked her.

The shy, icy-haired girl nodded as she glanced at him. "Hear rumours," she said quietly. "Kane... clear out the village years ago."

"That's right," Julian said with a nod. "I heard about it. Kane wiped out that entire town after one game hunter's trap broke the paw of one of his wolves."

Irritated, disgusted murmurs travelled around the room.

"Lots of narrow paths underground... dangerous," Lumi said.

"Here's what we do," Cyrus said loudly, silencing everyone. "If Kane plans to lure us into the mines, he's likely already got wolves setting up down there. So, we smoke them out. We fill those tunnels with wolfsbane smoke—a low dose so the worse they'll get is a cough for a day or two—and then I challenge Kane."

Jackson frowned and asked Daimon, "Why do we need to smoke the other wolves out?"

"Because every wolf has to be present when a challenge for power commences," Cyrus called.

With a startled flinch, Jackson sharply turned his head and set his eyes on him. "R-right," he mumbled.

"Sebastien and Maleki, you'll be handling the wolfsbane," Cyrus said as he glanced at the elf-vampire and the white-haired demon. Then, he looked at Raphael, Elias, and Amos. "You three will take your teams and work on rounding up all the stragglers." He set his sights on Daimon. "And Daimon, you're with me. We'll need to contain Kane until I'm ready to challenge him."

Daimon nodded.

"Everyone else is on cadejo duty. You watch the perimeter and make sure that no cadejo get past. That's the last thing we need," Cyrus ordered. "We're going with formation A. All of you who aren't mine, find one of my guys and stick with them."

Jackson could feel Ethan's eyes on him *still*, and he glanced up at Daimon to see a conflicted look on his mate's face. He was pretty sure that Daimon didn't want to leave him alone because Ethan was likely going to use that time to try and apologize for what he did, but Jackson didn't want to hear it. He wasn't ready to talk about it.

Cyrus loudly clapped his hands together. "All right, everyone group up and get ready. We're leaving in ten."

Everyone started leaving the room.

"Who should we stick with, chief?" Tokala asked Daimon.

"Anyone," the Alpha replied. "But stay in pairs. And Remus, you're staying here."

Remus sighed but nodded. "Okay."

"Let's go," Daimon mumbled and started heading for the door.

Jackson was relieved that Daimon didn't ask *him* to stay behind, but he was sure that was because he knew by now that he'd persuade him to change his mind. He followed beside his mate—

"Jack, wait," Ethan called and reached out to grab his arm.

Daimon immediately pulled Jackson back and shoved Ethan away from him. "Keep your filthy little hands off him," he snarled as the pack stopped behind him.

"Don't you fucking touch me!" Ethan growled angrily as he lunged at Daimon—

The Alpha lunged at Ethan, too; Tokala *and* Jackson tried to stop him, but Daimon broke through their grip and grabbed Ethan's throat. Daimon was stronger, and he forced Ethan back until he hit the wall; Ethan tried to pull Daimon's hands away and even kicked his legs, but Daimon kept his grip and started choking him.

"Daimon, stop!" Jackson insisted as he barged past the still, silent pack. He grasped Daimon's wrist and tried to pull him off, but he wouldn't let go, and Ethan's face was turning blue.

"I fucking warned you," Daimon growled, glaring into Ethan's eyes. "But you just couldn't help yourself, could you?"

"Get off!" Ethan choked.

"Daimon!" Jackson exclaimed, but no matter how hard he pulled, he couldn't get the Alpha to let go.

Julian went to speak up, but Tokala silenced them. *No one* did anything, and Jackson knew that it was because they weren't supposed to mess with their Alpha's business or something like that, but if someone didn't do something, Daimon was going to suffocate Ethan.

But when he opened his mouth to speak, Ethan grunted something through his struggled breaths, and then he abruptly shifted into his tiger form. He roared and threw Daimon off him, and the Alpha collided with his pack.

Daimon didn't waste a moment. He morphed into his Prime form just in time to grab Ethan when he leapt at him; he threw the tiger across the room, and the pack quickly dispersed to get out of the way.

Jackson didn't want them to fight again—they were going to kill each other! "Stop!" he shouted. "You—"

Tokala grabbed his arm and pulled him out of the way as Ethan and Daimon collided. "There's nothing any of us can do," he said.

"They're gonna kill each other!" Jackson insisted worriedly. "I have to do—"

Ethan landed on the floor in front of him with a thump and a growl. He tried to scurry to his feet, but Daimon grabbed his back legs, and with a vicious growl, he swung the tiger around and launched him across the room once again. The tiger hit a glass display cabinet filled with antique blades; glass and metal flew everywhere, and one knife impaled Ethan's leg. But Ethan didn't seem to care. He snarled angrily and yanked the blade from his leg with his mouth, and then he threw it towards Daimon.

The Alpha dodged the blade as he charged at the tiger, and Wesley pulled Dustu out of the way before the blade could hit him; the knife impaled the wall behind the pack.

Daimon and Ethan collided again, and this time, they remained locked in a bloody, horrifying battle. Jackson watched as they snapped and swiped at each other; Daimon yelped when Ethan sunk his huge teeth into his thigh, and Ethan shrieked when Daimon's claws impaled his waist. Their blood and fur splattered onto the floor, and neither looked as if they were going to back down any time soon.

Jackson's heart raced in his chest. He *had* to do something—

But all the commotion *finally* lured help into the room—someone who was capable of doing more than Jackson ever could.

Raphael snarled irritably as he barged past the pack with Sebastien and Cyrus following. The orange-haired man stormed towards the brawling lycans and snatched Ethan's scruff without a hint of fear or struggle on his face. He pulled him away from Daimon, and Cyrus grabbed Daimon's huge arms and kept him from trying to lunge at the struggling tiger. Ethan attempted to escape from Raphael's grip, but when Raphael slammed him down on the floor and held him there with his foot, the tiger soon gave up, his wounds bleeding.

"Enough!" Cyrus yelled and pinned Daimon against the wall. "What the fuck is wrong with you?!"

"What the hell is going on in here?!" Raphael then shouted, glaring over at the pack and then at Daimon.

"Get the fuck off me!" Daimon yelled at Cyrus.

"How about you calm down fir—"

"I have every right to kill that piece of shit!" the Alpha growled.

"You can fucking try all you want!" Ethan shouted back.

"Shut it!" Raphael warned, pressing his foot against Ethan's neck a little harder.

"Will somebody please tell us what the hell this is about?" Sebastien questioned, looking around at everyone.

No one answered. The pack shot unsure, confused looks at each other, and eventually, their eyes landed on Jackson.

But then Ethan snarled, "He's a fucking psycho, that's wh—"

"I said, shut it!" Raphael snapped.

Daimon growled angrily in response and tried to pull free from Cyrus, but like Ethan, his strength didn't match up.

"Jackson?" Sebastien then asked, staring at him.

Jackson shuffled around uncomfortably. It was hard enough telling *Daimon* what happened... but to tell *everyone*? His heart raced, and his legs started to feel numb.

"Well?" Raphael demanded impatiently.

"Jackson?" Tokala asked.

He took a deep breath and tried to steady his nerves. He looked at Daimon, who kept his hostile glower on Ethan; Jackson then shifted his sights to the tiger, who was starting to look worried. Jackson didn't want to tell everyone what happened... but he *had* to... didn't he? He couldn't think of a lie—he couldn't put together some story to make Daimon and Ethan's fight make sense, and he didn't want to risk getting punished for trying to hide the truth.

With another deep breath, he looked down at the floor to try and hide his nervous expression. "Ethan kissed me," he revealed. "And I didn't want him to."

The mixture of stares and murmurs that floated around Jackson made him feel even worse. Some of his packmates snarled, others mumbled their support for Daimon's attack—a few even said that they'd *help* Daimon kill Ethan if they had to. Of course, these people had been wolf walkers all their lives; they had laws and rules which Jackson was only just starting to *barely* understand, and it was made even clearer to him that Daimon had a right to murder his friend, but despite what happened and despite the malice which quickly filled the room, he didn't want to let it happen. He was angry—*furious*, in fact—but he'd never wish death on a man who'd been his best friend for as long as Ethan had.

But then Cyrus said, "It's your problem."

And Jackson's heart dropped into his stomach.

"But we ain't got time for it," Cyrus continued. "Raphael, take him back downstairs and make sure he's got a guard on him *constantly*. You can deal with this shit when we get back."

"Get the fuck off me!" Ethan then yelled as Raphael grabbed his scruff again.

"I'm not finished with him!" Daimon shouted angrily, trying to pull free from Cyrus.

"You *are* unless you want to spend the next week locked up," Cyrus growled at him.

Daimon didn't reply; he just snarled and huffed.

Ethan kept trying to escape, though, but he was no match for Raphael, who dragged him out of the room as if he were a screaming toddler.

Jackson's worry was soon accompanied by dismay. He didn't know what to do or say anymore. He asked Daimon not to do this, but he went and did it anyway.

"Have you calmed down?" Cyrus mumbled to Daimon.

With a roll of his eyes, Daimon shifted out of his wolf form and lightly shoved Cyrus away.

"Now I don't wanna see another one of you at *anyone's* throat until Kane's six feet under. Got it?" Cyrus growled.

Everyone muttered their reluctant replies.

"Good," he grumbled. "Now get the fuck outside." He stormed out of the room, and Sebastien followed him.

Jackson waited and watched as each of his packmates filed out of the room, and when Daimon came over to him, he lost his despondent stare and glared up at him. "I asked you not to—"

"Was I supposed to just let him attack me?" Daimon exclaimed.

His glare turned into a scowl. "No, but you didn't have to almost kill him, Daimon. You could have just...just restrained him or something until someone else got here, but you were trying to kill him!"

"Well, I'm sorry," he said with an irritated scoff. "I couldn't just stand around knowing what he did to you, Jackson. He's a narcissistic, manipulative piece of shit, and if someone doesn't put him in his place, he won't stop at forcing a kiss on you."

It felt like a dagger was plunged through his heart as he struggled to respond. He didn't know *how* to reply. He didn't want to defend Ethan because he *did* force him to kiss him, but he couldn't let Daimon think that it was okay for him to try and kill his friend.

But...what if his mate was right? What if Ethan would go further? For a moment...when Ethan kissed him, it felt like he didn't care what Jackson wanted, and it horrified him to think about what might have happened if he hadn't been strong enough to push him away.

As his heart ached, he lowered his head and looked down at the floor. The thought of losing Ethan hurt enough, but the idea that he might not even know who his best friend *really* was cut deeper. Ethan had changed so much since he went missing; he'd constantly tried to warn him away from Daimon, and he wasn't the nerdy, supportive guy Jackson knew.

"I'm not going to apologize for defending and trying to protect you," Daimon then said. "But what I *am* sorry for is that this is hurting you," he said as he placed his hand on Jackson's shoulder. "If he wasn't trying to convince you away from me, I wouldn't have a problem with him, but he's been trying since day one, Jackson, and all I'm trying to do is protect you."

Jackson didn't want to think about it anymore. It hurt too much—it made his heart ache and his brain throb. They were about to leave to fight Kane and his pack, and he needed to focus on that. But he couldn't ignore it forever. He *was* going to have to choose between his mate and his best friend, wasn't he? He couldn't have both, and he wasn't going to try and convince himself anymore that he could. Daimon would never be comfortable with Ethan, and Ethan would never be comfortable with Daimon.

He shrugged Daimon's hand off his shoulder. "We should catch up with the others before they leave without us," he mumbled and turned around.

Daimon grabbed his arm. "Jackson, I—"

Jackson pulled away from him. "I don't wanna do this right now, Daimon. We need to deal with Kane." He then headed for the door and didn't look back at the Alpha. He didn't want to see the look on his face because he knew that it would make him feel guilty. He loved Daimon, and the last thing he wanted to do was hurt him, but he didn't have the energy to talk about what just happened, and he wasn't ready to make a choice, either—he wasn't ready to admit to himself that he'd already made one. He just wanted to get the Kane business out of the way so that he and the pack could continue their mission to get to the lab.

Chapter Seventy-Four

An Impending Choice

| Jackson |

Nobody said anything as the pack followed Cyrus and his wolves through the sunlit forest. Jackson kept his eyes forward because he knew that if he caught a glimpse of Daimon's face, he'd cave and let him try to explain why he was right to attack Ethan. He could also feel the stares of his packmates, and Julian glanced at him every minute or so, but he didn't want to talk to *any* of them; he just wanted to get this done with so that they could get to the lab and finish what they'd come out here to do in the first place.

"Hey," came Tokala's hushed voice. "You okay?"

Jackson turned his head and looked at the orange wolf, who'd caught up and was walking beside him. "Yeah," he lied.

"What happened back there…I'm sure it was kinda scary, and—"

"I really don't wanna talk about it," he interjected, cutting Tokala off.

The orange wolf frowned hesitantly. "Look, there's still *a lot* that you don't know about wolf walkers and the way we do things; the chief had every right to go for Ethan the way he did. There are very firm rules among *all* lycans when it comes to someone's mate, and if Alpha Daimon so much as heard a *rumour* that Ethan was planning on doing what he did, he'd have the right to defend your bond. You don't *ever* try something with a lycan who's already mated; it's literally the most disgusting thing a lycan can do."

Jackson sighed heavily. He didn't know what to say. What Ethan did was wrong in so many ways, but as upset as Jackson was, he didn't want to see his friend hurt…or worse.

"I'll leave you alone, but first…I should warn you about what's going to happen once we're done with Kane," Tokala said quietly. "You're going to have to choose between Alpha Daimon and Ethan; there's no way in hell Ethan's going to be allowed to stay around—he'd be a goddamn idiot to even try. The chief *is* going to exercise his right to kill him, and if you don't want that to happen…you're going to have to stop him."

With a horrified frown, Jackson shifted his sights to the orange wolf. "Stop him how?"

"Convince him. Make a case. Just try to persuade him to exile Ethan instead of killing him. That's the only way your muto friend gets to live." Tokala then left his side and returned to Wesley.

Jackson's heart broke a little more. He tried to focus on the forest around him as he followed Cyrus' pack, but he couldn't. Tokala was right. If he didn't do something, Daimon was going to kill Ethan. He scowled despondently and tensed a little as frustration surged through him. He'd come all the way to Ascela to find Ethan, and after everything he'd been through, he didn't want to lose him again, least of all be the one to tell him to leave.

But he couldn't have both, could he? It was either new a life with the man he loved—his *mate*—or back to his old life with the friend who'd been there for him for *fifteen* years. Picking Daimon would make him the biggest asshole of the century, wouldn't it?

Would it? He loved Daimon. Against all the odds in this dangerous, horrifying tundra, he'd found the man he was supposed to spend his life with. He found someone who protected him, someone who didn't treat him like a freak or unwanted garbage—someone who saved his life, and someone who he'd die for.

He huffed as his frustration overwhelmed him. His body was aching in response to his turmoil; he didn't *want* to choose. What if he got Daimon and Ethan to talk it out? What if he got Ethan to understand that he loved Daimon?

No…that would never happen. Ethan had made it pretty clear that he didn't and wouldn't respect his and Daimon's relationship, and asking Daimon to let Ethan stay would be an insult.

Cyrus' voice echoed from up ahead, "We're bordering Kane's location. We'll wait here in the cover of the trees until nightfall."

The pack came to a slow halt, and when everyone started sitting and resting, Jackson dragged himself away from the crowd and slumped down in the snow behind a hollow log. He wanted to be alone with his thoughts, but he knew he wasn't going to get that.

"Can we talk?" Daimon asked as he stood in front of him.

Jackson didn't look up at his mate; he glanced at the Alpha's paws before hiding his face under his own. "I'm not in the mood."

Daimon sighed and sat beside him. "I don't know what I can do to make you feel better, all I know is that seeing you upset hurts me, especially when I'm the reason."

He didn't reply—he didn't know what to say. He didn't have the energy to beg or question him.

"Jackson?" Daimon asked and nudged his neck with his muzzle.

"What?" he grumbled.

"I'm just trying to protect you," he said as he lay beside him and rested his head over Jackson's. "The fact that he's disrespectful enough to kiss a mated lycan is a dangerous red flag on its own; I don't want to imagine what he might try next. I know that you don't completely understand the way we do—"

"It has nothing to do with what I do and don't understand, Daimon," he said as he lifted his head and glared at him. "I've asked a million times for you to try and get on with him, and—"

"And he forcibly kissed you, Jackson!" he exclaimed quietly. "I've been right about him all along, and I'm not sorry for what I've done. *You* matter to me more than anything, and I'll do whatever it takes to protect you. I'm sorry that someone you thought you knew and trusted turned out to be this kind of person; I know that your friendship with Ethan was long and important, but—"

"Was?" he asked with a frown. "He's...still my friend, Daimon," he said, but he didn't feel as confident as he did the last time he said that. Ethan did something that made him feel very uncomfortable, something he didn't think his best friend was capable of, and it made him hesitate.

Daimon placed his paw on Jackson's. "Is he?"

With a reluctant, sullen frown, Jackson looked away and exhaled sadly. He thought about what Tokala told him and now was probably the only chance he'd get. "I don't want you to kill him, Daimon," he said firmly, and when he felt the Alpha tense up, he turned his head to look at him again. "If how I feel really does matter, then don't kill him."

The Alpha adorned an irritated scowl.

"Please," Jackson insisted. "Just...let me talk to him—"

"I'm not letting that piece of shit anywhere near you after—"

"*Please*!" he pleaded, staring into Daimon's conflicted, honey-brown eyes. "I don't wanna sit here and defend him, 'cause what he did was fucked up, but I don't wanna go making choices to exile him or whatever without hearing him out. I-I mean...he just had surgery or whatever, right? Maybe the drugs did something—"

"He seemed perfectly lucid in that meeting," the Alpha snarled.

He wasn't wrong. Jackson sighed defeatedly and looked down at the snow. "Just let me talk to him...please?"

Daimon's expression journeyed from aggravated to conflicted over the next few silent moments, and then it ended when a defensive frown contorted his face. "Not alone," he said sternly.

Jackson shook his head. "You'll just go for him the moment he—"

"Not me," he said, clenching his jaw, clearly trying to hold back his anger. "Tokala or Wesley—someone I trust to take action if he tries anything."

That seemed reasonable, so he nodded. "Okay. Thank you."

"But I swear to fucking God, if he so much as *touches* you, I'll have my wolves rip his hands off," the Alpha growled.

Jackson shuffled around uncomfortably. He wanted to assure Daimon that Ethan wouldn't try anything, but he didn't know whether that was the truth, so he looked down at his paws and sighed. It was probably best to change the subject; he didn't want to talk about it anymore. "Are you ready to go up against Kane?"

Daimon exhaled deeply. "I wish I could be the one to kill him," he grumbled. "What Cyrus plans to do is a mercy. Kane deserves to suffer for everyone he took from us, not to mention the mountain of other shit he's done."

He frowned and asked him, "Shouldn't he be like…tried for his crimes or whatever? Isn't there some kind of wolf walker prison like how there's a demon one?"

"Not that I'm aware of. I'm sure that if he did have to answer for what he's done, the Nosferatu would send him to a Caeleste-specific prison. But even that's a mercy," Daimon muttered.

Jackson went to reply, but he saw Raphael walking towards him, and the sight of that orange wolf made his mind go blank his heart beat a little faster.

"You're not planning on sleeping, are you?" Raphael asked as he stood in front of them both.

"Uh…" Jackson drawled. "I don't know."

"Well decide," he exclaimed irritably. "If I'm going to be babysitting you, I'd prefer to know if I actually need to do it."

Jackson couldn't believe he'd forgotten about the dream he had—that weird…vision or whatever it was called. The Holy Grail had tried to trap his soul in some sort of prison, and Raphael was there to ensure that didn't happen if they tried again.

He sighed and tried to keep himself from getting worked up about it. The Holy Grail *wouldn't* get a hold of him; Raphael might be horrifyingly scary and intimidating, but he knew what he was doing—Lord Caedis wouldn't have given him the job of ensuring Jackson's safety if he wasn't capable.

"Well?" Raphael snapped impatiently.

Daimon scowled irritably. "Caedis told you to watch him, so shouldn't you be doing it period?"

Raphael sharply turned his head and glared at him. "Watch your tone, Greyblood."

Jackson didn't want them to argue, so he said, "I could do with some rest, so I guess so."

With a roll of his eyes, Raphael slumped down ten feet away and watched Jackson like a hawk.

"It's not hard at all to tell that he and Lucian are related," Daimon mumbled under his breath.

Jackson couldn't help but snicker because he was right. Just like Heir Lucian, Raphael was a moody, entitled brat. He'd never say such a thing out loud, though. He didn't want another hour of inexplicable pain.

Daimon moved closer to him and rested his head on top of Jackson's. "Get some sleep. You're going to need it."

"You should, too," Jackson said as he let himself relax.

"Maybe," he said and exhaled deeply.

Jackson closed his eyes and tried to ignore the trepidation of Raphael's endless, piercing gaze. As he lay there, though, he started feeling nauseous again. It was like the world had to remind him whenever he was finally relaxing that he had a mountain of problems and secrets. But he couldn't let it consume him. There'd be a right time and place to tell Daimon. He just had to wait for it.

Chapter Seventy-Five

↤ ≼ ☽ ≽ ↦

Moving Out

| **Daimon** |

As the afternoon became the evening, Daimon sighed quietly, lifted his head from over Jackson's, and glanced around at the resting wolves. Some of Cyrus' guys were getting up and ready, and Cyrus was talking to Sebastien, who shifted into his hound form a few moments later and rushed off to help three others deal with a lone cadejo.

"Looks like we're getting ready to move," Raphael said.

Daimon turned his head and set his eyes on the orange wolf.

"He awake?" Raphael asked, nodding at Jackson.

The Alpha looked down at his sleeping mate and then back at Raphael. "No."

"Then wake him up."

Daimon snarled irritably but held his tongue; he wasn't about to start an argument with him. He nuzzled Jackson's neck and quietly said, "Jackson."

But his mate didn't respond.

"Jackson?" he asked as he nudged him.

He still didn't wake up.

Daimon started panicking. The last time this happened, Caedis had to wake Jackson before his soul was imprisoned by the Holy Grail. He jumped to his paws, but before he could speak, Raphael shoved him out of the way and shifted out of his wolf form. The Alpha watched him place his hand on Jackson's head the way Caedis had, and he muttered the same words in that strange language, too.

Jackson suddenly flinched and shot up to his paws. He looked around as if he had no idea where he was, but after a few seconds, he calmed down and stared at Daimon with a confused frown. There was also fear in his eyes, and his body was visibly trembling.

"What did you see?" Raphael asked him before Daimon could ask if he was okay.

As he slowly turned his head to look at Raphael, Jackson tried to compose himself. "The same as before," he answered shakily.

"The same guy?"

He nodded. "Is this... gonna happen *every* time I try to sleep?"

"Probably," Raphael said. "The Holy Grail are persistent; Strămoș Luca wouldn't have put me on babysitting duty if they weren't."

"Can't something be done?" Daimon questioned frustratedly. "I'd rather not have to have one of you around all the time after this mission is over."

Raphael scoffed. "I'd rather not be around you all the time, either. But we both have to suck it up and do what Strămoș Luca says, don't we?" He shifted his glare to Jackson. "Did you see or learn anything new?"

Jackson thought for a few silent moments. "I-I don't know," he mumbled. "The same bells... but they rang in sequences of three. Could that mean anything?"

The orange-haired man frowned as if he was pondering, and then he shrugged. "Maybe, maybe not. The number three could mean a lot of things: three hours, three days, three weeks—or maybe three tries and they give up or switch tactics."

Jackson looked like he'd seen a ghost. "Or... three dreams?"

Raphael mumbled, "Well, best not take any naps until we get back to the house, huh?"

Daimon scowled in hostility as anger and worry filled him. "This isn't a fucking joke," he exclaimed frustratedly, and the fact that he didn't even know the full extent of what the Holy Grail were doing and what they wanted made him feel worse. "These people are trying to take his soul; is it so hard for you to take it at least the slightest bit seriously?!"

The orange-haired man turned to face him—

"It's fine," Jackson said before Raphael could say whatever he was going to say to match the offended look on his face. "We can figure it out after Kane's dealt with... right?"

Raphael seemed hesitant to back down, but after a few moments of shifting his gaze between them, he half-nodded and said, "Strămoș Luca will get to the bottom of it." He turned around and walked off.

Daimon shook his head as he growled quietly. He wanted to yell... he wanted to *scream* to let his built-up anger and confusion out, but he felt aimless. Why did the Holy Grail want Jackson? Was it *really* because he was a created hybrid, or was there more to it? He wanted answers, but there was no way for him to get them—not yet.

Instead, he sighed away his fury and looked at his mate. "Are you okay?" he asked him quietly.

Jackson sat down. "I don't know," he said as confusion and fear fought for domination of his face. "I just... I don't know what to do or think or say." He shook his head and exhaled deeply. "Some cadejo Master wants me, and now the Holy Grail does, too. If this is what my life is gonna be like, I...I almost wanna use my reward from Lord Caedis to undo this whole hybrid thing."

Daimon moved closer to him and frowned as confusion outweighed his frustration, but before he could question *why* Jackson would want that, it hit him. He understood why Jackson would want to be free of all the perils that came with being what he was; often when he was a child, Daimon himself wished he wasn't a Greyblood, so he knew what his mate was going through. Instead of asking why, he asked him, "Do you think that's even possible?"

He shrugged. "I mean...if he can bring Sebastien's mate back to life, I'm sure he can undo whatever turned me into a hybrid." He then shifted his gaze to Sebastien, who was talking with Raphael and Cyrus. "Sebastien might know."

"But will he be honest?" Daimon grumbled.

Jackson frowned at him. "I don't know why he'd lie about something like that."

"He's Caedis' little stooge; telling people the ins and outs of his shady deals and contracts would probably get him killed. I mean, isn't that the point? Isn't the whole deal with the devil thing supposed to benefit Caedis more than the people he makes deals with?"

A conflicted expression warped Jackson's face. "I don't...know. Sebastien only got roped into serving him for life because he didn't read the terms properly, right? And *I* did. I read that contract over five times; we get to the lab...and we get whatever we want."

"I don't know," Daimon muttered unsurely. "It all feels a little too good to be true, especially after spending time around Caedis' little devil spawns."

Jackson laughed a little but quickly sunk back into a depressing gloom. "But I also wanna know everything that *he* knows about the Holy Grail; I want to find out what really happened to my parents."

Daimon felt the urge to offer to use his reward to give Jackson either one of his desires, but he wanted to use it to find someplace new for his pack to settle and be safe. "You might be able to get that information anyway," he said. "If Caedis is going to be figuring out what the Holy Grail wants with you, maybe you can get whatever you can out of him in the process."

"Yeah, maybe."

He moved his face closer and nuzzled Jackson's head. "If you can't get it out of him, we'll find another way to get it."

"Get what?" came Sebastien's voice.

Daimon rolled his eyes as he turned his head to look at the hound. "None of your business."

Sebastien frowned but didn't snap back. "We're getting ready to head out. Heir Zephyr said you had another dream thing; you okay?"

Jackson nodded, and before Sebastien could turn around, he said, "Can I...well...I wanted to ask you something about Lord Caedis."

"Okay...like what?" the hound asked with a wary expression.

"Can he...well...if I were to ask for it...could he undo whatever made me a hybrid?"

Sebastien looked a little bewildered. "Uh...I mean...maybe. He can unmake vampires, so...." He shook his head. "But it's a wolf walker thing, so I really don't know. Sorry." The hound then looked behind him at Cyrus' wolves, who were lining up ready to move out. "Look, there ain't time for any of this right now; we gotta get moving. Maybe I can help more on the way back or something."

Daimon couldn't help but feel suspicious, but he wasn't going to attack Sebastien—not yet at least. He'd question him later.

"Okay," Jackson said with a deep exhale. "I'm ready."

"Are *you*?" Sebastien asked Daimon. "Cyrus is relying on you to back him up."

The Alpha nodded.

"All right, let's go," the hound said as he turned around.

Daimon walked beside Jackson as they followed Sebastien towards Cyrus' wolves. Tokala and the rest of the pack joined them, and Amos and Elias started telling them where they'd be walking. Daimon knew that he was going to be separated from Jackson; he wanted to argue, but not only did he know that it was useless, but he also had to focus on the mission. He had to be with Cyrus to help him keep Kane from running off like the pathetic little coward he was.

He stopped in front of Amos, who directed Jackson to one of the groups who'd be dealing with cadejo.

Jackson turned to face Daimon. "So...I'll see you when it's over."

Daimon nodded and nuzzled Jackson's muzzle. "Stay close to your packmates, okay?"

"I will," he murmured.

The Alpha nuzzled his head a little and then stared into his mate's shimmering blue eyes. "I love you."

Jackson smiled and said, "I love you, too."

The Alpha watched him turn around and make his way towards his group. Seeing that he'd be with Wesley and his Epsilons made Daimon feel a little better, but he knew that he'd be worrying the entire time that something was going to happen to him.

"Greyblood," came Cyrus' voice.

Daimon looked over at him.

"Come on. Time to move out," Cyrus said.

With a breathy sigh, Daimon glanced at Jackson, who got in line behind Julian, and then he made his way to the front of the pack to join Cyrus.

Cyrus looked him up and down. "Look, man... I don't wanna be that guy, but I need to make sure you're ready. I can't have you up here with me fighting this guy if you're distracted."

Daimon snarled irritably. "I'm not distracted. I just want to get this shit over with so we can get to that lab."

With a nod, Cyrus stared ahead into the trees.

"Are we ready to go?" Maleki asked as he appeared beside Cyrus with Sebastien. "Time is money."

"Yeah, yeah, calm down. I'm sure Alucard'll compensate you *very* well for this," Cyrus sneered. "That's all that matters to you, right?"

The elf-vampire scoffed and crossed his arms. "At least I've got my priorities straight, dog."

Cyrus rose to his hind legs with a furious snarl—

"Okay, okay," Sebastien drawled as he used his wings to keep Maleki and Cyrus apart. "We're all colleagues here. Let's just get done what we're out here to get done and then we can all go home, yeah?"

Cyrus snarled and backed off.

Maleki, on the other hand, scoffed and adorned a revolted stare.

"Come on," Raphael then growled as he shoved past them all.

Daimon watched Maleki and Cyrus exchange hostile glares. He hadn't seen them at each other's throats before; their past exchanges seemed to be all banter and chortles, but they evidently had some sort of grievance between them. He didn't care to ask for details, though.

Cyrus huffed but looked back at everyone. "Let's move out," he called and started leading the way.

As he followed Cyrus' lead, Daimon glanced over his shoulder at Jackson. His worry was already increasing, but he couldn't let it consume him. He had to focus. The sooner Kane was dealt with, the sooner he and his pack could get to that lab.

And the sooner they got there, the sooner they could finally find someplace to call home.

Chapter Seventy-Six

Winner Takes All

| Jackson |

There were Etas *everywhere*; in the derelict houses, the watchtower, and the catwalk overlooking an oily ditch. Kane was well prepared, but Cyrus was, too.

Jackson watched as the huge white wolf commanded his pack, guiding them through blind spots and finding cover in places Jackson wouldn't have even thought of. They used the snow the same way Jackson and his packmates once used it to hide from cadejo, slithering through it like fish in water. Cyrus' elite wolves pounced on Kane's Etas before they knew what hit them, knocked them out, and dragged their bodies away before they were seen. It was like something out of a special-ops movie, and Jackson was in awe.

But the time to observe and revere was over. Everyone had their jobs, including Jackson, and when Cyrus gave the order, each wolf hurried to get into position. Jackson stuck with Julian, Wesley and his Epsilons, and one of Cyrus' Betas, and once they got into position on the outskirts of the abandoned mining town, they waited.

Jackson could hear the voices of Kane's wolves, and they all sounded either worried or determined to prove themselves to their Alpha.

"I, uh...I have a bad feeling," Julian murmured.

"Shh," Wesley snapped.

Julian shuffled around uncomfortably, but after a few seconds, they said, "Kane's smart—*really* smart. We may have gotten rid of his Amarok, but he *has* to have something else. He knows how to use the cadejo, so who's to say he didn't move some of the ones from the pit? W-what if he unleashes the *entire* pit on us?"

"Lumi would have said something, right?" Ezhno said.

"She had a lot of useful information, and she didn't mention other Amaroks or anything similar," Cyrus' Beta muttered. "Stop freaking out and wait for Alpha Cyrus' call."

"Yeah, but I didn't even know Lumi existed," Julian replied. "She can't have known everything being locked down in that meat dungeon."

Leon sighed irritably and said, "Just stop and concentrate. We're supposed to be looking out for cadejo, and we can't do that if you're yapping on and making us all feel anxious."

Julian went quiet but the nervous look on their face didn't wither.

Jackson wouldn't let *his* nerves get to him, though. For Cyrus' plan to work, he had to focus. He had to do his part. What if Kane *did* have a hidden weapon, though? Or what if Daimon and Cyrus weren't enough? What if Cyrus lost? He frowned but kept his composure. If Cyrus didn't *know* that he was a match for Kane, then he wouldn't have dragged everyone out there, would he? He wouldn't have sounded so confident when he talked about taking Kane on.

The shadow of Sebastien's dragon-like wings stretched across the snow and raced past where Jackson lay; he looked up and watched as the winged hound swooped down towards the centre of the mining town, and on the other side, another creature did the same. Its body looked like that of a bipedal, hairless wolf, but it had the face of a bat and the wings of a demon. It raced down towards the town, and after a blinding, white light lit up the darkness, a rain of blue smoke gushed down from the sky.

Horrified yelps filled the air, and Kane's wolves burst into action.

Cyrus' attackers raced out of the snow and swarmed the town as Kane's pack rushed around in panic. Those who'd been in the mines hurried out, coughing and gasping for air as the blue wolfsbane smoke that Maleki and Sebastien rained down on them poured out behind.

It was working. Everything was going just as Cyrus had said it would.

And just as Cyrus had also said, the cadejo started coming.

"Get ready," Wesley said as they all turned to face the incoming corpses.

Despite having faced cadejo multiple times already, Jackson hadn't gotten used to them. That smell, the sight of their rotting, mangled bodies. And knowing that one bite would turn his packmates horrified him.

But there was no room for fear. It was time to fight.

| Daimon |

Daimon stormed through the battlefield with Cyrus, searching for Kane. They assisted their allies on their way, scouring every building and tent, but the cowardly wolf was nowhere to be seen.

Cyrus grabbed one of Kane's wolves and lifted her off her paws. "Where's your Alpha?!" he growled, glaring into her terrified eyes.

The brown wolf choked and whimpered as she insisted, "I-I don't know!"

Daimon grabbed a wolf, too. "Tell me where Kane is!" he demanded.

With a guttural snarl, the wolf tried to fight back, but he was no match for Daimon's strength and was soon pinned down with nowhere to go.

"Tell me!" Daimon yelled furiously.

"Fuck you!" the wolf roared.

Daimon smashed his furred fist into the wolf's face, knocking him out. But then he saw something—a shimmer of silver in the corner of his eye. He sharply turned his head towards it, and when he saw Kane scurrying out of a building which Raphael had just crashed into and caused to collapse, a grin stretched across his face. There he was.

He burst towards him, charging through the crowds of battling wolves; he didn't care that he knocked down Cyrus' fighters. He was going to get that coward; he wouldn't let him get away again.

"Daimon!" Cyrus called, chasing after him.

Daimon ignored him. He raced across the battlefield, keeping his eyes on Kane, watching as he scampered around like a rat, avoiding the fight. What a filthy little coward.

He dropped to all fours so that he could run faster. As he vaulted over a brick wall, he snarled angrily and saw Kane heading for a tunnel entrance. *Of course* he was going for the mines.

But Daimon wasn't the only one chasing the cowardly wolf. A blinding flash of white light hit the rock face above the mine entrance; Kane stumbled to a halt as rubble fell and blocked the way inside, and he was forced to veer right and head for another shaft. But the winged creature—which could only be Maleki in some sort of vampire form—swooped down and threw another ball of exploding light towards the other mine entrance, blocking it off with rubble.

Kane skidded to a halt and looked around in panic, but there was nowhere for him to go.

Daimon charged towards him, and Kane had no choice but to fight, so he stood up on his hind legs and waited for Daimon to reach him. And Daimon didn't hesitate. He lunged at Kane, shoving aside any feeling he had other than his rage. When he collided with him, he avoided Kane's claws and sunk his teeth into his bicep. Kane shrieked and slashed Daimon's side with his claws, and although it hurt like hell, Daimon didn't let go. Kane's blood poured from the wound his teeth made, and he planned to bleed as much out of him as he could.

But not even a second later, a pair of hands gripped Daimon and pulled him away from Kane. He tried to fight, but he was no match for Cyrus' strength. Cyrus yanked him away from Kane, and then they both stumbled back together when Daimon tried to escape.

"What the fuck do you think you're doing?!" Cyrus yelled angrily.

Daimon snarled but didn't get to reply.

Kane laughed and growled, "Greyson. I wondered when you'd come back for round two."

Cyrus sharply turned his head and set his eyes on Kane.

Daimon wanted to attack—he wanted to lunge at *Cyrus* for pulling him away from Kane, but as much as he desired to hurt him, as much as he desperately wanted to avenge his packmates, he had to stick to the plan. So he set his eyes on Kane, too, and waited for Cyrus' call.

"Round two?" Cyrus questioned. "Did I hit you so fucking hard that you forgot I beat you?"

Kane snarled and snickered. "Beat me? Is that why I'm still here? Is that why we're *all* still here?" he asked as he held his arms out, gesturing to the battlefield.

"You're all only still alive because like you, your packmates are dirty little cowards," Cyrus snapped.

With a ferocious snarl, Kane stepped forward as if he were going to attack, but he hesitated and backed off. "Coming from a guy who hides behind ancient hybrids and disgusting vampires. You're a fucking disgrace to our kind."

"I've done more for wolf walkers than your line *ever* did."

Kane scoffed and glanced at Daimon. "You fucking Greybloods think you're so special. Ada is the true Wolf God; Greymore's just some immigrant wolf who came over from a dying world, siding with vampires and demons and all kinds of scum. He tainted the werewolf way; he tried to turn us into meek little dogs, errand boys for fags and fairies—"

Cyrus snarled; he was shaking, clearly trying his best to resist the urge to attack.

Daimon had to fight, too. He might not know as much about his lineage as Cyrus, but Kane was disrespecting his ancestors, and that on top of the hatred and desire to slaughter him was making it nearly impossible for Daimon to resist.

With a condescending scoff, Kane looked Cyrus up and down. "You're a disgrace."

"And you're on borrowed time," Cyrus growled. He stood up tall and bellowed, "Kane Ardelean-Blood, I challenge you…to the death. Winner takes all."

Kane looked stumped at first, but when the battle slowed down around him and his wolves stopped fighting to observe, he started to look desperate.

"You have no right," the cowardly wolf accused.

"I have every right," Cyrus replied confidently. "With your wolves and my wolves as witnesses, do you accept my challenge?"

Kane's twitchy brown eyes nervously shifted from Cyrus to Daimon and back again. The hesitant look clinging to his scarred face slowly contorted into a devious grin, and he scowled as he said, "You're going to wish you never said that." He burst forward in the blink of an eye and collided with Cyrus.

The force of their collision sent Daimon stumbling back, and when he caught his balance, he watched the two wolves tumble across the snow, snarling and slashing and biting. Blood sprayed in every direction, splattering onto the ice and against the rocks, and savage growls and pained yelps cut through the bitter air.

Daimon backed off towards his packmates, who stood among the crowd of wolves observing the gnarly battle. Every time Cyrus slashed or cut Kane, Kane managed to hurt him back just as badly. The white wolf grabbed Kane's arm and launched him into one of the nearby buildings, but the black wolf struggled out of the rubble as if the collision was nothing and clashed with Cyrus again.

But then the distorted snarl of a cadejo snatched his attention. Daimon turned his head towards the sound and set his eyes on a group of Cyrus' wolves; they were fighting cadejo, and when Daimon remembered that his mate was out there fighting those corpses, too, dread filled his racing heart. Cyrus didn't need his help anymore, did he? And he didn't have to stand there and witness the battle, either. That was between Cyrus' pack and Kane's.

Daimon didn't hesitate. As he left Cyrus to fight Kane, he focused on Jackson's scent and hurried to find him. Whether his mate needed his help or not, he was going to protect him, and he'd help make sure that no cadejo interfered with Cyrus' battle.

Chapter Seventy-Seven

⌒ ≼ ☽ ≽ ⌒

Antlers

| Jackson |

They just kept coming, almost as if they were spectres clawing their way out of long-forgotten graves. The eerie symphony of snarls and screeches echoed through the desolation, leaving a sinister undertone that mingled with the stench of decaying blood. As the cadejo horde advanced, it seemed as though the very earth had birthed them, an army of the damned racing towards Jackson and his packmates.

"On your right!" Wesley's voice shattered the frigid air, a desperate warning slicing through the night.

Julian swung around, colliding with a cadejo that materialized from the shadows. The creature's visage peeled away, its skin sticking to Julian's paw like a grotesque souvenir. With a furious snarl, the wounded cadejo lunged at Julian, but Jackson intervened—he crashed his body into the beast before it could bite his friend. The creature tumbled across the frozen ground, leaving behind a trail of rotten ooze.

Panting, Julian managed a strained, "Thanks," their eyes reflecting the horror of the unfolding nightmare.

The cadejo tried to get up, but Jackson shouted, "Stop!", and the zombie did as he commanded.

Julian tore the creature's heart out.

"Time and place, I know, but that's so fucking cool," Julian panted.

Jackson let himself grin in response. The cadejo listened to him, and he wasn't going to waste the potential that lay before him.

The relentless onslaught continued, a ceaseless tide of undead monstrosities overwhelming them. Cyrus' Beta, Clint, executed a fallen cadejo, and Jackson halted any incoming corpse with a single word, allowing his allies to execute them without struggle. When a group of at least ten corpses charged towards them at once, though, Jackson's command seemed to go unheard.

"Stop!" he demanded.

But the cadejo only reacted with confused snarls—they didn't stop or stumble.

Torn between the urge to unleash the formidable power of the inimă and the fear of losing control, Jackson chose to use his wolf's brute strength to assist his packmates. Each blow echoed through the night as he slammed his paws and tore with his maw, but it all felt like a futile attempt to push back the inexorable wave of death.

Jackson was made heavily aware that he could only do so much, and the cadejo were still coming. Could he only command one at a time? Two? Maybe three or four? He didn't know, but he had to be sure.

"Where the hell are they coming from?!" Wesley exclaimed.

More and more cadejo emerged from the forest's dark depths; this part of the woods seemed to harbour an otherworldly secret, releasing its macabre inhabitants with every passing moment. It made Jackson wonder whether Kane had unleashed the horde trapped in the canyon; it was the only explanation that made sense.

And if Kane *had* freed the pit of rotting creatures, then undead wolves were the least of their problems. Sirens, brutes, prowlers—and God only knew what else—would be among the swarm, and the very thought of facing variants sent a shiver down Jackson's spine.

But he couldn't become distracted. He stuck close to Julian, helping them take down any cadejo that came their way, commanding when and where he could. Wesley and his Epsilons were handling their line well, but panicked cries and pained yelps echoed through the forest, drowning out the savage tournament between Kane and Cyrus. The others were in trouble—Jackson didn't know who, but every wolf was his ally, and if he could help, he would.

A spectral burst of blue and white erupted, violently piercing the suffocating darkness. The twisted cries and distorted roars of cadejo echoed loudly, intertwining with the malevolent noise of the undead horde. Jackson's eyes widened as Sebastien descended from the shadowy heights; the winged hound conjured balls of sizzling blue flames from his jaws, each flicker a macabre dance of incandescent death. The azure inferno consumed an entire group of cadejo, casting grotesque shadows that writhed and contorted in the unholy radiance.

Across the desolate expanse, Maleki unleashed his eerie powers. A spectral white fire, as cold as the icy grip of death, surged forth, engulfing the cadejo on the opposite flank. The malevolent entities crumbled and dissipated like fragile illusions, their tortured forms obliterated by the relentless deluge of ghostly flames.

Yet, despite the intervention, an unsettling chill lingered in the air—a palpable reminder that the forces at play were beyond the comprehension of even Cyrus' elite wolves.

A monstrous presence slithered through the encompassing darkness, a sinister force that stirred the very shadows it traversed.

Jackson's attention was snatched from the chaos unfolding before him to the gloom behind the endless horde; he felt a primal unease gnawing at the edges of his consciousness, that feeling... that terrifying urge that something terrible was imminent.

Julian's urgent cry sliced through the disorienting haze, yanking Jackson from the depths of his horrified contemplation. Reacting on instinct, he lunged towards his friend's distress, sinking his teeth into the sinewy back leg of a cadejo. Brando emerged from the shadows, and together, they tore the beast apart, extracting its still-beating heart in a macabre ritual to free it from its tortured existence.

But then a harrowing growl bellowed through the battle. The guttural sound sent a shiver down Jackson's spine; lifting his head, he scanned the gloom, his senses on high alert, his heart racing.

A hauntingly familiar voice seeped through the darkness, calling to him, *"Harmonic... variant."*

And then he saw it. The looming silhouette of a colossal, mangled wolf, its horrifying face peering at him from between two trees. It towered enough to be a Prime—maybe a prowler—but its body remained obscured in the enveloping shadows, and with each passing moment, Jackson's instincts urged him more and more to flee.

To run.

To get the hell out of there.

He was in danger, and both his wolf and demon instincts seemed to quiver.

"Jackson!" came Daimon's voice, bringing immediate calm to Jackson's still body.

He turned to face his mate's call, and when he set his eyes on the white-furred Alpha, he exhaled in relief.

Daimon joined the battle; he seamlessly melded into the fray, each swipe of his formidable claws dismantling the cadaverous horde, his presence infusing his packmates with a newfound vigour—the strength they so desperately needed.

Jackson, fuelled by a renewed determination, wielded his raw power to stagger another cadejo; Daimon's colossal paw then pierced through the beast's chest to extract its putrid heart. And then they moved on to the next cadejo, and the next, and the next, working together to take them down.

But unlike a living pack, the undead remained oblivious to their inherent disadvantage, mindlessly persisting in their onslaught. The unwavering unity of the living countered each advance, rendering the corpses helpless. And although the cadejo kept coming, snarling and snapping their jaws, every single one was torn apart before it could get close.

In the midst of the relentless struggle, hope began to weave through the air, dispelling the once oppressive atmosphere like smoke in the wind. Their stoic Alpha radiated a quiet assurance that encouraged the once-struggling pack... but Jackson's feeling didn't fade.

Something else was out there in the dark. Something evil. Something dangerous. Something unlike anything the pack had faced.

And his instincts still urged him to run.

"What do we do, boss?" Wesley asked Daimon the moment they had a chance to breathe.

Daimon huffed and looked over his shoulder at the battle still happening between Kane and Cyrus. "We have to keep fighting until Cyrus wins."

"Heads up!" Clint called.

They turned to face the incoming cadejo.

"They just keep coming!" Leon exclaimed.

"Kane probably unleashed them all from the pit," Julian panted, their face riddled with terror.

"Which means we'll be facing more than just standard cadejo," Brando said.

Just as Jackson had told himself—just as he'd hypothesized—it might very well be true that the cadejo pit was flooding free like a broken dam. And he wasn't going to take any risks. "I saw something," he told them all. "I-I don't know if it was a prowler or some other kind of variant, but it was big, and it said something that the prowler I came across said."

"Could it be the same prowler?" Ezhno questioned.

But there wasn't time for a discussion.

"Fight now, talk later!" Daimon instructed and grabbed the throat of a cadejo which lunged out of the dark.

"Stop!" Jackson yelled at a zombie which was inches from Ezhno, and then he lunged at it and tore its heart out.

"Thanks, man," Ezhno breathed.

Jackson helped his packmates take down the corpses, but no matter how hard he fought, he couldn't dismiss the horrible feeling that something was coming. "I have one of my feelings," he warned Daimon, his voice barely audible over the gruesome sounds of tearing flesh and snarls. As they dismantled the decaying creature, Jackson's eyes darted nervously, haunted by a lingering unease. "I saw something in the woods just now. I-I don't know, but I think we need to hurry up and get out of here, Daimon. I can't shake the feeling that we're being watched."

Daimon's snarl echoed through the dense, shadowy forest as he ripped the heart from another cadejo. "Where did you see it?" he demanded, his eyes narrowing with predatory intensity.

Jackson pointed his paw towards the two gnarled trees, where the blurred visage had materialized. "Over there."

"Advance!" Daimon commanded, his voice cutting through the eerie stillness.

The fighting pack surged forward, relentless in their assault on the cadejo.

As they approached the trees, Jackson's heart raced, drowning out the sound of the battle; he moved hesitantly, his paws heavy with the weight of impending doom. Alongside Daimon, he assisted his packmates, tearing through rotting wolves. As they reached the trees, he steeled himself for a confrontation with the unknown, preparing to unleash the inimă.

However, to his bewilderment, there was nothing. No looming creature, no spectral presence. Only the relentless onslaught of more cadejo, casting an unsettling shadow over the desolate woods.

"There's nothing here, Jackson," Daimon said as he looked around.

"More undead!" Clint called.

Jackson watched his allies fight off the cadejo. He couldn't ignore the feeling, though—it was still there. He felt like something was waiting to pounce. But what? Where? He looked around, his instincts *still* insisting that he fled.

He had to find it.

He had to know what he saw between those trees.

After he helped Julian take down a cadejo, and once he stunned a trio of corpses by yelling, "Stop!", he stared into the gloom. With a determined huff, he rushed off, hurrying deeper into the woods. He swerved past the cadejo, avoiding their snapping jaws, and when he got so far away that he couldn't hear the battle anymore…he stopped.

The snow beneath his paws quivered, not from the wind but from an unseen force that sent shivers through Jackson's fur. His heart thumped in his chest as he glanced around; the air was thick with an unsettling stillness, broken only by the sharp, whistling breeze that carried the scent of death.

Jackson shivered in trepidation; the weight of unseen eyes made him feel vulnerable, exposed to whatever was lingering in the shadows. Each passing moment intensified the scrutiny, an invisible predator assessing whether to strike or wait for the opportune moment.

A sudden snap cut through the stillness, a branch breaking under an unknown force.

Something stirred in the darkness ahead, a subtle shuffling that sent a chill down Jackson's spine.

The silence shattered with a low, rumbling growl, a sound that seemed to echo from the depths of an abyss.

It was here.

That ominous voice whispered to him. "*Harmonic… variant Perfect….*"

It had to be the prowler, the one that had spoken to him before the arrival of Raphael and his team.

Jackson stared into the darkness, watching as a stream of breath cut through the cold behind the trees. Heavy footsteps thumped closer, the snow crunching beneath each step.

And then he saw it.

The humongous silhouette of a bipedal creature, grotesquely taller than its initial appearance. What might have seemed like an Amarok twisted by the cadejo curse now revealed itself with antlers on its head, adorned with dangling vines. The ground quivered beneath the creature's colossal form, and its breaths, deep and sinister, cut through the cold air, snarling with a maniacal excitement—a malevolence that seemed almost pleased to see Jackson.

"*Finally*," it breathed, gripping the tree beside it was its mangled claws.

It edged its face out of the darkness… and Jackson stifled a horrified gasp.

The vines dangling from its massive antlers weren't vines but long, spindling cuts of flesh. Its face had no skin, revealing a dark, rotting skull with eyes as red as blood inside its deep sockets, and between those eyes sat a strange sigil carved into its bone.

It had to be a cadejo variant; the creature reeked of death, and what patches of fur that clung to its rotting body were a contorting mixture of orange and black.

Jackson stared up at it, shivering as fear won control of his body.

The creature grinned, baring a jaw full of sharp, jagged teeth. And with a delighted exhale, it whispered, "Jackson."

Chapter Seventy-Eight

⇀ ≼ ☽ ≽ ⇀

The Perfect Vessel

| Jackson |

There were no words to explain the horror that gripped Jackson's soul. A spectral paralysis seized him, rendering his limbs immobile, his heart pounding an erratic cadence in the cavernous stillness. Before him loomed a grotesque entity, a twisted amalgamation of flesh and nightmare, a monstrous silhouette that defied the laws of reason.

The creature spoke not with vocal cords but with a malevolent aura that wrapped itself around Jackson's very essence. It said his name with an otherworldly familiarity, a chilling recognition that transcended the mundane. It required no verbal declaration to convey its sinister intent; the macabre desire emanated from its disfigured countenance.

A grin, not of joy but of unholy satisfaction, etched across its deformed visage. Its eyes, devoid of humanity, fixated upon Jackson with an eerie intensity that penetrated the depths of his vulnerability. The creature's utterance slithered through the air like a serpentine whisper, a haunting resonance that echoed within the recesses of his tortured psyche.

"You're perfect," it exhaled, the words carrying the weight of a sepulchral promise. The creature's voice resonated as a subsonic undertone, a spectral symphony that stirred the shadows. "The perfect vessel."

Jackson's primal instincts, silenced by the oppressive atmosphere, failed to guide him. The urgency to flee surged within him, yet his corporeal shell remained captive to the malevolent force that loomed before him.

In the oppressive stillness, the unspoken truth manifested—a choice between annihilation and assimilation. The impending doom clung to the air, leaving Jackson ensnared in a web of existential terror, unsure of whether the impending fate was to be his demise or a grotesque metamorphosis into something beyond his comprehension.

The creature inched closer, causing the icy ground to tremble beneath its measured steps. Strangely, it seemed cautious, as if uncertain about Jackson. Its movements were slow, almost hesitant like it half-expected him to snap out of his fear and put up a fight.

Jackson fought against his fear, but the inimă showed no signs of awakening and wrapping around his neck, and his senses failed to detect any living entity nearby. He didn't know how to explain it, but it was like he was caught in a field ensnared by an invisible blanket that negated all his strength and senses, like a city struck by an EMP, like the power had suddenly gone out, leaving the world in darkness. He was powerless against the monster before him, and there was nothing he could do to stop it.

With a guttural growl, the creature took another step closer, moving out into the moonlight which cut through the tree branches. It towered over Jackson, even in his wolf form; it was bigger than Daimon, bigger than an Amarok, and it horrified him more than the sirens did.

The moonlight showed Jackson more of its ghastly bipedal form, revealing that its body was scarred with more runes like the one carved into its skull. The creature reeked...but not of rotting flesh. An ashy smell clung to its fur like someone had burned wood and leaves just before it started raining. And although the creature looked like it should be dead, Jackson could hear a heartbeat; he could smell fresh blood inside its body, and he could feel the warmth emanating from it.

Was this thing a cadejo...or was it something else entirely?

"I have waited...*centuries* for this," the creature breathed as it reached one of its bony, mangled hands towards Jackson.

Jackson's body recoiled from the impending touch of the creature; the mere thought of its contact sent shivers down his spine. He attempted to pivot and flee; however, the creature seized him with speed that defied everything he knew and had come to learn. In an instant, he found himself lifted from his paws and ruthlessly pressed against the gnarled bark of a tree.

The creature's strength manifested in its ability to effortlessly subdue Jackson. His grunts of resistance were drowned out by the eerie stillness of the surrounding woods, and the cold touch of the tree bark pressed into his fur, an unyielding witness to his predicament.

Locked in a desperate struggle, Jackson's eyes met those of the antlered wolf. A haunting silence enveloped them as the creature stared into the depths of his horrified gaze. No matter how vehemently Jackson fought against the overpowering force, the creature's strength proved insurmountable, an ominous reminder of his vulnerability in the face of an adversary belonging to the Caeleste world.

The fight echoed through the haunted woods, the very essence of suspense clinging to each strained breath and futile attempt to break free. In the chilling dance between predator and prey, Jackson's feeble resistance only served to emphasize the relentless power of the antlered wolf, leaving him ensnared in the inescapable grasp of a malevolent force.

"Not this time," the creature growled, its breath carrying the scent of blood and sulphur. "You're alone, no one to save you," it sneered, tilting its head to the side.

Jackson choked and flailed his legs around, but all his attempts were futile. "S-stop!" he commanded.

But that only made the monster laugh. "I answer to no one."

The creature's grip was slowly depriving Jackson of air, and he could feel the strength fading from his limbs. His heart raced as panic quickly ensnared him, and his rapid breaths only carried him much faster towards his inevitable slip into unconsciousness.

But when he felt the creature's sharp claws pierce his skin, Jackson was struck by more than just pain. His vision blurred, and his eyes rolled to the back of his head—and then he saw it.

Them.

Flashes of places he'd never seen before.

The overgrown halls of an abandoned home, its shattered windows covered in moss, and weeds growing through the marble floor.

A dark, abandoned tomb with an altar in its centre and scorch marks covering the old, cracked walls.

And a murky forest plagued by mangled, twisted creatures that made his heart race faster.

Deer.

Wolves.

Foxes.

It all blazed before him, and every time he saw something he'd already seen, it looked just a little older or a little more *dead*. He had no idea why he was seeing it all, or what any of it meant, but when the giant wolf let go of him and stumbled back with what sounded like a frustrated grunt, Jackson snapped out of it, and his vision returned to him.

He wasn't going to waste his chance.

Jackson bolted into the woods, his paws pounding against the ice. The sinister thump of the colossal, antlered wolf resonated ominously behind him, an unrelenting echo that drew nearer with each panicked step. Casting a frantic glance over his shoulder, dread seized him as he realized escape was already beyond his grasp.

The monstrous wolf closed the distance with speed unlike anything Jackson had seen, its presence overwhelming any semblance of hope. Before he could summon a defence, the creature's massive claws ensnared him, a merciless grip that extinguished any fleeting thoughts of evasion.

With a furious roar, the beast hoisted Jackson from the safety of his paws, callously flinging him aside like a discarded plaything. A sickening crack echoed through the desolate woods as Jackson's body collided with the unforgiving embrace of a tree; pain surged through him, and the ethereal boundary between flesh and agony blurred as something within him fractured.

The wintry landscape bore witness to Jackson's agonizing descent, the snow beneath him offering no solace, only a frigid bed of torment. Lying helpless, he could only watch as the monster approached, a predatory silhouette prowling through the eerie silence. The world seemed to hold its breath as it closed in, casting an oppressive pall over the fallen prey, and the woods whispered tales of impending suffering.

There was nothing he could do. His body wasn't responding, but this time, it wasn't because of fear. His bones were broken. His blood was oozing from wounds he couldn't see, and as he watched the snow around him stain red, his horror and fear grew into something suffocating. His breaths became harder to take, his heart raced so fast that it felt like it was about to burst out of his body, and his head was throbbing.

He tried to call for help, he tried to summon the inimă, but he was truly, entirely alone.

Until blue flames lit up the dark and collided with the antlered wolf.

Jackson watched as the beast stumbled away from him and tried to wipe the flames off itself, grunting and snarling in desperation. Its skin burned, its fur helped the fire spread, and the monster had no choice but to drop to the snow and writhe around.

That was when Sebastien landed in front of Jackson. Although he couldn't hear what the hound was telling him, Jackson knew that he was there to help, and his terror was quickly drowned out by relief.

But Sebastien suddenly stopped trying to help Jackson to his paws. He *froze*, and when Jackson looked up at him, he saw that the hound was staring at the antlered wolf, which had already extinguished his fire.

"*You...*" the monster drawled angrily.

Sebastien was *trembling*. He looked as if he'd seen a ghost—his face possessed an expression that Jackson would have never thought he'd see on him.

The hound shakily responded, "It's...you."

With a snarl and a grunt, the beast stood up straight, and the cautious stare that Jackson had seen on its face when he first encountered it reappeared. "Give me the vessel," it growled.

Sebastien shook his head. "No."

The creature scoffed and an evil grin stretched across its mangled face. "Are you *still* that naïve little brat? You couldn't save Caleb, or the *thousands* of others who've died because of you; what makes you think it'll be any different this time?"

Jackson trembled as the pain in his body grew. It was obvious that Sebastien knew who or what this antlered wolf was, but there wasn't time for questions. That thing wanted him, and he wasn't going to lay there and let it take him. "S-Sebastien," he grunted.

Sebastien scowled and stood protectively in front of Jackson. "I've learned a lot since then, including how to put fuckers like you back where they belong."

The creature's grin grew as it prowled a little closer.

But then the sound of thumping paws cut through the tense quiet, and the antlered wolf lost its maniacal smile. It looked over its shoulder, scowled frustratedly, and then set its eyes back on Jackson and Sebastien.

"Better do what you're best at," Sebastien warned.

With one last snarl, the monster growled, "You're on borrowed time, Huxley," and then it dropped to all fours and raced into the woods, disappearing in the blink of an eye.

Jackson closed his eyes as he exhaled in relief.

"Are you all right?" Sebastien asked, placing his paw on his shoulder.

Pain shot through his body, and Jackson flinched.

"Shit, sorry," the hound stuttered.

He shook his head and opened his eyes, and when he saw his pack, led by Daimon, rushing towards him, the rest of his fear withered. But a terrible sense of dread remained. What the hell was that thing? How did it render him and the inimă useless? How did it know Sebastien? How did Sebastien know *it*? And who was Caleb?

"What happened?" Daimon demanded as he hurried to Jackson's side.

"It was some kind of variant," Sebastien answered.

Jackson frowned strangely at him, but he wasn't going to question him in front of everyone. There was probably a good reason why he wasn't telling them the truth—whatever that may be.

Daimon nuzzled his mate's neck. "Why did you run off on your own?" he asked quietly, both confusion and dismay in his voice.

"I-I wanted to find whatever that thing was that I saw," he said with a pained grunt as Daimon assessed his wounds. "It was…I don't know. It had antlers."

"Antlers?" Julian questioned.

"Like a deer?" Wesley asked.

Jackson nodded. "Sebastien chased it off," he said as he glanced at Sebastien, who looked relieved that he'd said that.

"Should we go after it?" Brando suggested. "If it's a variant we haven't faced before, wouldn't it be best to learn what we can about—"

"It was massive," Sebastien interjected. "And fast. We can't afford to chase after something right now; Cyrus needs us."

"Can you walk?" Daimon asked Jackson.

Jackson carefully moved his legs around; he could feel his body healing, and although the pain was still agonizing, he was able to climb to his paws without making it any worse. He stood up, leaning on Daimon, and then he looked at his concerned packmates. "Where's Tokala?" he asked, seeing that the orange wolf wasn't with them, and neither were Lance and Lalo.

"Back at the fight," Wesley answered.

"Can you take him to the rendezvous point?" Daimon asked Sebastien, gesturing to Jackson.

"Why?" Jackson asked, confused.

"You need to rest and heal. The rest of us can keep fighting," his mate told him.

But Jackson shook his head. He didn't want to rest—he didn't want to have to leave the battle. He could help, and his packmates needed him. "I'm fine," he insisted. "I can keep fighting."

"You took a pretty devastating blow," Sebastien said.

"I'm fine!" he exclaimed. "We're wasting time just standing here talking about it."

Daimon shook his head and quietly said, "You're bleeding."

Jackson looked at the wounds on his body. "Then just take me to Raph—H-Heir Zephyr; he can heal me."

The Alpha's worried, reluctant stare thickened.

"He *is* on healing duty," Sebastien said.

"I'll be okay," Jackson told his mate softly. "Come on."

Daimon huffed and pondered, but he clearly knew as well as everyone else did that the longer they stood there, the longer Cyrus' wolves had to hold off the cadejo alone. So the Alpha sighed and nodded. "All right. Let's get back."

"What about that variant?" Julian asked as the pack started heading back towards the battle.

"I'll warn everyone," Sebastien said and hastily took off.

Jackson watched him disappear above the trees. He couldn't help but feel skeptical; Sebastien knew something about that antlered wolf—they seemed to know *each other*, but the fact that Sebastien hid that from everyone made Jackson think that maybe it was some kind of Nosferatu business. But that monster wanted *him*, it called him a perfect hybrid, a perfect *vessel*, and he hadn't forgotten about the things he saw when that creature's claws cut into his skin, either. Whatever it was, he wanted to find out.

Chapter Seventy-Nine

⤺ ≼ ☽ ≽ ⤻

Victor

| Jackson |

The abandoned mining town lay still beneath the canopy of towering pines, the air thick with an eerie silence that echoed the anticipation of the looming confrontation. Kane, his black fur blending seamlessly with the shadows, moved with a sinister grace. His eyes betrayed a wicked intelligence as a subtle smirk curled on his maw. He circled Cyrus, who stood tall on his hind legs, his stoic demeanour belying an equal measure of caution. His wounds looked much worse than Kane's, but Jackson knew that was because his fur was white, the perfect canvas for the crimson dismay seeping from between his fur. Kane was bleeding all over the snow, leaving a trail as he prowled warily.

Jackson watched between the rubble of the building he lay in while Raphael tended to his wounds. The two monstrous wolves clashed in a dance of fangs and claws, each strike met with a counter from the other. A rain of red marred the ice as they exchanged blows, and the crowd, a sea of wolves divided between Cyrus' and Kane's packs, observed in breathless silence, seemingly oblivious to the storm of cadejo trying to breach their packmates' defences just a few feet away.

Unable to take his eyes off the fight, Jackson felt the weight of both packs' angst hanging in the frigid air. His breath escaped in shallow puffs as he anxiously observed, knowing that the outcome could seal the fate of the entire wolf walker species.

The fight raged on, each combatant seemingly evenly matched, until Kane, true to his crafty, cowardly nature, executed a sudden move that caught Cyrus off guard. He lunged at Kane, who instinctually moved to block his attack just as he had several times before, but Kane moved with speed he hadn't displayed before, and when Cyrus lifted his arms in defence, the black wolf curved his strange body and savagely sunk his teeth into Cyrus' thigh. He yanked back and forth as Cyrus yelped in agony, and when he tore a *huge* chunk of the white wolf's flesh from his body, a low growl of satisfaction escaped Kane's maniacal breaths.

A surge of panic rippled through the onlooking crowd. Even Jackson flinched.

"Don't fucking move!" Raphael growled.

Jackson fell still but didn't spare his healer a glance. He couldn't look away, not for a moment.

Cyrus stumbled back and hit the ground, grasping his thigh with both his huge paws. Kane cackled as he prowled around him, and then he burst forward and clamped his jaws around Cyrus' arm. As the white Alpha snarled and yelped, Kane started tugging, harder and harder as his pack cheered him on. No matter how many times Cyrus' fist met the cruel wolf's face, Kane didn't let go, and when the sound of tearing flesh cut through the roaring crowd, Jackson cringed and fought the urge to look away.

But he was glad that he chose to keep watching.

Just as hope seemed to wither away, something miraculous occurred. Cyrus, battered and seemingly defeated, summoned a surge of strength; despite the horrific injury on his leg, he managed to lift it and kick Kane's side, sending the black wolf stumbling aside. His white fur gleamed in the moonlight as he rose, and his wolves among the crowd, momentarily silenced by despair, erupted into gasps of disbelief and renewed hope.

With a roar that echoed through the snowy forest, Cyrus unleashed a torrent of power. His form seemed to radiate an otherworldly light, and the very ground quivered beneath him. Kane, caught off guard by the sudden reversal, was unable to withstand Cyrus' unleashed might; his desperate attempts to avoid and block each of Cyrus' devastating blows were almost laughable, and when he evidently worked out that it was over for him, he tried to turn around and run.

But Cyrus snatched him by his scruff and yanked him back. He then turned him around, grabbed his throat, and lifted him off his paws.

Jackson's racing heart seemed to stop beating for a moment as he watched the massive Prime decide whether he wanted to tear Kane apart or not. He knew it was awful of him to hope that Cyrus would rip that creature to shreds, but he didn't regret it. Kane deserved to die; he had to pay for every single wolf he'd hurt and killed. He deserved to pay for what he did to Julian, Alastor, Enola, Bly, and Rachel. And *Lumi*, too. And all those people he'd locked up in that dungeon. All the humans he'd killed—the ones that weren't hunters, anyway. And all the wolves' lives he'd made hell. It was time for him to face his crimes.

And Cyrus seemed to share that notion.

The white wolf roared ferociously in Kane's face. Kane started begging like the pathetic coward he truly was, but Cyrus clearly gave as few fucks as Jackson did. Without remorse, Cyrus gripped either of Kane's front legs, and with one powerful, *disgusting* pull, the black wolf's body tore into two, and as his insides started pouring out, Jackson grimaced and looked away. He'd seen enough.

He looked at his own injured body and watched as it slowly healed in response to Raphael's touch.

"Were you expecting any less?" the orange wolf muttered.

Jackson frowned. "What?"

"Kane didn't stand a chance against Cyrus. We all knew it."

"Oh…I mean I've never seen Cyrus fight, so I was a little worried, yeah," he admitted.

Raphael took his paws off Jackson's furred leg. "Lay there until you're told it's time to move out. Your body will do the rest on its own. You should also increase your blood intake to at least four or five times a week." He then turned around—

"Why?" Jackson asked with a frown.

The orange wolf turned to face him again. "Because demon offspring require it."

As embarrassment and dismay filled him, Jackson looked away.

"You did…know that you're—"

"I know," he snapped before Raphael could say the words. "I just…didn't know the blood thing."

"Well, I'm not surprised. You should probably book an appointment with Sinclair. He's the best guy to ask about this sort of thing."

Jackson half-nodded. "How do you…know? Is everyone gonna—"

"I know because I had to access your body's ethos to heal you. It's unlikely that anyone else will be able to tell, though; demon offspring are very hard to detect while inside their…parent." He then turned around and went over to one of the other injured wolves.

Being reminded that he was pregnant made Jackson feel dismay and dysphoria—it even made him feel a little sick. A part of him was glad that nobody would be able to tell until he was ready to explain it to Daimon himself, but he still didn't know when or if that time would come.

With a conflicted frown, he turned his head and peered through the rubble at the battlefield. Cyrus, triumphant yet exhausted, stood amidst the fallen snow. Every wolf began to bow their heads in recognition of his win, and it was then that Jackson realized that Cyrus' victory had saved *everyone*. Not just Kane's wolves, and not just his own or Daimon's, but every single wolf walker—all of Caeleste kind, even. Now, Daimon's pack could continue their mission to get to the lab, and hopefully, whatever waited inside would reveal the cure to the cadejo virus.

"Clear the cadejo out!" Cyrus' voice bellowed, his command reaching the ears of every capable wolf.

Jackson watched the crowd disperse and join the battle by the tree line. He wanted to get up and help, especially since Daimon was out there, but he knew that his mate could handle himself, and in his current state, he'd be nothing but a burden and distraction to Daimon. So he remained where he was and observed as Cyrus' *massive* pack took down the swarming undead.

But something sat upon the howling breeze.

A voice.

A feeling.

A *reminder*.

That antlered creature was still out there…watching, waiting. Jackson could feel its eyes on him, he could feel how desperately it wanted him, and he could feel its animosity among the twisting trees.

"*Jackson*," its voice echoed, sending chills down Jackson's spine.

His heart started racing again. He looked around the decrepit building, gawping at the faces of all the injured wolves. But it was Daimon who he really wanted to see, so he stared through the rubble again, hoping to catch a glimpse of his mate, a glimpse that would give him the feeling of safety that he desperately needed—

"Jackson."

Jackson flinched violently as he sharply turned his head and set his eyes on Tokala. The orange wolf stood a few feet away with a confused look on his face like he was waiting for him to reply.

"Are you feeling better?" he asked.

With a shake of his head, Jackson snapped out of it and nodded. "Y-yeah. Heir Zephyr healed me; he said my body would do the rest."

Tokala sat in front of him. "Wesley told me what happened out there. I'm sorry I wasn't there to help. We could've probably chased it down if I was."

"It's fine, I guess. You had to deal with other cadejo. At least we know it's out there, though."

"Yeah. I'm sure Cyrus or someone from the Nosferatu or Venaticus will deal with it."

Jackson glanced outside. "Is everyone okay? I feel stupid sitting here doing nothing."

"Everyone's fine," Tokala assured him. "The chief and Cyrus are rounding them up, dealing with the last of the cadejo. I think we'll be heading back to the house soon."

With a nod, Jackson set his eyes back on the orange wolf. "Do you think there's gonna be enough room in that house for all the wolves Cyrus just won from Kane?" he asked amusedly.

"Probably. I was looking around in our downtime; the place is massive."

"I kinda wanted to have a look around, too, but ever since that business with Heir Lucian, I've been, well…you know," Jackson admitted.

Tokala nodded. "Mmh. I know different Caeleste have different rules and traditions and such, but from what I've seen of demons so far, I don't think I'd survive very long as one," he said, chuckling.

"I'm just glad I'm with you guys. I don't think I'd make it very long with a demon pack, either," he said with a sigh.

Amos then peeked in through one of the gaps in the wall. "Hey, we're moving out. You all good to move?"

"Everyone's fine," Raphael said as he stopped healing one of the other wolves.

"You good, kid?" Amos asked Jackson.

Jackson nodded, and when he stood up, he stumbled a little, and Tokala helped him balance himself. "Thanks," he said.

The orange wolf smiled and asked him, "Do you need help walking?"

He shook his head. "I'll be okay. Thank you, though."

And then he saw Sebastien. He had so many questions, and he didn't want to wait to ask them, so he hurried past Tokala, out of the decrepit building, and towards the winged hound, who was watching while the wolves slowly gathered in the old town.

"Sebastien," he called as he approached him.

The hound glanced over his shoulder at him.

Jackson slowed his approach, and once he walked around Sebastien and stood in front of him, he noticed the *haunted* look on his face. Maybe now *wasn't* the best time to ask…but he was reluctant to wait. "Th-that thing with the antlers. I—"

"I don't wanna talk about it," he dismissed and turned his back on Jackson.

With a determined frown, Jackson moved around to Sebastien's front again. "You knew each other—you knew what that thing was."

Sebastien didn't reply.

"Is it some kind of variant? Like a prowler?"

He still didn't answer, but his haunted, irritated expression was worsening with every word that Jackson spoke.

"You said you knew how to put it back where it belonged, and then it said something about someone called Caleb, and—"

"Just shut up, okay?" Sebastien snapped angrily. "I said I didn't want to talk about it." He started walking away.

Jackson followed him. He wasn't going to give up yet. Sebastien was hiding something—something important—and he wanted to know what, especially since that antlered monster wanted *him*. "Why did it call me a vessel? It was trying to take me, and I have the right to know wh—"

"Actually, you don't," the hound interjected as he stopped walking and sharply turned his body to face Jackson. "This has nothing to do with you."

"But it tried to fucking take me; how does this have nothing—"

"Because you're just some kid, okay? Stay in your lane." He turned around and started walking again.

Jackson huffed frustratedly but didn't follow. As aggravated as he felt, he knew that he wasn't going to get answers out of him. Not yet at least. But whatever Sebastien knew, there had to be a reason why he was keeping it to himself, right? He wasn't sure, but if Sebastien didn't give him what he wanted, then he'd ask around. There *had* to be someone else who knew what that antlered wolf was.

"Jackson!" came Daimon's voice.

Relief flooded through Jackson as if storm gates had been opened. He turned to face his incoming mate, and when Daimon wrapped his wolfish arms around him, Jackson smiled contently and buried his face in the Alpha's thick, soft fur.

"Are you okay?" his mate asked quietly.

"Yeah," he replied, nuzzling Daimon's neck. "Heir Zephyr healed me up. I still feel a little wobbly, but he said I'll be okay."

"Good," Daimon said and started caressing Jackson's neck with his muzzle. "What were you chasing Sebastien for?"

"I was trying to get him to tell me what that antlered wolf is, but he's being super defensive."

"I'm sure we'll get answers once we tell Cyrus what we saw."

"I hope so," Jackson mumbled. He then lifted his head from Daimon's fur and gazed into his honey-brown eyes. "Are *you* okay?"

The Alpha nodded. "Fine, but a little surprised, if I'm being honest. The only casualty of this battle was Kane. These guys have obviously been at this kind of thing a long time; makes me feel like I'm putting the Greyblood line to shame."

Jackson frowned. "What? I don't think so. I mean Cyrus is *really* old, right? *And* he's connected to the Nosferatu, so of course he's gonna be this good. But that doesn't make you any less of an Alpha, Daimon."

Daimon smiled weakly and said, "Maybe. I'm just glad you're okay."

"I'm glad you're okay, too," he murmured and nuzzled Daimon's neck again. He'd find out what he could about that antlered wolf once they got back to the house. Right now, he just wanted to enjoy his mate's embrace and bask in the relief that came with Cyrus' victory.

Chapter Eighty

The Phantom

| Sebastien |

The *moment* Sebastien stepped through the manor doors, he pulled Raphael aside and asked him, "Where's Lord Caedis?"

"Still down in the conference hall somewhere," he mumbled. "Why?"

"I need to speak to him," he said as he morphed into his human form.

"Hmph," Raphael huffed and walked off.

Sebastien waited as patiently as he could, his legs trembling, his heart racing. Once everyone left the hall, he used his claws to cut his palm and smeared his blood on the very middle floor tile. The marble trembled and transformed, widening to reveal the staircase which led to the conference hall, and he raced down as fast as his legs would carry him.

When he reached the doors, he sprinted across the conference hall and to the door between the rows of seats. He pulled it open and navigated the narrow corridor to its end, and with a breathy, frantic huff, he pushed open the oak double doors—

He froze when he saw Lords Caedis and Zalith naked on the couch; Lord Caedis was on his hands and knees, and Lord Zalith kneeled behind him—they stopped fucking the moment Sebastien burst in and sharply turned their heads, setting their hostile gazes on him.

"Get zhe fuck out!" Lord Caedis yelled furiously.

Sebastien immediately darted out of the room and pulled the doors shut behind him. Seeing his bosses having sex was traumatizing enough but knowing that he was about to get the scolding of his life was worse. He knew that he was supposed to knock.

He shook his head as he walked back towards the conference hall, trying to unsee what he'd just seen, but he could hear their moans echoing down the corridor, and holding his hands over his ears wasn't enough to block out the sound.

When he got to the conference hall, he pulled out one of the seats at the table and sat down. He waited, tapping his fingers on the surface. But the longer he sat there, the heavier his angst became. Seeing that... *thing* out in the woods after such a long time horrified him. He couldn't shake the anxious chill that ensnared his tense body, and the longer he let the fear consume him, the harder it became for him to fight off the haunting, dismaying memory of *that* night.

The door behind him swung open with a loud bang—

Sebastien jumped to his feet and turned to face Lord Caedis just in time to see his infuriated face—and his fully clothed body. His boss snatched his collar and pinned him down on the table.

"'Ow many fucking times do you need to be told to knock on zhe fucking doors?!" Lord Caedis exclaimed, anger seething from his hell-fiery eyes.

"I-I'm sorry," Sebastien stuttered, meek in his boss' enraged gaze. "I-I really need to tell you so—"

"Zhen use a fucking phone!"

"It's the phantom!" he exclaimed, panting.

The furious look on Lord Caedis' face slowly contorted into a confused one.

"I saw it," Sebastien continued. "Antlers, red eyes, the runes."

Lord Caedis gradually released his grip on Sebastien's neck, and when he stepped back, adorning a concerned, pondering expression, Sebastien stood up straight and stared at him.

"It wanted Jackson—it *wants* Jackson," he said worriedly. "It almost had him, but we got there in time to send it running. But it was *him*, My Lord, I swear."

A tense silence fell over them as Lord Caedis wordlessly thought to himself. The expression on his face journeyed from concerned, to angry, to cautious. He then set his gaze on Sebastien and said, "Show me."

Sebastien admittedly felt nervous about sharing his memory with Lord Caedis, but he didn't have a choice. He slowly lifted his hand and edged it shakily towards his boss' face, but Lord Caedis hastily placed his middle and index fingers on Sebastien's temple and his thumb along his jawline, and then he grabbed Sebastien's wrist and made him put his hand on *his* face.

Once he positioned his hand correctly on Lord Caedis' face, Sebastien closed his eyes and concentrated.

"Show me zhe exact moment you saw 'im," Lord Caedis ordered.

Sebastien nodded and recalled the moment he saw the antlered wolf. He felt Lord Caedis digging around inside his head, like a snake slithering through his brain. But he stifled a whimper and stopped himself from grimacing, waiting for the moment the memory was over and Lord Caedis let him go.

But the seconds dragged on into minutes; Lord Caedis examined the memory over and over again, and Sebastien was beginning to get a headache. He held on, though; he knew better than to question his boss.

"Vhere's Jackson?" Lord Caedis suddenly asked as he let go of Sebastien and backed off.

As his skull throbbed, Sebastien rubbed his temples and groaned quietly. "Uh... he's upstairs... with his pack or something." He shook his head and frowned hauntedly. "It's him, right? From Alder Estate."

Lord Caedis nodded slowly. "Ve knew 'e vould show 'is vace again—vas inevitable. 'E needs a new body, and vould seem zhat 'e's chosen Jackson to be 'is vessel."

"What do we do? We've already delayed the lab mission so much already, but we can't send Jackson back out there with that thing, can we?" he asked anxiously.

His boss adorned the same expression he always did when he was thinking. Every moment that ticked by made the silence feel more tense, and when he finally spoke, his words were firm and decided. "Ve can't postpone zhe lab mission again. My gvandson vill be vith you, as vill several of Cyrus' volves. Ve know zhe phantom can't visk getting 'urt, so 'e von't come near Jackson if 'e 'as allies avound 'im. Zon't take your eyes off 'im; make sure 'e alvays 'as at least vive of you vith 'im at all times, and if you so much as see a *glimpse* of zhe phantom, you summon me. Understand?"

Sebastien nodded. "Y-yeah, I understand."

Lord Caedis pulled a small glass vial from his pocket. He cut his palm with his claws, and then he let his blood drip inside. Once it was full, he plugged the vial shut with a small cork and handed it to Sebastien. "You vemember zhe vords?"

"Of course, My Lord," he said with a nod as a shiver of trepidation shot through him. He'd only ever seen others summon a powerful deity, but he was confident that he'd witnessed it enough times to get it right.

"Go. Let everyvone vest vor zhe night. You vill leave at dawn vor zhe lab," he instructed, and then he turned around and disappeared through the double doors.

Sebastien looked down at the vial of blood. In his hand, he was holding what was probably one of the most precious things in this realm. Anyone who wasn't loyal to Lord Caedis could take it and wreak horrific destruction; someone who knew how to transmute could transform it into anything they desired—money, power, or even someone they'd lost to death. But not Sebastien. No. He'd do exactly as Lord Caedis instructed—if he needed to.

| **Jackson** |

While he lay on the couch with his head resting on Daimon's chest, Jackson tried to work out who to ask about the antlered wolf. He was already sure that Sebastien wasn't going to give him answers, but there *had* to be someone else around this place who knew *something*, right?

"If there's anything I'm gonna miss about this place, it's getting this stuff," Julian said as they greedily chewed their Slappy's burger.

"You know it's super unhealthy, right?" Lalo replied.

"So? It's delicious," Remus said and sipped loudly from his drink.

While everyone started arguing with Lalo, Daimon looked down at Jackson and asked him, "Are you okay?"

He nodded as he glanced up at him.

"Are you not hungry?"

"Not really," he admitted. Not only was he eager to get answers about that monster, but seeing everyone so relieved and content made him think of Ethan. Despite what happened, he missed his friend; however, he knew that their relationship was now likely at an end.

Daimon started fiddling with Jackson's hair. "Are you worried about that creature?"

Jackson sighed deeply. "Yeah... but I also need to talk to Ethan. I'm not ready to have to make a choice; I know I have to, though."

"You don't have to talk to him now," Daimon mumbled. "You could leave it until we're back from the lab."

He could feel himself about to consider it, but he dismissed the idea before it could take root. If he didn't face Ethan now and make up his mind, he'd never do it. "I can't," he said sullenly. "I need to do it before we go. I don't wanna leave him here for God knows how long while we go out there to find the lab."

Daimon looked disgruntled but muttered, "All right," in response. "Would you prefer Tokala or Wesley in there with you?"

"Probably Tokala," he answered.

"I'll go and tell him what's happening," Daimon said as he sat up.

"And I should probably find out where Ethan even is," Jackson said with a frown.

Daimon nodded and got off the couch; he headed over to Tokala.

Jackson got up, too, and when he saw Raphael pass the room, he hesitated. He didn't want to talk to him; he'd probably get snapped at... or worse. Maybe he could go and find Amos or Elias.

But just as he was about to head for the door, *Sebastien* stepped in.

The white-haired demon loudly cleared his throat, and when everyone looked at him, he said, "I spoke to Lord Caedis. You can all rest for the night, and we leave for the lab first thing in the morning."

"Like... right away?" Julian asked nervously.

"Yeah. Dawn," Sebastien confirmed. "Heir Zephyr's coming, and so are Amos and Elias."

"Why?" Wesley questioned.

"Extra protection for Jackson. That antlered wolf could still be out there waiting for a chance to snatch him, so Lord Caedis wants to make sure that doesn't happen. Now get some rest. We've got a long journey ahead of us tomorrow." He then turned around—

"Sebastien," Jackson called as he hurried over to him.

Sebastien sighed deeply and walked towards the door. "I already said, I'm not answering any questions about—"

"N-no, I actually just wanna know where Ethan is. I need to talk to him," he said, following him down the hallway.

The white-haired demon shot him an unsure glance. "Aren't you two having problems? It's probably best to leave it until you've got to the lab."

Jackson shook his head. "I already told Daimon; I don't wanna leave Ethan here with a bunch of strangers for God knows how long. I want to try and resolve all of this shit before we leave. I mean having him around would help, especially with that…thing out there, right?"

Sebastien stopped walking and sighed deeply. "I don't know, man. It's your call. He's in room twenty-three on the second floor." He then walked off, leaving Jackson alone.

Now that he knew where Ethan was, Jackson felt a little more nervous. But he wasn't going to put off their inevitable conversation; Ethan deserved better than that.

He made his way back into the lounge and joined Daimon and Tokala. "Well, Ethan's on the second floor," he told his mate.

Daimon's disgruntled expression thickened.

"So…we're going now?" Tokala asked unsurely.

"I wanna see if we can sort this out before we have to leave for the lab," Jackson said with a nod.

The Alpha huffed irritably.

Jackson didn't want to argue, especially not in front of everyone. If he and Ethan could come to some sort of agreement, then maybe everything would be okay. But if Ethan didn't calm down, then Jackson was afraid that he might have to choose between him and Daimon…and he already knew who he was going to pick.

Chapter Eighty-One

⌐ ≼ ☽ ≽ ⌐

It Will Always Be Him

| **Jackson** |

As Jackson approached the guarded room where Ethan had been put, his heart started beating faster. He felt anxious, dismayed, and a little angry; he didn't know what would come of the conversation he needed to have with his friend, but he hoped that he wouldn't have to cut ties. Despite everything...Ethan was still his friend.

Seeing the guards also reminded him that he needed to find who had stabbed Daimon. He considered enlisting Tokala's help, and it seemed as though it was the best idea; Tokala could sense people's intentions, and he'd be able to help him and Julian find whoever tried to kill their Alpha much faster.

"What do you want?" the man guarding the door suddenly asked when Jackson, Tokala, and Daimon stopped in front of him.

"Uh...to see Ethan," Jackson answered. "Sebastien told me where to find him."

The man's sights shifted between the three of them but quickly locked on Daimon. "Not you."

With an irritated huff, Daimon turned to face Jackson. "I'll just be down the hall," he said and kissed his lips.

Jackson smiled and nodded, and as his mate headed back down the hall, he did his best to calm his racing heart. "Can I go in?" he asked the guard.

"Why are *you* here?" the man questioned Tokala.

"To make sure that Ethan doesn't harm Jackson," the orange-haired Zeta answered.

"Hmph. Make it quick," he said and then pushed the door open.

Jackson nervously fiddled with his fingers, stepping past the guard and into the room.

Ethan, who was sitting cross-legged on the bed with a gloomy, hopeless look on his face, sat up straight the moment he set his eyes on Jackson, and a surprised but wary expression contorted his face.

When the door shut behind him, Jackson flinched, and while he tried to work out what he wanted to say, he gawped across the room at his friend.

"So…" Ethan started, "are you here to tell me to pack my bags…go back to New Dawnward?" he asked despondently.

Jackson frowned. "No," he said, moving closer. "Well…I hope not," he corrected, stopping a few feet from the bed.

Ethan scoffed and looked over at the window. "Right. That's why you've got a bodyguard, right?" He turned his head and glared at Jackson. "Afraid I'm gonna attack you or something?"

"No," Jackson said as his thrown thickened. "He's here because Daimon's worried for me."

"Daimon," Ethan snarled.

Jackson sighed deeply and shook his head. "Look, I wanna talk so we can move past this. I don't want to send you back to New Dawnward or wherever; I want you to stay, but only if you calm the hell down!" he exclaimed. "I told you how I feel, and if you can't accept that, then you can't stay here. All this fighting with Daimon isn't helping *anyone* and one of you is gonna end up killing the other."

Ethan went to say something, but he hesitated and glared out the window again.

Unsure whether Ethan was taking him seriously or not, Jackson moved closer to the bed and sat on the edge. "Ethan," he insisted.

His friend slowly set his gaze on him.

"Do you get what I'm saying?"

The muto scoffed. "Yeah. Stop trying to save you from that narcissistic piece of—"

Jackson shot to his feet. "This is what I'm talking about! Daimon hasn't done anything to harm or manipulate me, *ever*! And if you can't see that and get over this stupid hatred that you have for him, then we can't be friends anymore."

A look of utter astonishment slapped Ethan's face. "Why are you letting this guy get between us? You've known him for like a month, Jackson. What the fuck is a month next to our years?" he questioned, resentment in his voice.

"Because Daimon's my mate!" he answered frustratedly. "How many times do I need to tell you?"

"Right, your mate," he grumbled and looked away again.

Jackson felt his frustration evolving into anger. He wanted to snap, and something inside him was *urging* him to, but the last thing he wanted was to lose his temper. He exhaled deeply in an attempt to calm himself. "Wilson, if our friendship meant nothing to me, I wouldn't be here trying to work through this. I love Daimon, but I also love you—like a *brother*, okay? You're my brother; you always have been, and always will be. I don't wanna lose you, especially not now, but I can't…have you trying to kiss me or convince me that you're better for me than the guy I imprinted on."

Ethan didn't immediately answer. He looked like he wanted to interject several times, but he held back, and now that Jackson was finished, it seemed as though he didn't know what to say.

But Jackson waited. He stood there as the seconds ticked by, letting his friend process and think. However, he started to worry that he might have been too harsh, or that Ethan would think he didn't care, or that he just wanted to get rid of him to make his life easier. But that wasn't the case at all. If he could keep both his mate and best friend around, he would. The rest was up to Ethan.

The silence grew thicker with uncertainty, but after a few long moments, Ethan looked up at Jackson and frowned sullenly. "Why him, though? What did he do that made you decide you wanted to spend the rest of your life with him?" he asked hopelessly.

Jackson sighed and sat back down on the edge of the bed. "Because he just…I don't know. He gets me. Unlike everyone else around me, he didn't judge me for being who and what I am. He protected me, saved my life, and he came back for me when I was banished from his territory. He came back for me a bunch of times, actually. He helped me learn how to survive out here, and he makes me feel safe. He doesn't make me feel like all I'm good for is sex. He loves me, and I love him, and nothing you do or say is going to change that," he explained, and the more he said, the more he realized how much he really did love Daimon; it made him realize how much his mate meant to him, and how much he'd done for him. And if now was the moment where he had to choose…he wouldn't hesitate to tell Ethan that it was and always would be Daimon.

"I get you," Ethan mumbled despondently. "I never judged you. *I* protected you. What did he do differently? What did *I* do wrong? I don't understand."

"You didn't do anything wrong, Ethan," Jackson said, shaking his head. "It's just…different. I told you; I've always seen you as my brother, and I still want you in my life…just not in the way *you* want."

A look of despair covered Ethan's face as he looked away again.

Jackson knew that look. He knew that his friend was trying to hold back tears. He wanted to comfort him, but he wasn't sure if Ethan would appreciate it right now, so he waited for him to reply.

"I'll never be good enough," Ethan lamented, his voice breaking. "And I guess that's gonna have to be okay, isn't it?" he sniffled, gradually turning his teary face to look at Jackson. "I mean I've already spent our entire lives watching you love other people, haven't I? It's nothing new. I'll get over it—I don't really have a choice in the matter."

As Ethan's despair grew, Jackson began to feel guiltier. But he had to resist the urge to tell him that he was wrong; he had to resist the urge to comfort him with lies. This was how it was, and he couldn't change that. "I'm sorry, Ethan," he said sadly, slowly moving his hand over his friend's shoulder. "But I really mean it; I still want you here."

Ethan dragged his hands over his wet face and laughed derisively. He didn't say anything to match his chuckle, though. With a shake of his head, he cleared his throat and looked at Jackson. "Yeah. I mean what kind of friend would I be if I left you out here in zombie land, huh?"

Jackson wasn't sure whether he was being sarcastic or trying to shift to a less depressing atmosphere, but he suspected it was the latter, so he smiled a little and said with a small laugh, "Not a very good one."

The muto cleared his throat again and slapped his knees. "So...when do we go to this lab now that this Kane shit's out the way?"

"You heard?" Jackson asked as he took his hand off Ethan's shoulder.

"Yeah. I might be locked up, but I still have that lycan hearing. Did Cyrus really tear him in half?"

Jackson grimaced when he remembered the gory sight. "Yeah. Not gonna lie, I thought I was gonna throw up."

"Would've been cool to see."

"It wasn't pretty," Tokala chimed in.

Having forgotten that he'd been standing there the entire time, Jackson looked over his shoulder at him and said, "At least it's over, though." He set his eyes on Ethan again. "We're leaving for the lab first thing in the morning. Heir Zephyr, Amos, and Elias are coming with us."

"Great," Ethan muttered. "I guess Raphael's better than Lucian, though."

"Definitely," Jackson agreed.

Ethan smiled and glanced around. "Do you have to go back to Daimon?"

Jackson stifled a sigh and said, "Yeah. He's kinda waiting down the hall. And I mean it's late...and we should get as much rest as we can before tomorrow. We'll be heading to the lab, and hopefully, we all find the answers we're looking for."

A despondent frown flickered across Ethan's face, but he didn't argue. "Yeah. Maybe I'll find out where my parents went."

"I hope so," Jackson said. "And hopefully we find something there that can help the Nosferatu find a cure for the virus."

"Here's hoping," Ethan said unenthusiastically.

Jackson could feel the atmosphere growing awkward. He didn't want to let it get any worse. "Okay, well...thanks for understanding...and for not screaming at me and calling me an asshole."

Ethan laughed a little and looked away.

"I'm gonna go get some sleep, so...I'll see you in the morning, okay?"

"Yeah. Night," he said dismissively.

Jackson wasn't going to argue with him. He was certain that his friend needed space, so he was going to give it to him. He stood up and headed for the door, and when he looked back over his shoulder, he watched Ethan turn to face the window, sitting with his back to Jackson.

"Let's go," Tokala said as he opened the door.

With a nod, Jackson left the room, and as the guard closed the door behind them, he headed down the hall to where Daimon was waiting.

The Alpha immediately stood up from the couch he'd been sitting on and asked, "How did it go?"

"Fine, I guess," Jackson said with a shrug. He still felt guilty, and he was worried that his and Ethan's friendship wouldn't be the same—he already knew that it would be different... but not so different that Ethan couldn't even look at him for longer than a few moments anymore.

Daimon shifted his sights to Tokala, who nodded.

"He's gonna back off," Jackson told Daimon. "And he's gonna come with us to the lab."

His mate didn't look very happy about the last part of his sentence, but he didn't huff or snarl; Daimon exhaled deeply in what looked like an attempt to stay calm.

"He gets it," Jackson added. "I told him that it's always gonna be you, and he kinda just... backed down, I guess."

"Hmph. Well, what he says and what he does are two very different things," Daiimon muttered irritably.

"I believed him," he insisted.

Daimon sighed and said, "We'll see. We should get some rest."

Jackson nodded in agreement. He was exhausted more than anything else, and sleep was exactly what he needed right now. He just hoped that Ethan wouldn't decide to change his tone overnight; the last thing he wanted was to wake up to him and Daimon fighting again. But as guilty as it made him feel, Ethan *did* seem to understand; he sounded defeated, and he looked utterly heartbroken, but he hadn't fought with Jackson, which he took as a sign that maybe he finally accepted everything Jackson told him.

But the only way to be sure would be to see how he acted tomorrow, and Jackson couldn't help but dread what the morning would bring.

Chapter Eighty-Two

Guilt and Shame

| Sebastien |

The hours ticked by, and Sebastien couldn't sleep. He couldn't stop thinking about the phantom. Those red eyes. That gnarly, serpentine voice. And the harrowing reminder of what happened in the crypt where he first laid eyes on the creature.

He couldn't escape the memory of that night, the night Caleb died because of him, the night Sebastien had made a horrible mistake which would haunt him for the rest of his indefinite life.

Calling Clementine was the only thing he knew that would calm him down, but it was 5 a.m. in Uzlia, and he didn't want to wake his mate up so early just for a conversation that they'd had countless times before, especially since Clementine needed all the sleep he could get before his interview at the Uzlia Journal.

He tossed and turned in his bed, trying to find something else to focus on, but *nothing* grasped his attention, not even the fact that he'd seen his bosses having sex earlier. Something like that would drill its way into his brain and stay there for weeks, but not this time. The phantom claimed his mind, his senses, and even his sleep.

With a deep sigh, he sat up and slouched forward. He stared out the tall window to his left, watching as the snow fell from the moonlit sky, and it forced a depressing melancholy on him. Two centuries ago, the sky would be full of skyfish by now, enjoying the snow, taking a chance to swim down from above the clouds and bask in the light of lanterns and candles. But there wasn't a single fish in sight; their numbers had slowly withered since the middle of the great world war, and even after it was over, the creatures hadn't shown signs of returning. Sebastien suspected that it had something to do with how dark and dangerous the world had become... and it was all his fault.

To make things worse, the phantom was after Jackson, the one person who might be able to help the Nosferatu find a cure for the cadejo virus after so long without success. If the phantom took him, then not only would their chances of finding a cure wither, but so would any chance of saving the world from the mess the infection had caused—the mess that *Sebastien* had caused.

He started picking at the skin on his face, trapped in a web of anxiety, guilt, and dismay. The phantom needed a new body, and it had chosen Jackson as its vessel. If it was successful, if it managed to possess Jackson, then the phantom would become so strong that *no one* would be able to stop it…not even Lord Caedis. But his boss was right; the phantom couldn't risk getting hurt, especially not now, so it wouldn't take any huge risks to get hold of Jackson, would it?

Would it?

Sebastien scowled unsurely as he picked at his skin. How many more people were going to die because of him? How many had *already* died? He didn't want to think about it. He knew what he'd done, and he'd never forgive himself, no matter how many times he was told that it wasn't his fault.

The hand mirror sitting on his nightstand started humming.

He frowned and looked down at it, and when he saw that the glass had faded to black, he picked it up and activated the communication rune on the back. When he saw Clementine's face appear in the mirror, his guilt thickened, but he also felt relieved.

"Hey, are you okay?" his mate asked worriedly.

Sebastien groaned guiltily. "Did my stupid demon feelings wake you up again?"

Clementine laughed quietly. "Yes, but they're not stupid. I like being able to tell when you're feeling a certain way, 'cause you don't talk about your emotions as much as I'd like."

With a quiet sigh, Sebastien fell onto his back. "You should go back to bed, babe. It's early, and you have that interview later."

"I'll be okay. I've been pretty jetlagged lately, but I'm finally settling into the time zone. I was gonna wake up soon anyway." He laid down, too. "Now, tell me what's wrong, or I'll start guessing."

Sebastien huffed and started scratching his cheek—

"See, now I *know* it's something big. You only claw at your face like that when something's really eating you," Clementine said with that skeptical expression he always made when he was onto something—or at least thought he was.

But Sebastien didn't know how to tell him.

"Did something happen with Caedis or Zephyr? Or Jackson?" Clementine deadpanned. "Did your PTO request get denied?"

Sebastien sighed again and shook his head. "No, it's nothing like that. It's just…I…" he paused and looked away from Clementine's curious face.

"What is it?" Clementine asked, this time sounding unnerved.

He took a deep breath and closed his eyes. "I saw it," he muttered, his voice quiet and reflecting the dread building up inside him. "It's back."

"Saw... what?" Clementine asked unsurely.

"The phantom."

Sebastien could *feel* Clementine's horror, and when he looked at his mate's face, he tensed up; seeing him look so pale and afraid made Sebastien feel sick.

"Are... you sure?" Clementine asked anxiously.

He nodded. "Lord Caedis confirmed it, but... I knew the moment I saw it."

"But why? Why did it decide to show its face after a hundred and fifty years of hiding?" he questioned confusedly.

"It needs a new body," he told him, his heart racing in response to his angst. "And it's chosen Jackson."

Clementine sat up and looked down into his mirror at Sebastien. "I guess... it makes sense. Something like that would need a body like Jackson's, a body that can hold two different ethos types inside it without being torn apart."

Sebastien nodded as he sat up, too. "If it gets Jackson, it won't ever need to find a new body again, and it'll be able to grow beyond what we've seen. It's some sort of... I don't know—"

"Numen?"

"No, not that far. I mean... we all suspected that the cadejo might have some kind of shot caller, especially after what Jackson shared with the council about that prowler and its Master. Maybe... the phantom *is* the Master. I mean that's where these kinds of astrals get their power from—from the people who obey and believe. Like the Numen: the more followers and believers they have, the stronger they are, and with creatures like phantoms, the more souls they eat, the stronger they get. So if it really is behind all these cadejo, then I'm afraid that it'll get so strong that not even Lord Caedis can stop it," he lamented.

Clementine adorned a perplexed frown. "Now that it's shown itself, shouldn't the Nosferatu be trying to capture it? I mean, if the phantom is the possible original source of the virus, wouldn't it make sense that something in its blood might be the cure?"

"We don't know if it's the original source," Sebastien said, shaking his head. "We don't know where the virus came from, we only know that... what happened in Alder Estate is the cause for everything that's happened in Ascela," he said sullenly. "But I'm sure that Lord Caedis has already thought about all of this, so we're wasting our time."

With a quiet sigh, Clementine pulled his mirror closer to his face. "Stop blaming yourself for what happened. You couldn't have known who or what that phantom was; your mission was to find out what was happening in that house, to find out what was making all those people sick. You were just doing your duty. If it's on anyone's head, it's Caedis. *He* was the one who sent you out there knowing full well that you could talk to astral Caeleste—he *knew* that phantom was there."

"Yeah, but he didn't know that it was the same kind of phantom that lived in Aldergrove Academy. *I* did. I should have stopped, I should've known that—"

"But you didn't know, Sebastien," Clementine interjected, shaking his head. "It is *not* your fault. Maybe it isn't even Caedis' or the Nosferatu's. Whoever created this virus is to blame, okay? If you didn't let the phantom out, someone else would have, or it would've eventually found its own way out of that crypt."

Sebastien exhaled deeply and hung his head in shame. "But it was my fault that Caleb died. I could've stopped it from taking his body; I could have offered my own body and taken it to hell with me, ended it all before it even started," he mumbled.

"Yeah, but if you did that, I'd still be dead, and we wouldn't be together. Demons don't go to the same place as humans do after we die," his mate said matter-of-factly. "And not just that, think of all the people you've helped since then."

He wouldn't let himself feel any less guilt. He knew what he'd done, and no amount of Clementine's consoling would help. However, he didn't want to seem ungrateful for his help, so he smiled as best he could and said, "I guess."

"When are you guys leaving for the lab?" Clementine then asked.

"In the morning—well…" he said and glanced at the clock, "in about six hours."

Clementine frowned disapprovingly. "You should be sleeping."

He shook his head. "I can't settle. And I miss you."

"I miss you, too," Clementine said despondently. "*Did* you ask Caedis about getting time off?"

"No, not yet. I kinda forgot with everything that's been happening. I'll ask him in the morning or something, I…" he dragged out the last few words of his sentence and cringed. "I burst in on him and the Zenith earlier."

Clementine sighed deeply. "And he yelled at you again? You gotta start knocking on doors, Sebastien. I've—"

"It was an emergency, but I really wish I *had* knocked," he grumbled.

His mate frowned. "What happened?"

Sebastien scoffed and muttered, "I saw them fucking."

Clementine stifled a laugh. "Really?"

"It was like walking in on my dad getting railed by his co-worker who we all thought was just his best friend," he replied, lying back down. "Which doesn't really make sense because everyone knows they're married, it was just…I don't know. Caught me off guard."

Snickering, Clementine shook his head and laid on his side. "I imagine he was furious, then."

"If I wasn't so scared about the phantom, I probably would've pissed myself when he pinned me on the table," he admitted.

"You're lucky you're his favourite errand boy, or I'm sure he would've done much worse," Clementine said, a combination of concern and amusement in his voice.

Sebastien let out another long sigh and relaxed his body. "Maybe he'll give me a little extra time off than usual if I really am his favourite."

"Mm, a long vacation," his mate said contently.

"Somewhere warm."

"With a beach."

"And no snow. No wolf walkers or cadejo or illegal hybrids," Sebastien muttered.

Clementine laughed a little. "Don't worry. I'll make sure your time off is genuine time off, even if I have to swat Nosferatu messengers away myself."

Sebastien smiled and murmured, "Thanks, babe. I love knowing that I can always rely on you."

His mate then frowned a little. "You're gonna be okay, right? If that lab really does have answers that could help find a cure, I can't imagine the people behind its creation would be too keen to let you in."

"We're taking Heir Zephyr and the twins with us, so if anything is waiting to try and stop us, we'll be fine getting through," he assured him.

Clementine didn't look entirely confident, but he nodded and said, "Okay. And you're gonna stick close to Jackson, right?"

He nodded. "I won't let that phantom anywhere near him, and I'm sure Daimon won't, either."

"Just be safe. I want you back here in one piece," he said sternly.

Sebastien smirked at him. "Don't worry. You'll soon have every part of me to yourself."

His mate smiled contently. "All right, get some sleep. You're gonna need it."

"I'll try," he said quietly. "Good luck with your interview. I know you'll get it."

"Thank you. They seem pretty eager to have me since I've done interviews with all those gods and kings and celebrities," he said smugly. "Mostly thanks to some white-haired kludde demon who Lord Caedis apparently holds rather dearly," he teased.

Sebastien couldn't help but smile and rolled his eyes. "Being my mate does have its perks, huh?"

"So many perks," Clementine said with a sultry tone. But then he shuffled around and sat up. "Okay, go to bed. And call me as soon as you get back from the lab, okay?" he said firmly.

As much as he didn't want to have to say goodbye, he really should try to get some sleep. Now that he'd spoken to Clementine, he *did* feel a little better, so maybe he'd be able to stop tossing and turning while sinking into guilt and anxiety.

He nodded in response. "I love you."

Clementine pulled the mirror closer and kissed it. "I love you."

Sebastien stared into the glass, and when it faded to black, his heart sunk into his stomach. He missed him already. But once the mission was over, once they got to the lab, he'd be able to take some time away from work, and he'd spend a long vacation with Clementine. *That* was all he wanted right now, and the thought of it was what would get him through tomorrow.

At least he hoped so.

Chapter Eighty-Three

⌇ ≤ ☽ ≥ ⌇

Mate

| Jackson |

The memory of the antlered wolf plagued Jackson's sleep. All he could see were its glowing red eyes, its rotting body, and the runes etched on its skin.

Its gnarly voice.

Its strange, sickening smell.

And in his nightmare, Sebastien didn't turn up to save him when the monster started dragging him into the woods.

He woke up with a sharp inhale, fear and confusion overwhelming him as he frantically glanced around the room he lay in, but when Daimon stirred and tightened his warm embrace around him, Jackson let out a deep, calming exhale and relaxed.

That creature might scare the shit out of him, but he'd much rather have a nightmare about that than be trapped in another dream by the Holy Grail.

"Hey," came Daimon's tired voice.

Jackson turned his head to look at him. "Hey," he replied when his gaze met Daimon's. "Sorry if I woke you up. I had a nightmare about that…thing," he mumbled and looked up at the ceiling.

"Are you okay?"

He nodded. "Yeah. I just kinda wish I could unsee it, you know?"

"I know," his mate said sympathetically. "Don't worry. I won't let it hurt you—I won't let *anyone* hurt you," he said firmly.

Jackson smiled and turned his head to face him again. "I know," he said and moved his hand to the side of Daimon's face. He then guided his fingers down to his neck and fiddled with the string that he wore with the ring Jackson gave him on it.

Daimon kissed his lips, and when he ran his fingers through Jackson's hair, they kissed again.

But Jackson already knew where it was going; he could see that look of desire in Daimon's eyes, that need for more. While he might usually feel enticed, he didn't right now; he felt…anxious—probably because they'd be leaving for the lab very soon, and probably because he knew that he needed to tell Daimon that he was pregnant, but he still didn't know how.

"What's wrong?" Daimon asked as Jackson turned his face away.

With a deep sigh, he shook his head and dragged his hand over his tired face. "I'm just worried about today. Getting to the lab, dealing with whatever's out there. I kinda feel like there's gonna be something else to get in our way, especially since seeing that antlered thing last night."

Daimon rolled onto his side, leaned on his arm, and looked down at Jackson. "We'll be okay. Kane's dead, so there aren't going to be any hostile wolves for miles. As for cadejo, it's nothing we haven't dealt with before, and if we come across sirens or prowlers or some other variant, we have *you*, and we have Raphael as well. We're going to make it."

Jackson glanced and smiled as best he could at him.

The Alpha's gaze wandered down Jackson's body, which was covered by the blanket. "Have you thought more about what you're going to do once the mission is over?" he asked, but he sounded as if he was hesitant to hear the answer.

However, Jackson didn't feel conflicted about his response. Talking to Ethan last night made him realize how much he really loved Daimon, and how much he didn't want to lose him. He'd saved his life more than once, he helped him learn how to survive, and he taught him about and helped him adjust as best he could to this new world—a world that had been shrouded from his memory.

He knew that he had to decide whether he wanted to go back to his life in New Dawnward or stay in Ascela with Daimon, and as much as he enjoyed his job, his mate was more important. Life in a place far from civilization made him nervous, but he knew that he'd make it with Daimon to help him; he knew that he could get used to it, especially with the man he loved at his side.

"I have," he told Diamon.

His mate shifted his gaze to his face, waiting for him to continue.

Jackson smiled contently and said, "I wanna stay with you."

Daimon's sleepy face lit up with relief and happiness. "In Ascela?"

He nodded. "Yeah."

The Alpha's smile grew, and he pulled Jackson into a tight embrace. "You have no idea how happy that makes me."

Jackson held him tightly. "I just wanna be with you, wherever that is," he said quietly.

Daimon nuzzled his neck as he rested beside him. "I know it must have been hard to choose to leave your old life behind."

"I mean…it makes me feel a little anxious, yeah…but I don't really have anything back in New Dawnward. I can help people out here; I don't have to be a journalist to do that—and if I end up missing it, well…I'm sure I can work something out, right?"

"Yeah," the Alpha said with a light nod. "But what about Ethan?"

Jackson sighed heavily. "He's still my best friend, but after I told him how it was, he kinda just…pushed me away. I don't know if he's going to go back to New Dawnward or not if he finds his parents, but what I *do* know is that I wanna be here with you. I love you."

Daimon kissed his neck. "I love you, too."

Hearing those words filled Jackson with a warming serenity. Of course, he knew that Daimon loved him, and he'd heard him say it before, but for some reason, it was different this time.

Everything felt different this time.

That warm, content feeling intensified, and Jackson suddenly felt as if something inside of him was waking up. He panicked at first, worried that it might be his wolf or demon instincts, but before anxiety could infect his serenity, he felt something else.

Something he'd been waiting to feel for a *long* time.

That gaping, empty hole inside his heart…was healing. He felt the deep, clawing loneliness and nauseating feeling of loss withering, lifting from him like a persistent fever finally breaking.

And for some reason, everything inside him urged him towards Daimon.

He turned his head to look at his mate, but the moment he set his eyes on him, the panic managed to burst through the strange feeling of bliss. He watched as a snake-like black mark slithered across the left side of Daimon's body, breaking into forks and wrapping around him. It extended over his chest, around his arm, and even up his neck and over his face, and when the entire left side of his body was covered in black, serpentine markings, an orange glow emitted beneath it, like it was burning into Daimon's skin. But Daimon didn't react; he lay there staring at Jackson with a confused frown.

And then it disappeared, fading into the Alpha's skin as if it had never been there.

"Jackson?" Daimon asked insistently as if he'd asked several times before with no response. "What's wrong?"

He shook his head as he stuttered, "I-I…I don't know." He nervously edged his hand towards Daimon's arm. "I…saw something."

"Saw what?" he asked with a frown.

Jackson's heart started racing as his anxiety and confusion grew. "I-I don't know, it was this kind of…I—"

A knock came at the door, and Sebastien called from outside, "Get up. We're leaving in ten."

He stared at Daimon's arm, waiting to see if the serpentine mark would show up again, but the longer he waited, the thicker his worry became. Had he done something to him? He felt like he had, but he didn't know what, and the confusion and uncertainty was overbearing. What if he'd done something terrible? What if what he just did was going to hurt Daimon?

Jackson didn't know what else to do; he burst out of bed and hurried over to the door, ignoring Daimon's confused questions. He pulled the door open and leaned outside, and when he spotted Sebastien, who was knocking on *everyone's* doors, he called in a panic, "Sebastien!"

The white-haired demon and his packmates who had stepped out of their rooms sharply turned their heads and set their eyes on Jackson.

"What?" Sebastien asked.

"I-I…something happened to Daimon, a-and I don't know—"

"What happened to him?" Wesley called in concern.

"Something's wrong with my dad?!" Remus exclaimed worriedly and tried barging past Sebastien. But the white-haired demon ushered the kid towards Tokala, who kept him from running over.

Sebastien pushed his way through the crowd as everyone stepped out into the hall. "What happened?" he asked, reaching Jackson.

He shook his head as he stepped back into his room. "I-I don't know! It was some kind of…mark!" he said and turned to face Daimon, who was sitting on the bed inspecting his skin with a confounded frown.

"Mark?" Sebastien questioned. "What mark?"

Jackson huffed, trying to calm down, but his heart was racing, and his body was trembling. His eyes shifted to the crowd outside the door, and then to Daimon, who shot an utterly confused stare his way. "It was like…a snake," he said to Sebastien.

"A snake?"

He nodded. "Like…stretching up his arm," he explained as he dragged his hand up his own arm. "And it was like…forking out and wrapping around him and stuff—it even went up to his face!" he told him. "D-did I do something? I didn't mean to, and I wasn't even thinking about anything, we were just talking!"

Sebastien lost his concerned glare and laughed quietly.

Panting, Jackson scowled in confusion. "W-what?"

The white-haired demon roughly patted Jackson's shoulder and shook his head. "You just imprinted on him, kid. Nothing to get this worked up about." He patted his shoulder again and said, "It finally happened, huh?" He smirked and turned around, heading for the door. "All right, show's over. Go and get ready," he called sternly, trying to break up the crowd.

"Imprint?" came Daimon's voice. "Demon imprint?"

Jackson's racing heart didn't slow, but his fear was replaced with *euphoria*. He imprinted on Daimon? His *demon* imprint? Daimon really *was* his demon mate, and he didn't have the words to explain how happy and relieved that made him feel. All he could do was let a relieved, content grin stretch across his face, and when he looked at Daimon, he couldn't resist the urge to go to him. He raced over, flung his arms around him, and held him tightly as he laughed in relief.

Daimon laughed, too, and pulled Jackson with him as he fell back.

He'd been so conflicted and worried about who his demon mate might be; he'd worried that he might never find them, that they might be someone he didn't even know. But he was wrong, and all that worrying was for nothing.

It was Daimon.

It had *always* been Daimon.

"I love you so much," he told the Alpha, tightening his embrace around him.

Daimon kissed the side of his face and said, "I love you so much, too."

He hugged him for a few more seconds, and as his racing heart started to calm, he let out an amused, relief chuckle. "I thought I did something bad to you, like some kind of demon thing that I didn't know anything about."

The Alpha laughed quietly. "Well, it *was* a demon thing, but a good demon thing."

Jackson smiled and lifted his head to look down at him. "I knew it was you," he said. "I just...I wanted it to be you so bad, like I knew it had to be. And it was."

Daimon placed his hand on the side of Jackson's face. "I'm not going to lie, I was worried that it might not be. Most of the time, a demon's mate turns out to be another demon."

"Well, Sebastien's mate isn't a demon, so...that gave me hope," he admitted. "But I don't really know the ins and outs of demon imprints...or wolf walker ones, to be honest."

"I can help you with the wolf walker part, but you might have to ask Sebastien if you want to know more about demon imprints."

"Yeah," he said with a sigh.

"What's wrong?" Daimon asked.

"Nothing, I just wish we had time to celebrate. But we need to get ready."

The Alpha exhaled deeply and nodded. "The sooner we get to the lab and find what the Nosferatu wants, the sooner we can get back to our own lives."

"It kinda feels like we've been doing this *forever*. I know it hasn't been very long at all, but...I don't know."

"I feel the same. But it's almost over," Daimon assured him. "Come on, let's get dressed."

They both got up and took new clothes from the dresser. Once they were dressed and grabbed their things, they left their room and headed downstairs, following behind

Brando and Leon. Everyone was waiting in the entrance hall, and once the four of them joined the crowd, Sebastien came downstairs with Raphael, Amos, and Elias.

Jackson spotted Ethan standing by himself away from the others; he felt the urge to go over there and ask him if he was okay, but he felt as if giving him some space right now was the best thing to do, so he stayed where he was and watched the white-haired demon walk towards the front door.

"All right," Sebastien called, stopping by the door and turning to face them. "Listen up. Once we reach Greykin Valley, I'll be leading the way—"

"I thought I was doing that," Ethan interjected.

"Heir Lucian shared the location of the lab with me," Sebastien said irritably, glaring at the muto. He then set his eyes back on everyone else. "We've had a few of Lord Caedis' căutător scour ahead, and they recorded *a lot* of cadejo activity; it's only gonna get worse the closer to the valley we get. The good news is that they didn't spot *any* variants, not even prowlers, but Lord Caedis is lending us two of his căutător to watch over us and warn us of any danger we might not see coming."

Jackson frowned curiously; he'd not actually seen a căutător yet. "What are căutător? Like...people?"

Sebastien held his arm out. A shrill, distorted screech cut through the air, and when a shadow raced overhead, everyone looked up, but they didn't see the creature until it landed on Sebastien's forearm.

It looked like a hairless, crimson-skinned ferret with tiny, claw-like horns between its black, soulless eyes and a pair of bat-like wings. It was no bigger than a ferret, either, and as it looked around at everyone, it almost seemed as though it was reading each of Jackson's packmates like pages in a book.

"*This* is a căutător," Sebastien said.

Another căutător glided through the air and landed on Raphael's extended arm.

"If you see one, don't try to kill it," the white-haired demon warned.

"You don't wanna find out what happens when you accidentally run one over with your truck," Amos muttered.

A few amused chuckles came from the crowd.

"Anyway," Sebastien called with a sigh. "We must be quiet, careful, and smart. Nobody can afford to let their guard down, especially not with that antlered creature out there."

"Any news on what it is?" Tokala questioned.

"No," Sebastien answered.

But for some reason...*somehow*, Jackson knew that he was lying. Why?

"Is it a variant?" Ezhno questioned.

"We don't know," Sebastien snapped. "Just keep your eyes peeled for it. No wandering off, always stay in groups of at least five, and Jackson, you're going to have a security detail from the moment we leave this house until we get back. Don't try to ditch them or ask for a few minutes alone, understood? This is for your own safety."

Jackson didn't like the idea of being watched 24/7, but Sebastien was right. That antlered wolf wanted him, and he had no plans to let it take him. "Okay," he said with a nod.

Raphael then stepped forward. "I'm only going to ask this once, and you've had all night to think about it, so be honest. Do any of you want to stay here? It's a dangerous, risky mission, and we won't blame you if you'd rather stay behind than be a burden to the rest of us."

Jackson stifled an irritated frown. These people really didn't hold back, did they?

No one raised their hand or stepped forward, though, and nobody looked hesitant. They all had the same determined or vacant expressions on their faces, even Dustu, Julian, and Remus, who Jackson suspected might choose to back out.

"All right," the orange-haired man said. "Let's get going." He looked at the căutător on his arm. "Go," he told it.

Both ferret-looking creatures took off and raced out the open window.

Sebastien shifted into his winged hound form, and then everyone else quickly morphed into their wolf forms, and Ethan into a tiger. And as Raphael and Sebastien led the way, the pack followed.

Jackson did his best to remain calm, but he was quickly overwhelmed by a tsunami of emotions the moment his paws touched the snow. Anxiety, excitement, dread, determination. This was it. They were heading to the lab, and once they got there, the mission would be over.

Chapter Eighty-Four

Sequoia Point

| Jackson |

Raphael and Sebastien forged a path through the oppressive silence of the forest. The farther they ventured from the sheltering embrace of Reiner Manor, an unsettling eeriness seeped into the air. A profound stillness hung like a shroud, with no avian melodies to grace the atmosphere—only the disconcerting gaze of the elusive căutător creatures.

In the desolate woods, the absence of familiar forest denizens intensified the unsettling ambience; no chirping birds, no scampering rabbits, and no rustling leaves beneath the paws of foxes. Jackson, gripped by a heightened sense of vigilance, scanned his surroundings with an almost desperate intensity. Every shadow became a potential harbinger of unseen threats. The looming presence of the rotting cadejo or the antlered wolf lingered in the periphery of his consciousness, a spectral menace that heightened the already palpable tension in the air.

"I don't know what I hate more," Julian muttered, shattering the silence. "When it's dead quiet, or when there's cadejo nearby growling and whatever."

"I hate the silence," Remus mumbled.

"Same," Brando replied.

"Shh," Raphael snapped.

They went silent.

Jackson wanted to ask how far the border to Greykin Valley was, but he didn't want to get snapped at, nor did he want to be the reason that danger found them. So he remained hushed, constantly checking every direction for the slightest sign of movement. However, the fact that he didn't feel eyes on him or that something was coming had to be a good thing, right?

"Are you okay?" Daimon asked *very* quietly.

With a nod, Jackson tried to match his voice's volume and said, "Yeah, just…nervous. Do you know how far we are from the valley?"

"No," he replied. "Wait here."

Jackson watched his mate leave his side and head up to the front of the group. He listened in, ignoring Amos and Elias, who moved closer to him the moment Daimon left.

"How far are we from the valley?" the Alpha asked Sebastien.

"Several hours," the hound replied. "We'll be there by dusk."

Jackson exhaled in disappointment. Dusk was *nine* hours away. Were they really going to be travelling non-stop for nine hours?

Daimon returned to his side. "Nine hours or so—dusk."

"Are we gonna be like…stopping for a break?" Julian questioned before Jackson could.

"Once we reach sequoia point," Elias answered.

"What's sequoia point?" Lalo asked.

"The beginning of the sequoia forest that surrounds the border of Greykin Valley," Raphael answered. "Now be quiet, all of you."

They did as they were told and moved silently through the woods.

Jackson focussed on the contentedness that came with knowing he'd imprinted on Daimon, that Daimon really *was* his demon mate; it helped him escape the eerie silence. But when they left the cover of the trees and traversed an open tundra, he found it just that little bit harder to ignore the lingering unease. Despite the fact that they'd be able to see cadejo coming a mile off, the empty, desolate space emitted its own sense of danger. What if something was watching from the tree line in the distance? Or what if there was something beneath them? *Above* them?

He looked up at the clouds several times, but he only ever saw the căutător. Not one cadejo crossed their path, even when they headed back into the woods. He knew that he was being a little paranoid, but how could he not be? After everything he'd seen and everything he'd been through, he couldn't help but feel cautious.

But as they travelled further, the silence began to fill with the sounds of forest critters; birds and small mammals started revealing themselves among the snow, and it relieved Jackson to see that the only company they had was harmless.

Maybe he was getting worked up for nothing. After all, if something *was* out there, his instincts would tell him, right?

When they approached the sequoia forest tree line, Jackson stared in awe at the *massive*, towering trees. They were bigger than the redwoods he'd seen when he travelled across Nefastus to get to Ascela; they stretched far into the murk, spreading up the sides of mountains and above the clouds. The smell of oak and pine hung in the air, and the distant cries of moose echoed from inside the impressive forest.

"These things can grow as big as three hundred and twenty feet tall," Wesley said matter-of-factly, glancing back at everyone.

"Shit, man," Julian muttered, gawping at the trees as the group approached them.

"Yeah, but if the trees are that big, imagine how big the animals that live in there are," Lance said ominously.

Brando laughed a little. "Like what? Thirty-foot bears?"

"No," Lance snarled. "Ethos beasts."

"He's not wrong," Amos said from the back of the line. "Some really freaky things waiting in there."

"What...kind of things?" Remus asked unsurely.

"Shut up," Elias snapped at his brother, whacking him with his paw. "You're scaring the kid."

"What? I'm just saying," his twin complained.

"Nah, I wanna know now," Leon said to them both. "What are we gonna bump into in there?"

"Nothing we can't handle," Raphael called from the front, slowing down as they got closer to the tree line. "Most of the inhabitants of this forest are herbivores. Everything else is an omnivore, save for the occasional Coyote or Delta wolf walker and your typical animals, like foxes and bears."

Julian looked around uneasily. "So, like...no giant lizards or monster birds or anything?"

Most of the pack looked at Julian strangely.

"Keunsae are native to Ascela and Avalmoor, but they're not going to try and make a meal out of us," Sebastien answered.

"What's a keunsae?" Remus questioned.

"Big, puffy ostrich-like birds," Amos said. "But people ride them. Super useful for mountains and shit."

They reached the tree line and stopped walking.

"We'll take an hour and rest here," Raphael said, pointing to several hollowed-out holes inside the huge, thirty-foot-thick sequoia tree bases. "Jackson, you're staying with me, Sebastien, Amos, and Elias. Daimon, you can come too. The rest of you, in there," he said, nodding at the hole in the tree opposite the one he was standing in front of.

Jackson expected Ethan to ask to stick with him, but he instead watched as the tiger followed Julian and the rest of the pack inside the other tree. He didn't blame him, though, and he'd already told himself that he'd give Ethan the space he clearly needed. So he turned around and followed Daimon into the tree.

As Jackson sat beside his mate, he watched Remus hurry into the tree, evidently having chosen to leave the others so that he could be with his father, and surprisingly, Raphael didn't argue.

"Have you never been this far out in Greykin before?" Amos asked Daimon.

The Alpha shook his head. "Greykin Valley is among the few places my pack and I didn't pass through when we were moving around to stay alive."

Amos nodded slowly as a sympathetic look appeared on his face. "It must've been real hard having to move around all the time."

"Well, we can't all have the security provided by gods and their children," Daimon muttered.

"Yeah...I guess not."

"It hasn't been easy for us, either," Elias grumbled. "We've lost too many friends and family to the corpses, people who we couldn't save no matter who lived under the same roof as us."

Raphael sighed loudly and said, "Can we just focus on the fact that we're closer than we've ever been to finding answers? Once we get to this lab, we could find enough to help create a cure, and maybe they can find a way to save people who've already turned into cadejo."

Jackson frowned at the orange wolf; that was the first time he'd heard a hint of *desperation* in his voice. Or maybe it was guilt. Whatever it was, it seemed as if Raphael had his own reasons for wanting to find a cure, or at least something driving him. Had *he* lost someone to the virus?

"Get some rest," Raphael then said as he stood up. "I'll check the perimeter."

They all watched him leave the hollow trunk.

Jackson waited a few seconds before asking, "What's up with him?"

Amos and Elias glanced uncomfortably at each other.

"You tell him," Amos mumbled, nudging his brother.

"No, you tell him," Elias replied irritably.

With a quiet huff, Amos set his eyes on Jackson and shrugged. "He lost someone to the virus."

Assuming it was one thing, but *hearing* it was another. Jackson was admittedly shocked to learn that someone as powerful as Raphael had lost someone to the virus. "How?" he blurted, confused.

"Just one bite, man," Amos said sadly.

"Who did he lose?" Daimon asked.

"His mate," Elias answered. "Might explain why he's such a dick sometimes—other than being the grandkid of a god and a demi-god."

Jackson's frown thickened. "But...he's so fast and powerful. How—"

"You turn your back for just a second, and it's all over," Elias said hauntedly. "We were out on a rescue mission; Alpha Cyrus caught word that there were some wolves trapped up on South Point, and he didn't wanna wait for clearance from Alucard to help them, so he made the call. When we got there, there were corpses *everywhere*. Hordes of them. We tried fighting our way through, but he had to eventually call for retreat."

"Some of our guys got stuck," Amos continued. "Raphael and Amelia, his mate, were part of the group that went back for them. Raphael was distracted trying to help

Jake and Nancy, and… it just all happened so fast. One minute Amelia was there, and the next, she was gone."

"We never found the body, either," Elias said sadly. "That just makes it a whole lot worse… knowing that someone you love is still out there, walking around as this *thing* stuck between life and death. It'd drive me insane."

Jackson now felt a little more sympathetic for the guy. If he'd known that Raphael had been through this before, he might not have thought so badly of him. But at least *now* it made sense.

"Dad?" Remus asked Daimon.

"Yes?" the Alpha responded.

His son adorned a despondent frown. "Do you… think that Mom and Rom are out there somewhere… as cadejo?"

A concerned and sullen expression appeared on Daimon's face, but he did his best to hide it from his son by pulling him closer. "No, Rem. Despite what we went through, your mother would never let anything happen to your brother."

"Will we see them again?" Remus asked sadly.

Daimon didn't look confident when he said, "Of course we will."

"I think that… I definitely want to ask the Venaticus or whoever to find them for us as my reward for this mission," Remus said, lifting his head from Daimon's embrace. "And then… we can all be together again, right?"

The Alpha smiled weakly. "I don't know, son. I'm almost certain that your mother wants me dead, and Caius even more so. But I'll make sure that you see your brother, don't worry."

Remus nodded and rested his head on his paws. "I can't stop worrying about him."

Daimon rested his head on Remus' to comfort him. "I know they're okay. Don't worry."

Jackson admittedly felt a little jealous that *he* wasn't the one in Daimon's embrace right now, but Remus was his son, and he needed him. He wasn't going to be so petty and selfish and ask a kid not to seek comfort from his parent. Instead, he shifted his sights to the forest outside. The sounds of distant animals relieved him, and although he felt a little nervous about the omnivores Raphael had mentioned, he'd much rather deal with living creatures than undead ones.

"So, we just have to get through this forest, right?" Jackson asked, looking at the twins. "And then we'll reach Greykin Valley?"

They both nodded.

"It's a *big* forest, though. We'll be travelling from here until dusk, maybe a little later," Sebastien said, his voice reminding everyone that he was there; they all seemed a little surprised by his interjection, not just Jackson.

"Raphael knows shortcuts, though, so we're technically getting there faster anyway," Amos added.

"What kind of shortcuts?" Daimon questioned.

"Fun ones," Amos said with a smile.

"Fun how?" Remus asked.

"You'll see, kid," Elias said amusedly.

Jackson was curious, and he wanted to ask questions, but based on their responses to Daimon and Remus, he was sure that he wouldn't get any useful answers. He didn't detect sarcasm in their voices, either, which was a relief. He just hoped that the journey from Sequoia Point to Greykin Valley would be easy and without peril.

Chapter Eighty-Five

⌝ ≼ ☽ ≽ ⌞

Shrieker

| **Daimon** |

The sun was setting.

Daimon stuck close to his mate as his pack followed Raphael and Sebastien through the sequoia forest. After cutting through a system of caves filled with bioluminescent butterflies and winged lizards, they were finally above ground again; but the tree line was nowhere in sight, and Daimon was beginning to feel impatient.

However, his skepticism outweighed his desperation to reach their location faster than possible. His sights shifted to Ethan every now and then; he was waiting for the muto to slip up—his distancing act wasn't going to fool him; the second he thought Daimon wasn't looking, he'd shoot Jackson a glance or try to speak to him, and the Alpha was waiting for that moment. He trusted Jackson, but he didn't trust Ethan. Someone like him wouldn't give up so easily, and Daimon wasn't going to let his guard down.

Knowing that Jackson had imprinted on him gave him not only a sense of relief and sheer joy but also a feeling of victory. Jackson was his through and through; Ethan wasn't going to come between them. He was curious to know what demon imprints did other than mark a person as a demon's property and mate, but now wasn't the time to ask.

He was also worried about Remus. His son was missing his brother, and as despondent as that made him feel, there wasn't much he could do until the mission was over. And even then, there were no guarantees that Romulus would choose to stay with them; he might want to be with his mother, whom Daimon highly suspected wouldn't want to merge packs and try to get along for the sake of their sons. He wouldn't be so naïve as to let himself hope that things would turn out any different, either.

A subtle, disquieting rustle echoed through the air, sending a shiver down Daimon's spine. His head snapped sharply in the direction of the sound, yet his gaze captured only the unsettling sight of an otherworldly magenta and lime green funnel-shaped plant. The colours seemed to glow with an eerie luminescence, casting an unnatural pallor over the forest around him.

Daimon frowned, fixating on the bizarre flora that now enveloped the spaces between the towering trees. As he continued to scrutinize the surroundings, a creeping sense of unease settled in. The once unnoticed plants had multiplied, weaving their unnatural tendrils into the very fabric of the forest. Glancing over his shoulder, Daimon traced the origins of this peculiar invasion, realizing with a chill that they had emerged insidiously, lurking in the periphery while he remained lost in his thoughts.

"What the heck are these things?" Julian asked, breaking the silence. They stopped walking and reached their paw towards one of the plants.

"Don't—" Amos grabbed their paw, "—touch that."

The pack stopped moving.

"Why not?" Jackson asked confusedly as he stood beside Julian.

Julian pulled their paw out of Amos' grip.

"They're shrieker plants," Sebastien said, escorting Julian away from it using his wing. "They react to touch and make the most disgusting sound; the last thing we need is you setting one off and calling every predator in the woods over here."

"Don't have to tell me twice," Julian said, shivering.

"Keep moving," Raphael called and resumed leading the way. "And don't touch *anything*."

The pack shot unsettled frowns at Daimon, but when he nodded, they started following Raphael.

Jackson glanced at Daimon, walking beside him. "So, screaming plants, huh?"

"I've never heard of anything like it," the Alpha replied.

"Rather that than screaming cadejo," his mate mumbled.

Daimon nodded in agreement.

But things only got stranger the further they walked. Daimon watched as a *huge* flytrap hanging off the trunk of one of the towering trees reached out and clamped its jaws around a luminescent crow, sending a rain of feathers down to the snow-covered ground. And then he saw brightly coloured, glowing creatures climbing the trees like squirrels, but they were as big as dogs and looked like feathered lizards.

"Uh…what the fuck is that?" Wesley asked, looking up at one of the feathered beasts.

"Tree drakes," Sebastien answered.

"Like…dragon drakes?" Remus asked excitedly.

"Yeah, they're a smaller species of dragon," the hound confirmed.

"Why is everything glowing?" Jackson questioned.

Sebastien laughed a little. "This is where having a nerdy boyfriend comes in handy," he said and looked back at the pack. "They're bioluminescent; some ethos beasts evolved the ability to use those kinda traits for like…communication or camouflage, and some have them to attract prey or dissuade predators."

"So...they can turn it on and off?" Julian asked.

"Some can, some can't," Sebastien answered.

"Those who can't make up most of the endangered species lists because they're easy for hunters to spot," Raphael muttered.

"Fucking hunters," Elias snarled.

"Scum of the world," Amos agreed. "Like...do you seriously have nothing better to do with your life? You just gotta go around trapping and hurting and killing innocent animals that just wanna live?" he shook his head and scowled. "I wish the Nosferatu would let me join that division; I'd love to take down hunters."

Raphael sighed loudly. "Strămoș Luca denied your *multiple* applications because you're a hothead. You need patience; a lot of the work in that division involves sitting around and watching. You don't get to kill hunters all day every day. There's a whole lot of legal involved, too."

Amos scoffed and muttered, "Whatever."

Something rustled behind them again. Daimon sharply turned his head, and this time, everyone else stopped, also appearing to have heard it.

"What was that?" Lance stammered.

"Probably just a glowing lizard, right?" Leon suggested.

Raphael moved through the pack and stood beside Daimon, examining the strange landscape around them with his eyes.

Daimon couldn't see anything among the shrieker plants and massive trees other than bioluminescent creatures. If there *was* something there, surely the animals would have fled. And those strange, ferret-like demon creatures watching from above would have warned them.

"Anything?" Sebastien asked Raphael.

The orange wolf shook his head. "No. Keep moving."

When they started moving again, Daimon looked at Jackson. "Do you feel anything? Sense anything?"

Jackson *did* look unnerved, but he shook his head. "No. I don't have any bad feelings or anything like that...I just feel nervous—but I always feel a little nervous about being outside...knowing what's out there."

"Like hunters," Lalo muttered anxious.

"And cadejo," Dustu added.

"All that's out here is glowing ethos beasts," Raphael called irritably. "This forest is protected by the Nosferatu; any hunter who tries to step foot past the tree line literally can't."

The pack looked confused.

And Daimon was undeniably intrigued. "Why can't they?"

"Wards, man," Amos answered. "There's a protective barrier around the place, and anyone with intentions to harm the animals here physically cannot get past the tree line. Pretty cool, right?"

Daimon frowned and asked, "If wards like that can be created, then can't wards be created to keep cadejo out of certain parts of the forest?"

"That's where shit's tricky," Amos said with a sigh.

"To create those kinds of wards, you need to *know* what you're trying to keep out," Elias continued. "We don't know entirely what cadejo are, just that they're undead. If we knew how they were created, then yeah, we could try. But right now, we don't have those answers."

Daimon heard it *again*. Something shuffled around behind him, but when he stopped to look, there wasn't anything stalking them or hiding in the teal bushes.

"What is it, chief?" Tokala asked, stopping beside him.

He frowned and slowly searched the space before him. "I don't know," he drawled. "I keep hearing something behind us."

"If something was following us, the căutător would warn us," Raphael called irritably. "Now move it. We're wasting time."

But Daimon felt reluctant. *Something* was following them; he was sure of it.

"Daimon?" Jackson asked worriedly. "What is it?"

"I feel like there's something following us," he told everyone.

Raphael let out yet another heavy sigh and barged past everyone. He stormed over to where Daimon was staring, looked around, and then glared at Daimon. "There's nothing here. This forest is home to literally hundreds of animals, some of them can even become invisible; what you're hearing is probably just some drake or frog foraging for food." He stormed to the front of the group. "Now let's fucking move!"

Daimon huffed irritably and turned around. He wouldn't let his guard down, but maybe he was being a little paranoid. Raphael was right; this forest was full of animals running around and foraging. He could just be hearing something harmless.

"I really don't sense anything, Daimon," Jackson said softly, walking beside him again.

He glanced at his mate and nodded. "Maybe I'm just nervous, too."

"I think we all are," Tokala said. "We're getting clo—"

An ear-piercing, harrowing shriek tore through the once-calm air. Its intensity reverberated within Daimon's skull, forcing him to halt alongside his pack. The sound assaulted his senses, a relentless attack that left him with no recourse but to cease and violently shake his head, as if attempting to dislodge the auditory invasion. Yet, the cacophony persisted, an overwhelming barrage emanating from every conceivable direction. Its pitch and volume mirrored the anguished cries of a suffering creature, but magnified a thousandfold, creating an unrelenting symphony of distress that seemed to permeate the very fabric of the surroundings.

"Who touched the fucking plants?!" Raphael's voice bellowed, barely audible through the relentless onslaught of screeching.

Daimon grunted and kept shaking his head, and when the sound started inflicting pain, he groaned and stumbled around, losing his balance.

"We need to move!" Raphael called. "Let's go!"

But Daimon couldn't move, and neither could his packmates. They all shook their heads, fumbling around; Julian and Dustu were the first to hit the ground, still shaking their heads, and Remus, Ethan, and Ezhno followed.

"Let's move!" Raphael yelled.

Daimon felt someone try to usher him forward; he did his best to follow, and he tried to glance around, but the sound was distorting his vision.

But that was when he heard it. Cutting through the shrieking, wailing cries, his senses picked up the sound of distorted snarling.

And the scent of rotting flesh.

Panic ensnared him, but he wouldn't let it overwhelm him. He stopped shaking his head and tried to find his footing; through his distorted gaze, he found his son, and he found Jackson. He could see Raphael trying to urge his pack forward, but everyone was stumbling and falling over their own paws.

He tried helping Remus up, but his strength failed him.

The wails dragged on, and Daimon's heart raced faster as the panic became heavier. He could still hear snarls, he could still smell rotting flesh; he knew what was coming, but no matter how hard he tried, he couldn't shake the disorientation.

And it was getting *louder*.

And *louder*—

The sound suddenly stopped.

Still disorientated but unrestricted, Daimon turned his head in the direction of the savage, distorted snarling. He watched as a cadejo burst out from behind a tree and grabbed the căutător, which had silenced the shrieking plant. The small creature screeched and cried, but the rotting wolf tore it apart.

And it wasn't alone.

Cadejo prowled out from behind the trees, grouping up around the monster which devoured the helpless căutător. They snarled and growled, baring their decaying, bloody teeth.

There were too many of them to fight, even with Raphael, and the orange wolf seemed to understand that.

"Fucking run!" Raphael yelled.

Everyone turned around and bolted, and the cadejo gave chase.

"Where the hell did they come from?!" Wesley called.

"No fucking idea!" Raphael called back.

"What do we do?!" Julian panicked.

Raphael led the fleeing pack to the right and up a hill as he called, "We'll lose them on the ridge!"

Ridge? What ridge? Daimon looked around, but he didn't see a mountain. "Where?!" he called demandingly.

"This way," the orange wolf called back. "Hurry up!"

The panting, panicking pack followed Raphael to the top of the hill. Daimon took a moment to look behind him, and when he saw a *horde* of cadejo, his panic intensified. Why were there so many? Where the fuck did they come from?

He shifted his attention back to the pack ahead, glancing at his mate and his son, who raced beside him.

"This way!" Raphael called as they emerged from the sequoia forest onto a snowy plateau.

Daimon spotted the ridge. Huge cracks cut through the ground, leading down into deep, dark chasms. He and his pack avoided each of them, but the cadejo weren't so smart. Yelps and whines cut through the tense air, and when he looked over his shoulder again, he saw several cadejo stumble and fall into the crevices.

"I hope all of you can jump," came Raphael's voice.

The Alpha saw the massive gap between the ridge and another plateau up ahead. It was at least twenty feet wide, but he wasn't worried; wolf walkers could jump twice as far as that, especially when running at full speed. "Let's go!" he called to his pack, trying to encourage them.

Raphael made the jump first, and when he landed easily on the other side, he skidded around to face the pack and waited.

Sebastien glided over without any effort.

Wesley, Brando, Ezhno, and Leon jumped next, all landing safely on the other side.

Ethan made it over, and so did Tokala, Lalo, and Lance.

Jackson jumped with Julian and Dustu, and relief struck Daimon when his mate landed on the other side without peril.

And then *he* jumped with Remus, Amos, and Elias.

When his paws landed on the plateau, he exhaled in relief and turned to face the horde—

"Dad!" Remus yelled in terror.

"Remus!" he panicked, rushing to his son, who held on to the edge with his paws—he didn't make it.

Everyone else rushed over and tried to help him up.

"Stop squirming around!" Raphael complained, trying to lift Remus with his paw.

"I got it!" Sebastien shouted and stretched out his wings. He swiftly took off, descended into the chasm, and grabbed Remus with his legs.

And just in time.

The frantic cadejo horde reached the edge; some of them tried to jump, but their rotting bodies failed them. They fell, some leaving splatters of blood and rotting fur on the ice when they collided with it, missing the ledge.

"Are you okay?" Daimon asked worriedly, holding his son, who bawled in terror, hiding his face against his neck.

"Why didn't the căutător see them coming?" Amos questioned as the pack took a few steps back, watching the cadejo pour down into the darkness.

"Is everyone okay?" Daimon asked, looking around at his pack.

They all looked their own kind of horrified but nodded in response.

"It's literally only gonna get worse from here," Sebastien said with a huff.

"Worse than *that*?" Jackson exclaimed.

"There's hundreds!" Julian added.

Raphael huffed and shook his head. "Come on. We need to keep moving." He turned his back to the thinning horde and started leading the way across the plateau.

Daimon ignored him and looked down at his son. "Rem?" he asked softly. "Talk to me."

Remus shook his head and shivered in his embrace. "I-I almost fell!"

"You're okay, you're okay," the Alpha assured him, nuzzling his head. "We've got you, Rem. You're okay."

"Come on," Raphael called as the last of the cadejo attempted to leap over but plummeted down into the abyss.

"Can you walk?" Daimon quietly asked his son.

Remus took a moment to respond, but he eventually nodded. "I think so."

Daimon helped him up, and once he was on his paws, he surveyed the plateau. It looked like it stretched on for a while, but there were mountains visible ahead, and he hoped that they were the entrance to Greykin Valley.

"How much further?" Julian asked as the pack began following Raphael and Sebastien.

"Those mountains," Sebastien answered. "That's the entrance to the valley."

Daimon was right, and although he was relieved, he was also afraid. Greykin Valley was *right* in front of him, but after being chased by that horde, he feared what else might be waiting for them. Whatever it was, though, his pack would survive—they'd get through it, and they'd reach the lab.

They had to.

Chapter Eighty-Six

Plan A, Plan B

| Jackson |

As Jackson fixed his gaze upon the foreboding entrance to Greykin Valley, a shiver crawled down his spine. The mountains loomed menacingly, their sheer presence casting elongated, inky shadows that sprawled across the tundra. Not a single tree broke the desolation, and the absence of cadejo or any living creature intensified the eerie silence that enveloped the place. The bitter wind howled through the barren landscape, whipping up flurries of snow that danced in a macabre ballet, and an icy, malevolent presence clung to the air, saturating it with a sense of impending doom.

"The lab's location is within a twenty-five-mile radius," Sebastien reminded the pack, looking back at them as he and Raphael led the way. "The căutător will fly ahead and look for structures while we work on getting deeper into the valley."

Jackson glanced at Ethan. He expected his friend to bring up the fact that he thought entering through the thin, narrow path was still the better choice, but he didn't say a word.

"Stay close and aware," Daimon called.

"As we said, the cadejo hordes are only going to get worse from this point forward," Raphael added. "We only fight if necessary. Understood?"

They all nodded and followed.

Jackson wasn't sure what might be waiting on the other side, but after getting chased by a horde not long ago, he felt nervous and on edge, and Raphael telling everyone that it was only going to get worse didn't help. Worse how? Would the hordes be bigger? Were there new variants that Daimon's pack hadn't come across yet? Or what if the antlered wolf was waiting in there for him? What if the lab was under guard? What if there were soldiers and tanks and helicopters? Or what if the Holy Grail was out there?

"Are you okay?" Daimon asked quietly.

Jackson glanced at him to make sure that he was asking him and not Remus, who was clinging close to the Alpha after almost falling into that abyss. When he saw that his mate *was* asking him, he nodded and stared ahead again. "Just nervous."

"Tell me about it," came Amos' voice.

"We're not going through until the căutător comes back with a survey of the land; stop panicking," Elias muttered.

"We'll rest here for a few minutes," Raphael said as he slowed and came to a halt. He then looked up at the single căutător creature and called, "Go. Tell me what's waiting on the other side."

The creature responded with a screech and raced towards the mountains, disappearing into the fog that ensnared their tips.

Jackson sat beside Daimon and took a deep, quiet breath. Before he could sink into his anxious thoughts, though, Julian sat beside him.

"I'm getting super freaked out, man," they muttered. "Like not even kidding. I kinda thought we'd never get here, you know? But now that we are, it's like… freaky."

He nodded in agreement. "I'm just trying to focus on the fact that we're so close to getting what we came out here for."

Julian sighed and made themselves comfortable. "*I'm* trying to focus on what I want as my reward."

"Any ideas?"

"I don't know. Like… I *know* there's things I want, but now that I can have any one thing, my brain is like… empty."

Jackson smiled a little in amusement; he glanced at Ethan, who was sitting by himself away from everyone else. He'd become so used to his friend joining these talks with Julian that it felt strange seeing him all the way over there. A part of him wanted to invite the muto over, but he still wanted to give him his space.

With a quiet sigh, he set his eyes back on Julian. "Yeah, I feel that." He then looked at Daimon, who was comforting his son. "Well, I decided that I'm gonna stay in Ascela, though," he told Julian. "I don't really have anything in New Dawnward to go back to."

Julian frowned confusedly. "What about Ethan? Is he staying here, too? I know you guys shared an apartment and all."

Jackson shrugged and felt despondent. "I don't know. I haven't told him yet."

"I think he'll stay, too. You two are besties, right?"

"Yeah, something like that."

Julian nodded and shuffled a little closer. "Have you, uh… got any leads yet?" they asked quietly. "Did you talk to Tokala or anyone?"

He knew that Julian was asking about his hunt for whoever stabbed Daimon, but with everything that was going on, he hadn't had time. "Not yet. It's probably going to have to wait until after we're done getting to this lab."

"Did you rule Dustu out yet?"

Jackson shook his head. "I need to get him alone and ask him."

"Right now?"

He thought about it; however, not only would there not be time, but he didn't want his babysitters hearing. He wanted to keep his investigation under wraps. "No. Probably not until we get back to the manor."

"Are we still working with Ethan?" Julian asked.

With a deep sigh, Jackson mumbled, "I don't know."

Julian nodded and glanced around awkwardly; they evidently understood that Jackson was starting to feel upset. "Well…I'll leave you and Alpha Daimon alone," they said as if they thought they were imposing. "Lalo's talking about some fishing trip he went on, so I'm gonna go listen to that."

After an amused scoff, Jackson nodded. "All right."

The silver and black-furred Omega stood up and wandered over to where Lalo was sitting with Lance, Dustu, and Tokala.

"Do *you* think Ethan will stay?" Daimon asked Jackson; clearly, he'd been listening.

He huffed and turned to face his mate. "I really don't know. He can go either way when he's upset, but right now, I almost feel like he's gonna go his own way once we're done at this lab. Whether he finds something about his parents or not, I don't think he wants to stick around."

Daimon looked conflicted. "And how does that make you feel?"

"I don't know," he admitted. "A little guilty, upset, maybe even kinda mad. But I'm not gonna force him to stay if he doesn't wanna."

The Alpha leaned closer and nuzzled Jackson's neck. "You have no reason to feel guilty."

He didn't know if that was true. He felt guilty, and every time he thought about what happened with Ethan recently, he felt worse.

"Heads up," came Sebastien's voice.

Everyone sharply turned their heads and looked at the hound, who was staring across the tundra. They all stared in the same direction as him, setting their eyes on a large, bear-sized creature in the distance.

Jackson squinted, trying to work out what it was. He watched it sniff the ground, walking with its head down; it looked sluggish and heavy, and it might actually be a bear. But he knew better than to let his guard down. He'd wait until someone confirmed what it was.

Barely a moment later, Elias called, "Urseis."

"What's an urseis?" Dustu questioned.

"An ethos beast," Sebastien answered. "It looks like a bear, but it has four eyes and eats mostly insects and berries."

"It's massive, though," Julian said with a frown.

Sebastien shrugged. "Giraffes are massive, but they eat leaves and shit. And elephants and rhinos. One thing you gotta remember when it comes to ethos beasts is that a lot of them look like they'd eat you, but they actually just think your hair is a bush."

Some of the pack laughed amusedly.

"Why do you know so much about ethos beasts?" Ethan muttered.

"Because my mate is a nerd," the hound answered. "And because I hang around Lord Caedis a lot. He's big on animals. Huge cat guy."

The pack looked confused and amused at the same time.

"He's a cat guy?" Jackson asked doubtfully.

"Believe it or not," Raphael chimed in, watching the sky. "Whenever I visited Strămoş Luca's place, this weird little hairless cat thing would always make a point of clawing up my shoes. I went through several pairs in just one month."

"Hairless cats are weird," Wesley muttered.

Jackson watched as Raphael held out his paw. The căutător demon descended and landed on his arm, and it started chittering quietly to him. Jackson listened, curious if he might be able to understand it, but he didn't get a word.

"All right, listen up," Raphael called as the creature flew off his arm and returned to the sky. "Once we get through the mountain pass, we're gonna find ourselves in an abandoned outpost. There are fences, so the cadejo outside can't get in. There's a fair few of them, but they're mostly congregating on the left near a broken turbine; it's making noise so they're trying to kill it," he explained, glancing around at everyone. "We can exit through a gate on the right behind a guard tower and use the cover of the abandoned vehicles on the road to get past. When we get clear of the outpost, there aren't any cadejo for two miles."

Although they looked unnerved, the pack nodded and waited for him to continue.

"As for the lab, it's eight miles from the outpost. We can follow the road there, but after two miles, there's a horde," the orange wolf continued. "Not only turned wolf walkers but turned humans, too. It's getting dark, so we'll be able to use that and the cover of the bushes to get around them. There's an oil tanker west of this horde; we're going to set it off once we're past; the sound and the light will lure not only them but any nearby cadejo, giving us more room."

"Can't we just set the oil tanker off instead of trying to sneak past this horde?" Brando asked.

"The light will give away our positions, and the cadejo will swarm us. The path we're going to take is the safest route, so we can't risk compromising it" Raphael answered.

Everyone nodded in understanding.

"And once we're past the horde?" Daimon questioned.

"We disappear into a small cut of forest. The road leads through it, and once out of the woods, it leads straight to the lab, which is a few klicks straight ahead," Raphael said.

"And the cadejo?" Tokala asked.

"None until we reach the lab," Raphael replied.

Sebastien looked at him. "And what's the lab looking like?"

"Surrounded. Hundreds, maybe even thousands of cadejo."

The pack looked around at each other with horrified expressions.

"However, there are plenty of opportunities to distract and kill them," Raphael said, clearly trying to assure everyone. "Several oil tankers, a siren we can activate from one of the watch towers, and the lab's security looks like it can still function; we just have to turn the generators on."

"What security?" Daimon asked skeptically.

"Automatic turrets," Raphael said. "They can be configured via the computer system to target specific signatures, so if we fill in the correct parameters, we can get the guns to take out most of the cadejo for us."

"Okay, and how do we get to the generators? And the computers?" Ethan asked before Jackson could.

"The generators are on the east side of the lab outside a loading bay. As for the computers, those can only be accessed from inside the lab," Raphael told them.

Everyone glanced unsurely at each other again.

"But I can fly ahead," Sebastien said. "I'll get the generators going, and I can get in there and work out how to change the parameters."

Ethan then scoffed. "Do you even know how to do that? Do you even know what a parameter is?"

The hound frowned at him. "I know enough."

"Right, enough to get us all killed," the tiger muttered.

Sebastien snarled at him.

"Look, I know computers," Ethan said, looking around at everyone. "Get me in there and I'll make sure it's done right."

Raphael adorned a pondering stare before sighing and nodding. "All right. Can you get him in?" he asked Sebastien.

"Yeah," the hound mumbled.

The orange wolf looked at the pack again. "While they mess with the turrets, we can all take cover in one of the intact buildings." He glanced at Sebastien. "Send the căutător when it's safe for us to start making our way to the gates." And then he asked, "Any questions?"

"Is there a plan B in case this doesn't go as planned?" Tokala called.

"Plan B for the first part of this journey is if the cadejo spot us, everyone climbs into the nearest vehicle for cover, and Sebastien and I clear a path. As for the second part, if we get spotted, you lot run while again Sebastien and I deal with the cadejo. I'll also tell the căutător to set off the oil tanker. And the third part, if the generators aren't functional, Sebastien and Ethan will manually control the turrets and distract and take out as many cadejo as possible, clearing a path for us," Raphael explained.

Julian shakily held up their paw. "And…a plan C?"

"No plan C," the orange wolf answered. "Any other questions?"

Jackson held up his paw. "Uh…well…if things don't go to plan, I can help," he offered. "I know how to use my fire, and—"

"No," Raphael denied. "Your only job is sticking with your pack and getting into the lab."

He knew better than to argue with him.

"Is that all?" Raphael asked.

No one else said or asked anything.

The orange wolf stood up. "All right. Let's get moving—and remember, stay close and alert. No heroics, no altering the plan," he said firmly.

Everyone climbed to their paws and nodded.

"Are you ready?" Daimon asked Remus.

His son murmured nervously, "Yeah."

"Stay close," the Alpha told him, and then he looked at Jackson. "You, too. Don't leave my side."

Jackson nodded. He had no plans to wander off in a valley full of cadejo.

"Let's move," Raphael called as he turned around and began leading the way towards the mountain pass.

Jackson followed beside Daimon. He did his best to remain calm, but a horrible sense of dread ensnared him. Knowing what was waiting on the other side didn't ease his worry; however, the fact that he was with someone as capable as Raphael made him feel a little better. That wolf knew what he was talking about, and he had a solid plan.

He wouldn't be so naïve as to think that everything would go perfectly, though. There were bound to be problems, but he trusted his allies to deal with them. Not only that, but *he* was capable of dealing with it, too. He had his fire, he had his demon strength, and he knew that he could command three cadejo at once, maybe more. He'd do whatever he could to make sure that they all reached the lab in one piece.

Chapter Eighty-Seven

Greykin Valley

| Jackson |

The pack navigated the serpentine mountain pass. Each twist and turn heightened the eerie anticipation that surrounded them as if the very air was thick with an unseen malevolence. The oppressive darkness of the encroaching night seemed to devour any semblance of safety, casting the jagged rocks and skeletal trees into ominous silhouettes against the moonless sky.

Jackson's imagination ran wild with the haunting possibility that at any moment, the abandoned outpost would materialize before them, and he'd have to face the horde of snarling, seething cadejo surrounding it. But he was ready.

As the winding path delved deeper into the darkness, the mountains loomed above like a colossal monument to isolation. The jagged peaks scraped against the ink-black heavens, shrouding the pack in an unsettling cloak of obscurity. The howling wind whispered through the narrow gaps, carrying with it an unsettling symphony of indistinct whispers that seemed to echo the unspoken fears dwelling within Jackson's mind.

The journey continued, each step amplifying the tension in the air; the oppressive blackness swallowed the landscape, leaving the pack to rely solely on their wolf senses. In the impenetrable void, every rustle of leaves and snap of twigs became a potential harbinger of impending doom. Jackson couldn't shake the feeling that the very shadows themselves harboured unseen threats, lurking just beyond the edge of perception.

As they pressed forward, the path became an intricate labyrinth of uncertainty. The pale glow of their wolf eyes barely pierced the dark, revealing only glimpses of the treacherous terrain ahead. Jackson couldn't shake the haunting thought that, in this lightless abyss, losing their way meant succumbing to the abyss itself—a fate far more sinister than what waited inside the valley.

But then a harsh breeze cut through the pass, carrying with it the burning scent of rotting flesh and the sound of savage, suffering snarls. They were getting close.

"Stay close," Daimon told Jackson once again.

Jackson nodded as he moved a little closer to his mate. He focused on the glow of moonlight up ahead, seeping into the pass through what must be the way out.

"Keep low," came Raphael's voice.

The pack did as he commanded and crouched, slowing and silencing their movements as they edged towards the end of the pass.

And when they reached it, everyone froze.

The abandoned outpost was shrouded in the shadows cast by the mountains, but the ground beyond the fences was lit by moonlight, and there were at least a hundred cadejo trying to reach the piece of metal dangling from the inactive turbine. A revolting choir of snarls and groans stole the silence, coming from every direction, and the cadejo that weren't trying to attack the turbine were lurking, dragging their twitching, rotting bodies around the perimeter.

Jackson followed beside Daimon as Raphael led the pack past the singed shell of a vehicle and towards the crumbling guard tower. He couldn't help but worry that something was going to go wrong; what if a brick fell from the tower? What if the cadejo finally managed to silence the turbine and turned their attention to the outpost? Or what if there was something lingering in the dark waiting for them to leave the safety of the fence?

No. He couldn't let his anxiety consume him. Raphael was an asshole, but he knew what he was doing, and so did Sebastien; if they believed that this plan would work, then it would work.

When they reached the gate by the guard tower, Sebastien very carefully and slowly pushed it open with his wing. Then, Raphael led the way out. The pack followed him through the gate and towards the long, winding road packed with abandoned jeeps, cars, and tanks. Just as the orange wolf had told them, they used the vehicles for cover, following the road further and further away from the outpost.

The sound of the undead faded with every few steps, and as they put more distance between themselves and the horde, Jackson began to let himself feel relieved.

It went just as smoothly as Raphael suggested it might.

Jackson exhaled quietly and glanced at Daimon, but what he saw past the Alpha snatched his attention. Beyond the thinning mass of abandoned vehicles, he saw a caribou... but there was something not quite right about it. The creature, standing out in the open despite the nearby cadejo horde, was twitching and writhing; its eyes shone red in the dark, and the longer Jackson looked, the more he noticed what was unnatural about it.

Gaping holes in its flesh.

Chunks of missing fur and muscle.

And black, rotting blood seeping from its eyes, ears, nose, and mouth.

It looked just like the twisted, rotting animals he'd seen in the visions forced onto him when the antlered wolf grabbed him, and it sent a shiver of mortification through him. He wanted to warn someone, but he didn't want to call for Raphael or Sebastien in case the creature somehow heard. So he said, "Daimon."

His mate glanced at him.

Jackson nodded in the direction of the rotting caribou.

Daimon shifted his sights to it. A confused frown warped his face, and after telling Tokala, who was in front of him, to pass it on, the entire group soon turned their attention to it.

But it was Sebastien's reaction which grasped Jackson's intrigue. He looked *traumatized*, but he didn't say anything. No one did.

"What the hell is it?" Jackson questioned quietly.

"Infected," came Raphael's hushed voice. "Keep moving."

Jackson frowned unsurely. The virus was affecting ordinary animals now, too? He had questions, and he felt desperate for answers, but he kept silent. He wouldn't risk giving their position away.

Raphael led them away from the outpost, and once they were clear, just as the căutător creature had reported, there were no signs of any nearby cadejo, giving Jackson two whole miles to try and get some answers.

"Why was that caribou infected?" he asked quietly.

"Yeah. Is the virus passing to normal animals?" Julian added.

Elias was the one who answered. "Not that we know of—at least not the widespread virus."

The pack murmured uneasily.

"Wait, there's different versions of the virus?" Wesley questioned.

"Yes and no," Amos said.

"The Nosferatu ran experiments on a whole bunch of captured cadejo, but none of them could turn ordinary animals," Elias continued. "And the infected animals that they captured were different to the cadejo."

"So…what does that mean?" Julian asked.

"Well, they theorized that there are certain variants that they just haven't discovered yet that can turn animals, or that the original version of the virus is responsible, the raw virus, not the kind that's transmitted through bites and such," Amos explained.

An unsettling chill ran through Jackson's body. "Where would they come into contact with that, though?"

"Out here," came Raphael's voice. "There's a Lyca Corp. lab nearby, and the fact that there are infected animals here could be a sign that we're on the right track—that what we'll find at this lab could help us find the answers we need."

Sebastien nodded in agreement. "If the raw virus is being kept there, then there has to be like... experimental notes and shit like that."

That would make sense. But not only did that make Jackson feel hopeful, it also made him feel terrified. If the raw virus could turn a caribou, then what else could be out in this valley? He didn't want to let his mind wander.

"Let's pick up the pace," Raphael called.

The pack silently followed him deeper into the valley. Eventually, the jam of vehicles disappeared, and only the occasional car or bike remained on the road. The moon climbed higher into the sky, reflecting a little more light onto the world below, and by the time it hung directly above the valley, the pack reached the massive horde Raphael had warned them about.

And it was *huge*.

The tsunami of snarling, seething undead stretched as far as Jackson's eyes could see. Rotting wolves and rotting humans, lurching aimlessly in every direction, stretching from one side of the valley to the other. It almost seemed like a purposely placed blockade, and it would deter anyone, but not the pack.

Raphael led them to the right towards the mountains; when they reached a scree dotted with large boulders and dead trees, they began their slow, careful path around the swarm.

Jackson did his best to remain calm, but his instincts warned him to turn back the further he walked onwards. He glanced to his left; every glimpse of the cadejo horde terrified him a little more than the last, but the pack had the cover of the dark and the occasional rock. They were fine.

They *were* fine, weren't they?

Of course they were. Raphael knew what he was doing.

He focused on the orange wolf, who fearlessly led them forward. If something happened, he and Sebastien had a plan; no matter what happened, they were going to make it to the lab.

There was something up ahead. The cadejos' snarls grew louder and more savage, and once Jackson passed a jagged boulder, he set his eyes on a flipped-over jeep a hundred feet from the scree. The cadejo had torn the doors off, and those that had managed to get inside were picking what tiny amount of flesh remained on the bodies of the four people inside. The stench of gasoline hung in the air, and when Jackson saw that it was leaking from the jeep, his frown thickened.

How recently had the cadejo flipped that vehicle? How old were the bodies inside? They didn't look rotten, and their blood smelled fresh—Jackson caught the scent from where he walked, even over the overwhelming pungency of the horde.

"Looks like we aren't the only ones trying to get to the lab," Amos muttered.

That all but confirmed Jackson's suspicions. But who else was trying to get there? Lyca Corp.? The Holy Grail? The Diabolus? He wasn't going to panic himself, though. The căutător demon had made it all the way to the lab and didn't report seeing anyone else there, so the only thing waiting for the pack were cadejo…right?

They kept moving, navigating the foot of the mountain, silently and invisibly making their way past the humongous horde. The closer they got to the now visible end, the faster Jackson's heart raced. They were getting nearer, and the cadejo horde was starting to thin out.

Raphael's plan really was working.

"Go," the orange wolf said to Sebastien.

The winged hound swiftly took off, ascending into the sky and disappearing above the clouds.

He was going to set the oil tanker off, wasn't he?

Jackson tensed up; knowing how close they were to the lab made him feel both nervous and excited. He was eager to find what they'd been sent out there for so that it could all be over, but he was anxious about what was waiting for them.

However, as they approached the end of the horde, a thought he tried to ignore lingered in the back of his mind. It all felt a little *too* easy, a little *too* perfect. Raphael was experienced, sure, but could his plan really be *this* foolproof? When they were dealing with cadejo, something *always* went wrong; a zombie always either saw them or caught their trail, but that hadn't happened despite the alarming number of undead.

But maybe he was overthinking. He didn't want to wonder why nothing had gone wrong and cause something to happen—he didn't want to curse his pack or tempt fate to turn the tides.

The sudden, distant explosion of what must be the oil tanker snapped Jackson out of his thoughts. He sharply turned his head in the direction of the orange glow, watching as the cadejo horde began swarming towards it. Then, he looked ahead and spotted the forest that they were due to disappear into.

He shifted his sights to the departing cadejo.

"What's wrong?" Daimon quietly asked.

Jackson frowned at him. "Nothing," he replied.

But the Alpha's concerned expression thickened. When they passed the tree line and followed Raphael into the woods, he asked him again, "What is it?"

With a hesitant sigh, Jackson looked over his shoulder to see if any of the cadejo had spotted them, but they hadn't. "I don't know. It just… feels a little too easy," he answered.

"Don't fucking jinx us, man," Amos complained.

Jackson shook his head. "I'm not trying to. It just…I don't know how to explain it."

"Do you have a feeling?" Daimon asked him.

"No, I...I don't think so," he said confusedly, and when he stared ahead, he caught Tokala looking back at him.

The orange wolf chimed in, "Raphael's plan is good. He's been doing this how long?"

"Over a century," Elias answered.

Tokala nodded and said to Jackson, "It admittedly feels weird for everything to be going okay, but...maybe it's just because we're with people who've been doing this much longer than us."

Maybe he was right. Jackson was probably overthinking.

But what if he wasn't? What if something was waiting for them up ahead? What if something had purposely let them get this far?

No...he *was* overthinking. After all, he didn't have one of his feelings. He didn't *feel* like there was danger waiting for them.

"How far is the lab?" Julian asked.

That was when Sebastien returned. The winged hound landed beside Raphael and continued leading the way with him.

"A few klicks," Raphael answered. "About thirty minutes."

"I think we should rest before we reach it," Daimon called.

"Yeah, I agree," Elias said. "If we're gonna be dodging cadejo hordes and machine guns, we're going to need as much energy as we can get."

Raphael shook his head. "Everyone can rest while waiting for Sebastien and Ethan to activate the generators and configure the security system."

Daimon snarled irritably but didn't argue.

"It's okay, Dad," Remus mumbled to him. "I don't need to rest."

"Yeah, we're good, chief," Tokala added, and the rest of the pack nodded in agreement.

Evidently, they were *all* just as eager to get to the lab.

Jackson tried to focus on that; he tried to dismiss his suspicions and concentrate on the fact that the lab was just thirty minutes away. *Thirty minutes.* After everything they'd been through, after all the danger and disaster that had gotten in their way, they were finally on the lab's doorstep. All they had to do was get past another horde.

One more horde and the mission would be complete.

Chapter Eighty-Eight

The Lab

| Jackson |

There were cadejo *everywhere*. Hundreds, maybe even *thousands* looming around the lab like a sea of groaning, suffering corpses. But their sheer numbers weren't what had the pack on edge; there were prowlers and brutes among the ocean, more than any of them had ever seen in one place.

The lab, an imposing structure with obsidian-tiled walls stretching over a mile in diameter, sitting at the bottom of the hill that the pack were standing on. Every window bore protective shutters, glistening silver under the moon's glow. Towering layers of metal fences, adorned with sinuous coils of barbed wire, encircled the compound. Sentinel guard towers loomed on each corner of the hexagonal enclosure, overseeing the formidable expanse.

Two helicopters occupied helipads visible from Jackson's position, and the ground below bristled with the presence of tanks and gun-mounted jeeps neatly arranged in the parking lots. It struck him more as a fortress, reminiscent of a prison, than a medical facility. But then again, it *was* Lyca Corp., and they'd require this kind of security with what they got up to, wouldn't they?

"So...we gotta go through that?" Wesley questioned uneasily.

"It's a lot more than I thought," Tokala hauntedly replied.

"We've got a plan," Raphael snapped dismissively. "See that watch tower right there?" he asked, lifting his paw to point to a tower two hundred feet away and on the outskirts of the sea of corpses. "That's where we'll wait out the turrets. Those things are made of mungdenite; no metal is getting through."

"Something tells me those huge fucking guns are gonna get through," Ethan exclaimed.

He had a point. Those guns were *massive*—each turret on the *triple* turreted weapons was bigger than a wolf walker. "The bullets have gotta be like mortar shells," Jackson agreed.

"That's 'cause you're looking at the canons," Amos told them. He directed the pack's attention to a deep dent in the building wall. "That's where the turrets are. We gotta get the power on to get the shutter to come down."

"Okay, so why not just use the mortars?" Lalo suggested. "Blow the fuckers up."

"Because the mortars are meant for long-range attacks; setting one off here would not only kill us even inside the tower but would also blow up half of the lab," Elias answered.

Raphael then snarled irritably. "We're wasting time. Sebastien, take Ethan and get those guns online."

Sebastien nodded and turned to face Ethan. "You ready?"

"Sure," the muto mumbled and shifted into his human form.

"You got this," Julian assured him.

"Yeah," Jackson agreed with a nod. "You know more about computers than anyone else I know."

Ethan responded with an awkward grunt and faced Sebastien. "Let's go."

Jackson watched as the winged hound took off, grabbed Ethan with his front legs, and then carried him up into the sky.

"Are you all ready?" Raphael then asked the pack.

Everyone shared the same anxious expression, even Daimon. But the Alpha quickly adorned a vacant stare and glanced around at his packmates. "We all know the plan. We reach the tower, and we wait inside until the security system is up and running and firing at the cadejo," he told them.

The pack nodded, and although their nervous stares weren't entirely lifted, they *did* look a little more confident.

Jackson tried to match their energy. He was worried about Wilson, and he was worried about *everyone* and what might happen once they left the hilltop and headed down into the cadejo swarm. But it wasn't like they had to get through the horde; the guard tower was two hundred feet away, and there weren't many cadejo in their path to get there. They just had to be careful.

Very careful.

"Stay close," Daimon told his pack. "And stay low."

With a deep exhale, Jackson dismissed as much of his worry as he could. It was time to go.

Raphael began leading the way down the hill, using every boulder, bush, and tree for cover.

Every snarl and distorted growl forced Jackson to shift his sights to the cadejo horde; he knew that staring at it wouldn't do him any good, but he couldn't ignore it—he couldn't act as if they weren't there.

And neither could anyone else. His packmates glanced at the swarm every few seconds, all with the same nervous expression. The only one who didn't look anxious was Raphael; the look on *his* face was one of determination. He fearlessly led the pack to the bottom of the hill, waited behind the cover of a tank until everyone grouped up behind him, and then he began the journey towards the watch tower, guiding the pack using the cover of abandoned vehicles, rubble, and the occasional tree.

They got closer and closer, but the nearer they got to the tower, the deeper into the horde they traversed. There weren't just a few stragglers on the other side of the rubble now; there were gatherings of at least twenty cadejo per group, and those numbers rose as the pack passed the rubble and reached the cover of an old jeep.

But the pack kept moving, following Raphael past the jeep and under a fallen tree leaning against a tank. Once they passed a van, though, Jackson noticed that they were running out of cover. The oil tanker ten feet ahead was the last thing they'd be able to hide behind, and the watch tower was still thirty feet away. Were they going to have to run for it?

He tensed up as dread gripped him in a tight, suffocating hold. They were going to have to run, weren't they? In the midst of a cadejo horde, they were going to have to run for the door—a door that might not even be open.

"What's wrong?" Daimon asked worriedly, his voice barely a whisper.

Jackson turned his head to look at him—

A loud thump cut through the snarling and growling, and when the pack abruptly ducked down into the snow, following Raphael's action, Jackson crouched, too. He frantically looked around, searching for what made the sound, and when he set his eyes on the twisted, rotting form of a prowler, his dread skyrocketed.

The lanky creature lurched through the ocean of cadejo, barely ten feet away from the oil tanker; Jackson watched through the space between the wheels as the monster sniffed around, jerking its head as its body twitched and convulsed.

And then a horrifying, "*Some... where...*" echoed around inside Jackson's head.

Was it looking for them? Did it know that they were there?

Jackson tried to keep calm, but the last time a prowler hunted him and his packmates, it knew that they were hiding under the snow, and this time, they were out in the open.

"*Here...*" the prowler drawled, turning towards the oil tanker.

Jackson's instincts urged him to run just as they always did, but he wasn't going to give in. He could tell that prowler to leave, or he could use the inima to take the monster down. He could give his packmates the time they'd need to get to the guard tower.

No. That was stupid. *Foolish.* He'd get everyone killed. He'd attract all the other cadejo, and he couldn't control or fight *that* many.

He had to do *something*, though.

The prowler was getting closer, dragging its rotting paws through the snow, sniffing around as it moved through the horde.

Jackson looked at Raphael, but it didn't seem like he was going to do anything. Was he just going to let it find them?!

"*Here...*" the creature breathed, inching nearer and nearer and—

A ground-shaking, deafening explosion lit up the darkness on the other side of the horde.

Jackson flinched in startle but didn't cover his ears like everyone else. He kept his eyes on the prowler, watching as it turned around and began racing in the direction of the fire along with all the cadejo around it.

"Wait..." came Raphael's voice.

Taking his eyes off the departing corpses, Jackson stared at the orange wolf. His packmates stared at Raphael, too, waiting for his signal.

"Wait..." the orange wolf said again as several cadejo raced past the oil tanker, oblivious to their presence.

And then a few more scurried past.

"Now!" Raphael ordered and burst out of cover.

The pack immediately followed, shadowing his every move as he raced forward, jumped over a rock, dodged a dead tree, and approached the watch tower.

When they reached the door, Raphael slammed into it with his body, and it gave way. Everyone hurried inside, and once they were in, the orange wolf used his strength to jam the door shut behind them.

"That fucking prowler was getting so damn close—*too* close," Wesley exclaimed, panting along with everyone else.

"Where'd that explosion come from?" Julian questioned.

"The căutător are useful for more than delivering messages and overwatch," Raphael answered as he sat by the door and let out a deep exhale.

While the pack caught their breath, Jackson glanced around the circular interior of the tower. It smelled of dry rot and ash; a hint of pine hung in the air, probably coming from the distant forest, and there was nothing inside but a steep spiralling staircase leading up to the top.

"Did Sebastien and Ethan make it?" Ezhno asked.

Raphael nodded. "They made it."

"How do you know? Did they say?" Brando questioned.

"They made it," Raphael repeated firmly.

No one else asked anything. Instead, they either sat or lay down and rested.

Jackson did his best to relax, too. He felt like an idiot for considering being reckless; Raphael knew what he was doing. How many more times did he need to remind himself of that?

"Are you okay?" Daimon asked him.

He nodded and slowly laid down. "Yeah, I just…got spooked when I saw the prowler."

His mate nuzzled his head. "Don't worry. We've got this."

Jackson nodded again and then closed his eyes. Daimon was right. They had a plan, and it was working. All that was left to do now was wait until the guns were online.

| Sebastien |

When he reached the lab with Ethan, Sebastien landed on a balcony several floors up and let go of the muto. He shifted out of his hound form and followed Ethan to the balcony door, which wasn't hard to force open with his demon strength.

"Where's the security room? And the generators?" Ethan questioned as they stepped inside, finding themselves in a conference room.

"We're on the east side, so we just need to find the loading bay," Sebastien answered, heading over to the door. "You find the security room and I'll find the generators—we'll get shit done faster that way," he instructed, stepping out into a long, dark hallway.

Ethan scoffed as he followed him out. "Suppose there's cadejo in this place. What if I get bit?"

"This place has been on lockdown for years; there aren't any cadejo inside—at least not on this level."

"How do you know that? You've never fucking been here!"

Sebastien sighed irritably and turned to face him. "No, but I've seen plenty of places like it. They keep the experiments below ground level and everything else up here to make it look like a legitimate workplace. You're not going to run into any—"

A distorted, clicking sound echoed from the hall up ahead.

They both sharply turned their heads and stared at the double doors at the end of the corridor. Squelching footsteps clawed at the silence, and as they got closer, Sebastien and Ethan watched the silhouette of a man stumble and limp through the door's foggy windows.

"On second thought, yeah, let's stick together," Sebastien muttered.

Ethan went to shift—

"No, stay in your human form," Sebastien said, snatching his wrist. "These corridors are narrow, and you won't be able to move around as much."

"Okay, but I can't shoot blue fire or anything. What am I supposed to do to defend myself?" he questioned irritably, and there was a hint of angst in his voice.

Sebastien didn't have an answer for that. "Just stick close," he said as he started walking towards the doors.

"Why are you going that way?" Ethan exclaimed quietly. "Let's go the way that the fucking zombie *isn't* in?"

With a quiet sigh, Sebastien waved his hand towards the directory signs on the wall. "Loading bay is this way."

Ethan rolled his eyes like a stroppy child but quickly caught up to him. "Why don't we just follow the balconies or fly?"

"Because the loading bay can only be accessed from inside; there's a roof over it, and the gates are blocked off by the horde," Sebastien explained as they approached the doors. "Don't be a hero," he instructed, and then he pushed both doors open; one door hit the infected human, which tripped over its own feet and fell, and before it could try to get up, Sebastien plunged his hand into its chest and crushed its heart.

"Oh, fuck yeah," Ethan said excitedly as he yanked the rifle off the corpse.

"Do you even know how to use that?" Sebastien questioned as he stood up straight and wiped his bloody hand on his trouser leg.

Ethan examined the weapon with an unsure frown but eventually figured out how to detach and check the magazine. It was loaded. "Yeah, don't worry, man," he answered, clipping the magazine back in.

Sebastien rolled his eyes but didn't tell him to put it back. He'd rather he had something to defend himself with if he needed it. "Let's go," he said as he headed down the hallway towards the doors at the end.

He led the way to the end of the hall, carefully pushed the doors open and checked for infected, and then hurried to the right towards the stairs. Once they reached the bottom, they emerged in a large indoor courtyard. Lifeless, rotting corpses were sprawled over the empty fountain, medical supplies and weapons lay everywhere like rubble, and several dead cadejo lay on the tiled floor. Something happened here; Sebastien wasn't sure what, but something made this place shut down, and the traumatized part of him suspected that it might have something to do with the phantom.

"What happened?" Ethan questioned as they crossed the courtyard and headed towards the metal shutters. "Looks like a war went down."

"I don't know," he mumbled, reaching the shutters, which were made of vendite. He grunted irritably and looked at Ethan. "Help me lift this shit. It's gonna burn like fuck."

Ethan put the rifle strap around his shoulder and moved closer. "Can't you just burn it?"

"I can't do shit against vendite," he muttered.

When Sebastien gripped the bottom of the shutter, it burned his skin immediately, but he did his best to ignore the searing pain and the stench of his own burning flesh and started lifting. He grunted and groaned painfully, as did Ethan, but they didn't stop trying to lift it.

After his skin started sticking to the metal, though, Ethan let go and flailed his arms around frustratedly. "This isn't gonna work!" he exclaimed.

Sebastien let go of the shutter and stared down at his burned palms. Against vendite, their strength meant nothing; it rendered them just as weak as humans. But he couldn't give up. There was no other way to get in, so he was just going to have to keep trying. "Come on," he said as he took his jacket off and wrapped it around his hands as best as he could.

Ethan, who looked reluctant, sighed and rolled his eyes as he pulled his hoodie off. He wrapped it around his hands, and when Sebastien gripped the bottom of the shutter again, so did he.

They both strained as they pulled, and after a few more tugs, it finally gave way and began lifting. But as it gradually opened, the metal clicked and creaked, echoing through the empty halls, and it didn't take long for the infected to come crawling, drawn to the sound like moths to a flame.

Snarls and guttural clicks came from every direction.

While he lifted, Sebastien glanced to his left; he saw two infected humans sluggishly lurching towards them from the other side of the courtyard. Three more came out of the broken door behind Ethan, and another fell off the balcony above and landed beside the fountain.

Ethan panicked and let go of the shutter. "Holy fuck, man," he said as he turned to face the slowly approaching corpses.

The shutter was wide enough for them to fit through, but Sebastien knew that he should deal with the infected before they grouped up. There weren't any cadejo in the loading bay, and he knew next to nothing about generators, so he looked at Ethan and said, "Go and get the power on. I'll deal with them."

With a hesitant frown, Ethan glanced at him and then frantically shifted his sights between the infected. "You sure?"

"Yeah. Go. And keep that handy in case you need it," he said, nodding at the rifle in his hands.

Ethan turned around, ducked under the shutter, and disappeared into the loading bay.

Sebastien shifted into his hound form and burst into action. He fired a ball of blue flames at the two infected he saw first; when they combusted, he spat two more balls towards the three infected moving towards the shutter. And finally, he shot one last ball at the infected which had fallen from the balcony.

But it wasn't over.

The commotion attracted more, and as the rotting humans filed out of the doors in lab coats, suits, and military fatigues, Sebastien tensed up and adorned a determined but cautious frown. He quickly glanced behind him under the shutter to make sure that Ethan was fine, and as far as he could tell, there weren't any cadejo out there, so he turned his attention back to the ones coming for him.

He got to work. As he propelled himself into the air with his wings, he spat fire at as many of the infected as he could until he had no shots left. Then, while letting his ethos recover, he swopped down and mercilessly plunged his paw through the chest of one corpse, executing it. He swerved around, glided over to another, and forced his paw through its body, destroying its decaying heart.

Once he had enough ethos again, he shot another ball of fire at a group of infected. He landed in the centre of the courtyard, watching as all the flame-consumed infected slowly fell still and silent, and when they were all dead-dead, he waited a moment to ensure that more weren't coming and then hurried outside to find Ethan.

He scurried under the shutter and down the few steps into the loading bay. As he moved past the parked lorry, he looked around for Ethan; he spotted the brown-haired kid by the generator fiddling with wires. "What are you doing?" he asked as he raced over.

Ethan glanced at him. "Shit's shot to fuck," he muttered. "I had to take it apart."

Sebastien watched him work, checking his left, right, and rear for infected every few seconds. "Do you need anything?" he asked.

"Like what?" Ethan muttered, and when he tied two wires together, they sparked, and the generator rumbled for a moment before falling silent. "Fucking hell."

"I don't know…tools?"

"I don't see a toolbox lying around here," Ethan said, glancing around as he pulled the two wires apart. He put one wire down, picked up another, and tied it with the first. The generator groaned again, but this time, it started up, and it didn't fall silent. "Got it," he said with a grin, letting go of the wires. "Let's go."

The loading bay lights started flicking on; the sound of whirring machinery echoed around them, and a very loud metallic clicking came from above. Sebastien looked up, setting his eyes on two turrets—

"Move!" he shouted, pulling Ethan out of the way as the gun powered up.

But it didn't fire at them. The moment it beeped and activated, bullets rained from its barrel, but it was firing at the cadejo swarm outside.

"Get off me," Ethan grunted, shoving Sebastien away. He then looked at the gun, watched it mow down cadejo, and frowned at the hound. "I thought I was supposed to program them to do that?"

Sebastien's frown thickened. "Yeah, me too."

"I guess they already had them set up for shooting the cadejo; saves us a lot of time."

Seeing that the guns *had* indeed been programmed to fire at cadejo already furthered Sebastien's suspicion that whatever happened here had something to do with the cadejo—something to do with the *phantom*.

Several similar beeps echoed from every direction, and as more and more turrets started firing, the noise became so loud that Sebastien couldn't hear Ethan over it.

He had to get a message to Raphael, though. "Come!" he called, and moments later, the căutător creature descended, wriggled through a hole in the fence, and flew over to him. "Tell Heir Zephyr it's done!" he shouted.

The creature heard him and nodded before flying off.

Sebastien then patted Ethan's shoulder. "Let's go!"

Ethan followed him back inside, where it was much quieter.

"We need to find the entrance," Sebastien said. "We're gonna have to let them in."

"All right," Ethan agreed.

Sebastien led the way through the building. The hard part was over. All he had to do now was find the doors and wait for Raphael to lead the pack inside…and then they could find the answers they'd been hunting for *years*.

Or at least he hoped so.

Chapter Eighty-Nine

↔ ≪ ☽ ≫ ↔

A Sea of Red

| Jackson |

The sound of the turrets firing clashed with the noise of the horde; the undead screeched and snarled and howled, defenceless against the weapons mowing them down. But the stench of rotting blood and decaying flesh quickly polluted the air, and it made Jackson feel sick.

His packmates gagged in revolt, some holding their paws over their noses while others hid their entire faces beneath them. However, the only one who didn't look disgusted was Tokala. A concerned frown sat on his face, and it looked as though he was deep in thought.

In an attempt to escape the stench of the carnage, Jackson went over to him and asked, "Are you okay?"

The orange wolf snapped out of his thoughts and set his sights on him. "Huh? Oh, yeah. I'm fine. I'm just…anxious, I guess. We're so close to getting in."

Jackson nodded as he sat beside him. "Yeah, I'm anxious, too. A part of me thought we might not ever make it here."

"Me too," Tokala mumbled. "But here we are."

"And once we've found whatever's inside, we can get away from all this Nosferatu and Venaticus stuff," he said confidently.

Tokala turned to face him. "You've decided to stay in Ascela?" he asked, looking surprised.

"Yeah," he said with a nod. "I wanna be with Daimon, and all of you guys…well, you're like a family to me now—better than any I had growing up," he said with a sullen laugh.

The orange wolf laughed a little, too, but it was laced with tones of despair. "Yeah, I understand that. I didn't have much of a family growing up; I was a part of the pack, sure, but a lot of them disdained my mother and me because we're Redbloods. It wasn't until Alpha Daimon inherited the throne that I was treated like an equal."

Jackson frowned sympathetically. "I know too well how that feels…to be treated like an outcast."

"But now you've found your pack; you've found people who accept you for who and what you are," Tokala said with an encouraging smile.

"Yeah," Jackson agreed. "But I gotta admit, I'm not sure I like the whole demon side of things. I even considered asking Lord Caedis to take the demon part of me away, but—"

"Why?" Tokala blurted, confused.

Jackson frowned a little. "Because demons are scary," he said with a nervous chuckle. "I don't wanna be a part of a society that breaks bones when you hurt someone or say the wrong thing."

"It's not much different than wolf walkers," the Zeta said with a shrug. "But Alpha Daimon doesn't believe in physical punishment; that's why you haven't seen it happen with us."

"Well, either way, I just wanna be with you guys," he said, looking across the room at Daimon, who was holding his son.

The thundering gunfire started dying down.

Everyone stopped talking, pricked their ears up, and stared at Raphael.

With a frown on his face, the orange-furred wolf pressed his ear against the wall and listened.

Moments later, the căutător creature slinked in through an unseen space above and glided down to Raphael, who held out his paw. The creature landed, chirped at him, and then took off again when Raphael lowered his paw.

"Let's move," Raphael said as he went over to the door. "Stay close and keep your eyes peeled."

"Is everyone ready?" Daimon asked.

A mixture of determined and anxious expressions clung to their faces, but the pack nodded and grouped up with their Alpha.

"This is it," Tokala said as he and Jackson joined the pack.

Jackson smiled nervously in response. This *was* it. All they had to do was get to the lab.

Raphael yanked the door free, and then he slowly pulled it open, peering outside. After a few seconds of checking if it was clear, he opened the door all the way and led the pack outside.

The smell was even worse there; it was so bad that Jackson gagged, and so did everyone else. The snow was painted red and black with blood and rotten organs; *hundreds* of cadejo lay still in several pieces, torn apart by the turrets, and not one corpse was left standing, not even the prowlers or brutes.

Jackson set his sights on the lab. Most of the lights had come on, illuminating the dark valley centre; the turrets were rotating left and right, scanning for cadejo, and spotlights were combing the graveyard.

"Let's move," Raphael said and began leading the way through the thick tide of blood and guts.

"This is fucking vile," Julian complained. "One time, Kane made me and three other Omegas swim through this swamp, and it wasn't just mud, man…. Anyway, this shit is *worse* than that—I'd take a swamp full of God knows what over this."

"Shh," Raphael snapped.

Julian went silent.

As they moved forward, Daimon looked at Jackson, who smiled as best as he could at him in response, letting him know that he was okay—as okay as he could be in a sea of rotting insides.

The pack dragged their paws through the mess, getting closer and closer to the lab. When a cadejo suddenly burst out from beneath the carnage, it attempted to run towards the pack, which stopped to face it, but the turrets activated and gunned it down a mere second after it emerged.

"Fucking hell," Wesley muttered as the pack continued forward. "This is the kinda shit the Nosferatu is dealing with?"

"Yup," Amos called. "Lyca Corp. has labs and shit all over the world, and some of them are a lot more well-equipped than this."

"I don't think I could do that," Julian said, glancing around. "You know, be a military person."

"Me neither," Dustu agreed.

"It's not all bad," Elias called from the back of the line. "Especially when you're on a stealth squad. I envy those guys."

Raphael snarled irritably and looked back at everyone. "Less talk, more moving!" he exclaimed.

Wesley rolled his eyes.

"What do we do once we're inside?" Tokala asked.

"We clear the place out if Sebastien hasn't done it already, and then we check *everywhere* for information," Raphael replied.

"What if there isn't anything here?" Leon questioned.

"Yeah. What if we came all this way for nothing?" Lance agreed.

"We didn't come all this way for nothing," Raphael grumbled. "Now I'm not going to tell you all again. Less talk, more—"

An eruption of savage snarls and growls drowned Raphael's voice out, a cacophony of horror that shattered the eerie silence. From the depths of the massacre, a horde of seething, rotting cadejo burst forth just feet away, their malevolence palpable as they lunged at the pack. The guns, the once-reliable guardians, now remained eerily silent, adding to the mounting anxiety.

"Why aren't the guns firing?!" Amos bellowed, his frustration mirroring the chaos surrounding them.

As the pack battled the relentless onslaught, the cadejo exhibited a sinister intelligence. With chilling precision, they closed in on Tokala, who was isolated amidst the malevolent horde.

"Tokala!" Jackson's desperate voice cut through the pandemonium.

The pack rushed to Tokala's aid, the urgency heightening with each passing second. Tokala fought valiantly, kicking and slashing at the encroaching creatures, but the relentless advance of a prowler changed the course of the battle. Its lanky arms ensnared Tokala, dragging him away from his pack, the desperate cries for help echoing in Jackson's ears.

"Tokala!" The collective panic of the pack rose, and Raphael's immense strength became a beacon of hope as he battled alongside them. Yet, the sea of red churned with an unending tide of cadejo, forming an impenetrable barrier between the pack and their Zeta.

"Tokala!" Jackson shouted, kicking away the cadejo in his path, and as he fixed his sights on the prowler, he yelled, "Stop! Bring him back here!"

The prowler's eyes locked with Jackson's, and it stopped. But then whispers carried upon the wind, and the prowler quickly snapped out of its trance and continued dragging Tokala.

"No!" Jackson yelled. "Stop! Stop!" he called, trying to run after it. Why wasn't it listening?!

The orange wolf's desperate gaze met Jackson's terrified eyes, and he pleaded for help, his voice crying out Jackson's name.

Without hesitation, Jackson reached into his bag, his body trembling as he grabbed the inimă—their last resort.

But horror struck as the guns, silent until now, roared back to life.

"Get down!" Elias's urgent command sliced through the chaos.

Panic surged anew as Jackson, refusing to abandon Tokala, edged the inimă to his neck. But just as he was about to take action, Daimon crashed into him, a forceful collision that sent them sprawling beneath the deadly onslaught. The deafening whir of the guns and the explosive bursts reverberated, drowning out all other sounds; Jackson's heart raced, pounding in his ears as he struggled beneath the oppressive weight.

"We can't leave him!" he pleaded, desperation etched in every word.

"We can't do anything!" Daimon's response, laden with the same distress, echoed the futility of their situation.

The world around Jackson descended into chaos, and all he could do was watch, pinned down beneath his mate.

And then the guns went silent.

The only sound came from Jackson's panicked packmates, who were calling Tokala's name.

Jackson wriggled free from Daimon's protective hold and stood up; he searched the desolation for the orange wolf, but the only orange his eyes found was Raphael. His racing heart ached as dismay and denial gripped him tight. Tokala couldn't be gone—how could Tokala be gone?!

"Tokala!" he joined the desperate calls. "Tokala?!"

"Tokala!" Daimon called.

"He's gotta be here somewhere!" Wesley insisted. "Start searching!"

The pack began looking through the carnage at their paws, but the silence was once again stolen by snarls and growls, and they were getting closer.

Jackson stopped searching the massacre and glanced at the tree line; another horde was coming. "We have to hurry up!" he called desperately. "Tokala? Tokala?!"

But then Raphael shouted, "We have to keep moving!"

"We're not leaving him! He's here, he's gotta be!" Brando yelled.

Remus started crying, and his tears shattered the determined looks on everyone's faces. They all adorned horrified stares as if realization had hit them.

But not Jackson. There was no realization to be struck by. Tokala was somewhere among the carnage, and he needed their help. "Tokala!" he called again, using his paws to push cadejo corpses away. He was alive, he was here—his instincts told him so, just like they insisted that he was right about someone attacking Daimon. He wasn't going to ignore the feeling. "Tokala?!"

"Jackson," Daimon said regretfully as he hurried to his side. "We can't stay here. We—"

"We can't leave him!"

"He's not here!" Raphael shouted. "He's fucking gone!"

"We need to go," Daimon insisted with dismay in his eyes. "We have to go."

Jackson shook his head as his throat tightened, and tears formed in his eyes. "W-we can't...leave him out here!" he pleaded despondently. "He's here. He—"

Daimon shook his head, scowling in despair. "We have to go," he repeated.

His tears started falling. "N-no," he denied painfully. "W-we...he can't...I—"

The Alpha nudged him towards the pack. "We have to go," he said once more.

Jackson trembled as dejection enthralled him. But fear shot through him when he noticed the cadejo getting closer, and his instincts began urging him to run. How could he, though? How could he just leave Tokala? He *had* to be there somewhere; how could someone like Tokala just...die? No. He wasn't dead. He couldn't be—

"Jackson!" Daimon insisted.

"Let's fucking go!" Raphael yelled.

His body heavy with despair and horror, Jackson shook his head and tried his best to get a hold of himself. He wanted to keep searching, but he wouldn't get anyone else killed, nor would he let the cadejo take him. He snatched the inimă from where it fell when Daimon crashed into him, and as Raphael led the way, he followed his fleeing pack towards the lab gates.

The guns started firing again, mowing down the pursuing horde.

"Why did they stop back there?!" Elias exclaimed.

"I don't fucking know!" Raphael yelled back. "Maybe we were too close to the cadejo; maybe they don't shoot when other bio signs are nearby."

Their conversation drowned out, and a disorientating ringing filled Jackson's ears. It started hitting him…the realization. The reality. They couldn't find Tokala…because Tokala wasn't there, was he? He was gone.

And what made it worse was that they didn't know whether he'd been killed or turned, and if he *had* turned, they wouldn't be able to set him free.

"Inside!" Raphael's voice cut through the ringing.

Jackson followed his packmates through the open gate; Elias and Amos heaved it shut behind them, and Raphael led the way towards the lab's trio of front glass doors.

Sebastien pushed the middle door open from the inside; the pack hurried in one by one, and once they all passed him, Sebastien closed and locked the door.

They were in.

Chapter Ninety

⌐ ⋞ ☽ ⋟ ⌐

Black Files

| Jackson |

The weight of Tokala's death bore down on Jackson's shoulders like an insurmountable burden, an oppressive force that stifled the air in the hall. The atmosphere lay shrouded in a suffocating silence, a haunting stillness that mirrored the emptiness left in Tokala's absence.

No one dared to break the quiet. No words offered solace, and no movement disrupted the collective grief that hung in the air. The pack stood motionless, each member encapsulated in their individual prisons of despair. Their Zeta, their second-in-command, and their beloved friend—gone. Taken right in front of them, his life extinguished like a flickering flame. The reality of the situation weighed heavily on every heart, and the shadow of grief loomed large over the pack.

Even someone as powerful as Raphael had been rendered powerless in the face of the tragedy. His strength, normally an unyielding shield, had failed to save Tokala from the clutches of death. The unspoken realization of their vulnerability and mortality hung in the air, a bitter taste that lingered on their tongues.

Jackson's gaze drifted around the hall, seeking solace or understanding, but there was none to be found. The absence of Tokala's presence echoed louder than any spoken words could convey. The once-unbreakable bond and unyielding determination of the pack now felt fragile and frayed, the threads of unity unravelling with each passing moment.

The ache of loss settled deep within Jackson's aching chest, a searing pain that resonated with the hollow emptiness of the lab's entry hall. In the quietude, the weight of grief pressed upon their collective souls, and the realization that they couldn't turn back time or undo the irrevocable shattered Jackson's heart.

As the stillness lingered, an unspoken understanding passed through the pack—a mournful acknowledgement that life had been forever altered, and they were left to grapple with the harsh reality that their Zeta had been taken from them, leaving behind a void that seemed impossible to fill.

"We need to start the search," Raphael said, breaking the silence.

"Just give them a few moments, man," Amos muttered.

"We don't have a few moments. The longer we wait, the more ammo those turrets use up; eventually, they'll run out, and the cadejo will breach the fences."

Jackson wanted to yell at Raphael—he was such an insensitive asshole—but not only did he not have the strength, he also knew that if he did that, he'd get another broken leg.

"Hey," came Ethan's voice.

Jackson sharply turned his head and set his eyes on his friend, who was in his human form and carrying a rifle.

"Are you all right?"

Jackson hung his head in shame.

Ethan frowned and said, "I'm sorry, Jack. I know he was your friend."

"Move along," Daimon then snarled, appearing at Jackson's side.

For a moment, Ethan glared at him, but he didn't argue. He turned around and walked over to Sebastien.

Jackson didn't have the strength to argue with his mate, either. He didn't have the strength to do *anything*.

"Come on," Raphael called as he shifted into his human form. "We need to start searching."

"There's an elevator that'll take us to the lower levels," Sebastien said.

"Now," the orange-haired man insisted.

The pack didn't move.

But Daimon let out a deep, despair-ridden sigh and adorned that stoic expression he adorned when he needed to be strong for his wolves. "Come on," he said to them. "Tokala wouldn't want us to mope around and waste time. Let's get what we came for."

Jackson didn't want to move, but when the pack started reluctantly following Raphael, Daimon nudged his side, and Jackson walked beside him.

Once they reached the elevator doors, everyone shifted into their human forms and filed inside.

It felt like all their eyes were on Jackson…like they were thinking the same thing that he was. It was *his* fault, he could have done more—he *should* have done more. But….

"The prowler didn't listen to me," Jackson said sullenly. "I told it to stop, and…it *did*, but only for a second. I don't…know why."

"It's not your fault," Daimon replied, slipping his hand into Jackson's. "It's no one's fault."

"It's the fucking guns' fault," Wesley uttered despondently.

"Why didn't you tell us from the get-go that they'd stop firing if we were too close to the cadejo?" Brando questioned Raphael, who pressed the elevator button.

The orange-haired man scoffed as the doors closed. "Because I didn't know. I don't know every damn little thing about everything, believe it or not," he grumbled.

"We're sorry," Sebastien interjected before several of Jackson's packmates could respond, all of them with furious scowls on their faces. "If I'd known, I would have told you guys. But I didn't. If you wanna blame anyone, blame me."

Daimon shook his head. "Let's just... focus on getting what we came for," he repeated, but he was clearly struggling to maintain his composure; Jackson could feel his hand trembling.

The elevator carried them down as they stood in silence.

But then Wesley grunted, "We should've looked for him. We just left him out there!"

"Stop," Daimon said firmly.

The Gamma shot a glare at the Alpha but didn't say anything else.

"Up front with me," Raphael said to Sebastien as the elevator approached the basement.

Sebastien squeezed past Lalo and Leon and stood beside Raphael.

Jackson knew that he should prepare for whatever waited once they arrived, but his grief and despair kept him trapped in a state of hopelessness. Even when the elevator arrived and the doors slid open, he stood there with a despondent stare on his face; he didn't start walking until Daimon, who was still holding his hand, led him out into the long, dark corridor, following Raphael and Sebastien as they slowly navigated the way forward.

"So... where do we go first?" Ethan questioned.

"Every Lyca Corp. building has a central information room," Raphael muttered, cautiously leading, checking every door and window they passed.

They silently followed him; the tense air was still thick with grief, and it felt as if either no one knew what to say or were afraid to speak their mind.

"How do we get whatever we find back to the Nosferatu?" Ethan asked, breaking the silence again.

"Heir Zephyr will deal with that," Sebastien answered.

They turned right and followed another corridor, went through a pair of double doors, and crossed an empty, dark hall lined with laboratory doors.

"Over here," Raphael said, hurrying over to another set of double doors, but they were sealed shut, requiring a card to open. But instead of foraging around for one, the orange-haired man threw himself at the doors, and they gave way to his immense strength, swinging open.

Everyone waited outside behind Sebastien while Raphael checked for cadejo, and once they were given the all-clear, they followed the white-haired demon into the room.

The left wall was lined with shelves of books; the right had several maps pinned to it, and the one ahead had boards of pictures, documents, and drawings hanging from them. Filing cabinets took up most of the floor space, along with computer desks and bookshelves. The desks had old laptops and computer screens on them, as well as tablets, phones, and recording equipment.

"All right, everyone, start looking," Raphael ordered as he headed over to one of the computers. "Look through *everything*. Find anything that talks about how the virus was being used here, any experiments they were doing on it—anything virus-related, honestly."

When Daimon nodded, the pack did as they were told. Wesley, Brando, Ezhno, and Lance went to the left side of the room; Julian, Dustu, Ethan, and Lance went to the table in the middle of the room, and Leon and Lalo went over to the computers with Sebastien.

Jackson went with Daimon and Remus to the right and started looking through one of the filing cabinets. He tried to focus, but he couldn't get Tokala's face out of his head—he couldn't stop thinking about his begging, pleading cries. Why didn't that cadejo listen to him? Why wouldn't Daimon let him use the inimă?

"Hey," Daimon said quietly, placing his hand on Jackson's shoulder. "Listen to me, Jackson. It wasn't your fault, okay?"

He frowned sullenly and flipped through the files. "Yes, it was."

"It wasn't," he said firmly. "We couldn't have known that those cadejo were under there, and—"

"I should have done more," he interjected, shaking his head. "I could've used the inimă, I could've—"

"Even if you did use it…it was too late," Daimon said despondently. "All we can do now is finish what we all came out here to do."

Jackson shook his head again as his dismay and guilt grew. "And what if we don't find anything useful?" he questioned as he stopped looking through the drawer. "It's all just fucking employee names."

Daimon rubbed his shoulder. "Hey, it's okay. Just search another drawer; there's plenty of them."

He scowled frustratedly and shut the drawer. Once he opened the one beneath it, he looked through the files inside, and Daimon took his hand off his shoulder.

"Yo, what about this?" Julian called.

Jackson stopped searching and looked over at them.

In their hands, Julian was holding a black file.

"That's good," Raphael agreed and turned to face everyone. "Get all this off here," he said as he started shoving everything off the table in the middle of the room. "I want everything we find put on here."

Julian put the file on the table and went back to searching.

"Hey, there's another one here," Lance said, holding up a similar black file.

"Should we just be looking for black ones?" Dustu asked.

"No," Sebastien said as Raphael returned to the computer. "The black ones are classified files, so we want all of those, period. Everything else, stick to the list Heir Zephyr gave you."

Everyone nodded and kept searching.

Jackson didn't find anything in the second drawer other than more employee files. He closed it, opened the third, and searched it, and when he found a black file, he frowned and pulled it out.

"What is it?" Daimon asked.

"It says…subject zero-zero-nine," he said, reading the file name.

"Add it to the pile," came Raphael's voice.

Jackson tossed the file onto the table and got back to searching.

Black file after black file, the pile on the table quickly grew. When Jackson found another, he went to add it to the collection, but he hesitated when he saw 'Caleb Henning'.

Caleb? The same Caleb the antlered wolf mentioned?

Jackson glanced over his shoulder to see if he was being supervised, and when he saw that Sebastien and Raphael were busy downloading files onto an external hard drive, he discreetly opened the file.

A black and white photo of a man who looked either eighteen or nineteen was clipped to the first page, and written on the paper was information about where he lived, who his parents were, etcetera, and when he died.

1177, one hundred and fifty-five years ago.

He flipped to the next page, and when he saw Sebastien's name, he frowned and read on.

Undecim 30th 1177, Sebastien Huxley, Nosferatu agent, travelled to Alder Estate in DeiganLupus to investigate a plague killing townspeople. While investigating, Huxley recruited Caleb Henning to assist.

Huxley's investigation eventually led him to the Alder catacomb, where the phantom, otherwise known as patient 0, was imprisoned. Huxley freed patient 0 under the impression that it would save the townsfolk, but patient 0 possessed Henning's body and was able to escape Alder Estate.

After capturing Henning in 1198, we began researching the virus his body contained, a virus capable of turning animals into undead. After years of work, we were able to weaponize the virus using the blood of Thomas Greymore and Bennet Morgan in 1225.

However, Henning began showing signs of degradation. His body got weaker, as did the virus in his blood. We—

"What are you doing?" Sebastien snapped, snatching the file from Jackson's grip.

Jackson scowled at him and tried to snatch the file back. "I was reading that!"

"You're not supposed to be reading shit," Sebastien growled, yanking it away from him.

"Calm down," Daimon warned him as everyone watched the altercation.

But alongside his anger, Jackson felt skeptical. He knew that Sebastien was hiding something, and after seeing his name on that page, he wasn't going to let it go. "I saw Greymore's name in that file," he told Daimon, who he knew would want to know more.

"What?" Daimon questioned.

"It's confidential!" Sebastien argued.

"Add it to the pile," Raphael ordered.

But then Wesley said, "Nah, Greymore's Fenrisúlfr, isn't he? I wanna know why his name's in there." As he moved closer, his Epsilons followed.

Sebastien scoffed. "You'll know what you need to know when Lord Caedis decides," he said and tried to place the file on the table, but Ethan snatched it from him. "Hey!"

Ethan read through the file as he backed off; Sebastien and Raphael tried to reach him, but the pack got in their way—that was until Raphael used a little more strength and barged through the crowd. He grabbed the file from Ethan and tossed it on the pile.

"Back to fucking work," the orange-haired man ordered.

"Why's that file talking about that Henning guy or patient zero or whatever needing a new body like that antlered wolf?" Ethan questioned—he'd obviously gotten further in than Jackson managed.

"What?" Daimon snarled, glaring at Sebastien and Raphael.

"Who's Henning?" Dustu asked.

"Patient zero?" Lalo questioned.

"Get to wo—"

"We're not doing anything else until we get answers," Daimon interrupted Raphael. "We're not your employees or your servants, and we have a right to know what it is exactly that we're dealing with. Why is Greymore's name in that file with Sebastien's name?"

"And Caleb," Jackson revealed. "I heard the antlered wolf mention him to you," he said, looking at Sebastien, who looked *horrified*.

Neither Sebastien nor Raphael answered; they shot each other unsure stares, and then they glanced around the room at everyone. But when it looked like Raphael was about to answer, Sebastien shook his head.

Raphael didn't respect his wish, though. "A hundred and fifty-ish years ago, Sebastien was sent to Alder Estate in DeiganLupus to investigate a fast-spreading plague taking out townspeople. During his investigation, he found undead animals...and a phantom, an ancient, trapped spirit which feeds on the souls of those who die on the grounds it's chosen either willingly or not as its home. He worked out that the phantom was the cause of the undead animals; its energy was so strong that it was affecting the world around it. It managed to convince Sebastien that releasing it would solve the problem, and since all Sebastien was sent to do was solve the problem, he freed it."

Sebastien snarled uncomfortably. "Can you just—"

"Sebastien dragged a kid, Caleb, into his investigation," Raphael continued, talking over him. "Phantoms are the strongest kind of astral Caeleste; when powerful enough, they can manifest a physical form, but they need the body of someone living to do it, and in this case, it was Caleb. The phantom took his body and fled, disappearing without a trace. The plague was eradicated in DeiganLupus, but it started popping up again a few years later. We investigated, and we found the phantom there—or as he's been referred to in that file, patient zero. We suspected that the cadejo virus was linked to him, but we didn't know for certain because the virus the phantom was carrying only infected animals. But now we know that Lyca Corp. is responsible for its evolution, and for it infecting Caeleste," he explained, glancing at the file Jackson had been reading.

"And what does that have to do with Greymore?" Daimon asked.

"Exactly what the file said: they've been using his blood along with a demon's to reconstruct the virus—to weaponize it," he answered.

"This…whole time, Lyca Corp. had him?" Amos asked, his face smothered with despair. "For *a hundred and fifty* years?"

Jackson wasn't sure how to react to everything Raphael just said. "So…the antlered wolf…is patient zero?"

"Yes," Raphael confirmed. "And he needs a new vessel. These bodies that he's used over the past century and a half can only harbour his ethos for so long, and they eventually begin to die. That's why he wants you, a perfect hybrid, a body that'll be able to harbour his ethos without being slowly torn apart."

Horrified, Jackson swallowed hard and glanced around at his packmates' confused faces.

"But he can't risk getting hurt because while his body is dying, it doesn't heal, and a fatal wound would banish him from the flesh, and Sebastien could send him to the Underworld," Raphael said, glancing at Sebastien again.

The room went silent for a moment. It was like no one knew what to say—even Jackson didn't know what to say.

But then Ethan broke the quiet *again*. "Okay, well…we can't let him get Jackson, can we? And from what you're saying, it sounds like the only way to keep this patient zero from getting what he wants is to either lock Jackson away—which we won't be doing, I'm telling you now—or kill the fucking thing. So let's fucking kill it!" he exclaimed.

"This thing eluded the Nosferatu for over a century—"

"Actually, technically, he didn't," Amos said, cutting his brother off. "He was here. Lyca Corp. had the phantom; that was why the Nosferatu couldn't find him."

"Even so, we have no idea where he is…or who he is," Raphael said. "Let's just focus on what we came here for: the cure."

Nobody obliged.

"Wouldn't it be in the files?" Brando suggested. "Maybe we can find something to help the Nosferatu find and kill it, as well as stuff about the cure. Two birds, one stone, right?"

"I mean I bet *you're* dying for revenge, right?" Ezhno said to Sebastien.

But the white-haired demon didn't answer. He looked stricken with grief…or guilt. Maybe both.

Raphael shook his head. "Lord Caedis will decide what to do with all this information, not us. Now get back to work."

"No," Daimon said firmly. "You've kept us in the dark with far too many things and it's about time we got some answers. Jackson's life is in danger, and I won't stand around cluelessly while there's some antlered wolf out there looking for him!"

The pack nodded in agreement.

Raphael scoffed—

"I agree," Sebastien said, finally speaking up. "I wanna know, too. That thing killed Caleb because of me—it's *out* because of me. I want to know who else it's using to get around."

"We're not looking through the files," Raphael denied.

"Lord Caedis is just gonna tell us all anyway!" Sebastien argued.

Raphael looked frustrated. His sights shifted from Sebastien to the pack and back to the white-haired demon. With an irritated huff, he waved his hand in dismissal. "What the fuck ever. It won't be on my head."

Ethan immediately snatched the file that Jackson had been reading while everyone else slowly approached the table, eyeing the mountain of folders and files.

Jackson stared at them, unsure of which one he wanted to take. He was far too overwhelmed with trepidation and grief; he knew that the antlered wolf wanted him, but now that he knew the details as to why, he felt a whole lot worse. He felt vulnerable. And he felt like a liability. What if the antlered wolf got a hold of him? It would be over, wouldn't it? It would be a whole lot harder for the Nosferatu to stop it if it never grew weak.

But not if they got to it first. He looked at Ethan. "Does it say who the antlered wolf is?" he asked.

Wilson flipped through the file. "I dunno. All I'm seeing at the moment is Caleb."

"Hey, there's something in here about wolfsbane," Wesley said, holding up the file he'd chosen. He then read, "Wolfsbane has shown promising results slowing down the progression of the cadejo virus." He lifted his head and looked around at everyone. "Could this have something to do with the cure?"

"Wolfsbane?" Lance questioned.

Jackson wanted to chime in, but he saw the intrigued expression run away from Ethan's face, replaced by a pale, horrified stare. "What?" he asked.

Everyone looked at the muto.

"Uh…" Ethan drawled. "Guys, I…isn't…" he paused and turned the file around so that everyone could see the profile pages he'd been reading. "Isn't that…Tokala?"

"What?" came a flurry of confused voices.

Everyone moved closer, gawping at the blurry black-and-white photograph.

Jackson stared at it, and when a choir of disbelieved, confused murmurs echoed around him, his guilt-ridden heart seemed to stop for a moment.

The man in that photograph…*was* Tokala, and he didn't look a day older than he was now. The file even said 'Unknown Redblood'.

"It's gotta be someone else," Wesley insisted, shaking his head. "Someone who looks like him."

"You're fucking kidding, right?" Lalo exclaimed fearfully.

"It…can't be," Dustu breathed. "He's our friend!"

Jackson's frozen heart started racing as horror and realization struck him tenfold. It *was* Tokala. Patient zero, the phantom, the antlered wolf—it was him, and it had been this *entire* time.

Chapter Ninety-One

Patient Zero

| Jackson |

The pack's initial grief for Tokala's death twisted into a harrowing mix of confusion, despair, and horror. In a cruel turn, they discovered that he had not been their fallen ally but a clandestine adversary all along. Tokala, once a beacon of unity, had concealed a web of lies, orchestrating the demise of their packmates. The mourning that gripped them now echoed not for an external threat but for the treachery within their ranks, an unimaginable betrayal that left them teetering on the edge of profound despair.

"No..." Daimon denied shakily, stepping away from the table. "I trusted him. We...*all* trusted him."

The pack hung their heads in dismay, and the revelation quickly consumed the entire room.

"You're telling me it's been your Zeta this entire time?!" Raphael exclaimed angrily.

Jackson scowled despondently. It all made sense.

That was why the cadejo always seemed to know where they were.

That was why Tokala had been so nice to him from the very start, and why he'd gotten close.

That was why so many of their packmates died.

That was why...Daimon got hurt during Ethan's extraction. *Tokala* stabbed him, didn't he?

And that was why Tokala screamed for Jackson's help when the cadejo dragged him away.

It was all a part of Tokala trying to get him away from the pack. It was all a part of Tokala trying to pry Jackson's protectors away. It felt a little too coincidental that a knife impaled Daimon's back in the *exact* place that even surgery might not fix; that was Tokala's attempt to get rid of Daimon so that Jackson would be easier to take, wasn't it?

This *whole* time...it was Tokala. *Everything* was Tokala. That was why he avoided the Great Lake grounds, wasn't it? Because they'd expose him for who and what he really was. And that was why Tokala wasn't with the pack when they'd come and rescued him from the antlered wolf.

"The antlered wolf had orange fur," Jackson said, wide-eyed and stricken with despair. "And every time we were getting somewhere, the cadejo always seemed to know where we were."

"But...he's been with us for years!" Brando exclaimed. "He...I...how can he...I don't—"

"He's been playing us this whole fucking time," Daimon growled as he snatched the file from Ethan. "He's orchestrated *everything* that's happened to us since we found Jackson, all in feeble attempts to take him."

The pack gawped at their Alpha for a moment.

But then Wesley broke the silence. "Dirty...little fucking coward," he growled, clenching his fists.

"He's still out there," Sebastien said hauntedly. "That whole getting dragged away by the cadejo thing was another attempt to lure Jackson away from us. He'll be waiting."

Ethan scoffed and shook his head. "How did none of us see it?"

"He was so nice to Jackson even when we all hated him," Lalo said.

"What the actual fuck, man?" Julian breathed. "What...the *fuck*?"

The pack exclaimed and muttered their astonished, furious reactions to the revelation, speaking over one another, shaking their heads, and passing the file around to get a closer look at the photo of Tokala.

"Dated 1290," Brando read when he took the file from Leon. "That's fifty fucking years ago—he's not even that old!"

"The phantom doesn't age," Sebastien said, his voice laced with trepidation and dismay. "Kinda just...freezes the body it possesses."

"But Tokala knew things!" Ezhno insisted. "Stuff that only wolf walkers know—stuff that only Redbloods know!"

"Dad?" Remus abruptly asked, his shaky voice cutting through the pack's tense exchange of reactions.

Daimon looked down at him. "What?"

Remus lifted his trembling arm and pointed out at the hall. "W-what's that?"

They all looked in the direction he was pointing in, and when everyone saw the pair of glowing red eyes shrouded in the darkness on the other side of the hall, they tensed up and stepped back.

A horrible, *terrible* feeling of dread struck Jackson like a blade to his heart—to his *instincts*. Those red eyes.... He knew them, and they knew him.

Daimon protectively pulled both Jackson and Remus behind him, and the pack took their defensive positions.

But a deep, cruel laugh sliced through the murk, ricocheting off the walls and creeping into the room like a cold breeze.

Jackson tensed up, his heart racing, his instincts urging him that it was time to go. But where could *any* of them go? The only way out was exactly where those eyes were shining.

"It's...it's him," Sebastien said with a horrified look on his pale face.

"Everyone get back!" Raphael ordered.

But no one moved.

"Get back!" he insisted again.

Still, everyone stayed where they were, watching as the pair of eyes began to move closer, and loud, thumping footsteps bellowed through the tense, cold silence.

That deep, cruel laugh echoed again. "Little Zephyr Redblood," it spoke, its voice serpentine and disembodied. "Always trying to prove himself, never enough."

Raphael scowled and gritted his teeth, but as he stepped forward, pairs of glowing red eyes began shining in the dark—three pairs, ten pairs, twenty, more. Seething, snarling corpses prowled out of the shadows, twitching and growling.

And when the monstrous, antlered beast emerged from the darkness, Jackson froze and stifled a breath. It was so huge that it couldn't even stand on its hind legs; it edged towards the room, a wicked grin on its rotten face. The runes on its exposed skin and bones glistened orange in the gloom, and the torn, stringy flesh hanging from its antlers dragged along the floor, leaving a trail of black rot.

It stopped thirty feet from the door, and the cadejo stopped behind it. "I'm only going to tell you once," it drawled, its eyes shifting from Raphael to Daimon, who Jackson hid behind. "Give me Jackson...and I'll let you all live."

Daimon reached behind him and gripped Jackson's arm. "Fuck you," he snarled.

"I-it doesn't even sound like him," Lance insisted. "M-maybe it's—"

"Why?" Wesley blurted, cutting his Epsilon off. "We trusted you."

The antlered wolf laughed again, snarling as it did.

"Answer me!" the Gamma yelled, lunging forward—

"Don't," Elias warned him, grabbing him before he could attempt to attack the monster.

"Better listen to him," the beast growled and set its eyes back on Jackson.

Jackson's heart was still racing, so hard that it was starting to hurt. Why didn't his instincts tell him that it was Tokala? How did he not know that someone who was sleeping and living and eating mere feet from him every day was the creature who wanted to use his body as a vessel? The creature that had caused the deaths of his friends and of *countless* wolf walkers and Caeleste for *years*? Why, when he needed it most, did his apparent prophesising instincts not tell him that the phantom was Tokala?

"Well?" the antlered wolf growled.

"Stay behind me," Daimon mumbled to Jackson.

Raphael then scoffed and slowly moved around from the back of the table. "What did you think was going to happen?" he asked as he gradually approached the doors. "Did you think you'd come down here, spook us with a couple corpses, and we'd hand over your key to immortality?" He laughed a little and stopped in the doorway. "You're even fucking stupider than I—"

The antlered wolf lifted and waved its right paw, abruptly propelling Raphael to the side with an invisible force; he hit the wall, which cracked and crumbled, and when he landed on the floor with a thump, he lay still and silent.

"Raphael!" Amos exclaimed, but as he took a single step, the antlered wolf launched him across the room, too; he flew back, crashed into the computer desk, and hit the floor.

"Amos!" Elias panicked, and just like his brother, he was thrown across the room by a single wave of the antlered wolf's paw.

"Anyone else?" the antlered wolf tested.

The pack, just as frozen as Jackson, didn't utter a word. They all looked to their Alpha for answers, but Jackson felt Daimon tense up, and he wasn't sure whether the conflicted look on his face was because he was trying to work out what to do or because he really had no idea. But what *could* they do? There was no way out.

"You're not taking him," Daimon growled, gripping Jackson's wrist.

"No?" the beast snarled. It held out its hand and pulled it back—

Remus shrieked and grabbed onto Daimon, who grasped his son's wrists before he was propelled forward towards the monster. Everyone else burst into action and grabbed hold of either Remus or Daimon, struggling and grunting as the boy was pulled by an invisible grip.

Jackson helped too, using all his might, but the pack were struggling, their feet scraping along the floor. He tried summoning more strength, but when the antlered wolf snarled and pulled harder, he noticed something.

A faint, black mist-like aura seethed from the surrounding cadejo, floating like snakes towards the antlered wolf, soaking into its mangled body. As the beast tugged, trying to pull Remus towards itself, Jackson saw one of the cadejo behind it drop dead, and the aura began seething from another one.

Were they the source of the antlered wolf's power? Was that why it had run the first time Jackson confronted it…because it had no cadejo around to feed off?

Another corpse dropped as the monster struggled, snarled, and gradually pulled the entire pack closer—so close that they were now passing the doors.

Jackson had to act fast; he grabbed the inimă from his bag, and when he pressed it against his collar, the amulet wrapped around him like a starved serpent, and the consuming, drowning, *overwhelming* power surged through him, forcing him into his demon form.

The second his wings and horns appeared, Jackson burst forward—

"Jackson, no!" Daimon shouted in panic.

The antlered wolf stopped trying to tug Remus away when Jackson collided with three of the cadejo on its left. With a vicious snarl, the massive monster tried to grab Jackson while he tore the three cadejo apart with his bare hands, but it missed, its huge paw slamming down on the ground just inches from him as he lunged towards the next few corpses.

That was when the cadejo stopped lurking and charged towards the pack, reacting to the antlered wolf's roar. Jackson tried to grab and execute as many of them as he could, but they weren't interested in him.

"Jackson," the antlered wolf snarled as it lunged towards him.

Panic fused with the power raging through Jackson as he leapt out of the way, barely escaping the huge monster's grip. As he skidded along the floor, he caught a glance of his pack fighting the cadejo in their wolf forms, but the antlered wolf was no longer drawing power from them, and if Jackson was correct in assuming that it was weaker without them, then maybe he could kill it.

Jackson dodged the beast's paws again, propelling himself away with his wings. Then, he held out his right hand, and once a ball of crimson fire formed in his palm, he threw it at the antlered monster—but it missed and hit the wall behind it.

"Come here, you little shit," the beast snarled, trying to grab him.

Jackson dodged again, his heart racing, his body trembling as the overwhelming power struggled for control. But he wouldn't let it rule him. The power belonged to *him*. He threw another ball of fire, but it hit one of the cadejo lunging at Lance.

Sebastien left the pack and joined Jackson; he jumped at the antlered wolf and sunk his teeth into its leg, making it shriek and roar.

"Get to cover!" the hound ordered, but then he grunted when the monster grabbed his wing and yanked him off; it threw him across the room, and when he hit the wall, Sebastien whimpered and struggled to try and get up.

Jackson scowled desperately as the beast went to execute Sebastien. He threw another ball of fire, and when it hit the monster's arm, it swung around to face him. But despite his attempts to make it do so, the fire didn't spread and engulf the creature, it just sizzled out, leaving not even a scorch mark on its skin.

A cruel grin stretched across the beast's face, and as more cadejo burst in through the stairwell doors behind it and headed for the struggling pack, the monster prowled towards Jackson, drawing power off the increasing swarm.

Jackson's pack needed him, especially with Sebastien, Raphael, and the twins down, but they wouldn't stand a chance if the antlered wolf wasn't distracted. What was he supposed to do, though? His fire was useless, and he was barely able to dodge its lunges. His instincts were still telling him to run, but he wouldn't leave his pack—he *couldn't*.

He snapped out of it in time to dodge the monster's swipe, but before he could skid to a halt and turn to face it, the beast snatched him with its other paw, ensnaring him in its tight, crushing grip.

"Jackson!" came Daimon's horrified voice.

Jackson struggled and gasped for breath as the antlered wolf lifted him off his feet and pulled him closer to its mangled, rotting face. But no matter how hard he tried, he couldn't break free—he couldn't even cut its skin with his claws.

"I've waited *centuries* for this," the monster growled, and up close, its distorted voice sounded more like Tokala's.

"Get off me!" Jackson choked, his body beginning to go numb as his breaths were harder to take.

The monster laughed, and as the pack snarled, growled, and panicked, it turned its head to look at them. "You could have avoided this, Jackson, if only you'd given yourself to me willingly. And it would have been a lot less painful for you, too," it said, slowly turning its head and glaring into his horrified eyes.

Desperation and terror filled Jackson to the brim. He panicked, trying to escape, his instincts screaming and begging, but there was nothing he could do. "We trusted you!" he shrieked, his heart racing so fast that it felt like it was about to explode. "We all did! You were our friend, Tokala! You—"

"Tokala died a long, long time ago," it breathed, its grin of rotting teeth widening. "The Redbloods sufficed as vessels for a good fifty years, but I need a body like yours, one that won't fail my true form." It squeezed Jackson tighter, depriving him of even the struggled gasps of breath he'd managed to take. "You were never meant for anything else but this." It widened its huge, putrid jaws, edging its teeth closer to Jackson, who writhed around and tried to use what little strength he had left to escape.

But it was useless.

There was nothing he could do. The power of the amulet was silent in the monster's grip, just as it had been when he first crossed paths with it. He couldn't save his pack, and he couldn't save himself.

The gaping jaws neared his body, and as his strength faded, his head began to spin—

"Get the fuck off him!" came Daimon's furious voice.

Jackson was suddenly tossed free from the monster's grip, and when he hit the floor, he watched as Daimon, in his Prime form, clashed with the antlered monster.

The Alpha slashed the beast's face with his claws, but as the antlered wolf drew power from the few remaining cadejo, the wounds healed immediately. But Daimon didn't let that discourage him. With a furious snarl, he slashed his claws at the beast again; the monster roared and tried to grab Daimon several times, but the Alpha skilfully dodged.

"Get out of here!" Daimon yelled as he dodged another of the monster's attacks and then slashed its neck with his claws.

As the monster stumbled back, the pack finished off the last of the cadejo; Jackson watched them try to help Raphael up, but the orange-haired man wasn't responding.

Jackson tried to get up, but pain shot through his broken body when he moved, making him grunt in response—and that distracted Daimon. The Alpha glanced at him after dodging the antlered wolf's swipe, and the monster seized its chance. It slammed its paw into Daimon, launching him across the room and crashing into his pack, and then the beast charged at Jackson.

With a panicked whimper, Jackson tried to scurry away, but just as the beast was about to reach him, Daimon threw himself at it again, shoving the creature away from Jackson.

But when the beast stopped stumbling, Daimon wasn't able to recover as fast, and there was nothing that Jackson could do to help. The antlered wolf grabbed Daimon with a vicious snarl, pulling him up off his feet, and after a cruel, evil grin, it yanked the Alpha closer to its widening jaws—

And then everything happened so fast.

Daimon's blood splashed to the floor, and a deafening rumbling came from every direction.

The building shook, and with a blinding flash of crimson light, a massive explosion knocked the antlered wolf off its feet.

Daimon landed on the floor with a thump, and a blur of red and black burst through the ceiling. A snarling creature collided with the antlered wolf, sending blood splattering in every direction.

But Jackson didn't care who or what was fighting the monster now. He moved as best as his body would let him, dragging himself over to where Daimon lay as his racing heart shattered in his chest. "Daimon?!" he cried painfully as he reached him, and the gaping wound on the Alpha's shoulder made Jackson feel like he was being crushed again.

His mate writhed and whined in agony, red and black veins spreading from the antlered wolf's bite as the infection spread.

Jackson scowled in dismay, tears streaming down his face as he stared at him. He placed his hands over the bleeding wound as if to save him from bleeding out, but that wouldn't stop the infection. That wouldn't stop him from turning.

"Daimon!" he wailed, staring down at his mate's horrified face.

Sebastien then appeared at his side and gripped his arms. "Jackson, we gotta go," he insisted, trying to pull him away.

"No!" he yelled, shoving Sebastien away. He then desperately shifted his sights to the pack—maybe there was something in the files that could help him save Daimon—but that was when he saw what was fighting the antlered wolf.

A huge, dragon-like creature with two pairs of wings and a crown of horns fought with the beast; the monster tried to sink its teeth into the dragon, but its armour was too thick, making the beast snarl frustratedly.

At the same time, *the Zenith*, in his demon form, was helping Raphael up, and several other demons were assisting the pack.

"Somebody help him!" Jackson shouted, pulling Daimon's head into his lap. "Somebody do something!"

Sebastien grabbed him again. "We need to go!" he insisted. "We can't do anything for—"

"I'm not leaving him!" he refused.

"Jackson, he—"

The antlered wolf crashed to the floor mere feet away from Jackson, snarling and roaring; it made an attempt to grab him, but the dragon creature clamped its jaws around its arm and yanked it away from him.

"J-Jackson," Daimon then grunted, trembling in his arms.

Jackson looked down at him, and when he saw his mate's honey-brown eyes fading to red, he scowled in despair.

"You…have to go," the Alpha breathed and closed his eyes as an agonized expression contorted his face. "P-please," he pleaded painfully.

But Jackson shook his head. "I'm not leaving you!" he cried.

"You…have to," Daimon grunted as he started panting. "There's nothing—"

"There has to be something!" he interjected and desperately looked at Sebastien. "There has to be something!"

Sebastien adorned a sorrowful stare and shook his head. "There's—"

The antlered wolf landed close to Jackson again after getting kicked across the room by the dragon, but before it could attempt to grab him, the other creature clamped its jaws around its leg and pulled it away. It swung the antlered wolf to the side, sending it crashing through the wall and into another room.

"It's time to move!" came the Zenith's voice.

"Come on!" Sebastien insisted to Jackson.

"No!" he cried, holding Daimon as tightly as he could. He wasn't going to leave him. He couldn't live without him. How could he live without the man he loved? The man he was supposed to spend his life with, the man who rescued him from despair and dismay, and the man who'd become his entire world? He couldn't—he *wouldn't*. There *had* to be something!

"Please," Daimon begged weakly, his voice fading. "You have…to go."

But Jackson didn't listen to him. His broken heart raced, and his aching body shivered as the world around him went quiet. There *had* to be something that he could do. He'd survived several cadejo bites, and the Nosferatu believed that he was a key part in finding a cure. If *he* was immune… then his blood had to do *something*, right?

He stared at Daimon's face; he was getting paler, the infection was spreading like wildfire, and he could feel his mate's body giving in. His trembles got weaker, and his panting breaths got slower and became stifled. Jackson was losing him.

As his tears streamed down his face and splashed onto Daimon's skin, he scowled in despair. He *wasn't* going to lose him; he wasn't going to lose the man he loved.

Jackson gave in to his instincts, letting them guide him. He tore a wound into his wrist with his fangs, and then he placed his wrist against Daimon's lips, using his other hand to widen the Alpha's jaw.

"What are you doing?" Sebastien questioned, but there was worry in his voice. "Jackson?"

Ignoring him, Jackson made sure that his blood dripped into Daimon's mouth, and then he gently moved his mate's head from his lap. He laid the Alpha down, leaned towards his neck… and sunk his fangs into his skin.

Daimon responded with a weak, pained and confused grunt, flinching.

Jackson bit down a little harder, injecting his venom into Daimon's bloodstream, and once he was done, he sat up and stared down at the Alpha's pale face. "Daimon?" he pleaded.

But there was no response.

"Daimon?!" he whined.

Sebastien shook his head and gripped Jackson's arms. "We have to go *now!*"

It didn't work. The life faded from Daimon's face, and along with it, Jackson's strength to fight withered. Just like he'd failed to save everyone else, he couldn't save his mate, and he'd lost him forever.

He gave in, letting the white-haired demon pull him to his feet—

A cold hand abruptly gripped Jackson's wrist.

Jackson dropped back to his knees, staring at the hand—*Daimon's* hand. His racing heart beat faster as he let himself hope. "Daimon?" he asked quietly, shifting his sights to his mate's face.

But Daimon didn't respond.

"*Please,*" Jackson begged, placing his hand on the side of Daimon's face. "Don't leave me."

"Jackson," Sebastien said once again, trying to pull him away.

Jackson held on to his mate, leaning forward and resting his head on his chest. He listened to Daimon's heartbeat gradually fade, his tears still trickling down his face.

What was he supposed to do now? What was the point of anything anymore? What was the point in his life if he didn't have Daimon at his side? He didn't want to live that kind of life. He didn't want to go back to how things were…empty, pointless, and alone.

He didn't want to live without Daimon.

But then he felt Daimon's grip on his wrist tightening.

He heard the Alpha's weakening heart begin to speed up.

And a strange, sulphuric smell contorted his mate's scent.

Jackson lifted his head and stared down at Daimon's face.

His colour was returning, and the infection spreading from the massive bite was receding—the *wound* was healing.

"Daimon?" Jackson breathed.

With a confused, painful grunt, Daimon opened his eyes—his blood-red eyes. He stared up at Jackson, but as blood oozed from his mouth, he turned his head to the side and spat something out.

Jackson set his eyes on two of Daimon's teeth, which lay in the blood which seeped from his mate's mouth, and when he shifted his sights back to the Alpha's face, he watched him confusedly open his mouth and lift his right hand to it.

Where Daimon's canines once were…there were now fangs, and when the Alpha realized it, a look of horror struck his face.

And beside Jackson, with a pale, mortified look on his face, Sebastien hauntedly asked, "What have you done?"

GREYKIN VALLEY
Greykin Chronicles | Volume Two

THE GREYKIN CHRONICLES

Greykin Mountain
The Greykin Chronicles | Volume 1
❋
Greykin Valley
The Greykin Chronicles | Volume 2
❋
Greykin Depths
The Greykin Chronicles | Volume 3
❋

[And more…]

THE NUMENVERSE
OTHER SERIES/STORIES

The Numen Chronicles Series One

Set in the year 957. A reclusive, former god-hunting vampire lord and a promiscuous warlord demon who comes from old money are forced to work together to save endangered vampires. As they collaborate, their hate starts to wither; Alucard's quiet life is turned upside down, and Zalith's 600 years of meaningless conquests appear to be at their end.

※

Aldergrove Chronicles

Set in the year 1176 after Aegisguard's second world war. After being told he has only six months left to live, Clementine decides to track down his sister's murderers, leading him to Aldergrove Academy, a place where a hundred students must fight to the death to earn their right to travel to the New World. But he soon learns that the students aren't the only ones prowling the corridors at night in search of blood.

※

Where The Wild Wolves Have Gone

Set in the year 1330. Following Luan, a young transman werewolf who belongs to a pack owned by Lyca Corp., a military-focused organization. The pack have served them for generations, but after a mission goes sideways, Luan begins to learn the horrifying truth about the people they serve.

※

The Numen Chronicles Series Two

Set in the year 1335. While hunting for his missing friend, Elijah stumbles upon a fiery journalist, who so happens to be looking for the same people as him: the doctors who experimented on him when he was a child. But when the two are forced to go on the run together, Elijah's healing wounds are opened, and he realises that Lyca Corp. took more than his childhood.

To stay up to date with future releases, follow the author through their website!

www.numenverse.com/

GREYKIN VALLEY
Greykin Chronicles | Volume Two

Milton Keynes UK
Ingram Content Group UK Ltd.
UKHW041234251124
451300UK00022B/19

9 781917 270113